The Vampire Files

VOLUME TWO

P. N. ELROD

ACE BOOKS, NEW YORK

THE BERKLEY PUBLISHING GROUP
Published by the Penguin Group
Penguin Group (USA) Inc.
375 Hudson Street, New York, New York 10014, USA
Penguin Group (Canada), 90 Eglinton Avenue East, Suite 700, Toronto, Ontario M4P 2Y3, Canada
(a division of Pearson Penguin Canada Inc.)
Penguin Books Ltd., 80 Strand, London WC2R 0RL, England
Penguin Group Ireland, 25 St. Stephen's Green, Dublin 2, Ireland (a division of Penguin Books Ltd.)
Penguin Group (Australia), 250 Camberwell Road, Camberwell, Victoria 3124, Australia
(a division of Pearson Australia Group Pty. Ltd.)
Penguin Books India Pvt. Ltd., 11 Community Centre, Panchsheel Park, New Delhi—110 017, India
Penguin Group (NZ), Cnr. Airborne and Rosedale Roads, Albany, Auckland 1310, New Zealand
(a division of Pearson New Zealand Ltd.)
Penguin Books (South Africa) (Pty.) Ltd., 24 Sturdee Avenue, Rosebank, Johannesburg 2196, South Africa

Penguin Books Ltd., Registered Offices: 80 Strand, London WC2R 0RL, England

THE VAMPIRE FILES: VOLUME TWO

PRINTING HISTORY
Art in the Blood: Ace mass-market edition / February 1991
Fire in the Blood: Ace mass-market edition / June 1991
Blood on the Water: Ace mass-market edition / June 1992
Ace trade paperback omnibus edition / September 2006

Ace trade paperback ISBN: 0-441-01427-5

An application to register this book for cataloguing has been submitted to the Library of Congress.

PRINTED IN THE UNITED STATES OF AMERICA

10 9 8 7 6 5 4 3 2 1

CONTENTS

THE VAMPIRE FILES

VOLUME 2

ART IN THE BLOOD

*A special thanks to
my friends at ORAC.
I couldn't have done it
without you.*

*And for Ben Beagle Elrod,
for your patience, courage,
and all the joy you so
freely gave. Ten years
was too brief a time.
Sleep tight, little guy.*

Art in the blood is liable to take the strangest forms.

—Sherlock Holmes, in *The Adventure of the Greek Interpreter* by A. Conan Doyle

1

HUNGRY and careless, I'd opened the vein more than necessary and the blood slipped past my mouth and dribbled down the animal's leg. I shifted my right hand above the wound and applied pressure, which slowed the flow, and continued with my meal, siphoning off more than usual because I'd been on short rations the last few nights. I drank my fill and more, the excess partly due to curiosity; I wanted to know if I'd swell up like a leech or if I could get away with fewer feedings per week. The cow didn't mind, she could afford to spare a quart or more—there'd just be that much less to spill out when they finally slaughtered her for someone else's dinner.

I drew away, a handkerchief immediately at my lips so as not to spot my clothes, and tightened the pressure on the leg. It worked, and the bleeding eventually stopped. My hand looked the same, at least—no puffiness there. I wondered how long it would take for the red to fade from my eyes. The usual time was only a few minutes, but there was no way to tell. These days I preferred to avoid useless mirrors and their many complications.

To spare my shoes from farmyard-style damage, I went incorporeal to get out and flowed past the wood corrals and their complaining occupants. It was a disorienting state, but I knew the route well and was soon back on the open street again, doing my best imitation of a normal man out for a walk. My car was parked less than a block away, but I always varied my route into and out of the Stockyards. Few people believed in vampires these days, but it never hurt to be careful.

The first aid to the cow had stained my fingers somewhat, so I took a swing past Escott's office with a mind to borrow his washroom. His lights were on, which surprised me, for only yesterday he'd mentioned a dearth of business. I didn't feel like his company just then and kept walking, but silently wished him luck as I passed. He detested being idle. A dripping tap in an alley down the street provided all the cleanup I needed, and I tossed the stained handkerchief into a trash can. Escott's laundry service, which I shared now, had once asked if his houseguest suffered from frequent nosebleeds.

The car started up without fuss and I drove aimlessly, turning when the mood struck me and obeying the stop signals like a good citizen. I pulled up and parked near the Nightcrawler Club up on the north side and pretended it was only an impulse that took me there, and not some inner need.

They had a new man out front. He looked askance at my ordinary clothes, but let me in when I asked to see Gordy. The hatcheck girl was not new, I rarely forget dimples, but she didn't know me from whosis, and put my plain gray fedora next to the flashier silk toppers with a friendly if impersonal smile.

I knew the place had been raided by the cops at least once since my last visit, and Gordy had taken the temporary shutdown as an opportunity to redecorate. The walls were bright with fresh paint, and the tables, chairs, and bandstand were now shiny black with gleaming chrome trim. The only thing unchanged were the costumes on the girls, which remained black with silver-sequined spiderwebs patterned on the happily short skirts. The leggy details were enough to keep me occupied until Gordy showed up.

He was puzzled to see me, maybe slightly wary as well, but when I stuck my hand out he took it. He was a big mountain of a man with a solid, but not crushing grip. He had no need to prove his strength against anyone, taking it for granted people could figure it out for themselves.

" 'Lo, Fleming, what's up?"

"This and that. Got a quieter place than here?" I gestured at the band across the dance floor below. They were just starting off another tune for the patrons.

He nodded, not one for much wordage, and led the way through a door marked PRIVATE. The soundproofing did its job and we were in the casino room, up to our eyeballs in stale smoke and the tight atmosphere of prolonged tension. Gordy nodded to a couple of tough boys in tuxedos guarding the money cage and threaded through the craps and roulette tables to the back exit. We took a short hall and some stairs up to an office I remembered very well. The redecorating had gotten this far with a new rug, paint, and paintings. His deceased boss's boats had been replaced by green-and-brown pastorals. A canvas depicting a lush forest covered a section of the wall where six slugs from a .38 had embedded themselves one memorable night.

"Nice picture, huh?" he said, noticing my interest. There was a very slight humor coming from his eyes. "I like to look at it."

"That's what they're there for." I noticed it was not an ordinary store-bought print, but a real oil with a decent frame.

"Yeah."

He pointed at a deep leather chair and settled into a wide matching sofa, taking up most of it. He wasn't fat, just big, and I knew from experience he could move fast and light when he wanted to; the present slowness was all part of his camouflage. Large men were supposed to be slow and stupid, so Gordy cultivated that image and thus kept a lot of people off balance. In his business an edge always came in handy.

"Want anything?" he asked, meaning refreshments.

I shook my head and with some caution removed my dark glasses. From his reaction I could tell my eyes were still quite red from the feeding.

"You look like you had a hell of a weekend."

"I did."

"You're not the social type, Fleming, at least for places like this and mugs like me. You got a problem?"

"Yeah."

He apparently recalled the last time he'd seen my bloodred eyes. "Trouble with Bobbi?"

"No."

"Another woman?"

I couldn't tell if he was being perceptive like Escott or if it was simply the next logical question for him to ask. "Yeah, you could say that."

"What kind of trouble?"

"I killed her."

The news didn't exactly send him into a panic. "You need protection, a cleanup job?"

"No, nothing like that."

He had one of those phlegmatic faces under his short-cropped blond hair; great for poker or making people sweat. "You need to talk about it?"

My instinct to come see him had been right, and I nodded, inwardly relieved.

"So talk," he said. He wasn't the soul of encouragement, but he settled back into the depths of the sofa to listen. I gave him a short version of how I'd killed the young woman and why I'd done it, just stating bald facts and not bothering with any defense. During the story he stared at yet another painting above and behind his desk, his eyes hardly blinking the whole time.

"I'm sure Charles knows about it, but he hasn't said anything. I don't think he ever will."

"Smart guy, then," he approved. "What about Barrett?"

"He apparently took the suicide at face value."

"He probably wants to. How are you taking it?"

"I feel like . . ." But I couldn't finish. I couldn't put words to what I was feeling.

He raised a hand to call off the question and tried another. "You remember the war?"

"I was in it."

This confused him, since I didn't look old enough, but he continued. "You fight? You have to kill?"

"Yeah, I see what you're getting at. This was different."

"Why? Because it was a woman and in a nice house and not out in a field of mud with the noise and cold? She was killing people. You had to stop her. What's the problem?"

"Living with it. Why me?"

He shifted his sleepy-looking eyes from me back to the painting. It was a soft overview of a farm near sunset, in one corner a boy was leading two plow horses back to the stable. "When I was a kid, I once knew a retired hangman. I asked him about it. He knew how to do it better than anyone else but he didn't think much about it, it was just a job to do. I can't say he enjoyed it, but he knew he was doing his part in making things cleaner."

It seemed an odd statement coming from him, considering how he came by his living. "Yeah?"

"Yeah. You either learn to live with it or you go crazy. Make up your mind."

"Is that what you've done?"

He glanced over, again with faint humor. "I'm just a businessman."

"That's what Capone used to say."

"Huh. He never talked about the dirty side of the business, not where he could be overheard. He'd pretend it wasn't there. Maybe that makes him crazy. I know it's there, I don't enjoy it, but I'm good at it. And I'm not crazy."

The humor was more pronounced, but under it was something hard and very cold. The base of my spine went stiff as I suppressed a shiver.

A few days, or nights, later I was just coming down from the upstairs bath when I heard Escott let himself in the kitchen door. His arms were full with a newspaper, raincoat, and several small cartons, and the latchkey got stuck in the lock again. When he started to jiggle it loose he nearly lost the cartons. Drawing a breath to say hello I caught a strong whiff of Chinese food and rushed to rescue the soggy white boxes before his dinner ended up on the floor.

"Thank you," he said as I transferred them to the counter by the sink. He extracted his key and glared at the lock for exactly one second, tossed his coat and hat on the table, and stalked into the dining room. He was back almost immediately with a screwdriver and small oil can, and began an energetic assault on the rusty mechanism.

"Your dinner'll get cold," I said, leaning against a doorway to watch the show.

"A distinct possibility, but I'd rather it be cold than suffer the indigestion this recalcitrant lock is likely to cause me."

"You almost make me glad I've given up eating."

His mouth twitched, whether from amusement at my remark or frustration at the job was hard to tell. Something gave, and he seized the oil can and attacked the breach in the lock's defense while it was vulnerable. He experimented with the key, grunted with satisfaction, and put things back the way they were.

"Good evening, Jack," he said, standing and dusting his knees off. It was his way of starting things over fresh. "How are you tonight?" His suit coat joined the raincoat on the table and he turned on the hot water in the sink to wash his hands.

"Fine. You look tired."

"Thank you so much. I can assure you it is not from overwork."

"You were busy the last few nights."

"Yes, but that little—extremely little—job is resolved and I've nothing to do now."

"Boredom?" I knew how exhausting that could get.

"Inactivity. I never allow myself to become bored, but inactivity may strike at any inconvenient moment."

"There's a difference?"

He registered mock surprise as he toweled dry. "Most certainly. One cannot help inactivity, but boredom is a self-inflicted disease. I firmly believe there is a special Providence watching us all for signs of boredom, the moment we declare ourselves in that state some disaster will occur to take our minds right out of it. The last time I was bored was the year 1920. I was carrying a spear, so to speak, in the court of King Claudius. . . ."

I looked blank.

"Hamlet?" he suggested, by way of clarification.

Dawn broke. "You were on stage in front of an audience and bored? I'd be scared to death."

"Given time, one can become used to anything. I'd grown all too familiar with that particular scene in that particular play and thus declared myself bored. The next thing I knew the trapdoor we used for the Ghost to enter from under the stage gave way and down I went. It was one of my more spectacular exits."

"Were you hurt?"

"A bruise or two when I landed on the platform below had me limping for a week. It seems the fellow playing the Ghost forgot to latch the trap properly after his last scene."

"Did you kill him?"

"He was terribly embarrassed so I thought it more vengeful not to put him out of his misery." He pulled out a few clean plates and emptied the cartons onto them. "Since then I've schooled myself to patience when it comes to inactivity. I've completely sworn off boredom."

I shoved his things to one side of the table to give him room. "So work is slow?"

"I more than caught up on my reading." He nodded at the crumpled newspaper.

"Not even a divorce to turn away?"

His thin lips curled in distaste. "Please, I am about to eat."

"Sorry."

"What social event are you off to tonight?" he asked in turn as his long fingers snapped up a set of chopsticks with practiced ease.

"How did you—"

"You've taken more care than usual with your hair, that is a new shirt and tie, and I believe Miss Smythe will be quite impressed with the after-shave and shoe shine."

"Looks okay, then? I can't really tell."

"Mirrors must be a considerable source of annoyance to you these days."

"You can say that again," I grumbled.

"The event?" he repeated, just before plunging into his chow mein or whatever it was; the smell was making me vaguely nauseous, but that was my usual reaction to solid, cooked food.

"Some kind of party. Bobbi and Marza got a job singing and playing background music, and their boss said it was okay to bring a date."

"It sounds an odd mix of the formal and informal."

"Yeah, bunch of artists up along the north shore. One of them's loaded and wants plenty of people along to celebrate a show he's having at his fiancée's gallery."

"His name?"

"Leighton Brett."

His right eyebrow bounced once and he indicated the paper with his chopsticks. "Page eight."

I uncrumpled it and opened to the page. It was a splashy article placed above the fold with lots of photos. A picture of Brett standing with some people took up most of the space. It was a standard pose of him shaking hands; in the background was some kind of landscape painting. The caption said he'd won the Lloyd A. Farron Medal and five hundred dollars for a painting called *Homeward Bound*. Brett was a big man, towering over the others by a head. He had a long, solemn face, dark, curly hair, and serious eyes.

Another photo of him with his fiancée Reva Stokes had them standing before his portrait of her. He was accurate and had caught her looks exactly right, but somehow softened and sweetened them so at second glance it seemed like a different woman from the cool-faced blond next to him.

The article went into detail about Brett's award presentation and the opening of his own gallery. Reva would be managing the sales; his job was to keep the place filled with new work. The between-the-lines message indicated he was destined to be one of art's new masters and consequently a good investment for collectors.

I went back to the first photo, drawn by something familiar in the painting. It looked very much like the farm scene hanging above Gordy's desk. This one still had a boy leading two plow horses, but the stable was gone, replaced by trees and part of a dirt road.

"This painting"—I pointed out *Homeward Bound*—"Gordy's got an almost identical one in his office."

"You've been to see Gordy?" He was mildly surprised.

"Just to say hello. I'll have to ask him who the artist is."

"It could be Brett, I understand he's quite prolific."

"But why paint the same scene twice?"

He shrugged. "You could ask him. More than once da Vinci did two versions of one scene. *The Virgin of the Rocks* comes to mind, and *La Gioconda*." He rolled the foreign word out with dramatic relish and attacked his rice.

"La what?"

"The *Mona Lisa*, my dear fellow."

"There's only one *Mona Lisa*."

"In the Louvre. There's another sitting quietly in a bank vault in New York. It's a shocking waste."

"You're pulling my leg."

"I assure you it is absolutely genuine."

"How come no one's ever heard of it, then?"

"Because the owners want no part of the attitude of disbelief, which you are presently displaying with such clarity, or to attract the attention of potential thieves."

"How do you know about it?"

"I read a lot," he said, but I picked up a note in his voice that indicated he was skirting the truth. Before I could jump out with another question, he glanced up at the kitchen clock. "Perhaps this is forward of me, but I noted in the story about Leighton Brett that the party he is having tonight begins at eight, and it is just now—"

"Holy shit." I ran down to the basement and grabbed my hat and coat. To save time I vanished and reappeared in the kitchen, a stunt that often unnerved Escott. It worked. He nearly choked on his bean sprouts, but recovered beautifully.

"Shall I leave the latch off?" he asked dryly, knowing full well I had no problems with locked doors.

"Nah, but don't wait up for me."

He tossed my wry look back and saluted me out with a wave of his chopsticks.

Traffic wasn't good, but I was less anxious for my own lateness than Bobbi's; I had no wish to cost her a job. I rounded the last corner to the front of her residence hotel and saw them already outside looking for me; Bobbi, her accompanist Marza Chevreaux, and Marza's date, Madison Pruitt. Bobbi opened the passenger door and swooped inside to plant a quick kiss on me before Marza could scowl disapproval.

"Sorry I'm late," I said.

"You're timing's always been perfect for me," she whispered with a little smirk, and then Marza and Madison were piling into the backseat. Marza did have something acid to say about my lateness, but Bobbi's last remark had my head swimming, so I didn't hear any of it.

Bobbi brought out a much-folded scrap of paper and called directions, while Madison tried to engage me in a political discussion. He had taken great stock in last Wednesday's rumor that Hitler was planning to retire and turn the chancelorship over to his air minister, Goering. I didn't see that it would make much difference, but all the way along Michigan Avenue he argued passionately in favor of keeping Hitler in charge of things.

"I thought the Communists didn't like Hitler," I ventured when he paused for breath.

"We don't, but Goering would be worse. He's better educated and a trained military leader. As soon as they finish practicing in Spain his air force is going to be bombing Paris next. Don't forget the German army moved into the Rhineland Zone only last March—"

Marza finished for him. "—and next thing you know they'll be using the Eiffel Tower for target practice. We've heard it all before, Madison."

"But Jack hasn't. Have you?"

"I'm always interested in hearing people's opinions."

In the mirror I saw Marza shoot the back of my head a look that would have done Medusa credit, and Madison continued with his political observations for the rest of the trip. Occasionally, he even seemed to make sense. Bobbi kept us on course until we were in the middle of what I would call a rich neighborhood, and counted off house numbers. The one we wanted took up an entire block and was lit up like New Year's.

"Look at the cars," said Marza. "We're late."

"They're early," Bobbi corrected. "Reva said there'd be some hangers-on from the gallery opening."

"I'll drop you at the front and park the buggy," I suggested. "No sense in all of us taking a hike."

"They should have hired some valets," said Marza, still wanting to stew.

Madison snorted. "And lose their image as unworldly artists?"

"Darling, anyone who lives in a pile of such proportions has a very clear idea of how the world works, and it certainly would not have stretched their budget much to provide a little basic comfort to their guests." Marza had apparently forgotten she was at the party to work, not play. Bobbi glanced at me and managed to keep a straight face.

The exterior of the house was comfortably ugly, built of large slabs of gray stone in the shape of a mock castle, complete with a crenelated roofline. The grounds were formal and well kept, with only a few early leaves skittering in the wind over the gray brick driveway. I paused under a huge covered entry to unload the others, then rolled out again to find a parking space. Space found, I strolled back up the drive with a few other arrivals. Some were in formal clothes and looking smug about it; another group was dressed for an afternoon in the yacht basin and looking equally pleased with themselves. I overheard one of the formals also complain about the lack of parking valets, but no one else seemed to mind.

Bobbi was waiting in the entry for me and slipped a possessive arm through mine.

"What happened to—" I started.

"Madison spotted some friends and dragged Marza along inside. For all his dad's money you'd think he could afford to buy some manners."

"Or even rent them. Don't worry about it, Madison's still a kid."

"He's over thirty."

"There are kids and then there are kids. Have I told you how gorgeous you are tonight?"

"Not out loud, but feel free to—oomph . . ."

She said to feel free, which is why I grabbed her and kissed her, garnering a few whoops of encouragement from a clutch of passing guests. Despite the distractions, Bobbi didn't put up any fight and gave as good as she got.

"When does the party end?" I asked.

She took a deep breath. "Five minutes from now would be too long, but hold that thought."

I grinned back, and we assumed a more sedate posture and walked inside.

The windows were wide open, but insufficient to the task of cooling down the rapidly crowding room. Brightly clad bodies, cigarette smoke, and the steady rumble of conversation filled all the corners, and this was just the front hall. I automatically looked for a familiar face and was mildly surprised to spot one, though I'd never met her before. Reva Stokes, slim, self-possessed, and carefully dressed in a shade of chocolate brown that matched her eyes, broke away from a conversation, extending a long hand at Bobbi.

"So glad to see you, Miss Smythe." Her voice was smooth with a touch of throat to it. Bobbi introduced me as her date and asked where she was to sing.

"The long hall, I'll take you there." She turned and led the way, talking over her shoulder. "It's the largest room we have, but I'm afraid the acoustics are terrible. Leighton refused to have the piano moved."

"I'm sure it will be fine. The gallery opening went well, I hope?"

"Oh, yes, just wonderful." She sounded anything but enthused.

Bobbi was nerved up enough to hold my hand all the way there. The long hall had fewer people in it, but the twenty-foot ceiling and bare floor turned it into a cross between an echo chamber and a bowling alley. I never did notice the walls for all the humanity in the way.

Folding chairs and music stands were arranged to one side of a grand piano the size of my Buick. Several men in tuxedos were sorting through some sheet music and tuning their instruments. Reva asked them to start the background music as soon as they could and told Bobbi she could pick her own program. A white-haired man in the back spotted Bobbi, broke into a smile of greeting, and came over to kiss her cheek.

"Bobbi, you look wonderful as always. Now who's the tall fellow getting so jealous?"

"Titus, this is my date, Jack Fleming. Jack, this is Titus Noble, leader of the band."

Noble pretended to wince. "String quartet, my dear girl." He glad-handed me. "I remember you from Bobbi's housewarming party. Marza said you were in the rackets."

"Titus!"

"Bobbi, if I don't ask questions, I'll never learn anything. The hard part is surviving the answers. Well, Mr. Fleming?"

"Jack," I said automatically. "And sorry if it disappoints you, but I'm not."

He craned his neck to one of the other musicians. "Teddy, you owe me a beer. Then what do you do besides escort beautiful young singers around to places like this?"

"I'm a writer." My answer popped out naturally and hopefully covered out-of-work journalists like myself.

"Ohhh." He nodded a bit vaguely, then leaned close to Bobbi's ear. "Don't marry him until he has at least three best-sellers under his belt."

She cuffed his arm playfully, then they started hashing out the music program for the evening. They didn't get far before realizing they'd need Marza. I volunteered to go look for her and started weaving through the knots of chattering people and waiters balancing silver trays.

She was with Madison, who was holding forth before a group of Bohemian types on his favorite subject: the unfairness of the world in general, and how Marx had given them all a blueprint on how to make things work. Marza looked bored to death, and if she didn't exactly welcome my interruption with open arms she had no insults ready, either. I told her where Bobbi was and she walked off—rather quickly. I listened for another minute to the political lecture, decided he'd ceased to make sense again, and drifted back to the main hall to watch the show.

It didn't take long for Bobbi to get things straight with Noble, who led off the music with one of those chamber things that all sound alike. I was surprised at the volume coming out of their stringed instruments, and it had an immediate quieting effect on the people closest to the players. Titus played a violin with the apparently easy concentration of a true professional, but I found it difficult to sit and listen, for some of the high notes sounded like nails on a blackboard. He was expert enough, but now my ears were just too damned sensitive to listen with any comfort. After a few minutes I was getting to the limit of my duration, but then the music abruptly wound up to a self-satisfied finish and everyone started applauding.

Marza gave him enough time for a decent bow, then attacked the piano keys with her maroon talons and Bobbi launched into one of her club numbers. It was a light love song and apparently a favorite, as a few more people squeezed into the room to see who was singing and then stayed because Bobbi's looks matched her voice. She was quietly dressed in a high-necked, long-sleeved gown of midnight blue, but it was some kind of soft, clingy fabric that floated and moved with her body. I was hypnotized along with the rest and didn't make a sound until she was finished and bowing to her share of the applause.

Titus took another turn, a somewhat longer piece with not much violin to it, so I was able to tolerate things. Bobbi edged away from the piano and came over to see me.

"You bite a lemon or something?" she asked.

"The music's fine, I just can't listen to it." I explained my sensitive ears and she sympathized.

"I'll tell Titus, then, or he'll think you won't like his playing. He's been worried enough about whether Reva's brainstorm would work."

"What's Reva's brainstorm? Mixing you and Titus together?"

"Right, the idea is to give everyone something they like. I think it's supposed to reflect her husband's painting style."

"Any of his stuff hanging around? I'd like to see it."

"Probably. Find a wall if you can and follow it. I'll have a break in about thirty minutes. . . ."

"I'll be back."

She squeezed my hand and returned to the chair reserved for her next to Marza, who was pretending to study her sheet music.

Madison appeared next to me, a disappointing and depressing substitute at best. He shook his head at the general direction of the players and sighed. "What a waste of money."

"People gotta have music."

"Don't you see, though? Look at the way the world is and tell me we couldn't fix things if we could develop a classless society to spread the wealth around."

"Probably," I agreed with caution. "But it would only work if everyone was in it on a voluntary basis and stuck to it."

"That's what I'm trying to do, only sometimes it seems impossible."

"You get that as long as you deal with people. Everyone's got an opinion and they generally think theirs is right."

"But I *am* right!"

"Keep your voice down, you don't want to get thrown out and us with you."

He calmed down very little, grinding his teeth in time to the music. "You hungry?" he asked, lighting on a fresh subject, no doubt inspired by the close passage of a waiter with a tray.

"Nah, you go ahead." And he was gone before I'd finished speaking. The quartet piece ended and Bobbi was up again, this time singing three in a row, finishing up with a version of "Melancholy Baby" that would stop traffic on a hot day. The hall was full up by now and more were more trying to crowd in. Bad acoustics or not, Reva had a success on her hands, if you could tell anything from the applause.

Titus started up another chamber piece and Bobbi slipped away. We couldn't get together because of all the people in between, so she pointed in the direction she planned to go and I nodded over the mass of heads.

The air got considerably cooler because a bank of French windows leading into the back garden were wide open. Bobbi went out one on her side, I used mine, and we met in the middle on the back porch.

"Thought I was going to suffocate," she said, grabbing my arm. "Let's take a walk, I need the air."

"You need a medal, you're just the greatest."

She smiled and glowed and I felt that pleasant stab hit me all over again because she was so beautiful and we were together. We didn't bother with talk and followed a winding cement path on a slow stroll. I hardly noticed the garden, getting only an impression of thick, high hedges, faint Japanese lanterns, and cast-iron furniture at convenient spots. She picked a wide seat trimmed in white-painted grapevines and sank onto it with a sigh. I sat next to her, holding her in the crook of my arm in case it was too cool for her after the pressing warmth of the hall.

"I'd like to have a place like this," she said. "A garden so big you lose yourself in it, and someone else to bring me breakfast in the afternoon."

"Don't you mean morning?"

"Not with the hours I keep. Did you mean that when you told Titus you were a writer?"

"It'll do until something else comes along."

"What do you write?"

"Your name across the sky in diamonds."

She laughed at the image, no doubt expressing her good taste.

"Would you like some?" I asked.

"What, diamonds?"

"Yeah."

She sobered. "What girl wouldn't?" But her tone was off.

"You don't like the idea?"

"I like the thought behind it, but I don't want that kind of gift—not from you."

"Why not from me?"

"Because of the way it used to be for me. I took things like that from Slick, like a fancy payment—you know I was no angel—but I don't want anything like that from you. Things are different with you, and I want them to stay that way."

She looked uncertain on how I was going to react, but I didn't have any choice in the matter. I pulled her tight and close and didn't stop kissing her until she insisted on coming up for air by thumping the back of my neck.

"Like I said," she continued, "hold that thought."

"I'll do more than that," I said, and started exploring her lips again. Her heartbeat was way up, along with her breathing.

"On the other hand, why wait?" she asked, and I paused.

"What?" Sometimes I can be pretty dim, but I caught on fast when she did something with her collar and it dropped several inches. "Oh, you can't mean here and. . . ."

"Why not? I'm ready for you now and I don't want to wait till after the party. I'll be too tired to enjoy things."

I could see her point, but felt suddenly vulnerable. The alcove we occupied didn't seem all that private. I could still hear voices uncomfortably near. She put her mouth on mine again and her arms went up my back to pull me closer.

"It's really very dark here," she whispered. "No one can see and if they do they'll just think we're necking—won't they?"

She was certainly right about that—in more ways than one—and I couldn't stop kissing her anyway. The pumping of her blood was as hypnotic to me as her voice, and I gradually sank lower along her neck until I was just over the two small marks left by our previous encounters. My canine teeth were already out and ready, but it was a new angle for me and I had to twist around a little more so I wouldn't hurt her.

She kept silent as I broke the skin, but her body went stiff and then shuddered, and she held me harder than ever as the pleasure rolled over her again and again. I drew it out for both of us, taking one seeping drop at a time. The thunder of her heartbeat and her now-languorous breathing drowned out all other sounds for me. There was only the shimmering woman in my arms and the taste of her life enriching my own.

2

BOBBI said my eyes were still flushed red, so I could only walk her partway back to the house. As soon as we got close to better lit areas and more people, she broke away with a smile and wave and went in to start another set. I returned to the cool solitude of the garden, found our bench again, and sat down, feeling peaceful and mellow about the world in general and quiet excitement over Bobbi in particular.

Sounds from the house drifted over the tailored grounds, the usual murmur of conversation, and the piano, then Bobbi's voice rose in plaintive song. She was having a private joke kidding me: the tune she'd chosen was "Red Sails in the Sunset." When the applause settled down, Titus Noble took over with a high-pitched string number that made the inside of my head itch. It was all part of the internal change; when I'd been a daylight walker I'd had no trouble with violin music. For self-protection I drifted farther from the house, putting trees and more hedges between my sensitive eardrums and the noise.

Sounds of another kind soon caught my attention, low voices, male, and I instinctively knew they were trying to be secretive. Their whispers were almost up to conversation level and punctuated irregularly by muffled laughter.

They were gathered at the foot of a massive fountain where a nearly naked stone woman dumped water endlessly from a jug. The big paper lanterns in the court gave them just enough light to see. A few glanced up from their circle at my approach, then turned back to the hot game of Harlem tennis they were playing against the fountain's marble base.

A youngish man with dark, sandy hair combed forward over a high brow puffed air into his fist, said a short prayer to Lady Luck, and tossed the dice with a practiced hand. They clicked and clattered on the pavement, hit against the low wall of the fountain, and bounced to a stop. The man crowed, others groaned, and money was swiftly collected, exchanged, and put down for the next toss.

Grinning broadly, he swept up the dice and breathed on them again, rubbing them between his hands with something like love.

"They're hot enough, Evan," someone complained, followed by an impatient chorus of agreement.

Evan tempered his grin and threw with an expert twist and follow-through, giving out a muted yell of triumph. More money was passed, and the rumpled stack where he knelt grew. The general opinion was that his streak couldn't last another roll and the bets were down. Evan went through more breathing exercises, rolled his eyes, and grimaced as though to transfer his hopes and energies into the dotted cubes. Silence fell on the restive group for the few seconds it took until the dice stopped and the resulting shouts of outrage and glee were enough to travel back to the house.

Just as he was collecting another rift of bills and congratulations, another man grabbed the dice over Evan's surprised protest. They scuffled, but the losers in the game got them apart, apparently aware there was a reason behind the breach of etiquette.

"What is it, Dreyer?"

The man walked under a paper lantern and looked at the dice carefully. I could almost hear him growling. He bounced them in his palm a few times, then rolled them at the base of the fountain.

"It's not your turn," complained Evan, who was just beginning to sweat.

Another man examined the results of the roll, then tossed them twice more over Evan's objections. By now Dreyer wasn't the only one growling, and Evan was facing a ring of hostile faces.

"Just a little joke, boys . . ." he said with a sick smile, hoping against hope someone would laugh.

Dreyer punched him in the stomach. He doubled over and would have fallen if not for all the supporting hands. It signaled a general free-for-all aimed at Evan and a fast scramble to recover the money. The milling bodies totally buried him for a moment, then his vague cry floated up clearly from the guttural profanity. The mass lurched and something large splashed into the fountain.

Until the punch in the stomach, I'd followed the proceedings with some amusement, good entertainment being a rare thing. After the punch I debated on just how to step in, but the splash got me moving. I was all too well acquainted with getting beaten to a pulp and dumped into water. Cheat or not, Evan had an ally.

I shoved flailing bodies out of the way to get to the fountain. It was shallow, but Evan's torso was underwater and destined to remain so as long as Dreyer held his legs up. I pushed him to one side, grabbed Evan's shirt and tie, and hauled him out like a drowned kitten. His thin hair streamed and water sputtered messily from his nose and mouth, but he didn't look ready to die yet. He was just settling onto the ledge of the fountain for a coughing fit when someone grabbed my right shoulder and spun me round to meet a fist.

The impact was a distant thing, after all. I hardly moved, though Dreyer must have put everything he had into it. Now he was hunched over his sore hand and glaring at me, probably working up to try again with the one he had left.

"Let it go," I told him.

"He cheated," he stated flatly.

I was the center of attention now and all of them looked one word away from beating me up for interfering with their fun. There were too many for me to influence, but it didn't seem necessary to try. Dreyer was the leader and would be the one to convince.

"So don't play with him," I suggested.

"Go to hell," he snarled back.

He looked ready to take another swing. From the stink of booze on his breath he might be just drunk enough or dumb enough to try. If so, then I'd make damn sure he lived to regret it.

"Forget it, Dreyer," someone from the rear said. "Let's get the money and go."

A few of the more practical ones broke away to count cash, but kept a wary eye open to watch any developments. Dreyer didn't move.

"*C'mon,* he's not worth the trouble."

Dreyer seemed to be having an internal debate over that point, then abruptly straightened from his near crouch. Before he could think twice about things, I caught up Evan and hustled him out of the war zone.

No one followed as we threaded through the maze of hedges. Evan had got his breath back, but still held a hand to his sore face where a beaut was forming on his left jaw.

"Thanks, buddy, I owe you one. They were really going to kill me."

"Just one of them—and you're welcome."

"Yeah, Dreyer's a real bastard. Come on back to the house, I'll buy you a drink."

He was more in need of it than I, but there was nothing better to do until Bobbi was finished. He knew the place and directed me around to a side entrance that opened into the kitchen. It was another enormous room and equipped with enough food and utensils to serve Wrigley Field during a sellout. We both winced at the bright light and bustling staff until a tubby young woman in white spotted us and came over, hands on her hips.

"Good grief, is that you, Mr. Robley?"

"What's left of him, Jannie," he shot back with a smile, and then winced at the action. "Got an ice pack?"

She sighed and shook her head at the wreckage and motioned for me to drop him in a chair next to one of the sinks. She found a towel and began to sop up his excess water. "What happened this time?"

"Well, there was this swimming contest—"

She dropped another towel over his face and rubbed briskly, his pained protests overriding his story. "Walt!" One of the white-coated waiters hustled over, grinning from ear to ear. "Go get a robe from the bathhouse storage and then try and find Miss Robley." He nodded and left, no doubt happy to be the one to pass the news along.

Evan fought his way out of the towel. "There's no need to bring Sandra into this, this is the first break she's had in a month of Sundays."

Jannie ignored him and made an ice pack with his towel and lumped it firmly against the sore side of his face. He yelped, but held it in place while she returned to direct some business on the other side of the kitchen.

"Women," he moaned. "They're all sympathy until you really need some. I get into the least little bit of trouble and they automatically think it's my fault."

I nodded and pretended to agree.

"Jannie's nice, though; a little bossy, but she's got beautiful skin tones. A little white, a touch of umber . . ." He saw that he'd lost me and made a writing motion in the air. "For painting? You know—art?"

"You're an artist?"

"One of the few genuine ones at this party."

Jannie returned with something that looked like a sheet with sleeves. "Start taking them off, Mr. Robley."

"What—here?"

"It's warm enough with the stoves," she pointed out with easy practicality.

"Warmth isn't what I'm concerned about." He indicated some of the female staffers.

"They know what a man looks like, and you more than most."

He was close to blushing. "This isn't fair—"

She smiled down at him. "I said the same thing to you on that so-called modeling job you gave me, so shuck 'em."

"That was art, this is . . . is . . ."

"Revenge," she concluded sweetly.

Some of the other girls gathered around in a scene disturbingly similar to the one we'd faced by the fountain. I backed away, he was strictly on his own this time.

"Perhaps you'd like some help, Mr. Robley. . . ."

"No, thanks, I know how it's done," he said, inspiring a burst of giggles. Grumbling, he started peeling off his coat. When he wrestled free of it and his shirt he grabbed up the huge robe and belted himself in before unbuttoning his pants. Jannie gathered it all together in a basket.

"What about the rest?"

"My socks aren't wet."

"I mean your—"

"They're dry, too," he insisted grimly, and sat on the chair to preclude any attempt to remove his last shred of dignity. Jannie passed the basket on to another girl with instructions to dry things out.

Walt returned, ushering in a tall young woman dressed in rich green satin. Her russet eyes swept the room and fastened on Evan, who hunched a bit lower in his robe, looking supremely miserable. She came over and regarded him with amused tolerance.

"I was told you'd had an accident," she said judicially.

"Er . . . yes, something like that." He was definitely blushing by now. "There was a roughhouse, see, and I got caught up in the middle of it, and if my friend here hadn't stepped in and saved my life . . . well . . ."

"Oh, *Evan.*"

"I did *not* throw the first punch, I swear." He held up his hand, which was hidden by half a yard of sleeve. He noticed, quickly lowered it, and fastened on me as a distraction. "Sandra, I'd like to introduce you to . . . uh . . ."

"Jack Fleming," I said, rescuing him again, and we shook briefly.

"Thank you for taking care of him. You're not hurt?"

"Only a little damp, Evan took the real damage."

"But I'm fine." A few shards of ice from the towel fell out as he struggled to free his hand from the sleeve. "Evan Robley," he said to me, "soon to be famous—along with my lovely, understanding sister, of course."

"How so, famous?"

"Because a lot of artists only become famous after they're dead," she put in significantly.

They had the same coloring, sharp features, and paint-stained fingers. His sandy hair was straight, hers was curly and a deep russet like her eyes. She had a slender build, but the fragility was offset by her long, firm jaw; tough looking, but not unattractive.

"Do you want to go home?" she asked him.

"No, not at all. Jannie'll have my clothes back in two shakes. Why don't you two go on and enjoy the party?"

"I can't just leave you—"

"I'll be fine." He appealed to me. "Take her back to the party and make her have some fun. Please?"

Her head tilted to one side in challenge. Sandra wasn't the type who could be made to do anything she didn't want. She noted my hesitation with amusement and suddenly smiled in approval. Sometimes my easy-to-read face could be an asset.

"Stay out of trouble?" she told him.

"Don't I always try?"

Sandra slipped her hand under my arm and led the way out of the kitchen.

"It just keeps finding me, is all," he muttered under his breath.

I glanced back in time to see Evan begin an animated conversation with one of the maids.

"Are you here with a date, Mr. Fleming?"

"Jack. Yes, I am, and yourself?"

"Evan's my escort. He wandered off rather early. What happened this time?"

"Cra—dice game. Some of the boys didn't like the way he was throwing them."

"Not those loaded ones *again*?"

"He'll have to get new ones, he lost them in the struggle."

"The sad thing is he probably will. He never seems to learn."

"Like a drink?" I offered as a waiter approached. She nodded and I swept a glass off for her. "Does Evan sell much of his art?"

"Hardly any, his work is too different for conventional tastes, but I manage to sell some things now and then."

"Beauty, brains, and talent. Congratulations. What do you paint?"

"Anything that sells, I'm afraid."

"Isn't that good?"

"For money, I suppose it is, but it's not always good for artistic integrity."

"What do you mean?"

"Do you know anything about art?"

"I'm learning now."

She finished her glass of champagne and deposited the empty on another passing tray. "Come on, I'll give you a lesson in the basics." She took me away from the mainstream of the party into the more sparsely populated areas of the house.

"You know this place pretty well?" I asked, trying to keep track of the layout.

"Oh, yes, we're very good friends with Leighton and Reva. I've sometimes spent as much time in Leighton's studio as my own."

"I thought artists were always in competition with each other."

"To a certain extent that's true, but we also exchange ideas and critiques. Of course it usually depends on the artist. Evan and Leighton have totally different styles, so they appeal to different tastes. Now look at this one, something you could hang anywhere in the world, in almost any house."

We paused in front of a landscape of mountains with a flowing, cloudy sky. There was a lot of detail to it, the colors were pleasant to look at, and it was very similar to the rural scenes in Gordy's office.

"What do you think?" she asked.

"I'm not sure, I don't feel qualified to judge."

"Do you know what you like?"

"Yes . . ."

Her attention sharpened. "But what?"

"I don't know, maybe it seems just a little too perfect."

She took my arm again. "Let me show you some more."

We explored the open areas of most of the downstairs rooms, squeezing close to all the walls and studying enough canvas to support a small museum. Leighton Brett's style was distinctive to himself, but for some reason I couldn't get into his paintings for more than a minute or so. I couldn't imagine buying one to look at for years at a time. Sandra was delighted.

"What's this about?"

Her smile had a definite softening effect on her face. "You are one of the few people I've met who've spotted it."

"What did I spot, then?"

"Leighton's artistic manipulation."

"What's that?"

She gestured at the painting, this one of a vase of flowers. "See the colors, very bland except for this touch of red here and here, which gives it all balance. I'm not denying he has a great deal of technical skill, but it's all very carefully planned, as you said, just a little too perfect." Her attitude was more amusement than jealousy, like a teacher instructing a pupil and enjoying the interaction for its own sake.

I looked at the flowers again and knew that with or without Sandra's information I still wouldn't like it. "What do you paint?"

"The same sort of things as Leighton, only I don't get paid as much.

I was lucky enough to get in on the WPA program to produce art for federal buildings, which certainly helps at rent time."

"I didn't know the WPA even had a program for artists."

"Oh yes, and it's saved more than a few lives."

"Do you paint what you like or what they tell you?"

"A bit of both. Remember what I said about artistic integrity? They don't really dictate what they want to me, but I am expected to paint something acceptable. Leighton's a great help to me there, he has a knack for knowing exactly what people expect, and then gives it to them. Whenever I think I'm going dry, I come over here for a refresher course."

"How does he feel about that?"

"He doesn't know about it," said a dark-haired man, turning around from his own station near the still life. "And since Sandra is quite tactful, he never will."

Sandra flashed a very devastating smile on him and touched his arm with an impulsive hand. "Alex! I'm so glad you came. How are you?"

His response to her obvious affection was minimal. His body went stiff at her touch and then relaxed visibly, as though he had to consciously remember she was a friend. "I'm well enough."

He didn't look it. He held his body straight, but his clothes were loose from weight loss and the skin on his face was dull. The impression was not so much ill health as neglect. The term "walking dead" had a more meaningful application to him than to myself. His suit was expensive but unpressed, and his collar and cuffs frayed beyond saving. He noticed my assessment and a slight spark of resentment lit his dark eyes for a brief second, then went out. He didn't give a damn.

I understood why when Sandra introduced us. Alex Adrian: one of the very few who had become famous outside artistic circles. In the last ten years hardly a week went by that his work didn't appear on some major or even minor magazine. He was in demand for snob advertising, illustrative work, society portraits, you name it. His talent crossed all boundaries and had kept him at the top. But this year, in January, the work stopped, and with enough notoriety to make headlines in more places than Chicago.

We shook hands briefly to obey social convention and then he pulled back into himself, hands held in front, the fingers of the right slowly twisting his wedding band around. I was interested to note he still wore it, perhaps as silent defiance to the rumors he'd murdered his wife.

"How is your WPA work going?" he asked Sandra.

"As well as possible, I'm working on a series for a civil-service building in Rockford."

"What are you doing?"

"Mountains, flowers, and sunsets; I don't know what the building looks like so I'm assuming the workers there would be glad of a little color."

"No doubt. Has Evan sold anything lately?"

"Another nude to Mr. Danube, and too far below the asking price."

"Tell him to stop having those pre-negotiation drinks with his buyers. What about that gallery deal?"

"It fell through. I was hoping to talk with Reva about carrying some of Evan's more restrained work."

"Why doesn't he do it himself?"

"You know how it is, Alex. He just can't seem to manage; I've tried. I pushed him in the right direction tonight and he ended up in the back fountain again."

Adrian almost looked interested. "Again?"

"Jack fished him out this time. He's in the kitchen waiting for his clothes to dry."

"Perhaps I'll check up on him, if only to protect the virtue of Brett's hired help."

"The hired help are perfectly able to look after themselves," said Evan, breaking in. His hair was combed, if a little flat, and though his clothes were still damp and wrinkled, he was cheerful. "You're looking awful, Alex, you should drink more." He held up a glass as an example and drained half of it away.

"No luck with Jannie?" said Sandra wryly.

"Not with Jannie, no. What are you all talking about me for?"

"We'd exhausted the conversational possibilities of the weather," said Adrian.

"But not drying paint," Evan shot back. "Done anything lately?"

"No."

Adrian's tone was not encouraging. Sandra noticed it and changed the subject. "Evan, I saw Reva in the small drawing room—"

"That's a good trick in this crowd."

"Evan—"

He held up a placating hand. "Peace, dear baby sister, I'll take care of it in my own way."

"When?"

"On a day when Reva doesn't have hundreds of people around her, all wanting one thing or another. This isn't the right time. The day after tomorrow, maybe."

"Why so long?"

"Because if she feels tomorrow the way I plan to feel, she'll need her rest. The day after, she'll be recovered a little from the shock but still be tired and fairly vulnerable to suggestion. That's when I'll tackle her on the gallery."

"Promise?"

"Word of honor. But tonight I'm planning to make every effort to enjoy myself so that when I tell Reva what a wonderful hostess she is, she'll know I'm sincere and not merely flattering her. Now, would anyone else like a drink? No? Then I'll just help myself." He finished the rest of his glass and went off in search of more.

Sandra half started after him, but Adrian gently caught her arm. "Let him go, you can't live his life."

Sandra glared at him a moment, then her face softened. She had a lot of things to say about the subject and managed to pack it all into that one look before nodding agreement. "All right, but I am going to see he eats at least one sandwich before he starts his debauch." She went after him.

"She's his younger sister?" I asked.

Adrian continued to twist his ring. "Yes, but a good deal more responsible, so she seems older. I'm sure he'll get his work into Brett's gallery, his plan for talking to Reva was sound enough. Sometimes he's not as foolish as he appears."

"And other times?"

Adrian abruptly smiled, showing a row of large but perfect teeth. "He is exactly as he seems." The smile vanished just as abruptly as though it had never happened. "How did Evan manage to end up in the back fountain?"

I briefly recounted the crap game and fight.

"Dreyer?" he interrupted.

"You know him?"

"I've heard of him, he's not exactly polite society. I'm surprised you were able to handle him; generally the man's a maniac. It's just like Evan to try cheating him at his own game."

"He's a gambler?"

"I'm not certain. Chicago seems to specialize in his type, if you know what I mean. I wonder why he's at this party, but then a lot of other unsavories are here as well. Money and manners don't always go together."

I remembered Madison Pruitt and could see his point.

"Are you connected with the art world, Fleming?"

"Not really, my girlfriend is singing here tonight and wanted me along."

"Bobbi Smythe? You're very fortunate. I heard her, she has a lovely voice."

"I'll tell her you said so." And that's when the idea clicked in my head. "Alex, how does one go about commissioning a painting?"

"I couldn't say for other artists. For myself, I decide what I want to work on. The general rule is half payment in advance and half on completion. Why do you ask?"

"I wanted to get a special present for Bobbi, she won't take trinkets from me, but I don't think she could turn down her own portrait."

"Especially one by Alex Adrian." He wasn't boasting, but simply aware of his talent and reputation.

"Would you consider taking on a commission?"

He did at least think it over before shaking his head. "I have to say no. It's not the subject or you, I just haven't the time. I'm sorry. Perhaps you could commission Evan or Sandra, they're both very competent. Evan in particular, when you can get him to do realism. I warn you, though. Go along with Miss Smythe during the modeling sessions. Evan rather enthusiastically fits most people's cliché ideas of an artist. I think if he had no talent at all he would still be an artist, if only to exploit the popular reputation involved."

"You're certain you won't take it?"

"Very certain. Sorry."

He excused himself and moved back into the crowd. He was puzzling, because I was positive for a moment that he was going to say yes. The dullness had left his face, and even in the packed room, I'd heard his heart hammer a little faster. He'd been genuinely interested and then the walls had come up, visibly and quite sudden. I glanced around to see if anything had inspired the change. The only thing in his direct line of sight were people, none of them known to me, but then a woman moved her head and I saw Reva Stokes, smiling and playing hostess.

She caught my look and nodded, then came over, graceful, smooth, and with a warmer attitude than before now that she was certain of the success of her party. "Are you enjoying yourself, Mr. Fleming?"

"Yes, thank you."

"I saw you talking with Alex. Are you friends?"

"Just met him tonight, I take it you know him, too."

"Yes, he and Leighton are good friends. He was over here a lot before . . . before Celia died."

"Celia was his wife?"

"Yes. It was suicide, he found her in their garage. She'd shut the doors and started the car and just sat there and let it happen. What a horrible way to die."

"The papers were less than kind to him, I suppose."

"Those disgusting rags. One of the reporters all but broke into his home for an interview. Alex threw them out, and that's when they started writing those awful stories. They were clever about it, they didn't print anything they could be sued for, but the innuendo was nearly enough to ruin him. He's had to change his phone number several times because of the terrible calls, and once some kids stoned his studio and broke windows. People can be so awful."

"He did seem withdrawn."

"You can hardly blame him. He's been a complete recluse since then; I'm hoping his coming here means he's getting back to being his old self."

"Does that also mean getting back to painting?"

"I hope so. I know he hasn't done any work for months."

"He must have loved her a lot."

"Oh, yes," she agreed, absently distracted because a large man came up and put a friendly arm around her shoulders.

"How are you holding up?" he asked with good humor. He had a drink and cigarette balanced in his free hand and looked comfortably happy about the world in general. Like Reva, I knew his face from the photo in the paper.

"Just fine, Leighton," she replied. "And you?"

"I can do this for hours yet." He removed the arm from her shoulders and extended a hand at me. "Leighton Brett, guest of honor of all this madness."

"Jack Fleming."

He was larger and even more solid than the newspaper photo implied. It only hinted at the rich, curly brown hair and had left out the laugh lines round his eyes. There was no hint of the planned calculation his paintings showed, and I wondered if Sandra had just been pulling my leg.

"Mr. Fleming is here with Bobbi Smythe, Leighton."

This garnered a broad smile. "She's doing a wonderful job in there."

"I'll be sure to tell her."

"Did you know that Alex was here tonight?" Reva asked him.

"Yes, I finally talked him into coming. It's about time he got back to normal again. He's had too much of his own company and needs to remember life goes on."

"We were just talking about Celia—"

"Not where he or anyone else could hear, I hope. You know he's just coming out of it, the last thing he needs is for all that gossip to start up again."

"It won't be repeated," I said.

"I should hope not," he rumbled, and Reva looked uncomfortable. A subject change again seemed in order.

"I had a question for you on one of your paintings—"

"Certainly, go ahead."

"The farm scene in the paper that won the award, have you painted any duplicates of it?"

"Certainly not. What do you mean, 'duplicates'?"

"I happened to see a very similar painting once before in someone's office, and I'd heard that artists sometimes make copies of their own work."

"If I want copies I do a print or an engraving. Where did you see this?"

"In a private office, three fairly big paintings. The owner got them through a decorator, but I don't know the name."

"Reva?"

She shook her head. "I don't remember selling three of that size to any one person or company, not all at once, anyway. It could be an imitator, there are a lot of them around."

"Far too many and you're being too kind, girl. Those bastards are little more than forgers, as far as I'm concerned. A man works for years to get his style, and then they just jump in and make a fortune off all my efforts. I want to see these paintings. Where are they?"

It did not strike me that Gordy would appreciate having an artist of even Brett's reputation barging around his office and asking questions. "I'm not at liberty to say, but I can ask the owner permission for you to—"

"Ask permission? Look, if someone is cheating me and the public out of my work, I want to know about it." His voice rose; apparently he was very unused to getting no for an answer.

Heads were turning and Reva had backed away, flushing beet red with embarrassment. I did what I could to keep my voice calm and even. "I can't tell you now, but I'll look into it for you, I promise."

He paused, blinked, and seemed to realize he was on the verge of making a scene. He chose to ignore it altogether. "Good, call me as soon as you know anything." His good humor returned an instant later. Reva's color evened out again, but her tone was a little forced as she drew my attention to a still life on the wall. The people around us gradually went back to their own conversations. I stuck it out and made some kind of comment or other. Brett responded well to my inexpert praise, and even indulged in some modest self-critique.

"Yes, but it's a bit old now, at least to my eyes. I've learned a lot since that one was painted. I suppose we ought to sell it off and replace it with something better."

"It looks fine to me," I said, hoping the remark didn't sound as false to him as it did to me.

Reva stepped in. "Brett always says things like that; every artist knows his next painting will be better than the last."

"And it's always true," confirmed Brett. "Have you been by the gallery yet?"

The safe and sane small talk continued until someone else claimed their attention and I could decently slip away. It was past time for me to return to the long hall and see how Bobbi was getting along.

The sound of the music was my guide, Bobbi was singing again, another slow club number that could make a statue weep. The place was as crowded as before but I managed to squeeze through and catch her eye. She gave me a discreet nod without pausing in her song of hope and heartbreak.

The crowd had backed off to create an impromptu dance floor, and couples swayed to the slow music. I was a little surprised to see Adrian among them. He didn't seem the sort to indulge in frivolity, but perhaps Sandra had talked him into it. She was one of those rare ones who could do that without seeming pushy. Her head rested contentedly against his shoulder and neither of them were in any pain.

Someone appeared abruptly at my side, Walt from the kitchen. He was looking anxiously at the dancers.

"Something wrong?" I asked.

He recognized me. "Well, yes, sort of . . . Mr. Robley . . ."

"He needs to see his sister?"

"No, sir, I think the last person he'd want to see is his sister. He mumbled something about Mr. Adrian."

It sounded ominous, but I didn't want to break in on them. All the world loves a lover and all that, and I had more than one romantic bone holding up my carcass. "He's busy, let's see if I can substitute."

Relieved, he led me out by another door to a hallway and eventually to a linen closet. Evan was at the bottom of it with blood on his face.

3

HE moaned as the hall light hit him.

Walt said, "I was getting some more towels and found him. I thought he was just sleeping one off until I saw he was hurt. He wanted I should get Mr. Adrian to help take him home."

I knelt next to him and felt his arms and ribs. Since he didn't yell any objections, I assumed nothing was broken. "Evan? Can you tell us what happened?"

"Truck with fists," he mumbled. There was a small cut over one eye, but most of the gore was seeping gently from his nose. I borrowed one of the towels, held it to his face, and told him to tilt his head back.

"There's a bathroom just next to us," Walt offered helpfully.

We gave Evan another minute to get his breath back, then I all but carried him out. He sank gratefully onto the closed lid of the toilet and sat quietly while Walt and I cleaned off the worst of the mess. In addition to his already-bruised cheek, his left eye was swelling shut. The first real sign of life was his shocked yelp when I dabbed antiseptic on the cut.

"Who did it?" I asked.

"Dreyer—what're you trying to do, top him?" He pushed the swab of cotton away petulantly. "One of his boys must have followed me around. I've never known such a sore loser."

"I think you're the one that lost."

"Walt, be a pal and find me something for the pain."

Walt obligingly searched the medicine cabinet until Evan made it clear he wanted his painkiller in a glass with ice.

I resumed cleanup on his face. "You want to go home?"

"Yes, I think that would be a very good idea."

"What about Sandra?"

"Oh, God . . . tell her I got an unexpected date and went home early. She'll understand. I hope."

"You have a way home?"

That stumped him, so I offered him a ride, which he woozily accepted. When Walt returned I told him to keep Evan in one place while I went back to the long hall.

Bobbi was singing "Gimme a Pigfoot" to the raucous delight of the crowd, and Titus Noble's quartet was attempting an impromptu accompaniment. Sandra was still with Adrian, no longer dancing, but standing on the edge of things and clapping in time to the music. Adrian's enjoyment looked a little forced, but the hesitant smiles he gave Sandra were genuine enough. I elbowed over and passed on Evan's message to her.

"A date?" she puzzled. "Who with?"

I shrugged. "He didn't want you to worry about him, he said."

"There's a first time for everything," commented Adrian, not too helpfully.

Leaving them, I scribbled a quick note to Bobbi explaining I was driving home a drunk guest and would be back for her before the party was over. Since I couldn't interrupt her, I opted to give it to the cello player, who wasn't doing too much at the moment. I didn't trust Marza to pass it along.

Evan was anything but enthused over moving. The bruises were stiffening up, and now he insisted he'd be happy enough spending the rest of the night on the bathroom floor. When Walt offered to check with Reva about the loan of a bedroom, Evan changed his mind. One question would lead to another and eventually involve Sandra. He had no wish to listen to another sisterly lecture on the virtues of moderation and the avoidance of rough company.

Walt guided us out by a side door and would have helped us the rest of the way to my car except for Jannie's piercing shout. The spare towels were long overdue by now. I told him to go back; Evan was a handful, but nothing I couldn't manage.

I was wrong.

The pounding on his stomach combined with that last drink ended in a predictable way. The cold night air hit Evan like a bag of cement, he went green, made a green noise in his throat, and doubled over. I was just quick enough to aim him at the flower beds before he lost it all.

"Ridiculous, isn't he?"

Adrian was in the doorway watching the show and not quite grinning.

"I've seen worse," I said truthfully. "I'm taking him home. Dreyer got to him again and he didn't want Sandra—"

"Evan never fails to be considerate of others, at least after the fact. Need some help?"

"Yeah."

When it was over we hauled Evan past the long line of cars and loaded him into the back of my Buick, where he promptly fell asleep.

"You followed?" I asked Adrian.

"Of course. Your story to Sandra didn't sound like Evan at all. When he falls in love for the evening, one generally doesn't know about it until the next afternoon. He's in no condition to give you directions now, I'll come along if you don't mind."

"Hop in."

I started it up, carefully backed out, and only remembered to turn the headlights on by correctly reading the growing alarm on Adrian's face. We rolled slowly down the drive to the distant street, and he guided us from there.

"This happen to you often?" I asked.

"If you mean taking Evan home in such a condition, yes. I've done it more than once."

"The guy that found him was looking for you at first. Sorry this had to interrupt your evening with Sandra."

"We'll be back soon enough."

"I had an interesting talk with her about Leighton Brett's art . . . do you agree with her views?"

"I'm not certain what they are."

"I thought his stuff was too perfect, she said he planned it to be that way."

"No doubt she is right. Leighton insists on a great deal of control in his life, there's no reason why his art should be different."

"Doesn't that limit creativity?"

"That depends on your approach. All good art requires control, the real skill is not letting the control itself show."

"It should look easy? Like anyone could do it?"

He glanced over once, approving. "Exactly. You end up with a thousand students going in for art. It looks easy, especially the more modern schools. That's how Evan got started. He thought that anyone could slop paint over a canvas and call it art, but he surprised himself and a few other people. He's one of the few with a true talent for the expression of an idea as well as the work."

"But what about Brett's control?"

"He paints what the public wants to see and he does it so well. Not many of them notice what's missing."

"What's that?"

"Leighton Brett."

"Yeah?"

"Art is often a process of self-revelation, but he's a careful and private man, and his work reveals nothing of what is within him. He paints what's popular and saleable and enjoys the honors involved, such as they are. All you'll know about him from his paintings a hundred years from now was that he was a competent draftsman with a streak of bogus sentiment."

"What will people know about you a hundred years from now?"

"Probably the same thing, but without the sentiment."

"I doubt that."

"Why?"

"I've seen your work—nothing bogus there."

He looked at me sidewise. I'd meant it to be a compliment; he decided to take it as such. "Are you an artist as well?"

I hesitated, considering his past associations with reporters. "I write a little, so I can understand the creative process from that angle."

"What do you write?"

Nothing so far, but you don't say that to people. I decided on the truth and if he didn't like it, too bad. "I used to be a journalist, a paper in New York, but I had to get out."

"Had to?" he asked after a long pause. "Why?"

"I didn't like what it was turning me into so I stopped and became something else. I'm free-lance now."

His voice would freeze fire. "And is this an interview?"

"No. We're just two guys driving another home and having a talk about art."

I don't think he took it at face value, but then he had no real reason to trust me. Except for his terse directions, conversation lagged, but he wasn't ready to bolt from the car yet.

We ended up in a lower-class neighborhood of tired brick buildings, cheap rent being the only obvious asset of the area. We dragged Evan from the car and got him up the steps of his house. Adrian struggled with the keys while I kept us more or less vertical.

Inside the narrow entry hall were the usual doors and stairs, which we went up, or tried to; Evan was so far gone as to be a danger to our collective balance. I had Adrian stand back, then hoisted Evan onto my shoulder in a fireman's carry.

"The strength of youth," he said, and led the way up to the second floor and opened the door of the Robleys' flat.

The front room was obviously a work area, its length running along one wall to take advantage of the north-facing windows. Two large easels were set up, one with a light cloth covering a work in progress, the other with its colorful canvas on display. The place was stuffy with the smell of linseed oil and harsh turpentine. The furnishings were sparse and unpretentious: some simple chairs and a table with a lumpy bronze sculpture as its centerpiece. A few unframed paintings clung to the walls, mixed in with a family photo or two. One of them was of two young men grinning like devils, hamming it up at some kind of carnival. A slender girl stood between them and their arms were around her. It was Sandra, a young teen just starting to bloom into a woman. One of the men was Evan, who hadn't changed much in looks or attitude. The other was Adrian, who had. A lot of years and life had come between the carefree face in the photo and the solitary, saturnine man who stood next to me.

Adrian turned on the lights and pointed me toward the back, where I found Evan's bedroom. I eased him onto the bed and threw a quilt over him. I was just debating whether to remove his shoes when I heard an oddly familiar slap-and-grunt combination and hurried out to investigate.

Adrian was doubled over, holding his stomach. A man in a cheap, gaudy suit stood just inside the front door and had apparently just walked in and punched him. A second, much larger man bulled his way past, grabbed Adrian's elbows from behind and hauled him upright with a sharp jerk. Cheap Suit laughed and landed another fist before he noticed my presence.

I grabbed the larger man from behind in his turn and pried his arms free. Adrian all but hit the floor, still trying to get his lost breath back. The big one shook an arm loose and swung it backhanded at my face. A couple of months earlier I'd have been flattened, but now I was just annoyed. I was about to let him know just how annoyed when the suit jumped in between us waving a knife under my nose.

He was grinning because he knew he had me cold, a wild-eyed maniac with bad skin and cartoon eyebrows. I released my hold on his friend. They were moving slowly now, but only because I was moving that much faster. His mouth dropped open in sluggish shock when I plucked the knife out of his hand and snapped the blade and handle in two like a dry twig. By the time he started to recover, Adrian grabbed both his shoulders and spun him around to pay his own respects.

The big one tried hitting me again. He was a solid piece of muscle and had had some sparring experience. His punches were short and controlled but I wouldn't let him get close enough to connect. This put him into a bad temper, but I wasn't feeling too kindly about things, either. I stepped into his right, trapped his arm under my own, and much to his surprise wrestled him against a handy wall, thumping his head for good measure. When we locked eyes I went in there as well, feeling righteous satisfaction when his expression went blank.

"Fall on the floor and stay there," I told him, and stepped back out of the way. He landed hard, like a tree trunk, without putting his arms out to cushion the impact.

Adrian was too busy to notice. I'd gotten peripheral glimpses of his fight, but nothing really clear. Now it was obvious he had one hell of a temper and had just lost it. He held the man up by his loud necktie and was systematically hitting his face and gut with hard, vicious punches. His teeth were bared in a parody of a smile, and breath hissed between them each time he connected. He backed the man up to a wall, then caught his throat and started squeezing to kill.

I had to step in then or end up with a pop-eyed corpse. Adrian ignored hearing his name, but I managed to work his hands loose without breaking anything and pulled him away. The suit, considerably rumpled, sank to the floor, too battered to even moan.

Adrian suddenly became aware of things and shook me off with a muted growl. He glared at the man, puffing from the exertion, his lips peeled back wolflike, as if he'd welcome an excuse to start over again. He glanced at me, his eyes bright. The barriers were down for a moment and I wasn't sure I liked what they'd been hiding.

"Who are they?" I asked.

He checked both faces carefully, contemptuously. "Damned if I know. Probably more of Evan's friends."

"Dreyer again?"

"Perhaps."

I stooped and felt around for Cheap Suit's wallet. The Illinois license identified him as Francis Koller. He was carrying nearly eight hundred dollars, which I showed to Adrian in passing. Adrian searched the pockets of the other man.

"His name's Toumey. What's the matter with him? He looks like he's in a trance."

"Glass jaw," I said, and shoved Koller's wallet back in his pocket. He didn't look in any condition to remember his own name, much less answer questions, so I left him and knelt over Toumey, tapping his mug a few times for effect. "Hey, come out of it."

It worked faster than I expected. His eyes lost their fixed stare and got wider. He made an abortive attempt to get up, except I got a grip on one shoulder and leaned a knee into his stomach. My fingers were very strong; he winced and tried to writhe away, but Adrian was on his other side and held him down as well.

"Okay, Toumey, you tell us all about it," I instructed.

He went slack and staring again.

"Why did you come here?"

"Shake 'im up."

"Who?"

"Robley."

"Why?"

"Owes money."

"Give me a name."

"Dimmy Wallace."

I looked at Adrian. He shook his head. "Who's Dimmy Wallace?"

"*Shut up, Toumey.*" This from Koller, who was still flat on his back and trying to talk through battered lips.

"He must be the brains of the outfit," I commented to Adrian. "Toumey, you stay right where you are until I say otherwise, got it?" Toumey nodded, his eyes glazed. Adrian had begun to notice something odd going on, but if necessary I could fix that, too. We switched to Koller. He was just starting to roll over to get to his feet so we each slammed him flat again, and none too gently.

"Dimmy Wallace," said Adrian. "Talk."

He told Adrian to go somewhere and do something. I grabbed Koller's chin and forced him to look up at me. "Think about it, Francis, it's two to one now and you're already bleeding on the canvas. You want I should let my friend here finish the job he started on you?"

"Don't call me Francis," he muttered, but contact was established and he was under my influence for the moment.

"Who's Wallace?"

"My boss, best in the city."

"What does he do?"

"Big man, does it all."

"Gambling?"

"The works."

"A mob?"

"The biggest, the best there is."

"One can't fault him for his loyalty," Adrian remarked. "So Evan owes money to Dimmy Wallace, the one mobster in Chicago who hasn't made the papers yet."

"To judge from his hired help, I doubt he ever will. My guess is these saps don't even know what Evan looks like."

"You mean they mistook me for . . . ?" his lips thinned with disgust. "Now *that* is adding insult to injury. What do we do with them?"

"Kick 'em down the stairs?" I suggested.

He considered it. "What about informing the police?"

It was a little surprising that he would want to drag them in, especially if he still had a cloud over him because of his wife's death. To me, the cops meant charges, arrests, court appearances. Daytime stuff. "Hardly seems worth the trouble," I said, hoping I wouldn't have to talk him into it.

"Perhaps you're right. Let's throw them out."

"Hey!" was all Koller had time to say before we hauled him through the door and downstairs. I made sure he was shaken up, but not seriously hurt when we finally dropped him in the gutter outside. He started up with the obscenities again along with dire threats against the Robleys and everyone that knew them. While Adrian watched from the doorway I picked Koller up by his necktie and pushed him backward over a handy car hood.

"You got a bad mouth on you, boy, so shut it before you lose it. Go back to your roach hole and tell your boss to use the phone the next time he wants to collect on a bill. You or Toumey show up here again and—"

I didn't finish the threat, it was unnecessary. Koller saw exactly what he never wanted to see in my eyes. I gave him just enough to scare him, then let him go. He stumbled once, regained his footing, and ran down the block like hell was after him. He never looked back.

Adrian's expression was closed and watchful again. "I wish I had your way with people."

I shrugged. "Let's get the other one."

Toumey was more quiescent than his partner, content to be led to the exit and shoved out, again with the instructions never to return. We got back to the flat and checked on Evan, who had slept through the party.

Adrian stripped away the quilt, picked up a bedside carafe, and poured what was left of the contents on Evan's face. What all the roughhouse and noise failed to do a half cup of water accomplished: Evan shot awake, flailing and spitting.

"You'll drown me!" he wailed.

"Not unless I strangle you first. Wake up." Adrian went to the bathroom off the hall and brought back a towel for him.

Evan vaguely blotted at the water, confused and muttering. "First there's Dreyer, then Sandra, then Dreyer, and then you. What's the matter with everyone tonight?"

"We've all had to deal with you. Who's Dimmy Wallace?"

"Who?" he said, a little too innocently.

"Two of his people were just here," I informed him. "And we both took a beating that was meant for you, so you owe us."

"What?"

I repeated the story until he said he understood things, but his comprehension might also have had something to do with Adrian refilling the carafe.

"All right," he grumbled, "but Sandra won't like me showing the dirty laundry."

"That's never bothered you before," Adrian pointed out.

Evan snarled blearily at him. "In your ear."

The carafe began to tilt.

"I didn't mean it! Dimmy's my bookie, sort of."

"We're listening."

"That's it—really. He gave me some credit on my losses, said he'd wait until I sold something. Well, I sold something, but then he said I owed him interest as well. I told him to wait until I sell another painting, but he's not the patient kind—"

"And the longer it takes to pay, the more your interest increases?" I put in.

"Exactly."

"You've paid the original debt, though?"

"And then some."

I had a deep and very sincere stab of sympathy for Sandra.

Adrian was simply exasperated but willing to take action. "Get your toothbrush, Evan. Sandra's as well."

"Huh?"

"I'm not leaving her alone in this house while people like that are after you."

"But *I'm* here!"

"As I said, she's not going to be left alone."

Maybe I could have assured him the toughs wouldn't be back, but someone like Dimmy Wallace would have others to take their place. "Okay, you guys pack the toothbrushes, I'll drive."

About ten minutes later we were in the car, making a circle back toward Leighton Brett's neighborhood, but not quite. The mirror was clean, no one had followed us.

Adrian directed me to a less pretentious area of quiet houses with demure picket fences and regular streetlights. His home was a long one-storied structure, with a closed garage on one side. On the paving in front of it was an oil stain marking the spot where his car usually stood. Somehow I wasn't too surprised he no longer used the garage for its original purpose.

Evan was installed in a long-unused guest room and went thankfully back to sleep with a soft groan. Adrian threw a blanket on him and shut off the lights.

"He might be disoriented when he wakes up," I cautioned.

"It won't be a new experience for him."

I followed him into the kitchen. Perhaps it had been a bright place once; cheery little feminine knickknacks decorated the walls and cupboards. Now they were dull with dust, and the once-fluffy white curtains hung limp and dejected. The usual litter of inexpert cooking and casual cleanup cluttered the counters, and a plate with its dried scraps rested on the table where Adrian had eaten the latest in a series of solitary meals.

He rummaged around in some half-opened parcels on the table and brought out a box of headache powders. He mixed a double dose in a glass of water and drank it straight down. "Need any?" he offered.

"No, thanks."

He edged the glass in with a dozen others by the sink. The sad atmosphere of the house was uncomfortable. It seemed to ooze from the walls, or more likely from Adrian. Either from his wife's death or by his natural temperament, he'd turned everything inward, and though too polite to obviously show it, he did not like having a stranger in his home, especially an observant ex-journalist.

When we got back to the party his posture relaxed slightly. He'd gone from being on guard to something else I couldn't quite read, and was twisting his wedding ring around again.

"Thank you," he murmured. "I'll find Sandra and tell her what happened."

"Anytime," I said to his departing back as he disappeared into the crowd.

Bobbi was still in the big hall, but taking a break, or trying to. I could hardly see her for all the men grouped around, offering her enough drinks for a chorus line. One of them was Titus. He was close to Bobbi but facing outward, and doing a reasonable protection job by keeping the worst of the interlopers at bay. I squeezed my way to the center to relieve him. Without a word he took her hand and gave it to me, an exaggerated gesture, but necessary considering the tipsy state of most of the men. A few backed off to give us room, and we escaped into the garden again.

She drew a deep breath and laughed a little. "Thought I was going to smother. Titus tries his best, but he's not as tall as you."

"Things did look a little crowded."

"Marza says they're like a pack of dogs following a—" She suddenly blushed. "Never mind, I had one glass of champagne and it's making me rude."

"You get my note?"

"Yes, who'd you take home?"

"Some artist I met here. He had a little too much party so we took him to Alex Adrian's house—"

"*The* Alex Adrian?"

"Absolutely. I met him tonight."

"I had no idea he was here. What's he like?"

"Distant. The sort of smoldering type women go crazy for, except in his case I think the fire's gone out."

"Must be because of his wife."

"What do you know about it?"

"That she committed suicide, maybe, or was murdered, maybe. You met him. What do you think?"

"The jury's still out for me. Are you on a break or is the party over yet?"

"I'm on a break. My contract expires at one A.M., and then you can take me home and put me to bed."

"With great pleasure, but I thought—"

"You thought right. I *am* tired, so I'm very glad I decided to seduce you earlier. Do you mind just tucking me in?"

I pulled her close and let her know exactly how I felt on that subject.

Rather than let her out of my sight again, I sat in the hall, gritting my teeth through the string quartet pieces until I could take her home. It was twenty minutes to quitting time when Sandra Robley drifted in, spotted me, and came over.

"Thank you for helping Evan," she said as I stood.

"You're welcome."

"Would *you* please tell me what happened?"

"Alex clam up on you?"

"It's his specialty. He said there was some trouble, but won't tell me what kind or why it means Evan and I have to stay at his house for the night."

"He thought it might be safer." I briefly outlined what had happened at her flat. "We didn't break anything, hut he wasn't about to leave you and Evan alone with those goons on the loose. You know about Dimmy Wallace?"

"Only that Evan owes him money."

I had an idea or two on how to help them, but decided to wait before committing myself.

"It's unbelievable that these people think they can just walk in—and neither of you thought to call the police?"

"Well, I—"

She made a dismissive gesture. "At least I know how Alex's knuckles got scraped. Honestly, sometimes he can he so infuriating. You as well. I'm grateful about Evan, but should it happen again, just tell me the truth, no more stories on last-minute dates."

I raised three fingers. "Scout's honor, ma'am."

She melted a little and flashed a muted version of her smile. "Thank you. Now I'm going to talk to Alex about his overprotective attitude."

It must not have been a long lecture, for about ten minutes later they both turned up again. Sandra was on his arm and he almost looked relaxed as they listened to the music.

"That's good to see." Reva Stokes appeared next to me, watching them with contentment. "No, please don't get up, I'm just passing by and wanted to check on things."

"They're special to you?"

"Very special friends. When Celia died we thought Alex might do the same thing, but tonight he seems to be coming out of it. I'm glad Sandra's there for him."

"Sandra seems pretty glad about it as well. I wish her luck."

"With a brother like Evan, she'll need it. I haven't seen him for a while, I hope he's—"

"Alex and I took him home earlier. He was tired."

She made a wry face. "Is that what you call it?"

"When in polite society, yes. Thank you for having me along, it's meant a lot to Bobbi."

"You're welcome. Are you in the entertainment business yourself?"

"In a way. I'm a writer."

"What do you write?"

Good question. I gave her a song and dance about a novel I'd started in high school and she lost interest quickly enough. It's probably the reason I never finished the thing and went into journalism instead.

One o'clock finally came and Bobbi launched into one last song, its theme concerned with saying good night and goodbye. A few of the more sober guests took the hint and drifted out, and Reva vanished to see them on their way. Bobbi finished and took her bows, and I felt free to intrude on the stage area before various young swains flooded her with offers of a ride home.

"Fleming."

It was Adrian. Sandra was busy for the moment talking with a trio of gaunt-looking women dressed in black velvet.

"Everything okay? I had to tell Sandra about—"

"Yes, that's all fine now. I wanted to clear some business up with you . . . about that portrait commission."

He had my full attention. "Yeah, what'd you want to clear?"

Adrian didn't quite meet my eye, but it seemed more from diffidence than anything shifty. He was like a man unsure of the thickness of ice under his feet. "Did you still want to engage me for the commission?"

"Yes, certainly, but—"

"Do you think you can afford it?"

I couldn't fault him for his honesty—or at least bluntness. "How much?" He named a figure I could live with and I told him so. "Is it a deal?"

He didn't answer right away, apparently still testing the ice within him. "Yes . . . I think so. The usual procedure is half down and half on delivery."

"Fine. I can get it for you tomorrow, if that's okay."

"One thing, Fleming. I—I'm not sure I can do it. . . . If I find I cannot, I'll return the money."

I nodded. "Fair enough. And if you can?"

"Then you get your portrait and I get the balance, of course."

"Deal." I held out my hand. He didn't seem to understand what it was there for at first, then hesitantly shook it. "What made you change your mind?"

From his wallet he gave me a business card with his name and number. "Call me sometime tomorrow and we'll work out a schedule for the sittings. Good night." He turned and went back to Sandra.

Bobbi broke off her chatting with Titus and came over. "What was that all about? Who was—"

I slipped an arm around her. "*The* Alex Adrian, and that was about my Christmas present to you."

"I see what you mean about smoldering—what Christmas present?"

"Well, it might take that long for the paint to dry."

"Jack—"

"You said you didn't want diamonds, but what about your portrait done by—"

She gave out a soft shriek of pure delight and threw her arms around me in a stranglehold.

4

IT was nearly two-thirty by the time I'd dropped off Marza and Madison, saw Bobbi safe into her hotel apartment, and said good-bye. I had hours yet before dawn and these were always the hardest to fill. Bobbi invited me to stay, but she was exhausted, so I left her to her well-earned sleep.

The streets were fairly empty: only the odd carload of party goers hooting past and an occasional lonely figure wrapped against the night and out on God knows what business. I was driving north again and for the second time that week parked close to the Nightcrawler Club and walked up the steps past the big doorman. He nodded once at me, perhaps because someone had clued him in on Gordy's preferential treatment. It was his version of a polite greeting.

There was a new singer working with the band, a pretty brunette with a feisty manner. Whoever did Gordy's booking knew talent. I passed by the club and went through to the casino without trouble. The games were still going strong and would continue until either the money or the night ran out. I recognized a slab-faced blackjack dealer and sat at his table for a hand or three.

His mug was immobile, but he couldn't control his heartbeat, which I was able to hear well enough. It thumped just a little faster whenever he got a good hand. I didn't consider my listening in on his reactions to be cheating. This was just using my unnatural abilities to help ease the odds in my favor. Not all the cards were good, but when I left the table I was a sweet two hundred ahead. It'd make a nice Christmas present for my folks when the time came.

The man in the money cage said Gordy was in his office, maybe. I didn't bother to ask for an escort through the back door of the casino into the halls beyond, but one of the boys followed—just to make sure I didn't get lost, he told me.

"You gotta 'pointment?" he asked, eyeing the lines of my suit for hidden weapons. He wasn't sure if I required a frisk or not, my level of importance to his boss had yet to be established.

"Didn't know I needed one just to visit."

He looked vaguely familiar and I wondered if he'd been one of the boys who put a knife into Escott last month. I was about to ask, but the office door opened and Gordy told him to get lost. It was just as well.

"What's up?" He motioned me in and I took my usual chair.

"Nothing much, had a question or two."

"Maybe I'll answer." He sat behind his desk this time and I studied the rural landscape behind him. It certainly looked like Leighton Brett's work to my uneducated eye.

"Know anyone named Dimmy Wallace?" I asked.

"Small-time bookie and loan shark."

"Doesn't sound like much."

"He isn't. Why you want to know?"

"He's squeezing a friend of mine dry with interest on a debt he's already paid."

"It's a tough world."

"You know where I can find him?"

"I might. Who's your friend?"

"Some artist, not much sense and less money, but likable."

"Gambler?"

"Yeah. He's losing money he doesn't have."

"Name?"

"Evan Robley."

Gordy socked the name away into his memory, that much passed over his deadpan face. "You won't have to find Dimmy, I'll get the word out."

"What'll you do?"

"Tell Dimmy he's screwing 'round with a friend of mine and to lay off. I'll let some others know Robley's a bad credit risk, make it harder for him to place a bet in this town. I don't need my own bookies stretching themselves on a mark with no bucks. They got enough troubles as it is."

"Thanks, Gordy, I didn't expect you to—"

" 'S nothing. How's Bobbi doin'?"

"Just beautiful, finished a job tonight at a swank home by the yacht basin. Marza did the piano and they had a string quartet for in between sets."

"Marza, huh? That broad's like sandpaper on a cut."

"I know what you mean. The guest of honor was this big-time artist, I think he may have done the paintings you have here."

Gordy's gaze traveled the walls automatically. "That'd be something, wouldn't it?"

"He doesn't remember doing them, though. I sort of promised I'd see if he had or not."

He lifted a hand. "Feel free."

I did. None of them had Brett's distinctive signature. I turned the woodscape over and just saw the name of the framers. "Did you get them from a gallery?"

"The decorator's. They had a stack of these in a bin and I picked what I liked best."

"An oil like this was in a bin?" Even I could see some work had gone into it.

"That's what I wondered, but the lady there said people pick art to go with the color of their sofa. You figure it."

"It's too screwy to figure, I'll pass." But it did sound pathetic and I could visualize hundreds of would-be Rembrandts daubing away to produce acres of mediocre canvas for the public just to make their rent payment. The difference in Gordy's case was the quality of the work. These were something I could live with, and I hadn't liked the stuff in Leighton Brett's home.

"What decorators?"

"Place downtown, they're in the book."

It was another swank outfit, but then between the club and casino Gordy could afford it. At this hour of the morning it was very firmly closed, not that that stopped me. I had nothing better to do. Going to an all-night movie or tiptoeing around the house so as not to wake Escott had no appeal at the moment. I slipped inside the street door of the decorator's and scented the air.

No watchman, but it wasn't exactly a bank. The average thief isn't interested in pieces of fabric or carpet patterns, and the chances of cash on the premises were slim. I prowled through pseudo-living rooms, looked at pictures on display, and found the bin of oil paintings Gordy mentioned. Several bins, in fact: unframed canvases of all sizes, with every kind of art style from every period, they were determined to please everyone. A few were signed, but most were anonymous, which bothered me. Either the artists were too modest or not proud enough. One or two were interesting, but I didn't find any that resembled Brett's style.

The office was locked, which was no problem; I just slipped inside. The desk drawers were also locked. Problem. Breaking the drawers open wouldn't be very nice and I didn't have Escott's talent for undetectable burglary. One of these nights I'd have to ask him for a few basic lessons. My curiosity wasn't that urgent, though, and neither was Brett's, as far as I was concerned. He could have the name of the place and run his own investigation.

Escott wasn't home when I woke up the next night, but he'd read my note and gotten the requested cash from his hidden safe. Because of the big crash, neither of us trusted banks, and because of his association with me, we'd both ended up with a parcel of money that needed a cache. His solution was to purchase an extremely solid safe and then carefully hide it.

He had a passion for secret panels, hidden doors, and similar camouflage, and the skill to indulge himself. The original basement steps were made of wood, hardly more than a scaffold running along the wall. He thought they were too rickety for regular use and had a crew come in and build something considerably more solid. He was careful to choose bricks that matched those on the outside of his house and then went to some effort to age them so that they would look like part of the original construction. He supervised the whole thing and even tried his hand at bricklaying, then paid off the workmen before they had finished the job.

He lugged the safe into the dead space under the stairs and started building up the courses. By the time he was finished, the safe was sealed in for the life of the house, but by pushing on a certain brick, four square feet of a solid-looking wall pivoted open, giving one complete access to the combination lock and door. He piled a few pieces of old furniture around the stairs to complete the effect of a derelict area. It was a neat job and he was proud of it.

I had the combination, but usually had him play teller whenever I needed money because he was particular about preserving the dust around the opening. When I checked, there was no evidence he'd touched the area in months, but the cash was in an envelope on the table next to my earth-layered cot. I switched the money to my wallet, picked out some clothes, and went upstairs to call Adrian.

Sandra answered.

"I thought you might be home by now," I said after identifying myself.

She had an unmistakable smile in her voice, which was very interesting. "No, Adrian insisted we stay a little longer, just in case. I don't mind."

The way she was looking at Adrian last night certainly supported that statement. I told her I was dropping by in an hour and to let Adrian know about it. She said yes, hung up, and then I called Bobbi.

"Want to meet the man who's going to immortalize you?"

"I've only been waiting all day. No offense," she added.

"None taken, I'll be right by."

My last call was to Leighton Brett, and I left the name of Gordy's decorator with one of the maids. From there on he was on his own.

Bobbi was dressed in a beautiful cream-colored suit with touches of brown velvet on the lapels and wrists. The hemline was low enough to be in fashion, but high enough to maintain a man's interest; the neckline deep, but not scandalous. She looked perfect, and all I wanted to do when I saw her was rip off the wrappings and carry her to the nearest couch for some serious fooling around. I settled for a kiss of greeting for the moment and escorted her down to my car.

We were both full of talk, the kind of happy nonsense that all lovers indulge in. She was still flying high from her job last night and her agent was arranging yet another radio spot.

"Will it be national again?" I asked.

"I don't know yet, but I've got that local broadcast next Saturday. Will you come to the studio and watch?"

"Just try and stop me. Need a ride there?"

"Of course."

"Marza, too?" This was less enthusiastically offered.

"Not this time, she has a job elsewhere that night."

"Gee, that's too bad."

"Admit it, Jack, you're ready to turn handsprings."

"Not really, I'd have to stop the car first."

I parked in Adrian's drive just behind his black coupe and opened Bobbi's door. "You nervous?"

"A little. I can't help but wonder about his wife."

The thought had occurred to me as well, but there wasn't much I could do about the situation. We walked up to the front door, which was immediately opened by Sandra. She'd exchanged her party clothes for some wide-legged slacks and a bright scarf to keep her curly hair in place. She had a dust cloth in one hand, a spotted apron around her slim waist, and looked very domestic except for the impishness in her eyes. She let us in and I did introductions.

"You're just in time for fresh coffee." She led the way to the kitchen, which had changed considerably since last night. The curtains were clean and the clutter cleared. You could actually sit at the table and see what it looked like. "It's funny, but it's so much easier to clean someone else's place than your own. Cream and sugar?"

Bobbi had a cup, I politely begged off. "I hope this wasn't too disruptive for you."

"What? Getting yanked out of my own home in fear for my life? Whatever gave you that idea?"

I thought of telling her it was all right to go back, but decided it would be best to let Evan know first. He may have had a rough time from Sandra today about his shortcomings and would be glad for some good news to give her.

"It hasn't been so bad, and I think the company's been good for Alex, but I'll want to go back soon."

"Too much housework?" asked Bobbi.

"Not enough paint. I never feel good about myself unless I paint a little each day, and cleaning isn't very spiritually fulfilling, if you know what I mean."

Bobbi commiserated, then I asked about Adrian.

"He's in his studio. He's been getting things ready since he got up this morning. I'm so happy to see him starting work again. This is what he's needed for so long."

"I should think the magazines would still want his art."

"They do, but since the . . . since his wife died he's refused their commissions. He'd shut himself away for so long we were afraid he'd never come out. I hope this will help him to do it."

"So do we. How's Evan doing?"

"He's got some awful bruises, but seems to feel all right. He's in the studio helping Alex. The place has been shut tight since January so there was some cleaning to do."

"If we've come too soon—"

"Not at all. Alex said this was the business meeting and he'll want to set up a schedule for the sittings with Miss Smythe. I'll take you through now."

The studio was just off the kitchen, a very large room seamlessly added onto the original lines of the house. A bank of high windows ran along its north wall to catch the light. They were open even now but covered with long white curtains that moved with the night breeze like lazy ghosts.

Except for an overstuffed couch and chair in the center, all the furnishings were geared toward Adrian's work. On one end were two slanted drawing tables, one with a light arranged beneath it to shine up through its translucent top. Other, more obscure equipment lined the walls and a huge bank of shelving held his supplies and finished work. In the center of the room was his easel, heavier and more complicated than the ones the Robleys owned. I felt like an intruder in a sorcerer's cave.

"Jack!" Evan looked up from his beer and hobbled over. His eye was still swollen shut and the area around it was gorgeously colored. "Recovered from last night, eh? Boy, was that a party or what?"

"Bobbi, this is Mr. Robley . . ."

He took her hand and tenderly kissed the back of it. "Evan to you, my sweet, and I'm your slave for life."

"Which is hardly an asset," said Adrian, stepping forward. "I'm Alex Adrian, Miss Smythe. I enjoyed your singing at the party very much." He neatly slipped her hand away from Evan and shook it, then mine. "Please come in." He gestured at the sofa and pulled up an old chair for himself. He looked different from last night; less formal and guarded. His manner with Bobbi hinted at the possibility of some considerable personal charm.

Sandra disappeared and Evan puttered in the background of the studio while we worked out the less artistic details of creation. There was some discussion on the size of canvas to be used and how to pose Bobbi.

"I'm not sure," she confessed. "You're the expert. Have you a rec-ommendation?"

"Yes," Evan said promptly.

"Be decent for once," Adrian warned.

"What I recommend is a neoclassic version of Goya's *Maja Desnuda* with less surrounding background."

"I told you to be decent."

"Well, she can leave her clothes *on,* of course! It's the *pose* I'm talk-ing about—that air of sensual relaxation. If you don't pick up on that, Alex, I swear I'll come in and paint it myself."

"You may try."

"*What* kind of pose?" asked Bobbi, carefully separating the words.

Adrian smiled. "Evan is suggesting I do a full-length portrait of you reclining on pillows. The choice of what to wear or not wear is entirely up to you, though."

"Oh, good," she said in mock relief.

The next point to work out were the sittings, something I'd have to miss since they'd be during the day for the sunlight. Evan's input had its effect and Bobbi asked if it would be all right if she could bring a friend along to watch. Adrian had no illusions about her wish for a chaperon, but then he had no objections, either.

"Three sittings, then," he announced. "An hour or so each should take care of it."

"But shouldn't it take much longer? I thought these things went on for weeks."

Evan broke in again. "Not with an expert like Alex and his style of work. What you're paying for is all the training he soaked up in the fancy French art institute he went to."

"And you should go there, Evan."

"There's a difference between an institute and an institution, no, thank you. Besides, I don't speak French."

I gave Adrian his half payment in an envelope. He seemed to approve of the straight cash and made out a receipt, which concluded the busi-ness meeting.

"If you've the time," he said, "I can make a preliminary sketch right now, just to block in the general form."

Bobbi glanced at me. I shrugged and nodded. Adrian had me move off the couch, produced a pillow, and told Bobbi to get comfortable. She suppressed a grin and relaxed back on the pillow. Adrian stood off a few feet, returned, and adjusted the position of her arm and backed off again.

"There's some strain on the line of the neck," Evan observed.

Adrian took the suggestion and tilted Bobbi's head a little. When he was satisfied he pulled one of the drawing tables from the wall and went to the storage shelves for a huge sheet of clean paper and a stick of charcoal. He made a half dozen sweeping lines and added a few precise strokes for details.

His face was totally different now that he was focused on the work. I saw serenity as well as concentration. Evan and I no longer existed for him; all that was important was his eye, his hand, and the model.

He reached a stopping point and had Bobbi come over for a look. Evan and I crowded in as well. The sofa had turned into a chaise lounge covered in plump pillows, but not so much that they overwhelmed Bobbi's reclining figure. She was languid but with an alertness in her eyes that seemed to dare the viewer to come closer. Her clothes were more suggestive of sweeping robes than the smart suit she wore, but anything else would have been inappropriate for the mood he was setting up.

"Is that what you see?" she asked.

"On a good day, yes. Will it do?"

"Absolutely. If this is the sketch, I can't wait to see the finished painting. This is like magic."

"Evan, I've some prepared canvas somewhere. . . ."

"Yeah, I put them . . . I'll get them." He rooted around and produced several sterile white canvases, already stretched and nailed over wood frames. Adrian chose the largest and put it on the massive easel.

I thought he'd repeat the sketch on the canvas, but instead he took a pin to the paper and punched tiny holes through it along all the major lines.

"What's he doing?" I whispered to Evan.

"It's how he transfers the sketch," he whispered back. "When he's got enough holes in it, he'll position the drawing where he wants on the canvas, then hit at it with a small bag of charcoal dust. The holes allow the dust to leave a guide mark for him to follow."

"Why not just draw on the canvas?"

"Too hard to clean off if you should change your mind about something."

The sketch drifted to the floor as he shifted his attention to the canvas, and I could see now how he was able to keep up with the demands the magazines had put on him. Only a few more minutes passed and he added in all the necessary details. Bobbi's face appeared out of the blankness, taking on expression and life.

He stood back again, studying it with a critical eye, but was apparently satisfied. "That will do for tonight, tomorrow I'll see to the underpainting, and you can come by the day after for the first sitting."

"I still can't get over the speed," she said.

Adrian found a rag and scrubbed at the charcoal dust clinging to his fingers. "Most of the time involved has to do with allowing the paint to dry—at least that's how it is for the way I work. All I ask is that after the final varnish dries you take it to a decent framer."

"We wouldn't do anything less."

Bobbi was looking with interest at some of the painted canvases stacked in slots and asked to see them, and Adrian obliged. Evan said he wanted another beer and invited me for one as well. I again turned down the offered drink, but tagged along to the kitchen.

"I've got some good news for you," I said as he searched the icebox. "I talked to a friend of mine and he's telling Dimmy to lay off on the interest payments."

He stopped cold. "Say that again."

I repeated it.

"Who's your friend?" he asked with amiable suspicion.

"Someone with an interest in art. He knows Dimmy and said he'd fix it. You and Sandra can probably go back home now."

"Honestly?"

"True blue."

"How in the world did you do it?"

"Well . . ."

"Never mind. Perhaps it's better I don't ask, you shouldn't question miracles, they're too few and far between." He popped the cap from a brown bottle. "This is great, really. I don't know what to say—except thanks—and that I don't plan to go home just yet."

"Yeah?"

He glanced around to see if anyone was in earshot and lowered his voice. "It's Sandra. You see, she's, well . . . it's her and Alex. You know . . . last night." He took a swig off the beer. "I was a bit out of things, but not that far out. Maybe I'm supposed to get upset since she's my sister, but she's a big girl now and—"

"Why should you stand in the way of romance?"

"Exactly! To tell the truth, I'd like to see her safely married or whatever to whoever—or is it whomever? Anyway, having Alex for a brother-in-law can't be much worse than having him for a friend, and she could do worse herself. Besides, it would get her out of *my* hair, that awful little walk-up we live in, and into *his* hair and a very cozy house, which is just what she needs."

"I hope it works out for you."

"Same here, so I won't come out with the glad news for a while yet, and I'm going to be fairly well oiled or at least look like I am before I turn in tonight to give them plenty of opportunity for more innocent sinning."

"Very considerate, but if you don't mind a personal question—"

"You've saved my life, so feel free."

"I was wondering about his late wife."

"Oh. That." His face fell. "What d'ya want to know?"

"Why did she kill herself?"

"Oh, I thought—" He caught himself and started over. "There you have me, friend. It took us all by surprise. I mean Celia and Alex had their rough moments like any other couple, but when she . . . well, it left us all flabbergasted. She seemed very normal and all. Normal, you know? It fairly tore Alex up. He looked like death himself for a while. I think that party last night was the first time he's really been out of the house since it happened."

"She leave a note?"

"Yeah, she said she just couldn't go on any longer. It was next to her on the car seat. You know how she died?"

"Yes, Reva mentioned it to me."

"Reva." He smiled. "Lovely girl . . . It shocked her, too. She and Celia were very good friends; they were both models. Celia married her artist, and Reva's about to, so I suppose they had a lot of notes to compare on the subject, not that Alex or Leighton are even remotely alike."

"How so?"

"They both paint and wear clothes and eat food, but beyond that they're night and day, stylistically and temperamentally. Like all that business in the studio, it was taken care of with a minimum of fuss and bother in about a quarter hour, right? If you'd gone to Leighton for the work you'd still be talking—and talking. He's more showman than anything. If someone comes to him for a commission he puts them to a lot of trouble so they think they're getting their money's worth. Then he'd have your girl sitting for a couple hours every day for two or three weeks so you think he's really earning his fee."

"That's what we expected with Alex."

"And he didn't give it to you. Art is a business with both of them, but Alex just gets on with it, and if people are disappointed with the lack of show, the finished product makes up for it."

"I'll say. That sketch he did was really great."

"And you don't need to worry about the painting, he'll do something to knock your eyes out."

"How did you two get together?"

He laughed. "It's been so long I hardly remember, we both go so far back. His family had money and mine didn't; he had the polish and I had the spit. I used to get him into a lot of trouble taking him off to pool halls and other fun places, then he'd show me how to look at things and draw them. We both had watercolors down by the time we were out of grade school. He'd won a few prizes and me, too, and then one day I sold something. It convinced me this was a way of making a living without working—that and the occasional crap game."

"And if you left the crap games alone you *could* make a living," said Sandra, coming in with a broom and dustpan. "Is he telling you the sad story of his life, Jack?"

"Not so sad," defended Evan. "I enjoy every moment." To illustrate, he drained off the rest of the beer and raided the box for another. Sandra rolled her eyes in mock suffering and left for the studio.

Evan grinned beatifically. "Before yesterday she'd have given me a five-minute lecture on gambling, drinking, and other forms of peaceable sport. Now she's so occupied with Alex it takes the pressure off me. Isn't love wonderful?"

I had to agree. "She and Alex have known each other just as long?"

"Not really. He was my friend mostly until we got older, then he went off to study in Paris for a couple of years. When he returned she started to notice him, but then he was off to New York getting established. He came back just after the crash; famous, quite thoroughly married to Celia, and off Sandra's eligible list."

"That's a funny way to describe a marriage."

"It applied to them. I liked Celia well enough, but she was a bit self-centered—no, that's not the word. . . ." He eyed the dwindling contents of the beer bottle. "I think this stuff is starting to get to me."

Before he could decide on his definition, Bobbi, Sandra, and Adrian walked in. Bobbi was pulling on her brown velvet gloves.

"All finished?" I asked.

"Jack, you should see the things he has in there, it's absolutely wonderful. Alex should have it in a gallery or museum. They're all too beautiful to be shelved up out of sight."

"Maybe you could talk to Reva," said Evan.

Adrian shrugged it off. "Another time. You're going to see her tomorrow, aren't you?"

"Yeah, sure, first thing, but I'm having my doubts."

"You promised, Evan, so don't try to get out of it," Sandra told him.

"I wouldn't do that, it's just I won't be held responsible if Reva says no. She'll be thinking of Leighton—"

"And Leighton thinks of himself," Adrian concluded, twisting his ring around again.

"Well, it *is* her gallery, of course she'll want to be selling his work and Reva might think my stuff would take away from his sales."

"Even though the gallery gets a commission should your work sell?"

"Not as much as they'd get from Leighton. He's very popular just now, you know."

"We know, but we also know your work is quite different from Leighton's and would attract a different audience. Reva will certainly want to widen the pool of prospective buyers."

"Not that wide . . . Can you imagine someone like Mr. Danube walking in for a look?"

Adrian apparently could and wisely shifted the point of his argument. "Sandra expects you to try."

"I *will* try, I've said so, but . . ."

"Yes?"

"Nothing, just but."

Sandra had her arms crossed and was leaning against a counter, watching the exchange with amusement. "Alex, he's just having a case of the shakes."

"Odd, that usually doesn't happen until the morning after the debauch."

Evan sighed dramatically. "They're talking like I'm not in the room anymore, which means I've become invisible again. If I could learn to control it I'd go on stage and make a fortune."

Sandra came over to put her arm around Evan. "You don't have to worry. Even if Reva says no, it won't diminish your work. You're a wonderful painter; sooner or later more people than just Mr. Danube will realize it."

"Sooner, I hope."

"Right now Leighton is popular with the public, but these things come in cycles. Your turn will come. Look at Impressionism; when it first came out everyone hated it, but now look what it's going for."

"Right, but aren't those artists all dead by now?"

She groaned. "Don't be so morbid, Evan."

5

"So what did you think of the higher arts?" I asked as Bobbi finished off the last of her vegetables.

"Not so high. It's a business, just like everything else. But I'm not saying that's bad. Artists have to eat, you know, speaking of which, thanks for supper."

We were in Hallman's, one of Escott's favorite haunts. It was a fancy place with potted palms and a staff that, in their bright uniforms, looked like fugitives from a Russian opera. Though the greatness of its food was forever lost to me, it was still a hell of a good place to impress one's girl-friend.

Bobbi did proper justice to her meal, which somewhat compensated things for our waiter. To keep from insulting him or the chef, I said I'd eaten earlier and pretended to nurse a cup of coffee.

"Sure you don't want a bite?" She offered a forkful dripping in rich sauce.

My throat constricted. "Not of that, no."

"You don't eat anything?"

" 'Fraid not."

She caught the look on my face. "Have I said the wrong thing?"

"Not you, sweetheart, you've a right to ask questions. I just don't know if this is a private enough place for me to answer them."

"You really think anyone here would take it seriously?"

"Why take chances?"

"Okay." She shrugged and changed the subject. "What was all that talk you and Evan had in the kitchen?"

"I was just letting him know some of his financial worries were over." I explained about the roughhouse with Dimmy Wallace's boys the night of the party. "Now you know why Sandra and Evan were camping out with Alex."

"How did you get the shark off his back?"

"I talked to Gordy about it and he did all the hard work. Guess I owe him a favor now."

"Maybe. He might not collect."

"Yeah? Why not?"

"Because of all that business with Slick. I think he still feels bad about slugging you around."

"I never felt a thing."

She didn't look convinced.

"Honest, he hardly laid a hand on me."

"Now you're sounding like Evan."

"Let's hope he's not catching. What were all those paintings like that Alex showed you?"

"It's hard to say, you just have to see them. He had everything: mountains, cities, there were dozens of portraits that he'd done for mag-azines—really famous people."

"And now you're going to be one of them."

"You think having Alex Adrian do my portrait will make me famous?"

"More likely the other way around."

"Why, thanks! But he's already famous."

"And he hasn't worked since January. Sabbaticals like that can ruin a career. You have to keep producing or risk being forgotten."

"Not this guy. His stuff ought to be in a book or something. With someone like him I'll bet hundreds of galleries would jump at the chance to exhibit his work."

"Maybe you can mention it to him during your sittings. Who you taking along for moral support?"

"You were my first choice."

I nodded a modest acknowledgment of my status with her. "And your second?"

"Probably Marza."

"You sure she won't curdle his creative process?"

"She's okay, except where you're concerned."

"Tell me what I've done this time."

"Nothing, as usual. Once Marza has an idea lodged in her head about someone, it's impossible to get it out."

I waved a playful fist. "I know a great way to—"

"It's a lost cause, Jack. She'll either have to get used to you or lump it."

"Lump it," I concluded. "Is it just me or does she hate all men?"

"Well, there's Madison, but I suppose he's so tied up with his politics he doesn't really count. She's not really a man hater, she just hasn't met a nice guy yet."

And with her attitude it seemed likely she never would. Where Marza was concerned, charity was not one of my stronger virtues.

"I think I'll ask Penny instead of Marza," she said thoughtfully. "She's a giggler with nothing in her head but clothes talk, but meeting Alex Adrian might keep her subdued."

"She's the skinny redhead I met at your housewarming?"

"Slender. And yes, that's her. You've got a good memory."

"She nearly dropped her drink on me. I tend to keep track of potential disasters. Just keep her from tipping Alex's paints over, he's got a temper."

"I don't doubt it."

"Why's that?"

"When he was showing me his canvases he came across a portrait of a woman and sort of froze. It was like I was next to a block of ice and I could feel the cold coming off him."

"And you think it was anger?"

She nodded. "Then he shook out of it, shoved the painting back, and brought out something else as though nothing had happened. I wanted to ask him about it, but it wouldn't have been polite, so I pretended not to have noticed. He was aware of it, too; damn social games."

"A portrait, you said?"

"I think it was his wife."

"Why?"

"Just a feeling from the way he acted. It's like those times when you say Charles can read your mind."

Escott was no swami, he just had his own method for figuring out people by the way they talked and moved. It was all based on deliberate and analytical observation and could sometimes be pretty spooky if you're not used to it. Bobbi wasn't as scientific minded, but I could put as much stock in her intuition as Escott's logic. Both were pretty reliable.

The evening ended very pleasantly at Bobbi's and I almost didn't need the elevator to float down to the lobby and out the door. The euphoria was enough that I hardly noticed the ghost-town streets during my leisurely drive to Chicago's huge library. I parked under one of the multi-globed lamps and made a cautious sweep of the area for watchers. The last thing I needed was a beat cop taking notice.

Things were clear and I slipped inside. Literally. Vampirism has disadvantages, but sometimes it can be fun. The whole place was mine, no interruptions, no distractions; all I had to do was remember to get home before dawn, which was hours away yet.

I headed for the newspaper section and located their morgue, searching out all the editions from the previous January. They were very informative about the usual New Year's celebrations and stories on the first babies born after midnight.

The Celia Adrian suicide made the front page on the afternoon of the third. Details were sparse: her husband, the famous painter and magazine illustrator, Alex Adrian, had found her slumped in their car in their closed garage early that morning. The car had apparently been started and left to run until the gas was gone, but by then it was long over. He'd called an ambulance, but efforts to revive her were futile; she'd been dead for some hours.

It gave a few more crumbs about Adrian's career and that was all—no hint of suicide, much less murder.

ADRIAN TURNS VIOLENT! screamed the next day's paper. On the surface the story was of a man so beside himself with strong emotion that it came boiling out onto the streets of his peaceful neighborhood with an attempt to assault a member of the press. Read between the lines: the reporter had gotten too nosy and Adrian had kicked him out the door.

A day later in one of the tabloids was a picture of Adrian and Celia with the headline question: IS THIS THE PORTRAIT OF A KILLER? The story went on to report again on Celia's death, with heavy emphasis on innuendo. Adrian was not available for comment, the police were keeping quiet, and there was a possibility of further startling developments in the case. The question in the headline was clarified down at the end of the article as they puzzled over the tragedy of Celia Adrian and why she may have killed herself. There was no by-line, which was hardly a surprise.

It was an unfortunate piece, escalating things enough so that the more respectable papers noticed and joined in on the smear. A story on the coroner's report appeared in one, most of it padding. Celia Adrian had died on January 3, between the hours of midnight and four A.M., of asphyxiation caused by carbon monoxide exhaust from her car. The note found beside her on the car was such as to indicate that she had killed herself. No other evidence was available to the contrary, but the tabloid strongly suggested that the police were being lax in their duty. Later I found an editorial with the theme of there being a different kind of justice for the rich and famous as opposed to the poor and oppressed. Stirring stuff, but not so noble when in conjunction with their apparent campaign against Adrian.

There was one last story a day later on Adrian's house being the focus of an innocent prank by some schoolchildren. It vaguely alluded to a broken window that may have been the result of an off-course baseball and condemned Adrian for wasting the resources of the police department in calling their assistance to the scene. This one had a by-line, somebody named Barb Steler, which I noted down before looking for more of her work.

Yesterday's tabloid carried her name, so it wouldn't be too hard to find her, something I had an inclination to do. I wanted to know why she had it in for Adrian.

Flipping back to the screamer headline, I studied the grainy shadows of the photo. It was obviously a file shot, taken at some social function. Adrian was in a tuxedo, the woman next to him wore a shiny evening gown. Celia had a model's aristocratic face; short, light hair; and beautiful, searching eyes. I tried to see if there was a hint of self-destruction in them, but whatever I saw was inevitably my projection onto her. This was a picture in a newspaper, not a crystal ball or even a mirror.

The tabloid offices were larger than I'd expected, but it probably took a large and imaginative staff to keep their pages filled with more than ads for invisible lifts and rejuvenating face creams. It was getting late, but there was still a skeleton crew working the phones and typing up tomorrow's scandals. At the receptionist's desk a large man with a morose, leathery face noticed me come in and stopped eating his horse burger long enough to ask what I wanted.

"I'm looking for Barb Steler."

"Gotta 'pointment?"

"Get serious, at this hour?"

"Then why try here?"

"Thought she might be working late."

"Maybe, but not this shift. Tomorrow she might be in."

"I want to find her now."

"You got that in common with a lot of guys, but I can't help you." He sounded all broken up about it, heaving a sigh and giving me the bracing benefit of the raw onions in his dinner. He made it easier by looking me square in the eye, daring me to start something.

I smiled and leaned in closer. "Listen to me, this is very important . . ."

Like I said, sometimes it can be fun. A minute later I had Barb Steler's home address straight from their personnel files and the advice that she wouldn't be there, but in a boozer down the street called Marty's.

"What's she look like?"

"You'll know her. Only real broad in the joint."

I thanked the man and told him to go back to his meal and forget he ever saw me. He did so, and by the time he shook it enough to be able to notice me again I was out the door.

Marty's was a dark, comfortable place, and its proximity to the tabloid offices must have made it the main watering hole for the workers there. One of the deep, padded leather booths was loaded with a group swapping lies over their drinks. I could tell they were newsmen a mile off because I used to do the same thing. A big brown case on the floor identified at least one of them as a photographer. They'd sooner be hanged than part with their Speed Graphics, on or off duty.

I was about to ask the bartender for help when I saw Barb Steler. Her co-worker had been right when he said I'd know her, and it wasn't just because she was the only woman in the place. No mental image I had conjured would have fit the reality.

She was in the booth with the boys, blowing cigarette smoke with the best and holding her own in the conversation. She wore a severely tailored suit, a mannish hat, and a worldly expression. Her bronze eyes were very large and predatory rather than vulnerable. Her skin was the palest I'd ever seen, but didn't look unhealthy. It set off her short jet black hair and generous bright red mouth.

I must have been gaping; she saw me and those seeking eyes flicked up and down and then turned to one of her party.

"Friend of yours, Taylor?" she drawled in a husky voice that could carry. She had meant it to do so.

Taylor gave me a once-over and shook his head. "You got a problem, buddy?"

"Barb Steler?" I said, making it less of a question than a statement. I ignored Taylor because I hate drunks.

"Give the kid a nickel," said Taylor, and got a chorus of approval from the audience.

"Who wants to know?" she asked.

"My name's Jack Fleming and I'd like to talk to you for a moment."

"You and half of Chicago," added Taylor. More hilarity.

"About what?" There was a hint of a smile, but it was a distant hint.

"I'd rather not say." Weak, but it was the best bait I could come up with under the circumstances. The way I'd said it indicated I had something interesting to tell and that she might not want to share it with her gin-soaked colleagues.

She tilted her head to one side, studying me with amusement. I studied her right back and she didn't seem to mind.

Taylor got impatient at all the eye play. "Ya want us to throw the bum out, Barb?"

This didn't speed up her decision; she'd already made it by then, but it did give her an excuse to act. She gestured with one hand, the way queens do when they wave at their subjects, and damned if every one of the guys there didn't give way to it. Two of them made haste to clear the booth so she could slide out.

I expected her to be tall; it had to do with her long, graceful neck and the way she moved. Again, I thought of royalty.

The boys were watching us with some resentment. She knew it but left the next move to me. I tried a cool but polite smile and nodded at some empty booths at the far end of the joint. She matched the smile and preceded me slowly, giving me plenty of time to evaluate the body under the suit. There wasn't a thing wrong with it.

She eased into a booth and I took the other side, facing her.

"Drink?" she asked.

"What would you like?"

"It was an offer, not a request."

"Thanks, but I'll take a rain check. You need anything?"

"Not to drink, no. What is it you wanted to talk to me about, Mr. Fleming?"

"Last January did you cover the story on Celia Adrian's suicide?"

"Among others. Why do you ask?"

"I was interested in why your paper maintained that it might not have been suicide."

The amusement spread from her huge eyes down to her mouth. She had absolutely perfect teeth. "Because a simple suicide does not sell papers."

"And courting a libel suit does?"

"Of course." Her cigarette burned out and she made a point of thoroughly crushing the butt in the table ashtray. "Now, why are you so interested in such old news? Surely you're not a lawyer?"

"No, I'm a journalist. I'm working on a book about famous unsolved cases and I thought the Adrian thing might be something to look into."

"It sounds very ambitious."

"It fills in the time."

"What paper do you work for?"

I gave her the name. "Except I don't work for them anymore. I came into a legacy, decided to quit and go free-lance." It was the truth, more or less. I was a crummy liar.

"Aren't you the lucky one? That's a New York paper. . . . Why are you out here?"

"Because this is where the story happened. What can you tell me about it that didn't get past the editor?"

She made a business of lighting another cigarette and blowing the smoke from her nose. It was quite leisurely and gave her plenty of time to think. "Very little, really. It was a fairly simple case, as I remember, but this was months ago. You probably know more about what I wrote than I do if you've been into the old files."

"I guess so, but that's not quite the same as listening to someone who's been there. What were your impressions of Alex Adrian?"

"The husband? He hardly left any."

Somehow it was oddly comforting to know I wasn't the only bad liar in the world. Her answer complicated things, but I had all night. "Too bad, I was really interested in hearing something solid. I guess I can check the police records tomorrow."

"Yes, there's always tomorrow, isn't there?" She was smiling again and part of me felt like a lone fish in a shark tank.

"I suppose I should leave you and let you get back to your friends."

"They can wait, Mr. Fleming."

"My name is Jack."

"I know, and mine is Barb." She locked those wonderful eyes onto mine again.

This opened things up for a little flirting, but not much—she was a very decisive woman. She stood up soon after and went back to the boys long enough to toss a dollar on the table to cover her drink, and we left together.

"Think she'll let this one live out the night?" Taylor muttered to the others as the door closed behind us.

The pretext we'd established between ourselves was for me to give her a ride home. We walked to my car and I helped her in; it was all very formal and polite. I never liked playing games like that, but this time I didn't mind because I wanted her information.

She had a nice apartment in a nice building. Thankfully she didn't pause at the door for more games on whether she should let in me or not. She opened it and let me make up my own mind and smiled again as I let it snick shut behind me.

"I suppose you think I'm fast?" she said, tugging at the fingers of her black kid gloves. She tossed the empties onto a chair along with her purse and hat.

"I think you know what you want," I returned.

She vanished into the kitchen and I heard the clink of ice on glass. When she came out the top few buttons of her coat were undone, revealing a little more milk white skin. Her very short hair and the harsh lines of her suit perversely emphasized her femininity. It was the same kind of effect Marlene Dietrich got in a tuxedo.

She handed me a glass heavy with ice and bourbon. "Bottoms up?"

It was less a toast than an invitation. She sipped, watching me over the rim, then eased onto her couch and watched me some more. I let my lips touch the edge of the glass and was hard put to hide the spasm of rejection my stomach sent up.

"You don't have to have it if you don't like it." Innuendo was her specialty.

"Thanks." I placed it on a low table and sat next to her. We weren't quite touching.

She put down her drink and rested her arm along the back of the couch, her fingers lightly rubbing the fabric of my coat. "You know, most men your age would either be all over me at this point or rushing out the door in a desperate attempt to preserve their virtue."

"Which do you prefer?"

"Neither, that's why you're here. You act older than you look."

"Maybe I am."

"Are you really a journalist?"

"Not anymore."

"Perhaps you thought by coming here I might talk a little more freely about Alex Adrian?"

I laughed a little. "Not much gets past you."

"No, indeed. I'm afraid you'll find me quite useless, as I've nothing to tell you. Nothing at all."

We had moved closer together somehow. "That's too bad."

Her mouth curled. "What would your girlfriend think if she saw you like this?"

"Who says I've got a girlfriend?"

"I do. I can smell her perfume on you. Winter Rose. It's very expensive."

She pressed the length of her body against mine, and I won't lie and say she wasn't having her effect on me. My symptoms were familiar enough: tunnel vision, heightened hearing and smell, and of course my upper canines were pushing themselves out of their retractable pockets. Mixed in with Bobbi's perfume and Barb's perfume was the all-too-tantalizing scent of blood. I stopped breathing but couldn't shut out its soft rumble as it surged through the veins in her throat.

She sensed at least part of what was happening to me and brought her lips around to cover mine. It lasted only an instant and left the possibility open for more if I wished it. I did, but pulled back.

"You don't have to do this."

She smiled with infinite patience. "How many times do I have to convince a man that it's not a question of 'have to'? I want to and that should be enough. Now lie back and enjoy yourself." And she pushed herself against me a little and started undoing my tie.

I let things go until she stopped to smile at me again. She slipped into it easily; it was so subtle I was only aware she was under by the slightly glazed look in her bronze eyes. Her hands dropped away and her head went sleepily back, drawing the skin tight over her unblemished throat. I stroked it gently, feeling the vein working under my fingers and noting the soft warmth with a great deal of regret.

Getting to my feet, I walked around the living room until things settled down internally. A few gulps of fresh air from an open window helped clear my head and before long my teeth were back in their place again. Barb Steler was one of the most desirable women I'd ever met, and I certainly wanted her, but she wasn't Bobbi and there was no way in the world that I would ever intentionally hurt either of them.

With that firmly in mind I went back to the couch and sat next to her. Her eyes were wide open, but she was asleep, and taking no notice of me now.

"Barb, close your eyes and think back to last January. I want you to tell me about the story you did on Alex Adrian."

Her eyes drifted shut. It was more for my comfort than hers, because I hate that empty look they get.

"Tell me about Alex Adrian."

Her face twisted. "Bastard."

For a second I wondered if she was talking about him or me, but she was still safely under. "Why is he a bastard?"

"He doesn't love me."

I didn't quite whistle. "You love him?"

She made a low noise in her throat. That was one question she didn't want to answer.

"Okay, never mind. Where did you first meet him?"

"Paris."

"When he was a student there?"

"Yes."

"Tell me about it."

It took quite a while because I had to prompt her with questions. It was a simple story but she'd buried it down deep.

She was a society deb on a continental tour with some friends when one of them dared her to model for an art class. She took up the dare and so met Alex Adrian, a promising art student. Long after her friends returned to the States she was still living with him in a little hotel on the Left Bank. Things were idyllic, from her point of view at least. There had been talk of marriage for a time, but it had fallen through.

"He didn't really want me," she sighed. "He didn't. It was his art first, always his goddamned art."

Their fights became more frequent as she demanded more attention from him, and he pulled away to concentrate on his studies. She finally left for home, returning to her own study of journalism. She was smart enough and good enough to work for any paper in the country, but preferred the style of her tabloid. She had a lot of venom in her system and it only increased when Adrian returned from New York with his new wife.

I shook my head, not liking my next question. "Do you think he killed her?"

"No . . ."

"Barb, tell me, did you kill her?"

"No."

"So it was suicide, after all?"

"Yes."

"And all those stories in the paper?"

"He deserved it. He hurt me. Bastard."

From under her closed lids a tear slipped out and trickled down her heart-shaped face. I touched it away.

"You tired, Barb?"

"Yes."

"I don't blame you. I want you to get up and get ready for bed as usual. All right?"

Her eyes opened and, still unaware of me, she walked into her bedroom and began removing her clothes. It took some effort on my part to remember I was a gentleman. I stayed out in the living room until she'd finished her bath and climbed into bed. The springs creaked as she settled into the sheets and pulled up the blanket.

She wore an ice white satin gown that left her shoulders bare and defined her breasts. She didn't see me standing in the doorway, but stared at something next to it. I came into the room. Hanging on the wall was an oil portrait of her. She was younger, her hair was different, but the artist had left no doubt to the world about her beauty. The signature at the bottom was Alex Adrian's.

"Bastard," she whispered.

I walked around the big double bed and pulled back the covers from the empty spot next to her and climbed in, clothes and all. It was the only way I could think of to convincingly leave the impression we'd slept together.

"Barb—"

"Barbara. My full name is Barbara."

I put an arm around her and drew her close so she was leaning against me. "Barbara."

"Yes?"

"You hide it very well, but you hurt a lot because of him."

"Yes."

"I think you should let go of the hurt, don't you?"

Until she crumpled, I hadn't been aware of the tension in her muscles. I murmured things to her, soft words meant to soothe, and they seemed to work. When her eyes were dry again, she really was ready to sleep. I shifted position, sitting up and facing her and easing her back onto the pillow.

"You had a good evening, Barbara," I told her. "You don't have to remember talking to me about Adrian, but thinking about him doesn't hurt now. Understand?"

She nodded.

"Now you have a good night's sleep. When you wake up in the morning you'll feel a lot better about things."

The covers rustled as she turned over. I carefully got out of bed and studied the portrait a moment longer before shutting off the light. A minute later I locked her apartment door, slipped out into the hall, and walked quietly downstairs so as not to disturb the other tenants.

The car seemed to make more noise starting than usual, but only because I wanted it not to. I shifted gears gently and drifted down the dark and empty morning streets, my head full of complicated thoughts and feelings. Instead of the road I saw a heart-shaped young face in an expensive frame.

The sad part was that she'd been dead wrong about Adrian; no one could paint a portrait like that and not be in love.

6

THE kitchen phone started jangling just as consciousness returned and my eyes popped open. Escott caught it on the third ring and I could tell by his end of the conversation that it was Bobbi. I threw on a bathrobe and decided to spare his nerves and walk up the basement steps in the regular way. He handed over the earpiece and went back to the front room to finish listening to his radio program.

Bobbi was anything but calm. "That rat backed out!" she stated, her voice vibrating with fury. "He called me up this afternoon to call off the sittings."

She'd said enough for me to identify the rat in question. "What happened? Did he say why?"

"He just said he tried and couldn't get into it, after all, some stuff about not being ready to get back to painting yet."

"That's ridiculous, after the way he was last night?"

"I know. First he can't wait to start, now he dumps the whole thing. What's the matter with the man?"

The thought flashed through my head that Barb Steler had remembered our talk last night and somehow made trouble with Adrian. It was worry making, but extremely unlikely. I'd been very careful with her. "Give me time to dress and I'll pick you up. We'll go over for a little talk and try to straighten things out."

"Are you sure you want me along? I feel like strangling him."

"Fine, I'll probably help."

Escott's voice drifted in after I hung up. "Problem?" he asked casually.

I shoved my hands in the robe's pockets and hunched into the front room. He was at his ease on the long sofa and stretched out a lazy arm to turn the radio down. I spent a minute or so explaining about the portrait commission and Adrian's sudden refusal of it.

He cocked a philosophical eyebrow. "Artistic temperament, perhaps? Perhaps not. He's probably far too professional to indulge in such games."

"I don't know. I'm taking Bobbi over to find out."

"A suggestion?"

"Yeah?"

"Take along your receipt—just in case you can't change his mind."
His hand swung back to the volume dial again.

With him it was a suggestion with double meaning, a nudge for my
conscience to kick in, as if it needed much help. I *had* been thinking of
influencing Adrian, but recognized with some sourness that Escott had a
point, at least for the moment.

Bobbi was dressed for war in a severe black suit with a slash of bloodred
color on her compressed lips. She was already waiting in the lobby, and
as soon as my car stopped she shot out and yanked the door open.

"I'm mad," she said, quite unnecessarily. Anyone in a fifty-yard ra-
dius could figure it out easily enough.

"We'll see what's going on."

"He chickened out, that's what I think." She crossed her arms and
glared out the front window. "And it's just not fair."

I got the car rolling again and listened as she talked herself down
from a long afternoon of anger and frustration. By the time we reached
Adrian's she'd calmed somewhat and was willing to hear his side of
things, if he had one.

He took his time answering the door and there was a change in him.
The relaxed face we'd seen last night had been replaced by the guarded
go-to-hell-and-so-what expression I'd noted at the party. It took Bobbi
by surprise; she was all wound up to ask an obvious question or two, but
one look and she knew it was a lost cause.

He let us into the entryway, but no farther. On a table rested the envelope with the money, which he handed to me, meeting my eyes, expecting a reproach and not caring.

"I can't really explain it," he said. "I just know I can't do the job,
after all."

"Why not?"

He'd been ready for that question, and the answer came out easily
enough. "Do you ever get a writer's block, if that's what you call it? I've
the same thing, but for painting."

It wasn't something I could argue with; you can't force a person to
create against their will. You also can't ask them why when they don't
want to talk. I couldn't, not with Bobbi looking on. I gave him his receipt
without another word. He stared at it, something crossing his face as if it
were the end of the world, then shoved the piece of paper into his pocket.

"I'm sorry to have put you both to so much trouble," he said tonelessly. He was saying what was expected of him; whether he meant it or
not was anyone's guess.

Bobbi shot me a brief look of alarm, her instincts were doing over-
time. I nodded back, we'd talk later.

Adrian opened the door for us and we were back on the porch with it closing quietly behind. I heard his steps retreating deep into the house.

"We sure read him the riot act, didn't we?" she said. "He looked positively sick."

"He was like that when I first met him, but he perked up when Sandra was around."

"You think they had a fight?"

"You think it's really our business?"

"No, but I'd like to find out."

We got into the car and I drove half a block and parked by a small neighborhood grocery at the corner. "Would you mind waiting here for a little while? I want to go back and check on him?"

"Because he might do something?" Apparently, she had the same idea about suicide as I did.

"I just want to check." And make sure there were no dangling ropes or sleeping pills within reach. Bobbi said she'd be all right and I got out and walked back down the street, trying not to look conspicuous. It still felt as though every window had a face in it and that every barking dog was reacting to me alone. Passing under an especially large tree, its trunk thick with shadow, I disappeared.

Adrian's house was exactly on my left. I willed myself in that direction and pushed against the light wind until stopped by a wall of wood. I pressed harder and was through the wall, floating in the still air of his front room and drifting around to find a safe place to solidify. Invisibility is not as much fun as you'd think: with my sight gone and my hearing a joke, all I had was extended touch, which could be deceptive. After a minute of covering the four comers and not getting any sense of another presence, I decided to risk it and materialize.

The risk paid off, for the room was empty and dark. I listened hard and could just pick up the sound of his breathing elsewhere. Cautious and as silent as possible, I edged into the hall. The rooms that were in view were also dark, except for the kitchen, which had a small light burning wanly over the stove. Beyond the kitchen was his studio.

I vanished again and floated in. He seemed to be lying on the couch. By moving close I could tell which way he was facing and was able to get behind him and out of his line of sight. I solidified in a crouch, though, just in case I threw a shadow from the banks of windows behind me.

The only light came from a small work lamp caged from one of his tables. Its gooseneck was twisted so the illumination fell on a canvas clamped onto his easel. It was a portrait of Celia Adrian. The newspaper photo had been a decent likeness at least of how she looked—Adrian had recorded who she had been. The style was the same as Barb Steler's portrait, but more mature and assured.

I saw guarded happiness in the blue eyes, a hint of selfishness around the mouth, and an unearthly beauty in every stroke of his brush. It was truth and idealization all at once. Her faults were there, but accepted as part of the whole. He'd loved her dearly, but not blindly.

The figure on the couch moved only a little. He was smoking slowly, thoughtfully, and I could spend all night speculating on those thoughts. For now he didn't seem on the verge of doing away with himself or anyone else. My curiosity was satisfied to some extent, but with Bobbi waiting, there was no time for a more thorough investigation. Maybe later I could pay him a less hurried visit.

She'd left the car for the grocery. Through the sign-covered windows I could see her nodding and listening to the middle-aged woman behind the counter. After a few minutes Bobbi picked up her package and joined me.

"You're not the only one who's a detective," she said, sliding into the car.

"I'm only an assistant to a private agent. You call Charles a detective and he'll come out in hives."

"Whatever. I got the lady inside talking about Alex and his wife's death."

"So was it suicide or murder?"

"About half and half. She used to wait on his wife, 'a tall, pretty lady who'd give you the time of day when you asked,' and can't imagine she would have done such a wicked thing. On the other hand, living with an artist can't be all that easy."

"Did you ask her about the day when it happened?"

"She said she saw the ambulance and wondered what the fuss was about and was terribly shocked to learn Mrs. Adrian was dead. She'd read all the papers and when they started saying Alex murdered her she was ready to believe it. He came into her store about a week later and she was ready to throw him out until she saw his face."

"Like death warmed over?"

"You heard?"

"He had the same effect on us tonight, remember?"

"Vividly. I was ready to kill him and then it just seemed so pointless, there was nothing there to argue with."

We both nodded in silent agreement. "What now?"

She looked surprised. "We go see Sandra and Evan. I didn't buy this just for my voice, you know." She shifted the bag and I caught the subtle clink of beer bottles inside.

Our knock on Evan's door got no answer, but I was sure I heard a voice and a soft thump.

"Think they're out?" Bobbi asked.

"Someone's there." I put an ear to the door but couldn't really distinguish much through it. We knocked louder and got no answer. "Maybe Francis came back to try and beat him up again, after all."

She tried the knob, but the door was locked. "The super might have a key—"

"You ever see my vanishing act?"

"Your what?"

"It makes Charles nervous and I didn't want to give you heart failure."

"You mean you can just . . . ?" She made vague gestures. I'd done it once before in her presence, but it had been dark and rainy and she may have missed it, having other things on her mind at the time.

"Yeah, wanna see?"

She was a game girl. "Okay . . ."

Then I wasn't there anymore. As though wrapped in cotton, I heard her gasp of surprise. I slipped inside, went solid, and unlocked the door. She jumped when it swung open, but her short blond hair wasn't quite on end.

"Yeeps! How'd you do that? I thought you were supposed to turn into a fog or something."

I pointed an accusing finger. "You've been reading Stoker again, haven't you?"

"Never mind that, why'd you never tell me about this?"

"You never asked."

"But—"

"Shh, I want to listen."

Now that we were inside, neither of us had much trouble hearing things. Somewhere in the back Evan laughed and a girl's voice responded, "That's right, now I'll hold it here and you shove it in."

Bobbi's mouth popped open and she blushed a bright red.

"No, not that way!" the girl complained. "Smoother . . . get that flap as well."

Flap! Bobbi mouthed the word.

"It can wait a minute," said Evan. "I thought I heard something out front."

"You just don't want to do a little honest work," was the retort.

Evan strolled in wearing a baggy set of mustard yellow golf pants, red shoes, and orange-and-green argyle socks topped off by an ancient paint-smeared shirt. His surprise from seeing us quickly translated into a smile. "Jack! Bobbi! Welcome to my extremely humble home, come in."

"If we're interrupting anything—"

"Nah, it's too late for that or I'd have kicked you out. I thought I'd locked the door anyway, oh well. My friend Sally was just helping me with the linens. It seems I don't know how to make a proper hospital corner."

Sally also strolled in, a petite girl with rich brown hair and a lush figure under her light print dress. She was the maid Evan had been chatting with in the kitchen while his clothes dried. It looked as though the party hadn't been a total disaster for him, after all. Evan introduced us and Bobbi brought out the beer.

"This is great, what's the occasion?" he asked.

"Call it a homecoming gift," said Bobbi. "Where's Sandra?"

"Out somewhere, probably with Alex."

"We were just there, she wasn't with him."

Evan shrugged. "Shopping, then, or at one of her girlfriends' talking about shopping. She'll be back before long. It's all right, she doesn't like beer." He found an opener and popped some caps. Just in time I stopped him from wasting one on me.

"How was Alex when you left today?" I asked.

"Rancid as ever. Why?"

"Because he called Bobbi this afternoon and canceled the portrait commission. When we went by he looked—"

"Like death warmed over," completed Bobbi.

"Really? You mean he decided not to do the painting, just like that?" I nodded. "We thought you might have an idea why."

"Me?"

"Or Sandra. Did they have any disagreements, stuff like that?"

"No, pretty much the opposite, from what I could tell. They keep going the way they are and I'll have this rat palace all to myself in another month." Rat palace or not, he seemed very pleased with the prospect.

"Evan, I had an idea that Alex may have taken on the commission in order to help you out with Dimmy Wallace."

He shook his head. "He wouldn't have to do that, he's got plenty of savings. If I asked him for help he'd just give me the money but I haven't asked him for help. Cheating the bookies is one thing, but Alex is my friend, more or less."

"He said he had a painter's block—"

"Not him . . . well, maybe him. There's a first time for everyone, I suppose."

"Sandra said he hadn't painted since his wife died."

"There's a difference between a block and just choosing not to work. He's been sitting around feeling sorry for himself and wondering if he could have made things different for Celia. You ask me, you should go back and give him a kick in the pants and tell him to paint."

"You really think he'd respond to that?"

"Of course he'd respond . . . but I'd want to be there to see the fight."
He looked like Sandra for a second with the impishness in his eyes. "This
isn't like him, you know. I've never known him to back out of a commission once the money's down. I really can't say what's wrong with
him. . . ."

"We could go back and ask this time," suggested Bobbi. "Could you
come with us?"

He thought about it, but shook his head. "I'm not too comfortable
about that; he's a friend, but this isn't really my business, after all. I'll be
honest about things: if Alex turns down the commission, I might have a
chance to take his place. . . ."

If anyone else had said it they might have sounded grabby, but not
Evan.

"Of course it won't be an Alex Adrian, and I can't charge his price,
but it'd be the best I could do."

I shrugged reasonably. "We'll see what works out."

It was enough for him. "Great, now I've got to put on a cleaner shirt
and walk Sally home."

"We can drive you—" I offered.

He held up a hand. "Thanks, but we really would like to walk. Why
don't you take Bobbi to dinner in the meantime. She's looking a little
peaked and you don't want to lose those skin tones."

Sally shifted and looked jealous until he put an arm around her and
squeezed.

"Keep 'em enthralled, darling," he told her. "Show off some of my
paintings." He ducked into the back of the flat for his shirt.

"I don't know if I can tell you much about them," Sally confessed.

"Paintings usually speak for themselves. If you have to explain them
then the artist needs a new job." I was practically quoting what I'd
learned from Sandra.

She smiled and laughed and led us to a corner of the room, where
dozens of odd-sized canvases were stored vertically in a home-built shelving unit. We pulled out one after another and I got a pretty good idea
why Evan wouldn't be making much money on his work. It was beautiful stuff, the colors were rich and all over, but for the most part you
couldn't make out what they were representing.

He had a few of what I would call regular paintings. He could indeed
please the public if he wished, but he was more comfortable creating his
own inner world than recording the one around him. Bobbi discovered
an especially large work and tilted it against the wall so she could stand
back and get a good look. Sally joined her and both their faces were
pinched with puzzlement. All I saw were swirls of fleshy pinks, darker

reds, and other warm colors. It looked like another abstract to me. Evan came out, tucking in his shirt.

"That's my favorite, too, ladies."

"What's the title?" asked Bobbi, who was also trying not to ask what it was.

"No title, really, but it is a portrait of a dear old friend of mine. It represents his joy to be meeting another friend he likes very much."

"I don't really see it," said Sally.

"There's a trick to it, actually. You have to stand at a specific spot for the meaning to become clear." He put an arm around each of their shoulders and pulled them back about ten feet from the canvas and stepped away. They stared at it, then suddenly broke into twin shrieks of laughter and outrage. Evan beamed.

I was about five feet from the painting and stepped behind the convulsing girls to get a look—and saw nothing but colors.

"Now you're too far away," he told me, and urged me forward another foot.

It said a lot for his technical skill as a painter that he was able to create such an effect. Too close, it was nothing but colors, too distant and it was more of the same. Stand exactly ten feet away and you could see it for the large-scale and quite rude self-portrait it was.

"He's got very good manners and never fails to rise in the presence of a lovely lady. It's one of my best works," he admitted without a trace of modesty. In the case of this painting, modesty would have been totally out of place.

Bobbi turned down a second night at Hallman's, stating she was too hungry to wait for things to simmer. We found a less pretentious eatery and she made short work of a basic plate of meat and vegetables. This time I didn't bother pretending with a cup of coffee and watched her with enjoyment. She was still snickering about Evan's masterpiece.

"I don't know where he got the nerve to paint it."

"Perhaps he was inspired."

"It certainly explains the number of nudes he had."

"Offended?"

"Nah, that kind of stuff doesn't bother me, it just takes a little getting used to. I may take one of my girlfriends over, she might want to buy it."

"Who is she?"

"None of your business. She's a man-eater and you're the last person I want her to meet."

"What, you don't trust me?" I sounded wounded.

"I trust you, I also have to protect you. She runs through men like I run through silk stockings and leaves them lying around torn up and ready to be thrown away."

"You're more tidy than that."

"Stinker. What's the time?"

"Nine-ten."

"We better not leave it too late."

"I'm ready when you are."

"I know," she said with some smugness, which did wonders for my ego.

For the second time that night we pulled up to Adrian's house. His car was gone.

"A person could get tired of disappointments like this," Bobbi growled.

"Feel like waiting a while?"

"Like for a stakeout?"

"I dunno, I've never been on one of those before."

"Wonder why he left."

So did I, and her question hung uncomfortably in the air between us for the next few minutes.

A car turned down the street, its headlights flashing across the rearview mirror. It slowed and swung into Adrian's driveway. He got out, a carton of cigarettes in his hand, glared at us, and slammed the door of his coupe. He seemed to debate whether he should ignore us and go on in the house or face us and get it over with. We got out of our car and saved him the trouble of deciding.

He waited until we were close enough for him not to have to raise his voice. Along the street curtains had twitched with the slam of the door.

"Yes?" Very polite and ice cold with irritation.

"We came from Evan's," I said.

He blinked. The opening didn't make sense and he had to shift mental gears trying to figure out what I was talking about.

"He said we should come back and kick you in the pants and tell you to start painting again."

He shook his head with exasperation. "Yes, I'm sure he did. Evan needs to learn to mind his own business." He moved past us and unlocked his front door, but indicated we would not be welcome past the threshold. "I've explained myself and tried to apologize. As far as I'm concerned the subject is closed."

Inside his house the phone started ringing, an excuse to leave us, which he gratefully seized. I was feeling pigheaded, though, and followed him inside, with Bobbi right behind. If it came down to it, I was prepared to put him under, even with her looking on. Hell, if we were intimate enough for sex she could survive watching me hypnotize someone.

He glared at us from the phone stand in the front hall, his attention divided by our presence and the need to hear the voice on the other end of the wire.

"What? Yes, what's wrong?" He focused on the phone, his glare shifting back to irritation. "No, I can't now. . . . Then, tell me what it is—oh, all right. I'm on my way." He dropped the receiver onto the cradle in disgust. "That was Evan," he said. "There's some kind of trouble, but he won't say what. I have to leave now."

"Dimmy Wallace?"

He shrugged. "I don't know, but he was very upset." Without another word he pushed past us and held the door long enough for us to get out, then locked it and went to his car.

"Are we going, too?" asked Bobbi.

"Yeah, but if things get too hot, you stay in the car and keep down."

We piled into my Buick and followed him to Evan's house. I was annoyed at the interruption as well. Though I hadn't been able to pick up Evan's side of the conversation, some of the stress-filled tones of his voice had leaked out; enough to make me uneasy.

Evan was sitting on the steps outside, his hands hanging slack and his head down. Adrian was out of his car and striding up to him before I'd set my brakes. By the time I was out Adrian was already going up to the flat.

Bobbi got out with me. I checked both ends of the street, but didn't see anything remotely resembling a bookie's collector. We hurried up to Evan, who took no notice of our arrival. A strong fist closed around my gut and more than anything I wanted to take Bobbi and get out of there.

Evan began to shake his head. A thin keening sound rose from his huddled form and put my back hairs up. Bobbi looked from him to me, her face dead white with alarm.

"What . . . ?"

I spread my hands a little and gestured at the house. Answers would be in there, not with Evan. We went inside and then I told Bobbi in no uncertain terms to stay on the bottom landing while I went up. She didn't argue and kept an eye on Evan.

The stairs creaked with each quick step. In other parts of the house the tenants made their noises of living: a baby gurgled somewhere in the back, on my left a radio blared an ad for a cold remedy. Drifting down from the floors above was the hiss and smell of frying cabbage and bacon. I could not sort out Adrian's individual sounds from the others yet.

The door to the Robley flat was wide open and the lights were on. Now I was able to focus down and heard Adrian's quiet breathing and nothing else. The background of the flat's front room was unchanged:

Evan's portrait still leaned against a far wall and a few empty beer bottles cluttered a low table.

New details impressed themselves into the overall picture: some packages carelessly dropped on a chair, a glove on the table, another on the floor, her purse on its side, a tortoiseshell comb fallen from it.

Sandra was on her back in the center of the room, her head turned to one side, her eyes and mouth slightly open.

Adrian was on one knee next to her. He slowly looked up as I entered. He saw me and forgot me because the shock had firmly closed over him. His face was utterly blank and the physical wall I'd seen and felt once before was back, perhaps this time to stay. Walls had their uses, and shutting out unbearable pain was one of them.

He turned to her and with a steady hand gently stroked back a lock of her russet hair. Blood came away on his fingers, but he didn't seem to notice.

7

HE didn't respond to his name, not at first, and I didn't want to have to go in and pull him out.

"She's dead," he stated faintly.

"I know, Alex. Please come away." God, it was surprising how calm I sounded. "Alex. Now."

His hand stopped, hovering just above her still face. I thought he was going to shut her eyes. The fingers drew back. Delicately. He abruptly stood up and swung toward me, or rather the door. I moved aside to let him pass and listened as he went downstairs. Bobbi asked him a question and got no answer. It was a very strong wall. I couldn't blame him for it.

I backed out and followed, utterly heartsick and with knees like jelly.

"Jack?"

Bottom of the stairs. Bobbi's arms. Her warmth, her living warmth. I said something to her, answering her question, and held on to her a little longer. When the worst was over, I was just able to talk.

"This is going to be a mess. Do you want to go home?"

"I can't."

"You can. You haven't really seen anything. The police—"

She shook her head firmly. "I need to be here."

And I was the one who needed her. I pulled her close again, then reluctantly broke away to knock on the super's door down the hall. He was a little peach-colored man with flyaway gray hair clinging to the back of his scalp. I told him that I had an emergency and needed to use his phone. He looked at me and at Bobbi standing forlornly next to the stairs. He seemed about to ask something, then shrugged and let me in. He got all the answers he needed as he listened to my end of the conversation.

The first to come were two uniformed cops; a few minutes later Escott arrived. I'd called him first, but he had the longer drive. Before the uniforms knew he was there he slipped inside the building and was upstairs for a quick look. He came down more slowly, his face somber.

"What do you know?" he asked.

In low tones we told him what we could of the evening, which didn't amount to much, as far as I could see. Just as I finished, one of the cops came up and asked for our story. His partner was trying to question Evan, who was still huddled out on the steps shaking his head. Adrian watched them both, his face expressionless. I repeated it all again, but more simply, and Bobbi corroborated. By the time he'd finished taking notes a car with two detectives pulled up.

The cop went out to talk to them, then held the door as a well-built man in expensively cut clothes stepped out.

Escott glanced at me, one brow raised.

"Thought it'd be a good idea to call someone we know," I said.

"It cannot hurt," he agreed.

I'd specifically talked to Lieutenant Blair despite the fact that the last time I'd seen him he'd been one short step away from booking me for murder. We'd worked things out, sort of, but he had no memory of how I'd convinced him to let me go. He only knew we were friends. At the time I'd felt like a heel for artificially inducing the friendship, but now it seemed more like a good investment.

Blair walked around Evan, looked Adrian up and down, then came over to us. We didn't shake hands, it wouldn't have been appropriate. He nodded at Escott.

"Charles. Thought you might turn up since Jack phoned it in."

Escott nodded back. "I'm here solely as moral support."

"Sure you are." He went to one side with the cop who questioned me and listened to him, then made the pilgrimage upstairs. More uniforms appeared and followed, keeping emerging tenants out of the way and asking more questions.

Hours later they were still asking them, but not making much progress. They'd taken over the super's flat. He didn't seem to mind; it was the most excitement he'd seen since Lindbergh landed.

Evan sat in the borrowed kitchen, his eyes hollow and staring at nothing. He was as cold sober as the stale cup of coffee in front of him, and still in shock. Adrian was the same, but able to respond to things in a slow way. Some time earlier he'd formally identified the body, his voice flat and soulless as he pronounced her name. Now he stood bolt upright with his arms crossed and his back pressed to a squat icebox, watching Evan, but not really seeing him.

Escott, Bobbi, and I had found a corner and quietly talked. I filled him in on the fight with Francis Koller and Toumey and all the business of the portrait and some of the business with Barb Steler. The latter had been judiciously edited since Bobbi was listening, but I would have done that anyway.

"And you say he must have gone out for cigarettes?" Escott murmured, carefully not looking at Adrian.

"That's what he had in his hand when he drove up. I know what you're thinking, Charles."

"It's just a thought, and certainly not the only possibility open to us, but all have to be considered."

"Let's try considering something else," said Bobbi. "He may have had the time to do it—it was at least an hour between us leaving with Evan and getting to Alex's—but you're short on motive."

"For Adrian, but motives may also be found in the best of families." Escott's eyes flicked in Evan's direction. Bobbi gave him a look that would have burned through steel. He took it stoically enough but did not retract the suggestion. "The police are well aware of that fact and are of the opinion that she *did* know her killer. From the little Lieutenant Blair has shared with me—"

Her eyes flared again. "But he *couldn't*—look at the poor man—"

"I know, but it might be interpreted as guilt, mightn't it?" Before she could reply he mitigated it all with a brief, dismissive gesture. "I'm only looking at this from their point of view. As yet, neither they nor we have enough data to work with, a circumstance I am more than willing to remedy. When the police are finished questioning the other tenants, I'll have a turn. Jack, you might find a conversation with Lieutenant Blair to be profitable."

"He'll be wanting to talk with us anyway. I'll see what I can get."

"Good man."

He started to say something else, but there was a muted commotion in the hallway and all eyes except Evan's turned toward the open door. Two beefy men were thumping heavily down the stairs. No one spoke as they carried the long wicker basket past the door and out into the night. I felt Bobbi's slim hand grip my arm tightly and she gulped breath back as the reality of Sandra's death hit her all over again. Bobbi had taken it all quietly enough when I'd broken the news to her, but there's a big difference between hearing and seeing.

She continued to hold on to my arm and stare long after they'd gone. Her reaction troubled Escott as well, and he covered the back of her other hand lightly with his long fingers, waking her from it.

"I'm very sorry," he told her.

Bobbi had been dry eyed until now. Escott's compassion tipped things for her and her lips trembled and twisted. I offered my handkerchief and she dabbed at the tears that suddenly spilled out. It was all very quiet and over in a minute; she'd wait for more privacy before really letting go with her grief.

Lieutenant Blair had followed the body down and now stood in the doorway, his dark gaze traveling and pausing on each of us. He murmured something to the cop who was watching things, and both of them moved in on Evan. Blair sat at the table across from him while the other cop took Adrian to one side, just out of earshot.

Blair spoke to Evan for several minutes. Evan could only shake his head mechanically to the gentle questions. In his bright and totally ridiculous clothes he looked like a sad-faced clown left stranded by his circus. Blair gave up for the time being and crossed to Adrian to hear his brief version of events. Then it was our turn.

Unasked, Escott slipped quietly away and Blair took his place in our corner. We went through it all again, but no amount of talk could change the facts or soften them. He was interested in Evan's connection with Dimmy Wallace and the scuffle Adrian and I had with his stooges. He noted it all down, but kept his conclusions to himself.

Bobbi asked to be excused and disappeared into the bathroom. It was more diplomacy than body need or wanting to repair her makeup. She knew I could get more out of Blair alone and I silently blessed her brains and tact.

Blair followed her departure and turned his attention back to me. "Bad business, her getting involved in another murder so close to the one during her radio broadcast. And before that, it was those two at the Nightcrawler Club. Death seems to follow that young woman."

"That's why I'd like to keep this short, I want to take her home as soon as I can."

"Of course. Now, what can you tell me?" He put on the kind of manner that invites confidences, but I wasn't having any because I'd already told him everything.

"You know as much as I do, Lieutenant. I only met this bunch a couple of days ago. God knows I want to help, but I really can't add anything more."

"What about the names of their other friends at this party? They might provide us with more information on the Robleys' personal lives."

"There's Reva Stokes and Leighton Brett. There's also a tough named Dreyer who was at the party. He took a few swings at Evan over a crap game . . ."

We went around on the business for a while until I was repeating myself. Unlike our last meeting I was trying to cooperate, as this time I had nothing to hide.

"What now?" I asked when he looked ready to end the interview.

"Now we try and get Mr. Robley upstairs to see if anything was stolen."

"In his condition?"

"We haven't much of a choice. You only just met him and Mr. Adrian has stated he hasn't been here in some months. We just want him to take a quick look. If there was a robbery it will affect our investigation."

From that angle I could see the sense of it, but before he could start, another uniform came in and whispered in his ear. I heard it quite clearly but pretended not to. Blair looked at me, cocking his head slightly.

"Well, you speak of the devil and watch what happens. Miss Smythe's been making some phone calls."

Bobbi had long since emerged from the bathroom and was standing protectively close to Evan. "I felt I had to. They *are* friends of the family."

"That's all right," he assured. "I'm glad you did." He sent the cop off and a moment later Reva Stokes and Leighton Brett walked tentatively in. Reva looked shaken and was very white except for the red rims of her eyes, and she was hanging on to her fiancé like a lifeline. Brett had his arm around her and simply looked grim. Bobbi went to them and spoke in discreet tones, gesturing to Evan in explanation. Reva shook her head—in sadness, not refusal—found some strength within herself, and went over to take Evan's hand.

At this touch, he slowly raised his lost gaze. The muscles under his skin twitched a little, and he seemed ready to cry as he looked at her. I was hoping he would. He needed some kind of release; his blank silence was much more disturbing than Adrian's.

I glanced around for him, but at some point he'd left the room.

Blair introduced himself to Brett and explained the need for Evan to go up and see if anything was missing.

"The man hardly knows where he is, how can you expect him to help you?"

Diplomacy came easy for Blair, but then he was used to handling all kinds of belligerents in his job, and Leighton Brett was just another voice in the crowd. "He's the only one who can do it. I would appreciate your help." He was polite, but there was an edge to his voice even Brett could not ignore. Growling and sullen, he went to Reva and told her what was wanted.

As though acting as translator, Reva spoke to Evan and somehow broke through the fog that was holding him. He nodded listlessly and the chair scraped over the faded linoleum as he found his feet. Blair proceeded and said nothing as Brett and I followed the slow parade upstairs.

A chalk outline and a little blood on the floor were the only indications of what all the fuss was about, unless you wanted to count the fingerprint dust everywhere. Evan identified Sandra's purse and nodded to confirm that the smaller change purse that would have carried her money was gone.

"Two dollars," he said clearly.

"What about two dollars?" asked Blair.

Evan searched his mind for the answer. "She doesn't carry more than two dollars. We don't have much, you see—"

"Is anything else missing? Did you keep any money or valuables?"

"We don't have much, you see." Evan was drifting again. He wandered around the room, blinking at the familiar now become horrible and unable to absorb the change. "You see . . ." He stared at the stacks of oil paintings in their storage slots against the wall.

Brett bulled his way past the cop at the door. "That's enough, the man needs a doctor, not pointless questions. If you're through—"

"Yes, I'm through, get him out of here."

Evan was now looking at the outline on the floor, a place we had all carefully stepped around. He was breathing faster, the air chopping in and out of his lungs in silent gusts. His mouth sagged shapelessly and a line of spittle spilled over the right corner in a fine thread. He began that terrible keening again, hopeless and frightening to hear.

Brett stepped forward to take his arm and the smaller man shook him off with unexpected strength. He rocked slightly from the waist, as though from cramp, and the keening grew louder.

The uniform next to me was gaping. He was young and had never seen anything like it before. I nudged him out of the spell. "You got a doctor here?"

His attention shifted reluctantly. "Yeah, maybe he's still—"

"Then go get him and make sure he's got his bag. *Move.*"

He moved, clattering down in his regulation shoes.

Brett tried to guide Evan out again, talking to him in a low voice. Evan stayed rooted to his spot and shook him off again. I stepped forward and motioned Brett to keep back. I looked into Evan's straining face, but couldn't quite reach his eyes. He wasn't seeing me or anything else in the room but the pathetic marks on the floor where his sister had fallen and left him forever.

I called his name, loudly. He matched it with more sound, which was beginning to rise into a full scream. I tried to focus onto him, but it was like squeezing quicksilver; he just wasn't there. He was lost in a place I could not follow. Sending men into madness is one thing; bringing them out of it was another and beyond even my powers at the moment.

Evan's scream died away for want of breath. No one touched him. We were waiting for him to go berserk, for him to start breaking things up so he could be restrained, but nothing like that happened. We could do nothing but wait, and it seemed like forever before a thin man with a black bag appeared. No one needed to explain what was needed. He quickly dug into the bag and prepared a syringe.

"Lieutenant Blair, make sure he doesn't kill me," was all that he said. He approached Evan as though the man were an unexploded bomb.

We moved in a little closer as the doctor slid the shoulder of Evan's coat back and freed one arm. With a pair of scissors, he cut open a section of the shirtsleeve below the elbow, swabbed the bare skin with cotton, and sank the needle into the vein. Evan never knew he was there.

It must have been a pretty massive shot, for within a few minutes his staring eyes began to glaze over and his heart and breathing slowed. As the tension leached out of his muscles, it seemed to do the same for the rest of us and we all visibly relaxed to a certain degree.

The doctor put his stuff away. "He's going into the hospital, Lieutenant, at least for overnight observation."

"No objections," said Blair. He mopped at the sweat on his forehead with a silk handkerchief.

"My fiancée and I are his friends, we want to take care of him," Brett offered.

The doctor shook his head. "He needs professional help for now. You can check on him in the morning if you like."

Evan could have complained about being invisible again, because they were talking as though he weren't in the room. In a way, he wasn't.

The drug in his system took him a few steps further along to oblivion and he swayed a little. I got to him just in time and swept him up before he hit the floor. By now he was utterly limp, a deadweight in my arms as I carried him to his room and put him onto the bed. The coverings were still unfinished from Sally's interrupted housekeeping lesson. Only a few hours ago the world had been normal.

The doctor came in and took his pulse. "Help me with the blankets," he said. "I want to keep him warm."

I pulled the bedclothes out from one side and folded them over Evan, then added a crumpled quilt that had been thrown over a chair. "He gonna be all right?"

"He's got enough stuff in him to keep him out for some hours yet. Ask me then. Has he a relative or friend who can come with him to the hospital?"

Adrian, perhaps, if I could find him. He was in only slightly better emotional shape than Evan, but perhaps having something to do might help him. "I'll see."

Brett was trying unsuccessfully to pump Blair for information and barely concealed his annoyance at my interruption.

"I'm taking Miss Smythe home, Lieutenant," I said.

"Right." He looked at the young cop and told him to clear me with the others, then returned his attention to Brett.

Bobbi had reheated the coffee and was pouring some for Reva when I came down. Both had heard the scream and both had questions on their faces. The answer seemed inadequate to the experience.

"He's going to the hospital," I told them. "I thought Alex would want to go along."

"I'll find him," Reva volunteered, and gave her hot cup to me.

I looked at it stupidly, wondering what to do. A faint smile ghosted over Bobbi's face and she took the cup back.

"Can we go home yet?" she asked.

"As far as I know. I want to talk to Charles."

"He can call you at my place."

It sounded good to me. I told the cop on duty where we were going and walked out into a blinding burst of light.

Reporters. Of course. The kid with the camera knocked out the used flashbulb, quickly replaced it, and yelled at me to look at him. I spun Bobbi around and hustled both of us back into the house.

"*Damn.* Where's the back way out of this dump?"

The cop pointed and we followed his direction, but two reporters were waiting in the alley behind the house, kicking idly at the spillage from the garbage cans and smoking. It was a hell of a way to make a living and at the moment I was hard pressed to believe I'd been one of them only a month or so back.

"Let's just go on," said Bobbi.

But I dug in my heels, feeling the anger surfacing and badly needing to do something about it. "Wait here a minute, I'll take care of them."

She nodded and let me go out the battered screen door. They were on me like flies on fresh meat, shouting questions over each other and threatening to bring more people in with their noise. I held up a hand and achieved a pause in the barrage.

"Okay, fellas, one at a time." I pointed to the older one. "You first. Come over here so you can see what you're writing."

"That's fine, I just wanna know who's talking."

He backed me over to the door, where we could make use of the light from the house. His crony hung close enough to listen, his notepad ready and pencil poised over it. I ignored him and froze onto the older man's eyes.

"I want you to stand very still and not move for five minutes. You won't see or hear anything during that time and you won't remember me."

It helps when they're off guard. His partner's cigarette sagged in puzzlement, but it only lasted as long as it took for me to give him the same instructions. I went in for Bobbi and we walked past them, two improbable statues on display in a dank setting.

Bobbi was all wide-eyed. "They'll burn themselves—"

"Good point." I went back and thoughtfully removed the cigarettes from slack mouths, dropping them into a handy puddle.

"You . . . I mean, you hypnotized them?" she asked. "You *really* hypnotized them?"

"It comes with the condition."

"That's just like in that book."

"No, that's just like me."

"Do you do it a lot?"

"Not often."

"How do you do it?"

"Beats me. Watch where you step, sweetheart."

We picked our way out of the alley and came up to my car from behind. It was across the street from the house and as yet had not been noticed. I opened the door and slid across to the driver's side. By the time Bobbi was in I had the engine going and shifted it into first. We took the first corner right and headed for her hotel.

"Poor Sandra," she whispered. I only just heard her above the low rumble of the car. I took a hand off the wheel and covered hers briefly. It felt very small and cold.

"You want to stop somewhere for a drink?"

"No, I just want to be home. I want my own things around me."

It was a natural reaction to head for the safety of one's own nest. We said nothing for the rest of the trip. The silence held until I unlocked her door and turned on the living-room light. She was spooked and I obligingly checked all the rooms of her apartment before she took off her jacket and sat down. A brief raid on her liquor cabinet produced a medicinal shot of brandy, which she gratefully accepted. ·

"You all right?" she asked.

"I was wondering the same about you."

"I'm just scared and shaky."

"It'll pass."

She nodded absently and went into the kitchen to put her empty shot glass in the sink. When she came out she didn't settle back on the couch with me again, but wandered around the room touching and straightening things. Blair's words about death following her floated annoyingly through my mind.

She poked at some nonexistent dust on her Philco and rubbed her fingers clean. "I think I'll get out of this stuff and have a shower. Will you keep me company? Talk to me?"

"Anything you want."

I watched her take her clothes off, her movements unselfconscious and automatic. That fist gripped my gut again as I thought of the young girl I'd killed. She'd been the same way.

While the water hissed on the other side of the protective curtain Bobbie and I talked of God knows what, about anything except what had happened tonight. She shut the water off and I handed her a towel.

"I guess there is an advantage to short hair," she murmured, dabbing at the damp ends the shower spray had caught. She dried off and I helped her slip into her white satin robe. She tied off the belt and put her arms around me, resting her head on my chest. Her skin was warm and smelled pleasantly of soap. This lasted a minute and she broke away to go back to the living room.

She curled up on the couch, tucking her bare feet under the folds of the robe.

"Tell me what's on your mind," I said.

Her eyes dropped. "I'm trying not to think. It's what I feel and I feel guilty for feeling it."

I shoved some magazines to one side on the coffee table and sat on it to face her. "I know what it's like."

"I know you do. Were you scared when it happened?"

"What? Tonight?"

"No, back then . . . when . . . when they killed you."

This wasn't what I had expected.

"I'm scared, Jack. I'm scared of dying and I thought if you could tell me about it . . ."

She'd watched them carry Sandra out and had seen herself in that long basket.

"Tell me what scares you," I said.

"All of it. I'm afraid it might hurt or take days and days, but mostly that it won't make any difference, that I'll just not be here and no one will notice. I know you would, and Charles, and some of my friends, but the world will go on and I won't be here to see it. I don't want to be left behind. I don't want to leave you."

"You won't." But my heart was aching already. With care and caution I could live for centuries, but Bobbi . . . I shied away from that agonizing thought.

I moved to the couch and cuddled her into my arms. Maureen and I had faced the same decision, though the circumstances had been very different. I'd chosen out of love for her, not fear of my own mortality.

As though reading my thoughts, Bobbi said, "I love you, Jack. I can't bear the thought of leaving you. That's what scares me the most."

"What did you say?"

"I love you, I don't ever want to leave you." She turned to look up at me, her hazel eyes searching mine for a response. "The only other thing that scared me was telling you that, but after tonight I knew I had to."

"You were afraid of telling me . . ."

"It's an important word to me and everything that goes with it is frightening—at least for me."

That was true; it was frightening and exhilarating and the best and the worst all rolled together, and I'd been afraid to say it, too. We could go to bed and make love, but say nothing about it before, during or afterward. It was ridiculous.

"You don't have to be frightened," I said, my voice shaking. "At least you don't have to be frightened to love. . . ." And for the next few minutes everything got gloriously, radiantly incoherent.

Bobbi lay contentedly back in my arms, her breathing normal again, her eyes sleepy. "Are we awful?" she asked.

"How so?"

"To do this after poor Sandra—"

"It's normal. You get close to death and you want to reaffirm life. That's why a lot of babies are born during wars."

"What we do doesn't make babies."

"The instincts are still there, though."

"According to you it doesn't make vampires, either."

"Not unless we exchanged blood. Your famous book at least got that right."

"Stop picking on my book."

"Okay."

She was waking up a little, one hand stroking the spot on the vein under her jaw where I'd gone in. "That's been on my mind, you know."

"Exchanging?"

"We talked about it before."

"I remember." We'd talked about it, but not nearly enough. It was a hard subject for me to open up on.

"You said that's what Gaylen wanted, but you didn't want to give it to her."

"She was insane. It didn't show, but part of me must have known. That's why I didn't want to do it."

"What about to me?"

"How do you feel about it?"

She shrugged. "I don't think I know enough yet to tell you."

"That's a good answer."

"It's not easy for you, is it?"

I drew a breath and sighed. "It's just at times all I see are the disadvantages. My life is limited in a lot of ways, ways I'd never thought about until it was too late."

"Like what?"

"For one thing, I miss socializing over food, and I'm really beginning to hate mirrors. Sunlight blinds and paralyzes me, and if I don't sleep on my earth I have the most god-awful dreams. Going to the Stockyards is a real pain. I often leave it till late so I don't have the cattle smell on me all the evening and can wash it off when I get home."

"Did she feel the same way?" She was referring to Maureen.

"She let me know what to expect, but she never complained, except about mirrors whenever she bought new clothes." But Maureen had had decades to adjust to things and I was still grass green. Maybe in time . . .

"Then why did you want to change?"

"I loved her."

"Don't you believe I love you just as much?"

"Yes. I see what you're getting at, Bobbi, but you need to know there are no guarantees. We could do it, but it might not work."

"And then again, it might. I don't see it as a promise or even as insurance, but it *is* hope. That's all I really want, Jack, just that piece of hope."

I thought long and hard about it for maybe two seconds. She had a serious decision ahead, though I was sure she'd made up her mind already. When I'd talked things out with Maureen, I'd been the same. I'd loved her and we both wanted the hope in the background of our lives that it would continue. Now I loved Bobbi and life was repeating itself.

"Look, you need to see exactly what it's like for me. I want you to know the worst of it, and then if you still feel the same—"

"What are you talking about?"

"I want to take you to the Stockyards. I think you need to see what it is that I have to do every few nights."

"You want to show me how you eat?"

Things twisted inside. "I don't eat, Bobbi. I open up a vein in a live animal with my teeth and drink its blood."

She shifted around a little and crossed her arms, prepared for hostilities. "Are you trying to put me off?"

"I'm trying to give you an idea of what it's like to live this way."

"And painting anything but a rosy picture about it. Don't you think you're being too hard on yourself?"

"Well, I—"

"And passing that attitude on to me is hardly fair to either of us."

"Uh . . ."

"Exactly," she said. "Now, how about some straight honesty? Is what you do really so horrible? What happens to the cow after you're through with it?"

"Well, nothing. I don't drain them dry, you know."

"I didn't know, but I'm not too surprised or you'd have to have a hollow leg. As for the cow, she hangs around in a smelly pen until driven to the slaughterhouse, then some guy smacks her between the eyes with a sledgehammer. Depending on how she's processed, sooner or later she ends up on my dinner table. Does that make me better than you just because I pay to have someone else do the dirty work?"

I'd thought the whole business out before, but had never applied such logic specifically to Bobbi. She had me cold and she knew it. She smiled as the dawning finally broke on me.

Somehow things didn't seem so hard, after all.

8

WE spent a little more time talking and decided to postpone our Stockyards visit for some other night. Bobbi was physically and emotionally exhausted and I wanted her to sleep on things. My own trip there could not be put off, though. I was getting nerved up and had to concentrate on simple tasks—indications that I badly needed my long drink. After seeing her to bed, I drove straight over.

I'd purposefully overfed last time and it had bought me an extra hunger-free night. The tiny amounts I took from Bobbi also helped to some degree, but were really insufficient to maintain me. Earlier, when my lips were on her throat, it had taken a conscious effort on my part not to go in a little deeper. The temptation had certainly been present, and this time it had been very difficult to end things and pull away. When hungry, my body only knew that blood was blood, whether acquired by feeding off cattle or through sex with Bobbi. The very real possibility existed that I might lose control and continue taking from her past the point of safety. To prevent that, I wanted to be well supplied from a less fragile, more bountiful source.

Again, I parked on a different street from my last visit, ghosted in, and did what I had to do. Bobbi's logic floated through my mind as I knelt and drank. Talking things over with her made one hell of a difference; tonight was the first time I admitted to myself that I enjoyed the taste of the animal's blood. It *is* different from human blood, like the difference between milk and champagne: one nourishes and the other leaves you high as a kite. Tonight I'd had the best of both.

The feeling lasted until I was back on the street again and walking to my car. I was walking, seeing things, thinking thoughts, and Sandra Robley was dead, her inert body awaiting its turn for the autopsy table. Some *bastard* had shut her down. God knows why; there's never a good reason to be a victim.

I got in and drove half a block on an impulse. It paid off. The lights of Escott's second-floor office were glowing. Parked near his door, just behind his own huge Nash, was one of the newer Lincolns. It was really too late for him to be interviewing clients, so his visitor was probably connected with the murder investigation in some way. I shut down my motor and softly approached the building. Beneath his window, open to catch the night breeze, I could listen in on their conversation.

". . . anything, absolutely anything at all, I would be very grateful to know about it."

"Do you wish to retain my services, then?" Escott asked.

"Inasmuch as you are connected with this . . . this terrible business."

A drawer slid open. "Very well. Here is my standard contract. It's fairly straightforward. I cannot make you any promises, and in a case such as this I am under strict limitations. If I should find evidence pointing to a specific person's guilt I am legally bound to turn it immediately over to the police." He sounded extremely formal and was uncharacteristically discouraging, an indication he was not happy with his latest employer.

"You mean you think Alex did it?"

"I have no opinion one way or another, I merely follow a line of inquiry until all questions are answered."

I lost the reply, because by then I was walking up the covered stairs to the office. Two raps on the frosted glass of the outer door seemed sufficient to announce me, and I was inside, matching interested looks with Leighton Brett. His big frame and expensive clothes made him look out of place in the institutional wood chair opposite the room's equally plain desk.

He was puzzled by my showing up, but it shifted into acceptance when Escott greeted me and explained I was an associate.

"I thought you were a writer," said Brett, turning it into a friendly jibe.

"Only on my days off. This is what puts bacon on the table."

"Mr. Fleming was the one who originally called me in," said Escott.

"I'm glad he did, you were the only one there talking any sense."

It seemed more likely that Escott had been the only one there willing to listen to him.

"How did things wind up?" I asked. There was no other place to sit so I hitched a leg over one corner of the desk.

Escott moved a heavy glass ashtray a little to give me more room. It contained only one dead cigarette and no pipe dottles. They hadn't been there long. "Evan Robley is in the hospital—Miss Stokes is sitting with him now—and Alex Adrian has gone missing."

"What do you mean? Is he out on a drunk or just not home?"

"The police are waiting for him to turn up at his residence."

"To arrest him?"

"Possibly. Lieutenant Blair is being especially close about his plans, but Adrian's disappearance from the crime scene does not look good."

"It stinks to high heaven, Charles, and we all know it." I turned to Brett. "You know him best, where would he be?"

He spread his large hands. "I haven't had much contact with him since Celia died. Evan might know, but with the condition he's in . . ." He didn't have to finish, but thinking about Evan gave him another idea. "I could call Reva at the hospital, she and Sandra . . ." Again, he did not finish.

Escott pushed his desk phone toward him and we waited as he went through the motions. While he struggled to locate Evan's hospital room and consequently his fiancée I quietly asked for more information.

"What did you get from the other tenants?"

"The people on the same floor were out all evening. Those above did hear a man and woman arguing, thought nothing of it, and turned their radio up to drown the noise. The rest were a singularly deaf and incurious lot with problems of their own. A quarreling couple is not an oddity in that neighborhood."

"And nothing on who the man was or what the fight was about?"

"Nothing at all. No one is even sure if the argument is even connected with the crime; it could have been quite another couple fighting."

"What do you think?"

"That I need more information. There was one thing which you might enlighten me about: one of the reporters there was asking after you by name."

Oh yeah?

"Extremely female, tall, with dark hair and light brown eyes; very well dressed and quite striking."

"Barb Steler."

"The journalist who knew Adrian in Paris?"

"The same. Wonder what she wanted."

"An interview?"

"No, thanks. As it was, Bobbi and I barely made it out of there. She probably spotted me when that photographer popped a flash right in my kisser."

"I wonder if you left an image on the negative," he mused in a very low voice so Brett wouldn't hear.

"I hope not. The last thing I want is my mug plastered all over the morning editions."

Brett hung up and shook his head at us. "Sorry, but she said she couldn't think of anyone or any place Alex would go to. She's hoping he'll turn up at the hospital to check on Evan."

"If he left prior to Mr. Robley's breakdown, he won't know to go there," Escott pointed out.

"Yes. *Damn,* how could he go tearing off like this?" Brett smacked the desk lightly with the flat of his hand, then got to his feet. "I have to leave now, Reva made it clear she doesn't want to be alone anymore."

"Of course, and if I should learn anything . . ."

It reminded Brett of the business contract on the blotter. "I think I'll take this along for reading material. You'll hear from me in the morning."

We all said good night and Escott let him out the door. He didn't speak again until Brett's Lincoln rolled off and cleared the street.

"You've an idea?" He made it more statement than question.

"Just a small one. This assumes that Alex didn't kill her and that before he disappeared he was able to get some kind of sense out of Evan."

"Concerning Dimmy Wallace?"

"Jeez, Charles, why do I bother to think with you around?"

He took it as a compliment. "Our problem is to locate Wallace."

"No problem," I told him.

A smile briefly crossed his bony face as he understood the reference. "My phone is entirely at your disposal."

I entirely made use of it. The call took almost as long as Brett's, but I finally got through to Gordy.

"This is Fleming. I need an address."

There was a pause, because Gordy survived through caution. "Whose?"

"Dimmy Wallace."

"He making trouble again?"

"No, but I'm trying to prevent it. Someone I know might be gunning for him. I want to stop it."

A longer pause, but I knew Gordy wasn't one to waste words or time. The line was empty for a few seconds, then he came back with an address, which I wrote down. "You never called me for this, got it?"

"I never even heard of you—and thanks." I hung up and turned to Escott. "He says it's an all-night gas station."

He glanced at my scribble. "It's on the south side—enemy territory for our benefactor, if I recall the current gang political situation correctly. His wish for anonymity is well placed."

"Wallace isn't there all the time, he's usually on the move, but we might be able to talk to the people there."

"Most assuredly *you* will be able to communicate with them. Please allow me a moment to prepare before we leave, though." He opened the door behind his desk and made use of the inner room it served. There he kept an old army cot and some spare clothing, among other things. When he finally emerged, he looked slightly heavier and sported an unmistakable bulge beneath his coat under the right arm.

"Ready?" I asked.

"As I shall ever be. We'll take my car."

And no chances; he wanted his bulletproof vest, gun, and the armor plating of the Nash between himself and the unknowns that Dimmy Wallace represented. I approved. Chicago could play indecently rough at times.

Escott handled his big tank of a car, along with its extra weight in steel, the way Astaire danced with Rogers. He very obviously derived a lot of pleasure from driving and my guess was that if he loved anything, he loved his Nash, bullet dimples in the doors and all.

We were up to the speed limit, but he didn't seem to be in a hurry to arrive. That kind of urgency was missing from his attitude. We took a few turnings and though my knowledge of the city was still sketchy, I knew we weren't on a direct route to the south side.

"What's up, Charles?"

"Someone is following us," he said with quiet interest.

The hard blue glare of the streetlights struck his chest, traveled up to his chin and vanished as our car moved forward. It reminded me that whoever was behind us would see my outline if I turned around to look, so I didn't.

"Can you tell who they are?"

"Unfortunately, no. Their headlights are in the way."

"What d'you want to do about it?"

"There are a number of options open to us."

"I'm all ears."

His eyes flicked up to the rearview mirror, then back to the road. "I can lose them . . ."

"Aren't we a little too big for that?"

"Shoe Coldfield did somewhat more than add special glass and armoring when he owned this particular vehicle. There were some slight modifications to improve engine efficiency as well."

"Why is it that I'm not very surprised?"

"Haven't the faintest. Now the problem with losing them is that we may never know who they are, and such antics are liable to arouse the curiosity of the local constabulary."

"What other options have you got?"

"We can pretend to be unaware of them and lead them to a spot convenient to us, and—as it is so colorfully put in westerns—get the drop on them."

"I like that one. Got any particular spot in mind?"

"Yes, I'm heading for it now."

"Had it all worked out beforehand?"

"More or less, but it seemed best to keep moving until I'd discussed things with you. I'm so glad our decisions are in accordance."

"What if they weren't?"

"I'm not sure, but since they are, it hardly seems relevant to speculate over might-have-beens."

That was true. I was just nervous and he was being polite and not pointing it out to me—not in so many words. Escott ought to have been the nervous one, as he was physically far more vulnerable than I, but he liked this kind of work. He seemed to feed off tension the way I fed off cattle.

"I plan to rely on your speed and other special abilities," he told me.

"Okay."

"I'm going to take a turn into an alley ahead and go slow enough for you to get out. When the other car comes through, I'll have stopped at the far end. Chances are they will also stop, and you can improvise from there."

"And if they don't follow you in?"

"Then we'll go to plan B."

"Which is . . . ?"

"I'll let you know when I think of it."

I shook my head, but it didn't matter much. If this stunt didn't come off no doubt he *would* think of something else.

He made a leisurely turn into a narrow space between two long buildings. Dark walls of brick and useless, soot-stained windows slipped past and slowed as he took his foot from the gas and shifted gears. There was enough room to open the door, but I didn't bother. When we were down to ten miles an hour I dematerialized and slipped out.

Smack in front of me was the solidity of the right-hand building, which I used to orient myself. Turning and pressing my back (such as it was in this state) to the wall, I very slowly eased into the world again, but only a little. I was mostly transparent, which meant that unless I moved around or lost concentration and went whole, the party in the other car couldn't easily see me. On the other hand, I could still get a very good look at them.

Their headlights were dark as they turned into the alley. They saw Escott's car far ahead of them, but slowed to think things over. It gave me a good chance to identify the driver.

Escott had said to improvise, right now I was torn between anger and curiosity. When the first wave of it passed, they were halfway to me. I could wait for them, rush in, and do my Lamont Cranston imitation, or I could find Escott again and tell him to get us lost. Both were equally tempting.

Now they were within ten feet of me and sailing slowly past, so I made a decision, materialized, grabbed the passenger-door handle, and yanked it open.

In the crowded confusion of the front seat of the car, I wasn't sure who screamed the loudest at my sudden appearance: the young photographer clutching his camera or Barbara Steler clutching the steering wheel.

Out of reflex, she hit the brakes and the engine stalled. The kid with the camera made an abortive attempt to push me out, but I got my left arm inside in time and pushed him against the seat hard enough for him to lose his breath. The arm remained, to hold him up and to give him something to think about.

Barbara tried the starter, but their car was flooded now. She looked up—fear flashed through those huge bronze eyes for a second until she recognized me—then she slammed her hands on the steering wheel.

"*Damn* it! Where in *hell* did you come from?"

I'd meant to give them a good scare and couldn't keep the grin off my face. "Ask my mother, she knows all about it."

"You never had one, you bastard."

"Temper, temper. Maybe you'd like to tell me why you're following us around."

"You used to be in the business. Figure it out." She put a palm to her forehead and tried to slow her breathing. The adrenaline surge caused by my entrance had them both shaking.

"Barb . . ." this from the photographer, in a slightly strangled tone. My arm had slid up to his neck. I eased the pressure but kept the same position.

She saw what had happened and suddenly threw her head back and laughed. The kid joined in, but not too enthusiastically. When she recovered, her body was less tense and she had an air of being in charge of things. She opened her door and got out, walking around to wait in front of the car. I told the kid to stay put. He was still wobbly and content to do as he was told without any special influence on my part.

Barbara was in somber black, right down to her kid gloves and silk stockings. It brought out the ivory of her skin and made me want to see more of it than was decently possible under any circumstances. Her full lips were softly curved into the kind of smile a woman gets when she correctly reads a man's mind.

"This is hardly the perfect place to talk," she began.

"Good, because you won't be getting any interviews."

"Darling Jack, don't be offended, but I don't want to interview you, I just want you to help me arrange one."

The endearment was interesting, considering what hadn't happened during our last encounter. "Who did you have in mind?"

"Alex Adrian, of course."

"And you think I know where he is?"

"Or your friend, Mr. Escott. He must be getting impatient waiting for you down there." She indicated the far end of the alley. "Why don't you run along to him and continue on your errand?"

"Only if you back out and go home."

"But it's such a long drive from here, I couldn't possibly return empty handed."

"Force yourself."

"My dear, you of all people should know I *never* force myself."

The alley suddenly felt very close and warm. "Yes, well, there's a first time for everything, Barbara—"

"I mean it, Jack, I want to see Alex." Her manner shifted to a more serious tone and I wondered if she were lying again. This time I couldn't tell.

"Why?"

"Because the police are after him for walking out on the scene of a murder. I talked with them. He's in very serious trouble. He needs help—" She stopped and straightened, as though she'd said too much for her own comfort and regretted the words.

"You still love him?"

She wasn't happy that I knew that and her eyes flared, then shifted away. "Think what you like, but please take me along."

"Women who love Alex always seem to come to a bad end. Are you sure—"

She moved as fast as a striking snake, her palm cracking sharp and loud. Outrage rolled from her like a wave, more tangible to me than the slap. She looked ready to add a verbal insult to the injury but was too mad to think of one acid enough to suit the occasion.

"I guess you're sure," I said, rubbing where she'd hit my cheek. It hadn't hurt.

She turned on her heel to go back to her car.

"Barbara, wait a minute."

"No."

"I'm sorry I said that, but I had to know where you really stand."

She paused at the door. "I'll find him myself."

"Not alone, you won't."

"How else, then, if you—"

"Maybe I will help you."

That stopped her cold.

"I'll talk to my partner."

It was my turn to walk away and I felt her eyes on my back all down the length of the alley. Escott had the motor running, ready for us to bolt if necessary. He shut it down when I came up on the driver's side and started talking. He wasn't happy about my request.

"I'm reluctant to involve anyone else in this, especially a member of the fourth estate."

"She wants to come for her own reasons. Her paper has second place this time."

"I understand that, but are her personal motives going to get in the way of things? I've no wish to expose anyone to unnecessary risk."

"She could also act as backup for us. She can drive and be safe enough in your car. That sporter they're in wouldn't hold up to a good rainstorm."

"A good point, but are you sure you couldn't tell her to go home?"

"I could, but I don't want to."

"Is she immune or something?"

"No, I just want her along."

Humor and frustration mixed in his expression and then vanished with a shrug. "Very well, but no photographer. That's the prerequisite I place upon her coming with us."

I ducked out before he could change his mind.

Barbara accepted the offer with ill-concealed astonishment. "Why— I mean—after I—oh, never mind, we'll be right behind you."

"Hold on, Charles said only you could come, so don't insist on having a saddle with your gift horse."

She looked ready to contend the point and visibly worked to change her mind. It took a little more than logic to talk the kid into it, though. He was anything but crazy about letting her run off to parts unknown with two strangers; that was his main argument. Unspoken was the simple fact that he didn't want to be left out. Barb smiled, though, ran a well-calculated finger down the side of his face, and all his determination melted into an ineffectual puddle in less than a second. He took over the driver's side and solemnly promised to take the car back to the newspaper offices for her.

She kissed her fingertip and tapped it on his nose, and that made his whole week. Then I stepped in and caught his attention. I didn't do much more than repeat his promise back to him, but from the slackening of his expression I knew for certain he'd keep it.

"My, but you're suspicious," she commented as we watched him back the car out of the narrow space. "Did you think he doesn't understand plain English?"

"Like you reminded me, I used to be in the business. Neither of us would want a breach of trust at this point, would we?"

"Darling, it's the farthest thing from my mind."

"Good. Keep it there."

She slipped a friendly arm into mine as we walked up to Escott, who got out to meet us. When I introduced them, she flashed him the kind of smile that could knock over a bank vault. They exchanged pleasantries as though we were at some fancy tea party and not a dank alley just off the river with God knows what lurking around the next corner. Escott was apparently not immune to the charm of someone he'd described as "extremely female."

"We must have some ground rules," he said, finally bringing up business. "It is not likely we'll even find anything tonight, but if we do, you follow our orders."

She murmured agreement, maybe a little too readily for my peace of mind, but if it became necessary, I could enforce things as I did with the photographer.

He held the door for her and she stepped into the backseat like a queen going on a tour. "Lock the doors and if we tell you to duck, don't ignore it," he suggested.

Something in his tone got her attention and she banked the charm down for the time being and nodded seriously.

I got in, Escott got in, and we moved back out onto the street. He put a few extra turns in our route south, just to make sure no other cars had been waiting for us. None were, so he made a beeline to the address.

The gas station we wanted was a solid-looking cinder-block structure sloppily coated with dirty white paint. It sported two battered pumps out front and a garage on the left of a tiny office. Parked in front of the garage door was a well-dented open-bed truck. The fenced back area contained a broken-down carriage, dozens of rusting fifty-gallon drums, and stacks of balding tires. It wasn't the kind of place a mother would take her kid to for a rest stop.

Escott pulled in and we waited for someone to emerge and sell us some gas. I got out to do what I hoped was a passable imitation of a man stretching his legs. Barbara remained quietly where she was, her big eyes wide open and watchful.

A cadaverous old man with half a cigarette growing from the corner of his mouth squinted at us from his sanctum by the cash box, perhaps deciding if it were worth his while to leave it. He finally concluded we were staying and levered to his feet. As he drifted past, I could almost hear the pop and creak of his joints. He leaned into the driver's window and muttered something in a rusty-saw voice that might have been a question. Escott apparently had a gift for translating obscure dialects and asked for a few gallons of gas. The old man hawked and spat—without losing his dead cigarette—and did things with one of the pumps.

He kept a cold eye on me as I wandered around. A suspicious person might think I had designs on the cash box, so I avoided the front office, if not the suspicion. The garage part was closed off, but something about it had my attention on a gut level and I moved closer to listen.

The wide door had two filthy windows. They were dark, but only because of the black paint smeared on the interior side of the glass. Maybe the station owner had a legitimate reason for such aggressive privacy. Maybe.

I moved along the front of the garage with my ears flapping, but between the wind stirring things around and the gas pumping away I couldn't pick up anything on the inside. Escott was trying a little friendly conversation with the old man and kept him busy checking the oil and cleaning windows. While they investigated something or other under the hood, I went around the corner and pressed an ear against the building.

What I got for my trouble was a dirty ear. If there were any people inside, they were so quiet about it that I'd have to go in to find out.

Brick walls are no real trouble for me—I'd found that out the first time I discovered how to vanish—but filtering through one like coffee in a percolator was not my idea of fun. High up, just below the roof overhang, was a long row of fly-specked windows. It would be easier to slip through any existing gaps in their casements; they'd be small, but better than the wall. Once I'd gone transparent and floated up, I could see from all the rust that they hadn't been opened in years, and the corner of one of the panes was beautifully broken away. Grateful at this piece of luck,

I disappeared completely and slipped through the three-inch opening like sand in an hourglass.

My hearing wasn't much better inside than out, though I thought I heard some kind of scraping sound. In my immediate area I was lodged between the wall and a series of thick surfaces curving away from me that I couldn't identify. The ceiling was only inches above, and down where my feet would be I couldn't feel anything but air. I hate heights.

Then I definitely heard voices and forgot about mental discomforts.

"Lay that off, you dummy."

"But it's gettin' thick."

"So put in more water."

The scraping stopped. "Why don't he get rid of 'em?"

"Shuddup."

It was like trying to listen through a load of blankets. One cautious degree at a time I sieved back into the real world, just enough to hear and see and hopefully not be seen. The curved things turned out to be a rack of old tires and I was hovering between them and the wall. The more solid I became, the heavier I got, and it took no small effort to maintain my half-transparent state. Being fifteen feet over a cement floor without any other support than air and willpower did not help my concentration.

The garage had two doors: the big one in the front for the cars and a regular one that served the office. The remaining three walls were lined with rows of tires, and below these were greasy workbenches and a confused scattering of tools and supplies. A man had the office door open a crack and was keeping an eye on the outside. His back was to me, but I was sure I didn't know him. He wore a dark purple suit with orange pinstripes, and nobody I knew outside of a circus would have been caught dead in such a getup.

Standing just behind him, trying unsuccessfully to look over his shoulder, was Francis Koller. Since the other man was bigger, Francis gave up and went back to stirring a shovel around a large, flat container shaped like a shallow horse trough. He was trying to be quiet about it, but the shovel would sometimes go its own way and scrape along the bottom. The viscous, cold-looking gray stuff in the trough was cement.

"I said to lay off," the other man hissed, not turning around.

Francis laid off.

"Where the hell is the other bozo?" he griped.

Francis deduced it to be a rhetorical question and didn't bother to answer.

The other bozo had to be a reference to myself. Until I returned to Escott's car, whatever they were up to would have to wait, but Escott would be running out of stalls by this point. There were only so many he could try before they became too obvious.

I shifted a little, taking care not to bump the tires. My view of the garage widened.

The center of the floor was broken up by the grease pit, its wide rectangular opening covered by a metal grid. Standing against the opposite wall were a half dozen rusting fifty-gallon drums with various faded labels on them. One of them had been pulled out from the rest and its cover removed. It was positioned exactly under a heavy-duty block-and-tackle arrangement used to lift motors out of cars. A thick, taut chain ran from the supporting framework above down to a steel hook. Attached to the hook was a knotting of rope and hanging from the rope by his wrists was Alex Adrian.

His slack figure was motionless and his head drooped down on his chest. I couldn't see his face. The toes of his shoes dangled just over the open mouth of the metal drum. Enlightenment came with a fast and sickening twist of the gut. I suddenly knew what they were going to do with all the cement.

9

THE air was foul from the stink of spilled gas by the car. When I materialized I had to steady myself against one of the pumps because the sickness had followed me from the garage.

At that distance I couldn't tell if he was alive or dead. If dead, then we could take our time; if alive, then we had none left to spare. And if they put him alive into that drum . . .

With the pumps and car between us I knew the man watching from the station couldn't see me, and no one had noticed my return. Escott and the old man were still poking at things under the hood and Barb was watching the spot where I'd gone around the far corner of the garage. I tapped on her window. She whirled and slid over to roll it open.

"What's the matter?" she whispered, too worried to question how I'd gotten there. "Did you find anything?"

I could only nod and realized it would not be wise to get too detailed. "They've got Alex. They're—"

"Is he all right?"

"I don't know, I couldn't see that much. There're two men inside, and they've got him trussed like a turkey." She made to move and I stopped it with a short, hard gesture. "*Don't,* they're watching us right now. They're only waiting for us to leave—"

"But we can't—"

"Yes, we will. You and Charles are going to drive off and find the nearest phone. You call the cops and get them here as fast as you can."

"What about you?"

"I'm staying here to keep an eye on them."

She dived into her purse and brought out a beautiful nickel-and-mother-of-pearl derringer, pushing it into my hand. "Here, you'll have two shots. You have to remember to cock it first before pulling the trigger . . . you *do* know how to shoot?"

"Yeah, but—"

"Just in case," she said, and I knew it would be easier to pocket the thing than argue with her.

"Okay, thanks. You get the cops here fast, got it?"

"Yes—"

"And an ambulance, too."

"Ambulance?" The word moved on her lips with no sound behind it.

"Just in case." Adrian might need it if he was still alive, and if not, then his killers most certainly would before I was finished. "Has Charles mentioned me at all while he's been keeping Chuckles busy?"

Her expression flickered as she shifted thoughts and tried to remember. "I don't think so, he's been talking about the car the whole time. Why?"

"You'll see." I hoped Escott would follow my lead.

The old man glared at the engine with contempt and shook his head at Escott's latest question. "I jus' pump the gas, I'm tellin' you I don't know nuthin' 'bout these things."

"But just listening does not require any mechanical skill, and I'm sure if you did so while I pressed the accelerator, you'd be able to hear it as well." Escott was using his most persuasive voice and sounded like an amiable idiot. He looked up as I approached. "Oh, hello, I was trying—"

"Just wanted to say thanks for the lift," I interrupted, holding out my hand. He'd picked up the cue without batting an eye and we shook briefly.

"You're not coming along?" he asked.

"No, this is where I get off. I already said good-bye to your missus. See you around."

He wished me well and continued to argue happily with the old man for another few minutes, long enough for me to take to the sidewalk and stroll away out of sight. I blessed the actor in him, vanished again, and doubled back.

The sidewalk was my prime landmark. I followed its flat, hard surface, keeping low out of instinct rather than necessity. In this form, body posture is meaningless, but the illusion of it in the mind is a comfort.

My second landmark was the old truck parked in front of the garage door, where I turned left, moving forward until I felt the wall of the garage itself. Floating upward, I quickly found the window with the broken pane. The last faint outside noise I heard was Escott's Nash starting up. Pouring inside to the spot behind the tires, I faded enough of myself back into the world to see and hear things.

They hadn't moved. Francis held his shovel in the trough of cement, the man at the door kept watch, and Adrian hung motionless from the ropes. After stuffing him into the oil drum and filling the leftover spaces up with cement, they'd probably load it onto the back of their truck. North of us was a perfectly good lake with miles of coastline; finding a deserted spot to dump their problem wouldn't be too hard.

"You took your time," the man complained, holding the door for the old geezer to come in.

"They din' wanna leave and so what? He's gone now."

"What about that other one? Where'd he go?"

"Off. Hitchin' a ride and got hisself unhitched."

"You sure?"

"I seen him walk."

Francis resumed scraping at the cement. "This shit's starting to set, Dimmy, we gotta *move*."

"Who's stopping you?" he snarled back.

Dimmy Wallace: bookie, loan shark, and new terror of the south side, but then Francis was easily impressed. I saw a middle-size, stocky man who badly needed to cut the limp blond hair straggling from under his hat. He had a pudgy face and colorless eyes with the kind of blank expression you usually find on infants or lunatics.

Francis took the hint with a short, relishing laugh and put down his shovel. "C'mere, Pops, gimme a hand." He went to a length of chain leading down from the pulley mechanism above, presumably so he could lower Adrian down into the oil barrel.

Pops thought it over sourly. "Nuh-uh. None o' this crap, I pump gas."

"I said I need a hand," Francis insisted, but apparently he was too much a junior member of the team to swing any authority. Pops turned around and went back to the tiny office. Francis tossed a comment about the old man's ancestry to his indifferent back and unhooked the chain from the wall in disgust.

Bringing Adrian's body down a few more feet was a strain for him. Dimmy Wallace made no move to help, nor was he asked. When Adrian started to double over, Francis reversed the chain to take in the slack. He strutted up, hands on his hips, the owner of a brand-new toy.

"Do I kill him now or wait and watch him squeal?" he asked Wallace.

That was the best news I'd heard all evening. It gave me a whole new set of worries, but at least I knew Adrian was alive.

"Do what you want, but just do it. We ain't got all night." Wallace was bored with the business.

"We got till Toumey comes back."

"You got till the cement sets. Remember?"

Francis did, much to his disgust. He wasted no more time and poked at Adrian's downturned face. "Hey, Mr. Hot Shit. C'mon, you don't wanna miss any of this."

"Give 'im some air," Wallace suggested.

Francis moved faster than thought. A knife appeared like magic in his hand and the blade slashed at Adrian's throat and caught on something. When his hand came away he was holding the knife and Adrian's tie. I sagged inwardly with sick relief.

He showed it to Wallace. "That's a fancy one, ain't it? These hot-shit rich guys like the good stuff, don't they?"

I shifted a little more to the right to get a better angle on Francis. It would be steep and fast and I'd have to judge it just right when to—

"And lookit these fancy buttons. . . . But maybe they ain't good enough for such a nice shirt. Maybe they oughta be solid gold instead." He dropped the scrap of tie and neatly sliced away a collar button. "Come on, hot shit, I'm talking to you—wake up and lissen."

The point of the knife jabbed Adrian lightly in the side and he jerked, swinging a little from the rope.

"Yeah, hot shit, have a good look at things. You 'member trying to fight me? This is how I pay you back, you see? You *see?*" He laughed at whatever he saw on Adrian's face.

Adrian mumbled something I couldn't catch. Francis looked at Wallace.

"He wants to know if you killed some broad, Dimmy. You kill anyone today?"

"Not that I can remember," said Wallace, his voice flat.

"How come you don't ask *me,* hot shit? Maybe I did it, maybe I walked in and did her good. Maybe she let me in and wasn't friendly enough. That's the sister, huh? Robley's sister? He keeps quiet about her, but we know all about her, and we know all about how to make a girl real friendly. Hey, Dimmy, he's telling me to shut up. What do you think of that?"

Dimmy was bored again and expressed no opinion.

Playing, Francis jabbed the knife at Adrian's face. "That's what I think of shutting up, Mr. Fancy Hot Shit."

I moved a little lower. It would have to be from below. The rack of tires ran all along the wall's length and there was no room to go above them.

"You know you're bleeding? Maybe I should just open it up a little more . . ."

He was very close to Adrian, it was going to be tight.

". . . slip it right between the ribs. I can do it fast or slow—how thick is your skin, Mr. Hot Shit?"

I was nearly too solid. Gravity tugged at me as I pressed my feet against the wall and launched across the open space of the garage like a swimmer into water. I felt the resistance of the air slow me down and countered it by growing more solid. Solidity gave me weight and speed, and when I slammed into Francis with a full body tackle I'd completely materialized.

We crashed into the stacked oil drums, bringing them down with a stunning amount of sound. One of them fell right on me, cracking my head, and I couldn't move for a moment. With some disgust, I belatedly realized I could have vanished right after hitting Francis and saved myself the discomfort.

A hand plowed in and grabbed the collar of my coat, hauling me out of the mess. I sprawled backward, throwing my arms out for balance, but my rescuer dodged out of range, not that I was in shape to do him harm. My head felt like a small firecracker had gone off just under the spot where the barrel had landed. The metal wasn't as bad as wood, but the pure kinetic shock of all that weight required some recovery time.

Pops appeared from the office, gawking at the chaos and then at me. "Thas one of 'em—the hitcher with that feller who wouldn't leave."

"What?" demanded Wallace.

"I seen 'im walk. How'd he get in here?"

Dimmy Wallace had more cause to wonder about that himself, having witnessed my miraculous appearance out of nowhere. I rubbed the sore spot on my skull and got reoriented. Francis was facedown in the middle of the overturned drums, not moving. I hadn't killed him, but he wouldn't be functioning for some time to come. In front of me was Pops and on my left and coming around to the front was Wallace.

He had a stubby black revolver in his hand. From the tiny size of the barrel opening it looked to be only a twenty-two. They could do damage and could certainly kill, but you had to know how to use them. Since I didn't know what kind of shot he was, I'd have to assume he was an expert and handle things from that angle. Adrian was my prime worry; we were both on the wrong end of the gun, but he'd be the one to get hurt if I weren't careful.

He swung a little against the confines of the barrel. Francis had been so close to him when I came hurtling down that he'd been bumped by the rush. His face was guarded as always, but flushed with a new alertness at my arrival. His eyes were sharp, dark pinpoints, full of sudden questions and something I interpreted as fear.

"You okay?" I asked.

His eyes widened slightly and his mouth twisted open—into an awful gasping laugh. He shut it down almost as soon as it was out.

"You!" This from Wallace. After that he couldn't seem to think of anything else to say. He'd seen me literally come out of thin air and was having a lot of trouble handling the event. His eyes kept bouncing from me to the rest of the garage, searching for some hiding place that I might have sprung from.

"Looks like Francis is a little flat," I said conversationally. "You want I should pick him up?"

The words didn't really register, which was too bad, as I wanted to distract him from his uncertainty and speculations.

"He was with that car?" he asked Pops.

"I tol' ya," came the confirmation.

Wallace shifted from me to Adrian and back again. "The other guy'll bring help, you can bet on that."

"Then I'm gittin' gone."

"Yeah, go start the truck."

Damn. I'd been hoping to stall him a little longer. I was ten feet away from the gun. Wallace had judged that to be a safe distance to keep me from trying anything. It couldn't be helped, I wasn't about to let them take a free walk out.

I moved a step to the right, widening the space between myself and Adrian. The gun muzzle swung and centered on my chest. Pops froze, his mouth slack and the bottom gums showing, as he waited to see what happened.

"Stay *put,*" said Wallace.

His eyes were still blank and I didn't like what wasn't in them. Off to the left Adrian expelled another short hiss of air. I couldn't tell if it was laughter, pain, or fear.

Then Wallace moved one finger. He was fast; there was no way I could have stopped him in time.

The bullet lanced my chest like a white-hot needle, its impact and effect all out of proportion to its size. His aim was perfect, precise as a top surgeon's. It went in just left of my breastbone, slipped between the ribs to clip my heart, and tore out my back.

Time slowed and movement along with it. As a sound separate from the shot, I heard the flat *tink* of lead on steel as it struck one of the barrels behind me. Before the finger could tighten on the trigger again I was on him. His lips peeled back as I wrenched the gun away, a mirror of my own pain. The bullet's tearing flight through my body had nearly knocked me down from the fire-red shock. I wanted him to feel the same hurt, I wanted him to know about death. . . .

A short, curse-choked scream.

Adrian's voice shouting my name.

White darkness clouding my sight.

Din-filled silence jamming my ears.

Sound flooded back into my consciousness as though I'd never heard it before. Time had slowed and then vanished altogether from my mind. It returned, trickling unevenly as I woke out of the cold rage that had taken me down to . . . to . . .

I shied away from what lay within me. My body trembled. The first time this had happened, it hadn't been so bad. Understanding had come with experience, but that didn't make it any better. If I'd still been a normal human, I'd have staggered to the grease pit and been sick.

Dimmy Wallace was on his side at my feet, curled fetuslike around his broken arm. Pops was gone and distantly I heard the rough thrum of the truck outside starting up. He'd be well away by the time I ran out front. The cops could worry about him, I had troubles of my own.

I turned Wallace over gently, as though to make up for what I'd done. He mewed out, crying over his ruined arm. His colorless eyes opened, squinting as though simple sight caused him pain as well.

Then he bared his teeth and started calling me every foul name in his ample street vocabulary.

The world shifted abruptly back to normal, and his cursing washed over my fear and dissipated it. He called me more names, thinking my laughter was at his agony, then the eyes widened a little more as he decided I was crazy. I had been, for one brief, awful moment. Now I was deliriously thankful I'd not passed the insanity on to him.

"You're staying right where you are, understand?" I made certain he would obey but didn't bother putting him to sleep. I had, after all, wanted him to feel pain.

Francis was well and truly out, but I collected his dropped knife and put it in my coat pocket. It clattered against Wallace's gun. Another small tremor fluttered against the base of my spine because I couldn't remember picking the thing up.

I finally stepped clear of Francis and went to Adrian, pulling the knife out again. We locked eyes as I reached above him and cut at the rope. He said nothing, but his gaze dropped after a moment to the hole in my shirt. He'd been awake. He'd seen and heard it happen.

"Bulletproof vest," I said.

"Yes . . . of course," he murmured.

The last strand broke away and he collapsed forward, biting off the agony of release. We had a clumsy moment as I alternately pulled and lifted him from the oil drum. When he was out flat on the filthy floor, he groaned gratefully at the change of position.

"Your hands?" I asked. The skin was swollen and red where the rope had cut into his wrists, but his fingers were still moving a little.

"Can't feel a thing yet. It's my shoulders and back—" He broke off and the creases around his eyes and mouth deepened as he dealt with the inner protests of his body.

Outside, a car rolled up, nearly silent. I only just caught its tires crunching over the road surface. The driver must have cut the motor and coasted in. I told Adrian to keep quiet and cracked open the office door for a look as Wallace had done before me.

I saw a narrow piece of the station and some of the street beyond. Parked across the street, opposite the pumps, was Escott's big Nash. In the distance and coming closer I heard the first siren rise and soar into the pale night sky. I sighed relief and went out to meet them.

Lieutenant Blair had been up all night as well, but suffered the effects more. I was tired, too, but in a different way from him.

"And you say that when you drove off in the car, Charles just slipped into the garage and surprised them?"

"Yeah. I wanted to go in, but he was in charge and said it was his place to do it himself. Somebody had to drive the car away as a distraction and to keep an eye on Miss Steler, so I got the job."

The uniformed cop who took down my original statement had listened to it twice-over now with mild interest. His current entertainment came from watching Blair trying to swallow it all. He sat at our table in the hospital canteen, his notebook and pencil on standby in case I decided to change anything. Blair was across from me and fastidiously ignoring the stale cup of coffee someone had brought him.

The canteen was empty except for a woman behind the counter minding the coffee machine and a pile of donuts. She looked more interested in the donuts than us. It was a big hospital for a big city; maybe she was used to cops interviewing people at ungodly hours of the morning.

"Dimmy claims that he shot you," he said.

"Uh-huh." I sounded doubtful. Who was he going to believe, some crook or me? On the other hand, this could prove to be quite a strain on our induced friendship. "If he wants to put a nail in his coffin, that's his business, but it was Charles he shot."

"Really?" It was Blair's turn to sound doubtful and he leaned forward, lacing his fingers together. "And just how did *he* survive?"

"He's got a bulletproof vest. He said Wallace looked pretty rattled when he didn't fall down, maybe that's why there's a mix-up about who got shot."

Blair had done a quick inspection of my clothes and found no trace of a bullet hole. Earlier, Escott and I had hastily switched shirts in the men's room while everyone had been busy with Adrian and the others in emergency. I carried my punctured coat over my arm.

"So Dimmy shot him and it sort of slipped his mind?"

"He's not the type to get worked up about a thing like that."

The cop at the end made a noise and Blair glared at him, then came back to me. "Well, yes, I can see how that could happen, he must get shot several times a week. I'm sure he's used to it by now."

I shrugged good-naturedly. "You'll have to talk to him about it, I missed all the fun."

"I'll bet." He couldn't quite resist putting in some sarcasm, but he was at a dead end and knew it. A change of subject was next. "All right. Now, as to how you knew to go there . . ."

"The gas station? That was Charles's idea."

"Was it?"

"Yeah. He thought maybe Adrian might have gone after Dimmy Wallace because of Sandra—which is how it turned out—and he's got a few connections around town. . . ." Some truths, some falsehoods, they were mixed up enough for me to get away with them.

"What connections?"

I shrugged. "You'll have to ask him."

"I will. How did that reporter get involved?"

"She followed us and wouldn't leave, you know what they're like."

"I know what that one's like," he muttered, and the cop made a noise again and got another glare.

A third cop came in and said that Francis Koller was awake. Blair told me to get lost and went to yet another interview. My old suggestion of friendship was definitely wearing thin.

When they all walked out and left me alone I put my head on my folded arms and felt old in heart, cold in spirit, and tired to the bone. It was a mental weariness, harder to deal with than the physical kind. You can go to bed and rest the body, but the burden of your own emotions can take years to lift, if ever.

"Would you care to go home?" Escott stood in the doorway, hands in his pockets, head cocked to one side.

"Like a week ago. What's the time?"

"A little after five."

Dawn was still too far away. I wanted oblivion now.

"Headache?"

"Yeah, but all over, if you know what I mean."

"Indeed I do. How did things go with Lieutenant Blair?"

"Pretty much as you expected."

"I'm pleased to hear that."

"Said he'd talk to you later."

Escott gave in to an extended and luxuriant yawn. "You take the car, then. I'll find a cab after he's finished his questions with me. Come on, I'll walk you out."

My chair squawked loudly against the floor as it scraped back.

"Will the suggestions you gave to Miss Steler about who did what hold?" he asked.

"I don't think there'll be any problem."

"Let us hope so. With your condition you could hardly put in a court appearance if and when this mess comes to trial."

"Maybe if it were a night court . . . ?"

He smiled. "What about Koller and Wallace?"

"I was able to talk to Wallace before they put him in the ambulance. He didn't kill Sandra but he couldn't say yes or no for Koller. The white coats chased me out before I could tell him what kind of story to give."

"What about Koller?"

"Him I'll have to talk to later, or maybe the cops can sweat it out of him today. I don't think he can back up Wallace's story. I came in so fast he never knew what hit him."

We'd only gone a few yards down the hall when a large nurse stepped from her station and blocked the way. "Mr. Fleming?" She glanced back and forth between us.

"Me," I said, halfheartedly raising a hand.

"One of my patients asked to see you before you left."

"Isn't it past visiting hours?"

"It certainly is," she said wearily. "But he was very insistent."

"Alex Adrian?" I'd been expecting this and dreading it.

"Right this way." She led off without checking to see if we followed.

Escott politely waited outside as I went into Adrian's private room. He was sitting stiffly against a bank of pillows on the high bed, wearing a flimsy hospital gown and a disgusted expression. Two big wads of bandages covered his wrists and I couldn't help but think of Popeye the Sailor.

"Something amusing you?" he said.

"Just glad you're all right."

"That's one man's opinion."

"The nurse said—"

"Yes, please come in."

His face was drained and gray against the white pillows, and the cloudiness in his dark eyes suggested drugs. In deference to his wrenched shoulders and arms, he was careful not to move his head too much. I took a metal chair next to the bed and turned it around to face him.

"Cops talk to you?" I asked.

"Oh yes. Quite thoroughly and at great length, then that lieutenant told me I'd been damned lucky and to leave police work to the police from now on."

"Nothing like adding insult to injury."

"The insult is that they're not telling me anything. What's to happen to Wallace?"

"I don't know. Last I saw, they'd knocked him out to work on his arm."

"Is anyone watching him or Koller?"

"Yes." I didn't like this turn of the conversation. "Stay away from them, Alex."

He said nothing. A sullen red fire glowed far back in his half-lidded eyes.

"They're in custody and that's enough for now. You can press charges—"

"I already have, for assault and attempted murder, but it is not nearly enough."

"It'll have to be."

He looked straight ahead to the blank white wall in front of him. "If it had been Miss Smythe, what would you do?"

That one hit me hard, as he'd meant it to. Once my gut reaction eased, I realized it had taken a lot out of him to say that, to admit Sandra had made him so vulnerable.

"Same as you, want to tear them to pieces."

His eyes shut, his voice dropped to a gentle whisper. "That's exactly what I want to do to them, and I want to do it with my own hands."

I couldn't hold that against him. I knew exactly how he felt. More so, because in the past I had acted on those feelings and killed.

"Thank you for coming after me," he said in the same quiet tone. The darkness within and around me lessened a little.

"You're welcome."

His breathing evened out and deepened. Whatever they'd given him was getting a chance to work now. "Did it hurt very much?" he asked.

"Did what?"

"When he shot you."

Hell.

"I once saw a magician shoot at a deck of cards and hit only the ace of spades. . . . Perhaps Wallace had a magical bullet that only puts holes in clothing and not in people."

"What do you want?"

The question surprised him enough to open his eyes. "Nothing, really—only confirmation of what I know I saw. You came diving out of thin air from an impossible angle, then took a smash in the skull that should have knocked you cold for hours—or even killed you."

"Maybe you were a little feverish from hanging there for so long."

"Yes. Perhaps I was, but I'm not now." He looked away from me, a faint glitter coming from beneath his lashes. "I saw you fade and flicker back, like a light bulb losing and then regaining its power. I saw you. I did not imagine it."

Hell and damnation.

"The barrel came crashing down and you dropped under it, and then it rolled away because you weren't there anymore. Wallace only saw you coming out of nowhere, he missed the rest. The other barrels were in the way for him. By the time he'd waded through, you were back again, and solid."

I bit my tongue and waited him out.

"And you got up seconds later, asking *me* if *I* was all right." He laughed faintly, like a ghost. "I might have blacked out then, I might have imagined it all, but not the shot. I was quite wide awake. I saw you take it point blank, I saw the exit hole in your back." His look dared me to contradict him.

I didn't and confirmed things by turning away.

"I thought you were rushing him on momentum alone, that you'd fall at any time, but you didn't. You got to him and he screamed."

"I was breaking his arm."

"It was more than pain; it was like what you did to Koller the other night when you frightened him."

"Maybe I've just got a way with me."

"Yes, you do. I wanted to see your face then, I wanted to see *why* he screamed."

His voice was still low and gentle, but somehow filled the sterile room with vibrations of his . . . hate? That wasn't the right word, it wasn't large enough to encompass the emotions quietly seething from him. I knew and had felt all that he was going through: the rage, the need to do something about it, and the ultimate helplessness when that need is denied. It was different for me; I could free myself, but only at the cost of someone else's sanity. Adrian did not have that terrible luxury. He could only talk, which was why I was so ready to listen.

"I didn't tell the police any of this, of course," he said. "And I can understand why you asked me to lie to the police about you and your friend."

"They'd just think you were crazy, coming at them with a story like that."

"They certainly would."

It would only take a moment and he was more than half-under now. A moment of shifting his thoughts around, a few suggestions, and I'd be safe.

"I won't tell anyone."

He didn't have all of it, just enough to question, to be dangerous.

"You moved very fast, you know—when you went after him. You seemed to flow and merge with the air." He was starting to drift already.

Only a moment to convince him of a false memory, to tell him what he should think. I hesitated, because this acceptance was suddenly very important to me.

"It's quite . . . beautiful." The creases on his skin smoothed as the muscles beneath relaxed.

A touch, a freezing of his mind and a simple command . . .

". . . beautiful . . ." The glitter submerged under his lids.

I went out quietly so as not to wake him.

"What did he want?" asked Escott, falling into step with me.

"To say thanks."

10

A long day's rest restored my tired body, if not my peace of mind. When the sun went down and darkness released me for another night, all the same problems were there, only they'd had time to ripen.

Alex Adrian's name was on the front page of the lesser papers again and even the major ones had placed the story above the fold. They carried virtually identical accounts of Sandra's murder. Later editions mentioned that two suspects were in custody, but Barb Steler had scooped them all with her report on how they'd been captured.

"I find it odd that she does not give your name," said Escott. He was stretched full length on his sofa in the parlor, the papers neatly stacked over his legs and a stiff brandy within easy reach on a table. "Or perhaps it's not so terribly odd, after all."

I'd just come up from the basement when he started talking as though continuing an interrupted conversation. His brain was always working and sometimes he expected people to keep up with him. By now I was used to it, but it usually threw others off balance.

"We had a little talk at the hospital when I was giving back her gun," I said.

"She did a credible job of minimizing your role in the incident. No bright lights and fame for you?"

That one didn't even deserve an answer. The radio was tuned to Escott's usual station, giving us an earful of violins playing Mozart. With the volume down low, the higher-pitched notes were almost bearable.

He folded the last paper, adding it to the stack on his knees, then inhaled a few molecules of brandy. "I appreciated her free advertisement of my business, but am rather annoyed at being called a 'private detective.' "

It just meant he'd be getting more requests to do divorce cases. He could handle turning them down.

"Learn anything new today?" I asked, sitting across the table from him.

"I was able to glance at the autopsy report."

That had to have taken some doing. Blair hadn't exactly been in a sweet mood when we'd last seen him.

"Sandra Robley had some bruising on her face and the left side of her skull was smashed in by a very powerful blow. The forensic man was of the opinion that she'd first been struck by a fist and then hit with something much harder while she was down. The police found a heavy bronze sculpture by the sink in the Robleys' kitchen. They think the killer took it there to wash away the blood and fingerprints. It was next to a damp towel and quite clean."

"Very neat of the bastard."

"Except for her change purse, nothing else seems to have been stolen."

"You think it was a blind?"

"Yes. Probably the best the killer could do at the time. They had no valuables in the place unless you count their paintings. Except for confidence tricksters or forgers, who are rarely so violent, very few criminals are interested in the fine arts as a source of money."

"What do the cops think?"

"They are of a similar opinion, that it was a blind, but murder for the gain of a few dollars is certainly within their experience. Today they've been questioning Sandra's friends and business acquaintances on the theory that the crime was committed for a personal reason rather than gain. A personal motive is often easily found out—proving one in court is the tricky bit."

"What about Evan?"

"He's recovered enough to give the police a coherent statement, but is still in hospital and under mild sedation."

"He's all right, then?"

"As well as he can be, considering his circumstances."

"What'd he say?"

"That he walked his lady friend home, returned to his own house about an hour later, and discovered his sister's body. He remembers calling Alex Adrian, but has no memory of anything afterwards. His doctor says the amnesia is not unexpected, he may recover or he may not."

"Do the police believe him?"

"They confirmed the times of arrival and departure with the lady, which was also corroborated by her roommate. Both vouched for his good character in the most sincere terms and also stated that Evan was in a lighthearted, very humorous mood. Of course, the man could be a consummate actor or a liar who so believes in his own fantasies that he is able to convince others."

"He doesn't strike me as the type, if there's a type for him to be."

"I'm merely covering all possibilities. As for practicalities, he had the means and opportunity, but no readily apparent motive. I'm not saying the police have entirely ruled him out as a suspect, but thus far they have yet to arrest him."

"That's something at least. How's your new client doing?"

"Mr. Brett came to the office long enough to drop off his contract and to listen to an expurgated version of how we found Adrian. He then signed a check and left for the hospital to see Evan."

"He paid you already?"

"For one day's—or rather night's—work. He's satisfied that Wallace and Koller are responsible for Sandra's death."

"Are you?"

His gaze was firmly fixed on his brandy snifter. "They do seem to be tailor-made for the part, and their violent response to Adrian's intrusion was most incriminating. Since Wallace is not powerful enough to challenge Gordy directly, their motive for murder could be a form of reprisal against Evan Robley."

"Shaky, Charles."

"I know. From what you've told me, they would have been more likely to want to frighten the Robleys and thus intimidate Evan into continuing payment on his canceled debt. Murdering his prime source of income is certainly carrying things too far. Wallace and Koller are denying all knowledge of it."

"They'd have to. Any news on the old geezer from the garage?"

"The police located him later that morning, he's assisting in their inquiries—oh yes, they also found the other fellow, Toumey."

"Yeah?"

"He'd taken Adrian's coupe around to a certain garage to sell to the

less-than-honest operators there. They have, or rather had, a highly lucrative stolen-car business. The police alert to pick up Adrian included a
description of his vehicle and its license number, and a passing patrol car
happened to be in the right place at the right time. Several birds were an-
nihilated with the casting of that particular stone."

"So Adrian's off the hook with the cops?"

"Yes, for the time being."

"You think he did it?"

"I think we lack information." He'd stare a hole in that brandy
snifter if he wasn't careful.

"And you figure I should talk to him?"

He nodded once, but remained silent, letting me think. Damn the son
of a bitch. The Mozart stuff ended and was replaced by some kind of
modern vocal piece that sounded like stuttering, lovesick cats. I heaved
to my feet.

"I'll see you later."

I didn't take a direct route but dropped by Bobbi's hotel to check on her.
I'd tried calling from Escott's, but her phone was busy.

Piano music came through the walls, which meant Marza was visiting. I grimaced, but then no one ever said life was fair, and knocked on
the door. The music faltered over a few notes and then continued on with
determination. She usually kept the mute pedal down for the sake of the
other hotel tenants, but shifted her foot from it as Bobbi let me in.

We hugged hello and Bobbi asked her to stop playing so we could
talk.

Marza put on a sweet smile, utterly lacking in sincerity. "I'm sorry,
was I disturbing anyone?" She pretended to busy herself by lighting one
of her noisome little cigars. To protect my own sanity, I grabbed Bobbi
and dragged her out into the hall and firmly shut the door behind us.

"Rude, isn't she?" I asked.

"Absolutely," she answered, and then we gave each other a proper
kiss.

"Your phone's been busy," I said when she came up for air.

"It started ringing when the papers came out this morning. I'm just
famous enough locally to bring every crank out of the woodwork, so I
had to take it off the hook. Did you see one of those rags? 'Singer Stum-
bles Over Slaying.' I just hope they don't cancel my spot this Saturday."
She pulled me tight, needing reassurance. "This is awful, thinking about
myself with all this going on."

"No, it's not. You couldn't be awful if you tried, unlike some people
I know." I nodded significantly at the door and Marza's direction and
eventually got a smile.

"I'm sorry about that, she thinks you've dragged me into a situation that will hurt me. Marza's terribly protective."

"She's terribly something. Are you doing all right?"

"Yes, I'm just fine, really. Did you have anything to do with finding Alex?"

I gave her the quick version of events and covered the points all the papers missed. "Anyway, the heat's off him for now."

"What about poor Evan? I've tried calling the hospital, but they just said he was stable, whatever that means."

"Charles says he's all right, he just doesn't remember much from last night."

"Probably just as well. Look, I'm going to kick Marza out so we don't have to hang around the hall."

"Sorry, baby, but I have to go talk with Alex about some things."

"Like whether he—"

"Yeah, that and some other stuff."

"I don't know whether to wish you luck or not. Can you come back by later?"

"As soon as I'm free."

"Good. I'm still going to kick Marza out. She's been with me almost all day and I need a break."

"Atta girl."

At the hospital, the nurse on Evan's floor told me only thirty minutes were left for visiting.

"Is he still under medication?"

"Yes, a mild sedative to relax him."

That was convenient. "Has he had any other visitors?"

"Some of his friends are with him now." Her phone rang before I could ask which ones.

I opened his door quietly and was not too surprised to see Reva Stokes and Leighton Brett. Reva was concentrating on her talk with Evan and didn't notice me, but Brett looked up in time. He was a big man, but still managed to ease out soundlessly, giving a relieved sigh as he joined me in the hall. He smiled grimly and pumped my hand.

"Good of you to come by like this," he said. "I hope you don't mind waiting, but Reva's just gotten him to talk a little about Sandra, and an interruption now might spoil the mood."

"I understand. How's he doing?"

"Better than he was last night. I forgot to thank you for your help. When he started to go off the deep end—"

"We were just lucky that doctor was still hanging around. Is Evan's memory any better?"

" 'Fraid not. I'm hoping Reva can help him, but if it comes to it I'll be looking around for some kind of psychiatrist. I don't know about you, but that breakdown he had last night scared me to death, and I'm still worried about him."

"How so?"

"He might do something crazy if we don't watch him. He and Sandra were very close. They genuinely liked each other. Now, I like my own sister, but if she got killed—God forbid—I wouldn't do anything desperate to myself out of grief. Anyway, that's how Evan's worrying me."

"Does his doctor know about this?"

"I've talked to him. He's keeping Evan sedated for the most part, but whether that's doing him any good . . ." Brett finished with a shrug.

"How long will he be here?"

"He gets out tomorrow and then he's coming to our house. I'm not letting him go back to that apartment and stay there alone."

"I'm glad to hear that, but I thought since he's known Alex for so long . . ."

He snorted, but not unkindly. "Alex is hardly fit to take care of himself, much less Evan."

"He's survived."

"At the cost of his soul, if you ask me. He gave up when his wife died. All we're seeing now is the walking corpse."

Brett had a point there. The first time I met Adrian I thought the same myself. "He seemed pretty lively last night."

"Oh, he still has some anger in him. That's what sent him off half-cocked and nearly got him killed. I think anger is all that's really keeping him going these days, which is not a good way to live. I'd like to get *him* to a psychiatrist, but you can't cure a man's mind unless he wants help in the first place."

"I can understand him being angry about Sandra, but—"

"About his wife? It's been there, all mixed up with his grief. The man can twist himself up so much he could meet himself coming around a corner. Alex was working in his studio the night Celia—the night she died."

"And if he hadn't been painting, he might have stopped her?"

Brett nodded. "He's angry with himself and sometimes it's thick enough to cut with a knife. Evan was able to put up with it because he's known him for so long and is so easygoing he can't stay mad at anyone for more than a minute."

"Has Alex been in to see him?"

"I don't know. He was released earlier today and isn't answering his phone."

That sounded familiar. Brett excused himself to look in on Reva and a few minutes later they both emerged.

"I'm glad you've come by," she told me, taking my hand briefly. "He's still very sleepy."

"I won't stay long," I promised, and wished them a good night. When they were well down the hall, I went into Evan's room.

He was motionless on the high metal bed, his lank, ash-colored hair clinging damply to his pasty gray forehead. One lamp burned in a corner, its shade tilted so the light wouldn't bother him. He didn't notice I was in the room until I sat down next to him and lightly touched his hand.

He started slightly and his eyes dragged open. "Wha . . . ?"

"Hi, remember me?"

Recognition tugged at the corners of his mouth. "Where's that pretty lady of yours?"

"I had to leave her home, I've heard of your reputation."

"You and all the nurses on this floor. Any water around?"

I found a glass on the bedside table and filled it for him. He sat up for a sip and fell back, exhausted. "They pumped me full of something I don't like. Everything tastes awful, even the water."

"How do you feel?"

"Dunno . . . wrapped up in cotton, all over. When I'm out of here I'll find something else to do the job."

Brett's fears were still fresh in my mind, but I had the feeling Evan was referring to the kind of emotional painkiller you get from a bottle of booze. "Cops give you a hard time?"

His eyes went vague for a second. "I don't think so, it's all so fuzzy."

"I know."

"This is real, isn't it? She's gone, isn't she?"

I nodded.

His hands formed into helpless fists and went slack again. "Why?"

"I don't know, Evan. I'm very sorry."

Not unexpectedly, tears started out of his eyes and trailed down the sides of his face. He was unaware of them.

I'd seen him start up like this before and neither of us would be the better for a repeat performance. "Evan . . . listen to me . . ."

First I calmed him down and then we had a quiet talk. It didn't take long to reach through to his blocked memory and find out he'd told the complete truth to the police. At least I had my own private confirmation that he hadn't killed Sandra and knew nothing about it. The last thing I did before sending him off to sleep was to make sure he had no thoughts about suicide.

I stood and turned to leave—and stopped short. Adrian was standing just inside the door. His mouth was slightly open and he was twisting his wedding band around. I'd been focused entirely on Evan and had heard nothing.

"Hello," I said, hoping it didn't sound as awkward as I felt.

"I was wondering if you might show up," he stated neutrally. He was casually dressed, his shirtsleeves rolled back to accommodate all the bandaging on his wrists.

"How are you?" I asked.

"Well enough."

"Been there long?"

"Oh, yes."

"I'd like to talk to you."

"I rather thought you might. Shall we find a more comfortable place to do so?"

Not waiting for a reply, he led the way down the corridor to a spacious room with one wall composed mostly of windows. Chairs and tables dotted the polished floor at frequent intervals, and a row of wheelchairs were stored in a far corner. During the day the place would have been flooded with sunlight, but now it was gloomy and strangely isolated. He didn't bother turning on the high overhead lamps and was content to remain in what for him would be darkness.

"It's like your studio, isn't it?" I asked.

He arrested his move to pull a chair from a table and glanced around. "Yes, it is . . . I'd wondered why I liked this place."

"And you prefer sitting in the dark?"

He got the chair the rest of the way out and sank gratefully into it. His movements were slow and careful, an indication of the stiffness lingering in his shoulders and back. "I don't mind. It softens reality and makes the impossible more acceptable."

"Me, for instance?"

"Yes." He brought out a pack of cigarettes and tapped one onto the table, but didn't fire up his match. Perhaps even that tiny spark would have made things too real for him. "I meant what I said last night, I won't tell anyone about you—or about what I just saw."

"Thanks."

"I have a lot of questions, though," he added.

"I might not answer them."

"You've a right to your privacy." He played with the cigarette, turning it end over end between his index finger and thumb. "Were you born with your abilities or were they acquired?"

"Acquired."

"Are there others like you?"

"I know of only two others."

"What are you?"

I considered that one seriously for a few seconds, then started to laugh. I couldn't help myself. Adrian looked vaguely insulted at first, then broke into one of his sudden smiles. It was brief, on and off again, but he meant it.

"Sorry," I said.

He shrugged it away and finally lit his cigarette, blowing smoke up into the still air. "Yes, I can see I'm ridiculous."

"Not you, the situation. Wanna change the subject?"

"By all means."

I broke away from the door and took one of the other chairs at his table. "Sandra."

Muscles on both sides of his neck tightened into iron. "No."

"Have to."

"Why? No . . . never mind, it's all too obvious. As with Evan, you want to know if I murdered her."

"You need to be eliminated from a list of possibles."

"Same thing, nicer phrasing." He looked directly at me, his eyes and voice like ice. "Ask."

I did and got the answer I expected. While I had his attention I asked my other question. "Did you kill Celia?"

His reply was slow in coming, so slow in fact that he woke out of my influence in his fight to hold it in. His walls were back up again but not as solid as before. When he took a puff from his cigarette I noticed the slight tremor in his hand. "I did not kill my wife," he whispered. "Not directly."

"How, then, indirectly?"

He was quiet for so long I thought I'd have to give him another nudge. "My work," he said finally, his tone so faint I might have imagined the words. "Always my damned work."

I waited until he'd smoked another half inch. "Your work?"

"What I have is not artistic talent, it's addiction. It's always been there, all my life. The silence and total solitude are utterly necessary for me to produce. Not many people can understand that, least of all Celia. She did try, and God knows she loved me, but it must have been the bitterest thing of all for her to realize she would always be second to the art."

I knew how bitter it had been for Barb Steler.

"I believe that all people have the need to create, and consciously or not they find outlets for it. They paint or write, they marry and have children. Celia had no such outlets for herself, but the need was there, so eventually she found one."

"What do you mean?"

"Another man. I really don't know how long it went on. She had the most miserable excuses for being out and sometimes she couldn't keep her stories straight. Even now I'm not sure if I was being selectively blind or just stupid, probably a bit of both. She wanted me to find out, like a child who does something bad for the sake of getting attention."

"Did you?"

"Yes. Sooner or later every sleeper wakes. I think she was glad when it happened. It was quite an explosion on my part, but it proved to her I could still be hurt—that I still loved her." Some of his inner agony welled up, constricting his throat, thickening his voice. "Two days later she went out to the garage and started the car."

He drew deeply on the cigarette to distract himself and coughed a little on the smoke. If there was a suppressed sob hidden in that cough, I pretended not to notice.

"I was on the other side of the house in the studio and heard nothing. I'd been avoiding her by working on another damned magazine cover. We'd talked divorce; neither of us really wanted it, but we didn't know how to return to each other. I didn't know how to forgive her. She broke it off the only way she felt she could." He stared out the tall windows, seeing nothing. "That's how I killed her."

"Did Sandra know about this?"

"No. I wanted things to be different for us. She would have always been first—I would have made certain of it. We never had the chance."

"Who was the man?"

"Celia never told me."

"Could it have been Evan?"

He was almost amused. "No, of course not. He talks a lot of charm to a lot of women, but has the sense to stay away from the married ones. Besides, at that time he was happily involved with a little blond model named Carol."

"Have you ever figured out who it was, or guessed?"

He shook his head and stubbed out the cigarette in a tin ashtray. "I used to think of nothing else and now it hardly seems to matter anymore."

"You've no idea?"

"None." He ticked at the ashtray with an idle finger and nearly sent the dregs flying. "I think I'll look in on Evan now."

"He's going home with Reva and Leighton tomorrow."

"I thought they might make the offer, if only to spare him from my cheerful company. They did the same for me when Celia died, but I knew I'd smother beneath all their concern for my well-being. Evan's the type to respond to such care, though. Perhaps it's what's best for him."

"I hope so."

"Good night." He walked out slowly, hardly making a sound.

". . . so if Charles is still up when I go home he'll be getting an earful."

Bobbi half reclined on her couch, her feet curled under her and a small coffee in her hand. I sat opposite her on the edge of a low table, rubbing my right fist into my left palm.

"You think Celia and Sandra are connected?" she asked.

"They were both involved with Alex Adrian."

"He really got to you, huh?"

"Because of losing Maureen, I see myself in him. I know how he feels."

"You want to help, but you can't."

"In a nutshell," I said, sighing. "Your phone back on the hook?"

"Not yet, you need to use it?"

"No, I'm just noticing the quiet a lot for some reason."

"Stop carrying the world on your back and things will get a lot noisier for you."

She raised a smile out of me again. "Want to go to a movie?"

"How 'bout a western with a nice cattle stampede?"

That made me blink, until I figured out what she was getting at. "Been thinking about visiting the Stockyards?"

"All day."

"If you're sure . . ."

"Not yet, but you said I should watch what you do."

"I know. I think you have less problems handling it than I do."

"We can find out."

"Okay. Go put on something you don't mind getting dirty. That place ain't exactly Michigan Avenue, you know."

Ten minutes later we were cuddled up in the front seat of my car. Bobbi wore some battered Oxfords, a dark sweater, and a matching pair of wide-legged ladies' trousers. Her bright hair was covered by a black cloche hat she said she hated, but hadn't gotten around to throwing out yet. We didn't talk much, but it was a companionable silence. I drove sedately and parked fairly close in.

The air vibrated with the lowing of hundreds of animals, and their stench flooded over us. Normally I wouldn't have parked downwind, but it was convenient. The car air would clear out when we left. I glanced at Bobbi to see if she was ready to chicken out. She seemed to read my mind and shook her head with a smile.

"How do we get inside?"

"I usually disappear and float in, like I did the other night through Evan's door. This time we'll climb a fence."

She opened her handbag and pulled out a tattered pair of black cotton gloves. "Just as well I came prepared. I don't want to pick up any splinters." She pulled them on and tossed the bag under the car seat. "Ready?"

"You been studying for this?"

"I had a lot of time to think about it."

Picking a long, dark stretch between streetlights, I led the way in and helped her climb up and over. No one was near enough to notice our intrusion, but I didn't want to take any chances by hanging around too long. We went to the closest occupied pen and scrambled over its thick timbers.

Bobbi stared at the three cows huddled in the far corner and they stared unenthusiastically back. "Big, aren't they?"

"They stink, too."

"But you put your mouth—"

"Baby, I get so hungry, it just doesn't matter." A lazy stream of wind from a distant slaughterhouse carried a breath of the bloodsmell over us. Bobbi couldn't pick it up, but I could and it stirred dark things within me.

"Are you hungry now?"

"I'm getting there." I'd fed last night, but a person can be full of food, walk past a restaurant, and still salivate. The same principle applied now. I made myself breathe regularly to catch more of the smell and centered my attention on the nearest animal.

The process of hypnotizing people is fairly simple, but different rules apply to animals because they have less intellect and better defensive instincts. I didn't entirely understand how to make an animal stand still for me, it was on the same level as my ability to disappear: I'd think about it and it happened, like flexing an invisible muscle. Maybe the animals could sense it somehow; it didn't matter much to me as long as it worked.

I closed in on the cow and ran my hand lightly over a big surface vein. The animal remained still, as though I weren't there. Bobbi tiptoed closer to see things better.

"This is where I usually go in," I told her, keeping my voice low and even. She nodded her understanding.

"What about your teeth?"

My canines had not yet emerged. I wasn't really all that hungry, nor was I sexually aroused to any great degree. "I'm having a problem there."

"Maybe I could help?" Her intuition was working again. That, or she correctly read the look in my eye.

"If you don't mind a little smooching in a cattle pen . . ."

She didn't.

A few minutes later I had to pull away from her. "I should have brought you along sooner, it's a lot more fun like this."

"Just as long as you don't feel the same way about the cow."

"Good grief, no."

The animal hadn't moved. I crouched next to it, careful to keep my knees out of the muck, and centered in on the vein. Not so very long ago I'd been quite squeamish about the whole business, now I cut straight through without any fuss—and I drank.

Bobbi crowded in to see. I finished and wiped my lips and she patted the cow. "Nothing shows, at least nothing I can see now," she said.

"They get worse battering on the trip in."

"Maybe you should keep one as a pet."

"Charles hates cattle, too messy for him. So—what do you think?"

She shrugged. "It's not what I expected."

"And what was that?"

"I'm not sure . . . maybe that you'd sprout horns or something or start foaming at the mouth. Actually, you looked like you were enjoying it."

"Maybe I should start selling tickets."

"Get an agent first. Shall we go?"

"Thought you'd never ask."

We went back to her place and she shucked out of her old clothes while I flushed some soap and hot water over my face. When I came out of the bathroom I immediately noticed the lights were out and that she hadn't bothered to get dressed again.

"Something on your mind?" I asked innocently.

"I'd like to take up where we left off in the cattle pen." She slid her arms around my neck and fastened lightly onto my lips. "That is, unless you think you've already had too much for one night . . ."

She stifled a shriek as I picked her up and carried her to the bed. We fell into it, laughing, and proceeded to do some delightfully indecent things to each other. Between the giggles and gasps, we talked of love and, eventually, consummated it.

Bobbi dozed a little and I stared at the dull white bowl of her overhead lamp, drifting in a pleasant haze of good feeling. Our legs and most of my clothes were tangled up in the sheets, but at the moment it seemed like too much trouble to straighten things out. Elsewhere in the hotel two radios played, each at a different station, but faint enough so as not to be annoying. Outside, traffic sounds oozed in through the windows.

"What are you smiling at?" she murmured.

"You were right. The world isn't so quiet since I put it down and started listening."

"I'm a font of wisdom," she agreed, and stretched luxuriously.

"Have you thought about what comes next?"

"You mean about changing me?"

"Uh-huh."

She snuggled in closer. "Well, it's kind of scary, but then so's love."

"How can love be scary?"

"It just is; the most important things always are."

"You scared of me?"

"Never, but you're still important."

"That's good. What do you want to do?"

She propped up on one elbow and looked at me. "I want to spend forever with you, or at least try."

Damn if I didn't start to get a lump in my throat. I pulled her close and couldn't let her go for the longest time.

"Jack . . . ?"

"Mm?"

"You may not breathe, but I still . . ."

I opened my arms a little and she emerged, smiling, her hair as rumpled as the sheets. "What do we do?" she asked.

I stroked the whole length of her body as though for the first time, making new discoveries, tasting new tastes. They say when you make love to produce a child it's different, more intense and vital. I felt that now and savored it. This was something to always be remembered and I wanted it to be the best of all possible memories for both of us.

She moved against me and on top of me, her warmth soaking into my own flesh. With her I had no need of sunlight. I spread my arms to her and her hands generated new heat where they touched me.

Her lips plucked at my face, my chest, my neck. . . .

That felt wonderful. I encouraged her to continue.

Her blunt human teeth wouldn't be able to break the skin easily, but the touch of them was maddening. I caressed her long, smooth back and worked my hand around front, between us, to her flat stomach. She lifted a little and I moved my hand lower. Her sighs lengthened, matching my own.

The clean scent of her rose perfume filled me, the roar of her heart deafened me, the weight of her body on mine was a delightful burden I never wanted to set down.

She lifted her head, arching it back, her mouth open in a breathless cry as she accepted the climax I gave her. Her legs went stiff, her arms wrapped convulsively around me. Her hair and skin glowed in the faint light from the window. Dear God, she was beautiful.

My other hand came up, because I couldn't stand to wait any longer. With one of my fingernails I dug into my neck over the large vein. I felt no pain, only a sudden trail of scarlet fire seeping onto the flesh.

She saw—and understood. She kissed my lips once and then put her own to the wound. My sigh stretched into a moan as she took from me and as I gladly gave. I'd never had this kind of a climax before, not as a human, not even with Maureen. Like a storm, it rolled over and through and went soaring up to a peak lasting as long as she drew on my red life, taking its promise into herself.

11

"COME *on*, Jack, this isn't funny."

Something energetically tugged and shook my arm, hard enough to wake the dead.

"Wake *up*."

"Mmm?"

The shaking stopped. "Are you in there? Wake up and answer or I'll get a bucket of water and—"

"Mmm!" I was more affirmative this time and waved her off. " 'M 'wake already." My voice was slurred and it was an uphill battle just to open my eyes.

"So convince me," she insisted.

After a bit of concentration I managed to keep the lids up long enough for a glimpse at her face. Her expression was an interesting combination of anger and worry. "Whas the 'mergency?"

"You are. You haven't moved for hours. I thought I'd killed you."

I considered the heavy feeling of pleasure that still dragged at my edges. "What a great way to go."

"Are you all right? What happened?"

"Just having a little rest. I should have warned you that I might conk out afterwards. Is it very late?"

"A little after ten. You mean that's normal for you when we do it this way?"

"Yeah, but don't worry, it feels just great." I reached for her and pulled her close, craving her softness again. "I think it happens because of my blood loss."

"But you'd just eaten, sort of. I couldn't have taken that much from you."

"I think this had less to do with amount and more to do with sensation."

"Does it hurt you?"

"Anything but. How do you feel?"

"Fine, I guess. You just scared me with that stunt—I mean, you were so *still*."

"Maybe you wore me out."

"Is that how you sleep during the day?"

I nuzzled her hair again. "That's right. Having second thoughts?"

"It's a little late for that, this is just healthy curiosity."

"I'm all in favor of any kind of healthy activity."

"No kidding." She burrowed a little closer and a low laugh bubbled from her. "You know, one of my friends says sometimes it's so good for her she passes out. Is that what happened to you?"

"Yes, my sweet love. That's what happened to me. Accept it as a tribute to your talent and its effect on me."

"Wow."

And that said it all for some time and we held lazily on to each other until she stirred and stated she was starving—for solid food.

"Take you out?" I offered.

She stretched. "Maybe tomorrow; all I want are a couple of scrambled eggs and then I have to sleep. I've got to get up to rehearse at the radio station and then work out what I'm going to wear at this broadcast."

"How come you get dressed to the nines for a radio show? Your audience can't see you."

"The ones in the studio can, and so do all the people I work with. Another thing is that I sing better when I know I look good."

"Oh."

"Besides, the other women dress up and I'm not about to have any of them see me at less than my best."

"You dress for other women?"

"Oh, Jack, it's only showing a little competitiveness."

"And I thought I'd put you out of the running."

"You have, but I don't want people thinking I don't care how I look anymore."

"Bobbi, you'd look like a queen even in a gunnysack."

"I'm glad you think so, but I still wouldn't be caught dead wearing one. Now give me a kiss and let me go fix some food."

A short while later she was slipping some butter-yellow scrambled eggs onto a plate along with a slice of dry toast. "If I do change, I think I'm going to miss this stuff a lot. You said you missed the socializing but not the food?"

"That's right." I gulped queasily at the cooking odors and watched in fascinated horror as she dropped a dollop of ketchup on the plate. Even before I'd changed, I'd never liked eggs with ketchup; mustard, maybe, but never ketchup.

"If we do this exchange again, are you going to pass out the same way?"

I must have had a sappy look on my face. It wouldn't be the first time. "I certainly hope so."

"What, do it again or pass out?"

"Well, they both felt terrific. . . ."

She laughed and attacked her eggs while they were still hot, but she sobered again after a few bites. "One more question?"

"As many as you like."

"Was it this way for you with Gaylen, I mean when she . . ." she faltered. "Maybe I shouldn't have asked."

Something in my manner must have stiffened up and she'd noticed right away. "No, it's okay. I still have some scar tissue left, is all, it just isn't where you can see it."

"And with Gaylen?" she prompted, her brow puckered.

I closed my hand gently over hers and told the utter truth. "What you and I did together was make love. What she did to me was a kind of rape. There are a hundred hells of difference between the two."

Escott was still up when I got back home, which I half expected, as he often kept late hours himself. What I did not expect was the presence of a visitor as evidenced by a car standing in my usual spot in front of his house. I recognized it, parked farther down the block, and walked back, wondering if I should just barge in on them or not. Barb Steler had left him with quite a favorable impression of herself; if she in turn found him even a little attractive, my unexpected arrival might not be too welcome. My own ecstatic experience with Bobbi had left me mellow and wishing the same joy upon others, but on the other hand I wanted to know why Barb had come calling.

Curiosity won out and I used my key this time to go inside. If Escott found her irresistible, he was enough of a gentleman to take her upstairs rather than risk a fall from his narrow sofa. In that case I was prepared to become diplomatically deaf and leave the house for an hour or so.

But they were talking about the European situation in his front room and the thought crossed my mind that at times Escott could be an idiot.

". . . Spain is merely the testing ground in a larger game. It's certainly no secret now about Hitler supplying Franco with pilots as well as planes."

"And from this you believe that he has larger ambitions?" she asked, her voice all soft and throaty.

"Larger than any man in history has dared to imagine."

"Today Germany, tomorrow the world?" I could almost see her depreciatory smile. "It is an awfully *large* world."

"Filled with many who would only too cheerfully give up their right to think if they believed it would buy them a little peace and prosperity. It's what he's counting on."

"But think of the good that he's done—"

"Like hiding all the anti-Semitic propaganda for the duration of the Olympic games? Such extreme attitudes directed at a specific population have absolutely no place in an enlightened twentieth-century state, and yet this is the spoken policy of that state's leader. It is hardly a position appropriate for a reasonable and responsible society to take, and yet he has many followers on both sides of the Atlantic."

"Surely you don't intimate that I—"

"Ah, but you equate my general views as a personal attack on yourself and you needn't. Playing the devil's advocate has its appeal and makes for a better debate. I rather enjoy a good debate."

"And politics are a favorite subject?"

"Not in particular, but one may extrapolate from the larger overview politics provides and distill it down to simple motivations. Hitler's outstanding hatred for Jews most certainly has its root in some personal experience. The man is in sad and desperate need of some sort of mental counseling. He certainly has no business running a country."

"One might say the same for many other world leaders, mightn't one? But then who would be left in charge to run things?"

"The civil service, of course. They may be as slow to change as a bone into a fossil, but are generally more stable than fanatical, slogan-spouting dictators."

She laughed, low and musically, and I made some noise shutting the door. Escott called out from the front room.

"Jack? Come in and join us, my dear fellow, we've been having a most interesting talk on world affairs."

I stuck my hat on the coat tree and sauntered in. Escott was at his ease in his leather chair and Barbara was comfortably ensconced on the couch. Cigarette smoke swirled in the air above the brass lamp by the window and each of them had had at least one mixed drink. For a man of Escott's quiet personal habits, this was practically a New Year's blowout on Times Square.

Barbara patted an empty spot on the couch, smiling fondly at me. "Yes, do come in and help us solve everything."

"Well, uhh . . ."

Escott gave me a very slight high sign, indicating he wanted more company. Not only could he be an idiot, but he wanted a chaperon, too. To each his own, I thought, and dragged my mind away from carnality and myself into the room. I sat on the other end of the couch from Barbara and smiled easily at her. She returned it just as easily and still managed to inject it with a potent shot of her own special electricity. Some people are like that, and her more than most. I wondered why she buried herself working for a cheap tabloid instead of a larger paper.

"You're looking tired, Jack," she observed. "Are you all right?"

"I've been busy."

Escott was very interested, but said nothing because of Barbara's presence.

"Is this a social call?" I asked her.

"I like to think of all my visits as social calls, but not everyone is of the same mind on that."

"Miss Steler came by with some news concerning Dimmy Wallace," Escott prompted.

"What news?"

She shifted forward a little and lost some of her affectations. "He's still being held on other charges, but the police have dropped him as a suspect for Sandra Robley's murder."

I wasn't too surprised at that and said so.

"Then you don't think he did it anyway?"

"No, not really. Why did they drop the charges and what about Koller?"

"Both of them have an alibi for the time."

"What kind of alibi?"

"Wallace's car broke down on the other side of the city and a Father Philip Glover of St. Mary's and two other priests stopped to play good Samaritan. They gave him a lift to a garage and back again, then stayed with him to make sure his car was in working order. He's covered for the whole time of Sandra's murder and then some. Koller stayed behind, but went across the street to wait in a bar. There are several witnesses to confirm that."

"It's too good to be true. Are you sure about these priests?"

"Father Glover is a well-known figure and has served the parish for the last twenty years or so."

"What about the bar?"

"It's one of those little neighborhood taverns where everyone knows everyone else. That's why they noticed Koller; he didn't seem to fit in."

"What were they doing on the other side of town?"

"Minding their own business, they claim. Perhaps they were on a collection trip, but all that really matters is that their alibi is solid and now Alex is back as suspect number one."

"But he nearly got killed himself because he thought Wallace and Koller did it."

"Which doesn't matter to the police. All they know is that he was closely involved with Sandra and can't account for his time that night."

"And that he's under a cloud from another woman's death."

Her look lanced through me with the same kind of force and intent as Wallace's gunshot. Escott had been quiet before, now he turned to stone waiting to see what happened. She drew a deep breath as though to call me a few names, but changed her mind and let it out very slowly.

"I hope you will believe that I am trying to help him now. Or perhaps you're testing me again?" There was enough ice in her voice to start a new glacier, a suitable contrast to the fire in her eyes.

"We all need to be aware of what he's up against, that's why I mentioned it. I know you're trying to help, or you wouldn't be here."

The fires banked, at least for the moment, but she was anything but happy at being reminded of her past smear campaign.

"Are the cops planning to arrest him?" I asked.

"I think so, but word is they're waiting until they've finished talking with all of the Robleys' friends and business contacts. Unless they turn up something from that end . . ." She shrugged.

"He will want a decent lawyer," said Escott.

She turned on him. "And do you think he's guilty?"

He was looking at me. I shook my head. "No, but he is in deep enough trouble to require one all the same. Perhaps you know of someone who might be useful."

"I do, but what else can be done?"

"Little enough at the moment. We and the police require more information than is presently available."

"I suppose a signed confession from the murderer would be nice." She'd put an acid bite to her tone.

"It would be decidedly convenient. Who knows what the future may hold?"

Barbara did not share his optimism one bit. "Nothing more than a jail cell for the rest of Alex's life unless we do something for him." The sarcasm had no effect on Escott, which annoyed her. She got her gloves from her purse and started pulling them on. "Well, gentlemen, it *is* getting late. Jack, would you see me out to my car? The street might not be very safe at this time of night."

I remembered the derringer she carried and figured she wanted talk, not protection, but walked her out anyway.

"How *do* you put up with him?" she asked, turning and leaning back against the closed door of her car.

"It's mutual respect. Besides, he has to put up with me as well."

"That *must* be amusing."

"We're doing what we can about this, Barbara."

She smiled, just a little, and touched my cheek with one finger. "I know, and I'm being terribly ungrateful, especially after the way your friend charged in there to save Alex."

Last night's editing of her memory was still holding, so not everything was going down the drain. "Yeah, he's good at that kind of thing."

"What else has he done?"

"In general or about this case?"

"Both. I'm thinking of writing a feature article on him. 'The Lonely Life of a Detective' or something like that."

"First off, he calls himself a private agent, not a detective, and second, you need to talk to him about what he does."

"You think he might object to his name appearing in my paper?" My hesitation in answering did not insult her. "Don't worry, I have no illusions concerning the kind of rag I work for."

"Why work for them, then?"

"Why not?"

"Because you're too good for them."

"I'm glad you think so. The truth is that I like what I do and will continue to do it until something I like better comes along."

"*Is* there anything you like better?"

Her smile broadened and she traced a finger down the side of my face. "I think you know the answer to that, darling Jack. The problem with my little pleasures is that I don't want to earn my living by them, then they would cease to be so pleasurable."

I didn't know what to say to that and she thoroughly enjoyed my discomfiture.

"You *are* such a sweet man. Would you like to come by later for a drink?"

If she only knew what that invitation really meant to me. "Not tonight—"

"Yes, you do still look tired. What have you been doing?"

"Visiting friends." I started to laugh. "It can be draining."

She picked up on the humor, even if she didn't get the joke. "Another time, then"—she pecked my cheek, got into the car, and slid over to the driver's side—"when you're fully rested." It wasn't what she said, but the way she said it. As she drove off, I stood in the cloud of her exhaust and gulped a few times.

Maybe Escott wasn't such an idiot, after all; it probably had to do with his instinct for self-preservation. I quickly retreated into the house, locking the door for good measure.

He was still in his chair, only now he'd drawn his legs up so his knees bumped his sharp chin, and he'd lit a pipe. He broke off staring into space when I returned and flopped wearily on the sofa.

"A tiring night?" he inquired.

"More than you'll ever know."

"I have observed that when you employ your special talents it often leaves you in a depleted state. May I conclude that you had occasion to use them this evening?"

"Oh, yes."

"Miss Steler prevented you from speaking out, I'm sure, but if you are not too fatigued I should like to hear an account of what happened."

I gave him his earful on my hospital visit, but left out Bobbi and the new phase in our relationship, though he was unabashedly fascinated by my condition and anything to do with it. Hearing about our exchange of blood would no doubt interest him on a certain cold, academic level, but at this point the current state of my emotional life wasn't relevant to the Robley case, nor was it really his business.

By the time I'd wound down, he'd finished his first pipe and was busy reloading another. The air was getting too thick for talk so I got up, opened the front windows, and flushed out my clogged lungs.

"Do you plan to do anything about him?" he asked, successfully lighting up on the first try.

"Alex Adrian?"

"Insofar as he knows about you."

"I don't think he'll be any problem."

He accepted my judgment with a curt nod and closed his eyes against the curling smoke. "Tomorrow I shall make a nuisance of myself to Lieutenant Blair and see what his plans are concerning Adrian. He will have collected a number of reports on Sandra Robley's other friends by then, perhaps he will also have a better suspect upon which to focus his attention."

"I hope so."

"Indeed. I have serious doubts that the present judicial system would accept your unorthodox method of arriving at the truth as viable evidence."

"Especially since I'm not available during day sessions."

"I foresee another possible problem: You were with Adrian when he found the body. It is entirely possible you'll have to give evidence to that effect."

"Oh, shit."

"Or be held in contempt if you fail to show up."

"Couldn't I give a written statement or some kind of proxy?"

"I'm not sure, I'll talk to my lawyer about options. This was an occurrence I had not foreseen when I asked if you would like to work with me."

"Same here, but I was the one who asked you for help this time."

"I appreciate your confidence in me but fear it is misplaced this time. In essence, this is a tragic business, but of the sort that the police are best suited for dealing with."

"Even if they arrest the wrong man?"

He drew and puffed smoke, thinking carefully. "I doubt they will be able to scrape up a strong enough case against him to bring it to court. He has no alibi, to be sure, but he has that in common with a lot of people, including myself."

"Yeah, but you didn't know Sandra and you have no motive."

"True. Then who did? Who would want to kill such a woman? The violence preceding her death and the violent manner in which she was dispatched indicate that she aroused a great deal of emotion in her murderer. Who among her circle possesses such a temper?"

"Alex."

"Of course, always back to him, and you are absolutely certain of his innocence? Yes, then we must look elsewhere." He tapped the pipe against his teeth a few times and opened his eyes to look at me. "Do you fancy another outing tonight?"

"Where?"

"To the Robleys' flat."

"Any reason why?"

"Because I wish to have a better look at it. Circumstances were such that I had no chance for a good look 'round on the night of her murder."

Oh Lord, it looked like he was going into one of his energetic moods again. All I wanted to do was lie around the rest of the night and think about Bobbi. "Won't the cops have cleared away everything important by now?"

"I'm certain of it, but I wish to see what they deem unimportant." He put his pipe aside and stretched out of the chair, looking like a stork unfolding from its nest. "Charming as it was to entertain Miss Steler, I feel I've been vegetating here all evening. A drive in the cool air will do me a world of good."

"It's kind of late to be waking up the super in their building."

"I've no intention of disturbing that worthy man's rest."

"You need me along to go through the door and let you inside?"

"Not as long as I have my burgling kit. I would like your company because you had been there only a scant hour or so prior to the crime and can so inform me of any differences that might impress themselves upon your memory."

"After all this time?"

"You underestimate yourself, though I do see the point that for you, the period between has been amply filled with activity. Are you really that tired?"

An answer to that question might lead to a dozen other questions, none of which I wanted to go into at the moment. "I think I can last till morning."

"Excellent! I'll just fetch my keys—"

I stopped him before he got too far along. "Let's take mine, it's already warmed up, and I wanted to move it closer to the house anyway."

"Quite so. I daresay it will be less conspicuous in that neighborhood than my Nash." He tossed me my hat and settled his own at a rakish angle over his brow. Now that he had something to do he was impatient to be off, so I speeded up a little, but my heart wasn't in it. The next time Bobbi and I exchanged, I was going to make damn sure I had nothing else to do for the rest of the night but recover from the celebration.

Escott opened the front door and practically bounded down the steps. I moaned inwardly and did what I could to keep up.

We walked into the building normally. Escott was of the opinion that in this case stealth would draw more attention than if we acted like we belonged. No one bothered to poke their heads out as we climbed the stairs, and after a short moment of listening, I was satisfied no one would.

The police had sealed off the flat, which was hardly a barrier to me. I saved Escott the trouble of working with his skeleton keys and picks and went on through the door to open it for him from inside. He slipped in, shut the door quietly, and flipped on the light.

Sadness hung in the air like a fog. Things had been moved and shifted but not cleaned up. Fingerprint dust was still everywhere and the chalk outline still lay on the floor, a pathetic marker of her presence. Escott frowned furiously at it, shook his head sharply as if to clear his mind, and moved on to search the kitchen.

He did not take long and moved through the two small bedrooms and the bath just as quickly before coming back to the front again. "Does anything draw itself to your attention?" he asked.

"Evan's painting has been moved."

Apparently some fastidious soul had seen the big self-portrait at just the right distance and had turned it to face the wall. I reached for it.

"A moment." Escott had come prepared and gave me a thin pair of rubber gloves, the kind surgeons use. He was already wearing some himself, I just hadn't noticed when he'd put them on. I shook myself inwardly and tried to pull on an attitude of professional detachment along with the gloves. In this depressed state I was no good to anyone.

I tipped the painting out enough to see that it was undamaged and checked the other vertical racks and their contents. As far as I could tell, nothing was missing or marred, though as elsewhere, many of the paintings had fingerprint dust on them. Escott found that of interest and peered at the bright colors of an abstract through his pocket magnifier.

"It appears Mr. Robley used his fingers as well as his brushes to achieve certain effects."

"Sandra, too. Both of them had paint stains on their hands."

"Are these Sandra's?" He indicated another stack of stored paintings against the opposite wall.

"I guess so, we only looked at Evan's that night."

He sorted through them. "She would seem to be less prolific than her brother, as there is more than adequate storage space available—or perhaps she sold more?"

I nodded. "She said she was on some kind of WPA art grant. That was how they were able to live."

"Producing art for federal buildings?"

"Yeah. I think she also did stuff for interior decorators. There's apparently a market for genuine oil paintings."

"I've heard of it, assembly-line oils, pretty pictures for the masses at the cost of artistic integrity."

"Integrity is hard to afford when you don't have food in the cupboard," I pointed out.

"Yes, there are strong arguments in both directions, and who's to say where one may safely draw the line?"

That called for a second look on my part, but I didn't think he meant it as a pun. I flipped through Sandra's work with Escott looking over my shoulder.

"She would appear to have a wide range of styles," he said. "This one is after one school and this after another. I wonder if she ever had time to develop a style of her own. . . ."

"What do you mean?"

He set four different paintings out for view. "These for example: all are landscapes and all depict the same basic forms of hills, trees, and water, but they could have been painted by four different people. I'd be inclined to think so, too, but they are all out of the same palette." He darted to the other side of the room, where some painting supplies were kept, and drew out a thin flat of paint-stained wood, then held it up to the landscapes. The dominating colors of brown, green, and blue matched.

"You're sure about that?"

"I've had a smattering of art in my time. A painter's palette is often as identifiable as his fingerprints."

"Okay, so we know Sandra painted them all. Her work had to appeal to a lot of different people so she could sell. Is it important?"

"All information is important until proven otherwise." He returned the palette to its place and focused his attention on one of the big easels. "Is this one hers?"

"I think so."

He flipped off the dust cloth protecting the surface of the canvas beneath. The painting was an angular townscape in autumn, with wet streets and blowing leaves. Escott peered at it closely with his lens, then with his beaky nose practically touching the surface, sniffed. He backed off, puzzled, sniffed again, covering a wider area this time.

"What are you doing?"

"Checking the state of the linseed oil."

"Is it stale?" I asked, amused.

"Indeed." He swept the flat of one hand across the painting and held his clean palm up for inspection. "It's quite dry."

"Why would she have a dry painting on the easel?"

He didn't answer but went back to her store of paintings and flipped through them, rapidly pulling out three, all the same size. They showed the same angular street, with variations of color and light.

"Winter, spring, summer and the one on the easel is autumn, obviously a series on the theme of the four seasons. I suppose it is just possible she was doing a little touch-up work, but it hardly seems likely."

"Why's that?"

"Please note the top clamp of the easel: it stops a good five inches above the painting."

"Meaning that it was originally adjusted for a different size canvas?"

"Exactly. Now I wonder what became of that particular work?"

"She could have taken it out herself."

"Then where is it? There are no wet paintings in this flat and she could not have sold them in that state."

"The cops took them."

He shook his head. "No, I stayed here and watched the forensic men. They did not remove any paintings. So unless Alex Adrian broke in and took them to his home for safekeeping or out of sentiment—"

"You figure the killer is some kind of art lover?"

"I'm not sure what to think. They were taken for a reason and unless he's mad enough to want to retain a most dangerous souvenir of his crime, the only reason I can think of to justify his theft is—"

"That what he took incriminates him in some way. Then what was it, a quick portrait or something?"

He had no answer for me and flipped the dust sheet back onto the canvas, then turned and brooded over the chalk scrawl on the floor.

It blocked my sight for only a moment, but I saw Evan again, standing in the same spot and swaying at the waist; Blair watching in shock, and Brett reaching to help him. That inhuman keening went through me once more and I shivered as though someone had walked over my empty grave.

Oh God.

Sometimes it happens that way, your mind hits on an answer with a sudden bright burst of insight, but won't tell how it got there, and you're left fumbling for an explanation. It eventually came tumbling out of my memory: words, looks, gestures . . . all fell together, linked up, and formed into a solid composition.

"Oh God." This time it slipped out aloud.

Escott sensed something in my tone. His eyes snapped up, silently demanding to know what it was.

I told him.

He soaked it up without comment, having heard some of it before, but only presented as idle conversation, and mixed in with other events. In the end he could only shake his head.

"You have the answer, and if we find the paintings, we'd have enough circumstantial evidence for the DA to bring it to trial—"

"But I sure as hell can't come to court to tell it. The one thing I can do, though, is get the written confession you wanted."

"Before only a single witness?" he questioned, meaning himself.

But I had a second witness in mind even as he raised the point.

12

THE streets were dead and sheeted over with cold white reflections from occasional lights. It was after midnight and one look at the lead gray sky clamped hard over the city was enough to make you realize how far away dawn could get if it really tried.

Escott sat next to the door and pretended to look straight out the windshield. Between us was Alex Adrian, who was doing the same thing, only he wasn't pretending. The stuff inside his mind was keeping him too busy. His face was drained and white, even the lips. His hands with their bandaged wrists were curled protectively around one another, the right thumb and finger twisting his wedding band back and forth in slow, unconscious rhythm. Except for that and the motion of the car, he was perfectly still. He could have been a corpse, right down to the invisible wall behind his eyes.

I'd asked a lot of him, and before things were finished I'd have to ask more—the question was, how much could he stand. He was an unexploded bomb now and I didn't know the length of his fuse.

"Turn here," he said. I nearly jumped—you don't expect a corpse to talk. "It's the servant's drive, better access," he added, his voice soft and distant.

I turned into a narrow break in the curb line. Trees crowded overhead and we rolled slowly along the drive's smooth cement surface for a hundred yards.

"Stop now and get out."

It wasn't a command, only another unemotional direction to follow. I eased the car to a halt and got out, pressing the door shut instead of slamming it. Adrian slid over on the seat, worked the gears, and drove off with Escott. They would circle around to the front of the stone castle Reva shared with Brett and use the main door. They'd called ahead and were expected company. I was not.

I followed in their wake. The driveway ran by a long slate-roofed garage with four wide doors and then curved away out of sight, masked by the bulk of the main house. The garage had two stories, but no lights were showing in any of the upper windows, so no chauffeur had been wakened by the passing of my Buick. The plain cement gave way to a span of decorative brick in a pattern, which I crossed to get to the house.

Except for a subdued night-light in the kitchen, the rest of the place was as dark as the garage, at least on this side. I found my way to the back garden and the line of French windows that marked the long hall where Bobbi had sung. The place was quiet enough now with all the people gone and looked larger than I remembered. The wind stirred unswept leaves around my ankles and I was just able to pick up the soft rush from the fountain at the far end of the grounds. It seemed like a century had passed since the night of the party, when I'd dragged Evan sputtering from the water.

Pressing my ear to one of the doors, I only heard the slow tick of a clock somewhere inside. The quality of the sound muffled, went silent a moment, and returned sharp and clear as I slipped into the house and became solid again. Oriented, I turned left and walked quietly through a series of rooms and halls, my ears cocked and the rest of me ready to vanish at a second's notice. The bedrooms were all upstairs, though. I didn't expect to run into anyone else prowling around and did not.

Like Adrian, Leighton Brett placed his studio on the north side of the house to take advantage of the light. It was a much bigger room and filled with more stuff, but had the same air of organized chaos. A line of wet canvases mounted on different kinds of easels took up a lot of floor space on one side. They covered many subjects: landscapes, some flowers with a jug, and the start of a bowl of fruit. The air was thick with the smell of linseed oil and the sickening bite of turpentine.

Operating on the principle of *The Purloined Letter,* I made for them and took a good look, comparing the colors of the canvases with the leftover smears on a palette I found. I was anything but an expert, but they seemed to match, which didn't prove much one way or another—Sandra had used the same colors. We'd probably have to wait and work it from the fingerprint angle later on, just to be sure.

I caught the low voices and approaching footsteps in plenty of time to vanish. Something clicked after the door swung open, probably the light switch, and they walked into the studio.

"The kitchen really might be better for this," said Leighton Brett. "At least I could offer you coffee or something stronger. I don't keep any supplies here where I work."

"We want nothing," stated Adrian, his voice toneless as ever.

"Then why are you here at this hour?" The question held no exasperation, only reasonable curiosity.

I moved close enough to Escott to give him a shiver and let him know I was around, then floated off a pace. The door was shut, very firmly and quietly, and Escott said, "We must talk."

"All right. About what?"

He did not get a direct answer. They were probably staring at him, reluctant to start now that the moment had come.

"Alex, what is this about?"

"Sandra's murder." This time there was some expression to Adrian's voice, more than enough to put Brett on his guard.

"Jack." But Escott didn't really have to call me, I was already fading into the room.

Brett went comically slack-jawed at this. A whimpering sigh of fear rushed from him and his pupils dilated, turning his eyes to black pits. I clearly heard the jump and throb of his heart. He stumbled away from me, grabbing at the back of a fancy brocade sofa for balance. I kept still and did my best to hold his gaze. It kept dancing from me to Adrian, to Escott, and back as he tried to take things in. I didn't dare look away to see how they were doing, I was completely focused on Brett.

His surprise died abruptly as common sense took over. He'd seen something impossible, therefore he hadn't really seen it. My appearance had been some kind of trick. He was desperate to believe this, I could read it on his face like print on a page. When he looked at me for some kind of tip-off or confirmation of the joke I had him cold, and he went blank and wide-eyed as a store-window dummy.

I kept my voice low and even and told him to sit down on the sofa. He did so. He wore scuffed loafers and some old paint-spotted pants. Neither of them went with the embroidered Chinese dragons crawling all over his green silk smoking jacket. Maybe it had been a present from Reva for some birthday or other.

He was tractable now and it was safe for me to divide my concentration. Escott was on the other side of the studio examining the paintings on the easels. Adrian regarded me with caution, but he was not really afraid.

"This is what you did to Evan?"

"More or less."

"How are you able to do it? Why?"

Escott and I had speculated on everything from telepathy to simple hypnosis, which my influencing resembled, and had yet to find a clear answer for how. *Why* I could do it was directly linked to vampiric survival: it was easier to drain blood from a quiescent source, whether animal or human, than from one awake and fighting the process. I shrugged; now was not the time for a lecture on my changed condition. Adrian let it go and sank into a chair opposite from Brett to stare at him.

I joined Escott by the paintings. "The colors looked alike to me."

"And they appear to be painted in Brett's style."

"You spot anything that could help?"

He was bent down behind one of the canvases and was comparing it to another he'd taken from a storage rack. "Indeed, yes, while not conclusive, it is certainly worth consideration. The wet painting's supporting frame is of a slightly different construction than the others in this room. It's homemade, while these came from a commercial supplier."

"Sandra and Evan made their own," said Adrian, not looking up from Brett's face. "They couldn't afford to buy prestretched canvas."

Escott peered at the raw edges of canvas through his magnifier. "The weave pattern of the fabric is also slightly different, but I believe—yes, there are some fingerprints in the paint. That will give us the final confirmation at least of the circumstantial element. As for the rest . . ." He broke off and replaced the dry canvas on the rack and went to stand just behind Adrian. I sat on the sofa, close to, but not touching Brett.

"I want you to speak freely and answer some questions," I told him. "You will give us the complete truth. You will tell us everything we want to know." I licked my dry lips and nodded to Escott, who leaned forward.

"Brett, did you take some paintings from Sandra Robley?"

"Yes."

"Why did you take them?"

"They were mine."

That puzzled him. "They were *your* paintings?"

Adrian spoke. "He means they were done in his style."

Escott noted that with a quirk of one eyebrow and continued. "Brett, did you kill Sandra?"

"Yes."

He spoke without hesitation, no emotion, no change in his empty face. I looked away from him and kept watch on Adrian. He was also leaning forward from his chair, a sullen fire burning deep in his eyes. Maybe it was hot enough to set off his fuse, maybe not. I was there to make sure the explosion wasn't too destructive.

"Why did you kill her?"

"She was . . . stealing from me." Now a long shudder sieved through the big man's body and he seemed to shrink a little.

"What do you mean, stealing?"

"My life, all my work, taking it, using it."

Adrian stood up suddenly and crossed to the wet paintings. He glared at them, half reaching for them, then dropped his hands and swung back on Brett.

"You killed for this, because she imitated your—"

"Stole my vision and method, my ideas, and sold them for pennies," Brett whispered.

He stepped toward Brett and I tensed for the rush, but it did not come. It was less self-control than sheer disbelief that kept him from doing anything. He came closer, slowly, and stood over Brett. "Look up at me."

Brett looked up as ordered, with defiance creeping into his expression. My hold on him had slipped, but it didn't matter, he saw only Adrian. Escott and I were just part of the furniture.

"Try to understand, Alex, I worked hard to get here. It doesn't come easy for me, and then when I found out someone was imitating my style, capitalizing on it, using it, degrading it—"

"Stealing what you could have made on it?"

"Not just that—"

"No, it's worse for you, isn't it?" Adrian grabbed two fistfuls of Brett's silk jacket and hauled him to his feet, dragging him close to Sandra's paintings. "You wouldn't have killed her for just the money."

Brett didn't resist and only stared. Adrian released him, took out a landscape from the racks, and held it next to the one on the easel. Side by side you could see the difference. Brett's painting looked like the work of an imitator; Sandra's was the more expert piece.

"The money wasn't that important to you but your precious vanity couldn't take it. Anyone, even one with a crippled soul and no talent can see it. She copied your style because it's popular with the public, it sells, but she was *better* at it." He turned back to Brett. "She produced the kind of quality you could never hope to master, you knew it, you couldn't stand the thought of it."

Brett slapped the back of his hand at Sandra's canvas, missing it by a fraction. "She was embarrassed at first—and then she *laughed,* tried to make a joke out of the whole thing. She asked if I minded very much, that maybe I should be flattered. . . ."

The muscles in his heavy face knotted into something unrecognizable and I knew what Sandra had seen the second before he struck her down. Adrian saw it, too, and sensibly kept his distance.

"Flattered." He looked to be working into something I couldn't stop, unless I stopped it now.

"Brett."

The interruption distracted him just enough. He looked at me and most of the tension left him, but none of the bile. "You helped, you know. You told me about those other paintings and where they were being sold from. I got Sandra's name from them—"

Adrian cut through the smoke. "Don't shift the blame, Leighton, he never told you to kill her."

He didn't like hearing that and shook his head as though the words physically hurt him. "I didn't mean to, I really didn't—you have to believe that . . ."

Adrian said nothing and turned away. He stopped before the studio door. "The only things I or anyone else can believe are your actions."

"Alex, I am *sorry.* I lost my temper."

"I'm sure the jury will be more than sympathetic," he murmured.

Brett didn't hear. "It got away from me. I truly am sorry, it was like before, I just couldn't help myself."

Adrian's spine stiffened. "What did you say?"

"I . . . am . . . sorry."

I got Brett's attention. "We know you're sorry, now tell us what about."

His tone flattened from pleading to bald fact stating. "I'm sorry about Sandra . . . and Celia."

Adrian turned, his face all caved in, and hell in his eyes. *"Celia?"*

My influence had put the chink in the dam. Brett's conscience, what he had of it, did the rest, and the dam broke at last.

"She said she wanted to go back to you. I told her you wouldn't change. You're like nails, Alex, all sharp points and iron outside, and nothing inside but more iron. What woman could love that? I tried to tell her."

Adrian made a glottal sound and swayed, but stayed on his feet.

"You knew what she'd done, I told her she'd already lost you, that it was too late anyway. She was *mine* by then—she wouldn't listen to me. She wouldn't admit it to herself and she was *wrong,* and I hated her for . . . then later, when I saw how you took it, how much you *did* love her, I was sorry, more than you'll ever know."

"You killed her?" His lips barely moved.

Brett's eyes stabbed around the floor for an answer. "She'd written me a note breaking it off, said she couldn't go on any longer. I told her it wasn't good enough and that I had to see her. I really tried, but she was in an awful state, and we'd both had a lot to drink. She just would *not* listen.

"I couldn't stand it, I was so damned angry with her—I just couldn't help myself. It was quick, she was passed out drunk when I took her home. I left her in the car along with the note. She suffered no pain. . . ." He trailed off and finally shut his mouth.

Adrian backed right up to the door, bumped against it, and scrabbled for the knob with stiff fingers. It twisted and he got the door open and went out, leaving it to swing free; a gaping hole leading into darkness.

I got in front of Brett and froze him to submission and gave him some very precise orders. Escott had taken a step toward the hall, but paused when I said his name.

"Stay here with Brett, I'll go."

He nodded and looked at his charge with more contempt than pity. It was still fresh on his mind that Brett had hired him to keep tabs on the progress of the murder investigation, and being used like that galled his professional pride. He moved toward Brett and put him to work.

Adrian hadn't gone very far. He was in some kind of sitting room down the hall. In passing, I just glimpsed his silhouette against the gray windows.

His palms were pressed flat to his eyes, with his fingers curled up over his forehead. He held his body erect, but was trembling all over as he fought for control and sanity against his grief and rage. After an endless moment the trembling lessened and stopped. The tension eased from the set of his shoulders and his hands fell away to hang forgotten at his sides. The walls were torn down and realization had flooded in. Perhaps he had known about Brett on some subconscious level, but had found it easier to blame himself for his wife's death than anyone else; things not our fault always are.

There was a sideboard on one wall with a half-full decanter and glasses. I poured out whatever it was and took it over to him. He accepted it without comment and drained the contents as smoothly as a glass of water.

"Did you know?" he asked. The pale curtains had not been drawn against the night and his gaze drifted aimlessly in the dim light seeping through the windows.

"Not about Brett and your wife."

He placed the glass carefully on a table. "I had to get out, it was that or kill him—and you wouldn't have let me."

"No."

"You saved me that humiliation, at least. Do you like what you do?"

"No, but it has to be done."

"And by whom? What are you? Is there a name for what you are?"

"Too many, and all of them ugly."

"Nemesis comes to mind. It's the wrong gender for you, but appropriate on this occasion."

"I'm sorry."

"Oh God, please don't start parroting Leighton."

"We had to have you along."

"Yes, I was the ideal choice to witness your wresting the confession from him. I can keep silent about your methods. Was there no one else?"

"It had to be you. You needed to know, to see."

"Did I?" His head came up sharply, but his gaze faltered after a second and eventually turned inward. "Yes, you're right again. You told me what to expect tonight, but you could have hardly anticipated this."

"I'd been looking for him, though."

"For Brett?"

"For your wife's killer, if he even existed."

"Perhaps I'm being obtuse. Would you explain?"

"I've still got a lot of reporter in me and it sticks. I checked the papers, talked to Barbara Steler—"

"Barbara?" He went cold on me again, or even colder, if that was possible. "What did you learn from her?"

"A sad story. She still loves you, you know."

He didn't believe me, which was hardly a shock.

"We had quite a talk, only she doesn't remember any of it."

His mouth twisted, bordering on disgust.

"That's how I learned that all the stuff about you killing your wife was so much eyewash. Barbara had been hurt pretty bad, it was her way of getting back at you."

"I already knew that."

"I think she knows she overdid it. She insisted on coming along the night you took on Dimmy Wallace."

"I never saw her."

"She didn't want you to."

"It's probably just as well."

I let the subject drop. "Anyway, I talked to a few people about you and your wife. The one thing that really got to me was that no one who knew you or even casually met you could believe you'd killed her."

"How generous of them."

"Then the chance came up for me to ask you directly."

"And just like Leighton, I told you the truth. Well, it's too late now to be offended by your curiosity. How did you come to realize she'd been murdered?"

"I didn't and I never did. I thought it was suicide like everyone else."

"Then why pursue it?"

I didn't want to tell him how I'd slipped back to his house and seen the portrait he'd done of Celia. I'd seen her through his eyes and the truth he'd recorded about her. Alex Adrian really had no conscious inkling of how deep his talent ran or the emotional effect it could have on others.

He'd painted the whole woman: her beauty, the guarded happiness, and the thin line of selfishness lodged in one corner of her mouth. In ten years that line would have taken over most of her face; in twenty, she'd have been quite ugly. The girl I had killed had been selfish, and I'd taken pains to make sure her death had looked like suicide. The parallel between her and Celia had gotten stuck in the back of my mind, so far back I hadn't thought of it until now. I hadn't wanted to think of it.

"Why?" he repeated.

Because by finding the truth behind one suicide and freeing Adrian of his guilt I could somehow expiate my own crime, or at least learn how to live with it as Gordy had advised me.

Because in my experience—and by now I did have experience—selfish people don't kill themselves. They have to have help.

Maybe my reasoning was screwy, I was feeling tired again. That made it easier to lie. "I don't know why, Alex. I just did, is all."

By now his eyes had grown used to the darkness and he was studying me closely. "There's more to it than that."

He was as perceptive in his own way as Escott, damn the man. I nodded. "Yeah, there's more, but it's only important to myself."

He believed me this time and knew I wasn't going to talk about it. He shrugged acceptance and glanced past my shoulder. "What are they doing in there?"

I shifted mental gears to bring myself back to the present, to the house I stood in now, and the people in it. "Brett's writing. I told him to do a full confession—on both murders. Escott's keeping an eye on him."

"That's good." His chin fell to his chest with sudden exhaustion.

"Alex . . ."

"What?"

"I can take the pain away; the memory will remain, but it won't hurt so much."

He thought about it and even raised his head a little. He knew what I was offering and could appreciate that I sincerely wanted to help. He was also aware I was giving him a choice in the matter. "I don't doubt that you could, I may even take you up on it—later. For now I can stand things—I've gotten used to it after all this time."

"It's not the kind of thing you want to hold on to."

"It will be exorcised soon enough—I'm not planning to kill myself, if that's what you think. I meant when we take him in to the police. Will this mean the death penalty?"

"I don't know."

"I hope it does." His eyes glittered unpleasantly and his mouth curled into a dry and bitter smile. "Don't you?"

He misinterpreted the answer in my face.

"Or is it too bloodthirsty of me to want a little justice?"

"I was only thinking this is going to be hell for Reva."

"She'll be better off without him," he said, dismissing the shattering of her own life with a casualness I didn't like, but could understand. "God, but I'm sick of it all and it's only just begun."

"You need sleep."

"I used to know what that was. I suppose you could fix that, too, as you did for Evan."

"Yeah."

"Evan." Some of the hardness went out of his manner.

"He gets out of the hospital tomorrow," I reminded him. "He's expecting to come here."

He looked pained. "Of course he can't come here, not after this. I'll have to take him in for the time being and—" He froze. "Evan would have seen the paintings—unless Leighton planned to destroy them."

"If he wanted to destroy them he would have done so by now."

"Then why hasn't he?"

"You said the money wasn't that important to him. Maybe not, but Brett wasn't going to throw it away."

"He'd finish them and sell them as his own?" Adrian shook his head, trying to take it in.

"Evan wouldn't have been allowed to see them. Brett would have made sure of that. After the breakdown Evan had that night, no one would be too surprised if he took his own life. It's easy enough to arrange." I nearly choked on those last words, but he didn't know the real reason why.

"You knew all this?"

"Charles and I put it together as one of the possibilities. If the paintings hadn't been destroyed, we figured he had a reason to hold off. Greed was one of the ones we figured, it seemed plausible at the time."

"Leighton has everything already, how could he possibly want more? The money they'd bring in would be only pocket change compared to what he has. Why should he take such a risk?"

"Greed was just part of it. You hit on the real answer earlier. He doesn't have everything and he knows it."

He started to twist the wedding ring again, then stopped and looked at his hands. He held them flat, palms up. They didn't look like the hands of an artist, they were broad, the fingers blunt, but strong looking. Somehow they could transfer what he saw and felt onto paper and canvas in the manner that he desired. He could communicate his vision and emotion to others without spoken explanation. It was a gift, and perhaps by him it had been too long ignored or taken for granted.

"Sandra's talent," he stated.

"It's as you said; he'd finish them, sign them, and sell them—as his own. That's the key to all of it."

"Talent."

"Her paintings would have been his best work."

"The bastard," he said, with an odd uplift to his tone.

The DA got the verdicts he wanted, not that he had to work too hard with Escott practically handing him Brett's signed confession on a silver platter. Brett was found guilty of the first-degree murder of Celia Adrian and the second-degree murder of Sandra Robley, but avoided the death penalty in the end. He looked good in court and his obvious contrition impressed the judge and jury, if no one else.

Escott and Adrian were the prime prosecution witnesses, but they didn't have to work too hard at it, either. The facts concerning the murders were the bald truth, after all; the only lies had to do with how those facts were obtained. Escott gave the court a song-and-dance act about being suspicious of Brett's behavior the night Brett hired him to look into things. He later communicated his troubles to Adrian. When the two of them decided to ask Brett a few direct questions he quickly broke down and confessed. I'd made sure that Brett agreed with their story. It was a lousy one and I'd squirmed the whole time when we'd worked it out, but everyone swallowed it.

Escott wasn't too surprised. "They believe the most impossible things they hear on the radio and read in the papers every day. A simple little problem like this is hardly going to hold public attention for very long."

The papers were full of the story for a while, but mostly because of Alex Adrian's name. Escott and Adrian covered all the angles between them so my name never came into it, which suited me fine.

Brett's art at the gallery was sold off, and very quickly. The notoriety of the trial had drawn out collectors, thrill seekers, souvenir hunters, and other vultures. Because of the morbid competition, the paintings auctioned at premium prices. The money went to Brett's sister. Reva gave the gallery's commission to charity.

Things were tough for her, of course, though Escott was of the opinion she'd been more upset by Brett's affair with Celia than with his murders. After the trial, she went back east to stay with relatives until things cooled off, which they did, eventually. The next time we heard of her, she was re-opening the gallery, business as usual.

"What a resilient woman," Escott commented as he studied the article in the paper.

Evan came in with a tray of drinks. "And she's got good taste to boot. She's promised she'll take on anything I might have to sell." He put the tray down and helped himself to a glass. "Maybe I should rephrase that, it sounds a bit rude."

"We know what you mean," said Bobbi, and that made him smile.

"I'm glad to hear she doesn't hold anything against you or Alex—or vice versa."

"It's not her fault that Leighton's a . . . well, that he's the way he is, and we all know that. She's better off without him, if you ask me," he said, unknowingly echoing Adrian's opinion from four months ago.

Christmas was only a week away and we were at Alex Adrian's house to pick up Bobbi's present.

"Anyway, it should be a success. She's got a head for the business, knows everyone worth knowing, and has the two best artists in the country to supply her with goods." Evan had aged a little in the last few months but was looking better tonight. He said he had a date coming by later, so apparently old habits were asserting themselves again and I was glad to hear it.

"Well, here's luck to all of you." Escott raised his glass and indulged in a sip, and the others followed his example. I kept out of sight in the back and faked it.

Adrian walked in and managed a smile. It was faint and a little self-conscious, but sincere. He still wore his wedding ring, but had dropped his habit of twisting it at about the same time he'd broken his painting block. "It's ready for view," he announced.

We followed him back to the studio. All the lights were on, blazing against an organized explosion of colors from every wall. Adrian was a busy man again, as much in demand as ever, but he'd found time to fulfill one private commission, and I was anxious to see it.

Bobbi's face was lit up with pride and excitement as Adrian flipped back the dust cover from her portrait.

Evan had promised that Adrian would do a painting that would knock our eyes out and he hadn't exaggerated one bit. Bobbi's vibrancy, beauty, and sensuality crackled off the canvas like electricity from a summer storm. It was the kind of painting that made you realize why people loved art for its own sake, but then it was by Alex Adrian, and I had expected nothing less than a masterpiece.

The one thing I didn't expect to see was myself in the painting as well.

"What gives?"

Bobbi laughed at my puzzlement, and now I understood all her suppressed excitement. "Merry Christmas, Jack."

Jeez, I never know what to say at happy surprises and started mumbling I don't know what idiocies.

"I think words are not necessary at this point, old man," Escott chided.

He was right, so I grabbed Bobbi and lifted her high and spun her until she shrieked for me to stop. Then I gave her a kiss and we looked at the painting again.

As in his original sketch, Adrian had her reclining on a low couch, loosely wrapped in some timeless white garment that clung to her figure. She looked like a slightly worldly angel about to become more worldly than heaven might want to allow. One hand rested along the top back of the couch and was covered by one of my own. I loomed over her in sober black, but he'd somehow managed to make me look ghostly and ethereal in comparison.

The background was dark, neutral chaos with my figure emerging out of the swirling non-pattern. Where my hand touched Bobbi's I was quite solid and real. It should have looked ominous and threatening, but did not. This was what he'd seen that night months back in the garage when I dived out of thin air to save his life. He'd said it had been beautiful and here he'd found a place to record his vision.

I held my hand out to him. He seemed surprised at the gesture, but shook it and finally smiled again. This one had more confidence.

"How do you do it?" I asked.

He decided to answer with more than a deprecatory shrug. "We're artists. We see and understand more than most because we've had to look at ourselves first—and accept what we find there whether we like it or not."

"It still doesn't make us any easier to live with," added Evan. He stood back a little from the painting and compared it to the models. "I'm not sure I understand your symbolism, Alex, but it's certainly one of your best."

"There's no symbolism," Adrian assured him, keeping his face supremely deadpan. "I only ever paint what I see."

FIRE IN THE BLOOD

I was in the process of tearing away the top half of Olivia Vandemore's silver-spangled evening gown when Escott abruptly opened the basement door and called my name.

"Are you down there?" His voice was necessarily pitched to carry through a brick wall.

"In a minute," I growled back.

The last fragile strap gave way under feverish, brutal hands. A terrible shriek of pure horror rushed from her perfect coral lips and echoed throughout the dank stone passages.

"Jack?" He was coming down the basement steps.

Her warm, white body writhed helplessly on the carved stone altar—an altar stained black with the blood of uncounted victims hideously sacrificed to slake the unholy thirst of . . .

"Jack?" He rapped a knuckle experimentally against the wall of my inner sanctum.

. . . Sabajajji, the Spider God.

I hit the period and debated whether to turn it into an exclamation point. A quick look through the other pages confirmed that I hadn't used one for some time now, and it seemed appropriate for the scene. The reader was going to be far more concerned with the upcoming description of Olivia's writhing body than my punctuation. I backspaced, tapped the apostrophe key, and rolled out the sheet, adding it to the stack of deathless prose next to my portable. Further excitement would have to wait until after I found out what the hell Escott wanted.

"I was working, you know," I told him, emerging wraithlike from the basement wall and solidifying. It'd taken a couple of months, but he'd finally gotten used to such stunts from me—at least on those occasions when he expected it. This time he'd expected me to be behind a bricked-up alcove in his basement, so it was hardly worth his notice.

"Sorry," he said, his nervous fingers absently jingling his key ring. He was wearing his hat and coat.

"Something up?" I asked, tying my bathrobe. I'd started writing as soon as I'd woken up and hadn't bothered to dress.

"I believe so. I may have a job for us and thought you'd like to come along and meet our prospective client."

This wasn't his usual method of work, which was being a private detective, though he preferred to be called a private agent. Most of the time he'd have some job already in progress and only asked me in if he needed extra help. I always tried to keep a low profile and rarely saw the client. The fewer people who knew about me, the better.

"I'm kind of in the middle of something," I hedged, reluctant to be dragged away from Olivia's impending sacrifice and last-second rescue. "Or are you getting a fishy smell off this one?" Sometimes he'd have me come along to watch his back.

"Such niceties of personal judgment are most difficult to ascertain, especially since I've had no actual contact with the client. I can positively state that the gentleman is determined, if nothing else, and possessed of some degree of consideration, in that he was kind enough to send his chauffeur over to make sure I did not miss his requested appointment."

I followed the cant of his eyes up the basement steps to the hall door. As he spoke, the doorway—the entire doorway—was blocked by the presence of a uniformed Negro. He was built like an industrial-grade refrigerator. Escott couldn't really say anything in so many words, but this was definitely one of those times when he wanted someone to watch his back.

"So, what's the client's name?" I asked, all interest now.

"Sebastian Pierce," he said.

"Never heard of him."

"He was quite a large noise in Chicago some twenty-five years ago. After making a fortune from various investments, he then retired to enjoy it."

"We should all be so lucky."

"And this is his chauffeur, Mr. Griffin."

Griffin nodded once at me. "Good evening, sir." The amused look on his face indicated that he'd noticed the pajamas and bathrobe.

"Good evening," I returned, and tried to look dignified in spite of the unconventional surroundings. Maybe Escott had told him I was checking the furnace. "What time's this appointment?"

"Eight o'clock. We can just make it if you hurry." Escott turned and trotted lightly up the basement steps, pausing only a moment at the top so Griffin could vacate the doorway. He hardly made a sound. Maybe Escott wanted me to cover him, but who the hell was supposed to cover me? I gave an inward shrug and followed. For the time being Olivia would just have to wait at the altar.

Escott and I started rooming together a couple weeks after the night I woke up dead on a Lake Michigan beach. He owned a three-story brick relic that had been a bordello in less innocent days. It had plenty of space and we'd both agreed that it offered me more privacy than a hotel. We shared the bills and I had two rooms upstairs with my own bath, but when writing, the basement was my exclusive territory. The intervening floors served as soundproofing, so the clack of my typewriter in the wee morning hours didn't disturb what little sleep his insomnia allowed him.

I'm up so late and only after dark because I'm a vampire.

Just like the folklore says, I drink blood for sustenance—usually at the Union Stockyards every other night, depending how active I am. The cattle there don't seem to mind. Human blood has its own special appeal, but like most people, I keep my nourishment separate from my sex life.

I don't have any aversion to crosses, garlic, or silver, though I do have a problem with wood and crossing free-flowing water. I can't turn into a bat or wolf, but can disappear, float around, and even walk through walls if required. Most of the time I use doors—it's less conspicuous.

During the day I'm stretched out on a fairly comfortable folding bed that has a layer of my home earth sewn up in a long, flat sheet of oil-cloth. The bed is in Escott's basement, hidden behind a fire-resistant brick wall that he'd built himself. The tiny room beyond is located exactly under the kitchen, and Escott had thoughtfully fitted a trap into the floor there for emergencies. It was well hidden by his carpentry skill and a throw rug. I don't have a coffin. I hate coffins.

The room's pretty stark, but during the day I don't notice much of anything. It has an air shaft to the outside, electricity for the work light and radio, and a photo of my girlfriend Bobbi for decoration. My typewriter rests on a wide shelf attached to the wall. I enjoy the privacy when writing, but do my real living in my rooms on the second floor. There I keep my clothes and a comfortable scatter of magazines and books, and succeed in pretending that I'm no different from any other human. But the bed in the corner was for show only, and no mirror hangs over the dresser.

Tonight I picked out a plain dark silk tie to go with my second-best midnight blue suit. It was conservative without overdoing it, though next to Escott, I always look a little flashy. He feels the same way about double-breasted suits as I do about coffins and wouldn't be caught dead in one.

Escott and Griffin were in the parlor. Griffin was sitting on the edge of the big leather chair, his visored hat on one massive knee. He stood up smoothly as I came down. I couldn't figure his age, he had one of those thirty-to-fifty faces. Escott got up from the sofa and led the way out, locking up behind us. A minute later we were driving away in a shiny new Packard with Griffin at the wheel.

"Any idea where we're going?" I murmured to Escott, though there was a glass divider between the front and back.

He opened his mouth, shut it, and shook his head once, looking slightly embarrassed. "I asked all the usual questions, but Mr. Griffin deigned to answer only the most basic: the name of his employer and the time of the appointment."

"Nothing else, huh?"

"If his purpose was to inflict bodily harm upon my person, I think it would have happened by now. At least he had no objections to my request to have you along."

"If you feel so trusting, then why bring me at all?"

"I'm merely applying your own philosophy of not taking chances. Mr. Griffin did give me the impression that he wouldn't have been at all pleased had I refused his request to come."

He had a definite point there. I was much stronger than I looked because of my changed condition, but Griffin was not someone I'd cheerfully go up against just to see what happened.

"My belated apologies for dragging you from your work. How is it progressing?"

"Just peachy." I had a fanciful mental picture of the editor of *Spicy Terror Tales* breathlessly awaiting my latest contribution to the slush pile. Several years of background in journalism notwithstanding, my literary career at this point had been anything but lucrative, so my partnership with Escott was a financial necessity. Vampires spend money like everyone else.

Griffin drove to a quiet street with only one open business at this hour, a bar called the Stumble Inn. He parked in front, got out, and opened the car door for us.

"You'll find Mr. Pierce at the last table on the left," he told us.

"On the left," repeated Escott, as though such meetings were normal for him.

Griffin gently shut the door, folded his arms, and leaned against the Packard, causing it to tilt a little. It was a freezing night, but he seemed to be as indifferent to the cold as I. He was breathing regularly, though, which meant he was human, after all. That was a relief.

We went inside. The bar lined one long wall and the man behind it had his ear pressed to a radio that was giving out with more static than program. The place had tables, but no booths, and as promised, only one customer in the back on the left.

He stood up as we came close, a tall, weedy-looking man with a lion's mane of wavy white hair, brilliant blue eyes, and a monumental nose. His handshake was dry and firm.

"Well, I thought there'd be only one of you, but I don't mind the extra company if it'll get the job done," he said in a soft, gravelly voice. "I'm Sebastian Pierce, which one of you is Escott?"

"I am Charles Escott, Mr. Pierce. This is my business associate, Jack Fleming."

"Pleased." He nodded at me, then turned back to Escott as we sat down together. "English, are you? Is that a London accent?"

"Yes."

Pierce found it amusing for some reason and asked if we wanted a drink. I declined, but Escott said he'd have whatever Pierce was having, which amused him even more.

"Don't know as you'd like it, since it's only sarsaparilla. I got stinking drunk once in my life and swore never to repeat the experience."

"Sarsaparilla will be fine."

Pierce signed to the bartender, who brought over an open bottle and a glass, then returned to hunch over his radio.

"You think I'm some sort of lunatic, Mr. Fleming?" he questioned, reading my open-book mug correctly.

There were deep-set humor lines all over his face. It had been well lived in for the last sixty years or so, but they'd been good years. "I must know a hundred stories about what happens to the guy who walks into a bar and asks for what you're drinking," I said.

"Nonsense, you're only old enough to know two or three of those at the most."

I was in my mid-thirties, but looked a lot younger. I didn't bother to correct him and only shook my head a little.

"I happen to own this place," he said, moving his half-full glass around in smeary circles with long, flat fingers. On one of them, a huge ring made from chunks of cut-up gold coins winked happily in the dim light. "It's usually busier, but tonight I wanted some privacy, so Des here shooed out the regulars for the time being. Griff will make sure no one else comes in."

That was for damned sure.

Escott sipped his foamy drink without visible harm. "You mentioned a job, Mr. Pierce."

"Yes." He pulled out a photograph of a fancy-looking bracelet. It was covered in diamonds and some darker stones arranged in a spiral pattern. If the picture were life-size the bracelet would be about an inch wide. "I was in Paris before the war and had this specially commissioned as a gift to my wife for our fifth wedding anniversary. It was and is unique, and as you can imagine, quite valuable, both in terms of hard cash and soft sentiment."

"What is it made of?"

"Diamonds and rubies on platinum. When my wife died some years ago, I put all her jewelry in the safe until our daughter came of age. Marian had her twenty-first birthday last month and took charge of it all, according to her mother's wishes."

"And this piece?"

"Has been stolen. I want it back, but quietly. I don't want publicity, and I don't want the police."

"Have you an idea who took it?"

"Oh, yes. Marian's best friend Kitty has a boyfriend. Now, Kitty is a little doll, but it's a sad fact that the sweetest girls can hook up with the most rotten men, and that's the case with her and Stan. He can put on a smooth kind of charm and generally fool those too young to know better, but it's all show. I've met his type before and they're always out for whatever they can get away with. Anyway, the two of them were over at our house for a Christmas party last week and I expect that that's when the bracelet was taken."

"But you've no proof?"

"Nothing I can go to the police with, but I wouldn't go to them, anyway."

"A week is a long time, Mr. Pierce."

"I only found out about it today."

"He may have pawned or fenced it by now."

"You think you'll be able to trace it if he has?"

"There are no guarantees, but we can try, if he is the culprit. Who else was at this party?"

"Myself, Marian, her current boyfriend Harry Summers, Kitty Donovan, Stan McAlister, and the servants who were working that night. They've been with us for years, though. It was Marian's maid who first told me about it."

"The circumstances?"

"Marian usually leaves the valuable stuff lying around on her dresser mixed in with the rest of her costume jewelry. I know it's careless, I've nagged her on it more than once, but in our house it was safe enough until now. Her maid was cleaning and straightening today and noticed that the bracelet was gone. She asked me if Marian had finally put it in the house safe. We checked, but she hadn't, so we went over her room again."

"Marian did not wear the bracelet today?"

"No, or in the last week, we're sure of that."

"And she has not noticed it's gone missing?"

"No. As I said, she's very careless."

"Has anyone else been in the house since the party?"

Pierce shook his head decisively.

"Could Marian have taken it herself?"

"If I thought that I wouldn't have to hire you."

"What made you choose me?"

"I didn't, you're Griff's idea."

"Indeed?"

"He said you came highly recommended by a friend of his, Shoe something."

"Shoe Coldfield?"

"I think that was the name."

Escott glanced at me, one eyebrow bounced, and a smile tugged briefly at the corner of his mouth. Coldfield was now a gang boss in Chicago's "Bronze Belt," but he'd shared some lean times on the stage with Escott in a traveling Shakespeare company years ago. Once in a while he threw some business in our direction, just to say hello.

Pierce continued. "Normally I'd ask Griff to handle something like this, but we thought it better to hire someone a little less noticeable for the job. Griff is a bit . . . tall, and McAlister knows him."

"And if Stan McAlister should happen to mention the encounter to your daughter . . ."

"I'll be accused of doing all sorts of things for her own good," he concluded with a sigh of long suffering, and shrugged. "She's my daughter, but I'm damned if I know what's going on in her mind all the time. She would accuse me of being too nosy or something. She likes to think she's very independent and bitterly resents any implication to the contrary. If you have, or ever have children you'll know what I mean. All I want is to get the bracelet back. After that it's going into the safe until I'm gone, and then she can do what she likes with it."

"Assuming we're able to locate the bracelet, have you a preference for any particular method of recovery?"

"Since it was stolen, I thought you could steal it back. Stan wouldn't dare squawk."

"If he's fenced it already, we may have to purchase it—if it is still in one piece."

He grimaced. "I hope it is, or Marian's feelings or not, I'll have Griff fold the little punk in two the wrong way. The bracelet's insured for fifteen thousand, I'll go that high, but would appreciate if you could bargain things down to the lowest possible amount."

"We'll see what we can do. I unfortunately do not have any of my standard contracts with me."

Pierce pulled out a wallet and casually gave us each a hundred-dollar bill. It was a sumptuous retainer when compared to Escott's usual rate. "That's all the paperwork I think you'll need for now, Mr. Escott. If Griff trusts you, I can trust you. If the trust is misplaced, then Griff has ways of evening the score."

"Of that I have no doubts. We'll need a description of Mr. McAlister. In fact, I would like one of all the principals."

He was prepared and gave Escott a sheet of paper with names, addresses, and a list of McAlister's favorite haunts. He also produced another photo. "I took this at the party, it's a little harsh because I didn't get the flash right, but they're recognizable. That's my daughter." He pointed to a sleek brunette. "Fortunately for her, she took after her mother in looks. Unfortunately for me, she has my temperament and quite a lot of her own, besides. The handsome fellow next to her is Harry, and the two blonds are Kitty Donovan and Stan McAlister."

Escott carefully checked it over. "What does Mr. McAlister do?"

"Not very damn much, as far as I can tell. Stan has a taste for gambling and no inclination to work."

"Does Kitty work?"

"Yes, but mostly for amusement. Her parents left her with a comfortable trust. She augments it by designing hats for one of the big stores around here, custom stuff. She glues a few feathers and sequins to a strip of ribbon and charges a fortune for it. That's how she met Marian."

"What about Mr. Summers?"

"Harry's from a decent family. Not much money, but good people. Marian met him while he was working as a waiter at some party. He'd worked his way through school that way and now he's trying to start up his own business in radio repair, so I give him credit for some ambition."

"Does he also gamble?"

"No, Harry's pretty much of a tight fist with his money, which is sensible if you don't carry it too far."

"You think he does?"

Pierce nodded, amused again.

"You approve of him, though?"

"He's a cut above most of the lowlifes Marian's brought home, but I'm not taking it too seriously. She changes boyfriends as frequently as I change socks. She'll fasten onto someone else when she gets tired of going to the park and museums with Harry. They're free, you know."

"Does Marian work?"

"Has hell frozen over lately?"

Escott almost laughed. "Where may I reach you?"

Pierce mumbled and growled a little under his breath, and reluctantly parted with his home phone number. "But don't call if you can help it, I'll check with you every evening at about five."

We wound things up and left Pierce at the bar ordering another sarsaparilla. As Griffin drove us back home, Escott studied the party photo by the intermittent light from the street lamps.

"An interesting group, wouldn't you say?" he asked.

"I guess so. Funny how he's so leery of his daughter finding out about any of this."

"The extent that some fathers are dominated by their offspring would probably astonish you, and a man may go to absurd lengths in order to preserve the illusion of peace in his household."

"While disrupting others," I added.

"Yes, he did initiate this business in a somewhat unorthodox manner. At least it added a touch of interest to an otherwise commonplace case."

"That's what you figure?"

"This time, yes. The man didn't strike me as a fool. If he thinks McAlister took the bracelet, then it's likely to be true. We have only to find the fellow and verify things one way or another."

"Sure you need my help, then?"

"Most certainly. I could cover all of the places listed here alone, but it will go faster for your assistance. . . . Tell me, is Miss Smythe still head-lining at the Top Hat?"

"For another month yet." Two weeks ago Bobbi had landed the star spot singing in one of Chicago's best nightclubs.

"Now, that is most convenient. It's down here as a place frequented by Stan McAlister."

I could see what he had in mind a mile off. "Aw, now don't go asking me to mix Bobbi up with this business."

"Miss Smythe need not be involved. All you have to do is look the place over and see if McAlister is present. Don't you visit there each night, anyway?"

"Yeah, but only just before closing so I can drive Bobbi home. Her boss said no husbands or boyfriends during working hours for any of the girls, no exceptions. He thinks they take up valuable space."

"He can't object if you're a paying customer. Mr. Pierce's retainer should be more than sufficient to cover your expenses for now."

He'd made up his mind, so there wasn't much point arguing with him. Chances were, McAlister would be in some other joint and I could take Bobbi home as usual, with the added bonus of getting paid to catch her show. "Okay, I'll go have a look. What'll you be doing?"

"Checking some of his other haunts, and then I'll run by his hotel to see if he's in. If I find him, then I can sort things out right away."

Griffin dropped us at home and drove unhurriedly away, the Packard's exhaust a thick, swirling fume in the winter air.

"How you plan to handle it?" I asked Escott as I walked to my car and unlocked it.

"I'm leaving myself a wide range of options by not deciding that until I've met the man. If he's reasonable, I'll reason with him. If not . . ." He spread his hands in a speculative gesture and walked away, taking the narrow alley between his building and the next so he could get his Nash out of the garage in back.

Since my suit was good enough for the Top Hat, I could start right away as well. The sooner we got the bracelet back, the sooner I could return to the typewriter and rescue Olivia from a horrible fate at the hands of the dreaded spider cult.

My mind was busy with permutations on the story's ending as I made a U-turn and followed Griffin's route out of the neighborhood. I was halfway to the club before I noticed the car following me. A couple of turns later and I was certain about the tail; not a new experience, but decidedly uncomfortable. For the time being I did nothing and drove to the Top Hat. As I parked, the coupe drifted past, looking for a spot of its own. It was a neat little foreign job I'd never seen before, driven by a woman who looked vaguely familiar. Maybe she was some friend of Bobbi's, but I didn't think so. I left my car, walked in the club entrance, and offered my hat and coat to the check girl.

The claim ticket was hardly in my pocket when the other driver charged through the door, looking a little breathless. She spotted me looking at her, pretended not to notice, and marched past to toss a wide silver fox wrap at the girl. She made quite a business of putting away her own ticket in her tiny purse and then pretended a vast interest in a placard advertising the club's entertainment. I hung around the lobby, not making it easy for her.

A noisy group came in and she used them as an excuse to glance around, but I was still looking right at her. She flushed deep pink and went back to fiddling with her purse again, this time pulling out a cigarette case. I crossed the dozen feet separating us and fired up my lighter. Startled, her eyes flicked up to meet mine. They were huge, very round, and a pure and lovely blue. Her thick sable hair fell back freely from cream-colored shoulders. They were bare except for two braided metallic straps holding up the silver sheath of her evening gown.

"Thank you," she said, and lighted her cigarette. She briefly locked eyes again, made a decision, and blinked prettily. "What's your name?"

"Jack. What's yours?"

She giggled, schoolgirl seductive, and shook her head, letting her hair swing a little.

I recognized her now and wasn't happy about it. Sebastian Pierce had been very insistent about keeping his daughter ignorant of his business.

"You always follow strange men around?"

"Only the ones I might like."

"That can be dangerous, Miss Pierce."

Her head jerked in surprise, then her eyes dropped. "So I've been found out. Are you going to tell Daddy?" She looked up from under her bangs, as appealingly as possible.

"Depends. Why don't you drop the high school flirt act and we talk about it?"

Now she did blink. I might as well have smacked her face with a wet towel. "You—"

"You're right, and if you're so innocent, you shouldn't even know such words."

She took another breath, held it, and indecision flashed over her face. She would either cuss me out or smile. I got lucky and she burst into laughter; the genuine article this time.

"Drink?" I gestured to the bar in the lounge, a smaller, quieter room away from the stage show.

"Why not?"

As we turned to leave, I heard the orchestra finish its fanfare and Bobbi's voice soared up, filling the next room. I couldn't help but pause, and it was a physical effort to resist the urge to go in and see her.

"Something wrong?"

I was a man in love and bound to turn sappy at any given moment. "No, not a thing." Marian Pierce latched on to my arm and led off in the wrong direction. Not that she didn't promise to be attractive company and was part of the job at hand, but she just wasn't Bobbi.

A waiter read the signs right, at least the ones Marian was giving out, and seated us in the back, behind a row of short palm trees. She ordered scotch and water. I ordered only the water.

"Trust Daddy to find another teetotaler," she said, pretending world-weary disapproval.

"I drink, but not on the job."

"Oh, are you working or something?"

"Would you have followed me if I weren't?"

She puffed on her cigarette and thought it over. "Actually, I was following Daddy."

"Any reason why?"

"No."

It was going to be one of those nights. "Then you started following me. Any reason for that?"

She smiled, trying to charm her way out again. "I liked your looks better than your partner's."

And maybe she thought she could more easily get around someone who seemed to be closer to her own age. "I'll be sure and tell him."

"No, promise you won't tell anyone you saw me."

"Daddy wouldn't like it?"

Her eyes went down. "Something like that. Why did he hire you?"

"Your father is a client, which means I don't talk about his business.

You won't talk about yours, either. We're not going to get anywhere fast like this, Miss Pierce. One of us needs to go home."

"My name's Marian, but then if you're following me, you already know that."

"Why do you think I'm following you?"

"I really wouldn't know. Daddy . . . well . . . maybe he thinks I'm just a teeny-weenie bit too wild." She was back doing the vulnerable-little-girl act again. Any more of it and, job or no job, I'd leave to watch the rest of Bobbi's show. Escott could have my half of the retainer and good riddance to it.

"Why?" Impatience crept into my tone. It couldn't be helped, I was impatient.

"I can't really talk about it. But really, there's nothing to talk about."

"Well, that's too bad, then." I made to go and she caught my arm.

"No, please wait."

"For more runaround? Make up your mind, lady."

"All right. You can't tell me why you were hired, but can you tell me why you weren't?"

"Maybe."

"Did my father want you to spy on me?"

"No."

She sighed. "Well, that's something, at least."

"What are you hiding?"

"Nothing, but I do like to know what's going on around me. Daddy still treats me like a six-year-old." Her drink arrived and she put half of it away as though it were my glass of water. "How many six-year-olds can do that, Mr. . . . ?"

"Jack Fleming," I reminded her.

"That's a nice name. Why did you come to the Top Hat if you weren't spying on me?"

"My girlfriend works here."

"You would have a girlfriend, wouldn't you?" She pretended hurt. "Which one is she?"

"Let's never mind that."

Her face lit up with wicked mischief. "If you say so." She abruptly leaned over and fastened her mouth to mine like a lamprey on a fish. I could taste the scotch on her tongue. She fell back, looking flushed and triumphant, and finished the rest of her drink.

"Any reason for doing that?" I asked.

"Because I felt like it."

"That can be dangerous, too, you know."

"Oh, pooh, you're all right."

"Looks can be deceiving."

"That works both ways, darling. I could be a terrible vamp." She leaned back in the booth, crossing her arms to emphasize her cleavage.

"Then I'd better get out of here while my virtue's still intact."

"What?"

"Marian, you're a wonderful girl, but I have to be going."

"But why?"

"Uh-uh, we've already been down that street. I can't talk and you won't, and that makes for a dull evening."

She uncrossed her arms and moved in closer. I braced myself for another assault. This time I tasted the cigarette mixed in with the scotch. She released me, but didn't fall back. "It's about time you learned there's more you can do with your lips than talk," she stated, her voice husky and mature all of a sudden.

I showed my teeth and shook my head. It was safe enough to do this time; my canines hadn't lengthened by even a fraction of an inch. Like I said, she wasn't Bobbi. "Thanks, but maybe some other night, sister."

"Don't you like me?"

"Kid, you make a great first impression. I'm going to remember you for the rest of my life. . . ."

Then some bozo grabbed a fistful of my suit and yanked me from the booth onto the floor. What breath I'd drawn in order to talk got knocked out when I landed, not that he gave me much chance to say anything. Marian screeched a name, which I didn't catch, because the guy slammed into my ear with his knee. My head took a wild spin in the other direction, and I flopped out flat with the man towering over me like a building.

He got his balance fixed and carefully drew back one of his rough leather toes to kick my skull into the next county. I could disappear and let his foot sail through empty air, but this was the wrong place for that kind of fancy work—too many people and too many eyes. Just in time, I got my hand up and caught his ankle. He grunted at the initial shock and then gasped when I squeezed and twisted. He had to turn with it or suffer a green-stick fracture. Arms pinwheeling, he hopped once on his other foot and crashed into a waiter who had come up to stop the ruckus.

Both of them were on the floor in a sloppy football scramble. The guy that hit me started to hit the waiter, but I still had his ankle and gave it a sharp pull to remind him. He grunted out a very ripe curse, which upset some lady into calling for the manager at the top of her lungs. Another woman told her to shut up and a drunk said he would put ten bucks on the skinny guy in blue.

"Harry, how *could* you?" This from Marian, who had slid from the booth and was standing over us both.

Harry was in no mood to discuss motives and tried to kick me with his free foot. He hit my collarbone—hurting, but not breaking it—then he tried to slam sideways and get my other ear. I got my hand up in time again and twisted him pigeon-toed. He yelped, sat up, and tried once more to belt me, this time with his fists.

The waiter spoiled his aim by crawling out from under him just as another man was coming up. Together they tried to haul Harry away from me. I released my grip, still plenty mad, but content to let them handle him until it became clear they'd want help themselves. I got my feet under me, leaned over, and carefully pulled the punch I poked into Harry's gut. He only needed the breath knocked from him, not burst organs.

It worked. You can't fight if you can't breathe, and normal humans do need air on a regular basis. Harry stopped struggling with the waiters and rolled on his side, probably burning one of his own ears for a change as he scraped against the carpet. He made choking sounds trying to refill his lungs.

A man in a tux appeared, took the situation in with an experienced eye, and jerked his head toward the exit. The waiters picked Harry up and marched him away, presumably to throw him out. He didn't fight them, but his mottled red face was eloquent. If I wasn't careful, I'd be in for an ambush when I went out for my car.

"I apologize, sir, I trust you are not injured?" The tux was not a happy man. I told him I was fine, and then he apologized to the dozen or so people who had watched with varying degrees of interest. Two or three left, and the rest settled down to discuss the fight and wait for signs of more entertainment.

I straightened and dusted my suit, took Marian's arm, and made a decent exit myself as far as the lobby before stopping to square off with her. "Okay, who was he?" I already knew, but had appearances to keep up.

"Nobody important. Are you all right?" Her face was bright with excitement.

"Give me a name."

"Just some guy I used to date."

I kept looking at her.

Exasperation superseded the excitement. "Harry Summers," she snapped. "Is nosiness a part of your profession? No, forget I asked, the answer's got to be yes."

"I always like to get the name of anyone who sucker-punches me."

"Harry's got a jealous streak a mile wide. I'm really very sorry." Her apology was light, just words she was expected to say. Her mind was on something else.

"I think you should run along now, the management is figuring that we're bad for business."

She saw the tux talking with another tux and both were looking our way. "I'm not worried about them."

"I am. I don't want my girl to get canned because of this."

"They wouldn't do that," she said with the airy confidence of the unemployed rich.

"Don't bet on it."

"Then come with me. I know a very quiet place that Harry doesn't—"

"Excuse me, sir." It was the second tux and he knew me by sight if not by name. He'd seen me pick Bobbi up at the stage exit often enough.

"Never mind, I was just leaving."

"I think that would be best, sir."

I redeemed my hat and coat, Marian got her fox wrap, and we left with as much dignity as we could muster. It wasn't much; Marian started giggling before we were out the door.

"Did you see the look on Harry's face?"

"Yeah, we could sell tickets."

"My car's right over here." She steered me off to the left. I went along, keeping an eye out for Summers. Marian opened the passenger door, slid in first, and patted the leather seat for me to join her.

"Uh-uh. Time to say good night."

She shook her head in amused disbelief, then realized with a shock that I was serious. "But I want you to come with me."

"Not tonight, sweetheart." I shut the door on her. She flopped across the seat to try and open it again and, failing that, she rolled down the window.

"Jack, I *said* I want you to come with me."

"And it's the nicest thing I've heard all evening."

"But—"

"Marian, to tell the truth, you're just too much woman for me." I backed away and walked fast, putting a line of cars and a lot of darkness between us before vanishing into thin air.

Distant and muffled, I heard her door open as she charged out to chase me down. She called my name a lot, growing more and more frustrated as the minutes passed. I simply waited and floated free until she finally gave up. It took a long time, and even then she didn't go to her car, but back into the club. The clack of her heels faded and I returned to solidity again with relief.

I was crouched next to a Rolls and a Caddy and straightened with care. No one was in immediate sight, which was lucky. Pulling my vanishing act in a public place was strictly for emergencies only, but Marian more than qualified. As far as I was concerned, she was about as welcome as a case of warts—and as hard to lose.

Belatedly, I remembered that I was supposed to be looking for Stan McAlister. Maybe he was somewhere in the club and Marian had been putting up her best smoke screen to distract me. It would mean that she was in on the bracelet business, but nothing much would surprise me about that girl.

I'd been distracted, all right, but if McAlister was here, I'd find him. I started to go around to slip in by the stage entrance and had to stop cold. Harry Summers was coming across the parking lot straight for me, looking like a bulldozer on legs.

2

HE stopped about five feet short of me and glared, breathing hard. With wavy black hair and a strong, square jaw, he was matinee-idol handsome, but his hands were big and he looked as though he wanted to fasten them around my neck.

I was tired of him and he'd already put scuff marks on my suit. My conscience didn't chafe too much when we locked gazes and I told him to calm down. He was plenty upset, but soon stopped puffing so much, and the red mottling finally drained out of his face. He was unaware of what had happened; one minute he was ready to tear into me, and the next we were walking up and down the parking lot having a smoke like old friends.

"What was the donnybrook about, Summers?" I asked in a reasonable tone. "You must know I'm not interested in Marian."

Summers rumbled a curse and wearily leaned against a car, shaking his head. "I dunno. Something just comes over me when I see her look at another guy. She's crazy and she only makes me crazy. I wish I'd never met her."

I could sympathize. "You can't pick fights every time she looks."

His face was sour. "She was doing more than that with you. I saw it. Christ, the whole room saw it."

"Her idea, not mine."

"Then what were you with her for?"

"She didn't give me much of a choice. I'll level with you, Harry, I'm doing a job for her father and she only came on like gangbusters hoping I'd tell her about it."

"What's the job?"

"I can't say."

Like a lot of people, he ignored that fine point and pressed on. "Does it have to do with Marian?"

"Not really. What's she want to hide from her old man?"

He shrugged. "Me, probably."

"Something the matter with you? Pierce seems to think you're okay."

"Only because Marian doesn't let him look too close."

"Got a past, huh?"

Summers nodded. "Cops had me on a couple of assault charges."

What a surprise. "Like what you pulled on me tonight?"

"Yeah. Sorry. Nothing much came of it. I did some time and got out, but the records are there for anyone to find. Pierce won't think that that's okay."

"Tell him about it and see."

"I don't think it's worth it. Marian's flighty, she'll probably drop me for someone else after this. She doesn't forgive much of anything when she's crossed."

"She'll have to learn sometime or lose a lot of friends."

"With her dough, she can always buy more," he said bitterly.

I didn't gainsay him or offer advice or anything stupid like that. If he wanted to feel sorry for himself that was his business, doubly so if it had to do with Marian.

He tossed away his cigarette. It was only half-smoked and continued to smolder long after it bounced off the sidewalk. "I know I'm out of my class with her. She's as much as said she goes with me because I did time. I'm not the tough she thinks I am, all I got is a bad temper. But it makes her feel like she's breaking the rules herself. You know how that makes me feel?"

He didn't really want an answer, so I kept my mouth shut.

"She's got everything now and will have more of that when her dad goes. Maybe I'd have a chance if she didn't have so much."

"You don't want a rich wife?"

"The money doesn't matter to me, it's hers. I'd be working my own way no matter what. What it is . . . I dunno, it just gets between us somehow. Like with this." He gestured at the lavish front of the club. "I wouldn't come to a place like this in a million years, but she's here and she expects me to be here, so I come."

"No taste for the high life?"

"Too much of a good thing. I love strawberry ice cream, but I don't eat it till I'm sick. Marian would, and she'd insist that everyone else do the same."

The more I learned about Marian, the happier I was at ditching her, but Summers was genuinely miserable. He saw her faults and still wanted her, which could add up to a bleak future. We can't always choose whom we're going to fall for, and I felt sorry for the guy.

"Guess I'll be running," I said.

"Wait . . ."

"Yeah?"

"If you see her, tell her I said I was sorry."

I looked up at the brightly lit entry doors to the club. Marian was just starting to come through them. Her step was brisk and she wore a determined look on her delicate face. "Right, but maybe you should tell her yourself. See you around."

I ducked down among the cars before he could stop me again. In the general darkness, she might not have been able to spot me from the club. A second later, nobody could see me at all, and I floated off with the wind. When enough distance and time passed, I went solid and kept walking until I reached the rear of the building. At the top of some wooden steps was a metal fire door that could only be opened from the inside. I had to sieve in around the door, using the extremely thin space between its dense metal and the jamb.

No one seemed to be around. I materialized under a dim red exit light and dropped my nearly forgotten cigarette in a bucket of sand hanging on the wall. I rarely smoked the things anymore; my lungs didn't like them, but they made useful social props.

The band blared away in front of me, masked off from the backstage area by a silver curtain. It was flimsy enough to see through when the lights were up on the other side. A dozen girls wearing strategic bits of tinsel and tap shoes were trying to beat holes in the dance floor, an encouraging sight, because it meant Bobbi would be in her dressing room. I didn't waste any more time.

She said "Come in" to my knock. This time I turned the knob and walked through like a normal person. Bobbi was at the dressing table checking her makeup, a glowing oasis of platinum blond sanity in an otherwise screwy evening.

In the light-lined mirror she saw the door open and shut all by itself. Her wide hazel eyes blinked once in puzzlement, and then she broke into a smile.

"Jack!" She turned around so she could see me and opened her arms. I did what I could to fill them, half lifting her from the padded satin chair she'd been perched on. We were pretty incoherent for the next few minutes until she insisted on coming up for air.

"How's the show going?" I asked.

"Pretty good for a slow night. What are you doing up here so early?"

"On a job for Charles. If you have time, I'll tell you."

She glanced at a clock on the dresser. "I got five minutes."

"Okay." I gave her a very quick rundown on things, including Marian's attack on my lips, and the follow-up with Summers. Bobbi looked my face over and pursed her own lips critically.

"You run in rough company, buster. I didn't notice before, but that is definitely not my shade." She grabbed a cloth and briskly wiped my mouth. "The little tramp," she muttered. "Good thing you confessed or I might have clobbered you myself."

"What's to confess? I was just an innocent bystander. She was the one who got all the ideas, and then her boyfriend added a few of his own. He could have busted my eardrum."

Bobbi tossed the cloth on the table and swung around to sit in my lap. "Which ear?"

I pointed. She kissed it and tugged at the lobe a little with her teeth. "Does that hurt?"

"Keep doing that and you won't make it out of here in time for your cue."

"Ah, nuts," she complained, and stood up to smooth her dress. She was wearing some kind of sparkly black thing tonight. Everything important was covered, but it looked as though it had been painted on. "I get a thirty-minute break after this set. Will you still be here?"

"Sure. If I watch out for your boss, you think I can see the show?"

"If you're careful and stick backstage. The girls won't say anything to him, but tell them to keep their mitts off you."

"Yes, ma'am."

I followed her out and hung close as she wound her way to the stage. A dozen breathless leggy girls in rustling tinsel clattered past us. One of them gave out with a wolf whistle and the others laughed. Bobbi looked at me with mock jealousy.

"They must have noticed the tie," I whispered. "Real silk." I waved the end at her like Oliver Hardy and she playfully swatted it down.

The band started another fanfare. She pecked my cheek and made a smooth entrance to welcoming applause. The lights went out except for a single spot centered on her. It sparked off her gown and turned her hair into a molten blond jewel. My heart ached, she was so beautiful. I forgot about looking for McAlister, hiding from the management, and any other complications the world had to offer. Bobbi was singing and that was all the world I needed or wanted.

After the show, behind the locked door of her dressing room, Bobbi peeled out of the clingy gown. "I love having a live audience, but it's so hot under that light. Radio work is much more comfortable."

I reclined on an old chaise lounge that was jammed up against the wall, admiring the view. Bobbi rarely used underwear with her working wardrobe, maintaining that it spoiled the lines. All she had on now were her stockings, knee garters, and heels. All I could think was, *Wow.*

She hung up the gown, turned on a little fan, and stood in front of it with her arms raised, which did interesting things to her breasts.

"Maybe I should go outdoors for a minute, that would cool me off," she mused.

"Or heat up half the city."

"Is it warm in here to you?"

"Yeah, you could say that I'm feeling a little hot and bothered."

"I can open the door to create a draft. . . ."

"Don't you dare."

She dropped her arms and sauntered over to sit next to me on the lounge. "It's not fair, I've got my clothes off and you—"

"My hat's on the rack," I defended. "The way I'm set up now, I don't have to take 'em off."

"But what if I want to touch your skin, too?" One of her hands wormed under my coat and started plucking at my shirttail.

"Uh . . ." Now I really was too distracted to answer. She got under the shirt and ran her nails up my back, which made me squirm. I caught her arm and did a thing or two to return the favor. We had to keep the laughter down; the walls weren't that thick. Her other hand successfully unbuttoned my coat as she began crawling all over me.

It was absolutely wonderful.

Bobbi craned her neck in the mirror to get a look at her throat. "Good thing I'm wearing a high collar tonight," she said, her finger lightly touching the small red marks there.

"Is it bad?"

"It's never bad with you."

"I mean, are you hurt?" Since our method of reaching a climax required my breaking her skin in a very vulnerable area, her comfort was of serious concern to me.

"What we do never hurts, you know that. I was talking about the hickey around it. It'll fade in an hour or so, but not before the next show starts."

"Next time I'll show a little more restraint."

"Uh-uh. I like things just as they are. Besides, it gives me an excuse to buy more stuff like this." She shook out a red satin gown and let it slither down over her body. Watching Bobbi get dressed was as absorbing an activity as watching her strip. There aren't many girls around with that kind of talent.

Someone knocked at the door. "One minute, Bobbi."

"Gonna stick around for the rest of the evening?" she asked, touching up the powder on her nose.

"I'm *supposed* to be here to look for McAlister. Maybe I can slip out front, do a quick gander, and come back."

"What if you find him?"

"The one weak point in all my plans," I confessed with mock drama.

"That and getting spotted by my boss. He'll know all about the lounge ruckus and be in a wonderful mood. You stay back here and I'll ask around for you. Someone's bound to know this fella. Clubs like this thrive on booze and gossip."

"Well, I . . ."

But she only smiled and winked and flashed out the door, locking it behind her. She wasn't trying to keep me prisoner, only make sure no one else got in. That mirror over her table reflected nearly the whole room, and neither of us wanted to borrow trouble.

The band already had the next fanfare going and Bobbi made her cue just in time. I relaxed back on the lounge and listened to her distant voice through the intervening walls. Throughout her set, I pleasantly speculated over how many other couples had used the same lounge for their own romantic interludes. I had plenty of time to think about it, but when Bobbi finally came back she had news.

"I talked with Gloria—"

"The hat-check girl?"

"I was hoping you hadn't noticed her."

"What'd she say?"

"McAlister was here for a while and then left."

"What time?"

"I'm getting to that. He was here when you arrived and didn't leave until after the ruckus. Looks like little Marian was trying to keep you two apart."

"Why do you think that?"

"Marian came back after you lost her in the parking lot and made a beeline to McAlister's table off the dance floor. Tina was running the drinks in that section, but neither of them wanted anything. They had their heads together for a bit, and the next time she looked he was gone. Gloria said he got his coat, stiffed her on the tip, and took off. She saw Marian walk past a minute or so later."

"Charles ought to have you as a partner instead of me. McAlister's probably halfway to China by now."

"Maybe, but chances are, he'll stop to pack first. Where does he live?"

"He's got a flop in a hotel . . ." I fumbled out my notebook, where

I'd scribbled the address. It wasn't far; if I hurried I might get there in time to watch his dust settle. "Gotta go, sweetheart. If I'm not back by closing, get a ride with one of the girls."

She laughed when I kissed her and wished me luck.

The Boswell House was a cheap residence hotel in a tough neighborhood that hadn't quite made it to being a full-fledged slum, but was trying all the same. No clerk at the desk challenged me when I walked into the dusty lobby and looked around. The stairs were on the right; ancient wooden things full of more creaks and pops than an old man's joints. I double-checked the lobby to be safe, then went semitransparent and floated up over them, guiding myself along with a ghostly hand on the banister. In this form I could see and hear what was going on, but it could scare the willies out of anyone spotting me.

Either the timing was good or for once my luck was holding. I went solid just as a leggy gal in a bright kimono emerged from the room next door to McAlister's. She had carroty hair and hard eyes and looked at me looking at her for exactly two seconds before spinning on her bare heel to go back into her lair. I must not have been the man of her dreams, after all.

A moment of listening at McAlister's door confirmed that he wasn't at home. The door was locked, but no problem.

The small room beyond wasn't much: cheap, battered furniture at the edges, and a Murphy bed taking up most of the space in the middle. It hadn't been made in a couple of weeks; that, or he was an incredibly restless sleeper. I figured he slept alone, since I couldn't think of a woman born who would voluntarily lie down in those stale sheets. I lifted the end of the bed and closed it up into the wall to give myself a little working space.

Escott had taught me how to poke and pry without leaving signs, so I went through everything, taking my time. Chances were, McAlister would be back before I was finished, and then I could tackle him about the bracelet.

His clothes were still in the wardrobe and bureau, which was good news. A dented metal suitcase was tucked under the spindly legs of a washstand. Unless he had plans to buy clothes along the way, he hadn't skipped town yet.

I'd just lowered the bed again to check under the mattress when the stairs outside warned me that someone was coming up, a man, by the sound of his shoes. He was going slow, but the old wood announced his progress like a brass band. I eased the bed down the rest of the way and vanished.

He took his time at the door and then opened it slowly, as though he expected a problem was waiting for him inside. He clicked on the light, waited another moment, then closed the door up again. He made a quick circuit of the room, brushing right past me. He stopped in his tracks.

"Jack? Are you here?"

A clipped English accent. Escott.

I materialized with some relief and squinted. After working in the dark for so long, the room lights seemed painfully bright to my sensitive eyes. "Yeah, I'm here. How'd you know?"

He looked relieved as well. "I felt a sudden cold spot cut right through my coat. When that happens I am inclined to think you must be lurking nearby. Have you been here long?" He pocketed a worn leather kit that held a number of lock picks and skeleton keys. It explained the excessive time he'd spent at the door.

"Long enough for a search."

"Is it clean?" A fastidious man himself, he couldn't help wrinkling his nose at the place.

"Figuratively speaking, yes, but we may have a problem. . . ." I told him about my little square dance at the Top Hat with Marian and Summers and Bobbi's news on McAlister.

"Dear me, but Miss Pierce has thrown a spanner into the works by her misinterpretation of her father's actions. If McAlister is the guilty party with the bracelet, he'll have the wind up by now."

"Which is why I got over here. Bobbi figured he'd stop long enough for his clothes."

"I may put Miss Smythe on a retainer," he murmured. "I've just come from a betting parlor McAlister frequents. It seems we're not the only party looking for him."

"He lose big?"

"Almost two thousand dollars—"

"Ouch."

"—to a bookie anxious to take it from McAlister's hide if the money is not immediately forthcoming."

"Let's hope he stops here first."

"Indeed. If he's carrying the bracelet with him it could be lost to our competition to cover his debt."

"Want to wait here for him?"

"It's much warmer than the street below, though we should shut off the light." He relocked the door.

When he was settled in a wobbling chair, I hit the switch. The darkness washed comfortably over my eyes and they adjusted easily. The dim gray illumination coming from the room's only window bounced off the mirror hanging over the bureau and caught the edge of Escott's face.

"Can you see all right?" he asked.

"Just fine."

"Then perhaps you might answer a question for me."

"What?"

"Why do you need a light in your workroom if you can see so well in the dark?"

I'd wondered about that myself. "I think it's because the place is so totally sealed up."

"The darkness is absolute then?"

"Like a . . . cave." I nearly said "tomb" and changed it at the last second. "In most places there's always some kind of light available, like what's here now. It's more than enough for me to work with, but that room is the exception."

"What about your hearing?"

"You talking about the car that just pulled up out front?"

He nodded. We waited and listened. I heard a lot more besides the slam of the car door outside. Some guy was snoring two rooms down, and above us a happy couple were having an athletic engagement. The showgirl in the kimono must have been reading. I concentrated on the lobby below and picked out the clack of a woman's high heels quickly coming up the stairs. She paused at the landing and again just outside, then a key slipped into the lock and turned. Escott hastily vacated the chair and was crowded next to me behind the door.

It opened slowly and she fumbled for the light. She surveyed the room only a moment, killed the light, and left. When the door was closed, I quietly told Escott I was going after her, and vanished. I swept past her down the stairs and out the building, then materialized. She was just coming out as I came in, and I made sure we bumped into each other.

She was tiny, not much over five feet even in her heels, and despite the bulky lines of her coat I could tell the rest of her was built along the same scale. She automatically looked up when we collided, and I had a pleasant view of big blue eyes limned with golden lashes and a fringe of golden hair escaping the edges of her hat. Sebastian Pierce had said she was a little doll and he'd been perfectly right.

I stopped her as she started past. " 'Scuse me, but aren't you Stan McAlister's girl?"

"What?" She blinked at me, properly confused.

"Kitty Donovan?"

"Yes, what do you want?" She must have been concentrating heavily on something else. Her mind had to visibly shift gears to this new distraction.

"My name's Jack, I know your boyfriend." It was an exaggeration, not an outright lie, so I was able to get away with it.

"Oh . . . well . . . how nice," she said, a little blankly. I could have told her I was Teddy Roosevelt and gotten the same response.

"Are you looking for him, too?"

At this, her big eyes went very round and she broke into a kind of frozen smile. "Looking for him? Why, yes, but he's not here tonight."

"He's not? That's too bad . . . I really needed to talk to him. Do you know where else he might be?"

She shook her head. "No, I just thought I'd drop in and see, but no one's home."

"Isn't this kind of a rough place for a nice girl like you to—"

"I don't think it's really any of your business," she told me brusquely. She started to duck past. I caught her arm. "Lemme go or I'll scream my head off."

"No, you won't. You need to know why I'm looking for him."

She was ready to question that, but let me lead her back into the lobby. I kept a loose hold on her arm, as though to steady her. She unsuccessfully tried to shake my grip.

"You lug," she grumbled. I didn't argue with her.

Escott was just coming down the stairs. I nodded at him and he joined us, politely removing his hat when I introduced Kitty Donovan to him.

"A pleasure," he said, bowing a little. She didn't expect his accent or such a high polish on his manners; neither of them went with the neighborhood.

"What's this about?" she asked.

"We're friends of Stan and we're looking for him," I said.

Her lips curled in cynical disbelief. "I'll just bet you are."

Escott stepped in. "He was at the Top Hat Club earlier tonight, do you know where he might be now?"

Eyes guarded, she shook her head. I was pretty sure she was telling the truth, but Escott wasn't satisfied. He cocked an eyebrow, indicating a lounge area off the lobby. It was just slightly more private and out of immediate line of sight from the door. We walked her in. I sat next to her on a couch and Escott took a chair in front of us.

She was scared now and trying not to show it. "Listen, if you are Stan's friends, he won't like what you're doing."

"We're doing nothing, Miss Donovan, only waiting until such time as Mr. McAlister returns."

"He's not here. I was just up in his room, see?"

"Perhaps I do. I think you have us mixed up with two other fellows. My word of honor, we are not working for Leadfoot Sam."

"Leadfoot Sam?" I echoed.

"Mr. McAlister's annoyed bookie. I believe he earned his colorful appellation due to his driving style during Prohibition."

Kitty was all anxious attention. "What about Leadfoot?"

Escott tried a reassuring smile that she wasn't interested in. "Nothing about him—at least as far as I'm concerned. We are not his agents."

"Then who are you working for?"

He pulled out his investigator's license and she studied it for a longtime. "We're on an errand unconnected to Stan McAlister's debts and only wish to obtain some information from him."

"I'm sorry, but I can't help you, and I really have to go now." She started to stand, but I gently pulled her back.

"We require but a few minutes of your time," he continued.

"But *I* don't want to be here. Now, let me go or I'll scream the house down."

"Kitty . . ." First I got her full attention, then stepped up the pressure. Her eyes seemed to get bigger and bluer as I held them with my own. She was on her way to slipping under when the entry door opened and a dapper-looking guy with straw blond hair walked in. He distracted me and, worst of all, he distracted Kitty. Her gaze shifted over and she gave out with a little gasp, then drew breath for a full shout.

"Run, Stan! They're after you!"

He whirled in a flash and was out the door before she finished. Escott charged after him and I started to move, but Kitty made a tackling dive for my legs. She was tiny, but more than enough to trip me. I crashed backward into a chair and flipped up and over, feet flying in a clumsy somersault. The floor was wood and awfully damned hard to land on.

When the room stopped spinning, I slowly crawled upright. Kitty had recovered and stood facing me. She dug into her purse and brought out a gun, slipped off the safety, and leveled it on my heart.

"Aw, now, kid, don't do anything I wouldn't do."

Her hand was shaking, but there was a grim set to her mouth. "Back. You stand right back."

I raised my hands to show cooperation. She carried some kind of .22 automatic and knew how to use it or she might have forgotten about the safety. The live bullets it probably carried wouldn't kill me, but getting shot hurt like hell, and my suit had been through enough rough stuff for one evening. There were other ways to take care of her.

"Kitty, we don't want to hurt Stan. We just want to ask him a few questions."

She shook her head and told me to move back. I could try hypnotizing her again, but she looked too nerved up to easily respond. It would also be necessary to get closer and she'd already made a firm decision to keep me at a distance.

"Gonna keep me here all night?" I asked. "What will the management think?"

"Wha'd'ya think I'll think?" A middle-aged man who looked as tough as the rest of the place came around the check-in desk. His hair was sticking up in different directions and he wore a drab bathrobe over his shorts and undershirt. He carried a massive shotgun that made Kitty's .22 look like a water pistol.

Before I could answer, Kitty cut in. "I'm Stan McAlister's girl. This guy and his friend outside were trying to kidnap me."

"Is that what all the noise is about?" His unfriendly eye caught sight of the overturned chair. From his expression, you'd have thought it was his grandma's priceless antique.

"This is a misunderstanding," I said. "My partner and I are—"

"Trying to kill Stan," she blurted. "Please, mister, could you hold him here while I get away?" There were tears and a crack of fear in her voice. Whether they were real or not was anyone's guess, but the man was willing to buy it.

"Sure, little girl. You take off. He won't get out of here for a while." He hefted both barrels in my direction and looked confident.

She whispered out her thanks and was gone.

"Look, mister, my partner and I are detectives."

"Uh-huh. Got any proof?"

I hesitated. Technically I was just along for the ride; Escott was the only one with a valid license. The hesitation was enough to bolster any doubts and the man took a firmer grip on the stock. Outside I heard an engine gun and the whine of wheels as Kitty's car tore down the street. I wondered what had happened to Escott.

"What I said was on the level." I lowered my arms as though they were tired. It didn't seem to bother him.

"Yeah, yeah."

"She just got a little nervous, is all."

He shook his head in patronizing disbelief.

"Now, I don't happen to have my license with me . . ." I started to reach inside my coat.

He dropped the disbelief for a scowl, renewing his grip on the gun.

"But I do have my wallet . . . so maybe we can make a deal?" I opened one side of my coat so he could see where I was reaching.

He licked his lips. "Okay. Double sawbuck."

"Single."

"Double or nothing, buddy."

"Okay, okay." I pulled out the wallet and fumbled around with it, walking toward him. The change in my posture and attitude worked. His hold on the shotgun went slack as he came forward. His attention was on the money, but at one point he looked up at me.

His mistake.

A few minutes later he was peacefully snoring back in his office and

I was outside looking for Escott and McAlister. Kitty was long gone, of course, and there was no sign of her fleet-footed boyfriend. The street was empty and black and the infrequent glare of tall lamps only deepened the shadows they were meant to relieve. It looked cold and was beginning to feel cold, even to me.

A distinct gasp and cough caught my attention and drew me to the alley running between the hotel and a closed coffee shop. The bundle of clothes lying in the middle of it was Escott, curled on his side, trying to remember how to breathe.

He stifled a groan as I helped him sit up. The only visible damage was a cut above one eye.

"I almost had him," he complained.

"What stopped you?"

"His blackjack."

It seemed like a good excuse to me.

"He thumped me and broke for his car."

"Round one to Stan, then." I got him out of the alley and folded into my Buick. He groaned again at this, since Stan had also booted him in the stomach for good measure.

"If this keeps up, I shall certainly consider raising my basic retainer," he said, hugging the damaged area.

"You go right ahead. Kitty got away, too. She had a gun and the manager's sympathy."

He didn't seem too upset. "Straight on, then. There's still a chance we can salvage things."

"How so?"

"I'm speculating she will head directly for her own home."

"Yeah? You got a crystal ball?"

"Hardly, but seeking a place of safety after receiving a bad fright is a very strong instinct. If she should follow that pattern, then we'll have the opportunity to question her without interruptions."

Escott gave me the address from Pierce's notes. I got the car in gear and we took off.

Kitty's home was in a nice block of modern apartments in a nice part of town. We parked on the curb out front next to a has-been of a car. I'd hardly stopped when Escott was out and pulling off one of his gloves. He put one hand on the old car's hood to see if it had been running recently, and his lips thinned with satisfaction.

"Stan's?" I asked.

He opened the door and checked the registration, then nodded. While I nervously watched the street for beat cops, he did something under the hood to make sure it wouldn't start.

The apartment entrance required either a key or that visitors buzz. I saved us some trouble and slipped through to open the door for Escott. Kitty lived on the second floor at the end of a carpeted hallway. After trying her door and finding it locked, I did the same thing again, but slowly. Still invisible, I checked the room beyond to ascertain that no one was there. It was very small, probably no more than an entry with a coat closet. I reformed and spent a moment listening, but picked up nothing. I clicked the lock back as softly as possible and let Escott inside.

He already knew to be quiet and his manner was calm enough, but I could hear his heart thumping like a drum. He enjoyed this sort of work.

The living room was new looking, the furniture comfortably plump, but not fussy. A low table displayed drawing pencils, a battered sketch pad, and a stack of fashion magazines. Escott flipped a few pages of the sketchbook. It was full of stylized drawings of heads, all tilted to show off the crazy hats they wore.

The first bedroom was a work area. A couple of card tables in the middle were covered with a colorful scatter of ribbons, feathers, netting, lace, velvet, and similar junk. In the corner stood a small black sewing machine, and stacked next to it were different kinds of hat blocks. A wall full of shelves held samples of the finished product. Most of them looked awfully strange to me, but were probably just the thing for Bobbi to go crazy over.

Escott went down the short hall to the other bedroom and I followed. It was done up in pale blues with an eye for comfort, especially the central furnishing.

"That's a pretty big bed for such a small lady," I said. It looked nearly double the regular size, filling most of the room. I'd seen something like it once in a movie and had thought things like that only existed in Hollywood.

"Agreed." He went over to one of the nightstands and opened the top drawer, immediately pulling out several packets of prophylactics. "Well, well."

I shifted uncomfortably. The girl was entitled to some privacy and I didn't feel right about invading it on such an intimate level. Escott dropped them back and shut the drawer with hardly a raised eyebrow. To him it was simply information. He collected it in the same absent way other people collect string. He checked the closet and bath and came back right away, shaking his head to indicate they were empty. That left only the kitchen at the other end of the flat.

The dining room was clean and uninteresting. The door from it to the kitchen was shut. I listened and this time heard the faint sound of someone breathing within. Just as I touched the doorknob I jerked my hand back as though from an electric shock.

"What is it?" asked Escott.

It was unmistakable, but I drew another cautious breath just to be sure.

"Jack?"

I swallowed with difficulty, because my mouth and throat had gone bone dry. "Bloodsmell," I whispered.

He started to say something but caught the look on my face. He nodded, understanding, and slipped his glove back on to open the door.

A lot of different images crowded my eyes: gray-speckled linoleum, shining steel cabinets, white curtains with red trim. The trim almost seemed to accent the red pool at our feet.

Kitty Donovan had pressed herself into a corner formed by the steel cabinets. Her hands gripped their edges on either side with white fingers. Her mouth hung slack and her eyes were too big to be real, as though they'd been painted on her face. She was staring at Stan McAlister, who was sprawled on the floor in front of her.

He was on his back. His coat and shirt had been unbuttoned, their pockets turned out, and the contents scattered. There was a nasty bruise on his temple; bad enough, but whoever had hit him had wanted to be sure of things. The blood had oozed from at least a dozen wounds in his chest and one in the neck, where the carving knife was still embedded.

Kitty looked up at us, shivering violently from head to toe. Her lips moved, but only a soft hiccuping came out of them. Her eyes fastened once more onto McAlister's body, then abruptly rolled up in their sockets. With an audible sigh, she dropped gracelessly forward in a faint.

3

I moved toward her but Escott stopped me. His face was drawn and his lips had thinned to the point of disappearance.

"Mind where you step," he said in a low, carefully level voice.

He wasn't trying to be funny; he looked as sick as I felt. I nodded and took my time getting to Kitty. She'd just missed hitting the mess from McAlister's throat. I scooped her up and Escott followed as I took her out and put her on the oversized bed in the back.

"Still wearing her coat," he murmured. "She must have walked straight in and found him."

"I'm glad you don't think she did it."

"Of course, she could have knocked him out first and then killed him as he lay helpless. The physical evidence is against that theory, though. Except for this"—he removed one of her shoes and examined the smear of blood on its sole—"she is quite clean. The killer would most certainly have at least a spot or two on his hands."

He sounded pretty clinical until I realized that the cold detachment was his way of being able to handle the whole horrible business. He was still pasty white and his fingers twitched with more than his usual nervous energy.

"I have to make some phone calls. If she comes round, keep her back here and don't touch anything that will hold a print." He carefully placed the shoe on the nightstand. Almost as an afterthought, he swiped his gloved fingers over the drawer handle, and left.

Her skin was clammy and blue at the edges. I pulled the bedspread up and tucked it around her slight body. There seemed no point in reviving her; she'd be awake all too soon and have lots of talking to do for the cops. She was still out when Escott returned a few minutes later.

"Our employer is not at home and no one knows where he is. I should have liked to have given him some warning about this, but it can't be helped now, the police are on their way. I rousted the manager of this place. She's downstairs waiting to let them in."

"You call Lieutenant Blair?"

"Yes. He'll be thorough, which means you might not wish to be here. If this ends up in court . . ."

"I'll stick around. Tell him that I was waiting out in the car while you followed the girl inside. They won't call me into court if I wasn't here to see anything."

"And your presence now?"

"I got tired of waiting and followed you in—after you found the body. The only problem is Kitty, she saw us both."

He hardly glanced at her. "I doubt that she will be in a condition to remember, but if so, then it is something you can remedy easily enough. Now, before Blair shows up I want to check things again."

McAlister's looks hadn't improved while we were gone. Escott picked his way around the kitchen as though the pool of blood were part of a mine field. He'd once mentioned that he suffered from squeamishness; apparently it was under control tonight. I couldn't bring myself to go in, and hung back in the dining room, out of the way.

"Seepage rather than splashing," he said to himself in a voice that sounded borrowed. "He must have already been dead for this one." He indicated the blade in McAlister's throat.

"What about his stuff?" My own voice was thin.

He surveyed the scattered debris from the turned-out pockets. "His wallet—if he carried one—is missing. Perhaps we are meant to think the motive was robbery."

"Maybe it was, but for the bracelet."

"Which is not here, unless it's under him, and I've no wish to move him and see. Only we and Mr. Pierce know of it as being a possible motive for this terrible thing, yet these multiple wounds indicate . . ." He squatted on his heels, staring hard at them.

"What?"

He shook his head. He would talk when he was ready. He stood, casting around for something else to study, fastening his gaze on the stove and a heavy iron frying pan there. Instead of sitting square on a burner, it was tilted half-on and -off. Escott peered at it closely, keeping his hands well clear.

"Is that what smashed his head?" I asked.

"I believe so. It more than qualifies as a blunt instrument and is the only likely object in the room."

"What about his blackjack?"

"Yes, there's that, but I really don't see him as cheerfully handing it over for his killer to use. Also this was done very quickly. We weren't more than ten minutes behind Miss Donovan, and McAlister was less than five minutes ahead of her."

"So the killer must have been waiting here for him."

"Unless Miss Donovan is the killer."

"But you said—"

"I know. It is most unlikely, given her actions to aid him at the Boswell House, but it is just possible."

"You don't really think . . ."

He shrugged. "All permutations must be equally considered, especially the unsavory ones. Perhaps you can settle things one way or another when she comes round."

"You can make book on it."

"Yes, that's another factor to consider," he mused.

"What?"

"Leadfoot Sam, the bookie."

He quit the kitchen and I led the way back to her bedroom. The bed was empty, its spread tossed aside. The shoe on the nightstand was gone. A corner window with access to the fire escape was wide open and the thin curtains over it seemed to shiver from the icy air drifting inside. We both darted over, but she was nowhere in sight.

Escott allowed himself a brief and entirely American-sounding obscenity. "She'll make for her car."

"I'll go find out."

He didn't argue. To save time, I vanished on the spot and hurled out the window, using the uncompromising metal gridwork of the stairs as a guide to the ground. Re-forming, I heard a motor kick over and rushed around the building in time to see her taillights flare and dim as she took a sharp corner out of the apartment parking lot.

My car was on the other side of the place, of course. I was halfway there when the first of the cops rolled up and stopped. I waved at him in a friendly, hurried way, but he wasn't buying any. He'd been called to the scene of a homicide and spotted a man running away; it was more than enough to inspire his hunter's instinct. He was out and shouting for me to stop.

I didn't know if he had his gun in hand or not and had no inclination to find out. Quickly swerving under the deep shadow of a couple of trees, I vanished again, and kept going. He was still beating the bush when I bumped against my car and slipped inside. I was feeling pretty smug as I started up the engine. The feeling lasted until a prowl car roared in from nowhere and screeched to a halt right in my path. The first cop ran up, half crouching so he could see inside the driver's window. He did indeed have his gun in hand and it was pointed right at my chest. I decided not to move.

He bellowed at me to get out and I obliged. While he and his friends went through the farce of slapping me down and putting on the cuffs, Kitty Donovan sped merrily away into the night. I might have eventually been able to hypnotize my way out of it, but there were too many strikes against that gambit. The three of them were distracted and hostile, it was too dark for them to see me very well, but most of all I was just too dust-spitting mad to talk coherently.

A couple of unmarked cars rolled up and a medium-tall man in a belted leather overcoat emerged from one of them. We hadn't seen each other in several months, but I knew him right away. A young forty and dandy handsome, Lieutenant Blair was one of the best-dressed cops in Chicago, if not the rest of the state. He walked up slowly, studying things, and especially me. A broad smile of recognition appeared under his carefully groomed mustache.

"What have you got here?" he asked, addressing the cop who had a proprietary hand on my shoulder.

"Caught him running away, Lieutenant." The cop briefly described my capture.

"Uh-huh. Why were you running away, Mr. Fleming?"

"I was chasing someone."

"And who were you chasing?"

I didn't know how far Escott wanted to go in protecting his client's privacy. "Better ask Charles about that, I only came along for the ride."

Last fall, in order to avert a problem, I'd hypnotized Blair, planting the idea in his mind that we were friends. It had worked very well, but by now time and circumstances had eroded my suggestion down to almost nothing. Blair wasn't a bit amused with me.

"If you'd like to go for another ride, I'm sure we can arrange it."

The cop took a firmer grip on me as though to follow through with the threat, and that's when Escott made what I can only describe as a timely entrance. There were some smudges of grime on his clothes, indicating he'd also used the fire escape to exit the building. He was only slightly breathless, enough to give the impression that he was in a hurry.

"Lieutenant Blair, thank you for coming so quickly." He shook hands with Blair and at the same time got him walking back toward the apartments. He immediately launched into a succinct outline of his version of the evening, keeping me safely in the background until the last. Somehow he managed to avoid mentioning Pierce's name or how we broke into Kitty's flat.

". . . when we saw that she'd escaped out the window, Jack naturally went after her," he concluded.

"Naturally," he agreed, his tone bordering on sarcasm. "And just why did the young lady go out the window?"

"She was probably frightened out of her wits."

"Where would she go?"

Escott shrugged minimally, using one hand and an eyebrow.

As our parade reached the entry doors and the lights on either side of them, Blair noticed the souvenir Escott sported from McAlister's blackjack. "You been in a war or something?"

"Only a small skirmish, hardly worth the resulting headache."

Escott's offhand and deprecatory manner amused Blair long enough for him to have the cop release me. He had more important things to do than to push around the hired help. By the time we turned to go into the building his mood had gone sour again. It spread to the rest of the group, with the exception of the middle-aged woman in a bathrobe who let us in. For her, it was a toss-up between terror and curiosity. Murder can do that to people.

The next couple of hours were spent sitting on Kitty Donovan's overstuffed sofa watching a parade of cops turn the place over. Her neat little life was twisted inside out as they took photographs, dusted for prints, and collected anything that could be remotely connected with Stan McAlister's death.

Things wound their way down and the number of investigators thinned and left. Without ceremony or stir, McAlister was carried out in a stained and creaking wicker basket. Escott watched, his face carefully blank. One of his hands rested on the power switch of a table lamp next to his chair and he idly flicked it on and off until one of the cops told him to cut it out. He stiffened a little, not from the cop's annoyed order, but from some internal start. His pale gray eyes fixed on me, but he had no chance to say anything. Blair came over and started asking questions again, the kind Escott couldn't answer. I'd once been on the receiving end of one of Blair's interrogations and knew Escott's reticence would not be welcome.

A description of Kitty Donovan and her vehicle had been issued so the prowl-car boys could get in on the hunt. Blair hadn't made it any too clear whether he wanted her as a witness or a suspect. He'd listened to everything we could tell him, but had reserved judgment on our conclusions.

With the passage of time and the scarcity of facts, Blair's patience lessened in direct proportion to his growing temper. His olive skin got a few shades paler and his dark eyes were bright from all the internal heat. Push him too far and he'd explode. Escott didn't look very worried about it.

Blair abruptly stopped the questions when a muscle in his jaw started working all on its own. I thought the volcano would go off then and there, but he still had it well in check. His voice was smooth, almost purring. "Very well, Charles, I can admire your business ethics, but it's getting late and I've other work to do. I may need to call you in for more questions at any time, though, so I want you to hang around the station just in case anything new occurs to either of us."

"Are you charging me with anything?"

"Don't tempt me."

Escott had been carefully neutral since Blair's arrival and continued to hold on to it. He nodded, ruefully accepting Blair's terms, and I wondered what he was up to since he was fully capable of talking his way out of the situation. "Would you like to have my assistant accompany us?" he inquired politely.

"No, I would not. Your assistant can just get the hell out of here."

One corner of Escott's mouth twitched. Blair missed it or he might have reconsidered his snap decision. "Very well," he said, with only a hint of exasperation. "Jack, I was wondering if you'd look after my car before going home. I wouldn't want any pranksters bashing in the lights." He handed me the keys.

"Yeah, sure."

One of the plainclothesmen hustled him out.

"What's this about his car?" asked Blair.

"Nothing, Lieutenant," I said. "We had to leave it in a rough neighborhood, is all."

"Near the Boswell House, by any chance?"

"Yeah. What about it?"

"Just stay away from the place. My men are going over it now and you could get swept up and taken in along with anything else they find over there."

I shrugged, all innocence. "They won't even see me . . . I promise."

Escott had parked his Nash under the doubtful safety of a street lamp a little distance from the hotel. No one had bothered it; the weather might have been too discouragingly cold for anybody to try. I checked inside and found his notebook in the glove box, opening it to the last page. The paper with all the information on McAlister dropped out. Maybe that was what he wanted picked up, but I wasn't so sure. I put it in my own notebook and took a look at his lights, front and back. The whisper of city dust on them was undisturbed, so he hadn't left any hidden messages under the glass.

Half a block down were three cars too new for the area. One was a black-and-white, another unmarked with a tall aerial, and the third a slick-looking Cadillac. I sat in the Nash and waited until the cops finally came out, and drove away.

The driver waiting in the Caddy stayed put, but I wasn't much worried about him, figuring his employer was busy visiting some girlfriend. The street was dead quiet when I got out and walked across to the hotel.

The manager was awake again and had thrown on some clothes. He stood at the front desk narrowly watching a tall woman using his phone. Maybe he thought she'd walk off with it.

"Ten cents," he said when she finished.

"A nickel or nothing," she snapped.

"That's a business line. While you're calling for a cab, I could be losing money."

"Like hell." She dug into her handbag and stuck a cigarette in her freshly painted mouth. I stepped in and lighted it for her. She glanced up and nodded a brief thanks. The last time I'd seen her she'd slammed a door on me. Her eyes had lost a lot of their hardness and were puffy and red. She'd tried to disguise the lines with a layer of powder and almost succeeded. Her carroty hair was covered by a close-fitting black hat and she'd replaced the kimono with a dark dress and coat. The stuff looked expensive, but slightly shabby with age or a lot of wear. At her feet was a large suitcase.

"Moving out?" I asked.

"What's it to you?"

"Ten cents," repeated the manager. He concentrated on her, ignoring me because he didn't remember our earlier encounter at all. The suggestions I'd planted earlier were still strong in him. I fished out two nickels and tossed them on the desk.

"Hey," said the woman. "Don't do me any favors."

"Life's too short to spend time arguing, besides, I want to talk with you."

"Hey!" she protested as I took her elbow and steered her away from the desk. "I don't want to talk to you. Lemme go or I'll call a cop."

"You're too late, they just left."

She stopped fighting me, suddenly curious. "Who the hell are you, anyway?"

"A friend of a friend of Stan McAlister."

The name meant something to her but she pretended it didn't. "Who?"

"Your next-door neighbor."

"That lug. Well, he ain't my neighbor anymore. He ain't nobody's neighbor now. The cops—the cops said—" She broke off with an involuntary shudder.

"Yeah, I heard what happened to him."

"You a cop, too?" she demanded.

"No, I'm here for a friend of a friend. Remember? Why are you in such a hurry to leave?"

"That's my business. Why are you so damn nosy?"

"Because Stan got himself and my friend into some deep trouble tonight."

"I'd have never guessed with all the cops around."

"Are they why you're leaving?"

"So what if it is? I don't like cops, it ain't a crime. Look it up."

"I believe you. Look, I'm only trying to dig out some information on Stan."

Her hard eyes lowered in sulky thought. "What kind of information?"

"What people he saw, how he made his living, that kind."

She shook her head. "I can't help you."

"Not even for some extra cab fare?"

"I don't know nothing worth that much. A place like this, it don't pay to get curious about anything."

I could believe that. "You ever talk to him in the hall?"

She almost laughed. "He talked to me."

"What about?"

She looked at me with pity. "What do you think? Mugs like that are always on the make, but I wasn't interested."

"He have a girlfriend?"

"Yeah, there's always some noodle-brain around who'll fall for his kind of line."

"So he brought 'em here?"

She nodded and drew heavily on her cigarette, affecting boredom, but I could almost smell the fear rolling off her.

"You see any of them?"

"I'm not the housemother here."

"He have any other kind of visitors?"

Her eyes were less hard now than tired. "I already told all this to one of those goddamn cops. I don't know nothing, which means I can't say nothing. You want to know about the guy, ask the management."

"I will, but you're better looking."

She put on a thin, disillusioned smile. "Nice try, kid. Maybe some other time."

"Hold on—"

"I can't, my cab just pulled up."

"You hear of anyone called Leadfoot Sam?"

A little noise came out of her throat and she shook her head. She was plenty scared. "Please, I just wanta get out of here."

"I'll walk you out."

Her mouth dropped a little, but she was grateful for the release. I carried her heavy suitcase and put it in the trunk for her.

"Where will you go?" I asked, holding the door as she climbed in behind the driver.

"Anyplace where I can get an unbroken night's sleep. Hey, you don't have to do that."

I passed a five to her and shut the door. "Yeah, I know."

She rolled down her window. "You nuts or something?"

"Probably. Sweet dreams."

Her mouth worked and her teeth started chattering from more than just the winter air. She rolled the window up and the cab drove away. I waited till it made the corner then went back inside.

"What's her name?" I asked the manager.

"She's too old for you, sonny," he leered.

I quickly decided that manners and charm would be a total waste on him. Since there were no witnesses around now, I opted for my usual shortcut, and had him talking like a mynah bird in a very few minutes.

The guy said the woman's name was Doreen Grey and that she called herself an actress. A lot of girls called themselves actresses. I shrugged and passed it off. Life was tough all over. I skipped her and asked about McAlister and got some answers.

He'd moved in about six months ago and paid his rent on time, usually putting in a little extra on the side. He did the kind of entertaining that the management was content to ignore as long as the tips were good.

He had a lot of different lady friends; Kitty had been only one in a long parade.

I told the manager to catch up on his sleep and went to McAlister's room to see what the cops had left. It was about the same as before, but with the drawers pulled open. The bed looked dirty and depressing. I didn't like to think of Kitty ever being in it. Perhaps their assignations took place in her own room. The supplies stored in her nightstand lent some hopeful credence to that.

Escott's apparently idle play with the table lamp came to mind. I turned on the one overhead, once again wincing at the brightness. Two more lamps flanked the bed. I checked them over but found nothing odd. They were as cheap as the rest of the furnishings and had no hidden crannies for concealing expensive bracelets. They even worked. Their combined brightness made the dingy little room even more depressing. I shut them off and stared at the walls, trying to figure out what Escott had seen.

Across from the bed was the bureau and its mirror. As I ran an eye from one wall to the other, I noticed the crummy prints hung up for decoration. They had been left a little crooked on their wires by the cops; I'd been careful to leave them straight. They served to remind me that the mirror had been bolted to the wall. It was about the only thing in the place that might have been worth stealing. Because mirrors give me the creeps, I'd pretty much ignored it before, with my eyes purposely not focusing on its reflection of an empty room. I crossed over for another look. At each corner a bright new screw held the mirror's frame fast in place.

I gave one edge a tug and the whole thing snapped free with a sloppy crunch. The mirror was a fancy one-way job to hide a hole in the wall. The hole went right through the lath and plaster to Doreen Grey's room.

And I'd given her cab fare.

After indulging in a quarter-minute of intense self-recrimination, I put the mirror down and slipped through the wall to look around. Doreen's room was an appropriate reverse of McAlister's except the bureau had been pushed over a few feet. There were three faint dents in the bare floor beneath the hole, probably where she'd set up the tripod. Normal room light wouldn't have been sufficient for her photography, but she'd seen to that by giving McAlister some extra-bright bulbs to leave on during the show. They'd had a nasty little racket going, either for blackmail or pornography, but I could admire the planning involved.

None of it was any too good for Kitty. If McAlister had tried putting the squeeze on her, she'd have plenty of motive for killing him. She was a little doll, cute and demure looking as you please, but I was beginning to have serious doubts—the kind that send people to death row.

I shook out of them and finished searching the room.

Doreen hadn't missed a thing. Her wastebasket held wads of soggy tissues, indicating she'd suffered a bout of genuine grief for her partner's demise, but the rest of the place was clean. I speculated that both she and McAlister had lived ready to pull stakes and leave on a moment's notice. With the kind of business they'd worked, it would have been a necessity.

She could be on her way to Timbuktu by now and only the cops had the resources to find her—unless I got smart and called the cab company.

I went downstairs and borrowed the business phone. It was getting late and things were slowing down. They didn't have much trouble finding the driver who'd just picked up a fare from the Boswell House address. He showed up again about five minutes after my call and I went outside to meet him.

"Where to?" he asked when I got in.

"Noplace."

He threw a suspicious glance up to the mirror, missed me, and turned around. "What's the scam, then?"

"The woman you picked up here, where'd you take her?"

He hesitated.

"My intentions are honorable," I said, and pulled out a couple bucks for him to see, as if money could indicate a man's honesty.

He shrugged. It wasn't his business. He gave out with a street name and some general directions on how he got there.

"This another hotel?" I asked.

"Nah. It's a rough patch like this, stores and things. She paid me and stood in the street till I drove off."

"No hotels, apartments, stuff like that?"

"Nope."

"Were any of the stores open?"

"Nah. There was a bar doing business down on the far corner, but it looked like a lot of walking for her to do with that suitcase. She didn't want any help with it, I'm glad to say. That thing looked fifty pounds if it was an ounce, and my back's bad enough."

"Here, get yourself some liniment." I gave him the two bucks in lieu of a regular fare and got out. He shook his head, but grinned as he left. Crazy customers like me were always welcome. The exhaust had hardly settled when I heard the thunk of a car door as it slammed shut just up the street. A big bald guy stood next to the Cadillac I'd noticed earlier. He smoothed down the vast lines of his overcoat and started walking toward me.

He seemed harmless enough, at least at a distance. I was alone and not too worried about being able to take care of myself. As he drew near I started having second thoughts.

He was closer to being seven feet tall than six, with a massive, muscled body under the coat. He wasn't naturally bald, but shaved his head. He carried his hat in hand and swung it up in place as he came closer. I settled my own more firmly so it wouldn't fall off as I looked up at him. He stopped about a yard away and regarded me with a calm, confident eye.

"I want you should come with me," he said in an even, unhurried voice. He could have said something about the weather and it would have sounded the same.

A dozen smart-ass answers to that one popped into mind and just as quickly died away. He wasn't a cop, because I never heard of a cop driving a Cadillac. That left two other possibilities and I didn't think he was some kind of overgrown hustler.

"You work for Leadfoot Sam?" I asked.

He smiled, not showing his teeth, which was a relief. As it was, he was more than enough to scare Boris Karloff, let alone a solitary vampire.

"I hope it's not a formal occasion," I said, walking with him back to the Caddy. He didn't bother to enlighten me as he held open the rear door. I climbed in, sitting behind a gum-chewing driver who looked only mildly interested in what was going on. Sleepy eyed, he put it in gear and we rolled away as soon as the big guy had settled in.

It did occur to me early on that I could have turned down the invitation. I wanted to chase after Doreen Grey and get the details about her racket with McAlister. On the other hand, Leadfoot was another source of information, and he was going out of his way to make himself available. His method was unorthodox, but for the moment not too threatening.

The drive was short; we stopped at an all-night drugstore less than a mile away. My escorts took me around to the back entrance, used a key, and walked me in. We stood in a cluttered storage and pickup area, full of crates and all kinds of bottles.

"That you, Butler?" a man called from farther in and down.

"Yeah, Sam," answered the big guy, ducking as he came through the door. He carefully shut and locked it. The driver hung back and Butler urged me in the direction of a rusty spiral staircase.

I wasn't too sure the steps would hold our combined weight. They protested a little, but not alarmingly so as we trudged down to a dry, dusty room stacked with more crates. A metal-shaded bulb hung low over a table that must have been assembled from pieces, since it was too big for the stairway opening. A long, weedy man in his late thirties lounged in a chair at the far end with his feet up on it. He wore two-tone shoes, plaid pants, and a flowered vest. He wasn't following a fashion so much as trying to set one of his own.

Off to one side, he'd placed a straw hat, brim up, and was tossing cards at it with tremendous concentration. We had to wait until he'd finished out the deck. When the cards were used up, he stared at the hat with regret, then turned his attention to us. He had a narrow face, weak chin, and rather wide, innocent eyes. His brow furrowed, as though he were trying to remember something.

"Who's that?" he asked Butler, staring at me with sincere puzzlement.

"He was at McAlister's hotel. He put Doreen in a cab, goes into the hotel. I see lights come up in McAlister's room. The lights go out and he comes out. He calls a cab, but don't leave in it, just talks with the driver. I thought you should maybe want to talk to him, too."

"I'm Sam. Who're you?" he asked me.

"Leadfoot Sam?"

He was a study in blank astonishment. "You can't be. *I'm* Leadfoot Sam. Butler, take this man away, he's an imposter." Then he roared out with a room-filling laugh and Butler grinned.

I didn't know whether to join them or bolt out before it got worse.

"You're a killer, Sam," said Butler.

"That's right." Sam stopped laughing and stared at me meaningfully. "And don't anyone forget it."

If his game was to disconcert me, it was working. Lunatics always leave me unnerved.

He pointed at a chair. "Sit."

I looked to make certain he wasn't talking to Butler and walked over to take the chair. It was a plain wooden job with a worn chintz pad on the seat that didn't seem to belong there. Sam was blank eyed again, so I lifted the pad to see what was under it. He was visibly disappointed when I tossed his hidden whoopee cushion onto the table.

"Get us something to drink," he told Butler.

Butler located a crate and wrenched off the lid, nails and all. He pulled out a flat bottle of booze and set it down between us. Sam unscrewed the cap to let it breathe.

"No glasses," he apologized. "But this stuff should kill off most anything catching." He offered me the first swig.

The last time I'd swallowed something other than blood, I'd ended up heaving it into a gutter. Once again, I was trapped by the demands of social ritual.

He misinterpreted my hesitation and took a quick drink to show that it was all right. I accepted the bottle, put it to my lips, and held my tongue over the opening, pretending to drink. The drop of booze I did taste was bitter and burned.

"Is it that bad?" He really seemed concerned.

"I'm not used to the good stuff," I hedged.

He laughed, a single barking explosion. "Good stuff! Sonny, this is what we had left over after Roosevelt made it legal again. It's been sitting down here for—Butler, how long has it been sitting down here?"

"A long time, Sam."

"A long time."

I tried to look impressed. "You use to run this yourself?"

"I don't remember the cargos so much as the driving. It was a goddamn long haul from Canada to here, and you wouldn't believe the hours."

"Gave you a good name at any rate."

"Yeah, it gave me a good name. Now what's yours?"

I started to say Jack the Giant Killer and thought better of it, not being too sure of Butler's temper. I opted for my middle name and the name of my favorite radio hero. "Russell Lamont."

"Pleased to meet you, Russell Lamont." He took his feet off the table to lean over and shake hands. "You a cop?"

"No."

" 'S'funny, 'cause I'm getting a cop smell off you."

I showed him an old press card and covered up the name with my thumb. "I'm a reporter. Is that close enough to cop to get the smells mixed?"

He didn't like it, but was still too curious to throw me out. "How about telling me what your interest is in Sam McAlister?"

"He's a friend of a friend."

Sam shook his head, his narrow shoulders slumped tragically. "Aw, that's not nice, Russell. You come down here, drink my booze, and then fib. Shame on you."

"That's the best I can do unless there's something in it for me."

"What'd'ya have in mind?"

"Information on McAlister and Doreen Grey."

"Gonna write a big story and name names?"

"Nah, I just want to help some kid out of a jam."

It was the truth, but he didn't want to believe it. "Ever think that *you* might be in a jam?" His gaze flicked to Butler, who was still looming somewhere in the back.

"Nothing I can't handle."

That was a barrel of monkeys to both of them. I smiled, too, just to show them I was a good sport. I was still smiling when Butler appeared behind me, gripped the seat of the chair, and steadily lifted it and me to the ceiling.

"You sure about what you can handle?" asked Sam.

Butler bumped the chair up and down a few times so that my head brushed a ventilator conduit.

I couldn't help but smile again. "You should rent him out to carnivals. He'd make a great ride."

Sam nodded once, Butler grunted acknowledgment and without further ceremony, threw me and the chair across the room.

4

I'D been more or less ready for that one and went partially incorporeal the second he released me. Semitransparent and considerably lighter in weight and mass, I was able to twist around and gain control of my fall. The arrested spin wouldn't look natural, but I was banking on the visual confusion of my blurred movement to cover up the stunt. The bad light shining in their eyes would help.

The chair clattered as it hit first and skidded out of the way. When my feet swung under me I went solid again and landed upright on the concrete floor with only a mild jolt. My hand flailed and struck the far wall as I recovered balance, but it was much better than having my whole body smash into it.

As though nothing unusual had happened, I made a calm business of straightening my clothes. Under all the show, I was plenty mad and needed the time to cool down before turning to look at them.

Leadfoot Sam and Butler were rooted in place and openly gaping. Sam's fingers splayed out flat on the table in preparation to jump in any given direction. When I didn't move, he groped blindly for the bottle and drained away a healthy amount with a desperate swallow. It was terrible stuff; his eyes began to water. Butler came around the table, his mouth still open, and he studied me good and hard. His shaven head swiveled back to Sam.

"Did you see . . . ?"

Sam had no answer. Both of them had touched something totally outside their experience. When the world gives you that kind of a lurch it's hard to know what to do. Alter a long, long moment, silent except for their harsh breathing and thundering hearts, Sam gave out with a brief laugh. It sounded nervous and artificial compared with his previous efforts. Whatever control he thought he had of the situation was lost, and that sick little exhalation was his response to the painful truth.

I came forward and loomed over the table. Sam sat back in his chair, unconsciously putting distance between us.

"Tell Butler to take a break," I said. I used no influence on him; it wasn't necessary.

"Yeah." Not an answer or a question, the word came out of him all on its own, a meaningless sound. The jokes and threats were gone now. He was afraid.

Butler sensed it and didn't want to move. I fixed on his eyes and told him to relax. Some of the sap went out of him. Without further hesitation, he turned and trudged up the spiral stairs. Somewhere above a door closed, leaving me and Sam alone in the basement.

Sam's hands were under the table and I could guess why. He'd be packing a gun the way a shop girl carries her face powder; it was part of the daily uniform. I pretended not to notice and let him keep it if it made him feel better. I didn't feel like going to the trouble of taking it away.

"We need to talk, Sam."

He slowly nodded. I took my time picking up the chair and bringing it back to the table. It was a tough old hunk of wood and hardly showed any new scratches as I put it right and eased onto it again.

"Where you been tonight, Sam?"

The question was plain enough, but not what he'd expected. "I been around."

"Around where?"

"The Hot Spot."

"What's that, a bar?"

"Yeah."

"Anybody see you there?"

"Anyone who wants to bet on the game that's coming up."

"How long were you there?"

His answer left him well covered for the time of McAlister's murder. I was disappointed.

"Where was Butler?"

"With me."

"Now tell me about Stan McAlister."

He'd lost some of his fear and was almost comfortable. "What about Stan?"

"I know you were after him."

"He owes me money. What'd'ya expect?"

His use of the present tense wasn't lost on me. He hadn't heard the bad news yet, that or he was wasting time as a bookie when he should have been acting in the movies. "I don't expect someone like you to take bets on margin."

He was a little embarrassed. "It happens to the best of us."

"How'd it happen to you?"

"We were having a few drinks and I was just drunk enough to do it. I went over the records later, saw that he owed me big, and got Butler to start looking for him. I got a lot of people looking for him, but he must have heard about it because he's lost himself good this time."

"You got any people with a grudge on?"

"Say again?"

"You or your people want to bump him off?"

"Huh? Why should I do that? If he gets bumped, I can't collect my two grand. I'm not so rich I can shrug off that kinda loss. Is someone after him? Is that why you're asking all this?"

"You could say that. Who wants to kill him?"

"Not me. You ask around."

"I'm asking right here. What do you know about his business? Who'd he come in contact with?"

"How the hell should I know? I just take their bets; I don't care how they get their money. Why don't you ask him?"

"I can't. C'mon, Sam, give me a name."

"There's Doreen Grey."

"Uh-huh, who else?"

"He's seeing a little blond named Kitty, but I don't remember if she had a last name."

"What do you know about her?"

"Only that she's cute as a button. He takes her around, shows her the sights. I think she's too clean for him, but he's had others like her before."

"Yeah?"

"You know the type, girls that like to slum. They look peaches and cream on the outside but inside they got a taste for . . . well, Stan ain't exactly rock bottom, but he's pretty close."

"You don't like him?"

"I don't give a damn one way or another about him. He's a customer. All I want is the money he owes me." Most of his confidence was back. "Your turn: what's your game with Stan?"

"I already told you, I'm trying to get some kid out of a jam. You gonna call Butler down for another tumbling act?"

The reminder put him off a little, or so I thought. "Nah, I don't need to do anything like that. What kinda jam?"

"Nothing you need to worry about."

"Just trying to be friendly. You been asking a lot of questions and I been giving you the straight dope, so you at least give me one thing: where's he hiding?"

"He isn't. Tell me about Doreen Grey. If you've got Butler watching for you, why didn't he bring her in?"

"Huh? Doreen? She wouldn't know anything. She hangs around Stan, not the other way around."

He sounded so certain that I briefly wondered if McAlister himself had even known about the trick mirror—but only briefly. "She a girl-friend?"

"Her and a dozen others that think they are."

"You mean he's a pimp?"

"No, nothing like that, though I wouldn't put it past him. He's just got a way with him and women. I wish I could figure it out, I'd bottle it and retire rich and happy."

"Is Doreen Grey her real name?"

"Grow up, kid. Women like her never had a real name."

"Women like her?"

"She's a hustler, or was. Calls herself an actress or model. Do I have to tell you what kind of acting?"

"Does she do photography?"

"I heard she sits on both sides of the camera. She's got a little studio for all the dirty work."

"Where?"

It was on the same street where the cabbie had dropped her off.

"This studio got a name or number?"

"I dunno. A place like that doesn't advertise to the general public. It's over a grocer's, second floor, you can't miss it."

"You know a lot about it, ever been there?"

He only grinned.

I felt I'd gotten all the information I was going to get and stood up to leave.

"Uh-uh," he said. "You stay right there. We're not finished."

"It's getting late, Sam. I gotta go."

He brought his hands above the table. One of them held a fistful of black revolver. He was smiling all over his face again as he leveled it on me. "Not just yet, you don't."

I sighed, trying to be patient. "Okay, what is it?"

"Tell me where Stan is."

"With the cops."

"The cops? What for?"

"He was in the wrong place at the wrong time."

"Cut the crap and tell me what's going on."

If he'd been more polite, I might have answered without thinking.

There was no reason not to tell him about McAlister's death, but I have an inherent dislike of being pushed around, and he'd pushed me plenty already.

"You'll read it in the morning papers," I said, and moved to go up the spiral stairs. Behind me I heard the soft double click that meant he'd thumbed back the hammer.

"Hold it, Lamont, not unless you want one right now."

I paused and looked at him. "Brother, I've already had more than one. All they do is put holes in the suit and make me mad."

"Think you're tough?"

"Let's put it this way . . . do you really want to end up the evening with a hunk of dead meat on your hands?"

"I don't have to kill you," he pointed out.

"Yeah, you're too late for that," I muttered. He was getting on my nerves with the thing.

"You step back here and sit like a good boy."

That tipped the scales for me. He needed a lesson. I turned, made sure he was watching, and vanished. When I re-formed, I was right behind him. It only took a moment, not nearly enough time for him to understand what he'd just seen or to begin to react to it. I wrapped one hand over his mouth and clamped another around the revolver. The idea was to prevent it from going off by keeping the barrel from turning, but I'd forgotten that by cocking it, it had already turned. But the gun didn't go off when his finger twitched. The back of my thumb was between the firing pin and the bullet.

Ouch.

It wasn't nearly as awful as actually getting shot. The pain was best compared to a bad toe stubbing—brief, but of an intensity all out of proportion to the area involved. I knew now why they called it a hammer, since the firing pin had neatly nailed itself into me. My hand jerked away, taking the gun along, and I had to release my hold on Sam. I shoved him across the room and pried back the hammer to free my thumb from its painful trap. I must have looked like an idiot standing there alternately shaking my hand down and sucking the side of my punctured digit.

Then Leadfoot Sam gave me something else to think about when he caught his balance, turned, and broke out a nasty-looking switchblade. In his confusion over the last few seconds, he must have forgotten that I was the one with the gun. I still held it loosely in his direction and was grinning at him. Actually it was less of a grin and more like a show of teeth. My fangs weren't out, but the effect was just as satisfactory, if I could tell anything from his flinching reaction.

"Hold it, Sam. Start thinking twice."

He did, with his wild eyes staring at the revolver in an interesting mixture of rage and fear. His next move might be to call Butler down, but I didn't want any more witnesses. He needed distracting.

"See this?" I broke the cylinder open, pushed the extractor rod, and let the bullets drop out. He stared, wondering what the gag could be. I turned the gun upside down to get a firm hold on the grip and cylinder, then gave them each a hard twist in opposite directions.

The metal groaned quietly and snapped. I knew I was strong enough to damage the thing, but was pleasantly surprised at this development. I tossed the two pieces on the table. Sam's jaw dragged the floor again. I was still grinning.

"Sam?"

He appeared to be very sick.

"Do you know what evil lurks in the hearts of men?"

He made a sick little sound in his throat.

"Well, *I* do." At that, I reached up and flicked my index finger hard against the bare bulb of the room's single light. The glass shattered with a dull pop and plunged us into total darkness.

The sick sound began to descend into a prolonged whimper.

"So you watch yourself from now on . . . because that's what I'll be doing."

I couldn't see him—our complete insulation from outside light prevented that—but I could hear his heart banging away, and by now I could clearly scent the fear smell rolling off him like a tide. He'd recover soon enough, maybe even convince himself he'd been tricked, but he'd never forget it. I didn't care, as long as he gave me a wide berth from now on.

Dematerializing, I swept past him, making sure he got thoroughly chilled. Some spine-tingling laughter would have been appropriate, but I didn't trust mine to be sinister enough for the occasion.

Once up the stairs, I bumbled my invisible way out. Butler and the driver were still in the back storage area, quite oblivious to what had been going on in the basement. I didn't bother with them and seeped through the door into the rear alley, where the Caddy was parked. The keys were gone, but Escott had once taught me how to do a neat hot-wire job. I figured after all the trouble I'd been put through, they owed me a ride back. Neither of them made it out of the building in time to see me driving away.

I'd spent long enough on my forced detour and went straight to Doreen Grey's studio. The general location was a short cross street with "T" intersections at both ends. Down on the corner the bar was open, but everything else was dark. A single grocery store with hand-painted signs obscuring the dusty windows took up space in the middle of the block on the left side.

I parked the Caddy some distance away and walked. Next to the grocery's door, narrow stairs led up to the second floor. On the vertical part of each step someone had carefully painted advertisements for the businesses within. None of them had to do with photography.

Nothing to do but bull on and hope that Sam's information was as square as he claimed. The stairs brought me to a long, dim hall lined with doors at regular intervals. The hall went through the width of the building and ended with another identical opening at the far end that served the next street over.

I checked each door and its sign. Two of them were empty and for rent, and one of them had no sign at all, only a number painted onto the aging wood. It was sufficiently different from the rest to invite closer inspection. Listening, I could pick up no sound from the other side. With no change in my posture I sieved through, solidified, and straightened in an unlighted room. The darkness was thick even for me. A little seepage from the hall around the base of the door was barely sufficient for my eyes to use.

A table and some old chairs constituted the room's total inventory, unless you counted the dust in the corners. As a reception area, it was stark and discouraging. Opposite the entry door was another, firmly closed. I listened here as well, then passed through.

The room on the other side was as pitch black as my basement hiding place. Since my change, true darkness for me was rare, so this was not a comfortable thing to experience—especially when my ears told me I wasn't alone. I held perfectly still. If I couldn't see them, they certainly couldn't see me.

Odds were that the single set of lungs and swiftly beating heart belonged to Doreen Grey. She'd probably heard my footsteps in the entry and was scared to death.

"Doreen?" I asked, hoping to put her at ease.

My voice seemed very loud in the claustrophobic blackness, but not so loud as her brief, terrified scream and the gunshot that followed.

The muzzle flash fixed an image of the whole room in my eyes. I got a general impression of the layout of the furnishings and a specific one of Doreen crouched in a corner holding a pistol in my direction. Her eyes and mouth were wide open, her arms held stiff and straight. All that crowded onto my retinas to be sorted out later, since a split second after the shot I was too busy ducking to think about it. Bullets don't cause me any permanent damage, but I don't enjoy getting hit.

"*Doreen!* It's me—the guy with the cab fare!"

No second shot came.

"What?" Her voice sounded as shaky as I felt.

"I was at the Boswell House—cab fare—remember?"

"Wha-what do you want?"

"Talk, that's all. Put down the gun."

"No."

A sensible answer—if I were really dangerous to her. She was about three yards to my left and I was flat on the floor with no other cover within reach. Not having all the time in the world to talk her out of her fear, I opted for a more direct method and vanished.

I floated toward her, extending invisible arms until we touched. She was already shivering and gave out with a violent shudder at this freezing contact. I got very close, positioning what would be my hand over hers and her gun and making sure my thumb was well clear of moving parts. It might go off, but this time the noise didn't matter.

A good thing, too. She shrieked like a crazy woman when I re-formed holding onto her like a lover. She was ready to kick and fight till doomsday so I pried the gun from her hands and quickly backed off. Suddenly released, she stumbled away and scrambled for the door, sobbing all the way. She wrenched it open and escaped to the reception room while I was taking the gun off cock and slipping on the safety. I caught up with her again in the second she spent fumbling to unlock the outer door.

She screamed and kept on screaming when I slipped an arm around her waist to pull her back. I put a hand over her mouth and tried to talk her into calming down. Eventually she did—not from my efforts, but from simple lack of energy and oxygen. Her legs stopped thrashing and caved in. Propping her up seemed like too much work, so we both sank to the floor. I held her firmly but took away my hand so she could breathe.

She collapsed against me, still sobbing. Not knowing what else to do, I cradled her and told her everything was all right and hoped it would get through. When she seemed settled, I reached up with a questing hand and flicked on the overhead light. It hurt my eyes until they adjusted to the brightness.

"You okay?" I asked. A dumb question, but every opening can't be clever.

The sobbing had diminished to irregular hiccups. She twisted around to see me.

"Remember me now? I'm one of the good guys."

She shook her head in denial and struggled to find her feet. I let her go, being between her and the nearest exit, and stood up as well. She backed away to the opposite wall and turned to stare. There wasn't much of a show to see, all I did was dust off my knees and straighten my hat.

"How'd you get here?" she asked, her voice thick.

"I talked to your cab driver and he told me where he dropped you. Your former landlord gave me your name. Mine's Jack."

"What do you want?"

"Only to talk. I'm not going to hurt you."

She still wasn't ready to believe me. She kept her back to the wall and walked crab-wise to the other door and slipped into the next room, hitting the light. I followed and watched her pace nervously around, her eyes on the floor.

"Looking for this?" I held up her automatic.

She stopped dead cold, her heart racing fit to break.

"Take it easy, darling. I'll just keep it for the time being." I made a business of returning it to my pocket. "Why did you try to shoot me?"

"I didn't know . . . know that . . ."

"What? That I wasn't Leadfoot Sam? Why are you afraid of him?"

"Because it's stupid not to be."

If I'd been sitting alone in the dark, scared shitless from listening to approaching footsteps, I might have done the same thing. I could handle someone like Sam, but Doreen didn't have my unnatural advantages.

"It's a nice little gun. Did Stan give it to you?"

"It's mine."

"This place, too?"

"Yeah—yes."

A plain backdrop nailed to the ceiling covered one wall. Several different light stands were aimed at it. A stack of pillows cluttered the floor next to a dressing screen. Another closed door interrupted the rear wall. I checked it. The room beyond was a washroom converted to a darkroom, its single window made lightproof with a thick coat of black paint.

"Where's your camera?"

She didn't answer, but her eyes darted to her suitcase, which was parked by the pillows.

"What about your photos?"

"I don't have any."

"A photographer with no photos. C'mon, Doreen."

"Look, you just get out of here."

"It's too late for that." I circled around and shut the inner and outer doors.

She kept plenty of distance between us and ended up against the backdrop. A photo of her now would not be too flattering. Her carroty hair was in every direction and her clothes were thoroughly mussed about. Both knees on her stockings sported ladders. She became conscious of me looking at her and abruptly retreated to her purse to find a powder puff. While she repaired things, I brought two chairs from one side and set them down facing one another.

"Park it here, Doreen. It's time for a heart-to-heart."

She closed her compact with a decisive snap. "Is it?"

"Uh-huh. It's either me, the cops, or Leadfoot Sam. Take your pick."

She didn't like any of the choices. "Who are you, then? Why are you here? I don't know anything."

"Have a seat and we'll find out."

Her jaw settled into firm defiance. The tears and panic were gone and she was ready to deal with me. She glared, waiting for my next move.

Every little bit helped.

It took longer than usual. She was on her guard and I didn't want to overdo the pressure. This was different from the simple suggestions I'd shot at Butler and the hotel manager. A give-and-take conversation was more complicated, requiring greater subtlety and care on my part.

"You can relax, Doreen," I whispered.

After a long, long moment the tension leached from her posture.

"No one's going to hurt you."

Her lips parted and her eyes went glassy.

"Relax . . ."

Her face softened as her lids drooped and closed. She was asleep on her feet and as vulnerable now as she ever would be. I could get the answers I needed. All I had to do was come up with the right questions and listen.

While I thought on where to start, I noticed her body as though for the first time—her long legs and crown of fluffy red hair. I became very aware of her beating heart and the blood surging through it. I recognized the feeling stirring within me, but this time its irresistible intensity was startling.

Hunger.

Or thirst.

For a vampire they're much the same.

The red life I'd taken and exchanged with Bobbi was as deliriously fulfilling as any sex I'd ever experienced as a living man. The blood I drank from animals gave me the joy of pure energy and strength greater than I'd ever imagined. Now I was facing a combination of the two: to have human blood in quantity—and to take it from this woman.

The temptation was a very solid, thriving thing and much more difficult to put off than on other occasions when I'd faced it with Bobbi. I had always taken care with her and found it easy not to overindulge for fear of hurting her. The difference this time was the woman herself. She was a stranger to me, unimportant, nothing more than a small-time blackmailer and hustler.

Someone no one would miss.

Her scent filled my head. Human flesh, a trace of cheap perfume, salt from the dried tears on her face, and beneath them all, the bloodsmell.

The rest were like bits of flotsam floating upon its deep river. I licked my lips, my tongue brushing against my lengthening canines. To drink from that dark river . . .

I caressed her neck with the backs of my fingers; first one side, then the other. Lightly. Softly. She was utterly fascinating. It was as though, turn in turn, she were hypnotizing me.

Eyes shut, she responded with a slight tremor and sigh. I knew well how to give pleasure. She would love me for what I was capable of giving and doing to her. Because of the influence I was exerting she would not be able to help herself.

My arms wrapped protectively around her, pulling her body close. She swayed and rested against me, her heart quickening. Her head went to one side, exposing the tender white column of her throat. I tasted it with a slow kiss. The big vein pulsed rapidly beneath my lips. My mouth yawned wide, my teeth gently brushing over the thin barrier of her skin. We were both trembling. The blood suddenly welled up, pouring through me like scarlet fire as the first shock of ecstasy took us.

She would love me and I would love her. I *was* loving her.

Her heart fluttered against my chest. Her breath was full and warm as it whispered over my neck.

I had wanted her, I was taking her, and she was loving it. I drank from her and drank deeply. She was an endless fountain of shimmering strength.

Not endless.

It didn't matter. She clung to me; she didn't want it to stop. Besides, no one need ever know.

No one but me.

Conscience invaded craving. They mixed, separated, and tore through my brain like summer lightning.

I would love her to death.

I drew back, as though it were part of our love dance. She sighed again, turning it into a protesting moan. Two threads of blood trickled down her neck from the wounds I'd made.

To death.

But no one need ever . . .

Teetering.

I wanted her badly, more than anything else I'd ever dreamed of wanting.

To death.

I backed off until we ceased to touch. It helped. It helped more to picture her limp and heavy in my arms, her skin gray, her heart silent. I had killed before, but not for this, not for the convenient satiation of hunger.

The room was heavy with bloodsmell. I forced air from my lungs and did not replace it. I backed off another step.

The fusing of desire and appetite was nothing new and had conquered stronger men than myself. The absolute power I had over her—over anyone I wished—was an awful, frightening thing. I retreated from it, seizing on the quickest escape with a desperate will.

My body dissolved and floated free, tumbling a little from the inertia of its last faint movement. I remained in that state until the fever ebbed away and the grip of hunger eased and finally released me. Still, it was a very long time before I re-formed, and then only after I'd pushed far away from her. I drifted through the thin partitions of wood and lath until I stood in the outside hall of the building.

Air, icy cold and bitter, cut at my throat and lungs. I drew a second painful breath and a third. It was glorious. I felt like a swimmer unexpectedly breaking the surface after being sucked to the bottom of a whirlpool. My legs still shook, but eventually everything settled down as the world started spinning along its usual course.

I stood and stared at nothing, and tried not to feel what I was feeling.

I felt it, anyway.

Terror.

She could have died. I'd come that close to going over the edge with her. And I still wanted to finish what I'd started. My hunger was quiet, but not yet sated, and tugged at me to return to her.

Was it because of my changed condition, or had this always been within me? Was I a rapist or an animal fulfilling a physical need?

Or both?

I'd had lapses of temper and of sanity and had used them against people; I'd never before had such a lapse concerning hunger or had ever been so close to killing because of hunger. Until tonight I'd regarded myself as being a man with a condition that could be controlled—that *was* under control.

That safe and comfortable image was altered now, and I wasn't sure of anything anymore. I only knew I was scared.

And inside me, her blood fused with my own.

She was standing in the same spot when I returned, her face closed and defenseless with sleep. I made myself look at her, to see *all* that she was, all that I'd nearly destroyed. Her name was Doreen. She had a right to feel and learn and love, to choose for herself. She had a right to live.

She was human. I was not.

I went to the darkroom and wet my handkerchief under the tap there and used it to clean her throat. The marks were small and hadn't bled much. She might not notice them. I drew her collar up a bit, then touched her cheek, not with desire, but with a caring that had been missing before.

"Wake up, honey."

Her eyes flickered open.

"You okay?" I wasn't sure if she would remember anything.

She nodded. One hand came up to touch the spot on her neck where I'd kissed her, then fluttered away in confusion. "I think . . . I mean . . ."

I searched her face for the least sign of awareness of what had happened. The only thing I could see was puzzlement. I should have been relieved, but was just too emotionally hammered out to feel much of anything. Shoving my hands firmly in my coat pockets, I turned my back to her and took a few aimless steps. "There's a bar down on the corner. You think it's still open?"

"Yeah, it'll be open."

"I thought maybe I could buy you something." It was half statement, half question.

She accepted the offer with relief and gratitude. It went double for me.

She wrapped up tight and we walked across the street to a place with no name that I had noticed. Socially, it was somewhere between the Top Hat and the Stumble Inn. I bought a couple drinks at the bar and carried them to a booth in the rear, where we sat opposite each other. She put half of hers away in one needy gulp and fell back to catch her breath.

"All right?" I asked.

"Yeah. It was getting pretty cold up there in the studio."

"Cold?" I was worried about how much I'd taken from her.

"They practically turn the heat off at night. I guess the idea is to discourage tenants from doing what I was trying to do. They got ordinances against taking a flop in a joint zoned for office space."

"You have no place else to go?"

"I figured it'd be okay for one night, then I could look for another hotel."

"Tell me about Stan."

Her face clouded and started to crumple. "I can't."

"Yes, you can."

Our encounter must have left a few positive aftereffects somewhere in her mind. Either that or she really did want to talk. I kept my supernatural influences to myself and waited her out.

"It's just—the stuff I've done . . ." Tears ran out of both eyes and she blindly pawed the contents of her purse.

I gave her a clean handkerchief. I usually carried an extra. "It's all right, Doreen. I've seen a thing or two."

She brought the snuffling under control and cleared her throat by draining the other half of her glass. "Stan was the one with the ideas," she explained, finally jumping in.

"Like that fancy mirror in his room?"

"Yeah. He was already doing stuff, but only in a small way. He'd get love letters and use them—that kind of thing."

"Rich girls?"

"Not rich. He wasn't in that crowd, but he did go for ones that had money of their own and a reputation to keep. He could spot a spoiled brat looking for thrills a mile away, then move in and take them. He'd get enough money from them to live on, but not so much that they'd scream for a lawyer or cop. Stan was careful not to push too hard. If it looked like she'd kick up a fuss, he'd back off and find someone else easier to deal with."

"How did you two get together?"

"He needed a photographer."

"And . . . ?"

"He heard I did artistic photos, so he came around and asked if I was interested. He had everything all worked out about the hotel rooms. A place like the Boswell don't have any kind of house man, so it was easy to set up. We just moved in and I started taking pictures."

"He didn't mind being photographed?"

She smiled crookedly. "No, he enjoyed it. When he wasn't playing Prince Charming for the girls, he was just about the vainest creature on God's green earth. He used to flip through the prints I made, get himself pretty worked up . . ." She began to blush. I was glad that she could still do it.

I smiled wanly. "I know what it's like, Doreen."

"I guess we all do."

"What happened with Kitty Donovan?"

"She was just another mark."

"You get pictures of them together?"

"No. She liked her own place better. Stan never could get her into that hotel bed."

I was happy to hear it. "Then why'd he stick with her?"

"Because of the people she knew. She was his ticket into the good places and the people with real money."

"Like Marian Pierce's crowd?"

"Yeah, she was part of it. Stan thought she was ripe for picking, except he couldn't get past that crazy boyfriend of hers." The smile melted away. "Oh, God, I can't believe he's gone."

I was fresh out of handkerchiefs and gave her the drink I'd bought as window dressing. "You loved him?"

"I didn't have any reason to, so I guess I did. That'd explain all this, wouldn't it?" She gulped down a sob and got control again. "Look, would you tell me what happened to him? I couldn't ask the cops."

"And they didn't tell you?"

"Why should they? I was listening while they were in Stan's room. The way they were talking about him . . . I put it together that he was . . . was dead. I couldn't say anything, either. I was afraid they'd take me in if they found out about the racket we had going. It was horrible."

And what I had to tell her was no comfort. I kept it short. "Stan was killed at Kitty Donovan's place. Someone knocked him out and stabbed him. It was quick. He wouldn't have felt much."

She put her head down in her hands, moaning. I left the table to get another drink.

"Trouble?" asked the bartender.

"Death in the family."

He was sympathetic and pushed my money away. "On the house."

"Thanks."

"After this one, get her home, make her sleep."

"You know her?"

"She's been in a few times for a beer. She won't be used to the hard stuff. It'll hit her like a brick pretty soon."

"I'll watch out." I went back to the booth. "Doreen?"

She raised her head with difficulty and blew her nose into the sodden linen. "I'm . . . I'll be all right."

"Sure you will."

"Do the cops know who did it? Do they know why?"

"They're looking for Kitty."

"That little girl scout? She couldn't do anything like that."

"I don't think she did. You knew him. Who wanted to kill him?"

She shook her head and kept on shaking it. "Leadfoot Sam, maybe. Stan owed him a bundle. That's why I got out while I could. I didn't want him learning about me and Stan or he'd try and muscle it out of me. I don't have that kind of money, but he wouldn't believe that."

"I talked with Sam earlier."

"You . . ." she blinked against the tears with surprise.

I made a calming gesture. "He's not so tough once you learn how to handle him. Anyway, he doesn't know what's happened and I figure that that's the truth. He can't collect money from a dead man, so he's not really a suspect with me. Can't you think of anyone else? One of your clients?"

"Jeez, I just don't know. There were plenty of 'em sore as hell or hurt or embarrassed, but not enough to kill. He was careful, I said."

"Did he ever call one in?"

"What'd'ya mean?"

"The photos, did he ever use one and blow things for the girl?"

She was genuinely astonished. "Not that I know of. He only threatened, it wouldn't do him any good to push it that far. He'd just hold it over their heads. They'd either call his bluff or pay off. Almost all of them paid off. He knew how to pick and choose. If they didn't pay, he'd just let it go and find someone else to work on."

"Did he always take money?"

"Brother, that's all he would take."

"What about jewelry?"

"Too much trouble to hock or sell. He left that for them to do." She finished off the drink. "Y'know, maybe it was that crazy boyfriend of Marian's."

"Why do you think so?"

"Stan said the guy was nuts, even took a swing at him once."

"When and where?"

"I dunno. One of those fancy places. Stan ducked in time and laughed about it later. He said all he did was have a dance with Marian, then the guy comes in and goes berserk."

I could believe that. "When did this happen?"

She leaned her head on one hand, mussing her hair. "I dunno, I dunno. I'm too tired to think. Will you just take me back?"

"Did Stan have any hiding places?"

"Huh?"

"Where'd he put his valuables?"

"Noplace."

"He must have stashed things somewhere. What about the bank? Did he have a safe-deposit box?"

"No, nothing like that. He carried everything with him. Not that he ever had much."

I remembered McAlister's turned-out pockets. "Wasn't it risky?"

"Safer than leaving it at that fleabag hotel. Stan had a gun, too."

"All the time?"

"Of course."

Whoever had clobbered and stabbed him hadn't given him the chance to use it. "It wasn't on him."

The news didn't matter much to Doreen. Her head had slipped down onto her arms again. Those three doubles were having their effect.

"C'mon, honey. I'll get you home and put you to bed."

"You'n what army?" she mumbled, more than half-gone. I got her to her feet, waved a good-night to the bartender, and walked her out. The cold air revived her a little, but she leaned against me, as much for comfort as for warmth. We staggered up the stairs to the studio and I steadied her while she fumbled out the key and gave it over.

The entry was dark as before, but we'd left the light on in the inner room. Now it was off.

"Whatizzit?" she asked crossly when I wouldn't let her go in.

I signed for her to stay quiet and listen. The whole building seemed to be listening. Except for her own heart and lungs, I heard nothing. I went inside. When I turned on the light, she followed, tiptoeing unsteadily.

There weren't that many places to search, but the place had been thoroughly turned over. Her suitcase was open, the contents scattered, the pillows gutted, a file cabinet gaped in one corner. The darkroom was in the same shape.

"What did you keep here?" I asked.

She was too far gone to answer right away. "Photos, negatives, chemicals, nothing important. No cash."

"Maybe they didn't want cash." I checked some of the prints from the file cabinet that now lay on the floor. Girls striking different poses wearing little more than a provocative smile was the predominant theme. I recognized the backdrop and pillows.

Doreen knelt by her suitcase and methodically shoved the clothes back inside. She tenderly turned over the smashed remains of her camera, then left it on the floor. "They got all my negs."

"What was on them?"

She sniffled, found a dry handkerchief among her things, and blew her nose. "What'd'ya think? Stan's gone and now I got nothing. Absolutely, goddamn nothing. I'm leaving this town before they take even that away."

"To where?"

She shrugged and began to shuffle photos into a pile. I bent to help her, but a creaking floorboard in the entry caught my attention. I didn't have time to do more than straighten and turn before Leadfoot Sam walked in on us.

5

DOREEN looked up, blanched, and joined me in staring at him. The first to move was Sam. The second he recognized me, his hand jumped to his overcoat pocket and smoothly pulled out a gun. It was another revolver, identical to the one I'd twisted in two. Maybe he got them in sets.

"No need for that, Sam," I said, taking a long step away from

Doreen. If he planned to start shooting, I wanted her to be well clear of me.

"Shut up and hold still."

I held still. His voice was even enough, but the short nose of the revolver trembled, and he was nearly as white as Doreen. I'd made quite an impression on him earlier, but it hadn't been as effective as I'd hoped.

"Hands up and out."

I complied. It gave him a shade more confidence, which gave me more time to think. I could risk things and try controlling him with a quick suggestion, but he looked too nerved up yet for anything fancy. The wrong word from me and we'd all end up feeling sorry for what happened.

"Thought you had me going, huh?" he finally said, with just the barest hint of desperation.

"Going?"

"With that crap you pulled earlier off that radio show. You think I don't know a con trick when I see one?"

"Can't blame a guy for trying," I said sheepishly.

Given half a chance, people have a remarkable capacity for self-delusion, and if I could tell anything from the relief on his mug, Leadfoot Sam was proving to be no different from the rest. He'd really needed me to say something like that. Never mind that my generality was pretty meaningless, I had vaguely agreed with whatever explanation he'd invented for himself, and now all was right with the world. He relaxed by a single degree and smiled a thin, superior smile.

"It was a good one, wasn't it?" I asked, as though I'd been caught fair and square.

"How'd you do it?"

"I'll show you sometime. It works better in the dark."

He didn't take to that particular bait by obligingly turning off the lights, nor did he put away the gun. His gaze flicked away from me only once. "Hello, Doreen."

She'd sobered up quite a bit in the last minute and was probably wondering what the hell we were talking about. "Hi, Sam. What're you doing here?"

"I came to collect on a debt."

"What debt? I don't owe you anything. I don't owe anyone anything."

"Sure you do, sweetheart. You were partners with Stanley, weren't you?"

"I hardly knew—"

"Can it. I've just been over to Stan's room and found that sweet little racket the two of you had set up there. You must have raked in plenty. As I see it, partners are responsible for each other's debts."

"But, Sam . . ."

"Shut up. And you, Lamont—if that's your name—were you holding out on me so you could have first crack at her?"

"Holding out?"

"You never told me about Stan getting knifed, or did you do it yourself? Is there a picture of your girlfriend somewhere in Doreen's photo collection?"

"You're full of beans."

"Maybe you forgot to tell Doreen about it like you forgot to tell me."

"I see you still managed to find out."

"Oh, yeah, after a ton of time and trouble. The cops don't exactly give that information away to the public, you know." He turned a sour face on Doreen. "And what kind of line has he been feeding you, sweetheart? What do you know about this guy, anyway?"

She said nothing, but he'd gotten the wheels turning in her head—in the wrong direction as far as I was concerned.

"He's not here to get his picture took, is he? What's he want from you?"

"He don't—doesn't want anything," she said.

Sam shook his head sadly. "The world don't work that way, Doreen. You oughta know that by now. Everybody wants something. What'd he come to you for?"

She licked her lips, her tone guarded. "He was just asking about Stan, is all. Who mighta killed him, like that."

"And you never thought he mighta done it himself?"

She hadn't, and turned her doubts full onto me.

"Don't let him rattle you, Doreen," I said out of the side of my mouth. "Remember, I'm one of the good guys."

"Sez you," put in Sam.

"How about you tell us who did the redecorating here?" I asked, wanting to change the subject.

"I only just got here. Pin it on someone else, Lamont." He bent an eye on Doreen. "Is that the name he gave you? Russell Lamont?"

Her answer was easy enough to read. I'd lost her trust, at least for the moment.

"And what makes you a better bargain, Sam?" I countered.

His attention switched back to me. "Doreen knows what to expect from her old friends."

"Like a shiv in the throat?" I ventured.

"We'll see." He backed up to the door and whistled. A moment later a man that I recognized as Sam's driver walked in. He was followed by Butler, who had to duck his head slightly to miss the lintel. He took in the wrecked room, Doreen on the floor by her suitcase, and finally focused on me. He then raised the kind of smile you don't want to see in your worst nightmares.

"You took Sam's car," he stated flatly.

I said nothing, since it's pointless to argue with facts.

"Where is it?" Sam asked him.

"Just down the street. It seems okay."

Sam glared at me. "You better hope it is, or that'll be another one I owe you." He nodded at the driver. "Take her back to the joint. We'll follow in the Cadillac."

Doreen balked. "Where?"

"Just a quiet place so we can talk, sweetheart. If you're good, I'll buy you an ice-cream soda. You and I are going to cut a deal over Stan's outstanding markers."

"I don't have any money, Sam."

"Not yet, you don't . . . but you will. I'm just gonna make sure I'm around for my share."

"Please," she said to me. "Don't let him."

Sam centered the gun on her. "All we're gonna do is have a nice talk, Doreen. You kick up a fuss and I'll show you how mean I can get if I try."

"It'll be all right," I said. "Go on, sit tight and wait for me."

She looked at me as though I'd gone crazy and only needed a straitjacket to make it official.

"I'll come for you." I hoped she'd believe me.

Sam and Butler laughed at this. The driver hauled her up and dragged her out the door. The laughter did wonders for her confidence, but I was at last able to relax. With Doreen out of the way and relatively safe, my choices on how to handle the situation had increased considerably. The only thing I really had to worry about now was how to keep my suit in one piece.

"Ready to get down to business?" I asked once they were long gone.

Sam pretended to be impressed. "He still thinks he's a tough guy. Look him over, Butler, find out why he's so tough."

Butler approached, keeping out of Sam's line of fire, and slapped at me with big hands. I didn't quite fall over. He found Doreen's automatic right away. "This must be it." He grinned.

"Is that it?" Sam asked me.

"As far as you're concerned," I said.

He shot me a wary look and told Butler to continue. He pocketed the gun. My notebook, pencil, keys, and wallet were extracted and examined, the latter catching the most interest.

"It sez he's Jack R. Fleming." Butler squinted at my New York driving license.

Sam nodded, as though he'd known all along.

"He's rich, too." He held up Pierce's C-note.

"Put it back," I said softly.

With high good humor, Butler shook his head and stowed the bill away with Doreen's pistol. "Now what, Sam?"

"Now you teach him not to be so nosy. But go easy, Butler. I don't want to put him to bed with a shovel."

Butler looked me over, trying to decide where to start. He was a man with total confidence in his own physical capabilities and was probably taking my lack of fear for bravado. Right away I could tell he didn't like the smile I was showing him. He matched it with a nasty one of his own and followed it up with a fast punch.

He'd had some fight training in his past. Because of his height and massive build I'd been expecting a slow roundhouse-type swing that could be blocked with a raised arm. As it was, I only snapped my head out of the way just in time. His fist brushed my chin, but he caught me flat-footed with a lightning follow-up left that went straight into my stomach.

I doubled over and staggered with all the talking breath knocked out of me, falling backward over the ripped-up pillows. It was a soft landing, more or less. Butler stood away from the swirling feathers and waited for me to recover. I held a hand to the sore spot until it faded, and stood up, stepping clear of the mess. He totally missed the fact that I was not gasping for air or showing any of the other usual symptoms of such an attack. In fact, all I did was grin, and that really put me on his good side.

He had the height and reach on me, but the grin made him forget about those advantages and move in close. I let him back me up to a corner, left it till the last possible instant, and went transparent just as he struck. His fist tickled through my ghostly midsection and connected solidly with the wall behind me. The resulting howl of pain from him was almost deafening.

I immediately went solid again. If Butler had noticed me flickering on and off like a bad light, he was too occupied with his injured hand to think about it. Leadfoot Sam couldn't have seen much; I'd taken care to shift so that Butler's body blocked his view of the incident.

Butler tried another left. I was moving fast myself and his anger and pain were working against him. I caught his wrist in my right hand and returned his gut punch with interest with the left. He folded up like an old wallet. As soon as I let go of him he hit the floor and stayed there, gulping and gasping.

Sam knew his number was up because I was looking in his direction and still grinning. He showed his own teeth in a sticky grimace and raised his gun to fire.

"Aw, Sam, now do you want I should break this one in two as well?" I took a step toward him.

He made that sick little sound deep down in his throat once again and bolted for the exit. I flashed invisibly ahead of him and got to the entry first. He slid to a stop on his heels just inches away from me. While he was dancing to get his balance back, I popped him a light one on his chin. He dropped like a sandbag.

He was fairly stunned but made a halfhearted attempt to lift the revolver. I took it away from him, this time without puncturing my thumb. Grabbing a wad of his clothes in my free hand, I dragged him into the studio, dumping him on the floor next to Butler, who was still nursing his bruised gut. Sam's long bones thudded on the bare wood. His arms came up protectively.

"Sam?"

It took him a minute, but he eventually opened his eyes.

"Watch carefully, 'cause you musta missed something the first time around." I opened the cylinder, emptied out the bullets, got a good grip, and twisted as hard as I could.

Sam whimpered when it snapped.

"Next time it'll be your neck. You understand that now?"

He nodded a lot. I froze on his eyes and stepped up the pressure just enough for him to feel it. I wanted him good and scared.

"From now on you stay out of my way. You're gonna lay off on Doreen, too. You don't talk to her, you don't even think about going near her. You leave her completely alone. You got that?"

His jaw sagged. I knew I'd finally gotten through to him. I put the two pieces of his gun in each of his hands. Butler didn't fuss at all when I picked his pocket and retrieved my hundred-dollar bill and Doreen's automatic. I walked out, pausing long enough in the entry to flick off all the lights.

Somewhere behind me, Leadfoot Sam moaned miserably in the abrupt darkness.

Sam's remark about buying Doreen a soda hadn't been lost on me. Within a quarter hour I took the Caddy out of gear, cut the motor, and coasted to a stop across the alley entrance to the drugstore. A fresh-looking Ford stood next to it. Doreen and the driver were probably waiting inside for Sam and Butler to return.

A dim light gleamed in a single rear window of the building. I set the brake and got out. The place was silent, which could be good or bad.

I slipped inside the back way and went solid, listening hard. The easy whisper of soft breathing finally drifted to my ears from the direction of the spiral staircase. Sniffing instinctively like a hunting animal, I picked up a strong stench of booze and the heavy, familiar tang of bloodsmell.

The stairs led down to pitch darkness. I was reluctant to enter it and investigate; the hair on my nape was already on end. It was my own fault, since I'd shattered the overhead bulb myself.

I swallowed dryly, went transparent, and slowly coasted along the twisting metal rail into the basement. At the foot of the steps I was solid again with my nerves running on full. The breathing from a single set of lungs continued with the undisturbed regularity of sleep. I took a chance and lit a match. The burst of yellow fire flared and settled, revealing the room pretty much as I'd left it, except for the man sprawled senseless on the floor. He gripped a flashlight in one hand. It was on, but the batteries were exhausted.

His clothes were sprinkled with liquor and shards of brown bottle glass, and there was a hell of a bump and cut on his forehead. He was the driver who was supposed to be watching Doreen. She must not have expected me to return and had aced him herself when she got the chance. I couldn't blame her, but it was an unexpected nuisance. First Kitty and now Doreen . . . it was really my night for losing people.

I searched the rest of the store, but she was long gone. I left him to sleep it off, got in the Caddy, and drove quickly back to the studio. It was empty. Sam and Butler had pulled themselves together and left, hopefully for good. They were probably busy right now finding the driver in the drugstore basement.

Doreen's clothes were still scattered all over the place. I packed whatever I could find into her suitcase, then carried it away with me as I went to pick up Escott's car. Before leaving, I left a note for her hanging prominently from a slightly dented tripod. Chances were that if she had the moxie to smash a bottle over a guy's head, she'd eventually return to pick up her things. My note had Escott's office number and directions to call him for the stuff. I still had some questions for her and no doubt so would Escott after he'd heard about the evening's events.

His Nash had come to no harm sitting on the street, but I decided to take it home and pick up my more expendable Buick later. Though his concern for the safety of his car had only been a blind to get me here in the first place, it could do no harm to follow through with the ruse. Lieutenant Blair was a detail-minded man and I wouldn't put it past him to check up on me. I wondered if Escott had managed to talk his way out of his spot. If anybody could, he was the one to do it. I'd find out later; I had an errand to run now that I didn't dare put off.

The Stockyards were cold and quiet. The cattle huddled in their small pens and only rarely did one of them vocalize their collective misery at this late hour. The time was ideal for me, with no human eyes to watch as I crouched by an animal and sucked blood from a vein I'd opened with my teeth. It sounds pretty bad, but as Bobbi had once pointed out, I didn't have to kill in order to feed myself.

What had happened tonight, though, had shaken me from that confident complacency. I was running scared. The fusion of desire and appetite that I'd experienced with Doreen had nearly been too much to handle. After all these months, I thought I knew all there was to know about being a vampire, but circumstance and opportunity had proved me wrong, almost dead wrong, as far as Doreen was concerned.

I was *never* going to place myself or anyone else into that kind of a situation again.

The emotional temptation was easily avoided; all I had to do was swear off hypnotizing people. The intimate bond required for such deep hypnotic control was a two-way trap. Breaking free of the one I'd fallen into with Doreen had been one of the most difficult things I'd ever done. The next time, I might not be able to do it, therefore, there would be *no* next time. I would stick with simple and direct suggestions, nothing more.

As for the physical temptation, I was taking care of that by drinking deeply from a safe source. Usually I had only to drop by the Stockyards once every three nights, sometimes four, depending how often Bobbi and I got together. That would be altered to every other night. My hunger was inescapable, but easily remedied. To ignore it was to take chances with other lives.

I drank as much as I needed and more until the hot strength surged through and filled me with its red tide of life. Appetite and a shadowy mental bond that I barely understood had contributed to the incident; both would be under sharp control from now on. I only hoped that it would work.

Escott's office by the Stockyards was closed tight and deserted, so I moved on and purposely took a route home that led past Bobbi's hotel. Her living-room window on the fourth floor was visible from the street. It was just after three A.M., but her lights were glowing. She always spent at least an hour winding down from her work at the Top Hat; this was an open invitation for me to drop in on her. Without thinking, I found a place to park and went inside.

I took the elevator up and exchanged meaningless pleasantries with the sleepy operator. He opened the doors and I walked out as I had done a hundred times before. The doors slid shut behind me and the thing descended back to the lobby again.

I was halfway down the hall when I realized I absolutely could not go in to see her, at least not tonight. The truth of it was that I was still uneasy and Bobbi was perceptive enough to be able to spot it. She would want to know what was wrong and this wasn't something I could talk about. Especially to her.

What I was capable of doing and what I had done frightened me, but mixed in with the fear was a large chunk of guilt. It wouldn't matter much to Bobbi that I'd fed from Doreen as if she'd been one of the cattle in the pens. The simple fact was that I'd been with another woman. As I saw things, it was more than enough to destroy our relationship.

No, going in to see Bobbi tonight would be another big mistake. I needed time to settle down. Tomorrow night would be soon enough. I punched the button and waited for the elevator to return. The operator didn't ask questions about my change of mind, which was just as well.

The hotel lobby should have been deserted at this time of the morning. The night clerk often napped on the office sofa, and Phil, the hotel detective, usually hung out in the radio room when he wasn't making his rounds. Both of them were now at the front desk with two other men I didn't know and there was something about their collective posture that caught my attention.

Phil was a leaner. He leaned against pillars, chairs, tables, whatever was handy, and rarely put his weight on more than one foot at a time. Now he stood straight and alert with his hands at his sides and a look on his face that was no look at all. He'd blanked out all expression and not once did his gaze flick over to me, though he was certainly aware of the elevator doors when they opened.

The clerk was a slightly younger man whose name I'd never bothered to catch. He was also standing straight, with his hands in front of him on the counter as though he needed it to keep his balance. His eyes were wide and flashed briefly on me as I emerged into the lobby.

It was subtle stuff to pick up within the space of a couple seconds, but enough to make me pause.

One of the two strangers slowly turned his head in my direction. The other continued to face Phil and the clerk and didn't move. My pause became a full stop. Something was wrong, but I wasn't sure what to do about it.

The one looking at me took his time. He had a dark, unpleasant face with an expression to match, and both his coat and overcoat were unbuttoned. It was very cold outside and I could think of only one reason why a man would not bundle up against it.

The hair on my nape began to rise as he broke away and walked over. I waited for him.

"That your Nash out front?" he asked.

He already knew the answer, so I nodded. "Who wants to know?"

"Come with me and find out."

"You a cop?" I knew he wasn't and he knew I knew, and so on. It was part of the game we were playing. He shook his head. I checked on his partner, who was still watching Phil and the clerk. No one had moved an inch. "He coming, too?"

"Yeah."

"Then call him off."

"Rimik."

"Okay, Hodge," the other man answered.

He broke away from the desk, never once turning until he had enough angle and distance to cover us all. He wasn't showing any gun, you just knew it was there. The clerk was freely sweating now. Phil threw a silent question at me; I shook my head.

"You boys get on with things," I said. "Business as usual."

They had their own skins to keep in one piece, so no one said a thing as I walked from the lobby door under escort. It was an armed escort, but we were busy pretending that everything was normal.

As we stepped outside, a Cadillac with smoked-over windows pulled up. Its motor was so silent that all you could hear were the tires rolling over the pavement. These guys liked the classy cars, all right, but I was getting a different feeling from this bunch. They were as far removed from Leadfoot Sam as a tiger is from a tabby cat, and proportionately more dangerous.

I got into the backseat and Rimik climbed in next to me. Hodge sat in front with the driver. The car was in top shape; I barely noticed when we started to move.

Rimik was focused on the back of the driver's neck, but I had no doubt he was more than prepared to deal with any fast moves on my part. I kept my hands in the open and watched our route through the front window. I couldn't see out the side ones. There was a divider between the front and back, which was probably also opaque, but they didn't bother raising it. That could be good or bad. I was assuming the worse, but too curious to take action about it just yet. First I'd find out what they were after, then I'd think about getting away.

We drove over the river and into a familiar neighborhood, though I hadn't been through the area since last August, when I'd first arrived in Chicago. Nothing seemed to have changed, it was only colder and more empty than before. The cheap hotels and pawnshops gave way to long blocks of warehouses and inadequate lighting. The drive was half an hour of total silence. The last leg of it took us along a narrow street running between two huge warehouses built out over the river. We stopped at a side door.

Hodge was out first to cover things. Rimik signed for me to move.

"What's this about?" I asked, because it was time I showed some curiosity. I was also genuinely uneasy.

"Later," said Hodge.

The driver was ahead of us and opened the narrow door into the warehouse, then hit the lights. The place was still gloomy. It was full of crates of all kinds and the sharp odor of new wood, excelsior, and machine oil. It looked naggingly familiar. The stenciled labels on the crates identified their contents as machine parts. That tripped the final switch in my memory. I fought down an involuntary shudder that had nothing to do with the winter air.

Hodge sat on a crate, Rimik stood and stared at me, and the driver went to the office I knew to be out front. He returned several minutes later, nodded once at Hodge, then leaned against the far wall and fired up a cigarette.

I looked at Hodge. "It's later. What's this about?"

"You'll find out soon enough."

"I'll find out now, or I'm walking."

"You can try, kid."

From out of nowhere, Rimik had produced a big bowie knife and polished it with a soft cloth. He was still staring at me.

"You take me out with that," I said, "and your boss might not like it."

"You'd like it even less, Escott," said Hodge.

That shut me up.

Their mistake was a natural one. While I'd been talking with Bobbi they'd searched the Nash and found its registration and Escott's name.

"Take off the coat," he told me after a moment.

"It's cold," I reminded him.

"We'll give it back."

Rimik put the knife within easy reach—his reach—and came forward. His action distracted me, so I hadn't noticed Hodge pulling out a forty-five automatic. These boys were moving as smooth as oil and I didn't like the kind of teamwork that that implied.

He leveled the gun at my gut. "Take off the coat."

I took it off. There was no sense in forcing them to put holes in it or the suit. A shoot-out might force me to do other things as well. I knew what they wanted and stood by for yet another frisk. Rimik found Doreen's gun right off.

"Déjà vu," I said as he put it on the crate next to the knife.

"What?" asked Hodge.

"Nothing. Just French for 'here we go again'."

Rimik didn't bother searching my wallet or they'd have realized their mistake about my identity. They were looking for weapons, not enlightenment. He turned it back over with the other stuff, and I was allowed to put my coat on again.

"Who's your boss?" I asked.

Hodge answered readily enough. "Vaughn Kyler."

If he expected a reaction, he drew a complete blank. "What's he want with me?"

He carefully stowed the forty-five into its shoulder holster and let the edges of his coat and overcoat fall back into place. Unbuttoned.

"What does he want?"

He dug into a pocket for a cigarette and lighted it, paying no attention to my question. The temptation to make him answer was there, but I decided to wait. I had the time, and chances were his boss would tell me all about it. Right now they were playing a nerve game, but that only works if you can be intimidated. I sat on a crate and watched him smoke. Rimik picked up the bowie knife and slipped it into some kind of a hip sheath. I caught a glimpse of the gun under his coat as well. He was prepared for all sorts of weather.

Hodge smoked his cigarette down to a butt and tossed it accurately at a drainage grate in the floor. He looked ready to light another when we all turned in response to a distant noise from the office out front. The driver broke away from the wall, went into the office, and returned a moment later to usher in a new addition to the party.

He walked in without hurry, a medium-sized man in a vicuna overcoat with his hat pulled low. He paused in the penumbral area between the lights and checked things over before coming any closer. I had no problems making out his shadowed features, but he wasn't trying hard to conceal them. If he were really worried, he'd have taken more effective steps.

Every instinctive alarm God ever invented to help us survive the wide world had gone off inside me. The urge to vanish and whip out the door away from him was that strong; it was all I could do now to stay solid as he walked over.

His movements were as fluid and controlled as a dancer's. He had dark blue eyes and short black brows. His nose was long and fine lines led from it to a thin, hard mouth. His face was square, with dewlaps just starting to form, giving the illusion of a mournful look that was, indeed, only an illusion. The set of his mouth and stony eyes confirmed it. His pale skin was just a little puffy from soft living; he looked to be edging fifty. He had a fairly ordinary face, on the surface no different from a hundred others of the same general type. But there was something abnormal . . . about the man behind it that made my flesh crawl.

My own mug was easy enough to read. What he saw there didn't bother him. Maybe he was used to such reactions.

He looked me over good and close, then wandered past to see Hodge. I turned as he went behind me, wanting to keep him in full view.

"What?" he asked in a low voice.

"Spotted him going into her studio," said Hodge. "He came out with a suitcase, then drove to the Stockyards."

My spine turned to ice. I hadn't noticed anyone following me.

"He drove to a hotel off the Loop and went in. We got him coming out."

"Suitcase?"

"We searched it while he was in the hotel. Nothing inside but women's clothes. Must be hers."

"Name?"

"Escott."

"No," I said.

They each looked at me as though I had snot on my face. I was to speak only when spoken to. Well, to hell with that.

"The name they took from the car is wrong. My name is Fleming." I'd thought of giving them a phony, but it would be too easy for them to frisk me again. "Are you Kyler?"

"Yes." He studied me. "Where's the woman?"

We both knew whom he was talking about. "I don't know."

"Why do you have her suitcase?"

"I'm keeping it safe."

"When do you expect to see her again?" His voice was low, almost gentle, and had a slight East Coast accent.

"I don't know. Why are you after her?"

He ignored that one. "What is she to you?"

"Just a friend."

"Where is she?" he repeated.

My mouth is dry. "I'd cooperate better if I knew more about what's going on."

He didn't answer right away. The silence stretched out as he focused on me. It was meant to make me uncomfortable and was working to some extent. If need be, I could handle him, but he gave me the cold creeps.

"Doreen Grey has something I'm looking for," he finally stated.

"What's that?"

"No one's business but mine."

"Why should I help you, then?"

"I need information, not help. I will pay for it, if that's what you want."

What I wanted was to know exactly why this ordinary-looking man was so frightening. I tried to read something, anything, from him and could not. Maybe that was the answer.

"How much?"

He assessed me, my clothes, and other details. "One hundred dollars," he offered.

"You must have spent that on the hired help just to bring me here."

"Two hundred."

"Save your money. Tell me what you're after and I might be able to do something about it."

Kyler wasn't used to such treatment. Rimik, who hadn't said a word since I'd come in, shifted restlessly, perhaps hoping for orders to start committing mayhem. Hodge snorted. My nerves were acting up as well. My lips had peeled back just enough for the teeth to show.

"He thinks he's hot shit," observed Hodge. "We oughta show him better manners."

"You could try, gunsel." I didn't know if he went that way or not. It didn't matter, all I wanted was to make him mad and see which way his boss jumped.

Hodge jerked as though I'd touched him with a live wire. He closed the space between us in one step, his fist up and swinging. I blocked it by raising my arm then backhanding him, all in one move. He staggered bonelessly into a crate, bounced, and flopped to the floor. He stopped moving.

Rimik brought his knife out in the first second and swept it past me in a short arc to get my attention. He centered it with the blade at just the right angle to gut me like a fish. I held my ground and checked on Kyler out of the corner of my eye. He just stood there, watching the show, so I probably had a few seconds' grace.

His stooge was feeling playful. He tried an experimental thrust with the blade to get me to dodge back, only I didn't. I shot my hand out and caught Rimik's wrist, but the man was wise to that one and fast. He yanked his whole arm down, slipped away, and flicked the blade back up again.

White fire ran along my forearm. Now I did fall back, clutching the part just below my elbow where he'd neatly sliced things open. A few drops of blood splashed onto the concrete, the rest soaked into my shredded sleeve.

I wasn't badly hurt, metal wasn't as harmful to me as wood, but I had to pause a moment to keep from vanishing involuntarily to heal. The bleeding would stop quickly enough without such a complication and the pain would pass; at least I wasn't in the part of the warehouse that was over the river or I might not have had a choice.

What I couldn't stomach now was the uneven hiss of air between Rimik's teeth. He was laughing at me. It got me mad enough that I made another start for him.

The knife flashed like miniature lightning just under my nose. He was still playing, trying to give me a scar to remember him by. And he was still laughing.

I lost my temper then, and picked up the first thing that was handy; it happened to be a crate the size of a small suitcase weighing about forty or fifty pounds. We were no more than six feet apart and he had no room or time to duck. The look of gawking surprise that flashed over his face just as the crate caught him full in the chest was most satisfying.

Two steps and I was standing over him, tearing the crate to one side. My fingers had just closed over the handle of his bowie knife when I felt something small and solid bump inarguably against my left temple. It was followed by a soft double click that I recognized all too well. My grip went slack; I stopped moving altogether.

"Stand still," Kyler ordered in his gentle voice.

6

I'D overlooked the driver simply because he was the driver.

He'd thumbed the hammer back as a subtle warning to me. I wouldn't get another. All it needed now was a minimum amount of pressure on the trigger to go off. While I was very busy not moving, Kyler walked around just enough to check on Rimik.

"Lucky man," he said. Rimik was still breathing. "Chaven, take the kid over there." He nodded at another stack of crates that were too big to be thrown.

The driver, Chaven, bumped my temple again with the muzzle of his gun. I let go of the knife and straightened cautiously. He gestured in the direction he wanted me to go. I stepped away from Rimik's body and walked toward the crates. Two steps and I had to stop because the river below our feet was holding me back. Chaven put a hand in the middle of my back and pushed. It helped and got me past the point of no return.

"Turn around." Chaven had a voice like the edge of Rimik's knife.

I turned and was looking down the short barrel of his gun, noting that he favored a revolver over an automatic. Revolvers are simple tools, particularly the double-action type; there's no need to remember about the safety or chambering a bullet or clearing a last-second jam. All you have to do is pull the trigger and it goes boom. . . . In this case, it could go boom right through my skull. The shot wouldn't kill me, but it was an experience that I altogether preferred to avoid.

Now I knew how far Kyler was willing to go with things. He and his men were ready to kill, and kill casually for whatever they wanted. I was dealing with human garbage.

Chaven had a narrow, hatchet-hard face with no more emotion in it than the gun he held, so I watched his eyes. If he decided to do anything, I'd see it show up in them first.

"He's cold," Chaven commented to his boss.

Kyler hardly glanced up. "Only because he thinks I need him alive." He came over to stand next to Chaven and to look at me more closely. "Well, I don't."

The cut on my arm stopped burning and began to sting. I let my breath out slowly and drew another.

"Your last chance," he said, carefully spacing the words. "Where is the woman?"

I waited a moment before answering, just so that Kyler knew I'd understood him. "On the level . . . I don't know."

"Why do you have her suitcase?"

"For safekeeping."

"Then you expect to see her again?"

"Maybe. I don't know for certain."

"I will guarantee her safety. I will even pay her. She, at least, might appreciate some compensation for her time. She'll know me. She'll know I'll be fair."

"But I don't know you."

"I've already noticed and allowed for that, or you'd be dead by now. You're not stupid. Start asking around. You'll find out all you need about me and how I work."

I'd already gotten a pretty clear idea. Chaven still held his gun three inches away from my nose and his hand was very steady.

"I expect you to find her. When you do, tell her that if she leaves town before settling her business with me, she will regret it."

"I'll let her know."

"Do that, Fleming." Kyler's gaze froze onto mine. It was like standing in front of the cobra exhibit at a zoo, but without any protective glass in between. "Do it as though your life depended upon it."

Kyler returned Doreen's pistol—without the bullets—and had Chaven drive me to Bobbi's hotel, where the Nash was parked. It was another silent ride. I hugged my sore arm and bit my tongue to keep from asking him anything. They could learn a lot about me from the kind of questions I might have, and I didn't want any of them getting too curious. My best course was to keep a low profile; I was to be a messenger boy and nothing more.

Chaven pulled up next to the Nash, braking only long enough for me to get out. The Caddy glided away out of sight. I breathed a heavy sigh of relief, made sure the street was empty, and vanished.

It was swift and certain release from my pain. Through trial and a lot of error, I'd learned that going incorporeal speeded up the healing process. I floated around for a time and eventually sieved into Escott's car to rematerialize and take stock.

The bloodstains were alarming, but a little soap and water would clear them away. The seven-inch gash was already closed and had reduced itself to a nasty-looking red scar. It would fade soon enough. Too bad I couldn't say the same for my memory. He was out of commission for now, but one of these nights I planned to pay Rimik back in full, and take my time about it.

I considered going in to see Bobbi for a little cleanup and sympathy, but quickly decided against it. Kyler had made me paranoid. If his men were able to trail me from the studio to the Stockyards without getting spotted, they could still be on the watch. Walking back to the hotel might lead them to Bobbi, and I wasn't about to involve her in this mess.

Starting the car, I prowled around the streets. At this time of the morning, anyone following me would easily stand out. After half an hour of searching the mirror and seeing nothing, I felt reasonably safe and drove to Escott's office near the Stockyards. I parked the car, locked it, and walked away, going around the block to the next street over. Being reasonably safe isn't the same as being certain about it. I stood in a shadow-filled alley until the cold started to penetrate even my supernatural hide. Only one car came by, an old cab driven by a middle-aged man who looked both sleepy and bored. Not Kyler's style at all.

Vanishing again, I left the alley and felt my way two doors down the block, slipping inside the third one with heartfelt relief. The first thing I sensed after going solid was the rich, earthy aroma of tobacco. It was a small shop, jammed with all the usual paraphernalia needed for a good smoke. Escott owned a half interest in the place and used it for more than just keeping his favorite blend on hand.

I went around the small counter and up the narrow stairs. Woodson, the other owner, used the front section of the second floor for storage and never bothered with the back. The dust on the floor was undisturbed and I left it that way, choosing to float over it to get to the rear wall, where Escott had installed a hidden door. I didn't bother messing with the catch and just seeped through, re-forming in the washroom of Escott's office.

My eyes automatically skipped past the mirror as I walked into the back room, which was furnished with a few bare necessities. Once in a while his work kept him late and he wasn't above camping out here. His neatly made-up army cot was short on comfort, but adequate for an overnight stay. He also had a suitcase and a change of clothes on hand for occasional out-of-town trips. I opened the door to the front room.

Except for the blotter, phone, and ashtray, the top of his desk was clean. He was an extremely neat man, insisting on order and precision in every detail of his life, right down to the exact way his chair was centered into its well under the desk. I avoided moving it and sat in the other office chair.

I used the phone and tried reaching him at the house but got nothing. I dialed police headquarters and asked for Lieutenant Blair. He'd gone home hours ago. When I asked for Escott, they'd never heard of him.

He'd left no messages for me with his answering service. I wasn't sure if I should be worried about him or not. I decided not, and gave them a message for him to check his safe deposit box when he came in. It was what he called the hidden compartment he'd installed behind the medicine cabinet in his washroom. Now all I had to do was put something in it for him to find.

He had a Corona and a ream of paper on the top of his file cabinet. I brought them down and started typing.

It was a few minutes shy of dawn when I finally finished and put everything away. I tugged at the frame of the medicine cabinet and jammed the pages of my report into the narrow space there. Escott may have liked things tidy, but I was tired and in a hurry. I shut the cabinet fast before it could all fall out again and quickly walked through the wall to the tobacco shop storeroom.

Screened by a load of old crates and other junk was an especially long box that Escott had constructed for me as an emergency bolt hole. This was the first time I'd ever felt jumpy enough to want to use it. I slipped through and materialized inside its cramped confines. Like my cot at home, the bottom was lined with a quantity of my home earth in a flat oilcloth bag. It was secure, but far too much like a coffin for much mental comfort. Fortunately, the sun came up before claustrophobia overcame common sense, and I was asleep for the day.

There was no sense of waking for me, no coming up through the layers of sleep into full consciousness. When in contact with my earth, I'm either awake or not awake. It all depends on the position of the sun. I called my daytime oblivion sleep because it was a familiar word, not because it was accurate. Precisely at sunset the next night, my eyes opened, I remembered where I was, and wasted no time getting out. The box was useful enough, but I preferred being crammed into one of my steamer trunks.

In the tobacco shop downstairs a door opened and shut—either a late customer or Woodson himself closing things up for the night. He knew about the hidden door, but not about my long box or its supply of Cincinnati soil. Escott and I had figured that, like a lot of people, he'd be much happier not knowing.

No further sound came from below. I walked through to the rear of the office. On the radio that served as a nightstand was my typed report. In one corner stood Doreen Grey's cheap suitcase. Escott was lying on his army cot, a pile of newspapers within easy reach on the floor and a crumpled afternoon edition folded over his face. The deep regularity of his breathing told me he was in dreamland.

I really hated to wake him up. "Charles?"

The paper rattled. He was a light sleeper. He dragged the paper away and sat up. "Good evening," he said almost cheerfully. He did a beautiful double take. "Perhaps I should say good heavens. You look as though you've been busy."

"No need to be nice about it. We both know I look like something the cat dragged in. Can I borrow your razor?"

"Please do. Whatever happened to your arm?"

I'd omitted a few details about last night's activities from the report. "Kyler's boys play rough. Think your tailor can fix it?"

"Your arm?" he deadpanned.

"The clothes. My arm's fine." I peeled off my overcoat and suit coat. The blood had dried and all but glued everything to the skin. It looked terrible, but the damage beneath was almost healed by now. As I scrubbed off in the sink, I could see that last night's angry red line was now a long, white welt. Eventually, even that would disappear, leaving no scar. "Did you get things straightened out with Lieutenant Blair?"

He added his paper to the stack on the floor and stretched a little. "Yes, after I'd gotten hold of our employer and informed him of the murder. It gave him quite a serious turn but he came down to headquarters himself to see to things. Mr. Pierce is a formidable fighter. I was very glad that he was on my side. He managed to keep me free from any legal difficulties."

That was a relief; I'd been afraid that Blair would have Escott's license yanked for wanting to protect his client for a couple of hours. "I tried calling you. They have you down there all night?"

"No, it was Mr. Pierce who kept me so occupied. He insisted on buying me a late dinner to compensate a bit for the trouble I'd been to on his behalf, and then we got to talking."

"What was he doing while McAlister was getting murdered?"

His sharp gray eyes glinted with approval. "He maintains he was at the Stumble Inn for several hours, conversing with Des the bartender and cleaning out his stock of sarsaparilla. Pierce was terribly shocked at the news about McAlister, doubly so that the murder had taken place at Kitty Donovan's flat."

"The cops find her yet?"

He shook his head.

"What's Pierce think of her as a suspect?"

"He was partly incoherent, partly obscene, but wholly against the idea."

"What about Marian Pierce?"

"She was in the company of Harry Summers, who was trying to patch up a quarrel they'd had over you."

"Oh, brother."

"It seems you made quite an impression on both of them."

"That goes double for me."

"Which reminds me . . . Pierce went ahead and let his daughter know what is going on."

"I'll bet she was thrilled that I wasn't really following her like she thought."

"One wonders what activities she engages in to inspire such secretiveness."

"Smoking, drinking, and necking—those are the ones I witnessed, at least. I think she's just shy about having her daddy hear about them. He could take away her car keys. Have you heard from Doreen?"

"Not a word."

"Shit."

"But after such a harrowing evening, one can hardly blame her for wishing to keep out of sight."

"From Leadfoot Sam, you mean. She doesn't even know about Vaughn Kyler. If she leaves town before I can talk to her . . ."

"Indeed," he agreed. "I've made calls to one or two contacts I have. Since last night it has become common knowledge in Miss Grey's . . . ah . . . social set that he's looking for her. I daresay she'll discover that for herself soon enough. The police are also trying to locate her."

"Wonderful, just what she needs. How'd they get on to her?"

"I learned that they made another visit to the Boswell House and noticed the hole in the wall between the rooms."

After removing the mirror, I hadn't replaced it. They must have practically tripped over the mess. "What about her studio?"

"They searched it but discovered nothing of value, nor any clue to her whereabouts."

"But I left a note there with the office phone number on it."

He tapped the typed sheets on the radio. "So you said, but the police either ignored it, which is quite unlikely, or she got there before them and took it away."

"Or Kyler's men found it. They probably have the place staked out."

"And this one as well, if they troubled to trace the number down. You said they got my name from the car registration; I'm sure Kyler knows all about me and my little business by now."

I started to apológize or say something like an apology, but he cut it off.

"It's part of the job," he said with a dismissive wave of his hand. I'd forgotten that he enjoyed this kind of work. "I applaud your caution, but by now it may be superfluous."

"What do you know about Kyler?" I took it for granted that Escott would have some knowledge of the man, and I wasn't disappointed.

"Vaughn Kyler, as you correctly deduced in your report, has taken control of the gang formerly headed by Frank Paco. Kyler is not his real name and I've not been able to find it out. He is well educated, thought to be intelligent, and in less than six months has doubled the earnings off the rackets previously directed by Paco. We may reasonably conclude from this that he is ambitious and perhaps not a little greedy."

"The guy's a snake," I grumbled over the running water.

"He also knows how to efficiently deal with any rivals. His chief competitors for his position, Willy Domax and Doolie Sanderson, have been missing since last August, along with half a dozen of their lieutenants. No one seems to be too anxious to speculate on their whereabouts, either."

"What about Frank Paco?"

"He's still in the sanitarium. Apparently he is not considered to be much of a threat."

I could believe that. The last time I'd seen my murderer, he'd been drooling like a baby.

"Despite this, Kyler has a high reputation in the criminal community. People may not like to deal with him, but by their standards he is fair. If he has promised safety and monetary compensation to Miss Grey, I have no doubt that she will get it."

"Yeah, that and what else?"

Escott shrugged. "Now as for *why* Kyler wants to speak with her . . ."

"I figure it's either some photos she took or has to do with that damned bracelet."

"Probably the latter. It's the only obvious thing of value in—I take it that she didn't have it?"

"Not that I know of." I concentrated very hard on scraping away soap and bristles.

"Not that you—did you not ask her?"

"She mostly talked about McAlister."

"And you never thought to ask about the bracelet?"

"I had other things on my mind."

He looked at me as though I'd dropped out of the sky from another planet. He almost said something, stopped himself, and was silent during the rest of the time it took to finish my shave.

Inside me, memory twisted like a sword in my gut. Part of me wanted to talk, badly needed to talk, but a much larger part wouldn't allow it. I rinsed and toweled off. Only inches away from me, the mirror reflected an empty washroom. The sword twisted a little deeper.

"What is it?" He could sense that something was wrong.

"Nothing," I lied, staring straight ahead.

Escott loaned me one of his spare shirts from the tiny closet and a suit coat that didn't quite match my pants, but was free of slashes and bloodstains. There wasn't much I could do about my damaged overcoat; going without one in the middle of a Chicago winter was more conspicuous than wearing it as is. I'd just have to bluff through any questions.

Not that I was planning on leaving the office. I wanted to stick close to the phone in case Doreen should try calling. She might have had to hole up for the day herself, and I was hoping she'd feel safer now that it was dark.

Escott left to get something to eat; I filled in the time by reading what his paper had to say about McAlister's murder. The reporter had done a fair job; most of the facts were straight, and the names spelled correctly. Mine had been excluded, which was a relief. It was an odd feeling, too, considering my days on the paper in New York, when I'd once fought tooth and nail for a byline.

Blair had issued a standard statement that his men were looking for a suspect, but he remained cagey concerning that person's identity. Miss Kitty Donovan, the tenant of the flat in which McAlister's body was found, was unavailable for comment.

I folded that section of the paper and tossed it onto the rest of the pile. They were full of the usual insanity. Some big brain was recommending that people start using the word *syphilis* in guessing games and spelling bees as a way of breaking down the taboos concerning venereal diseases. He had an idea that if people started putting it into crossword puzzles it would cease to be so shocking. In theory, it sounded like a good idea, but I had at least two maiden aunts who would have swooned in their high-button shoes at the idea. Once recovered, I was sure they'd have hunted the guy down and shot him on sight.

The other papers I left unread; I wasn't in the mood to bone up on the the screwy workings of the rest of the world. My own little corner of it was more than enough to keep me unpleasantly occupied.

The blank white walls of the office offered no distractions. Escott liked them plain and for just that reason: so he could think. I stared at them and purposely cleared my mind of everything but white paint.

It worked for nearly a whole minute and then I was lost in the problem of whether or not to talk to Bobbi. I rarely mentioned my feedings at the Stockyards, no more than anyone would normally talk about how they brush their teeth. How I had used Doreen was on the same level—that's what I was trying to tell myself, anyway. I was desperate for some grain of comfort, for any excuse that would let me off the hook. Nothing worked, though. I'd lost control and that was it.

No excuses.

So I put off thinking about Bobbi. I wouldn't be able to decide what to do until after I saw Doreen again, which could be never. The phone wasn't . . .

Wrong. The phone just did. Twice, as I stared at it.

"Hello?"

"Hi, lover."

That damned sword twisted in me again. This was the first time I'd ever felt uneasy talking to Bobbi. "Hi, yourself." I sounded artificially cheerful in my own ears.

"You weren't at home, so I thought I'd try my luck at Charles's office."

"Yeah, I'm holding the fort while he puts on the feed bag."

"When you didn't come back last night I got a ride home with Gloria."

"Yeah, sorry. Things got busy."

"Did you catch up with that guy?" Bobbi hadn't seen the papers yet.

I ran a nervous hand over the dark wood of Escott's desk. "Yeah, Charles and I found him."

"What happened?" Her tone turned serious. She'd picked up something from my own.

"Someone got to him first. Killed him."

"Oh, Jack . . ."

She listened and eventually some of the story came out. I needed to talk, but even then it was only a sketchy account, especially the business with Doreen Grey. Mostly I spoke of McAlister's death, which had bothered me more than I'd realized.

He was a nobody, a vain and disgusting little blackmailer, but his death was hardly a good ending for even his sort. Any pity I felt stemmed from the fact that I, too, had been murdered. It gave me a unique, if personally horrifying, insight into things.

"What about Charles?" she asked. "Is he square with the cops?"

"He seems to think so. He knows how to take care of himself and he's got a sharp lawyer. He only wanted to wait until he could talk with Pierce first, to let him know the investigation's changed from theft to murder."

"And you don't think the girl did it?"

I shrugged, which she couldn't see. "She didn't do herself any favors running out like that."

"On the other hand, she doesn't know you or Charles. She must have been too scared to think."

"She handled herself pretty well at the hotel."

"Yeah, but seeing her boyfriend like that . . ." Bobbi got quiet, retreating into her own memories. I knew they weren't pleasant ones. I instantly forgot my troubles.

"God, I wish I could be there to hold you," I said.

"I know."

We didn't say anything, but then talk would have been superfluous. I waited her out, eyes shut, listening.

After a long time, she heaved a sigh as though to clear her mind of the dust. "Maybe you can make it up to me later. Will you be coming by tonight?"

"If I can, baby. But if I'm not at the club by a quarter till closing, then you'd better hitch another ride."

"In other words, I'll expect you when I see you."

" 'Fraid so."

"Okay. If you can put up with my hours, I can handle yours."

"Fair enough."

I'd almost sounded normal toward the end, but after the last goodbye, the restless worry flowed back like a cold tide against my heart.

When Escott returned I was hunched over his radio trying to find something worth listening to—a futile effort in my present mood. I wound the dial back to his favorite station and shut the thing off.

Since the phone call, I'd managed to make one decision, and that was to go looking for Doreen. If I hung around the place much longer, I'd be climbing his blank white walls and talking to myself in three different voices. I was about to tell Escott, but he interrupted before I had the chance to draw breath to speak.

"Get your coat and hat," he said. "They've found Miss Grey. She's in hospital."

He dropped an evening edition onto the cot. It was folded open to a story on the front page. The headline read, "Shooting Victim in Critical Condition." The facts were slim. A woman had been found lying in a drainage ditch of a city park with three bullet wounds. The police were still trying to identify her.

"This could be anybody," I said faintly.

"I called someone I know there and got a description of her. It matches the one in your report."

"Oh, Christ." I stopped wasting time and grabbed my stuff and followed him down to his car. He couldn't drive fast enough for me. When we eventually got to the hospital, I hung in the background, letting him ask the questions at the front desk, then followed again as he headed off down a corridor.

We were used to working like that by now; he dealt directly with the public while I stayed out of the way and went unnoticed. It worked until we reached the surgical ward. We had another desk to pass and no one was allowed through except family.

Escott started to make explanations to the nurse in charge, but I interrupted. "Look, I need to see the woman who was shot. I think she might be my cousin."

The woman asked questions. Other people had been calling the hospital and making inquiries about her patient. She wouldn't say who. I gave her a song and dance about Doreen not turning up for work today and her general description. The latter seemed to make a difference. The nurse's expression was grave as she went off to confer with her supervisor. Both returned with a doctor, who look us off to one side to hear things all over again. I'd always been a lousy liar; tonight it seemed to come naturally.

"If she is your cousin, you'll have to talk to the police," he told me.

"Fine," I agreed. Escott's eyes flickered, but he kept his comments to himself.

Under the eye of the supervisor and with the help of a large orderly, I was enveloped in a hospital gown that looked like a sheet with sleeves and given a cloth mask to cover my nose and mouth. This time, Escott had to stay outside and wait, but he was turning it into an opportunity. I glanced back before walking through the doors to the ward and saw him turning on the charm for the nurse at the desk. She didn't seem too cooperative, but he could work miracles with that accent of his.

The mask did not shut out the smell. It was always the same: a kind of death-sweet stink that I always associated with hospitals. The people who worked with it and the suffering that engendered it deserved Medals of Honor.

I was taken past a couple of beds loaded with silent human wreckage and shown a frail figure all but smothered under her bandages. A nurse stood close by, watching her breathe.

Until this moment, I'd held on to a vague hope that it would not be Doreen. As it was, I barely recognized her in this sterile setting. Her face was slack and colorless, the skin spread thinly over the sharp bones beneath. Only her carrot red hair stood out, a bright incongruity against the harsh steel and enamel fixtures. I put out a hand to stroke its limp strands.

"Is she your cousin?" asked the doctor.

If I said no I'd have protection from the dangerous curiosity of officialdom. It was also an easy escape from a responsibility I didn't want and could ill afford.

On her neck were the faint marks I'd left. Engulfed as she was with all the tubes and bandages, they were nothing, barely noticeable.

The doctor repeated his question.

"Yes," I said, hardly aware that I'd spoken.

He expressed sympathy and told me he needed information.

I anticipated the first question. "Her name is Doreen."

"Last name?"

"Grey."

The nurse wrote it on the chart at the foot of the bed without any reaction. Maybe she'd never heard of the Oscar Wilde book. I gave Escott's office address and phone number for a place of residence and made a guess at Doreen's age. If I didn't know an answer I said so. She took down the meager scraps of fact and then the doctor led me back out to the hall.

Escott looked up. He was leaning comfortably against the desk facing the nurse and she had a smile on her face. Both sobered and straightened when I emerged from the ward.

"It's Doreen," I told him.

He also said something sympathetic. I didn't really listen. For the next half hour, as I ran the gauntlet of answering questions for a lot of people in uniforms, I didn't listen to much of anything.

The doctor in charge of her case was named Rosinski. He seemed to know his business and was reluctant to make any optimistic promises. From the way his eyes shifted and how he answered my own questions, I knew he wasn't holding out much hope of Doreen pulling through.

"Her lungs were punctured, and one of them collapsed," he said. "I take it as a good sign that she survived long enough for us to get her into surgery, but that's it as far as it goes. She was very lucky that the bullets didn't bounce around her ribs and cause more damage than they did."

"What kind of bullets?" I asked.

"Very small; twenty-twos. The holes aren't much, but they're enough to do the job. The main problem now is to keep her breathing and hope that pneumonia doesn't set in."

"Was there much blood loss?"

"Her pressure and volume were low when she was brought in—"

"But she's not harmed from it, is she?"

"No more than one would expect in such a case."

"What do you mean by that?"

"I mean that her blood loss is something we took care of early on. Right now, she's got other things to worry about."

"When will you know anything?"

Rosinski would only shake his head. "We'll both have to wait and see on that one."

Earlier, I'd let Escott know I was willing to run my end of things for the time being, so he'd gone off to tend some business of his own, giving me room to work. He must have kept tabs on me, though, since he turned up not long after the questioning ended.

"This is hardly the place I'd expect to find someone with your particular condition," he said in a subdued voice, taking a seat nearby.

"It's quiet," I mumbled, staring at the floor.

I'd found refuge in the hospital chapel. The silence of the small room helped soothe my inner turmoil, and I won't lie and say that I didn't use the place for its intended purpose. Doreen needed all the help she could get; I just hoped that God hadn't minded hearing a prayer from the guy who may have helped to put her life in jeopardy in the first place.

"All the same . . ." But he didn't finish whatever he might have said about the oddity of a vampire being in a kind of church, and shrugged the rest away. He could see I wasn't in the mood for it. "I had to call Lieutenant Blair."

"What'd he have to say?" I wasn't all that interested, but wanted distraction from the stuff inside my head.

"Little that may be repeated in these surroundings. He dispatched a man to be here in case Miss Grey should wake up."

"Yeah, I remember talking to that guy. He may have a long wait."

"What did you tell him?"

"Just that we were doing private work for Pierce and that we'd also wanted to question Doreen about McAlister's death. He took it all down and left it at that."

"Was he not curious that you are listed as her next of kin?"

"Yeah, but I told him she really didn't have anyone else to look after her. When we talked last night I got the feeling that she really was all alone."

"Alone," he repeated thoughtfully. "Obviously not."

"What're you thinking?"

"I was only speculating about who might have shot her."

"Kyler or one of his stooges."

"Are you so certain?"

"Something's telling you different?"

"The circumstances of her assault."

"What about them?"

"Can you recall what caliber weapons Kyler's men possessed?"

"Chaven was using a thirty-eight, Hodge had a forty-five."

"I learned that the bullets taken from Miss Grey were from a twenty-two . . . an experienced criminal might prefer a larger caliber."

"There're always exceptions. Kyler or Rimik could have been carrying the right size."

"True." He started to dig for his pipe, remembered where he was, and changed his mind. "But if one is planning to kill a person, a small bullet is a poor choice for the job."

"Unless you want to be quiet about it. Back in New York I filed more than one murder story on the subject. Put a twenty-two right up next to a person and it makes less noise than a popping balloon."

"It was with that in mind that I managed to arrange and make an examination of the clothes she was wearing."

I shook my head. Escott could talk a tree out of its sap. "She was shot from a distance, right?"

"Correct. It's very possible that the person who shot her was an amateur."

"Just because it was a small bullet?"

"Because she was not killed outright. Did Kyler strike you as the type who would plan a murder and then botch the job?"

He had a point there. "Unless he wanted to make it look like the work of an amateur."

"The major objection I see against that is the fact that she did not simply disappear as did others before her. That's his usual pattern."

"Like Domax and Sanderson?"

"Hmm. A disappearance simply raises questions that may never have answers. Leaving a body to be found may result in the same situation, but one is at least certain of the violence involved and may work outward from that point."

"Okay, if we take Kyler out of things, who's left?"

"The same person who killed McAlister."

"I can figure that, Charles, but who?"

He shrugged. "We shan't discover that sitting around here."

"And Doreen?"

"We can always call the nurse on duty for any news concerning changes in her condition."

"What're you planning to do?"

"To get out and ask some questions. I suggest we start with Vaughn Kyler."

I nearly choked. "Great. Might as well start at the bottom and work our way up. How do we find him?"

"We won't have to. My researches today were most rewarding. . . ."

"You found out where he hangs his hat?"

"Not quite, but I've an idea on where to start. Care to come along?"

"Lead on, Macduff."

Escott winced. "That's 'lay on'."

"Sorry."

"The misquote doesn't bother me so much as your choice of play to misquote from."

Escott was not even remotely a superstitious man—except when it came to the theater. His particular quirk had to do with *Macbeth,* and he never would say why. I apologized again, respecting the quirk, even if I didn't understand it.

He shook his shoulders straight and drew in a deep breath. "Ah, well, perhaps our surroundings will cancel out any malign influences. We can hope so, at least."

"Amen to that," I said, and followed him out.

Not that I was taking his stuff too seriously, but I did insist on a quick stop back at the office to pick up his bulletproof vest and the Webley-Fosbery. Just in case. If we got close enough to interview Kyler, he'd probably be frisked and not allowed to keep it. On the other hand, if Kyler didn't want to see us, we would very definitely need some protection. I still had Doreen's automatic, but without bullets it wasn't much more than a weight dragging in my pocket.

Escott stowed his gun into his shoulder holster. With his suit coat and overcoat on top, it was invisible, even to experienced eyes. Now I realized why he favored single-breasted styling; they look okay unbuttoned and he'd left things that way to be able to get at his gun more easily.

We were all set to go when the low rumble of a motor drew my attention to the outside. From either end of the front window, we peered through the slats of the blinds to the street below. A flashy new Packard had parked just in front of Escott's Nash.

"It's Pierce's car," I said. "Wonder what he wants?"

He shook his head and watched with interest as Griffin lurched from the Packard and crossed the sidewalk to our stairwell. For a big man he didn't make much noise, even on those creaking boards. The door shook a bit as he knocked.

Escott let him in and offered a greeting.

"Mr. Pierce extends an urgent request that you come to his house immediately," said Griffin. There was a hint of humor in his eyes. He was very aware of the artificially formal tone of the invitation.

"Did Mr. Pierce state the reason behind his urgency?"

"I am not at liberty to say, sir, but you may rely on the importance of it."

Escott looked ready to toss the ball back again. It was entertaining, but I didn't feel like standing around all night just to watch. "C'mon, Charles. We'll follow in your car and take care of the other business afterward."

He'd been all wound up to tackle Kyler, so it was tough going for him to have to switch his intentions so abruptly. His curiosity was up, though, and that helped. A minute later and we were on the road in the wake of the Packard.

I expected Pierce to have a big place and wasn't disappointed. The grounds were well kept but informal enough so that the keeping wasn't too obvious. His house was a big brick monster that must have been stacked together by a piecework crew. It had a couple of turrets with flags, gables, and extensions out of the main building that looked like additions made by the architect after he'd sobered up. Ugly as it was, it looked friendly, and there were warm lights showing in the windows.

Sebastian Pierce emerged from the front door before Escott could set the brake and signed for me to roll down my window.

"I don't want the servants to know what's up," he said. "We'll talk in the guest house around back." Without waiting for a reply he trotted forward on his long legs and hastily slipped into the passenger side of the Packard. It was a very cold night and all he wore over his clothes was a bulky sweater.

Though much smaller than the main house and built of humble wood, the guest house was enough to do an average family proud. Its two stories were painted a fresh-looking white with dark trim. The porch light was on and a window shade upstairs twitched, indicating someone was waiting for us.

Pierce was out and striding up the walk as soon as his car stopped. Escott and I had caught some of his nervous energy and quickly crowded onto the porch. Griffin wasn't moving as fast but managed to arrive just as Pierce unlocked the door and ushered us into a tiny parlor. An arched opening on our left led to a large living room, where he settled us by the fireplace. There was a good blaze going and Escott peeled off his gloves, gratefully extending his hands toward it.

"Now where have they got to?" Pierce muttered, glaring at the empty room. Somewhere upstairs, a toilet flushed. He looked at the ceiling as though he could see through it and nodded with satisfaction. "Good. Excuse me and I'll bring them down. They're probably having a last-minute attack of nerves."

He darted from the room, leaving us to look at each other. Griffin's face was bland and not giving anything away. He removed his chauffeur's hat and asked if he could take our coats. Escott shrugged out of his and I did the same. Griffin had just hung them in a closet when Pierce returned with company.

Marian came into the room, looking troubled and sulky, the picture of a kid who had been caught red-handed at the cookie jar. She wore a dark collegiate sweater over wide trousers and sturdy walking shoes that had seen some use. Her sable hair was pulled back and sported a demure black ribbon; all she needed to complete the effect was a pair of Harold Lloyd glasses. It was quite a contrast to the sleek, sophisticated girl who'd tried to suck my tonsils out last night.

"Is she his daughter?" murmured Escott.

"Uh-huh. Guard my back, would you?"

He made a small sound that might have been a laugh.

A second person reluctantly walked in, urged on by Pierce.

"Holy cats," I whispered. "He's been holding out on us."

"Well, well," said Escott, his tone conveying agreement and delight. "Miss Donovan, how nice to see you again."

Kitty Donovan looked up from the section of carpet she'd been staring at. Her huge eyes went first to Escott, then to me. Her face crumpled, then seemed to swell from the pressure of all the emotion she was trying to keep in check. Then she broke down and burst into tears.

Escott quietly and eloquently sighed.

It was shaping into another long night.

7

PIERCE was right next to her and in the best position to offer a shoulder to cry on, or at least the middle of his chest, which was as high as she came on him. None of the rest of us leaped forward to take the job so he patted the back of her head and told her everything was all right and let her soak his sweater for a while.

Not knowing what else to do, I shoved my hands in my pockets and tried to look someplace else. The girl wasn't crying just to cry. The gusting, ugly sounds that came from her were the raw stuff of honest grief. She was in pain and there was nothing anyone could do but let her get through it.

Escott gave them a wide berth as he stepped over to whisper something to Griffin. The big man nodded and left for the back of the house, returning with a flat bottle and a shot glass. He poured some amber liquid out and passed it to Pierce. Though teetotaling himself, he apparently didn't believe in enforcing it onto others. He put the glass to Kitty's lips and got her to drink. She choked, hiccuped, and settled a little. Her sobs became less frequent and softer, but she still hung on to Pierce. He steered her toward the sofa and they sat down together. When she groped in the pocket of her dress and pulled out a sodden handkerchief, Pierce took it away from her and replaced it with a dry one of his own.

She blew her nose a few times and said she was sorry.

"It's all right, honey," said Marian, echoing her father's calming assurances. "You've been through the wringer. Nobody minds when a little water has to come out."

Kitty responded with something unintelligible and blew her nose again. Marian relieved Pierce of the shot glass and had Griffin refill it. Kitty finished her second drink more quickly and easily than the first, apparently welcoming its deadening effect.

"Would you gentlemen care for anything?" asked Griffin, lifting the bottle.

Escott declined. He wasn't exactly a cop, but sometimes considered himself to be "on duty." This was one of those times. As ever, I politely shook my head.

"At least some coffee, Griff," said Pierce. "A nice, big pot and very strong."

"Sinkers, too?"

"Yes, if we have them."

Griffin left the glass and bottle within Pierce's reach on a table and I presently heard him in the kitchen clattering around with things.

Escott sat on the edge of an easy chair opposite the sofa. "I'm very glad you sent for us, Mr. Pierce. What exactly is it that you require?"

"Some help, of course."

"I'll do what I can."

Pierce gave out with a good-natured snort. "I certainly hope so, or I'll want that retainer back."

The corners of Escott's mouth briefly curled and he leaned forward, going to work with a benign expression.

"Good evening, Miss Pierce, Miss Donovan."

Marian shot him a brief, meaningless smile and went to sit on the sofa next to Kitty. Kitty nodded and dropped her reddened eyes.

Pierce said, "I've convinced Kitty that she needs to talk with the police. But first I wanted her to tell you what happened so you can find out who did kill Stan. I'm hoping you'll be able to get her off the hook."

"Your confidence in me is most flattering, but I can make no promises."

"If you tried to at this point, you'd be going out the door right now."

"Fair enough. Miss Donovan, would you please tell us all that you did last night?"

It was slow in coming. The girl was obviously uncomfortable with everyone looking at her. Pierce nodded encouragement and once in a while Marian patted her friend's hand.

"Stan and I had a date," she said in a flat, lifeless voice. "I was waiting for him at the Angel Grill. I was there extra early—"

"Why was that?" asked Escott.

"I had some displays to arrange at a department store and finished them sooner than I'd expected. I didn't feel like going home just to go right out again, which was all I would have had time for, so I went straight to the Angel. While I was there one of his friends came over, a guy named Shorty."

"Has he another name to go with that one?"

"Shorty was all Stan ever called him."

"Describe him."

"Well . . . he's short," she said unhelpfully.

I envied Escott's patience. He tried another tack. "What sort of clothes does he wear?"

She was on firmer ground here. "Cheap and awful. They're good enough for him to get by, but he doesn't clean them. He had egg stains on his coat, and he smokes cigars—he just reeked from them."

By working off of the girl's emotional reaction to the man, he was able to get a fairly complete description. One detail led to the next. He produced a notebook and took it all down, then asked, "What did he want, Miss Donovan?"

"He was trying to tell me that Leadfoot Sam was looking for Stan."

"Trying?"

"He didn't just come out and say it, he kind of talked around it, hinting. I put him off and tried to ignore him, but he kept hanging around as though he wanted something, and kept *hinting*. I finally got the idea that Stan was in trouble and that I'd better let him know so he could avoid it. Stan wasn't due for another thirty minutes and Shorty had scared me. He said that Leadfoot knew where Stan lived and might be waiting for him there. I couldn't just sit around after hearing all that, so I left."

"For the Boswell House?"

"Uh-huh. That's when I ran into the two of you."

He smiled to let her know all was forgiven. "Now, tell me exactly what happened after you left the hotel."

"I went straight home. I thought Stan might go there, too. When I saw his car on the street out front, I knew I'd guessed right, and went inside."

"Was your door locked?"

"Yes. I unlocked it, went inside, and locked it behind me."

"You were still nervous?"

"I was still scared."

He nodded, not blaming her for that. "Did Mr. McAlister have a key to your door?"

She didn't blush and said yes in an even tone.

"Is that the only way one can get into the building?"

"I think so."

"No unlocked back doors?"

"I don't know. You'd have to ask the manager."

"Very well. What did you do after you were inside?"

"I called for him, but he didn't answer. I thought he might be in the bathroom, but he wasn't. I checked all over and then I went into the kitchen. I don't remember much after walking in. I know I saw him, but that's all. I know I saw him, but I don't remember seeing him."

"You were in shock, honey," said Marian, squeezing her hand. "Don't let it worry you. You're better off not remembering."

"But it *feels* strange."

Escott continued. "What is the next thing that you can recall?"

"Waking up in my room. I heard two men talking down the hall—you two. I was scared. I thought maybe you'd done it. All I wanted was to get out, so I took the fire escape and ran and ran. I just couldn't stand it. I had to run."

"That's where I come in," said Marian. "She drove over here to see me, but I hadn't gotten home yet."

"Then Miss Donovan talked to one of the servants?"

Kitty shook her head, probably more than she needed to, but the drinks were working on her now. "I didn't dare. I took the back road in to the estate and put my car in the guest house garage. Then I came in here and tried to call Marian on the phone."

"How did you get in?"

"I checked under the doormat for a key and got lucky."

"What did you do when you could not reach Miss Pierce on the phone?"

"Nothing. That is, I couldn't do anything. I had to sit in the dark or someone from the main house might look out and see the lights. It was cold. I couldn't build a fire because of the smoke, and I was afraid to change the furnace setting. It's only high enough to keep the water pipes from freezing. But I turned on the electric stove in the kitchen and left its door open and that helped. Then I found some blankets and wrapped up."

Escott looked sympathetic. "So you stayed here until you could reach Miss Pierce?"

"All night."

"It must have been most uncomfortable."

"I don't remember much of that, either. I had a little brandy and it went right to my head. I just fell asleep at the kitchen table."

Considering the emotional strain and the fact that she'd missed dinner, it was no surprise, but I could almost see the sneer on the prosecutor's face if she brought that story to court. Real damsels in distress were few and far between, even if they looked the part as Kitty did.

Griffin returned just then with a tray full of cups, milk, sugar, and the long-awaited coffee. A plate stacked with donuts was on one side of it and on the other was a smaller plate with a neatly made up sandwich. He put it all down on the coffee table and handed the sandwich plate directly to Kitty. She accepted it with some confusion.

"Eat," he ordered in a stern voice. Wide-eyed because he was nothing if not impressive, the girl picked it up and took a bite. A second later she remembered to chew and swallow. Once the process was started, she had no trouble finishing.

The food almost turned it into a social occasion, and Escott had to wait as cups were filled and donuts were passed. I declined offers of both and hung back by the fireplace. My hands felt cold. They shouldn't have, since I was fairly indifferent to anything but the most extreme temperatures now. Maybe it had to do with the question I would have to ask her. It wasn't so much the question, but the method I'd need to use to get my answer.

"Not hungry?" Marian came to stand next to me, a coffee cup in one hand.

"I had dinner just before Griffin came for us."

She looked me over. "I'll bet you're one of those men who eats like a horse and never shows it."

"Maybe I am." I was uneasy with the conversation. She seemed the type to insist I have something and take a refusal as an insult. A subject change was in order. "I understand you and Harry Summers made up."

Her blue-eyed gaze was still fastened on me. The pure color was lovely, but hard and cold, like a mountain lake with ice in it. It had probably been a bad move to remind her about last night. "Yes, Harry and I are all lovey-dovey again."

"I'm glad to hear it."

A hostile line appeared in the set of her mouth, then softened. "So's Harry. It was all his idea, after all."

"He said he was crazy about you."

"I know that. He only tells me so a hundred times a day."

"You could do worse."

"Like with you?" She smiled. It wasn't an especially nice one.

"Like with Stan McAlister."

She blinked, as though I'd smacked her on the nose.

"What did you tell him at the club?"

"Tell him? I don't know what you mean."

"Yes, you do. You were seen sitting at the same table and talking. He got up and left, then you did the same. What did you say?"

She blushed. Under her carefully applied face powder, it looked muddy rather than becoming. "Damn Daddy, anyway," she whispered, her teeth exactly on edge.

"Never mind that. What did you say?"

She put down her coffee cup because her hands were shaking. She was plenty mad. "All I did was say that I met you and that I thought Daddy had hired you to follow me."

"Why would that make Stan bolt the place?"

"It didn't. He asked me a lot of questions about the talk you and I had, and then he said that you weren't after me, but after him. That's when he left. I'd wondered why at the time, but now I know he was afraid because of the bracelet he'd stolen. He must have realized the theft had been noticed and that you were there to find him."

"Why would he talk to you, then?"

She looked puzzled. "Why not?"

"Since he stole the bracelet from you, I should think you'd be the last person he'd want to see."

"Not if he was trying to play innocent about it all. Stan only had to lie, you know. I'm sure he was good at it. He'd be able to stand up to me or even Daddy, but it must have all fallen apart for him the moment he thought someone was actually after him."

"Yeah, I guess it must. Did he say where he was going in such a big hurry?"

"No, but he had to have gone straight to his hotel. Kitty said that you and your partner scared him off."

"With some help from Kitty."

"Don't be so hard on her, she really loved him. She was expecting to marry him."

Oh, good Lord. "With your bracelet as a wedding present?"

She started to blurt out some kind of a retort and caught herself before any sound came out. She looked over at Kitty, a sick expression on her face. "Oh, my God, you can't mean it."

"I gotta look at things the way the cops would."

"But Kitty wouldn't do anything like that."

"Like what? Theft or murder?"

"Either one."

"Maybe you could be a character witness, but you'd better work on your delivery. Right now, it's not too convincing."

"You—" She bit the word off but I had a good idea about what she'd wanted to say. I'd been called worse. Name calling wouldn't have eased things for her; what she really wanted to do was to knock my block off.

"Who do you think did it?" I asked.

"Leadfoot Sam," she spat. "Whoever he is. Kitty knows a little bit about him. Not much, but enough to be scared."

"And if he didn't?"

"I'm sure I don't know, perhaps some one of Stan's other friends. He must have had others. Why don't you find that man Kitty told you about—Shorty—and ask him?"

"What about you?"

"I wouldn't know where to look."

"I mean did you do it?"

A soft laugh puffed from her. "Don't be ridiculous. Besides, I was with Harry."

"Then both of you were in on it, or maybe you talked him into covering for you. Or you're covering for him."

"Is that the best you can do? Why would either of us want to kill poor Stan?"

"I learned enough about 'poor Stan' last night to know that a lot of people might have wanted to kill him."

"Then go talk to them; I'm not part of that crowd." She swept back to the sofa to sit next to Kitty again. She glanced once at me with obvious distaste, then turned her attention to the others. Maybe she was hoping I'd just disappear as I had in the parking lot.

The short break had given her drinks time to really circulate into Kitty's system. She was a lot more relaxed when Escott resumed his questioning.

"Once you were able to get hold of Miss Pierce, what did you say to her?" he asked.

"I told her I was in a jam and to come see me here."

"Presumably without being seen to do it."

The girl nodded. "And then she got here and I told her everything that had happened . . . what I could remember of it."

"What time did this interview take place?"

"Sometime this morning," answered Marian. "Around ten or so."

"And when did you decide to mention it to your father?"

Pierce glowered at them. "They didn't."

"How did you find out?"

"My study window overlooks this whole area. When I saw Marian tiptoeing around in her own yard I had a feeling something was going on and came down to find out why."

"Which you did," said Marian, smiling as though chagrined at being caught. But her smile was a tight one and didn't reach her eyes. She clearly resented his checking up on her.

"Which I did," repeated Pierce. "And a good thing, too. These two innocents had some crackpot plan to hide Kitty out here until the fuss had died down, and then take off for Mexico. Lord knows what would have happened to them. . . . White slavers or worse."

Marian restrained herself and did not roll her eyes.

"Then you sent for me rather than inform the authorities," Escott concluded.

Pierce was scowling, but not too seriously. "I needed time to hear her side of things and figure out what to do next. I talked with my lawyer, but he's not a specialist in criminal law. Right this minute he's doing what he can to find someone who can help us."

"Once he does and after he's had a chance to talk to Miss Donovan as well, I think you should take her in as quickly as possible to make a statement. It might look better for her."

"It might look better, but would it be better?"

"To be honest, I don't know. Legally, you are required to do as I've suggested. There is a warrant out on Miss Donovan, and the longer you delay, the worse it can get. You and your daughter could end up facing charges for harboring a fugitive."

Pierce erupted from the sofa. The living room was really too small for him to decently pace off his anger. He vented some of it verbally, his colorful abuse aimed at the law in general and the criminal court system in particular. "I've half a mind to go along with your plan and put you on the next train out of town," he concluded, looking at Kitty.

"Then they would know I was guilty," she murmured. She was almost in tears again from his outburst and was shaking from the effort to keep them in. Marian was stone-faced bored. Perhaps she was well used to her father's tempers.

"Of course you're not guilty." He started to add something, then realized what shape the girl was in and put a lid on it. "I just want to do what's best for you. It's about time someone did."

If Kitty failed to notice what he said and how he said it, Marian did not. She was as stone-faced as ever, but her big eyes narrowed slightly.

"Miss Donovan?" I was adopting Escott's formal manner. It seemed right for the question I had to ask.

She looked up at me, glad for a distraction.

"Just to set the record straight for us, did you kill Stan?"

Pierce started to erupt again, this time his anger directed toward me, but Escott stopped him. Escott knew what I was doing and knew that I had to be careful not to let it be noticed. It wasn't hard, since everyone was looking at Kitty, waiting to hear what she said.

She didn't answer right away. I repeated my question, holding her gaze. When she did answer, it was with a negative. It even came out sounding normal—or as normal as a person could sound, given the circumstances.

I continued to concentrate on her. I wasn't seducing her, she wasn't seducing me. This was simple influencing to get at the truth. I had to remember that to keep myself steady, to stay in control.

"Do you have any idea who might have done it?"

"Leadfoot Sam," she said without hesitation.

I let up on the light pressure I exerted. The girl was unharmed and nothing else had happened. Memory and conscience still writhed inside me like bloated worms, but I could ignore them for now.

"Why do you think that, Miss Donovan?" Escott asked, picking up the slack before anyone knew it was there.

She displayed no awareness of my mental tampering. "Because of what Shorty told me. But I don't know why or how it could have happened at my place."

I had an idea or two, but kept shut about them.

"Have you been here all day?" he continued.

"Yes."

"Alone?"

"Yes, except when Marian was here."

"When was that?"

"This morning . . . after ten, wasn't it?"

Marian confirmed the time.

He shifted his attention to her. "How long did you stay here, Miss Pierce?"

"An hour or so, maybe a little longer."

"What did you do after you left?"

"I went back to the main house and tried to pretend nothing was wrong."

"Did you visit Miss Donovan at all throughout the day?"

"No, I couldn't do that or it might have looked funny." She broke off as her father nodded agreement, then resumed. "So I called her a few times to check on her, to see if she was all right. I'd let it ring once, then dial again so she'd know it was me."

"And she was there each time?"

"Yes, of course."

"And what times did you call?"

Marian shrugged. "I don't know, after twelve and again at two and three."

"You were at home when you made these calls?"

"No, not for all of them. I went out shopping."

"Shopping?"

"Kitty didn't have any extra clothes or even a toothbrush. I couldn't loan her any of my clothes since they don't fit her, so I went to get her a few things and some groceries."

"When did you do this?"

"At about one. I left after lunch."

"And returned?"

"Around four, I think."

"Is that not a long time to be shopping?"

"You don't know my daughter, Mr. Escott," said Pierce. "A three-hour trip means she's only just started. Why are you so interested in the time?"

Escott held silent a moment. I found myself holding my breath, even though I don't usually breathe. "There's been a shooting," he finally said. "It may quite well be connected to McAlister's death."

A little ripple of surprise went through them and the usual questions came out. Not all of them were answered. Escott kept shut about who was shot and where she was now. He only said that the person was a friend of McAlister's and left it at that, which left them all highly dissatisfied.

"The police are still investigating. I cannot give out any more information than that."

"But how is it related to Stan's death?" asked Pierce.

"I'm not certain at this point, though considering the facts we have, one may come to a logical conclusion. The more immediate problem for us is that Miss Donovan does not have an alibi for the time of the shooting."

"What time was that?"

"The police think it happened between three-thirty and four, when the victim was discovered."

"Where did it happen?"

"At a city park less than a mile from this very house."

"Oh, good God."

"But I was *here*," said Kitty.

"Have you proof?" he shot back.

The girl went white around the lips and shrank back into the couch.

"Miss Donovan need not have even used her car; it's but a twenty-minute walk both ways . . ."

Kitty made a sound halfway between a moan and a whimper.

"Shut up, Escott," Pierce snapped.

Escott ignored him. "Have you an alibi for the time, Mr. Pierce?"

Pierce opened his mouth to say something and left it hanging that way as the implications sank in.

"Does Mr. Griffin have an alibi, or your daughter?"

"Me?" Marian's eyes went wide and she groped for her father's hand. Griffin's brow puckered.

Pierce shut his mouth, shaking his head. "All right, I see what you're getting at, not that I like it very much."

"Neither do I," said Marian. "Why are you talking to us? Shouldn't you be checking on this Leadfoot Sam or Shorty?"

"I expect I shall be doing just that after I've finished with things here. Miss Donovan, do you still have the gun that was in your possession last night?"

Kitty looked blank. "Gun?"

"Remember in the hotel lobby?" I prodded. "Or was that a dime-store toy?"

The memory reluctantly returned. "I guess it's still in my purse."

"Where's your purse?"

"Upstairs, in the first bedroom."

Pierce volunteered to go get it, but Escott said no and sent me. The stairs were just off the parlor and went straight up without any turns. The first door next to the landing stood open and the room beyond looked occupied. The bed had been made up, but the covers were all wrinkled, and feminine clothing lay scattered around. The wastebasket was overflowing with tissue wrap and a stack of empty boxes stood next to the dresser, evidence of Marian's shopping jaunt.

On the dresser was Kitty's purse. Inside the purse was her little automatic. It was the one I remembered from last night and it was a .22.

I filched a handkerchief to pick it up and sniffed the barrel. It hadn't been fired. She could have cleaned it, but there was no evidence of fresh gun oil. I searched the room and could find no cleaning kit, but something like that could be anywhere in the house or out in the garage with her car. Kitty hadn't killed McAlister, and though I couldn't see her gunning down Doreen, either, my vision might not count for much. I could be nearsighted.

I came back down to a silent room. None of them seemed too happy when I exhibited the gun in its cloth nest. Escott took a close look without touching it and sniffed the barrel as well, then dismissed it.

"Are there other guns in this house or the main house?"

Pierce nodded. "I've a couple of hunting rifles and a Luger."

"What caliber are the rifles?"

"They're both .30-30s."

"You should be safe enough, then, though I would advise you bring them to the attention of your lawyer when the time comes."

"This person who was shot . . . is he dead?"

Escott went quite still, studying each in turn. I hoped that he was reading more from them than I."

"Yes, I'm sorry to say."

"Damn it. How does this tie in with McAlister?"

"The bracelet."

"Always that goddamned bracelet," he rumbled. He came to attention as a new thought hit him. "Did he have the bracelet? Was it . . . ?"

"The bracelet was not on the body." Escott bent his gaze on Kitty again. "Miss Donovan, were you aware that McAlister might have stolen Miss Pierce's bracelet?"

"Not until Mr. Pierce told me about it tonight. I feel terrible that I was the one to bring Stan into the house."

"Do you believe he stole it?"

She faltered. "Well, that's what Mr. Pierce said. . . ." She looked at him for support and got it.

"Of course he stole it," he told her. "But there's no need to worry about that. It's over and done with. Whoever killed him probably got the bracelet, and I could not care less."

"Do you, indeed?" queried Escott.

"What do you mean by that?"

"I cannot say, but may be able to tell you presently. What's needed now is to tell the police your side of things and make them believe it, something that's best done with experienced legal help."

Pierce took the hint with a heavy sigh. "All right. I'll phone and see if the old shyster's turned up a likely candidate."

He did some dialing, located his lawyer, and broke into a smile at the news he got. Arrangements were made for a meeting. Kitty would have to repeat her story, first to the new lawyer, and then to the police. I hoped that she had the stamina to last through the process. She had a long night ahead.

Escott was asked to come along, but declined. "Your lawyer is your best help there," he said. "Besides, you want the real criminal brought in, and I cannot work on the problem from the police station."

I also suspected he wanted to keep some distance between himself and Lieutenant Blair for the time being. Pierce accepted the point as it was given and didn't press things.

After we got our coats, Pierce excused himself and walked us out to the car.

"You don't really think that little girl did anything?" he asked Escott. Away from the others, his confident front wavered; his own private fears were more noticeable, now.

"No," he replied. "But I do believe she has been used and used wretchedly. Finding proof of it is quite another thing, though."

"Is that what you're going after?"

"I hope so." Escott got into the driver's side, started the motor and got us moving. It was at a snail's pace. His driving sometimes reflected his preoccupation with a problem: the busier his mind, the slower he drove.

"Good move back there," I said. "Were you hoping to find out something by making them think Doreen was dead?"

"I was, but not with any reasonable expectations. My primary purpose was to ensure some little safety for Miss Grey by assuring her attacker of her inability to talk."

"If he or she was there to hear it."

"Hmm."

"That bit about the key to the flat . . . McAlister didn't have one on him, did he?"

"No. His pockets had been turned out. His wallet was gone, and if he had been carrying his own key, it was also gone, no doubt taken by the murderer. Any prosecutor will hold that Miss Donovan must have let him in herself. We've only her say-so that McAlister possessed one."

"Which he probably did, since we know she didn't do it."

"It's a pity we cannot bring Lieutenant Blair into our confidence on that point. . . ." He caught my look. "Never mind."

"Leaving Kitty out of it means that Stan let in the killer. He either answered the buzzer or met him outside and they walked in together."

"And in ten minutes or less he is lying dead on the kitchen floor and the killer gone."

"Fast worker," I said.

"Why the kitchen?" he mused.

"It's loaded with weapons."

"So are most rooms in a house. Your conclusion implies a degree of premeditation, and the attack on McAlister looked impulsive to me. It was cold; perhaps they went there to find something with which to warm themselves."

"They get to arguing, McAlister turns his back, gets clubbed with a frying pan, and stabbed for good measure to make sure he's really dead."

"Something that I have noted is that if a woman is murdered, the violence frequently occurs in the bedroom, but when a woman herself murders, she chooses the kitchen as her stage."

"You're thinking of Marian Pierce?"

"As a possibility."

"What's her motive?"

"Unknown at present. Perhaps later you might talk with her and ascertain if one exists."

I didn't like this turn of the conversation at all. I wasn't ready to start explaining to Escott that I had given up hypnotic interviews. I tried for a

change of subject. "You said something about a logical conclusion. . . .
Wanna share it?"

One of his eyebrows bounced. "Yes, well, it has to do with Miss Grey
and the bracelet. I believe she had it all along."

I winced inside.

"And if she did have it, then perhaps she was shot for it."

He left unspoken the implication that if I'd bothered to ask an obvious question last night, she might never have been shot at all.

"It was not in her possession when she was found. One may presume
either a passerby performed a bit of impromptu larceny and escaped, or
that the theft was accomplished by the one who shot her."

"And you don't think it was Kyler?"

"I really haven't enough information one way or another concerning
his complicity to be able to make any kind of a judgment. He is most certainly involved, but we must determine the degree of his involvement."

"And maybe get Kitty off the hook?"

"We may hope as much. Her information was not utterly devoid of
interest." He pulled out a silver cigarette case and juggled with it. The
Nash threatened to cut a fresh road over someone's yard. I put out a
hand to steady the wheel. He took advantage of the break and quickly
drew out a cigarette and put it in his mouth. If we were at home or at the
office, it would have been his less portable pipe.

"Like the part about Shorty?" I asked.

"Hmm." He struck a match.

"You think you know him?"

"I believe I know of him, though I've never actually met the fellow."

"Who is he?"

"A dweller on the fringe, I expect."

I briefly wondered if his damned smoking set him off on a tangent or
if he only used it as an excuse to do so. Either way, the effect was the
same. "Want to explain that?"

"You've met his type before. They never seem to work, but somehow
manage to get by. They bounce from one unpaid bill to another and are
experts at the art of living off the charity of others."

"The crash made a lot of guys that way."

"People like Shorty have always been that way. Their prime concern
in life is usually centered upon their next meal."

"Or their next drink."

"There's that, too, though I believe the addiction to drink is but a
symptom, and not the problem itself. I've seen hundreds of them . . . sad
faces, angry faces, lost faces, and faces with nothing left in them at all.
One wonders where they've come from and where they will go and what
ruined dreams may lie behind their empty eyes."

"That's what I like about you, Charles . . . you're such cheerful company."

"I'm in a cheerful mood," he said.

"So are we headed for this fringe to look for Shorty or are you planning to tackle Kyler?"

"Oh, we shall interview Shorty first."

"Why? About all he can do is back up Kitty's story."

"And perhaps a bit more—if he is what I think he is."

"Some kind of stoolie?"

"An information salesman," he conceded, always one to put a polish on things. "I'm hoping he will give us a line on Kyler—or rather sell us one and thus save us a bit of time."

"So what was he doing giving stuff away free to Kitty?"

"I'm not so certain that it was intentional, but perhaps he was hoping his early warning might have generated some income from a grateful McAlister."

"How many stoolies have you met who were that dumb?"

He decided not to answer and focused his attention on the road and his cigarette. It was still fairly early and the amount of traffic reflected the hour. You'd think they'd all be huddled by their firesides, still gloating over their Christmas presents. If any. The last eight years had been starvation lean for too many people, and the realities rarely matched up with the cozy ideals in the magazine ads. I stared out the passenger window and watched the neighborhoods change from ritzy to nice, to good, to downright hostile, and back again. Escott finally slowed and parked the Nash in a borderland area of good that was starting to lose out to hostile.

Across the street a series of low buildings crowded close to each other, as if for warmth. On one of them hung a painted sign advertising the Angel Bar and Grill. One side of the sign was lighted, the other, with its broken bulb, dark.

Borderland.

"Looks like just the sort of place a guy like Stan would bring his girl," I said.

"One way or another, it would be certain to leave an impression."

A trace of rain hung in the air, just enough to dampen the streets and make us cautious of our footing as we crossed over and went inside. The place wasn't that big, but it was crowded and dim. Escott nodded once at me and went over to the bar. I peeled away and made a circuit of the room, looking for anyone who matched Kitty's description of Shorty.

A lot of unfamiliar faces looked back, reminding me of the ones Escott had spoken of earlier. I shook off the image and concentrated on the job.

Someone tugged at my coat from behind. "Hey, Jack."

I turned, mindful of pickpockets, and wondering who could possibly know me here. No pickpocket this time, just Pony Jones with his curiosity up. Pony did enough bookie business to keep himself, but not so much that he drew attention from the big boys. Escott had introduced us some months back when we were doing some other job. Pony always looked drunk, but never forgot a face or a name except as a dodge to trouble, then he became as vague as his appearance suggested.

Sitting next to him was his half-brother, Elmer, sometimes known as Elmtree Elmer since he was tall and about as tough. He had a brain deep inside that big body, but was lazy about using it, and usually content to let Pony do his thinking for him.

"What'ya doin' here?" asked Pony.

I could almost see all the ears swiveling in our direction. There was space at their small table, so I slipped into a chair opposite them. "Hi, Pony, Elmer. How's business?" As I drew breath to speak, I got a strong whiff of stale smoke, beer, and sweat.

"Good 'n' bad."

"Looks like the bad's winning."

Elmer didn't react at all, choosing to play dense tonight. Pony's crabapple face only crumpled a bit more. "Don't be a wise ass. You still working for that limey bastard?"

"Yeah, he's here with me."

Elmer grimaced. He liked Escott about as much as I liked sunbaths.

"Why are you sitting with your back to the door?" I asked.

" 'Cause my back can stand the draft better than my front. Who ya lookin' for?" His dark little eyes were avid. He knew I was off my usual track in coming to a place like the Angel.

"You wouldn't know him."

His mouth twisted. "C'mon, Jack, no need to dance around all night. Just say a name an' I'll let you know if I know 'em."

"Uh-huh."

"Flat fee, only a sawbuck."

"Try a buck, Pony." Over his shoulder, I saw Escott had finished talking with the bartender. I caught his eye and shook my head once so he wouldn't interrupt.

"Aw, c'mon, I got family to support."

"Fine, go get a regular job." I made to get up.

"Okay, a buck's fine, but only if I know 'em. Cost you more to find out more."

That always went without saying. "Guy named Shorty."

"My sweet Aunt Tilly, you know how many guys I know named Shorty? F'cryin' out loud, some jerkballs even call *me* Shorty."

I gave him my best and broadest grin. Though my canines were neatly retracted, it was more than effective. He tumbled right away.

"Aww, no, Jack . . ."

"Aww, yes, Pony."

Pony shrugged, flashed a yellow grin of his own, and rubbed his thumb against his fingers. I found a dollar and he made it vanish. He kept his hand out and tried to look like a hurt puppy.

"I said more will cost you more."

"This place is too crowded for talk."

He made a show of resignation. "Okay. We gotta flop close by, but I'd have to show you."

I caught Escott's eye again as I stood up. "Fine with me, Pony. I could use the exercise."

"What? Right now? It's cold out."

"Yeah, it'll probably be like that 'til spring."

Elmer was looking alert and damped it down when Pony shrugged at him. He'd accepted his fate and would go quietly. He stood, all five feet one of him a visible declaration of his least favorite moniker, and made a show of buttoning up his coat.

We walked to the door, Elmer leading. Pony behind him, and me ready for either of them to try anything. Escott was there ahead of us and held it open. Elmer paused to sneer at him and caused a minor bottle-neck.

Pony Jones was nothing if not an opportunist. He slithered around Elmer and, true to his nickname, bolted.

8

I got my arm out fast enough, but Pony dodged, and my fingers only brushed his collar. Without thinking, I went transparent and shot right through Elmer's intervening bulk. Maybe he'd attribute his rush of abrupt cold to the winter air. I only hoped that the Angel's other patrons would put the alarming vision of a ghost-man running through him down to morbid imagination and take care of it at the bar.

Pony was little and had some years against him, but he was on his home ground. Though only seconds behind him, I almost missed it as he ducked between buildings. Delayed as he was by having to go around, rather than through, Elmer, Escott was seconds more behind me. He'd just have to catch up when he could; I didn't dare wait.

Pony Jones's small form threaded out the other end of the alley and cut right. By the time I did the same he was out of view, but I heard the slap of his feet against concrete down another turning. When I'd made that one, he'd doubled back to another dank passage. A moment later his footsteps stopped.

I took note of that: they'd stopped, not faded into the distance. He was holding his breath somewhere, banking on the shadows to hide him. As far as I could judge the area was pitch dark—to human eyes.

I picked my way carefully down the alley, my footfalls as soft as I could make them. No doubt in his own ears Pony's heartbeat would drown out their minimal sound. At the far end was a disordered row of trash cans, the tumbled remains of a discarded armchair, and an unidentifiable bundle of odds and ends that might once have been clothes.

The bundle was breathing, very quietly, and its heart was racing. I reached into it, this time getting a good grip on the collar before hauling him up.

"Aww, Jack . . ." he whined, shedding rags and limp sheets of newspaper.

I got my bearings and found we'd all but circled back to the alley behind the Angel. Escott popped into sight less than fifty feet away. I called to him. He skidded to a halt, peering doubtfully in my general direction. It reminded me just how dark it was for him. I kept my grip on Pony's collar and marched him forward. Spill from a distant streetlight defined our figures as we emerged into view.

"Well, well," he said, straightening his hat. "Was there any reason behind your quick exit, Pony?"

Pony dropped into his first line of defense, which was to shuffle with a bowed head and mumble that he didn't know nothin'.

"I see. Then you aren't too terribly interested in increasing this evening's profits?"

Scenting more money, Pony raised his head.

Elmer trotted up, puffing. "Leggo a' Pony," he told me, expecting instant obedience.

Escott got in between us. "Hold off your rescue for just another moment, Elmer, we're conducting a business deal."

"Huh?"

"Deal?" said Pony at the same time.

"Money for information is the usual pattern, is it not?"

Elmer became surly as he cottoned onto the fact that Pony wouldn't allow him to beat up on a potential source of income. "Why'n'cha talk normal, so's a guy knows what you're sayin'?"

"I think we understand each other well enough, Elmer."

"Limey bastard," he muttered, echoing Pony's earlier comment. The last time Elmer had dealt with Escott, he'd spent a few days in jail. He wasn't the forgiving type.

Escott had a smile on his face—a rather serene one at that—when he abruptly hauled Elmer around by both shoulders and slammed him back first against a wall. Elmer yelped in surprise, shock, and pain, cramming it all into the same sound. The impact inspired him to fight back, and he brought a sudden fist up and threw a gut punch with as much force as he could muster. He missed the bulletproof vest by an inch, digging in just below the belt.

Escott hissed once through his teeth but kept his grip. He was still smiling when he bounced Elmer against the wall again. And again, very hard. The third time he let go, and Elmer slithered to the ground and stopped moving.

He'd startled me, because though I'd seen him angry before, I'd never seen Escott lose his temper.

He stared down at Elmer, immobile except for a slight tremor in his hands as the excess adrenaline wore off. His smile gradually disappeared, easing away by small degrees until nothing was left but an impassive mask. Considering the insult, his initial show of teeth was understandable, but the mask I saw now made me uneasy.

"Charles?"

He brought one hand up, fingers spread a little, the gesture a request for silence. I clamped my mouth shut and waited.

He turned slowly away from Elmer and faced Pony. The mask was still in place. If I was uneasy, Pony was definitely frightened. Escott plucked Pony away from me and pushed his back to the same wall, pinning his shoulders to it. Both glanced down at Elmer's semiconscious form and then at each other. They arrived at an obvious conclusion at the same time. Pony gulped unhappily.

"Why did you run?" Escott asked him, his tone dangerously reasonable.

Pony shook his head. "Just wanted to, that's all."

There was more behind it, but Escott let it pass. "Tell me what you said to Kitty Donovan."

"Who?"

"Stan McAlister's lady friend."

"But I don't know . . ."

Escott shook him once so that his teeth clicked, then leaned in close. "Jones, we got off on the wrong foot, though that situation may be easily corrected. What you must keep in mind is that *it can get worse.*" He let that sink in. "Do you wish that?"

Pony shook his head a lot. He'd never seen Escott like this before. His last bit of resistance faded.

Even in the dim light, Escott read it in his face and posture. "Good man. Now tell me what you did and said last night concerning Stan McAlister."

"It wasn't much," he said, licking his lips. "I saw his little twist walk in and park. Thought I'd go over and tell her that that clown Leadfoot had a head of steam up about Stan's owing him."

"Out of the goodness of your heart?"

"Don't be a—ahh, no, I thought I could get something outta her for it, but the kid's green as grass. She din' know what I was gettin' at or that it was supposed to be for sale. By the time I dropped enough hints on her, she'd put things together herself and ran out on me." He raised his eyes, looking for approval. He was disappointed.

"Was there a hit out on McAlister?"

"I dunno."

"How did you find out about McAlister's troubles with Leadfoot?"

"I keep my ears open, as usual."

"Exact information, Pony."

"But there ain't any. You know how it is. The news just goes around. I maybe heard it at the Imperial."

"Which is . . . ?"

"A pool hall. Leadfoot's muscle hangs around there. Sometimes they talk."

"And who else was there?"

"I dunno what you—"

"Who else was looking for McAlister?"

Pony shut his mouth.

"Was it Vaughn Kyler? Was it one of his men?"

"No! I dunno."

Escott's smile threatened to return. "Will I be able to find Kyler there?"

Pony was breathing fast, then he brought it under sudden control. His little eyes lit up with new confidence. "Yeah, you'll find him there— or at the Satchel. He keeps on the move, but you ask around and you'll find him . . . or maybe he'll find you." That thought cheered him—a lot.

"Then I'll be sure to tell him you said hello."

Pony dropped his grin and went six different kinds of pale. He struggled and pushed away. Escott let him go. Pony vanished around the next corner, content to escape himself and leave Elmer to our tender mercies. Maybe he'd return later to pick him up, but I wouldn't want to bet on it.

Not that it mattered much; Elmer was showing signs of waking and might be long gone before Pony got up enough courage to check on him.

"You fight dirty, you know that?" I said as we walked back to the car.

"Pah, the man was hardly worth the effort, but at least we got some names from him."

"Yeah. Which place do we start with?"

"The Satchel, unless you want to risk running into Leadfoot Sam again."

"Uh-uh. I've had enough of him for one lifetime."

"I daresay he might share the same opinion about you."

We drove to an unpretentious neighborhood with modest and respectable storefronts and stuffily closed businesses. The only lights showing at this hour came from an undistinguished two-story brick building in the middle of the block. Cars lined both sides of the street. One of them pulled away as we came up, and Escott pounced on the empty spot.

"You sure this is it?" I asked. "I don't see any sign out."

He set the brake. "An establishment like the Satchel hardly needs or wishes to call undue attention to itself."

That's when the dawn came and I sat up a little straighter. "How'd it get a name like that?"

"I believe it's related in some way to the satchel the collection man carries on his rounds. This particular place is used as a sort of bank; the various funds are added, divided, and dispatched from here."

"Where do they go?"

"My dear fellow, though this city is not very old when compared with others, it does have a quite lively and consistent history of corruption to make up for its relative youth. . . . Use your imagination."

I didn't have to use much, since I'd seen the same thing in other places. Vice flourishes best when it makes regular contributions in the right pockets. We went up the steps together and opened the double doors. Music was playing somewhere inside.

"Wait a sec," I said.

He paused and turned to look where I was looking. A new Cadillac with smoke-dark windows was parked not twenty feet from the entrance.

"I think we've come to the right place, Charles."

"His car?"

"Or one of his stooges. Keep your eyes open."

"With pleasure."

The foyer was conservative: simple white curtains, a plant in a big brass pot, and a square of carpet, but then this part of the house was visible from the street each time the door opened. Furniture was limited to a table holding up a lamp and a chair next to it holding up the bouncer. He had the kind of scar tissue you get from boxing, maybe a couple pounds' worth, and all the rest of him was hard muscle. He gave us a close and practiced look, nodded, and pressed a button on the little table. A buzzer buzzed and Escott opened the next door in.

The parlor was fancier. A big Christmas tree stood in front of the curtained window, buried under sheets of tinsel and glass ornaments. A wire was strung across the wall on that side, loaded with dozens of Christmas cards. At first it seemed odd, but then I thought, Why not? There was no reason why working girls shouldn't celebrate the holidays like everyone else.

In one corner was a phonograph, in the other a radio. Both were on and trying to cancel each other out with competing tunes. A short girl with thin legs was busy sorting through the records and hardly troubled to glance up. Two more were bent over the radio trying to listen, and four others were draped or sprawled over the lush furniture, flipping through magazines or talking. I took a brief—in this case, an extremely brief—inventory of what they were almost wearing and wondered why they even bothered.

Escott removed his hat and assumed a bland smile. I tried to do the same. It didn't impress the girls. None of them took notice when an older woman walked in through a curtained-off archway. She was in her forties, plump, and motherly except for the heavy powder and lip color. She smiled and welcomed us, asking if we'd like a drink.

"No, thank you," said Escott. "We're here to see Mr. Vaughn Kyler."

She shook her head, a study in polite confusion. "There's no Mr. Kyler here, or if he is, then he gave a different name."

One of the girls snickered.

"A pity, since it is most important that I see him. To be more correct, it is most important that he should see us."

Two blonds lolling on the sofa stopped pretending with their magazines and listened in. They'd caught Escott's accent and it was having its usual effect. The closer one put a leg on the coffee table in front of her and made a business of straightening her stocking. I watched the show with interest.

"I'd like to help you, but it's been a slow night," said the madam. "No one's been in here but a few regulars."

"It's early yet. Perhaps if you made inquiries with the gentlemen after they've concluded their appointments . . ." He produced a ten-dollar bill folded to the size of a business card. If my estimate was correct, he'd just bought each of us a pretty good time, or one of us a very good time.

She smiled, still polite, but with more sincerity now that he was speaking her language. "I'll see what I can do. In the meantime, make yourselves to home." She slipped through the curtains, leaving us in the company of a wide range of grinning possibilities.

"How appropriate," he said, quirking one eyebrow and apparently referring to the past of his own home.

"What's your name, honey?" The blond had finished one stocking and was busy with the other.

"Charles," he replied.

"Well, Charles, how 'bout you sit next to me and make yourself to home, like the lady said? You must be gettin' awful hot in that coat."

Her friend giggled.

"How kind of you to be concerned," he responded. "And your name is . . . ?

"Trudy."

"How do you do, Trudy?" He shook hands with her, which charmed her and the others to no end. He acted as though he were having high tea at the Vanderbilts, not in the middle of a brothel surrounded by half-naked women. The others closed in and insisted on introducing themselves as well. I suspected that they wanted to keep him talking. An English accent must have been quite a novelty to them.

I found myself outside the circle, though it didn't matter to me, I was enjoying the show too much to want to be a part of it. Escott went into high gear on the polish and manners. His eyes twinkled and the smile he displayed now was positively lupine in cast. The girls couldn't get enough of him and were visibly disappointed when the madam returned.

Her own smile had faded and her eyes were hard and humorless. "Up there," she said, jerking her head at the curtains. "Last door on the left."

Escott excused himself to the girls. The madam stepped out of the way at the last second and stayed in the parlor. Her gaze slid past me completely as I went by her into the next room.

It was a landing empty of people and short on decor. A table held a load of drinks and ice and a tray of sandwiches. It had one comfortable chair and a table with a phone and nothing else. Escott took it in with one glance and stalked up the stairs as directed.

The second-floor hall was lined with doors, some open, others closed. The varied activities going on behind the closed ones were quite audible, at least to me, and left nothing to my fertile imagination. It was very distracting.

Escott stopped at the last door as directed, raised a hand to knock, then thought better of it. He gave me an inquiring look and I nodded, taking his place. He may have been wearing the vest, but overall, I was

far more bulletproof. I knocked twice and a man on the other side said
to come in.

The room was bright and Spartan compared to the parlor. There was
no bed, but a long table with a double row of plain chairs took up the
middle of the floor. It was covered with some pencils, a ledger book, a
phone, and several thousand dollars in small bills. Standing over it, with
a gun out and covering us, was Kyler's man Hodge.

One side of his face was swollen and bruised up where I'd hit him
last night. From the expression that came over him when he saw me, it
was clear that he remembered the incident as well.

"So Hot Shit's come back for more?" All those bruises gave him an
unpleasant grin. Hell, it'd been just as bad before I'd marked him up. His
gaze dropped to the slash on my overcoat. "Rimik said he'd cut you
good. He's making plans to finish the job he started."

"We're here to see Kyler," I said.

"Yeah, that's what I heard. You got some news on that broad?"

"Maybe, but it's for Kyler."

"He don't have time to waste talking to punks. You give me your
news and get out while you still got legs."

"Oh, stop it, you're scaring me to death."

His grin broadened. "Now, that's an idea."

"Lay off the crap, Hodge. We want to talk to your boss and he'll
want to talk to us."

"He's busy."

"We can wait. The company downstairs is nice enough."

The muzzle of the gun twitched back and forth. "You and your pal
get your butts in here."

"First tell your friend with the asthma to come out from behind the
door."

He did no such thing, but his friend cautiously emerged. She had a
pinched face, thick glasses, and wore galoshes. Between them and her
baggy woolen clothes I could figure that she wasn't part of the house's
regular entertainment staff. She scuttled over to Hodge to stare at us. She
didn't look lethal, so we walked in. Escott's gaze was all over the place,
cataloging it before finally settling on Hodge.

"You . . . shut the door."

Escott obliged.

"Stand over there and keep your hands out. Opal, call the boss."

The girl grabbed the phone and dialed. It took a long time before
anyone answered and she sounded relieved when they did. In a breathy,
little-kid voice she asked for Kyler and mentioned Hodge's name. I
thought he might put the gun away to talk, but he and the girl worked

around that one. He held the earpiece in his free hand while she held the
mouthpiece up so he could speak into it.

His report to the other end was a brief statement of his situation,
then he listened for a time. The longer he listened the more he smiled.

"Okay, honey, put it away." She hung up for him.

"Good news?" I asked.

"You just wait here and see. Opal, finish what you started."

Opal plainly wanted to know what was going on, but was too timid
to come out and ask. She sat at the table and with a nudge from Hodge
began counting money. She quickly went through the stacks, put them in
order, and stretched rubber bands around the bundles she made. Each
bundle was recorded into the ledger. Escott was looking at that book in
much the same way a starving man would view a steak dinner.

Opal finished counting and loaded all the money and the ledger into
her huge purse. And I'd been expecting to see a satchel.

Hodge nodded approval. "Okay, now get downstairs and watch for
him. Lemme know when he comes."

"By myself?" Her face hardened with indignation.

"How else?"

"But those women make fun of me."

"So sit in the kitchen. G'wan."

She wrinkled her lip and nose in distaste and left. Hodge covered his
annoyance with a laugh.

"I swear, she's gotta be the only broad left in this town past the age
of consent that ain't consented yet. One of these days I'll have to screw
her just so she can start understanding all the jokes."

"Mr. Kyler's accountant, is she?" asked Escott with mild curiosity.

"No, his gardener. Who the hell are you?"

"An interested party."

"Gimme a name."

"Escott."

Hodge's eye flashed to me and back again. "So you're the one who
belongs to the Nash. How'd you know to come here?"

"I knew where to ask the right questions."

"Then somebody's been talking too much."

"On the contrary, not nearly enough. Mr. Kyler's made quite an impression on the community hereabouts."

Hodge didn't know whether to take that as a compliment or not.
Opal saved him the trouble by coming in.

"He just pulled up."

"Get the bag and stay behind me. You two go out first."

We paraded downstairs, but turned right instead of left and exited
the building through the kitchen. It faced an alley and we waited there

while Opal went ahead with the money. When she came back, her purse looked a lot lighter and thinner. Hodge told her to wait in his car, and she all but galloped away.

A Caddy rolled across the alley entrance. It looked identical to the one I'd spotted earlier, right down to the smoked-over windows. The front door opened. Chaven got out of the driver's side and came around to check that everything was clear. He joined Hodge and gave us each a quick slap-down search. He found Escott's gun right away and relieved him of it. He nodded to Hodge and we were urged forward.

The front passenger window facing us rolled down. Kyler was on the other side.

"What is it?" His blue eyes were hard and cold. My back hairs starting climbing.

"About Doreen Grey. Someone shot her."

If anything, his expression got even more remote. "I know. What about it?"

"Did you do it?"

Now he had no expression at all. I tried to focus down on him, to pin him fast with my own influence.

Nothing happened.

There was enough light for it to work, maybe I needed to concentrate more. I tried again. "Did you shoot her?"

"No." His gaze raked me, indifferent to the pressure I was putting on.

My muscles contracted all over. His response was completely wrong. He should have been slack jawed or dreamy or anything but in control of himself. On the edge of sight, I noticed Escott glance quickly at me. He'd sensed that something was seriously off.

In the alley behind us, Hodge and Chaven shifted on their feet.

"This one's Escott, boss," said Hodge, pointing.

Kyler's eyes narrowed. "I know."

Escott nodded. "We appreciate your personal attention in this matter."

"I'm off your suspect list for the woman," Kyler told him.

"To be sure, she was under your protection, but we had to be certain. Were you at any point ever able to make contact with her?"

"No. Someone got to her first."

"Do you know who that person is?"

No answer.

"Have you any idea at all?"

He turned his head to look at something in the backseat. When he turned back, his face was a little more animated with something that was a very distant cousin to amusement.

"You figure it out yourself, Mr. Private Agent."

Escott's chin lifted.

"Yes, I do know who you are. You crossed Frankie Paco once and managed to survive the hit he had out on you. You even bumped Fred Sanderson and shifted the blame to his partner."

The inaccuracy of fact was heartening to me. I felt marginally better knowing that Kyler was fallible on some level. On the other hand, it put Escott on the spot.

"That stuff's over now. After tonight, you stay out of my way."

One corner of Escott's mouth twitched. I knew him well enough to interpret it and felt my insides shrink. "Thank you for the warning," he said evenly.

"It's the only one you'll get. I want you to understand that I'm a lot better at this than Paco ever was."

Escott's eyes glittered. "Of that I have no doubt."

Kyler could tell he wasn't getting the reaction he wanted and it annoyed him. "Chaven."

Chaven took one step forward and buried his fist into Escott in a spot not covered by his vest—in this case, his right kidney. Escott bit back a sharp grunt of pain, but couldn't stop himself from dropping down on one knee. I moved toward Chaven, but Hodge still had his gun out.

"You just try it, Hot Shit," he said. "Give me an excuse."

It was enough to make me think twice about starting something that we'd all regret. I kept my movements easy and knelt by Escott.

I hissed in his ear, "You're an actor, goddammit, pretend you're scared."

He gasped a few times. Fortunately his head was down so it wasn't obvious that he was stifling laughter. "It's a bit late for that; he'd never believe such a show now."

"Maybe he'll believe it from me—I don't have to pretend."

"What could you be . . ."

But I lost the rest of it when Hodge loomed close and rammed a knee into my side. The breath washed out of my lungs. My back hit the cold, damp pavement and my head almost followed. I tucked my chin down just in time.

"That's for last night," he said.

I looked up, disoriented by my sudden roll from vertical to horizontal. Hodge was grinning, enjoying his chance to pay me back. His ability to really do damage was limited; my internal changes had toughened me up inside and out, but that didn't mean I was happy just to lie there and take it. In fact, I was pissed as hell and wanted to kill him. What held me back was Escott; I didn't want him getting caught in the middle, but he was already struggling to stand.

"No," I told him urgently. "Stay there and lemme—"

Hodge interrupted again. My teeth clacked together, barely missing my tongue. White light flashed behind my eyes. My body jerked and lay flat.

Vulnerable.

"That's for tonight. . . ."

He'd used his foot this time, and my head had been the football. I had to fight to stay conscious. If I blacked out for even a second or two, I'd vanish into nothingness for who knows how long. Hodge watched my efforts with hot interest. He was waiting until I'd recovered enough to fully appreciate his next trick.

". . . and this is for tomorrow."

He raised his foot, this time to bash it straight down into my groin.

I was tough, but not that tough. Terror and reflex took over. I didn't think about whether the place was dark enough for me to get away with it, or about the problems that might emerge; this was pure instinct. I disappeared a bare instant before contact. His foot plowed through empty air and slammed the pavement. He made a short cry, either from surprise or sudden fear; I couldn't tell.

Now I fought to regain solidity and won, by a narrow margin. My anger helped. I'd vanished for one long second, but reappeared in the same spot with my hips shifted well out of harm's way. Hodge's foot was still down, his arms waving as he tried to get his balance back. With such an opportunity presenting itself, I didn't have to think twice about taking it—the only rule in a gutter fight is to survive. Because of the awkward angle, I couldn't put much force into the punch, but it was enough to do the job. My fist swung up and smashed solidly against his groin.

His scream tore down both ends of the street and made flat echoes up the walls of the alley. He fell and rolled away, legs pulled in, hands cupping and cradling, his face twisted.

I got to my feet. Fast. Chaven had backed off a few steps and drawn his gun. It wavered equally between me and Escott.

A car door snicked open behind me. Kyler was out and holding a fistful of automatic. The expression on his face was a beaut: a cross between fear and anger. He'd obviously noticed my vanishing act and was trying to make sense of the impossibility of what he'd seen. He sure as hell hated the uncertainty.

The only defense I had now was to bluff it out and act normal—or as normal as possible given the circumstances. I hugged my side with an elbow, doubled over a little, and tenderly checked out my jaw, remembering to breathe heavily.

Chaven and Kyler didn't move, each waiting to see what happened next.

Escott understood what I was trying to do and made his own contribution to the illusion. "Are you hurt?"

"Yeah, I'm hurt," I snapped. "That son of a bitch went too far. I hope he's crippled."

Their attention shifted to Hodge, as I'd hoped. "Check on him," said Kyler.

Chaven crab-walked over, keeping us covered. Hodge's replies to his questions were pretty incoherent. Even with my hearing, I was only able to pick up "shit," "goddamn," and "kill 'em," spaced between pain-choked groans. I wasn't about to feel sorry for him, though. He was only going through what he'd had planned for me.

Escott was on his feet by now and cautiously joined me.

"Did Chaven see anything?" I whispered.

"I don't think so, I was in his way."

That was something.

Kyler moved abruptly and with an air of finality. For him, even a bad decision was better than no decision at all. His gun arm went straight and steadied, the muzzle sight aimed squarely at me. I stopped hugging bruises I no longer felt and shoved Escott away toward the possible cover of some trash cans. He was still too close to the line of fire, but if he ducked fast enough . . .

The kitchen door of the Satchel opened and the bouncer stuck his head out, investigating the noise. Curtains in the side window twitched and faces full of speculation peered at us. Opal appeared in the alley entrance and stared, one gloved hand to her mouth.

Kyler saw them and hesitated. They were part of his organization to one degree or another, but witnesses all the same.

There was a subtle shift in his posture and I knew hell was not going to break loose—at least for the time being.

"Chaven . . . get him out of here."

With Opal's nervous and clucking help, Chaven helped Hodge limp to his Caddy out front. Kyler kept us pinned the whole time with his gun and his gaze. I don't think he blinked even once.

Escott's expression had since assumed more serious lines, which was what Kyler must have wanted in the first place. Once Hodge was out of the way he walked over to get one more good look at us. No one was smiling.

"No changes," he said. "Escott, you stay out of my way. Fleming, I don't ever want to see you again. You can leave town or you can die, it doesn't matter to me. You have until tomorrow."

I focused onto his eyes, memorizing them, trying once more to break through their stone-hard surface to get at the mind beneath.

Nothing.

Chaven circled around to the other side of the car and opened the rear driver's door. He bent over some task for a moment. I heard a soft thud and thump against the road surface.

Kyler heard it, too, and started backing away until he reached the car. He opened the passenger door and slipped inside. Chaven was already in the driver's seat and had the motor running. The big Caddy glided off in near silence. Its twin, driven by Opal, followed a moment later. Hodge was in the rear seat and struggled up to the window for one last glare at me.

Good riddance.

Escott had nerves after all, and released the pent-up sigh he'd been saving. "You know," he said irritably, "that rat-faced fellow still has my Webley."

I had to swallow down a laugh that was trying to bubble up. If it got away from me now, I might not be able to stop. As a distraction, I checked to see what all our lifeguards at the Satchel were doing. Even as I turned, the bouncer withdrew and locked the door. The faces in the window disappeared. The lights still glowed, but the shades and curtains were in place again. With men like Kyler, curiosity was a shortcut to bad luck.

"You wanna go home?" I asked.

"That's an excellent idea."

Escott's stride was a little stiff. He absently rubbed his sore back as we quit the alley.

In the road before us lay a large, immobile bundle. I couldn't make it out at first; not until we walked closer, and saw that it had arms and legs.

A man's body.

Kyler had left behind his rubbish for us to clean up.

Escott cautiously turned him over. I caught the bloodsmell, sharp in the cold, damp air. The man had been put through the grinder. Twice.

His face was covered with blood, puffed, badly marked and recognizable.

"Jesus," I said. "It's Harry Summers."

9

ESCOTT'S hand dipped and held still. "He's got a pulse." When he tried to peel back an eyelid, Summers flinched.

"G'way," he moaned.

"Easy now, Mr. Summers, we're friends. I'm Charles Escott, we met yesterday—"

"Lemme 'lone."

"Harry," I said. "It's me, Fleming. Remember from last night? At the Top Hat?"

"G'ta hell."

"Never mind that, just tell us where it hurts."

"All goddamn over."

We spent a few minutes checking him for broken bones and bullet holes. Summers's answers to questions concerning his health were brief and grudging. The only time he showed any energy was when Escott stated his intent to take him to the hospital.

"Uh-uh. I'm not hurt that bad."

"You could have internal injuries, Mr. Summers."

"I've been in fights before. I know when to go in. I don't need to go in."

Escott decided not to press things. "Are you able to walk?"

"What's the rush?"

"We're all rather visible here. Besides, my car is infinitely more comfortable than the street."

The offer of a better place to rest penetrated Summers's somewhat dented skull and he allowed us to stand him up for the short walk to the Nash. We put him in with more care than Chaven had taken hauling him out, not that he was in any condition to appreciate our efforts. Once installed in the backseat, he heeled over on his side to hug his gut.

"You sure about not taking him to the hospital?" I asked.

"Humoring him will be much less difficult at this point. I'd also like to avoid official scrutiny until we find out how and why he ended up in Kyler's company."

"Okay, but if he starts looking really bad, he's going in."

"Absolutely."

Escott drove home and made good time getting us there. He parked out front for a change; the steps were broader and safer than the ones to the back door. I was thankful to see that he'd had my own car picked up and returned from the Boswell. I had a depressing idea that I might need it later.

Summers was reluctant to move, but we somehow got him out and into the house. Escott started the hot water running in the kitchen sink, then went upstairs for medical supplies while I settled our reluctant guest at the table. I made a quick raid on the liquor cabinet in the dining room. Summers needed no persuasion to drink down the triple I offered him.

"What happened?" I asked.

He snorted once as though I was a complete idiot and shook his head. He noticed the sleeve of my coat. "What about you?"

"I trimmed my nails and the scissors slipped. Why'd Kyler do this to you?"

He stared into his drink.

"What do you know about McAlister's death?"

"G'ta hell."

"What about Marian's bracelet?"

He stared at the table.

Escott had returned with an armful of stuff and was watching quietly from the hall doorway. He raised a questioning eyebrow. I shrugged. He walked in and dropped a load of towels, bandaging, and iodine on the table.

The water was running hot now, and Summers eschewed further help as he staggered to the sink to clean himself up. I ducked back to the dining room to find him another drink. Escott followed.

"Want one?" I asked.

"Please. The usual, but leave out the tonic this time."

I opened the gin bottle and poured generously, feeling a strong tug of regret that I couldn't join him. Physically, I could no longer tolerate the stuff, but the emotional need was still there; it'd been a hell of a night and I wanted to get drunk. I handed Escott his glass and tried not to watch as he took his first sip.

He looked past the dining room door at Summers, who was sluggishly washing his face. "He's not going to be especially cooperative," he said.

"I've already noticed that."

"You may have to nudge him along."

Occupied with Summers, he didn't notice my hesitation. "I think we'll get more from him if he works up to talking on his own."

"Unless it takes him all night."

"You in a hurry?"

"Possibly. It's Kyler that I'm concerned about."

"Because of Harry?"

He took another sip. "Consider this: Kyler could have dropped him at any point in the city he wished. Why, then, should he leave him with us?"

"It's a spit in the eye. He's sure he's got us pinned. We're all supposed to be too scared now to go running to the cops."

"And are we?"

He was serious, so I gave him a serious answer. "I'm still thinking it over."

"Are you, now? What about the ultimatum for you to leave town?"

"Or die. Don't forget that."

"Doesn't give one much of a choice, does it?"

"Yeah, and they're both lousy. Kyler must have been scared himself when I went out like that."

"Not that I can blame you for your action. Hodge's last assault was motivation enough for any desperate measure, and you certainly looked desperate. I must compliment you on your decision to pay him back in kind."

"Thanks, I spent hours thinking it over."

"Hodge might well be doing the same thing," he said with meaning.

"You're just full of encouragement, Charles. Hodge I can handle. I know his type: he's garbage, which means he's nothing—it's Kyler that's got me worried."

"Indeed?"

"I'd be a dunce not to be."

"Buy why? What have you to really worry about?"

He'd sliced right into it and wasn't going to be fobbed off with a light excuse this time. Mindful of Summers in the next room, I lowered my voice. "Last night I started showing off and pulled a couple of fast ones with Leadfoot Sam. Mostly I scared the shit out of him, because he didn't know what he was seeing—or wasn't seeing. All he wanted was to get away from me and stay there because he couldn't handle any of it."

"And Kyler is of a different sort than Leadfoot?"

"He's either smarter or dumber, depending how you want to look at things. Smarter because he knows I'm different and could be a threat, dumber because he hasn't the sense to leave it alone. You were standing right there, you saw what was going on."

"Then you did try to hypnotize him?"

"Three times. Nothing happened. I was going up against a brick wall and bouncing right off. The ball drops away and the wall just sits there and doesn't notice a thing."

"The only time that's ever happened to you was with—"

"Yeah, another vampire. I know."

"Is Kyler . . . ?"

"No," I said with much relief. "That's one of the first things I thought of, so you can bet your ass that I checked. He's got a nice, steady heartbeat."

"There's one other possibility—also a rather unpleasant one."

"You've got my attention already."

"It concerns Kyler's mental state. Do you recall the problem you had with Evan Robley a few months back?"

I did, and the memory of the experience was still uncomfortably clear.

"You tried to break through to the man and could not."

"Only because the poor guy went over the edge without a rope. I see what you're getting at, but aren't the situations just too different? Evan was going through a horrible emotional shock and had lost control; Kyler's his exact opposite. I never met anyone who was so totally sure of himself."

"Yes, each an extreme opposite to one another—but both able to resist your influence. It's probably not a conscious resistance either. Mr. Robley was so affected by his grief that for a time he was simply unaware of your presence."

"But that changed later," I pointed out.

"Because Mr. Robley was nearly recovered from his shock. He went over the edge, but managed to climb back. By contrast, Kyler is in a similar mental state, but able to function as though he were normal."

It sank in. Deep. And I didn't want it.

"I hasten to add that whatever is wrong with Kyler need not claim a severe emotional shock as its source, as in the case of Mr. Robley. Some people are born that way, or so it would seem."

"Charles, any way you look at it, Kyler's loony-bin material."

"Possibly. For now, all we may do is speculate, basing our speculations upon a single piece of negative evidence."

"What? That I can't influence him, so he has to be nuts? It sounds good to me."

"But there's also your personal reaction to the man, as well as my own. Earlier tonight you compared him to a snake. Having met him, I'm inclined to heartily agree with your assessment." He rubbed the spot on his back where he'd been punched.

"Which isn't exactly the kind of hard evidence you like."

"Ah, but I do set much store in instinctual reaction. We may have no conscious reason why certain individuals repel us but it is generally a good idea to give such inner reactions sober consideration. Time and again I have relied upon it and have thus far suffered no regrets."

Like the time he'd followed an amnesiac vampire around to see what made him tick. "Okay, no arguments from me there."

He finished off his gin. "No arguments, indeed. But you may yet end up having to do something to protect yourself from him."

"Are you trying to talk me into taking on Kyler?"

"I'm attempting to set out all the options in my own mind. Verbalizing them sometimes helps. As for having another direct confrontation with Kyler, that is your decision entirely."

I wasn't so sure about that. "I wouldn't even know where to find him."

"To quote our abbreviated friend Pony Jones, 'maybe he'll find you.' "

"Yeah," I said glumly. Which was what I was really afraid of, and anyone standing next to me could get caught in the cross fire.

In the kitchen, Summers had shut off the water and was gingerly dabbing his face with a towel. I finished pouring out a second drink for him and we went in.

Once all the blood had been washed away, the damage looked only slightly less alarming. One eye was swollen shut; the other had a cut over the brow. The rest of his inventory included various bruises in tender spots, a split lip, and a broken nose.

"If you are still adverse to the idea of a hospital, I know of a doctor you may see," Escott offered. He put down his used glass and stepped over to the refrigerator, pulling out an ice tray.

"I'll be all right," Summers insisted, dropping back into his seat at the table. "What d'you want, anyway?"

"You may recall that I was engaged by Mr. Pierce to locate his daughter's missing bracelet. Have you seen it, by any chance?"

Summers gave him a go-to-hell look. Escott ignored it and took the tray to the sink. He produced an ice pick from a drawer and began chopping. "Two people have died over this business so far, Mr. Summers. Vaughn Kyler is involved and I believe you know to what extent and why. We want you to tell us—"

"And get another going-over? No, thanks."

Escott scraped the shards of ice onto a towel, bundled it up, and offered the makeshift ice bag to Summers. He accepted with some suspicion, then cautiously held it to his closed eye.

"I've no wish," said Escott, "to involve the police just yet . . ."

"You leave them outta this, it's none of their business."

"If not, then it is most certainly mine, since Kyler was kind enough to drop you into my hands. He would not have done so if he were at all worried over the information you can give us."

"I don't know anything."

"Then you are at no risk in telling us about it. Why did Kyler do this to you? What did he want from you?"

Summers said nothing.

"Very well, then let's try it this way: Kyler was most interested in lo-cating a friend of Stan McAlister's, and so, apparently, was someone else. That friend was shot today, Kyler claims he did not do it. Perhaps you did."

"I dunno what you're talking about."

Escott's lips thinned and we exchanged a look. Summers was a poor liar. "You know enough to have tried to keep it to yourself; otherwise he wouldn't have expended so much effort upon you. And whatever it is, it's quite important, or you wouldn't have put up so much resistance."

Summers fiddled with the towel to pack the ice into a smaller bun-dle. The crunch and click were loud in the quiet kitchen.

"What did you tell him?"

"I didn't say anything, not to him and not to you."

"I see. So Kyler did not get the information he needed; that or he knew it already and only wanted you to confirm it for him, which you did in some way or he would not have released you."

"I didn't say anything."

"There are forms of silence that may speak volumes to the right ob-server, and I've no doubt that Kyler is an observant man. What did he ask of you?"

"Nothing."

Escott raised one brow at me to let me know it was my turn. The ten-sion that had turned my hands into fists now traveled up my arms and down my back. I was expected to give Summers the works, to put him under, and then steal from his mind. That had been our pattern in the past and I'd followed it freely enough and with little thought. A fast sug-gestion or a brief question for a simple answer wouldn't be good enough this time. Refusal would only prompt Escott to question me, and I'd ei-ther have to not answer or lie to him, and I didn't want to do either.

"If you're done, then I want to go home," Summers rumbled.

"Yeah, we're done," I told him.

Both of them looked surprised.

"We don't need him, Charles, any more than Kyler did."

Escott frowned for a long moment.

"Think about it," I said. "Kyler doesn't care who killed Stan McAl-ister or if Kitty gets the blame for it, that's not his business. All he seems to want is the bracelet. He puts out word that he wants to meet Stan's friend, who probably has it. He guarantees their safety and promises money at the end of things. But someone beat him to the meeting and the friend is shot. It makes him look bad, as though he went back on his word. He doesn't like looking bad. The bracelet's nothing to him now, he's going after the person who crossed him up. He can't get to Kitty,

Pierce, or Marian; they're too well protected, so he picks up Harry to get some answers. It's easy enough to figure out just what Harry knows."

Summers's bruised face got darker.

"Which takes us back to Stan McAlister. You *could* have killed him, Harry. You once took a swing at him for looking at Marian the wrong way."

"How did—" He clamped his mouth shut. He'd assumed, inaccurately, that Marian had told me all about it.

"Jealousy's a damn good motive. And though it's just possible that you could have talked him into letting you come up with him to Kitty's flat, Stan wouldn't have been dumb enough to turn his back on you. But you wouldn't have stood behind him and used an iron skillet and then a carving knife to make sure of the job, you'd have simply smashed his face in.

"But none of that happened. Someone else killed Stan. It wasn't Kitty, all she did was walk in and run out. Not smart, but the kid was too scared to think straight. The only others with a motive are the Pierces."

Summers's heartbeat, already high, jumped higher.

"Sebastian Pierce wanted the bracelet back; he hired us to get it. That could have been a move to provide him the cover he needed to murder Stan and avoid being a suspect. But I don't think he's the type to try anything complicated. Besides, he's got enough money and connections to order up anything he pleases and have the job done right. If his goal had been to kill Stan he'd have been a lot more efficient about it. That leaves us with Marian—"

"No it doesn't. She didn't do anything."

"Then it won't hurt if I speculate about it—just so we can eliminate her from things."

Summers subsided, all but growling, and glared at something inside him. He wasn't going to like what I had to say but hadn't worked up to the point of stopping me before I said it.

"This started out as a theft, with us hired to recover the goods, but Stan was a blackmailer, not a thief. Suppose he didn't steal the bracelet, but that it was given to him? You said last night that she went with you because you did some time. Marian likes to break rules, and going out with tough guys is part of the thrill for her.

"Now, Stan had a nasty little blackmail racket going. While he got into bed with any girl who had some money put aside, his partner was in the next room taking photos of all the fun and games. Later on, he'd show the results to the girl, making a convincing threat, and collect his living from them if they fell for it.

"He had a real talent for finding women who liked rubbing shoulders with his kind of lowlife. Maybe Kitty's one of 'em, I don't know, but he'd made friends with her and she had the kind of highbrow connections that took him straight to Marian Pierce.

"We'll leave out the details of how and when and just suppose that he started blackmailing Marian, but for once, instead of cash like before, he decides to go for something really big and demands her bracelet as payment. He gets it, but it's eventually missed. Her father suspects a straight theft, and we're brought in to recover it.

"But Marian's got her eyes open for trouble and spots us, picking me out to pump for information at the club. When she failed, she went to Stan and told him what was going on, and he ducked out. He didn't go straight back to his hotel, because he had a date with Kitty. I figure he went to the Angel Grill to find her."

"Could he have not broken his appointment and apologized later?" asked Escott. "The man must have surely been in too much of a hurry."

"You've got to include the stuff I got from his partner."

"What stuff is that, specifically?"

"That Stan had fallen in love with Kitty. As far as we've learned, she's the only one he didn't blackmail, though she certainly fits into the pattern he set with all the other women he's known."

"Negative evidence," he cautioned.

I shrugged. "Maybe so, but it accounts for why he didn't rush directly home to the Boswell to start packing. He went to the Angel, missed her or heard she'd left, then drove home. When he did arrive, Kitty warned him off, and he bolted for her place. Now he and Marian had their heads together at the club, but they didn't have much time for talk, and Marian probably had a lot to say. Stan could have let drop where he'd be and Marian decided to meet him there."

"Or Stan could have asked her to follow him."

"Yeah?"

"To obtain ready cash from her," he explained.

I nodded. If McAlister had wanted a quick exit from Chicago, he'd have had a hard time trading the bracelet for train tickets. "Okay, so when Stan turned up at Kitty's place, Marian was waiting for him. They go inside with Stan's key and eventually end up in the kitchen, probably looking for a drink. Now we've got two different things for them to talk about at this point: Stan could be demanding more money from Marian, or Marian could be wanting to get the bracelet back."

"Or both?"

"Either way it ends up in a fight. Stan makes the mistake of turning his back on her and she hits him with the first thing that comes to hand, which was an iron skillet. It must have killed him outright. She might not have known he was dead, but she was mad enough to kill him."

Escott shook his head once, not as a denial of what I was saying, but as a caution not to say it. Summers was hunched low over the table. He didn't need to hear the details of the knifing that had been done to make sure McAlister died.

"She searches the body and finds Stan's wallet and the gun his partner said he carried. She takes them and closes up afterward with his key, leaving Kitty to find Stan, and us to find Kitty. Then Marian runs like hell. She ran right to you, Harry, because she knew you'd give her an alibi. . . ."

Summers had at last worked up to his breaking point, only now he was far beyond just telling me off. He swung the ice-filled towel, using it like a cold, wet blackjack. I'd been expecting something like that and dodged. It hit my shoulder instead of my face. The towel came open and ice exploded across the kitchen. I made a grab for his arms, but he was too fast and, twisting the other way, made a lunge for the counter.

Correction: he made a lunge for the ice pick on the counter.

He got it.

He was too crazy to do much beyond blindly striking out at anything that moved, which included Escott. Escott aborted his attempt to grab at the ice pick and hauled himself back just in time to avoid a stab in the chest. Summers started after him.

"Harry!"

My shout got his attention. He turned and sliced air in my direction. His expression was fixed midway between red-faced fury and helpless frustration. With or without the bruising, he was unrecognizable. My idea of calming him down and talking him into dropping the ice pick was not going to work. He gave me no time to try, anyway, and rushed toward me.

The kitchen wasn't that big a room and only got smaller with the three of us playing tag around the table and chairs. The ice pick made the place positively claustrophobic. I was too busy watching it to see where my feet were going. My leg bumped a chair over while I backed away. It toppled in the wrong direction and I nearly fell on it. Summers turned my distraction into an opportunity for himself and went in under what little guard I had left.

The point of the damned thing missed the underside of my chin only because Summers's foot skidded on a piece of ice. I caught his arm just below the wrist, turned him fast so that I was behind him, and grabbed his other arm. He shifted his weight automatically like a dancer and rammed an elbow into my stomach. It didn't do me any good, nor did his heel when he raked it down my shin and onto my foot.

Escott cut in, fastening onto Summers's left arm. I let go and put all my concentration on the hand with the ice pick, using both of mine to slam it down hard against the old oak table. Nearly an inch of the business end embedded itself into the wood. Summers's hand shot past the handle. He let out with a roar of outrage when it connected with a muffled crack against the hard wood. The roar went up the scale, lost its force, and died off. His knees abruptly gave way and he sank to the floor. The knotted muscles in the arm I held went as limp as wet rope. The incident hadn't lasted more than a few seconds. His encounter with Kyler had left him too sore to fight for long and he was puffing like an Olympic runner. Between gasps, he called us every name he could think of, and a few more besides before finally winding down.

Escott was breathing hard through his teeth. It was more from anger than from physical need. He wasn't used to having homicidal maniacs tearing around his house. "At least we know just what led up to his beating earlier tonight," he said.

"Yeah, he and Kyler both have short fuses."

"I cannot say that I'm terribly sorry over it."

"Is that how it happened, Harry?" I asked.

"G'ta hell," he moaned.

I let go of my grip and stood away from him. He continued to kneel, leaning on the table as though in awkward prayer. Escott released him, curling his lip disapprovingly at the ice pick. With a slight effort, he removed it from the table to put it away in a drawer. He'd forgotten his compulsive neatness for once and the omission had nearly cost us both. Knowing him, he was probably more embarrassed than anything else. I decided to forget about it, since it was a cinch that Escott wouldn't.

"You were saying something about Marian Pierce?" he asked.

"Yeah." I looked down at Summers's bowed back. He was going through hell and I knew exactly what he felt like. "She killed him, Harry. And she told you all about it, didn't she?"

"It's not her fault," he insisted. "None of it was her fault. He was coming after her. The son of a bitch was tryin' to rape her, for God's sake. It was self-defense."

Self-defense. I glanced at Escott and saw confirmation of my own disbelief. It was just remotely possible. Summers had accepted her story, but then he was in love with her; he needed his illusions.

"And she asked you for an alibi?"

"She didn't have to ask," he snarled.

"No, I guess she didn't." I looked at Escott. "My best guess is that when she couldn't find the bracelet she went to the Boswell, but too many people were there first, and she could figure they were all looking for it themselves."

"And from the hotel, she began to follow Miss—McAlister's part-

ner." Escott was still throwing out a smoke screen to protect Doreen's
identity. I was glad of that.

"Or me," I added, "until I finally ended up at the studio. While the
partner and I were busy at the bar down the street, Marian broke in and
searched the place. Again, she came up with a blank."

"And this is where Kyler comes in."

"She needed help, so she called in a professional. We don't know her
connection to him yet, but I'm ready to start looking for it. What's
Pierce's number?"

Escott gave it, his brows drawing together and his mouth falling into
a hard, thin line.

I eventually got hold of the housekeeper, identified myself, and asked
a few fast questions. The news was good. Pierce, his daughter, Kitty, and
Griffin were with the police and had been for most of the evening. Lieutenant Blair was probably doing a thorough job on them, and for once I
had reason to silently bless his zealous attitude.

Hanging up, I drew Escott back out of earshot and filled him in. "I'm
going over to Pierce's. Can you meet me there later?"

"Certainly, but—"

I jerked a thumb toward Summers. "You'll have to take him in to the
hospital, after all. I broke his arm, only he doesn't feel it yet."

Escott looked surprised again.

Excuses always sound self-conscious. I cut off the one I was about to
make and stuck to cold fact. "It snapped when I slammed it on the table.
I felt it go."

The situation was beyond reasonable comment, so he didn't make
one. "Very well, I'll take him in. What are you planning to do at
Pierce's?"

"A little illegal searching. Kyler's had a big head start, but maybe I'll
get lucky. That's the other reason he dumped Harry with us—to keep us
busy while he goes after the bracelet. Odds are he'll want to go after Marian, too, so you'll have to call Blair, and fill him in so he can keep her safe."

"Arrest her, you mean."

Anger that I'd been unaware of and holding down flared quietly with
that possibility. "Yes, goddammit. If she's the one who shot Doreen I
want her put away."

Then his question was suddenly there again. It was the same one he'd
wanted to ask a few scant hours ago in his office when he first knew
something was wrong for me. Telepathy was not a part of my changed
condition, but I could almost hear his "why?" bouncing between my
ears. He was asking for something beyond the simple and obvious need
for justice; what he wanted was an explanation of my personal motive.

There were dozens, but the top dog of them all was guilt. If I hadn't been curious or been made drunk and stupid by the easy power the hypnosis granted me, if I hadn't . . . hadn't . . .

The room seemed very closed up. The silence added to my discomfort. I tried to ease it with talk. "While you're at the hospital, would you check on her for me? See how she's doing?"

Then his face went neutral. I winced inside. That bland front meant he was making all kinds of connections now. Once he saw her, he'd have all the proof necessary to turn them into conclusions. I might as well have tied a ribbon around it as a late Christmas present.

"Certainly," he promised, his voice also carefully neutral.

He had pockets of privacy for himself and was perceptive enough to recognize and respect them in others, but this particular one touched too close to our work to be avoided. He wouldn't let it pass, not later, when there was time for talk.

He watched my face. God knows what he made of the expression there. Probably a lot more than I ever wanted to reveal. I could have stood there all night telling him how I'd lost control, how sheer appetite and self-indulgence had brought me that close to killing her. The words only clogged in my throat.

And the worst part was that as much as the experience had shaken and frightened me, the insistent desire was still there, and it was very, very strong.

It wanted—no, *I* wanted . . .

Doreen had provided only the merest sample of what the full sensual potential must be. I'd cut off far too soon. She wouldn't have minded if I'd gone on; she wouldn't have cared.

She hadn't *cared. The overwhelming pleasure had been there for her as well.*

I wanted . . . to finish what had been started. The craving for her blood was like an itch inside my mind, one that I could reach but didn't dare scratch. Dear God, it wasn't enough that I'd raped the woman, I was ready to do it again until she died from it.

I palmed my car key and walked out.

Quickly.

I don't remember the trip over to the Pierce estate. One moment I was just starting my car and the next I was rolling through a lush neighborhood of tall trees and large, rich houses. It was like the kind of travel that happens to you when you dream, except I was sure I didn't dream anymore, at least not in a way that could be remembered upon awakening. No real sleep, no more dreams. I wondered if the lack could make me go crazy. Or maybe it was like the liquor in Escott's cabinet, with no true need beyond what was generated in my own mind.

If I could only apply that to Doreen.

No. I don't want to think about her.

I managed to blank her and everything else out long enough to get to the right address, then my mind shifted over to safer and simpler areas, like how to sneak onto the estate unseen. Easy for me, not so easy for my car—I wasn't about to leave it someplace and hike.

The entrance to the front drive had big stone gateposts to punctuate the ends of a long brick wall, but no gates hung from them. I ignored the opening and went on to circle the rest of the block. This property took up the whole of it. The brick wall was unbroken until I made my second turning and found another, narrower driveway. Small blue and white tiles set into the cement of the curb spelled out PIERCE LANE. A sign on a second, and less ostentatious, set of gateposts informed me that this was a private drive and to keep out. There were gates on this, the back door, but they'd been left wide open. It was a mixed blessing: I was able to sail right in, but it left me wondering if anyone else had done the same or was about to do so. Kyler was very much on my mind and I was realistically expecting him to be here ahead of me, and if so . . . well, I'd think of something.

For starters, I cut off my headlights and coasted forward, going easy on the gas pedal. I was anticipating a quick walk up to the main house, getting inside, and locating Marian's room. Once there, I planned to quietly tear it apart until I found the bracelet. But that idea got tossed out as I rounded a gentle curve and saw lights on in the guest house.

Some member of the household staff could be doing a little late cleaning up after Kitty's invasion, but I was too suspicious to take that on faith. I swung the wheel over. The car had just enough momentum to run up the curve in the drive and slot itself next to the guesthouse garage. At least it was out of view from the house. Anyone coming in by way of Pierce Lane would spot it, but cars and garages were a natural pair and hopefully the two blended together enough to be overlooked.

I remembered not to slam the door shut and took my time approaching the house.

The kitchen curtains were the kind that covered only the bottom half of the window. They were still effective, since the uncurtained top half was some eight feet from the ground. I got around the height problem by going transparent and floating up.

The lights inside were clinically bright to my night-conditioned eyes. It took a second to blink things into focus. I got a fast impression of the usual furnishings plus one guest sitting at the dining table.

Marian Pierce.

She was still in her collegiate costume; draped on the table was a dark overcoat and her purse. Next to them was an ashtray, and from the nervous way she was smoking, she'd have to empty it fairly soon. Everything about her tense, restless posture howled that she was waiting and impatient about it. As I looked on, she glanced twice at her watch, once to get the time, and again because she'd forgotten what she'd seen.

I could wait around outside until whomever she was expecting showed, but that course of inaction was dismissed as quickly as it came to mind. Instead, I went solid, dropped lightly to the ground, and knocked on the back door.

She probably jumped and froze for a few seconds; it took her about that long before her quick footsteps approached. A bolt scraped and the door opened a crack. I bulled in before she could see me and change her mind.

She backed up until she was stopped by the table and stared as though I were a new kind of fashion in unexploded bombs. "What are you doing here?" she demanded.

"Just checking up on things. What about yourself? I thought you were with the others talking to the cops."

She grabbed at the conversational opening with visible relief. "They finished with me. I got bored and took a cab home."

"So why are you here instead of home?"

"I'm just getting Kitty's things together."

"Uh-huh." I made no effort to sound like I believed her.

She bit back what promised to be a couple dozen sharp replies and decided to go for sympathy. "All right, if you must know, I'm here because this place feels less like a prison than the main house."

"Yeah, the poor-little-rich-girl problem. I know, I saw *My Man Godfrey*."

She ignored my mouth running off with itself and slid to one side until the table was between us. She tried to make it look like a casual movement and failed. She was a lousy actress.

The muscles in my neck went stiff when she dug into her coat pocket, but she only produced a pack of cigarettes and made a business of shaking one out and lighting it. "Carole Lombard had it easier. She was able to do whatever she liked."

"And you're not?"

"Not without everyone knowing about it."

"Everyone being your father?"

"Don't you have some secrets from your family?"

More than you could imagine.

She took a long drag on the cigarette and let the smoke flood upward. "You said you were checking up on things. What does that mean?"

"Driving around and thinking." Or not thinking, as the case had been. "I came up the back way and saw the lights."

"And found me," she concluded, with a stunning smile that put my back hairs up. Our last talk had ended on a decidedly sour note, and she wasn't the sort of person to forgive and forget. "Aren't you the lucky man?"

"That depends on whether or not you can come clean about you and Stan." My voice was going thick.

She didn't blink. She was a very good actress, after all, good enough to give me a serious twinge of doubt when I least needed it. "Stan?"

"You and Stan," I repeated.

No reaction. My doubt grew and shifted, like a large animal stuck in a small cage.

"Escott and I talked to Harry tonight. He told us everything."

"What about Harry?" she asked. Her tone held the perfect balance of puzzlement and irritation.

"Only that I had it right earlier. You got him to lie for you."

"I don't understand." Perfect again.

I was wrong and hating it. I needed to blame someone for Doreen, so I picked out a spoiled brat with bad manners instead of . . .

When I didn't reply, she broke away with a puzzled shrug. As she moved, her gaze swept past her wrist, checking the time again. Whoever was to meet her was overdue. We could be interrupted any moment.

I noticed her things on the table and gave myself a mental kick. She said nothing when I picked up her purse and turned it over, scattering its feminine clutter. The bag itself was still heavy. There was a pocket in the pale silk lining. From it I drew out a small .22 revolver. In the same pocket was a black velvet pouch. I shook it open. An explosion of red and silver sparks spilled into my hand.

Everything turned and returned. It happened that easily and quickly.

The bracelet felt heavy. One person was dead over it, maybe two, God forbid. The thing weighed a ton. I let it slip softly back into the velvet bag.

She'd almost stopped breathing. Her large eyes darted from it to my face.

I ignored the bracelet and opened the gun's cylinder. It held five shots. I pushed the rod. Two bullets and three empty shell casings dropped out, rolling a little.

That got a reaction, but not the kind you could see. It was as if a totally different person had dropped in and taken over her body. The change was sudden and complete; what was so frightening about it was that she still *looked* the same.

The floor seemed to swell under my feet, as though I were on a boat and the sea beneath it were fretful from an oncoming storm.

The doubt in me vanished forever.

I was staring at a killer.

10

"YOU bitch," I said, my voice low and gentle.

Her chin jerked. "I don't know—"

"You *bitch*." And this time it cracked and cut like a whip.

She whirled and ran from the kitchen, trying to reach the front door. I went right through the table and caught up with her in the entry parlor. When my arm snaked around her waist she began screaming. I smothered it off with one hand. She kicked and scratched. A lamp crashed over, followed by the spindly table that held it.

Lifting her clear of the floor, I swung her around, dropping her hard into a chair. Every time she tried to jump up and run, I pushed her back. She got the idea and stopped fighting.

"Daddy will kill you for this," she gasped, out of breath from her one-sided fight.

"Forget him. You're on your own."

"I—"

"*Can it.*"

She did and fell back in the chair to glare at me.

I wasn't impressed. "You're going to tell me the truth or I'll wring your neck. Take your pick."

Something in my face must have caught her attention, because I saw the first sign of real fear in hers.

"It's not that hard, Marian. You can start by telling me why you killed Stan."

"He tried to—"

"Not the crap you told Harry. The truth."

Fear won out over anger. "He had my bracelet," she muttered.

"Blackmail?"

"He had photos . . . of us. He was going to show them to daddy at the Christmas party. He said he'd trade them for the bracelet. So I did."

"But did he give you the negatives?"

"He said he would."

"You're not that dumb."

"He *said* so," she insisted. "I believed him then."

"Was he going to give them to you last night?"

"Yes, but for cash instead."

"At the Top Hat Club?"

"Yes."

"Until you spotted me."

"He put it off when he thought you were after him. He said to meet him at Kitty's and we'd trade there."

"What went wrong?"

She shook her head.

"Tell me."

"I said I had to have the bracelet back."

"He must have laughed right in your face."

"He'd complained before that he couldn't get as much as he'd expected off the bracelet. I told him he could make more money if I paid him in cash out of my allowance."

"And he wanted both?"

"Yes. He wouldn't give it back. I thought if I just knocked him out, I could . . . so I did. It wasn't in his pockets. I couldn't stand it, I—I don't remember what happened afterward." Her eyes were all over the place. Her memory was fine, she just didn't want to talk about it. "I was so angry, I had to have the bracelet back."

"Why?"

"I can't—"

"Yes, you can. Why?"

"I owe money to . . . to . . ."

"Vaughn Kyler? Is that how he's connected to all this?"

She nodded fearfully.

"How'd you manage that? More blackmail?"

She swung a fast arm and slapped me. I blocked her next attempt as though waving off a fly. "Come on, Marian."

"The tables," she hissed.

"What? Gambling?" So she had another little vice to add to her thrill list. "He let you run up a bill, right?"

"I didn't think it was that much, but added together . . ."

"And if you didn't pay it wasn't just showing photos to Daddy, it was things like broken legs and arms."

"That man with the knife . . . he said he'd skin my face."

"So you killed Stan to get the bracelet, only he didn't have it on him. Did you try his room?"

"I couldn't get to it. I had to wait, then I saw you talking with that red-haired woman outside the hotel. I remembered seeing her there before. Stan once said that she was a photographer and laughed about it. She looked scared when she left, so I followed her. I thought—"

"You figured right, she was Stan's personal photographer. What happened after you tore the studio apart? Is that when you called in Kyler?"

"I didn't. His men had been following me."

"You must have all made quite a parade."

"I told them that that woman had the bracelet. They said they'd get it."

"Except Doreen got away. How'd you find her again?"

"She called me. She said she'd trade the bracelet and the negatives for some cash."

"And you met in the park."

"But by then Kitty had come in, the papers were full of the story about . . . about Stan and the woman knew everything that had happened."

"Her name is Doreen," I said, almost to myself.

"I *had* the money, but sh-she was angry. She knew that I . . . I'd . . . that Stan—"

"Then you shot her."

"I—"

"No self-defense, no rape stories, you shot her, Marian."

"It *was* self-defense! She knew about me! She was going to take the money and tell the police no matter what. I could see that in her face. And the kind of person she was . . . the things she did . . . can you blame me? It's not as if she were . . . *she wasn't anybody important!*"

My hands spasmed into fists. A double dose of rage coursed through me like a jolt of electricity, half-aimed at her and half-turned upon myself. I backed away from her, fast. If I didn't, she'd be dead in seconds. To hear her mouth the same idiot's reason that I'd used to justify my own excess of appetite . . .

Not everyone likes a mirror; me, least of all.

In a burst of self-loathing I forced myself to stare at mine. Like all mirrors, she was unseeing and oblivious to what she reflected. With a terrible inner lurch, my rage transmuted into cold, sick horror. I looked at my mirror and understood perfectly all that was there.

"Yeah," I said at last, sounding lost in my own ears. "I guess she really wasn't, not to you."

The shift startled her, but she took it as a good sign, and was quick to land on her feet. "You have to help me, Jack. If you help me, I c-can give you anything you want. I mean that. I can give you anything. Tell me what you want and I'll give it to you."

She'd crawled up from the chair and stood before me, taking my silence for affirmation. I dimly felt the touch of her hands.

"Stop it, Marian."

"It's all right. Believe me. It'll be just fine. I want this, too."

I caught her hands and held them away from me. The action slowed the soothing flow of her promises. "But I don't."

"Maybe not yet, but I can—"

"No, Marian. It won't work this time."

First bafflement as she tried to understand, and then a flash flood of her own rage when she did. "You can't."

"I have to."

She shook away from me. "You won't."

"Get your coat, Marian."

Her initial response was incoherent, but I got the general idea. "I'm not helping you," she concluded. "You'll have to drag me out."

"If I have to."

"No one will believe you anyway. I won't tell them anything."

"You won't need to once they match the bullets up with the gun."

"I'll fight them and so will Daddy. It won't happen."

My head drooped. I felt very tired. "Maybe not, but we're still going in."

She backed up a step. "If you touch me again I'll make sure it shows, and you know what I'll tell them about it. Daddy will kill you no matter what."

My gaze fastened onto hers. She broke off and began again, like a record-player needle skipping over a bad groove.

"No matter what . . ."

I said her name and swept into her mind like a winter wind. Its cold tug pulled me along as well, the blast twining us tightly together.

This wasn't safe. I had to stop before it took us too far—before *I* went too far.

Then Doreen's face seemed to overlay Marian's. We were standing across from one another in her studio. Time had slipped backward to repair broken equipment, to stitch up the torn floor cushions; everything was in its place again.

Doreen wore a shapeless white hospital gown and walked toward me, arms out and eyes closed. Her lips parted, silently breathing my name, anticipating my next touch—the touch that would kill her. The vision was so strong and clear that once more the red taste of her blood lay like fire upon my tongue.

Her body was solid and warm as she clung to me; I traced the smooth, taut skin of her neck. To be linked to this woman, to any woman, to take until nothing remained of them . . . The mere sound of the blood in their veins was enough to seduce me—a single scarlet drop of it enough to damn me.

I kissed and kissed deeply, savoring the beautiful taste of that damnation. It flattened and dispersed and ultimately vanished, leaving behind the soaring desire for more.

She was laughing. Harsh and low, it kept time with her heartbeat.

What to do when she died?

What to do later, when the hunger returned?

A single drop was not enough for the *hunger*.

Laughter—silent now.

Heartbeat—fading.

Gone.

A dead weight lay in my arms and upon my soul.

I let her fall and stared at the wreckage. The hunger would return. It would always be there, ready to tear me apart, destroying others as it fed. An ocean of blood could not fulfill that insistent want. It would never be satisfied.

She was the first. She *had* to be the last.

"No," I murmured. "No more."

It could be controlled if I remembered to control myself. To do that, I had to close off this door forever and walk away.

The fire abruptly died and cooled. The ashes were bitter and dry but felt clean. Maybe I was damned myself, but I would drag no others down with me.

Marian's face jumped back into sharp focus. Her throat was unmarked, her eyes sharp and alert. Nothing had happened, at least not to her. We'd been under for only a few seconds, but time in a dream may be stretched to infinity's edge. I felt as though I'd been there and back again.

Dreams were not lost to me, after all, nor were the nightmares. They were somehow linked to the hypnosis. I'd driven men insane and all but killed Doreen because of it. But no more. The door was shut, and I was walking away.

Marian's expression changed to a curious mix of fearful hope and suppressed excitement. She was looking not at me, but beyond me. The weight of my own waking dragged heavily; the dream memory of a false past left my mind too sluggish to react to the shifting situations of the present.

When I turned, I turned slowly, which was just as well. A sudden movement would have set him off.

Hodge was in the room and held his gun level with my stomach. Marian's overdue guest had arrived at last.

"You're gonna die, you shit," he told me. His voice shook from sheer joy at the idea.

I said nothing and didn't move. Marian was behind but well to one side of me, fairly safe. I could trust him to hit a target six feet away. He could kill me if he liked. Others had tried. I felt oddly calm about the whole business; must have been leftover shock from the dream.

"You hear me?"

He'd come for the bracelet. Once Marian had found a little time to herself she'd let Kyler know she was ready to pay off her debt. It was a convenient payment since it also got rid of a telling piece of evidence against her.

"It's in the kitchen," I said. "In a black bag on the table." The lawyers could still make a case without it. Once the story hit the papers, though, Kyler might find the thing too hot to even break down to individual stones.

But Hodge didn't know what I was talking about. He was so wound up over me that he wasn't listening. His face was fever bright and slick with thin sweat. He was probably still feeling the aftereffects of my last punch. Maybe that was what had delayed his arrival.

Marian was moving, but I didn't look at her. It was best to keep Hodge's full attention on me.

"The bracelet's in the kitchen," I explained.

"You're dead."

"Kyler wants the bracelet, not me."

A chuckle twitched out of him. Kyler had nothing to do with this; Hodge was working on his own initiative. He raised the gun a little, just to dispel any doubts.

"He said I had until tomorrow, Hodge. Do you want to cross him on that?"

"Kyler ain't gonna find out."

"You don't want to take that chance."

Another twitch, this time without any humor behind it. He was thinking hard. I left him to it and wondered about Marian. I couldn't see her out of the corner of my eye anymore.

Hodge made his decision. He was going to chance things. The hard question for him now was where to put the bullet. A grin split his face up as he picked a target and lowered his aim. Considering that last punch, he was not only going to even the score between us, but permanently top it. I was awake now and ready. The timing involved for my vanishing would be close, but once he pulled the trigger, he was in for the surprise of his life. I'd worry about explanations later.

A crack and my head jerks forward.

Teeth rattle.

Darkness and light mix behind my eyes, canceling one another.

Knees strike the floor.

Arm hits something and twists out.

Face barks against the rough pile of the rug.

A spine-cracking thud.

This was wrong. It wasn't the quick, sharp pain of a bullet. It was far more deadly.

Another thud.

I try to crawl away from the agony.

Can't move.

God, my head.

Hodge yells something.

She keeps hitting me. Marian. With each strike, she gasps out some wordless sound. It's ugly, full of hatred and perhaps a lifetime of frustration.

I try to vanish.

Nothing. The pain is too much. I'm paralyzed from it.

Wood. She's using wood.

She's not stopping.

She won't stop until I'm dead.

Dead like Stan. She'd grabbed up a knife and struck out at him, venting God knows what fury onto his inert body when she couldn't get her way.

Dead.

Others had tried to kill me before.

Maybe this time would finally . . .

Finally . . .

"You crazy bitch!"

Hodge's voice. He seemed annoyed. I wasn't overly concerned. Marian's response was mumbled. "Yeah, he's dead, so lay off."

Bless you, my son. After that, pain distorted their voices past the point of understanding, and I drifted out of the conversation. I lay flat on my stomach with one arm awkwardly turned and the side of my face mashed against the rug. My left eye was partially open to a panoramic view of dark blue pile and a low slice of wall. Saliva oozed from my sagging mouth, making a wet place under my chin.

I'd had worse, but not recently, and past survivals give no comfort to current pains. For the time being all I could do was lie dormant until my nervous system decided to pull itself together. Too bad that Hodge had missed his chance at me; hit or miss, a metal bullet was nothing compared to wood. No wonder it was so popular for dispatching vampires.

Something dropped into my field of view with a clatter. I eventually identified it as the small table we'd knocked over earlier—Marian's improvised murder weapon, now discarded. It had looked so fragile then, not the sort of thing I'd choose for such a job. Who'd have thought—

Shut up, you're babbling.

The better to distract me from the pain, my dear. Christ, it felt like an elephant had used my skull for a batting practice.

"Get ready to go," said Hodge.

"Why?"

"Because the boss wants to see you."

"I can't leave. Daddy and the others will be coming back."

"And you want to wait here with the body?"

"Then get rid of it."

It. I'd been reduced to being an *it.* Coming from her, quite understandable.

"I don't work that way, honey."

"But I can pay you. I've got some money with me. It's yours if you help me."

Hodge coughed out a brief, shaken laugh. "Yeah, that's how it all works for you rich bitches. Wave some money and get someone else to clean up your garbage."

"Will you do it?"

He took his time answering and there was an edge to his voice when he did. "I'll do it. Now, get your coat."

"Where are we going?"

"Place by the river. Wrap up good, honey, it's cold out there."

"I'll have to be back soon."

"Don't worry about it." His tone was preoccupied. He was busy figuring out just what to do with me. I expected to be dragged to the trunk of his car, perhaps to wind up in the same spot as Willy Domax and Doolie Sanderson. Kyler probably had a regular assembly-line process for getting rid of troublemakers. Hopefully, it would take time, and by then I'd be in better shape to handle things. Hodge's big surprise would be only a little delayed.

As for Marian . . . she stirred up an army of black thoughts and feelings. Most of them were beyond voice, but not action. God help us both when I saw her again.

If I ever moved again.

Marian was in the kitchen; her heels clacked on the linoleum. Hodge prowled the living room. Something thumped and hissed. Marian returned, attracted by the noise.

"What are you—oh, my God, what are you *doing!*"

"Cleaning up the garbage. Now let's get out."

She started to make another objection, but he must have grabbed her to hustle her along. They went out through the kitchen, not bothering to shut the back door.

Without them for distraction, the pain in the back of my skull blossomed. I tried once more to crawl away from it, but my body was still frozen in place. Vanishing was impossible, negated by the use of wood. Damn it, why couldn't she have hit me with the lamp?

The damage must have affected my ears; something like radio static filled the air. I should have been able to hear their car as it drove away, though if Hodge was using that Caddy with the smooth motor . . . I hadn't heard him arrive, but then I'd been occupied with other things.

What had he meant by "cleaning up the garbage"?

Nothing good; even Marian hadn't liked it.

After a solid minute of effort, I managed to blink one eye. The right one that lay hard against the rug remained shut. I must have looked like Charlie McCarthy on a bad day.

There was a dry, dusty tang in the air. Well, that's what happens when you fall on a rug with your mouth hanging open. I spent another minute messily trying to work it shut.

Stick to blinking, it's easier.

A few years ago, I'd once suffered the all-time mother of hangovers. Even if I'd blanked out the drunken journey, the memory of arrival was still uncomfortably clear. Just short of my bed, I'd collapsed on the floor, spending an oblivious night on its hard, cold surface. In the morning, my joints were stiff and unforgiving, but it turned out to be a good thing not to have made it to bed, after all. When I woke up, my stomach's reaction to the excess abuse was instantaneous and awful. In acute physical agony, since my head felt like a popped balloon, I cleaned it up myself, too embarrassed to call the janitor.

The pain had been just as terrible then, but unlike tonight's fiasco, self-inflicted. Oh, for the good old days when I was too smart to hook up with a private detective.

Agent, Escott's voice automatically corrected in my mind.

This wasn't tracing stolen goods to be returned in triumph to the owner, it was destroying lives. McAlister dead, Doreen . . . maybe, and eventually, Marian.

Part of me was ready to kill her for doing this to me. I wasn't proud of that desire, but it was reassuringly human. No seductive draining of her blood figured in my mind, though. It would be up close and personal, a toss-up between strangulation or breaking her neck.

Babbling.

The radio static was louder.

I tried moving my fingers next. They were farther from my damaged skull. Maybe the nerves there hadn't heard the news, like a snake that keeps wriggling after the head is chopped off.

Queasy thought.

They felt like overstuffed sausages and were about as deft, but they faintly responded. As if in echo, my toes flexed a little. There was hope for me yet. Another month or so and I'd be tap-dancing on flagpoles. I'd embrace it as my new vocation. It probably paid better than writing and was safer than being assistant to a private agent.

Where the hell was Escott, anyway? Surely he'd have taken care of

Summers by this time, unless there'd been trouble at the hospital. If
something had happened to Doreen, he might be reluctant to deliver the
news.

The static had developed into an unmistakable crackling.

Fire.

Mind-numbing panic washed over me for a few uncontrolled seconds
before reason took hold. There *was* a fire, but in the fireplace. It had
been burning earlier, all during that interview with Kitty, and when Marian had returned, she'd merely—

Fire.

As if in confirmation, the electricity failed and the lights went out except for a soft glow reflecting off the slice of wall. My one working eyelid blinked at it stupidly.

They'd left me to burn to death.

Not to death, my mind continued idiotically, they thought you were
already dead.

Panic on top of panic as I tried to crawl out. A wave of heat washed
over the top of my head and down my body. I was pointed toward the
living room, the direction I had to go to get to the door serving the
kitchen. Behind me was the front door, a shorter distance, but it was
closed and perhaps even locked. Hodge and Marian had left the one to
the kitchen open. I had a wonderful vision of myself slithering through
it, tumbling to cool safety.

It was countered with harsh memories of fires I'd covered for the
paper in New York: bodies burned black, limbs stiffened into unlikely
poses of death. Would my brain burn up as well, or would it continue to
live on, trapped and insane inside a charred, grinning wreck?

My feet flinched but could not push me forward; my fingers grasped
but had no strength.

Vanish. Try to *vanish.*

Smoke flooded the room, dimming the firelight. Would anyone from
the main house have noticed by now?

The desperation to wink out and swirl away was strong enough to
fool me into thinking I'd actually done it. I felt the familiar disorien-
tation take hold; the heated air of the room would lift me to the ceiling, then with a swift mental push I'd melt through it into the open
air. . . .

Illusion. I might as well have been welded to the floor.

The place was oven hot and loud. I'd forgotten how deafening a fire
could be. Would anyone hear my screams? By the time the flames
reached me, I would, indeed, be screaming.

My legs trembled. If I could get my arms under me—my toes caught
on the rug, slipped, and caught again.

Move.

My arms spasmed, pushing me forward toward . . . oh, God, I can't go in there.

I was just able to raise my head briefly, long enough to see what hell looked like. Shifting, treacherous gleams of red, orange, and yellow-white danced along the living-room walls. The curtains were thick with flames; spinning clouds of smoke raced from them to the ceiling, filling the house. A forgotten magazine on the floor ignited and burned, the pages curling open one by one as though an invisible hand were swiftly turning them.

Half cursing, half sobbing, I urged my inert body to move before it was too late while begging for more time to recover. Another minute. Just one more minute and I could crawl. Please, God, give me that much.

I flopped and twisted, trying to roll away. The kitchen exit was blocked by the growing fire and my own limitations. I'd have to try for the front door and hope it wasn't locked.

Not enough time. The edge of the rug I lay upon was already being eaten away. The whole thing would soon catch and go up, enveloping my clothes . . . me . . .

If I could scream, I could move. Don't waste the energy on anything else.

Coordination was too slow to match my level of terror. I got a water-weak elbow under me and pushed. It slewed me to the right. The worst part was trying to lift my head; the neck muscles weren't up to holding it for more than a second or two. It dragged on the floor like an anchor.

Glass shattered somewhere, probably from the heat. I didn't really care; I was too busy.

Christ, the door was miles away. Maybe if I rolled toward it . . .

I writhed, thinking of that damned headless snake again.

Another glassy crash. Air rushed in, feeding the fire.

Someone shouted. My name, I thought, but I couldn't tell. My imagination had fooled me before.

More air. A sea of it rolled in; smoke dense enough to cut rolled out.

My name.

Someone coughing.

My name.

Blinded by the smoke, he blundered into me. Frantic hands clawed, randomly seized one arm, and tugged. I pushed in the same direction. Inelegant, but it worked. He cursed and coughed and damn near tore my arm from its socket. We made progress. The door loomed close, gloriously close. My head thumped against the threshold, reminding me of the original injury, but I didn't care anymore. We were out of the furnace. One last pull and he dragged me clear of the porch and onto the hard ground.

Inexplicably, he began beating on my ankles with his hat. I understood why when a whole new kind of pain shot up from them and blasted through the top of my skull. Stung to movement, my legs kicked and flailed and generally interfered with his efforts. In spite of this, he managed to smother the flames before they got out of hand.

He dropped next to me, doubled over with hoarse coughing.

God looks after fools, after all. Thanks, Boss.

"Are you talking to me?" Escott wheezed, his eyes streaming and red from the smoke.

I hadn't realized I'd spoken aloud. "Not exactly."

"Good God, what happened to you?"

Having no need to breathe regularly, I hadn't taken in the smoke and was better able to talk, only I didn't feel like doing much. "I was dumb enough to turn my back on Marian."

"Is she in there?" He made a half start toward the burning house.

"No," I said quickly, waving him down. "Got away."

"Where?"

Now was not the time for explanations. We had to be somewhere else and fast. "We gotta get outta here, Charles. Are you able to walk?"

"Are you?"

Details, details. "How far?"

He rubbed at his eyes and shook his head. I couldn't tell if he was coughing or laughing. "Hang about."

I wasn't in any condition to do much else. He staggered away, returning a short age later to improvise a new driveway over the grounds with his Nash. He parked a narrow yard from where I lay and opened the passenger door. After that, it was a simple matter of hoisting me inside.

"The Stockyards?" he asked, sliding behind the wheel. First aid for me always meant a long, healing drink.

"The river."

Which is full of water, he seemed to be saying. *Not your preferred draft, old man.*

"Just get us moving, Charles. I'll tell you about it."

He coughed again, but shifted gears and hauled the wheel around. As we passed the guesthouse garage, I nearly choked on a suppressed growl of outrage.

"That screw-faced son of a bitch stole my car!" A ridiculous reaction, considering what we'd both just been through, but it was one way of draining off some of the built-up stress.

"Which screw-faced son of a bitch?" he asked, managing to sound dignified despite his cough.

"Hodge. He came here tonight. When he left with Marian, they must have taken my car."

His face was one big question mark.

Right. I owed him—among many other things now—an explanation, or at least part of one. In a few short sentences I covered the disaster, omitting only the details of what happened when I tried to hypnotize Marian. It left a noticeable gap open to questioning, and Escott jumped straight into the middle of it.

"How on earth was Hodge able to sneak up on you?"

I shrugged, as though uncertain myself, and hoped that it looked convincing. "I was preoccupied with Marian, with getting her to talk."

He made a noise indicating that he understood and I belatedly realized that he thought I was referring to a hypnotic question-and-answer session. I let the misinterpretation stand. For the moment, it was better than the truth.

"She knew that I knew too much and jumped the gun—Hodge's gun, to be exact—by lambasting me with that table," I continued. "She couldn't have been listening to him. She went crazy like she did with McAlister. Hodge stopped her. I think it shook him up to see her like that."

"I daresay. Perhaps he even prevented her from inflicting more serious damage than she did."

"Or he was mad that she cheated him of the satisfaction of doing it himself. It would have been so much simpler if she'd just waited and let him try to shoot me."

"Most unfortunate that she did not. Are you better? You sound better."

I opened and closed my hands, evidence of my physical recovery. My singed legs *hurt*, but I'd soon be able to take care of them. The emotions would take longer, perhaps a lifetime, even by my changed standards. "I'm getting control again. It takes a little time and I didn't have any before. How'd you know I was there?"

"I didn't, nor did I look for you since I did not see your car. That may have been why Hodge stole it. As for why he set fire to the place . . ."

"To confuse and distract, like stirring an anthill with a stick. It leaves the ants running all over trying to put stuff back in order, and in the meantime they forget about the stick."

"Or its possible return."

"Okay, so if you weren't looking for me, then how . . . ?"

"I heard you," he said in a muted tone that made me feel quiet as well. My throat wasn't aching because of the smoke. "Then I saw you through the front window, which I had to break to open the door. I think you're aware of the rest."

"Thanks for pulling me out, Charles."

Shows of gratitude always made him uncomfortable. "Well, good help is hard to come by," he demurred. "I've but one request."

"Anything."

"Don't do that again."

I started to make a light reply, then for the first time noticed how tightly he gripped the steering wheel. His eyelids were jumping around and I could almost feel the nervous energy coming off him. He was putting up a calm front, but it was plain to me that I'd thoroughly scared the shit out of him.

"Scout's honor," I said humbly.

He nodded once, to close the subject, and switched to a new one. "You said the river. Do you think she's getting away via the facilities offered by the IFT warehouse?"

"That's my best guess. If she's not there, then I don't know where she'll be. And it's not a getaway or she wouldn't have questioned him. All she planned to do was to turn over the bracelet, then I showed up and threw a monkey wrench into the works. Hodge had orders to take her out. Since she didn't know what they'd done to Harry, she was just stupid enough to go with him."

"So Kyler could sort her out about shooting Doreen?"

"Yeah, only she might not survive the experience."

"Would he go so far?"

"What do you think?"

For an answer, Escott stepped on the gas.

11

THOUGH it had been a solid and busy six months since his last visit to International Freshwater Transport's warehouse, Escott's memory needed no prodding on how to get there. He picked out the fastest possible route, pausing only to chafe at stop signals. At this hour most of the intersections were empty, so the wait was doubly hard, but he wasn't about to attract attention by running through them. A curious cop was the last thing we wanted.

I was having trouble deciding if the tightness in my gut was due to Marian's assault or the situation we were walking into. Maybe it was a bit of both. Now that I had time to rest and take inventory, more aches stood up to be counted, especially along my spine. My lower legs and head were still the worst; I'd have to tend to them before anything else.

Eyes shut to concentrate, I tried to vanish. Except for a faint shiver running over my skin, nothing happened. My head throbbed in protest.

Damned wood.

I waited a few more blocks and tried again, failed, and waited some more. Each attempt got me farther down the line; on the fourth try, I finally melted away into the air.

Escott made a choking sound and the car swerved. It startled me back into solidity.

"What's going on?" I grabbed the arm rest for balance.

"Would you mind giving a fellow a little warning before you launch into that bloody Cheshire cat routine of yours?" he complained, looking very put out.

He usually held things in, but events were also eating him up from the inside. I couldn't blame him for letting it show for once. "Sorry. I have to do it again. Consider yourself warned."

He grunted and kept his eyes on the road.

I faded into a wonderfully numbing nothingness better than any salve, and stayed there. The only problem was trying to hover in one spot: I tended to keep moving forward whenever the car braked. The windshield glass and metal body of the car helped to confine me inside; the trick was remembering to hold in place on my end of the seat. It wouldn't do to distract Escott further by bumping into him with an abrupt rush of cold.

"We're here," he announced, his voice made distant by my invisibility.

I was reluctant to return, but when I did, things didn't hurt nearly so much. The skin on my legs had stopped burning and my head felt only slightly tender. A day's rest, a stop at the Stockyards, and I'd be . . .

"They're not exactly secretive, are they?" he commented, drawing my attention to the front of the warehouse.

"The gang's all here," I agreed.

Parked along the street were two identical Caddies and my Buick. In this drab neighborhood they stuck out like birthday cakes at a funeral. A light was on in the warehouse office, the rest of the windows were dark. If my heart had still been working, it'd have been trying to thump its way out of my chest.

"Anything wrong?"

I nodded. "Not twenty minutes ago I wanted to kill her; now I'm here to play Douglas Fairbanks and rush to her rescue."

"After what you've been through, your reluctance is understandable." Escott had one hell of a gift for understatement.

"It's more than reluctance. I'm ready to say to hell with it and leave her there."

"And will you?"

That question demanded more thought than I had time to give it. "I want to, but if I stay, then you'll go in instead, won't you?"

He said nothing, though for him it made for an eloquent speech. He'd go, all right, with or without me, and I wasn't about to let him do anything so crazy.

I laughed once, and not because I was happy, then started shrugging out of my overcoat. Escott's borrowed suit coat went, too. The cold wouldn't bother me for some time yet, and I wanted to be free to move. I tore off my rumpled tie and tossed it on the pile.

"Are you sure you're in shape for this?" he asked.

"Why? What do I look like? No, don't answer that. Let's just say that I'm in better shape than they think I am. You got a gun?"

"Yes." In addition to the stolen Webley-Fosbury, he owned a much smaller snub-nosed Colt revolver, which he started to draw from his coat pocket.

"Hang on to it for yourself," I told him. "If any rats get past me, you'll need it."

He saw the logic and kept the gun. "Good hunting."

"Break a leg."

We got out at the same time, swinging the doors shut, but not letting them latch. The plan was for me to go in first and scout around for the best opportunity to get Marian out. If it didn't exist, then I'd have to make one. Escott was to back me up if it became necessary. Knowing how crazy Kyler and his stooges got when crossed, I was going to be damned careful.

Though they looked deserted, I checked each of the cars to make certain of the fact. Escott followed and we ended up crouched in the same patch of shadow cast by one of the Caddies.

"I'd like to cut off their lines of retreat," he whispered.

"As long as it's quiet."

He flashed a rare smile or a rictus grin, I couldn't really tell, and eased open the driver's door. He felt under the dashboard a moment and something snapped in his hand. He darted to the other Caddy, performed the same operation, and returned. "That should put them in the shop for a while," he said.

"What about my car?"

"I'm hoping we may simply drive it out. Have you the keys?"

"Still in my pocket. Hodge must have hot-wired it."

Ideally, we wanted a clean getaway without any legal fuss. Escott was ready to use his gun, but it'd be better for us if he didn't. It was up to me to make sure things stayed quiet.

I crept up to the front door of the warehouse, feeling rather vulnerable in the dim light thrown out by its overhead bulb. I listened for some time, my ear pressed to the crack between the door and jamb and heard nothing. Shrugging a negative back at Escott, I pointed to myself and then toward the door. He gave me a thumbs-up in acknowledgment, turned gray, and ceased to exist.

Filtering through the same narrow crack was easy enough, then I made a quick sweep of the small room. It was empty and hadn't changed much since my last visit, as I discovered after materializing. An extra layer of grime and an oil heater had been added, but nothing more interesting. The second door leading into the warehouse proper was shut. I listened there for a time and eventually caught the faint sound of voices. One of them seemed to be Hodge's, but I wasn't sure.

I quietly unlocked the front door for Escott, then slipped through the inner door myself. I stayed invisible and felt my way around to what I hoped was a concealed corner and faded in slowly, eyes wide, and ears straining.

The place was vast and dark and the high ceiling caused the voices to echo deceptively, though I eventually pinned down their direction. I took my time approaching, half of it in a semitransparent state to avoid making sound myself. This lasted until I got a third of the way into the warehouse and ran into a familiar obstacle. The place was built well out over the river to expedite the transfer of goods to and from cargo ships. It was fine for the ships, but lousy for me with my inherent problem with running water. I'd be able to vanish easily enough; coming back again was the hard part. To do that, I had to be over land.

I went solid and tiptoed forward, then had to dig my heels in and really work. The resistance was like trying to push a long, heavy curtain back from the bottom, hard to get started and reluctant to keep moving. Once I was well out over the river I was all right, but as they say, the first step's a lulu. At least now my hearing wouldn't be handicapped.

They were at the far end of the long line of crates, using only a single work light, the kind with a handle and cord at one end and a hook on the other. They'd hung it awkwardly onto the lip of an open crate. It made a harsh fan of localized glare; odds were, they'd be fairly night blind outside of it. I moved closer.

Chaven was busy digging through the crate; stray drifts of excelsior littered the floor around him. He strained and lifted out a hunk of new-looking metal. I didn't know what it was beyond the fact that it looked like the internal part of a larger machine and that it was obviously heavy. He tossed it ponderously onto the floor with other, similar parts. The light on the crate shook as he worked. Shadows jostled one another.

"That enough?" he asked, straightening.

Kyler stood just behind the light and was difficult to see. "More."

"But that's over a hundred pounds."

"More. Those things get buoyant. I'm not risking a floater."

"Have a heart, my back's killin' me." But Chaven began digging again, pulling out piece after piece.

In the floor a couple of yards behind him gaped a trapdoor into darkness. Hodge sat on its edge, his legs resting on steps going down under the warehouse. I heard and smelled water. "You can help," Chaven said to him. "I've done my part." Hodge patted the spot under his left arm where his gun was holstered. I went very still and cold.

"If you want to stay here all night that's your business. There, that's two hundred pounds at least. Okay?"

"Take it down," said Kyler.

"Huh," Chaven bent, picked up a part in each hand, and walked up to Hodge. Hodge obligingly moved over to give him better access to the steps. Chaven grunted "huh" again and descended. He was gone for about two minutes, then returned empty-handed to take away two more parts.

I slipped back the way I came and made a fast and hopefully quiet round of the stacks. When I moved toward the light once more, I was behind Kyler, all but looking over his shoulder. The work light wasn't in my eyes so much from this angle. Now I could see Marian, a dark form in her long coat.

She wasn't moving. She lay on her side, huddled compactly at the foot of a tall packing case. It was the same one they'd backed me up against only last night. A ball of ice formed down in my stomach and rolled a little. Closing my eyes didn't help. She was still there when I opened them.

Hardly aware of it, I walked up to Kyler and gave him a solid punch in the kidney, one that Escott could appreciate. He dropped almost too fast for me to catch him, but I managed and held him up in front of me.

Hodge was alert enough to notice and react. He drew his gun and jumped to his feet, trying to squint past the light to his boss. Kyler almost jabbed my gut with his elbow, but he didn't have enough force or follow-through. In return, I slapped the side of his head. Once was all that was needed, then he had to have my full support to stand.

"Boss?" Hodge skirted the trapdoor. He saw me, or part of me. The light was still in his eyes, but he had enough of a target to aim at. He held the gun ready.

I made sure Kyler was entirely in his way. "Put it up, Hodge, not unless you think you can shoot through your boss."

"Who . . . ?"

"Besides, he said I had until tomorrow . . . remember?"

The stunned look on his face indicated that he did. "You go to hell," he said, but there was a crack in his voice. He was plenty scared.

"Not this time."

I pushed Kyler ahead of me. He tried to fight, but I had a solid grip on his arms and was practically holding him off the floor. Hodge took a better aim at me but Kyler stopped him.

"Get behind him, you jerk! Shoot him from cover!"

Hodge's reflexes were good. Two fast steps, and he was swallowed up in the shadows between the stacks. I dragged Kyler out of the fan of light and shook him the way a kid shakes a rag doll. He was too dazed to resist as I went through his pockets. Right away I found his gun and pulled it. I didn't have enough hands to use it and let it drop to the floor. In his inside pocket with his wallet was the black velvet bag. It still seemed to weigh a ton.

He recovered quickly and just enough to be inconvenient. I shoved the bracelet away and threw him toward the trapdoor. Arms flailing, he tumbled right into it with a brief yell. Another yell in another voice matched him for surprise and pain. Chaven must have been coming up the stairs when Kyler fell through onto him. They made a lot more noise rolling and crashing all the way to the bottom, and then they stopped making noise altogether.

I forgot them when Hodge fired his first shot at me. I was nearly deafened by the roar, but felt nothing. Seeing me come back from the dead must have left him with a bad case of the shakes. So much the better, since I wasn't ready to vanish just yet.

Gray smoke from the gun hung in the motionless air, giving away his hiding place. I went low and scuttled over to Marian. He fired again, missing completely.

"Boss? Chaven? You okay?" He sounded very worried. I didn't think it was for their skins, but for his own. Armed or not, he didn't want to face me by himself.

Neither of us heard an answer from the trap.

I turned to Marian, checking for a pulse, but I was way too late. It was harsh to think, but the only honest regret I felt was for her father.

"This is your work, Hodge," I heard myself shouting. The echoes filled the place, chasing each other into nothing.

"I did what I was told," he shouted back.

"Kyler gets his turn later."

Shot.

He'd moved. The bullet creased air next to my left ear and tore into the case behind me.

Shot.

But by that time I was moving as well and dropped flat.

Shot.

One in Marian's heart and five embedded in the crates. If he carried a round ready in the chamber, it meant he had at least two more bullets left, maybe a lot more if he had a spare magazine. Not that it mattered much to either of us in the long run. He could be packing a Thompson with a full drum and it wouldn't help him. But I couldn't afford to let myself be hit any more than a normal man could, not while I was over water.

No shot. He must have realized he was running short. Good. I didn't want to have to remind him and possibly tip my own hand.

Silence, except for his breathing, then came a stealthy step and a shifting of cloth. He was on the other side of the stack from me and creeping forward. He stopped for a long time to listen and perhaps puzzle out why I'd left Kyler's gun behind. I hadn't thought of it at the time, but now I could see that it was turning into an excellent piece of bait.

At the far end of the warehouse a door creaked open.

That had to be Escott, drawn in by the shooting.

Hodge jumped into the open, intent on Kyler's gun. I broke away from the stack and went after him.

He heard me charging up, whirled, and got off one more shot.

It went wild. Before he could trigger another, I tackled him, and we fell flat.

His head thumped against the floor and the whites of his eyes showed for a few seconds. He gagged, trying to recover his lost breath. He still had the gun, though, and enough presence of mind left not to use it until it could do him some good.

We were matched for weight, but I had him on raw strength and was able to immobilize him easily enough. His reaction was frustration, not surprise, as he kept struggling and got absolutely and utterly nowhere. I had one hand holding fast onto his gun arm. It'd be a simple matter to crush his wrist. . . .

Instead, I bent his hand around, forcing it in the direction I wanted. When he realized what I was doing, he thrashed and yelled, throwing all his desperate energy into a last scrabbling fight for life.

The gun was at half cock and as I found out when I pressed my finger on top of his trigger finger, had one round left. The sound was so loud I didn't really hear it, the muzzle flash blinded, the smoke burned.

I didn't know which I'd remember the longest: Hodge's terrified shriek, or the look on his face as it happened.

Limbs twitching and hands shaking, I stood away from him and swallowed back the laughter that surged up like a rush of bile in my throat. It helped when I turned my back to him. The exit wound was very bad and where most of the bloodsmell came from. Despite the evident and total finality of that wound, he still looked alive.

I will not regret this. If I had to, I'd do it again.

A few steps and I was leaning against a crate, hiding my eyes from it all. The laughter hung heavily in the back of my throat, threatening to either choke me or turn into a sob. It wasn't finished; more work remained to be done. There was yet one more suicide to arrange, maybe two.

First I groaned in protest, then, as though a switch had been thrown, everything shut down at once. The laughter died to nothing; the sickness forming in my gut faded away. I looked around with new eyes and found corners to be just a little sharper than they'd been before, and colors were brighter. The light from the lamp was both harsh and beautiful. I'd turned crazy cold—a mechanical man about to perform an unpleasant but necessary job. This wasn't vengeance—no more than a butcher is vengeful against the animal he carves up.

I drew a long breath and let it filter slowly out as I walked past Marian and Hodge and closed my hand over Kyler's gun.

"Jack?"

He'd come up softly. I was too wrapped in my own silent hell to have noticed his approach but was not surprised to see him. Escott was my friend and I could trust him to be sensible in an emergency. He saw Marian right away and went to her and learned what I had learned. He shook his head and said something, but I didn't quite catch it. Then he turned around and saw the rest of the place.

He stared at Hodge's body lying at the narrow end of a spray of blood and brains. The gun was loose in his hand now, but still pressed to his temple. That was wrong. I had to change the position slightly, to pull his hand back a bit to allow for the recoil of the shot.

"I'm taking care of it," I told Escott. "Don't worry about anything." In my own ears I sounded extraordinarily calm, as though I were doing a household chore for him. Like taking out the garbage.

Now he stared at me; I nodded back reassuringly and stooped to adjust Hodge's gun and arm. There, that looked more natural.

"We have to leave, Jack." Escott did his best to match my calmness, but I knew better. His heart was racing fit to burst. My own was, or rather, my own wasn't. . . .

Never mind that.

I smiled at him. "In a minute. This won't take long."

Cheerful. Almost. That's what it sounded like. I wasn't feeling at all cheerful, but then I wasn't feeling, period.

I walked to the trapdoor and started down the stairs.

Below the reinforced flooring of the warehouse were the dozens of thick cement pillars that supported it. They marched away in even rows in every direction, their tops wrapped in dirty shadow, their bases sunk deep in the water. The river had left them stained and stinking. The stairs led to a broad wooden landing that rose and fell with the lap of water. Tied next to it was a sleek inboard; on its deck sat an open crate. It didn't take much genius work to figure out where Chaven had put the heavy machine parts. Once the lid was nailed down, they had only to take a quiet cruise out to deep water and Marian's body would disappear forever.

The closer I got to the water, the higher my back hairs rose. For a few seconds I had to fight to stay solid, so overwhelming was the instinctual urge to vanish and draw away to the safety of land.

Kyler and Chaven were still sprawled on the landing. Chaven was groggy but trying to pull himself together. Kyler bled from a cut over one eye and was rumpled all over, almost comic in his disarray. He squinted up at me without recognition. The light was bad here for human eyes. To him, I'd be a silhouette against a slightly lighter shadow.

"Hodge?" he asked, doubtful.

"Hodge shot himself." Not quite true, but details like that didn't matter now. "You're going to shoot yourself as well, Kyler."

"What the hell . . . ?" said Chaven.

I raised my hand high so they could see what was in it. "I brought your gun along to do the job." Had I been capable of laughter, I might have laughed at their expressions.

Chaven woke up very fast and clawed inside his coat. I centered Kyler's gun on him.

"Jack." Escott's voice.

"In a minute," I called back.

"You've no time left to make a proper job of it," he reasoned. "We have to go while we can."

That made a lot of sense, but I hated to leave the work half-done when only another minute was all I . . .

Chaven got his gun out and fired. His aim was off because of the darkness and his own fear. The slug sang through my arm. Negligible damage anywhere else, sheer disaster here. I dropped Kyler's gun, staggered back against the rail, and forgot about everything but the necessity of remaining solid.

Shadows grew lighter, threatening to turn gray and vanish altogether. My hand was going transparent; I willed it back, ordering it to *hold* on to the stair railing, and not to slide through.

"Do you see? Do you see?" Kyler's voice. What the hell was he talking about?

I flickered back and forth between pain-filled reality and numbing dream. Escott shouted my name but I couldn't break my concentration to answer. Kyler and Chaven were limping away, stumbling into their boat, and I was helpless to follow. While Kyler fumbled at the ropes, Chaven took aim for a second, more careful shot. He hit his target, but for him the timing was ill judged, catching me in a semitransparent phase. The bullet whizzed right through my chest and smacked into one of the steps.

Before he could fire again, another gun went off. The roar so close above almost buried me in sound. It was all I could do to just hold on to the flimsy stair rail. I'd lost sight of everything except the bottomless black water that seemed to swell closer. . . .

Escott grabbed my shirt collar and hauled me back. Kyler and Chaven swung into view once more. They were both in the boat now and blue smoke belched from it as Kyler got the motor started. He was doing all the work; Chaven was hanging on to the box and not doing much of anything besides cursing.

Kyler gunned the boat and it glided rapidly away from the landing. He held a straight course between the tall pillars until he was free of them, then turned onto the river and was gone.

"You had time for another clear shot, Charles," I said. "Why didn't you take them?"

Escott gave no direct answer to my question. "We have to go, Jack."

The searing heat in my arm dissipated and with it the imminent threat of vanishing. Still sensitive to the pressure of the water all around, I was unable to do more than crouch on the stairs. Escott eased past me and retrieved Kyler's gun. He slipped on the safety and dropped it in his pocket. Coming back up, he held his hand out to me.

"Come along, old man. It's very cold down here or have you even noticed it yet?"

With his help, I found my feet and we trudged up and emerged from the trapdoor. He steered me well around the awful tableau framed by the work light, and we headed toward the distant front door.

"Are the cops coming?" I asked.

"It's best that we leave before we find out," he said, not really answering again. What was the matter with him?

The inner door was open and he left it that way. He did the same thing with the outside door, leaving it wide. We stopped at his car and he had me put on my overcoat. As he'd guessed, I hadn't noticed the cold. I felt nothing at all.

He took me to my own car and asked if I could drive it. It seemed an odd question, but I said yes and got in. He told me to go straight home and promised that he'd be following right behind if I needed anything. I shook my head, a little puzzled, but strangely touched by his obvious concern.

We drove off quietly, obeying all the speed laws and traffic stops. For me it was another dream ride like the trip I'd taken earlier over to the Pierce house. I pulled up to my usual curbside spot in front of Escott's old three-story brick house. Escott broke away to park in the narrow garage behind the building. He reappeared quickly enough to walk with me up the steps and unlock the door.

The place was warm and, after the fresh outside air, stuffy with the smell of his favorite pipe tobacco. We shrugged out of our coats; I draped mine on the hall tree, he put his on a hanger, and then put the hanger on an empty peg. After that we went into the parlor. I sat in the leather chair by the radio and noticed my hands for the first time. They were very dirty and smelled all at once of wood smoke, cordite, and blood. A sickening combination, but I did not feel sick.

Escott went into the kitchen and dialed a number on the phone. His call was very short and he'd swapped his English accent for a German one. He gave the address of the warehouse and in a frightened voice complained of hearing gunfire, then hung up. He made a brief stop in the dining room before coming in to sit on the couch opposite. He must have poured half the contents of his bottle of good brandy into the glass in his hand.

"I wish you could have some as well," he said. "If anyone needed it . . ."

"Is something wrong?"

"No, Jack." His answer was easy and reassuring. After a drink and a minute for the stuff to work into him, he said, "I expect what you really need is a very hot bath and some kip time."

I blinked a little, thinking it over. "That sounds good to me."

He must have been holding his breath, for he visibly relaxed. "You go on up and do that, then."

He seemed anxious for me to go, so I went to my room upstairs and peeled slowly out of my clothes as though shedding an old skin. Another layer came off in the hot water of the tub and yet another as I shaved. When I came downstairs again, my body felt better, but still strangely detached from my mind.

He was on the kitchen phone speaking in a low voice with a hushed shock that was only partly assumed. On the other end of the line it must have sounded sincere enough.

"I'm terribly sorry to hear that. . . . They do? . . . Oh, there's no question about it, I shall come over immediately. Yes, of course . . ."

And so on, until he hung up. "Pierce?" I asked.

He nodded. "Letting me know about the arson on his guest house. He thinks it's connected with his case and wants me to look at things. I don't know when I'll be back. Will you be all right?"

Again with the questions. "You want me along?"

"Not this time. Besides, you need the rest."

Maybe he had a point there. "Does he know about Marian?"

His face grew longer. "Not yet. The police may not have had time to sort it out yet. Anonymous calls don't always send them bolting off to an immediate investigation."

He left to get his coat. I noticed that he'd tidied the kitchen up from Harry Summers's visit. The empty brandy glass stood rinsed and drying with the others on the sink drain board. He wouldn't have wasted good brandy and I had no doubt that he'd properly finished it off, but his manner so far was stone-cold sober.

"I found this," I said when he returned to leave by the back door. I drew out the black velvet bag from my bathrobe pocket and put it on the table.

"Dear me." He arrested his move to put on his hat and opened the little bag instead. He studied the bracelet for a while, turning it over and over in his long fingers. I wondered if it felt as heavy to him as it had to me.

"I thought you'd want to give it back to Pierce."

He pursed his lips, managing to look thoughtful and horrified all at once. "No, I couldn't possibly—not at this point, at any rate."

"The warehouse, then. Plant it on Marian, where it belongs."

"We can't take that chance. As soon as the police get there, they'll be all over the place with their notes and cameras. It'd be impossible to smuggle it in, especially if Blair conducts the investigation."

"Then mail it to Pierce. We sure as hell can't hang on to it."

He balled the thing up in his fist, then poured it into the bag.

"For the moment, we shall do exactly that." He sounded like a man with an idea, but wasn't ready to share it yet, "You keep it for now until I have time to put it in the safe. It'll be all right in that vault of yours below stairs."

It'd be just fine, but I didn't want to have any part of it. I also didn't have the energy left to tell him, so I meekly stuffed the bag back in my pocket.

He locked the back door behind him and soon had the Nash out of the garage and was gone. The house loomed huge and empty about me. The place must have been warm enough, but I suppressed a shiver.

Without thinking much about it, I vanished and seeped through the floor to the walled-off alcove directly below the kitchen. It was so much faster than using the basement stairs and had the added attraction of taking me out of the world for a few moments. It was some time before I returned to solidity.

The room was hot and still. The lamp was on, just as I'd left it when I'd walked through the wall to find out why Escott wanted to interrupt my writing. Had that happened only last night? I squinted at the neatly typed sheets as though they were someone else's property. They were. I felt quite different from the earnest would-be writer that had typed them, different in that I wasn't feeling anything at all.

A tremor ran up my spine in the hot little room.

Bobbi's photo smiled at me from the makeshift desk. It was a studio portrait, done by the best in the city and glamoured up, though with Bobbi they didn't have to work very hard. She had one of those faces that the camera practically makes love to; all she ever had to do for a drop-dead photo was to smile.

I started to pick it up for a closer look and noticed my hand was trembling. I gripped it with the other, but it was just as out of control.

No regrets, remember?

The trembling spread from my hands to my arms and joined up with the tremor in my back. I couldn't seem to hold it down or stretch out of it.

No regrets, so why was every nerve in my body starting to scream? I rolled onto the cot and its layer of earth and shook and shook and shook and never once stopped until the sun came up at last and released me from the night's terrors.

▲ Epilogue ▼

THE fact that it was a whole different night when I awoke was of absolutely no comfort. It was still night, and some can be darker than others, as I'd come to learn, and I was starting this one with my equivalent of a hangover. My head and spine held fast to a residual ache and my muscles were cramped and tired and stiff as a . . .

Go on and say it, since it's true.

. . . corpse's.

I thought of a lot of unpleasant replies for that nagging voice in my head, but it hardly seemed worth the effort. If I felt bad, then no one could blame me for wanting to groan.

When I finally dragged myself upstairs to the parlor, I found Escott stretched out as usual on the couch smoking his pipe.

"Are you all right?" he asked in his most neutral tone, but studying me closely.

"Yes. I think I am, anyway."

"You sound better."

"How bad was I?"

"You were in some sort of shock. Last night your eyes looked like black pits with nothing in them. Most disconcerting."

Understatement was his specialty, but I didn't want to spend any time going over my troubles. Too much rehashing and they might come back on me. I dropped into the leather chair by the radio and asked a few questions about the events of the day and got an earful.

Soon after his arrival to view the smoking remains of Pierce's guest house, the cops came by with the bad news about Marian. Escott had gone with Pierce to identify her body.

"How's Mr. Pierce doing?"

"As can be expected, he's carrying a heavy load of grief. It's very hard for him, since he doesn't know all the details and I can hardly tell him. He will find full enlightenment, perhaps, to be of little comfort."

I couldn't help but agree.

The warehouse murders had opened up a whole new line for Lieutenant Blair to follow and he was good at his job. My efforts notwithstanding, he'd figured that Hodge's suicide had been a complete fake and was looking for the third party who'd arranged it. Escott suggested burning the clothes I'd been wearing at the time, especially the shoes. I'd left a fairly clear footprint behind. That they might trace it to me was unlikely, but why take chances?

"What do they call it? Accessory after the fact, or aiding and abetting?" I asked.

"I call it keeping a friend out of trouble."

The back of my neck prickled. "Charles, I murdered the man. I had a choice, and I chose to kill him."

"And we've been down this road before and survived. Would you do it again under the same circumstances?"

I dropped my gaze, giving him his answer.

"We may argue the fine distinctions between murder and execution if you like, but it will eventually come out that you no more wish to turn yourself in over this particular business than I do."

"It's just . . . just knowing that that kind of thing is inside me."

"It's in all of us, not just you. Last night you asked me why I did not take that second shot at them. Believe me, I truly wanted to."

"But you didn't."

"The idea was to get you out of there as quickly as possible. That was much more important than killing Kyler. Perhaps I should have risked complications at the time and done so, because there are sure to be more problems to come from it."

"Good God, he's going to be coming after you with an army."

"When he gets the time. At the moment he is far too occupied with avoiding the authorities."

The police had quickly traced the ownership of Kyler's Cadillacs and were trying to locate him to get an explanation of why they were parked in front of a murder site. Blair was also starting to turn up connections between Marian Pierce and Kyler and the gambling clubs he ran.

"I doubt much shall come of it, though." Escott sighed. "Kyler wields a great deal of power in this city, whether the city wants to admit it or not, and he's inherited some influential political allies from Frank Paco. There are threads to connect him to Marian Pierce, but I fear they are not plentiful enough or strong enough to twist into a rope for his neck."

"We're talking stalemate."

"For the moment." But he looked thoughtful.

"You thinking about the bracelet, Charles?"

"Hmm."

"Of using it somehow to nail him?"

"Somehow. But I haven't quite decided just how. It will come in time. I'm sure of it."

Doreen Grey was far from well, but the doctor was more optimistic than he'd been last night. She'd regained consciousness long enough to state in no uncertain terms who had shot her—and why. Though they couldn't prove by paperwork that the gun found in Marian's purse had belonged to Stan McAlister, his fingerprints were still on the bullets. The bullets taken from Doreen by the surgeons were matched to the same gun. Since Blair's original case against Kitty Donovan was too flimsy to hold up, he was dropping it altogether and backtracking Marian Pierce. His talk with Harry Summers more or less clinched things.

Sebastian Pierce's load of grief was proving to be very heavy, indeed.

Some of my own load lifted, though, at the news about Doreen. While Escott lighted a pipe, I trotted upstairs and dressed. It didn't take long and I was coming down again, in my best suit and another pair of shoes. Last night's clothes were tied up in a bundle under my arm. I'd snipped off the laundry marks and anything else I could think of and had stuffed those into a pocket.

On the way to the hospital I made several stops, twice at gas stations to flush away labels, then I detoured over a bridge to scatter the buttons in the river. The latter was the most difficult because of the water; the physical discomfort reminded me of the warehouse, and the warehouse reminded me of Hodge. I was glad to leave.

It was more luck than looking, but I found an incinerator still going at full blast in a backyard junk pile close to the Stockyards. The air stank of burning rubber and meat, but I was able to slip in and out without being spotted. Invisibility has its advantages. Shoes and clothes safely disposed of, I stopped next at the Stockyards and hoped that the drink I took there would clear away the last of the aches.

Visiting hours weren't quite over when I reached the hospital, but

Doreen was isolated from the other patients and the nurse was reluctant to let me do more than look through a window set in the door. Dr. Rosinski was with Doreen and I cornered him as he came out.

"She's doing as well as can be expected," he told me, which wasn't saying much. "So far there's no infection, which is a very good sign, but it will be awhile before she's past all the risks."

"Is she awake?"

"Partially. If you went in there, I doubt that she would really notice."

"Then it's all right if I go in?"

He could see that it was important to me, but the casual way he ordered up a mask and gown left me with a bad feeling. Perhaps he was taking all the precautions he could to help her, but he still didn't think much of her chances. He told me five minutes and repeated the same to the nurse.

Doreen looked smaller, more crushed somehow. Even the color of her hair was muted. I said her name a few times and touched a limp, cold hand. She stirred a little and her eyelids shivered open to half mast.

"Remember me, honey?"

The corner of her mouth curled slightly.

"No need to talk, I just came in to see how you were doing."

I suddenly felt incredibly awkward. There was no way I could say all I needed to say. I wanted to apologize to her like crazy, to tell her anything that would make it all better again, but it was impossible. The disappointment was a jolt; so much of a jolt that I finally realized why I was there. Sick as she was, I'd come to her to get comfort, not give it; to try to clear my own conscience at her expense.

The self-disgust I felt almost made me turn away, but I sat next to her and held her hand and smiled, though she couldn't see it through the gauze mask.

I kept up a one-sided conversation for another minute or so. Inane stuff, but she seemed to be listening. That, or I was fooling myself again.

"You . . ."

Her whisper was so soft I had to bend close.

". . . got away."

"From Leadfoot Sam? Yeah, I got away. He won't be bothering you, either."

"Yeah?"

"Promise. He's leaving you alone now. I made sure of it."

"Thas' good." Her eyes closed and opened. "Cops get her?"

It took me a second to work out that she was referring to Marian. "Yeah, she won't be causing you any more trouble. You're home free." God, I hoped that was true.

"What's your name again?"

That threw me until I remembered I'd given her one name and Sam another. "Jack."

"Then thanks, Jack."

I said you're welcome and left it at that.

"You got a nice girl home?"

"Yeah, you could say that."

She smiled a little. "Treat her good, huh? You . . . you're good people."

"I'm glad you think so, honey."

"Don' tell 'er 'bout us," she slurred out, her eyelids drifting shut. "You're the kind to c'fess, you don' wanna do that. Not to her."

"Doreen—"

"Lissen to me, I been there m'self. You tell her an' it'll change things. I know. If you got somethin' good, don' screw it up."

I wondered just how much she did know or remember about those few moments in her cold studio. Apparently it was a pleasant memory.

"Yeah, honey, I promise. You just rest for now and I'll take care of things for you."

And so on, until she was asleep again.

I'd gone in for comfort, decided against seeking it, and got it anyway. Doreen was some woman and I'd keep my promise to her. Not all confessions are good for the soul; some can even tear them apart. The last thing I ever wanted to do was to bring more grief to Bobbi's life, so I would be silent. I knew now that I could visit her tonight and feel comfortable about it.

The hospital parking lot was fairly empty as I walked out into the brisk air. In a few more minutes I'd trade it for the lot at the Top Hat Club and sneak in once again by the stage entrance to her dressing room. After that I'd try resuming my life again.

I pulled into the street and stepped on the gas. In the rearview mirror, I chanced to look back, and saw a silent Cadillac with smoke-dark windows doing the same.

Snake, I thought, and my hands began to tremble.

BLOOD ON THE WATER

1

It was war, then. The quiet kind that you notice only as an impersonal paragraph in the paper you read over the morning coffee or in the evening after work. Bold black letters might spell out: SHOOTING VICTIM FOUND, and then go on to give some sparse details of the person's age, where they lived and died, and that the police were following some promising leads. Most of the time you never learn if they turned up anything or not. Life moves forward and new paragraphs on other casualties appear in the paper. New, but with a dreary similarity to all the others, as in any war.

In my case I might not even get that much of an epitaph. Vaughn Kyler's enemies tended to simply disappear. Without an inconvenient body to trip over, the cops couldn't be expected to make an arrest.

I gripped the steering wheel more tightly to control the tremors in my hands and took a second look in the rearview mirror. The Cadillac was still there and following close enough to make it obvious that the men inside wanted me to know about it. The side windows were smoked over, but I could make out four vague figures through the windshield, though little else. Maybe one of them was Kyler but that wasn't very likely. The wide streets of Chicago, even at night, were far too public for him.

Last August he'd taken control of the Paco gang, and since Frank Paco himself was confined to a lunatic ward and his brothers and cousins were missing and probably dead, no one was around to object. In six months Kyler had doubled the earnings and spread the profits around so his position was that much more secure, but he was always on guard against any threats to his authority, which, unfortunately, included myself.

In no uncertain terms he'd ordered me to leave town or die. His attitude at the time indicated that he didn't really care about my choice as long as one or the other removed me from his sight. I suppose from his point of view he was giving me a better break than I deserved. That or he was just being careful. Sooner or later he could overstep things enough so that the cops would no longer ignore the situation and be forced to officially notice him.

But last night's many events had crowded his threat right out of my mind and I hadn't left, much less even thought of alternatives. On the other hand, he'd had a long full day to recover from that particularly busy evening and decide what to do about me. Sending some of his boys in one of his Caddies to play tag had to be part of it.

I made a few turns just to be sure and the big black car echoed my course in a leisurely manner. They had enough power under that hood to make mincemeat of anything my humble Buick could do. If I wanted to get away with a whole skin, it would have to be with brains and not speed. I just wished that I felt smart instead of scared. Kyler had that effect on me.

They didn't seem to be in much of a hurry to push the issue. I could figure that they'd planned out what to do and were only waiting for me to make it easy for them with a wrong move. They didn't quite hug my back bumper, but kept close enough to edge up my nerves. Not a good idea on their part; a nervous man is liable to do anything. It would have been far better to tail me at a discreet distance until I'd arrived at the Top Hat Club and then pick me off as I left the car. They wanted to frighten me before moving in; Kyler apparently had no reservations against letting his boys have some fun.

Even as the thought occurred, my hands abruptly stopped shaking. I drew a short breath, releasing it as a brief, taut laugh that flushed away my vague fears. I suddenly knew exactly how to handle them and had only to find the right spot for it.

The setup was important. I'd have to let them think they'd succeeded in rattling me. Shifting into the right lane, I cut a sharp turn at the next corner and put my foot down. The Buick had enough in it to accelerate away at a good clip, and I left them behind for a few hopeful seconds.

Traffic was light in the area, which was just as well since I didn't want any bystanders or cops getting in the way. I hadn't seen a patrol car yet, not that I was remotely interested in involving the law over this. If the men in the Caddy ran to type they'd have no qualms about bumping off a cop to get to me. I was content to leave Chicago's finest out of the immediate line of fire and take care of these clowns myself.

I continued the illusion of a chase for several long blocks. At one point I thought I'd genuinely lost them, but the familiar pattern of their headlights swung into view again and caught up. Losing them without having to try anything fancy would have been just fine, but that kind of luck wasn't working for me tonight. I took the next corner fast and tight, the wheels squawking until they bit the pavement with a quick lurch. The Cadillac easily kept pace.

The corner coming up was to be my last one. Sooner or later I'd have to run into a traffic stop that I couldn't beat through, and this was it. The driving lane ahead was blocked with cars waiting for the next signal change. The curb was lined with parked vehicles. Oncoming traffic prevented me from making a U-turn, so I stood on the brake and stopped just short of the guy in front of me. For effect, I tapped the horn, but no one bothered to move out of the way.

Since I was giving the impression of a nerved-up and frantic man, it was time to do something desperate. I cut the motor and launched out of the car on the right-hand side, sparing only one glance back at the Caddy. They'd been ready for that move; the front and rear passenger doors opened and two guys in dark coats bowled out after me.

I slipped between the parked cars and darted a dozen yards along the sidewalk. The street was well-lighted, but that didn't matter as long as I managed to get out of their sight for a few seconds. I ducked around the corner of a building and vanished. Period.

My forward movement slowed, stopped, and reversed, but by then they'd pounded past and were just starting to wonder what had happened to me. Their puzzlement wouldn't last all that long, so I whipped back the way I'd come like an invisible cloud, hugging the side of the building for guidance. I couldn't see at all, which made it hard to gauge distance, but tried my best guess. It worked out. When I re-formed into a solid man again I was twenty feet behind their car and in a position to do myself some good.

Vanishing was one of my more convenient talents—acquired, not inherent—though at first it had taken some practice to get it right. I'm one of the Un-Dead—a *nosferatu*—a vampire—pick your own name. Any one of them is close enough to the truth, but I tend to ignore them all because of the dramatically bad press associated with such words. In my own mind, I have a condition; terrible in some ways, great in others, but not something to be lightly dismissed.

I wouldn't show in their rearview mirror, but crouched anyway as I ran up to their right rear tire. The cold wind blew the exhaust right in my face, but I don't breathe much except to talk; it was annoying mostly because it made my eyes water.

Fumbling out my pocketknife, I buried the sharp point into the side of the tire with one strong jab. It deflated in a most satisfactory way, getting the immediate attention of the people inside. The guy in the backseat rolled down his window to see what had happened.

He wasn't Kyler, though it would have been nice. I popped his unfamiliar face once on the chin and he dropped out of sight without a sound. The driver said something, but I missed it when I vanished again and poured through the open window into the car. Just as he turned around to check on his fallen buddy I went solid. There was an even chance that he never knew what hit him. In this case it was my left fist, the punch pulled enough so as not to break his jaw.

The car started to drift forward and I had to scramble over the seat to grab at the hand brake. I killed the engine, yanked the key, and tossed it out the rear window into a pile of gutter trash.

The other two would be coming back any second now. I quit their car for my own, gunned it to life, and made that belated U-turn into the oncoming lane. Happily, no one got in my way, but I was beyond noticing such details, being in too much of a hurry to get back home again to see if Escott was still alive.

We were partners, sort of; he had a small business as a private agent, which meant that he didn't do divorce work, and I helped him out whenever he needed it. The last case had involved a search for a diamond-and-ruby bracelet worth fifteen grand that sparked off three, almost four murders. Escott and I still had the bracelet. We couldn't return it to its owner without implicating ourselves in two of the deaths. Escott was innocent; I wasn't, but he was my friend and doing what he could to protect me.

In essence, Kyler was at the bottom of it all, and Escott was trying to figure a way of pinning things to him. He was planning to use the bracelet in some way, only it looked as if Kyler wasn't going to give him the chance. As far as Kyler was concerned the bracelet and the money it represented belonged to him now, and too bad for anyone who happened to get in the way.

There's a deep cold well inside all of us where we keep our blackest fears. Mine had cracked open and was pouring stuff out like Niagara as I turned onto the last street and saw a twin of the Cadillac I'd disabled parked in the alley behind our house. This was a quiet little middle-class neighborhood where such cars are dreams just too good to be true. The smoked windows confirmed its ownership and the threat it represented.

I left my car on the street and tore around the empty Caddy to the back of the house. The narrow yard was silent. The garage was closed tight, but the roof of the Nash was visible through a side window. Escott had been home when they'd come calling. I vanished and seeped through the crack at the bottom of the back door and assumed a more or less vertical position just inside the kitchen.

Unable to see, I concentrated on listening, but heard nothing in the immediate area. I swept the room once to make sure it was empty and cautiously re-formed. Nobody stared back at me.

The place was wrecked. Every drawer and cabinet was open, their contents dumped out. Escott wasn't too interested in cooking or it might have been worse, but it was bad enough. The refrigerator was open and humming away, trying to keep its stripped insides cold. I shut the door very quietly, my hands shaking again. This time with rage, not fear.

A variety of indistinct sounds were coming from all over the house. There were at least two men on the ground flour and two others upstairs. Nobody talked much. They knew their business.

Peering around the edge of the door, I could look through the dining room to the front parlor, where I'd left Escott listening to his radio. He wasn't in sight, but I did catch a moving glimpse of a dark hat and coat that didn't belong to either of us. I dropped back.

The bedrooms were on the second floor and my instinctive urge was to take the high ground first. Any other time I'd have used the stairs; now I vanished again and rose straight up through the ceiling. The room I materialized in was my own. I was prepared for a mess and they hadn't disappointed me. The barely used bed was torn apart, my books and papers and clothes scattered to hell and gone. It was just my good luck and his bad that the thug who'd done the tearing was still there.

With something like joy I grabbed him by the scruff of his neck, lifting him away from the bureau he was ransacking. He was too surprised to cry out, and then he didn't have the chance to as I slammed him face first into the nearest wall. The one time wasn't satisfying enough, so I did it again, and once more because I was feeling mean. He left a bloody smear on the faded paper as he slid to the floor, a bundle of loose bones held together by his clothes.

It had made enough noise to draw the attention of his partner, whom I could hear in the bathroom next door.

"Arnold, what the hell was that?"

Arnold, being in no condition to answer, said nothing. The man in the bath emerged cautiously into the hall. He could see Arnold's fallen body from there. I waited behind the bedroom door for him to come in for a better look, only the guy was too wise to try that one. He crossed the hall to the top of the stairs and called down.

"Chaven, something's wrong."

Chaven's voice, familiar to me, answered, "Like what?"

"I dunno, but Arnold's out cold. The boss said to watch for anything weird and this is it."

I expected a derisive reply but was disappointed. "Okay, come down."

"But what about Arnold?"

"Come down, *now.*"

He did.

Shit.

It meant they knew more than what was good for me.

Their conversation drifted up from the foot of the stairs.

"What happened, Tinny?" Chaven asked.

"I dunno. I hear a thump and look in one of the bedrooms and Arnold's lying on the floor there."

"Out or croaked?"

"Jeez, I dunno. I din' like the feel of things so I stayed out."

"All right, we'll check on it together. You two stay back and cover us."

There was some shuffling followed by floorboard creaks as Chaven and Tinny slowly came up the stairs. I could have played more games, taking them out one at a time, but not knowing what had happened to Escott left me with a need to force the issue.

"Stop there, Chaven," I called from my room before he was halfway up. I made it sound as if I had a gun. I abruptly realized I did, since Arnold was sure to be carrying one.

The floor creaks ended. "Fleming?" Chaven's tone held equal amounts of caution and doubt.

"Yeah, and I've got your boy, so let's talk." I dug at Arnold's inert body, looking for the kind of argument that would be sure to work against these jerks.

Chaven used those few seconds to regain his balance, recovering too fast for my peace of mind. "Okay by me. Come out where I can see you."

"Sure." Maybe the ready answer surprised him since anyone else in my position would have been leery of getting his head blown off. But I finally emerged—holding the unconscious Arnold in front of me. Bullets can't kill me, but it hurts like hell to get shot, so I was only taking sensible precautions. I was also holding the gun I'd just salvaged.

Unimpressed, Chaven steadied his revolver on me, eye level. The sharp lines of his body and the set of his thin, hard face told me he was more than ready to use it. From ten feet away he wasn't about to miss. It flashed through my mind that I ought to go ahead and let him shoot since faking my death might get them off my back for a while.

Of course, Escott would then be stuck with them . . . if they hadn't gotten to him already.

Neither of our guns had gone off in the last five seconds but that could change if I even blinked wrong. I kept still and kept quiet. By letting Chaven be the first to speak it would give him the illusion that he was in control of things.

Tinny spoiled it by trying to be helpful. "I can get him from here." He was on the stair just behind Chaven.

"So can I. Lay off." Chaven never once looked away. "The bracelet," he said to me in the same annoyed tone.

"It's not here," I lied.

"Go get it."

"When you and your boys leave."

He had a sense of humor, if the noise he made was a laugh. "We go when I get the bracelet."

"What do I get?"

He thought about it for only a second. "Another chance to blow town."

"Like hell."

"Take it or die."

"Your boss has already decided that. Tell me another one."

"We can make it easy or hard, Fleming."

"You can't do anything to me or you lose the bracelet. Does Kyler think my hide's worth losing fifteen grand over?"

"You're worth nothing to him." But he was just talking to get the last word in and to think some more. "Besides, there's still your partner."

"Except he doesn't know where it is."

"He'll know, all right. He's too careful not to know."

"Then why don't you ask him?"

"With you here I don't have to. Now hand it over."

So Escott had managed to get away in time. They wouldn't have bothered ripping the place apart if they'd had him to question . . . unless they'd made a mistake and killed him outright. If they had, then none of them were leaving this house alive.

"Okay, but everybody get back. Crowds make me nervous."

At an invisible signal from Chaven, Tinny and the other two thugs retreated down the stairs to the landing. I could just see them through the banister. They still had their guns out and pointed in my general direction.

I hefted Arnold a little higher and took a step forward. Chaven didn't seem to notice that holding up all that extra weight with one arm wasn't bothering me much. He backed off a pace, but to the side, not down the stairs. His mind was on other things, then. We reached the same moment of realization, only I was just an instant faster as I pushed Arnold straight at him and ducked.

Chaven's gun roared out in the confined space of the upper hall. He snarled something and tried to bring the muzzle down, but Arnold was in his way long enough for me to get my feet set and launch toward him. For a few seconds it was all blind pawing, thick coats, and elbows, then I took a chance opening and clobbered Chaven in the head with the side of Arnold's gun. He stopped moving. I tore the revolver from his hand.

Tinny and his two chums came up out of nowhere. I shoved a foot into Tinny's gut. He grabbed at it, dragging me free of Chaven, but lost his balance and fell backward, his arms suddenly wide. One chum tried to catch him at the same time the second tried to get out of the way and they all tripped each other and took a partial roll down the stairs. By the time they got themselves pulled together, I was up again and looking like William S. Hart with a borrowed gun in each fist.

I suddenly had their full attention. Except for myself, everyone was breathing hard and red in the face, some more than others, as they realized I had them square.

"You! Put it on the landing."

Tinny knew I was talking about his gun without having to ask, which made him a bright boy. He did as he was told, and so did the others when it was their turn. I kicked everything through the open door into my room.

Chaven began to groan and push at Arnold as he came around. He snapped abruptly awake and glared. I expected him to start cursing once he took in the altered situation, but nothing came out. The look on his face and especially in his cold, stony eyes was eloquent enough. We both knew what we thought of each other.

"You stand up slow," I said, and he followed my directions carefully. He lifted one hand to check where I'd hit him. His fingers came away with a little red on them.

"Yeah," he said, as though agreeing with some inner voice.

I waved a muzzle at Arnold. "Get him. Everyone downstairs."

They got him, struggling clumsily with his uncooperative body. Chaven let the others work while he watched me, no doubt making plans on what to do at our next meeting.

I herded them through the kitchen and out the door. They slow-marched to the Cadillac and got in. Chaven was the driver; I made him wait until the others were settled.

"You can tell Kyler that I got his message about the bracelet."

"I'll do that, Fleming."

"You can also say that I want a better deal before I hand it over."

"What kind of deal?"

"I'll talk that over with Kyler. Have him call me here. The number's in the book."

That was the end of our business for tonight. I hoped. He got in the car and quietly drove away with the search party. He was visibly frustrated and anyone else might have expressed it in their driving, but not Chaven. He could have been out on a Sunday jaunt with his granny for all the care he took over signals and speed. Maybe he wasn't in such a hurry to return to his boss empty-handed.

Trotting back to the house, I checked the place from the attic on down. It was still a wreck, but unoccupied. The last spot I checked, primarily because it was so well hidden, was the walled-off section of the basement where I slept during the day. I disappeared, flowed through the familiar pattern of bricks to the alcove beyond, and re-formed.

The small room was in total darkness. My night vision is excellent except in those rare spots protected from all outside light, like here in my private sanctum. I usually left the lamp over my desk on for that reason, but now it was off. The complete claustrophobic blackness pressed on me as it would anyone else, and I instinctively started to back out again when a low, soft sound stopped me. A heartbeat.

"Charles?"

"Jack . . . thank God you're all right." It came out in a rush along with his pent-up breath.

With a click, the small light over the desk flashed to life. I winced and squinted painfully against the sudden brightness until my eyes adjusted. Escott was sitting in my work chair with my bathrobe draped over his clothes and a relieved expression on his bony face.

"You've been down here the whole time?"

He gave me a "what do you think" shrug and put the .38 he was holding back in his pants pocket.

"And with no light?"

"Out of necessity, I fear. It seemed preferable not to give them a lighted target if they chanced to find me."

Set in the ceiling above the folding bed was a trapdoor, visible on this side, but only a normal part of the kitchen furnishings on the other. It was centered under the old oak dining table and covered by a tacked-down throw rug. To unlock it, you had to open one of the cabinet doors back all the way. Once lowered, the trap automatically relocked. Escott had a penchant for such devices and the talent to design and construct them. Not for the first time was I glad that he'd indulged the theatrical side of his nature.

"You couldn't duck out of the house?" Given the choice of running or hiding in a dead-end bolt hole, I knew what my preference would have been.

"With them coming in both doors I was caught in a classic pincers movement. As it was, I barely made it down here. I'd just time to slide under the table and drop through the trap. It slammed down over me as they broke open the back door, then I had a few bad minutes waiting to learn if they'd seen or heard any of it. For a while I was beginning to feel altogether too close in kinship with the unfortunate fish trapped in a barrel."

"I see what you mean."

He glanced at his watch. "Heavens, I would have sworn that more time had passed than this."

"It was long enough for them to tear the place apart."

"Looking for that bracelet, no doubt."

"And not finding it. You put it in the safe, then?"

"I didn't have it."

"But I gave it to you last night." A little wave of cold puzzlement washed over me.

"And I returned it to you before I had to leave." He held up his hand as I started to object. He took off the robe and pulled a black velvet bag from one of the pockets. A fortune in diamonds and rubies linked together by bright platinum spilled out and twined around his long fingers.

"Jeez, I don't remember." Then again, I really didn't want to remember. Escott had mentioned that I'd been in pretty bad shape and I was ready to take him at his word and leave it at that, but the sight of the bracelet started to bring things to the surface. I recalled its weight in my own hand and the way the light made the rubies look like fresh blood. A whole new tremor ran up my spine. Escott noticed and slipped the thing back in its bag.

"I'm not in the habit of searching pockets that do not concern me, but when I borrowed this for protection, I couldn't help but find it." He hung the robe over the back of the chair.

"Protection?"

"Yes. Despite its proximity to the furnace, this . . . ah . . . haven of yours was a bit chilly for me."

"Is it?" Since my change I'd developed a certain indifference against most temperature extremes. "Guess I better get you out of here."

"I was rather hoping you'd say that. Would you object if I bought a folding ladder to store here against any future emergencies of a similar nature? Just in case I must make an unassisted exit."

I told him to go right ahead, then vanished to float up to the kitchen. I pushed the cabinet door back until the catch clicked, then hauled up the trap. The big table had to be shoved to one side this time to give us both room to work. Escott reached high and I was just able to grasp his wrist and pull him out.

"Good heavens," he said the second his head cleared the floor. It was for the mess, not the acrobatics.

He stood, his shoes crunching against a sea of spilled sugar, salt, coffee grounds, and milk. He walked slowly into the dining room and surveyed the broken liquor cabinet, the scattered bottles and glasses. He went on to the front parlor to find the overturned radio, tumbled furniture, and slashed cushions. I followed him upstairs, where the mess was worse. Drawers had been dumped, their contents pawed through. The books and souvenirs in his library/study were torn from the shelves. The overwhelming sick rage at the invasion hit me all over again; I could only imagine what Escott felt.

He was an extremely neat and organized man; Kyler's people couldn't have picked a better way to get him angry. He didn't show it much, only by the hardening of his eyes and the knife-edge thinning of his mouth.

"I'm sorry, Charles."

"Hardly your fault, old man. Looking at this, I can get an idea of what they might have done to me had I not been able to drop out of sight in time."

"I should have seen this coming. I could have stuck around and stopped all this."

He shook his head. "I wouldn't worry about it now. One cannot anticipate everything, otherwise life would be very dull, indeed. What *did* inspire you to return?"

I told him about the tail, how I'd slipped it, and what had happened when I found Chaven's party.

"You took care of all five of them? And by yourself?"

"With some help from Sam Colt." I pulled the guns I'd taken from my coat pockets. "There's more in there." I nodded in the direction of my room. That's when he laughed, actually laughed, out loud.

"I could almost wish to be a fly on the wall when Kyler questions his henchmen on this bit of business."

"They'll be back."

"I don't doubt it. I suppose he'll be calling any time now, unless he decides to forgo negotiations altogether after this. What will you say to him?"

"I'm still working on it, but I figure if he wants the bracelet this bad maybe we should give it to him."

"And you think you can convince him to leave us alone?"

I shrugged. "Unless you've got any better ideas?"

"Not at the moment, no. I see that surprises you."

"I thought you had a plan to plant it on Kyler and then call the cops down on him."

"Initially, yes, but I've had time to think it out. There's little chance of successfully pulling that off without drawing undue legal attention to ourselves. While I may be able to weather such a storm, you are ill suited to spending any time in jail."

"You mean you can't just make an anonymous call?"

"The authorities in this city would require something more than that to justify issuing a search warrant against someone in Kyler's position. Nor can I really approach Lieutenant Blair on this. He's far too intelligent. If either of us turn up waving that bracelet about . . . well, I should not care to dwell on the consequences. And if Kyler took it into his head to talk, even a partial telling of the truth of what happened last night would place us in a terribly precarious position."

"What do you call this? We're already there, if not with the law, then with Kyler."

Our problem was the fact that one of Kyler's lieutenants had murdered a girl and that I, in turn, had murdered him. It wouldn't take much for Kyler to twist the events around to suit himself, and he had enough power and influence to get away with it. At the very least, Escott would lose his license and probably serve hard time for his part in things. On the other end, Kyler could probably save himself a lot of trouble by having Escott just disappear like too many other people before him. At this time of year Lake Michigan made for an awfully damned cold grave.

"You might want to pack some stuff," I said.

"And run?"

"If I can't make a deal with him we're both up shit creek."

He nodded in reluctant agreement. He'd had plenty of time to think things through sitting in the darkness. "We might require a bit of breathing space before our next move," he admitted.

I started to ask him what he had in mind, but let that one lie for the time being. Neither of us could really do or plan anything until we heard from Kyler.

The call came about thirty minutes later. I was in the kitchen sweeping up some of the mess and answered.

I'd been expecting Kyler, but Chaven was on the other end of the line.

"Get a pencil," he snarled.

Escott always kept one close to the phone along with some paper. I snapped it up in time to write out the phone number Chaven dictated to me.

"You call there exactly at eleven o'clock, y'hear?"

"I hear."

He slammed down his receiver, but I'd been ready for that and was holding my earpiece a safe distance away.

Escott had come downstairs to listen to my side of the conversation. I showed him the number. "Probably to a public box," he commented.

"Yeah?"

"Lieutenant Blair is a remarkably efficient investigator; perhaps Kyler is worried about wiretaps on his lines in connection with last night's deaths. If so, then this is one call that neither of you will want to have overheard."

"Or traced. Think I better do the same thing. Just in case."

"And from another neighborhood," he added.

Chaven's phone call only traded one kind of waiting for another. Having a specific deadline to look forward to was slightly less nerve-racking, but in some ways it was worse. My concentration for even the simple task of sweeping up the kitchen was shot all to hell; mostly I moped around and peered out the windows. For a while I thought the clock was broken, but it matched my wristwatch minute for minute. Escott stayed busy upstairs. I wasn't sure if it was his way of handling the wait or if he was only avoiding my twitchy restlessness.

At one point I found myself dialing the number to the Top Hat Club to ask for Miss Smythe. I hung up on the first ring. Bobbi would be in the middle of one of her sets by now and the management might take a dim view of the interruption. Besides, what could I say to her that wouldn't leave her alarmed and worried?

She still didn't know that I'd almost died last night, permanently and horribly. She also didn't know how I'd gone over the edge and what had happened when I struck bottom. I could still feel the gun jump in my hand and see the blinding flash. It didn't quite blot out the man's last scream or the look on his face.

No regrets, remember?

Yeah, sure. Easy to say, hard to do. I was coming to realize that it wasn't so much that I had killed, but that I'd been out of control at the time. I was caught up in the not unreasonable worry that it could happen again.

Damn the bracelet. Damn everything and all its relatives.

I grabbed the broom and made an effort to finish the job. By ten-thirty the floor was clean of every grain and speck, but I was still sweeping for something to do. The mindless activity kept me from thinking so much. My thoughts weren't exactly comfortable.

Escott wanted to come along and I had no objections to offer, especially since he volunteered the use of his Nash. The big car was armored, with an engine powerful enough to match anything Kyler had. Much safer than the Buick.

Exactly at eleven, in an outdoor booth about two miles from home, I dialed in the last number Chaven had dictated to me.

"What do you want?" No introductions, no preamble. Kyler knew I'd recognize his voice.

"A truce."

"Terms." He made it a statement, not a question.

"You and your people leave me and all my friends alone. We do the same for you. For that, you get the item you want."

"What else?"

This seemed too easy, but I plowed ahead. "Your word on it."

"When?"

"As soon as possible. Tonight."

A pause from his end. In the background I heard muffled traffic noises, indicating that Escott had been right; Kyler was also in a public booth. For all I knew, we could be only blocks apart. "All right," he finally said. "And my word that we leave you and your friends alone."

"Good enough."

"Double-cross me and all bets are off."

"Okay."

"Come to the warehouse at midnight."

I covered the mouthpiece with one hand and hissed at Escott, who was just outside. "He wants to meet at the warehouse."

"Ask him why."

"Why the warehouse?" I said to Kyler.

"It's known to both of us. You'll be safe from me there. My word on that, also. Agreed?"

I didn't like it, but said yes. He hung up quietly, as though he'd eased a finger over the hook. The usual clicks of disconnection followed by the dial tone came a moment later.

"Not one for wasting words, is he?" Escott commented as I pried myself from the cramped booth.

"Yeah. And he was awfully damn cooperative. It makes me wonder what I just missed."

"He does seem to have you on the defensive. Why is that?"

"Why are people afraid of snakes?"

With no better way to spend the time, we went back home again. Escott hung his coat on the hall tree and disappeared for a moment, returning with a crumpled map of the city in one hand. I followed him to the kitchen, where he spread it flat on the table.

"I know where the place is," I said.

"As do I, but it is the surrounding area that requires my attention."

"You want to come along again, huh?"

"I have a more than casual interest in the outcome of this business."

A half dozen objections ran through my brain in as many seconds. Escott would have already thought of them all and then some and have counterarguments for each. "Okay, but I go in alone. If things go wrong, I'll need you in reserve to get us out of there."

We bent over the map. Escott was better at making sense of all the thin black lines and tiny letters and picked out a likely place to park. By eleven forty-five we were there. He rolled to a smooth stop on a side street about a quarter mile from the International Freshwater Transport warehouse.

"Good enough," I said.

"Not quite," he cautioned, and shifted into reverse. The car was now in an angle of shadow created by one of the many tall, ugly buildings in the area.

"You won't be able to see anything now." The high walls blocked all but a narrow view of the main street leading to the warehouse.

"Then, hopefully, they won't be able to see me."

Heavy winter silence closed hard upon us when he cut the motor. Each little tick it made while cooling down sounded like a firecracker to my sensitive ears.

"Have you a gun?" he asked.

"I've got the one I took from Chaven. I'm not planning to do anything with it, but can figure on a search; it'd be a shame not to give them something to find."

"And if anything should go awry?" His tone was matter-of-fact, but still expressed a reasonable concern.

I shrugged. "If I'm not back by half past, then assume something's fishy, find a hole, and pull it in after you. Same thing if it looks like you've been spotted. Take off and stay away from the house and the office. If that happens and we get separated, I'll leave a message with your answering service."

"Presuming that you are in a condition to do so," he muttered. He wanted to go along, but we both knew that on my own I stood a better chance of bringing it off and getting out with a whole skin. There wasn't much they could do to me, and, if necessary, I could always vanish.

"I'll be careful."

Escott handed me the black velvet bag. I checked the contents out of nerves rather than any lack of trust and shoved it deep into a pocket.

"Good luck," he said.

I got out, shut the door, and started walking.

2

MY rubber-soled shoes made soft padding noises on the pavement as I covered the quarter-mile distance in short order. I was dressed to blend in with the neighborhood and the night with dark pants, shirt, no tie, and an old pea jacket borrowed from Escott's disguise closet. A cloth cap was pulled low over my forehead and I'd wrapped a wool muffler several times around my face and neck. Since winter had set in I'd found it a necessary item to conceal the fact that I only breathed while talking. Most people probably wouldn't notice what was missing on cold, damp days, namely the usual dragon's puff of vapor, but why take chances?

This kind of worry coming from a man about to walk into a lion's den. Correction: snake pit. Kyler was anything but warmblooded.

I got within a block of my destination without seeing anything worth notice. One car went by, but I avoided it by slipping into a deep doorway until it was long gone. At the cross street I cut to the left, away from the river, then right at the next corner. Opposite the IFT warehouse was yet another large building and I was now walking behind it. The place had a back entrance for the heavy trucks; I hopped up on the loading platform and went straight for the nearest door.

It was locked, but I vanished and went inside anyway. My eyes adjusted quickly to the large dim interior once I re-formed. I took an experimental sniff of the place, catching the good clean smell of cut wood. Huge stacks of lumber loomed around me. So far, so good, as long as none of it avalanched down on my tender skull. I took great care not to bump into anything.

I crossed all the way to the front of the place but stood well back from the windows. They gave me an adequate, if somewhat grimy, view of the IFT warehouse across the street.

It looked empty. No cars were parked anywhere near the place and even the outside light over the office door was off. I could just make out the glint of a new hasp and padlock, probably installed by the cops to keep people away from the scene of last night's crimes. Perhaps Kyler planned to make our exchange in the street.

Something snuffled and growled behind me. Claws clicked over the bare concrete floor. Turning, I immediately spotted a large pair of glowing green eyes winking balefully in the faint light from the windows. They were spaced very far apart. Below them was an endless row of shark's teeth, and from a vast chest came a continuous rumbling like an extra-large diesel engine. That's about all I really noticed about the watchdog in the half second that passed before it charged.

I suppose I could have handled it, could have used my special influence to calm it down and make friends, but logical, friendly ideas like that are for people with the time to think them up. When a mastiff the size of a calf with a mouth like the Grand Canyon comes barreling down on you, the first thing you really want to do is try to get out of its way. My abrupt disappearance was more of a knee-jerk reaction than a planned escape, but whatever works.

The thing bored through the space where I had once been solid and I heard a muffled crash as it slammed into the front wall. The sound it made was more irritation than pain as it recovered from the shock and turned. It yelped in sudden confusion when it butted into me again and sniffed frantically, trying to pin me down. Its claws dug at the empty patch of concrete where I had stood, gouging up chunks of it for all I could tell; the damn thing was big enough.

I'm a dog lover, but know when I'm outnumbered. Rather than argue with it, I floated up until I bumped into a scaffolding about ten feet overhead, and sieved through. It was the floor to an upper office I'd noticed on my way in and it had the advantage of putting a locked door between me and the dog. The monster was still furiously investigating below as I became solid by slow degrees and in absolute silence.

By cautiously craning my neck I had the same view of the warehouse, just a slightly different angle, and could see more of the street. The wait was more uncomfortable since I didn't want to move around much. The dog was the persistent type, and if it got a clue to my location it would certainly follow. I didn't trust the door all that much, or the dog to be quiet about trying to break through to get to me.

With that comforting thought, I stood very still, indeed, and used my eyes and ears. The walls muffled my hearing somewhat, but some motor noises came to me. The vast dark bulk of the Chicago River supported some slow boat traffic, and thanks to my new perch I was able to see some of it. A couple of boats chugged lazily past and I did not envy their crews having to work on a cold night and at such a late hour. They reminded me that Kyler also had a boat and might even use it for his transportation, so I divided my watch between the street and the river.

At five to midnight I saw, but did not hear, Kyler's two Cadillacs pull up before the warehouse. The motors were very finely tuned; a cat's purr would have been loud by comparison. They cut the lights and I counted ten men as they emerged and crowded by the door. The cars blocked a lot of my view and I couldn't pick Kyler from the group. There was a brief pause as they did something to the padlock, then the door opened and they filed inside. So much for the police sealing the place off.

The outside light came on, then an inside one. Silhouettes bumped and thinned out as the men trooped through the office into the warehouse proper. I hadn't noticed any weapons, but all their lethal hardware would be easily concealed by their long, heavy coats. Kyler wasn't going to take any chances with me if he could help it. Maybe I should have felt flattered by all the preparations, but it was an honor I'd just as soon skip.

I pulled on a pair of gloves and checked the velvet bag again. The bracelet glinted, not evil in itself, but certainly an inspiration and a focus for the darkness in all of us. I polished it a little and hoped that it would be enough to buy me and Escott some freedom and peace.

Drifting down through the floor, I sailed past the dog, who was stubbornly on guard at the spot where it had last seen me. It whined once in puzzlement, but stayed put. I floated on a straight course between the stacks of lumber, brushed against the back wall, and was out again. It was just on midnight when I walked around the building and emerged onto the street.

No one seemed to be hanging around outside, which struck me as odd since Kyler was the cautious type. They were probably hiding somewhere, then. Yet another comforting thought.

The front of the warehouse was a blank, giving no clue to what was going on inside. Like the bracelet, it could be innocent or sinister. In my present mood I knew which one to pick. I walked slowly to the door and opened it. The mechanism sounded unnaturally loud to my keyed-up senses.

No one leaped out at me. So far, so good, again. Two hard-looking men I did not know stared back at me. One stood up from his seat on the desk, the other continued to lean a little too casually against a file cabinet. I kept the muffler in place. The fewer people who saw my mug, the better.

Neither of them moved. It was like a zoo when you walk past the exhibit with the big cats. You know the bars will keep them in place, but there's always that shiver of uncertainty in the back of your mind that they just might not be up to the job. The only restraints here were the invisible ones of Kyler's word.

I went through the inner door into the warehouse. The lights were on, but I was very aware of all the men I couldn't see. At least eight of them were lurking out there among the stacks of crates. One of them stepped into my line of sight. He said nothing as I moved forward. He waited for me and became my escort, leading me deeper into the building.

The line of crates ended, leaving free an open space, or it would have been free except for the ropes the police had left behind. Off to one side an abstract chalk design sprawled at the base of a crate. In the middle, near a closed trapdoor that led down to a river landing, was another. The latter was more recognizably the outline of a man's body, like a flat ghost. Next to the head was a spray of dark stain. In my mind I could still smell the cordite and blood.

I tore my eyes from the memory and made myself look at the man standing in the center of it all. Vaughn Kyler regarded me with equal amounts of tension and expectation.

He was in better shape than when I'd last seen him. The cut on his forehead had been neatly patched over, and either the vicuna coat had been cleaned or he was wearing a new one.

Chaven stood next to him, arms hanging free, his lean form all but vibrating from unspent energy. His forced retreat earlier had left him with a serious grudge against me.

The next few steps were difficult. The warehouse was partially built out over the river and the force of the free-running water below made an invisible but effective barrier to someone with my special condition. It was worry making. Kyler had warned his men earlier to beware of anything unusual when they'd searched the house. I wondered if he had chosen this spot because he'd sensed this weakness in me and wanted to test it further. I pushed hard against the opposing press of the water and hoped that it wasn't too obvious. Once past the first yard or so, it wasn't so bad, except for all my back hairs standing at attention.

Kyler, Chaven, and the guy next to me—now, where were the other five? Two of them closed ranks about twenty feet behind us. Another stood off to the left, partially hidden by some loading equipment. The two remaining were to the right, concealed by crates.

I kept going until only a few feet separated me from Kyler. From the very first, he'd given me the panicky creeps, and time had not mitigated that reaction. He looked ordinary, just another businessman nearing his fifties in well-dressed affluence. I was beginning to realize that it was the absolute *stillness* of the man's manner that made me think of poisonous reptiles, that and his cold, unblinking eyes.

"You bring it?" His voice matched his eyes, cold.

I nodded. My mouth was dry. He waited for me to make the next move. I slowly pulled the black bag from my pocket and held it high. "Straight deal?" I whispered, hardly able to work up enough spit to talk.

"Let's see it first."

Right. Any promise he might give at this point was dependent on his taking delivery of the thing, and we were both very aware of it. I opened the bag and turned it over. The bracelet flowed and twined around my fingers, catching the distant lights, turning them into silver and red sparks.

It was his turn to nod and he held out his hand to take it. If anything was to happen to me it would be now. I was expecting either gunfire or a guarantee, war or peace, when I turned it over; anything except what did happen. The only warning I got was Chaven's mouth curling into a nervous twitch of a smile as the bracelet finally slithered into Kyler's possession.

A blinding explosion of white light froze everything in place for that instant. It came from the left, from the guy by the loading equipment. It was incongruous, yet horribly familiar to someone with my journalistic background. My eyes seemed to take an age to recover, but I didn't have to see to know that he was slotting in another film plate for a second photo. He knocked the spent bulb free of the flash. As if in slow motion, it spun to the floor, scattering into a hundred glass slivers as it smashed against the scarred wood. The pop it made on impact acted like a signal for everyone to close in. The man next to me grabbed my arm.

They'd caught me flat-footed with this one. My instinct to vanish nearly took me out of things as it had before with the guard dog. I had to ice that for the moment, what with Kyler and all his men looking on. The two behind us crowded in and the other two on the right finally emerged from hiding. The medium tall one in the leather coat wore his hat at a dapper angle over his dandy handsome face. His unexpected presence here only added to my shock.

The deal was off, but then it had never really been on. It was a trap. Not Kyler's, though . . . the cops'.

The man walking toward me was Lieutenant Blair.

"C'mon," he said to the one holding me. "Let's have a look at him."

Oh, *shit*.

The muffler was still around my face. He hadn't recognized me and things were going to stay that way if I could help it. I savagely shook off the guy's grip and bolted to the left. The photographer was encumbered by the camera, but tried to block me long enough to hold for his pals. I bowled past him and tore to the right. I absolutely had to get out of sight, and my best hope was to circle around to the stacks.

They were wise to that one. Blair and another man outflanked me, the latter drawing his gun and ordering me to stop. I doubled back, making a feint for a side door on the other end. The photographer left his camera and tried to tackle me. I caught him before we both went off balance and swung him around sharply. He lost his footing and stumbled, blocking Blair's rush for a few precious seconds. I took the opening only to face two more men drawing their guns.

Cutting between them was not the best option, but the only one left. I was moving too fast to stop, anyway. A gun went off, probably by accident. I felt nothing and remained solid. Someone cursed and caught my arm again. I punched an elbow in his direction and got free. Blair shouted something, but I lost it as I gained the narrow opening between two long lines of crates. I was suddenly free of the uncomfortable pressure of the water below us.

At the far end and coming up quickly was one of the guys from the front office. Halfway along, he paused to pull out his gun and level it. Behind me, Blair and the others paused as well, abruptly aware that they were in each other's line of fire.

The crates stacked on either side were about four feet square, graduating to smaller ones on top like giant building blocks. I latched onto a narrow edge and heaved upward with desperation-inspired agility. Blair and his men suddenly closed in. One of them just missed grabbing my foot as I lurched up to the next tier. Blair ordered someone to run around to the other side of the stack to head me off.

I wasn't quite sure how, but I made it to the top of the wooden mountain about twenty-five dizzy feet up. A little belatedly, I remembered my fear of heights as I teetered on my uncertain perch. Blair yelled, telling me to come back before I got hurt. He stopped a man from following; evidently they were all cops except for Chaven and Kyler.

They were standing well back from the activity. Kyler had me in full view, still wearing a look of expectation on his normally blank face. He'd set me up good, and now I knew why.

Blair's voice cut through my disgust with the situation, reminding me that I had to keep moving. Fine, except that I was now limited to two directions, unless you wanted to count a sudden drop as a third. Cops were now on both sides of the stack, ready to nail what was left if that happened.

Fortunately, the boxes up here were small enough to be useful, as I discovered when I tipped one over and sent it crashing. The men scattered hastily as the thing tumbled down. Metal parts, shards of wood, and excelsior hit the floor like a bomb. Another gun went off—I couldn't tell from which side—and I ducked in reflex. Before he could get a second shot, I dropped two more boxes, one left, the other right, and then plastered myself flat. With everyone rushing to get out of the way I figured they'd be too busy to notice my disappearance. I also hoped that the angle and height of the intervening crates would help block Kyler's view of the stunt.

Two more random shots went off before Blair called for a stop, followed by a long, confused pause as they tried to locate me. I held my place, and figuratively held my breath, waiting them out. Confusion gave way to frustration, and a man was boosted up on the stacks for a look around. I flowed well away from any chance contact and let them get on with the search. After a time I eased my way down to the floor and tried to make sense of their shouts and rushing around.

"Where the hell is he?" was the most frequently repeated phrase. No one had an answer to it, either. Blair sent men to cover all the exits and to check the street. The rest circled and recircled the place. After several minutes of futile combing they began to realize they'd been skunked.

Blair shouted a question at Kyler. Between the distorting echoes and the natural muffling caused by my unnatural state I could hardly make it out, and neither could Kyler.

"What?" he called back.

I zeroed in on Blair's voice. "I said, did he get past you?" He was striding toward Kyler. I froze onto him and held tight, letting him carry me along. With his unknowing help I was able to move out over the water again. Despite the heavy leather coat, he began to shiver.

"We didn't see anything," Kyler answered. I hoped that he was telling the truth.

"If you're trying a double cross, you may regret it."

"Lieutenant, I was only doing my civic duty. As you can see, we got the bracelet back for you and I understand that it is a crucial piece of evidence in the case you are working on. This lunatic has killed twice, one of them a close friend and associate of mine. I have told you before how much I want to bring this man to justice; I think my cooperation tonight in informing your department of this meeting proves my sincerity."

"And were you able to identify him, then?"

Kyler let the pause drag out and I moaned inwardly.

"Were you?"

"I regret to say that I did not recognize the man," was his bland reply.

Now, what the hell was he up to?

"You're certain of that?"

"Yes, Lieutenant. He was wrapped up in that muffler, but I am positive that if I'd had any previous contact with him, I would have remembered it. I have a very good head for names and faces, you know."

Blair had nothing to say to that and called for a report from his men. The answers were all negative. He walked off to join them. I hung back to eavesdrop on Kyler.

"Where do you think he went?" Chaven asked him in a low voice.

"Who knows? He might still be here."

"This is crazy, Vaughn."

"But you saw what happened."

"I saw a guy go up who hasn't come down yet. What's with him? How does he do it?"

"I'm working that out. Are the boys in place?"

"Probably. Tinny was on his way just as the cops arrived for us. His girl's practically—"

"Shut up," said Kyler, not raising his voice, but still managing to express urgency.

As Escott sometimes said, *bloody hell.* I whipped away from them and threaded between the stacks and occasional cop, feeling my way toward the front. It was like blind man's bluff, except the goal was to avoid running into people.

I found the office almost by accident when I picked up half of a phone conversation. Blair was calling for reinforcements and giving out a description of me for the prowl cars in the area. He got the height and weight right and had noticed the clothes in detail, right down to the brown-and-blue stripe pattern on the muffler. Thank God he hadn't gotten a look at my face.

I slipped through the front door and bore left, moving fast over the flat plain of the street, using the curb as a guide. Whenever it curved sharply, it meant a corner, and I'd have to strike out for the other side and hope to hold a straight line. A car roared toward the warehouse; the buffet of wind from its passage threw me briefly off course.

A partial re-forming gave me fresh bearings and some much-needed orientation. I hadn't come as far as I thought and I was running out of time. Escott wouldn't wait forever and sooner or later a patrolman might pull up to ask him awkward questions. I dropped out of reality and sped along more recklessly than before, practically flying over the pavement.

The next time I went solid, I was within yards of his corner. Escott stood in a doorway covering the street and saw me melt out of nowhere.

"We're up shit creek," I said, slowing only a little. "Get the car in gear. We have to get to the Top Hat right away."

"Good lord, they're after Miss Smythe?" He darted around to the driver's side and threw himself in. I wrenched open the passenger door and chafed at the pause needed to start the motor.

"Something I heard from Chaven. Dammit, I thought she'd be safe from all this."

"No doubt Kyler has some excellent sources of information and an instinct for finding an opponent's vulnerable points," he said as he shifted and hit the gas.

"Hurry, but be careful. The cops are looking for me now." I tore off the cap and telltale muffler and dropped them behind the seat.

"What's happened?"

While he negotiated a route out of the district, I filled him in on things. "I guess you could say he kept his word; he didn't come after me, he only had to step aside and let Blair do the work."

"And yet he did not give you away to him."

"I think that whole fiasco was a test to see what I'd do when cornered. In one move he's gotten himself off the suspect list for the murders, shifted it onto someone else, and learned that much more about what I can do. He's probably figured there's no way to get a direct hold on me, so he'll try to get to Bobbi instead."

"Which indicates that he must want something of you."

"He wants me out of the way. Anybody who can do what I do is too dangerous to have loose. I'd just like to know what he meant about 'working that out.' "

"Perhaps he's researching the folklore section of the local library."

"Oh, great." I had a nightmare vision of Chicago's underworld searching for me, armed with crosses and draped in garlands of fresh garlic. It was just as well those items only worked at the movies. On the other hand, a hammer and stake were also part of the vampire hunter's traditional arsenal, and I knew from experience just how terribly effective *those* were.

"What about the photograph?" he asked.

I shrugged. "I'm not even sure I'll show up on the plate, but first things first."

"Absolutely," he murmured, concentrating on his driving. He beat through a couple of stop signals while I kept an eye out for patrol cars. The street traffic was mercifully light at this hour, but it still seemed to take a long time to get there.

It was the middle of the week, but the Top Hat Club had a good crowd if we could tell anything by the number of cars in the parking lot. Neon lights spelled out the name of the club against the clear sky and a glowing red top hat danced endlessly from side to side below them. Both caused confusing reflections on the windows of the cars, making it difficult to tell if any were occupied.

"I'll go check things inside," said Escott as he found a place to park. I started to object, but was interrupted. "They won't let you past the door dressed like that," he pointed out.

He was right and my regular clothes were inconveniently packed away in a bag in the car's trunk. We'd both prepared for the necessity of having to drop out of sight in case things went wrong.

"Besides, you could alarm the ones we're after if they should see you. Since they know what you look like, your sudden appearance could lead to an unfortunate incident."

"I'll do more than just alarm them," I growled, but saw the sense of things. I described Tinny as best I could. Escott took it in, then slipped out to go to the club. I got out on my side to make a more thorough search of the parking lot.

All I found were some courting couples in different cars who were generating enough personal heat to ignore the low outside temperature. They also ignored me, but then I was going out of my way to be quiet. I'd retrieved the cap and muffler from the back of the car and had wrapped up again. They linked me to the search Blair was conducting, but that was a few miles away, and I felt safe enough using them here. Nevertheless, I was quick to duck out of sight when a police car cruised past on its rounds.

A street ran behind the club and was where I usually parked while waiting to pick up Bobbi when she was through for the night. The manager and a few other employees also parked there, so I was familiar with their cars. The Olds on the end close to the back entrance was new to the spot, though, and there were two men sitting inside.

Maybe it was the jackpot, but I'd have to be sure first. There was no percentage in committing mayhem against innocent citizens. I assumed a casual walk and paused in front of it. The light was bad for them, but I gave them a chance to notice me and made a point of returning the favor.

The one on the driver's side turned on the headlights. The harsh glare was probably meant to discourage me; understandable, since I was more or less dressed like a suspicious character. I shaded my eyes against it and moved out of the way. The lights cut and they laughed a little. I nodded back in a friendly way and slapped my pockets for a battered pack of cigarettes, pulling one out.

"Gotta match?" I called so they could hear me through the windows.

Neither of them answered. I walked up to tap the driver's door and repeated my question. His hat was pulled low, so I couldn't see much above his hard jaw line. He rolled the window down and told me to scram. "Kyler sent me," I whispered.

He and his partner exchanged looks. "Who?" he asked.

"You heard me. He said to say the deal's off and to get out of here."

"I don't get it. You trying to make trouble?"

"Just trying to keep you out of it. Let the cops nail you if you want, it's no skin off my nose, but I wouldn't want the boss to think I didn't know how to listen to orders."

The driver frowned deeply and I wondered if he'd recognized me despite the muffler. By now I was fairly sure he was one of the mugs who had invaded the house. I was ready for a hostile response; instead, he leaned forward to start the car.

"What about Tinny and Chick?" he asked.

"They're leaving with me. It's safer."

He nodded once, shifted the gears, and pulled out of his slot. As soon as he turned into the main street, he hit the gas and didn't stop for as long as he was in earshot.

I gaped after them and indulged in a laugh of my own. This was almost too easy.

Escott would have the front of the club covered by now, but he might not have been able to invade the backstage area. I trotted up the steps to the rear door and slipped inside. A tall curtain blocked the audience's view of the utilitarian walls, but when the stage lights were on it was filmy enough to see through. I had a fine backseat for the floor show.

The band had just started up a bright and brassy fanfare, which brought on an abrupt burst of applause. I got a filtered view of Bobbi making her entrance for a novelty number. She was dressed like a feminized version of Frank Buck in white satin jodhpurs, matching bush shirt, patent leather riding boots, and a sequin-trimmed pith helmet. The explanation for the costume came when she launched into her rendition of "The Animal in Me." She charmed her way through the first chorus, skipped to one side of the stage, and pretended to hunt around for jungle dangers. As she returned, a line of tap dancers wearing tinsel grass skirts and strategic coconut shells followed.

They scattered across the stage to the delighted hoots from the audience and hammered out the number. A few bars later, the girls screamed and drew back in mock terror as a guy in a gorilla suit strutted out of the wings. He wore a white tie and collar and carried a walking stick. Bobbi sang more lyrics to the gorilla, then joined him in a little soft-shoe, hamming things up like crazy. The gorilla dropped to one knee to present her with a bouquet of fake flowers that magically appeared in his paw. Bobbi pantomimed a show of flattery, but decided to turn him down. The gorilla roared to his feet, grabbed Bobbi, and threw her over his shoulder. She gave out with another chorus from there as he carried her around the stage.

Just as it looked like the gorilla would run off with her, a second gorilla appeared in their way. This one wore an apron and carried a comically large rolling pin, which she used to threaten her "husband." He hastily put Bobbi down, mimed unconvincing innocence, and got bashed on the head for his trouble. While he was still reeling, his "wife" grabbed his ear and marched him offstage. Bobbi shrugged elaborately, then she and the dancers went into another chorus. She eventually made her own exit on a papier-mâché elephant pulled by an unseen member of the technical crew.

Even from my spot the show looked slick and full of fun. The applause didn't die down until she came back for a short reprise, sung from the back of the elephant. She made a final bow and rode away, waving and blowing kisses.

I couldn't hold still after that and worked my way around to her, arriving in time to watch her climb off the elephant by way of a ladder built into its upstage framework. The satin pants suited her admirably, especially from where I stood.

She was flushed and grinning, surrounded by the other girls for a brief moment until she caught a glimpse of me and stopped. I suddenly remembered to unwrap the muffler and her smile returned like a burst of light when recognition came. She threw her arms around me in a bear hug and I lifted her off the floor in delighted relief. All the pressures of the last few nights, all the fears, major and minor, dropped away from my overloaded brain at this expression of her honest, uninhibited joy.

For what seemed like a long time I'd been wandering blind and lost in one of the darker corners of my mind. I held on to her, feeling the warmth of her spirit and body soaking into my own. Maybe we both felt it, since neither of us was in much of a hurry to let go of the other. I kissed the top of her silky blond head, working my way down to her lips. When she finally came up for air my mood had undergone a considerable shift. My upper canines had started to bud.

She noticed right away. "Do I always have this effect on you?"

That raised a smile out of me, albeit a closemouthed one. "I've

missed you, baby." I caressed the soft skin of her neck. Now was
the time or place for that sort of thing, but soon, perhaps.

A couple of girls whooped and whistled at this unintentional sh
until the stage manager told them to clear off.

"You too, Bobbi," he said. "Get your boyfriend outta the way or it's
both our hides."

Bobbi's boss was not sympathetic to visiting friends, no matter what
the circumstances. I put her down again and she took my hand, leading
the way to her dressing room.

"Not that I'm not glad to see you, but why so early, and what's with
the getup?" she asked.

"Charles and I are working late and there's been some trouble."

"It's that bracelet thing, isn't it?"

"Yeah, sweetheart."

"What kind of trouble?"

"You ever hear of Vaughn Kyler?"

She stopped short, her big hazel eyes going wide. "Yes, I have. My
God, Jack, what have you gotten into?"

"Nothing I can't get out of, but he knows about you and I'm here to
keep anything from happening."

"Me? What's he want with me?"

I explained the situation in a few quick sentences. The blood drained
out of her face and the grip of her hand got tighter. "I already got rid of
two of them," I said, "but there are at least two more right here in the
club."

"Where's Charles?"

"Out front, I guess, but I'm not leaving you to go looking. He can
take care of himself. Whether your boss likes it or not, you've got a bodyguard for the time being."

"And who's going to bodyguard you?"

"I'm in no real danger; that's why Kyler's trying to get to you, honey.
We've gotta come up with a safe place for you to stay until the shooting's
over."

"You're not exactly inspiring me with confidence when you talk like
that. Are you serious about shooting?"

"Very serious."

She shook her head, not in denial, but with stretched patience.
"Okay. Let's sit down and see if we can figure out what to do next."

"In your dressing room, I want my back to a wall."

"I think that's where you'd rather have me," she said. The situation
may have been threatening, but she was still flying high from the show,
and detached her hand from mine to make a playful swat at my butt. I
took what was dished out and tried to return the favor, but she just

managed to dance out of the way in time. Laughing, we reached her dressing room door, but she sobered and stood back so I could look inside first.

It was well that I did. I was all but nose to nose with Tinny. He'd found another gun and it was ready in his hand. The mutual surprise froze us both for a second. Possibly as a distraction from the unpleasantness, I found myself noticing every detail of his plain face. Sometime tonight since the scuffle on the stairs at home, he'd acquired a road map of fresh scrapes. One of them was still oozing and I caught a whiff of the bloodsmell.

"Jack . . . ?" Bobbi couldn't see anything, but had picked up that something was wrong.

Tinny jammed the gun under my jaw. I decided not to move. He shifted a little, caught sight of Bobbi, and grinned. "Hold it there, cutie, or I make a mess."

Bobbi gasped once and held it, doing what she was told.

"Go get her, Chick," he ordered.

His big partner, who had been standing well behind him, nodded. "Three birds with one trip," he said. I wondered what the hell he meant by that, then put it together with Tinny's scrapes and immediately understood what had happened.

Chick started to shoulder his way past us to the hall. It wasn't deserted, but no one had noticed that anything was off, yet. Just as Chick came level with us, I snapped my left hand up and grabbed for the gun.

Tinny might have been expecting something like that, but couldn't have anticipated my speed. As I moved faster than their eyes could follow, their own movements seemed to break down for me. It was like watching a movie with the projector running the film a frame at a time.

Chick saw what was coming and had just enough instinct to duck back into the room. My hand closed over Tinny's and smashed it against the doorjamb. He grunted out a pain-filled objection, but didn't drop the gun. My other hand was still on the doorknob; all I had to do was pull on it. Fast. The edge of the door caught him sharply on the back of the head. The whites of his eyes flashed and down he went.

He was in the way as I forced the door open to get at Chick. The delay provided him a moment to do some reacting of his own. By the time I was through, he'd hauled out a blackjack as thick as a baseball bat and was all set to use it. He raised his arm for a short, vicious swing, then nearly lost his balance in his effort to stop. He let the blackjack fall and raised his arms high. The sound he made had no words, but somehow he was able to express surrender and a plea for mercy in one inarticulate, horrified gurgle.

I looked where he was looking. Bobbi had plucked the gun from

Tinny's slack hand and was aiming it steadily at Chick's crotch. Her
were showing, and it was not a smile.

"Back," she growled.

I knew she was on my side, but found myself backing up a step myself.

She came forward enough so no one in the hall could see what she
was doing. "Jack, pull this lug inside."

I carefully kept out of her line of fire and got a grip on one of Tinny's
ankles. Bobbi followed him in without taking her eyes from Chick or al-
tering the direction of the gun's muzzle. She shut the door, giving us some
very necessary privacy.

Chick started to babble out an idiotic explanation, reminding me of
the gorilla from the dance number. I told him to can it. My attention was
entirely focused on Escott's inert form. They'd dumped him onto the
chaise longue at the far end of the tiny room and had him trussed up like
a leftover Christmas package. While Bobbi kept Chick sweating, I
crossed to Escott in two fast steps and checked for a pulse, drawing in
and releasing a vast sigh of relief when I found one. He was groggy, but
breathing regularly and didn't seem to be bleeding anywhere.

I nodded an all's well to Bobbi, then fastened a look on Chick. "You
got lucky," I said to him. "Now I don't have to break your neck."

3

HE went white at the lips. Despite my assurance, he saw something in me
that frightened him more than the threat of Bobbi's gun. He started to
bolt for the door, but I was on him too fast. I caught his collar and swung
him against the wall, rubbing his face in it.

"Be careful, Jack," Bobbi warned. She wasn't worried about either of
us getting hurt, but that Chick might see more than what was good for
him. The mirror over her dressing table reflected all this side of the room.

I locked my gaze onto his. He had defenses up that he was unaware
of, but those quickly crumbled beneath the tidal force of my own anger
and fear. His pupils shrank to pinpoints and his mouth sagged as I began
to tear into his mind.

"Jack?" Bobbi's voice was troubled with the first hint of alarm.

Part of me knew what I was doing to him and that I should stop, but it was easier for that part to simply get out of the way and let the terrors within rush free.

"What are you doing? Jack?" She touched my shoulder, then shook it, trying to reach me.

His legs started to go.

"Jack?"

It was the dust-dry scent of her fear that finally broke through and saved him. I shut everything down, pulling back before it was too late, pulling back and turning away from her until I had myself under control.

"What is it? What's wrong?"

Three nights now of uncertainties, frustrations, deaths, and near death, and no end in sight; Bobbi's presence had only eased the darkness, not removed it.

"You all right now?" She ran her cool fingers lightly over my forehead. I caught her hand and pressed it against my cheek.

"Yeah, I'm all right." For the moment, but it was enough. I flushed out my lungs with a cleansing breath and felt the stuff ebb away, leaving behind only a faint shadow on my soul. It could return or not. The choice was mine.

"Then what . . . ?"

It was safe to look up. Chick was still conscious, but confused. I told him to close his eyes and go to sleep. He did and I let him slide to the floor.

She watched him go, biting the inside of her lip. "This is part of that kind of hypnosis you do?"

I nodded. "When I'm upset it can get away from me." I tried to say more, to explain it somehow, and couldn't.

"It scares you," she said.

"Yeah."

She left the borrowed gun on a table and came over to hold me, which was exactly what I needed. It didn't last long, because we had to see to Escott, but it helped. She gave me a final squeeze, then found a towel somewhere and wet it down at a tiny sink in the corner. I fished out my pocketknife to cut away the bindings on Escott's wrists.

"What is this stuff, anyway?" I complained, sawing through the fabric with some difficulty.

Bobbi tried unknotting Escott's gag. "It used to be one of my stockings. If they're this tough, how come they get runs so easily?"

"Don't know, but at least they did him up in style. You okay, Charles?"

He made a glottal noise that sounded like an affirmative, but wasn't all that convincing. One of his eyes was starting to puff up and his knuckles were scraped. He winced as Bobbi finally tugged the knot loose.

"Looks like you've been to the war, buddy." I broke through the last strands of silk.

"Several, I think," he muttered thickly, working his sore jaw.

"You want a doctor?"

He shook his head. Cautiously. "I'll be fine." Bobbi dabbed his face with the towel and he was content to lie back and let her fuss over him.

"What happened?" I asked when he looked up to answering.

"I'd come backstage for a quick look round and discovered Tinny waiting here, ready to accost Miss Smythe at the first opportune moment. I'd almost settled things in my favor when the other fellow turned up. After that . . ." He shrugged and touched the back of his skull, wincing again.

I looked at the discarded blackjack and figured that Escott had gotten off very lightly. "We're going to have to get out of here. Are you up to it?"

"You've got to be kidding," objected Bobbi.

"Don't I wish, but those other two mugs I got rid of could be back at any time with reinforcements, and they're going to be pretty sore. There's no law that says Kyler's going to be busy all night making excuses to Lieutenant Blair. If he and his crowd turn up, I don't want you or Charles caught in the cross fire."

"Fine with me, I don't like this kind of roughhouse, but Charles is still—"

"Capable of moving if necessity calls for it," he told her. "The sooner the better, if you please."

She gave him a look of mixed exasperation and affection, then got a bag and began stuffing her street clothes into it.

"It won't bother your boss that you're leaving early?" I asked.

"We just did the last show of the evening when you came in." She paused. "I can't go home, can I?"

"Not tonight. We'll find a hotel somewhere."

She considered the two of us with a raised eyebrow. "*That* should be cozy."

Escott sat up, rubbing his wrists. "Might I suggest a safer haven for all of us?"

"Suggest away," she said, sweeping some odds and ends from her makeup table.

"The Nightcrawler Club."

She stopped packing. That place had a lot of memories for her and the bad ones were still fresh.

Escott was well aware of them. "This is something of an emergency."

"I guess so," she admitted. "But for how long?"

Neither of us had an answer to that.

"And my job here?" She correctly read our faces. "Forget I asked."

"Sorry," I said.

She shrugged. "Don't be. It's better than being with Tinny and Chick. Staying there is a very good idea, I'm thinking maybe Gordy can help us out. If anyone in this town knows about Vaughn Kyler . . . but what do we do with these two clowns? We can't leave them here for the janitor to find."

"We could try questioning them," said Escott.

My recent loss of control had spooked me so much that the last thing I wanted to do was get involved in a hypnotic version of twenty questions. Besides, I'd made a private promise to myself about avoiding that particular mental trap. Now was not the time to inform Escott of my decision or the reason behind it.

I shook my head decisively. "Uh-uh. We've got to get out of here before their friends come looking for them. We'll pass them off as a couple of drunks who tried to get Bobbi's autograph. Where's the club bouncer?"

Bobbi had completed her impromptu packing and pulled on a coat. "I'll take care of it." She whisked out, her boot heels making no-nonsense clacks against the floor.

"As I've said before, what a very remarkable girl," Escott murmured.

"One in a million . . . and I just let her out of my sight." I hastily started after her, but she hadn't gone far. At the other end of the hall she was explaining things to the stage manager, jabbing a thumb in my direction to emphasize a point. He nodded with a grim but satisfied smile and quickly moved off.

Bobbi returned, looking smug. "He'll be back in a minute with Udo and Jürgens."

"Udo and Jürgens?"

"Busboys."

The stage manager soon reappeared with a couple of large young men who were enough alike to be twins. The seams of their white work coats were strained to the limit and I could have sworn that some of their arm hair was sticking out of the gaps. "What do they clear away, real buses?"

"*Shh,* they're really very sweet."

The trio lumbered past to stop only a moment at her dressing room. When they returned, Tinny and Chick were each dangling bonelessly from a massive shoulder. The stage manager brought up the rear, carrying their fallen hats.

"Drunken bums," he muttered. "We'll dump 'em outside, Bobbi. They won't be bothering you anymore."

The twins laughed and I was suddenly very glad not to be one of their parcels.

In the dressing room, Escott was on his feet again and working a dent from his hat. "This establishment certainly employs an effective cleanup crew. Those two fellows reminded me of the giants that built Valhalla."

"In *Das Rheingold?*" asked Bobbi.

"Why, yes. Do you enjoy opera, Miss Smythe?"

"If it's done right. Back in school I was in some Gilbert and Sullivan. . . ."

"Are we ready to leave?" I interrupted.

"Wait a second." Bobbi got her bag of clothes and paused long enough to stuff Tinny's gun and Chick's blackjack into her purse. "You never know when one of these might come in handy," she informed us, then led the way to a side exit.

Once out of the building, my feeling of vulnerability became more pronounced with the abrupt slap of cold air. We hustled to Escott's car, crowding together on the front seat. Despite his protest that he was fit, I insisted on driving and told him to keep his eyes peeled for tails. Our route north was an indirect one and in the end I was satisfied that we hadn't been followed.

I stopped in the service alley that ran behind the Nighlcrawler Club, cut the motor, and waited. The back door soon opened and a couple of mugs emerged to check on us. Escott rolled down his window and Bobbi leaned over to hail one of the men.

"Ernie? How you doing?"

The shorter man relaxed when he recognized her. "Hey, it's Bobbi. What're you doin' here, babe?"

"Come to visit Gordy."

"He's busy now, but he'll see you." Ernie made a point of noticing me and Escott.

"These are some friends," Bobbi explained. "They're okay."

He squinted, doubtful. " 'F you say."

"Can we park the car here?"

"Yeah, but not for all night."

"Good enough." At that, we piled out and Ernie escorted us into the building.

The kitchen was more or less familiar to me, as were the stairs and upper hall. About six months ago Slick Morelli's goons had dragged me over the same ground for a little rough questioning and the memory of the event was still strong. The circumstances were happily different this time, but I had a shiver of discomfort to suppress all the same.

Gordy, Morelli's lieutenant, had taken over the operation of the club and whatever else his New York bosses had an interest in; the Nightcrawler was only part of the iceberg. Most of the businesses were entirely illegal, but like any other, in need of good management in these hard times. He ran the operation efficiently, profitably, and with a minimum of trouble, exactly as required.

We were ushered right up to the office with its pastoral landscapes and comfortable leather furniture. Gordy loomed over a desk piled high with stacks of loose cash and canvas money bags: that evening's casino take. A huge, phlegmatic man, his eyes crinkled when he saw Bobbi, his version of a delighted grin. He nodded a greeting to me and Escott, then gave us all a second look, taking in Bobbi's flashy costume and bag as she removed her coat, my informal working clothes, and Escott's by now obvious battering.

"What's the problem?" he asked.

"Vaughn Kyler," said Bobbi.

Behind us, Ernie muttered something unintelligible. Gordy fastened his small eyes on him and jerked his head. Frowning, Ernie shut the door, his steps retreating down the stairs. Gordy gestured for us to take seats. Bobbi and I huddled together on the couch, Escott sank into its matching chair. Gordy came around the desk and leaned one hip on it, ignoring the bundles of cash as though they were so much confetti.

"Give," he said, never one to wait on ceremony.

By silent consent, I was elected storyteller. Maybe my past journalism experience had something to do with it. I went through all of it, starting with the original job Escott had taken on to recover the stolen bracelet, and ending with the disposal of Tinny and Chick.

"Right now, what we need is to drop out of sight for a while until we can figure out how to settle things with Kyler," I concluded.

"Don't see how you can do it. Kyler's gotten pretty big in this town. I can help some, but not that much. I don't want to risk a war and neither will my bosses."

"Can you at least offer Miss Smythe a place of safety?" asked Escott.

"No problem on that, same for you if you want it. Kyler's real target is Fleming and I can tell you he won't give up."

Bobbi didn't like his answer. "But what about Jack? You can't just toss him in the street to get run over."

"Gordy's saying that he doesn't have much of a choice," I told her. "If Kyler catches on to where I am—"

"Who's going to tell him?"

"Nobody," said Gordy. "He's able to figure it out for himself."

Bobbi read him right. "You mean he's already . . . ?"

"He called me about ten minutes ago."

Escott leaned forward. "Has he now? What was his purpose?"

"He wanted to know everything I could tell him about Fleming. I said I didn't know much, but he wouldn't have bought that. From what's been happening, I'm thinking he's got other places to go for news."

"And what has been happening?"

"You remember the *Elvira?*"

Slick Morelli's yacht. The scene of my murder. I remembered. Too well.

"When it went up for sale, Kyler bought it."

We all exchanged uneasy looks. "Why?" I whispered.

Gordy gave a minimal, but eloquent shrug. "He's after you, kid. That's all you need to know."

Bobbi wrapped her hands around one of mine. "Are we so positive that Kyler wants to kill Jack?"

When I'd summarized things for Gordy, I'd mentioned the death of Kyler's lieutenant, Hodge, but had been circumspect about the details. "Sorry, baby, but I'm stuck with it. He had a chance to call it all off tonight and didn't, and the proof is the easy fifteen grand he gave up in the trying."

"Then what will you do?"

Good question.

"Perhaps a little information gathering of our own is in order," Escott suggested thoughtfully. "Does Kyler still make his home at the Travis Hotel?"

"He's got the top floor all to himself," said Gordy. "If you're thinking on a visit, think again. He's turned the place into a regular bank vault."

"What may one expect to find?"

"Steel shutters on the windows, bulletproof glass, and an army of guys just looking for trouble to come their way."

"What does the management of the Travis think of their guest?"

"What can they think? He owns it."

"Convenient for him, I daresay."

"You got an idea, Charles?" I asked.

"No. But doubtless one will turn up. Some research is required first, beginning with what kind of questions Kyler had concerning you."

Gordy's gaze turned inward to his memory and he gave us a succinct recounting of the conversation. The more I heard, the less I liked it.

"He's too damned interested in what happened aboard that yacht," I said.

"Not to mention what you've done since then," Escott added soberly, letting all the implications sink in. "You haven't exactly led a quiet life lately. You've been fairly invisible to the papers and the police, but there are numerous other places to go for information, and Kyler would have gleaned each of them clean by now. I don't suppose you would consider allowing Kyler to go ahead and kill you?"

"I hope you mean that the way I think you do."

"Certainly. Arrange things in your favor so that he thinks you've been eliminated. You've done it before."

"By accident, and I only got away with it because no one was looking for anything unusual."

"That's for damn sure," said Gordy, who had been a witness.

"I can't count on Kyler to fall for that. If he has an idea about what I am, he'll know bullets won't do the job."

"And you weren't able to influence him, either," Escott said, referring to the attempts I'd made to hypnotize Kyler the night before.

"Nope."

"So forced persuasion or driving him insane may be eliminated as options."

"Yeah, though with him it would have been a short trip." Great. Now I was making jokes about it. Maybe I was getting used to the situation. Or maybe it was the way everyone was watching me, as if I had the easy answer.

Gordy shrugged again. "If you want any advice, I'd say change your name and get out of the country. That . . . or kill him first."

Bobbi's hands tightened over mine.

That was Gordy's easy answer, and the one I'd expected to hear. "Okay, say that I did it. I'd have to take care of his lieutenants, too, because they'd know who to blame and still be coming for me. Where does it stop?"

No answer.

"And I don't know if I can do it. Not cold. Not just walking in on him. Could you?"

His expression was unchanged, which made his reply that much more disturbing. "Yeah, kid, I could, but I don't want a war. This has got to stay between you and him."

Escott gave me a long, steady look, which I did not return.

"Does it bother you being back here again?" I asked, holding the door for Bobbi.

"Back in the club or this part of it?"

"This part." I gestured around at what had once been Slick Morelli's bedroom.

"It's just another place now that he's gone."

Some of the furnishings were still intact: the bed, a few pictures on the walls, tables, but it had the impersonal look of a hotel. Bobbi ignored it all to push open a second door leading to a smaller bedroom and went in.

"But this is where I'll want to sleep," she added.

It, too, had been stripped down, but didn't look quite so empty now that she was there. She put her bag on the dresser and let her overloaded purse drop next to it with a thud.

"They've got you backed into a corner, haven't they?"

I watched as she began setting her things out. "What do you mean?"

"First Kyler, now Charles and Gordy. It's like they're all pushing you into something you don't want to do."

"But may have to."

"It's already tearing you up. What happens to you afterward?"

I had no answer for her, not having one for myself.

She stopped unpacking and looked at me straight. "We can leave town like Gordy said. That would save everybody the most trouble."

"How do you figure?"

"I don't need to give you a list. Jack, you'll have come up with enough reasons of your own by now."

"Yeah, baby, and every one of them has an argument against it. We could take off and disappear, but then what happens to Charles? Kyler's after him as well. Say he decides to come along and we all start over some place else, we'll always have to be looking over our shoulder. I do enough of that already."

"Okay, but can you live with the other thing?"

"It wouldn't be any problem for me to float right into Kyler's steel-lined fort. He has no defense against that. If I know where he is, I can get to him. I've thought it all out."

"But . . . ?"

To kill. I'd done it before. Once by accident, while unused to my new strength, again, and quite deliberately for personal revenge, and again in a black moment of insanity. So much had happened in so short a time that I was afraid of that blackness returning, perhaps for good.

"But I think too much," I concluded.

"Just don't shut me out, Jack. I'm in this with you. No matter what happens, you're not alone."

I looked at her troubled face, remembering all the rough spots she'd pulled through, and felt something like a lump coming up in my throat. I drew her close, both of us clinging hard to one another and shaking a little. She started to speak, but I shushed her. "No more talk, sweetheart. I'm all talked out for now and running out of time. I just want to be with you while I can."

"Especially here?" she murmured. "Where we started?"

"We started downstairs in the casino hallway," I reminded her.

"And ended up here. Where we first made love."

"Not ended, I hope."

"Never."

I kicked the door shut. "Gordy better not shoot the lock off this time."

We suffered no inconvenient interruptions, during or after. We were quiet and intense, both needing the reassurance of touch, not speech. For me the little room filled with the sound of Bobbi's quickening breath and heartbeat and the susurrant whisper of my hands over her skin. As it often did for me, time seemed to slow between one beat and the next, my own movements slowing to match. Our leisurely dance took us to her bed once more and with no less passion than we'd known the first time.

I drew on her life, on all that she was and was willing to freely give. We drifted for ages, without thought or motion to disturb that perfection of sensation. When at last I pulled away enough to look down at her, she was shivering—not with cold or pain, she insisted, but from the aftermath of the pleasure.

"Your eyes are all red," she observed. We'd forgotten to shut off the light. "No, don't turn away. I like it."

"You sure?"

She chuckled. "My demon lover."

We settled against one another. Bobbi fell asleep in my arms; I stared at the ceiling and dreamed.

Times like this were the toughest.

Not that there was a lot of misery in my life, but now I would have given almost anything to be able to drop off to sleep—real sleep—with Bobbi and wake to see her in the morning sun. My condition gave me many advantages, but intertwined were restrictions that could never be ignored.

One of them was immortality. Or the next closest thing to it.

It sounds like a good idea, but what do you do in decades to come as your family and friends age and die while you stay ever the same? Life was so ephemeral—if not for me, then for everyone else. What would happen to Bobbi and me? We'd exchanged blood on many occasions. There was a slim chance she might change to be like me, but absolutely no guarantees, only equal amounts of hope and despair until the day she died.

And what then, if I lost her forever?

I held her, listening to the long sigh of her breath, to the fragile rhythm of her heart.

I held her and ached with the awful loneliness that I had come to realize was special to my kind.

I held her and could have wept from it.

These were the tough times. When it's the deepest part of midwinter night and you know you'll never sleep again, it's all too easy to fall into a bleak mood and think it'll last forever. Tonight I was especially vulnerable because I was contemplating another man's death and felt the memory of my own stir in fretful sympathy.

There wasn't much I could do about it, not here and now.

I faded away and floated clear of the sheets and blankets. The bed hardly creaked as my weight simply vanished and the covers caved in on the space my body had occupied. Bobbi lay undisturbed until after I reformed and bent to kiss her lightly on the temple. She smiled and snuggled more deeply into the pillows.

Demon lover, indeed, I thought as I dressed, shut off the light, and silently glided out.

Escott and Gordy were still in the office. Escott had turned up an ice bag and held it to his eye to bring down the swelling. The stacks of money were gone, replaced by coffee and sandwiches. The air was thick with cigarette smoke. The number of discarded butts in the desk ashtray indicated that they'd gone through at least one pack while I'd been saying good-bye to Bobbi.

"Any more calls from Kyler?" I asked.

Gordy answered. "No, but there's a couple of cars covering the club that don't belong out there. He knows what's going on."

That was a hint I couldn't ignore. "Okay, no sense dragging you into this more than necessary. I'll make sure they see me leaving."

Escott put the ice bag down. "You've decided what to do?"

"Yeah." Then there was a long pause as they waited for me to go on, only I didn't want to. "I'll call later . . . let you know what happens."

"Do you wish some company?"

I was tempted to say yes, but shook my head. Danger to him aside, something like this would have to be done alone. "Just keep an eye on Bobbi. Don't let those goons come anywhere near her."

No more questions after that. None were needed. I took the steps downstairs slowly, as though I were going to my own execution, not Kyler's.

The kitchen was deserted, so I didn't bother opening the door, and just seeped right through it. The outside air seemed harsher than before. Between the high black bulks of the buildings a gray slice of night sky pressed down upon me. The Nash was long gone, presumably parked in some safer spot than the club's back alley.

Covering the right-hand exit to the street was a black Ford. I studied it a moment and checked my immediate surroundings. It was dark enough that they probably hadn't noticed how I'd left the club. I drew in a deep breath of sharp air and puffed it out again, producing a long plume of vapor, then wrapped up in the muffler and walked toward them. I halfway expected—and maybe hoped—to see the passenger window roll down and a gun to poke out. It would be so simple to mime taking a fatal shot and let them charge eagerly back to Kyler to report their success.

But they weren't about to make it that easy for me and they'd be too suspicious if I returned the favor by directly approaching them. As soon as my foot hit the sidewalk I turned south and moved away rapidly, the back of my neck prickling. After I crossed the street and kept going, their motor whined and caught. I glanced back. They were keeping pace some yards behind . . . maybe setting me up for a hit-and-run? Well, I'd been through that before and survived, though a repeat of the experience was nothing to look forward to. The second car pulled up behind them. Better and better; I wanted us all well away from the Nightcrawler before the party started.

By the time I'd crossed another street to the next block they were ready to move in. I broke into a run, fast, but nothing the Ford couldn't easily overtake. They let me get halfway down, then whipped past and stopped square in my path. The second car closed in behind.

No cover presented itself. On my right was the brick face of a tall building, showing windows only, and those too high up for a normal man to break into. On the left was more of the same with a broad bare street between. They'd picked their spot well. I skidded to a stop and waited for them.

The two men in the Ford were the first out. Their guns were ready and covered me while two more emerged from a familiar-looking Olds. The driver of that car knew me right away.

"He's the one," he told the others. "Think you're a smart-ass, don't you?" He was still stinging from my successful con back at the Top Hat.

I offered no opinion as he slapped me down for weapons. I was clean. It wouldn't have made much sense to pack something only to have it taken away again. All he did find was a rather slim money belt that I'd thought to carry. It contained no money, though. In the event that I got caught away from my usual daylight sanctuaries, the narrow pockets of the belt were loaded with oilcloth-wrapped packets of my home earth. It was a sufficient quantity to keep the dreams at bay and allow me full rest. The man only recognized the belt for what it appeared to be and started to remove it.

"Never mind that," I said. "Let's just get going."

He paused, holding his gun steady on my gut. "Tough guy," he said, pretending to be impressed. Then I looked him full in the face and his sarcasm abruptly melted off. He automatically put some space between us.

"Your boss still want to see me?" I prompted.

That got him back on balance. "Yeah," he said. "He's been waiting all night to see to you personally."

He jerked his head toward the Olds. I was in no hurry and moved reluctantly in the right direction. Before I'd taken three steps, the rough murmur of a heavy motor drifted in on the wind. Another car was turning onto our street. Correction, it was a big paneled truck. Kyler's men paused and two of them turned away from the glare of its headlights, their bodies shielding their drawn guns from obvious view. Our whole group must have looked odd, but not enough to inspire any investigation. Probably just as well. The truck pulled around the parked Olds, gears grinding.

As it came even with us, it downshifted and the brakes suddenly squawked. The thing rolled another dozen feet, then stopped. The rear door was wide open, framing three men. All three were armed. The short one on the end took quick aim and fired. The man next to me gave out with a wordless yell and ducked. He got off a return shot that went wild and had no time for a second. Something invisible knocked into his chest and he spun to the pavement.

I dropped flat, eyes shut, and partially dematerialized. I didn't care who saw. Explosions and shouts roared above and around me for what seemed like a very long time but couldn't have been more than a few seconds. Ringing silence followed. I found myself solid once more, eyes blinking against the acrid smoke from their guns.

The men from the truck were out and checking the four bodies that sprawled around me. One of Kyler's men still moved, trying to crawl away. The small newcomer stood over him, taking precise aim at the back of his head. I stared and breathed in the sharp metallic warmth of the blood. I had to swallow hard to keep down the rising knot of bile in my throat. My flash thought that maybe Gordy had decided at the last moment to join in the war went away. None of these faces were familiar or friendly.

The wounded man sensed something and twisted to look up. He froze, his eyebrows high and his eyes popping. It would have been comical except for all the blood.

He started whimpering. "Please . . . I didn't . . ."

"Shut up, Vic," said one of the newcomers. "Jerk never did have any spine. Get him inside."

While the short one kept me covered, Vic was lifted and quickly loaded into the truck. Another of Kyler's men moaned and moved a little. We both noticed at the same time. One fast step and my guard was over him. Without hesitation, he pulled the trigger. The man's body spasmed in time to the blast of the gun, then quivered a few times after the echoes faded, but that didn't mean anything; he was dead.

The other two came out to check on the noise. Neither of them seemed surprised or very upset that their friend's action had taken away half of the guy's head. This was business as usual as far as they were concerned.

The guns were all pointed at me now.

More sudden silence as the one who'd delivered the coup d'grace gestured for me to climb in the back of the truck. I was given no chance to do anything else. The other two each grabbed an arm and hoisted me up. I was dragged in. The doors slammed, shutting us into near darkness, and the driver got things moving. The total elapsed time of the whole business couldn't have been more than forty seconds.

The short one turned on an overhead light and they all sorted themselves onto benches lining either side of the truck. Vic was curled into a silent bundle against the front wall. I remained on the floor, not so much because they wanted me there, but because I was still too stunned by what had just happened. I stared at each of them in turn, trying to separate them into individual faces rather than pale oval blurs that killed.

That's when the next shock set in as I realized that their leader was female.

She wore male clothing, except for the shoes, which were better suited for a tennis court. It was all a little large for her, but practical, once she'd pinned up the cuffs on the pants and overcoat. Her hair was covered by a flat cloth cap. Beneath it was a clean white face with a cupid's bow mouth; A small mole accented her left cheek. She had dark liquid eyes, and didn't look much older than twenty. She took her semi-auto off cock and tucked it into a shoulder holster as though it were something she was used to doing. She watched me watching her and didn't appear to be overly concerned about it.

The two men were older and more obviously tough looking, one with a badly broken nose, the other with a scar like an old burn marring his chin. He tapped out a cigarette and stuffed it in his face with one hand; the other was busy holding a gun on me. He offered one to his buddy and then to the girl, who took it absently, as if her mind were on something else. Probably me. She looked like a starved cat at feeding time and I was the first course.

"Gotta match, Angela?" he asked, not moving his eyes from his target.

She shook her head once, plucked the cigarette from her mouth, and gave it back to him. He took it without comment and returned it to his pack. His buddy produced a match and the air soon got cloudy as they puffed away.

If they meant to unnerve me with their combined stares, it was working pretty well, though once I became aware of my own reaction it lost some of its power. Cautiously, I got to my feet and sat on the bench opposite them. No one objected. No one said anything at all during the whole ride. We were sealed in without windows; I had no clue to our route or destination. Only by a few moments of uncomfortable pressure, mitigated somewhat by the close presence of my earth, did I know we'd crossed water. I could make a reasonable guess that we were somewhere west of the city. Maybe. I asked them no questions, figuring that that opportunity would come when we finally stopped.

So there were more guests at this party than me and Kyler. I could, of course, take care of these three if I chose. I was fast enough in a fight, or could just vanish. They gave me the creeps—hell, Angela was positively terrifying—but I was in no real danger unless they knew about my problem with wood. I was willing to take that chance to find out what they were after.

Our silent ride went on. I didn't bother looking at my watch, not wanting to drop my guard. We took a few more turns, enough for me to lose any sense of our direction and come dangerously close to one of my occasional attacks of claustrophobia.

Another turn. Our speed dropped and the road surface changed, growing rougher. My companions were as stone-faced as ever, but I got the feeling that we'd arrived.

The brakes whined for the last time and the motor stuttered to nothing. I'd grown so used to all the vibration that it still felt as if we were moving—that or I just didn't want to get out and face anything new. The one nearest the door opened it and jumped down. Angela jerked her chin at me and I shifted to my feet and followed, a little unsteadily. I kept thinking about how easily she'd killed off that wounded man. There had been deliberate thought behind it, but no feeling that I could see. Reflexive, like smashing a roach.

The third man dragged Vic out. He stumbled from the truck bed and collapsed on his face.

The driver came around to join us. He was a big mug with a lantern jaw who looked vaguely familiar. He checked me up and down once, but registered no return recognition, then helped pull Vic to his feet.

We stood on a white graveled drive next to the back door of a very large house. I made out two stories of expensive architecture that, again, was familiar. The driver, half carrying Vic, led us inside. Angela remained by me, on guard and looking like she wasn't. The other two brought up the rear. We walked through a plain entry—no frills for deliveries—took a few turns, and found a long hall lined with doors. It was dingy and our feet scraped against stiff, water-damaged carpet. We went through the last door. My stomach started to itch from the inside out as I began to realize where I was.

The room was a vast office, cleaner than the hall, and rich with leather and velvet furniture. The walls were lined with landscapes, traditional, solid, and giving the impression that money wasn't all that important to the people here. I drifted to a halt, Angela and the others pausing with me as I took in the office's showpiece: a larger-than-life portrait hanging behind the desk. The artist had painted to flatter, but I knew the stocky form and large, protruding eyes. In memory and—if I was caught away from my earth—in dark dreams his face haunted me with the recollection of shattering pain and death.

My death. I was standing in the home of Frank Paco, the man who had murdered me.

4

I stared sharply at Angela's profile, comparing it to the flat representation on the wall. The resemblance was sufficiently close to prompt my first question.

"Your father?"

Her eyes flicked quickly over to mine. She pointed to an overstuffed chair and one of her men gave me a nudge forward. The chair was too mushy and low for comfort, apparently designed to make a fast exit from its velvet depths difficult. I accepted it as part of their game and settled in for the time being.

Vic was dropped onto a sofa like a bag of laundry with legs. He moaned, clutching his left shoulder with a red-stained hand.

"Go get Doc," Angela told the driver, he grunted once and left.

Newton. That was his name. Six months ago he'd been guarding a phony laboratory in Paco's basement. He didn't recognize me, but he'd never had the opportunity for a good look. I'd gone in behind him then and knocked him cold. Not too sporting, but necessary in order to get him out before all hell broke loose. Reminding myself about good intentions and certain downhill roads, I wondered if tonight I'd end up regretting my past action.

Angela swept over to the desk and whipped off her cloth cap. Her sooty black hair had been scraped away from her face and pinned up. Without the additional head covering she looked somewhat smaller, but not at all vulnerable. She tore out the pins and stabbed at her hair with impatient fingers. Though a long way from beauty-parlor perfect, it more or less fell into place.

She hitched one hip on the desk, then changed her mind and paced the room, her fists shoved deep into the pockets of her man's coat. She stopped once to look out the door for Newton, then resumed, frowning at the thick rug beneath her soft shoes. The pacing did nothing to alleviate her restless energy or increase her patience at the wait. After her second trip to the door, she returned to the desk and shrugged out of the coat, tossing it onto the sea of oak in front of her. Beneath it was her shoulder holster, the black leather blending well over a dark blouse. Her gun had a bright nickel finish. It might have been a piece of fashionable jewelry the way she wore it.

The two men had taken up stations on either side of me. No one seemed inclined to start a conversation. Except for Angela, we all kept still and watched each other breathe for the next few minutes. As was usual in a very quiet room with strangers, I had to consciously imitate them to avoid attracting notice.

The place—or at least this part of it—must have been thoroughly scrubbed out since the fire. The house had not been totally destroyed, after all, and what was left had proved to be salvageable. There was no trace of the smoke damage in here, only the lingering smell of new paint. Furniture polish, overlaid with stale cigarette smoke and some faint perfume, filled up the corners.

Newton finally returned, bringing company. He held the door for an older man wearing slippers and a black-and-blue-striped bathrobe. His bloodshot eyes were puffy from disturbed sleep and he looked more than a little annoyed with Angela.

"Couldn't this have waited until morning?" he complained, making his unsteady way to her. There was a chair on one side of the desk and he sank into it with a long-suffering groan.

"We had to go when Kyler's boys made their move." She gestured at the sofa. "Fix him up."

He noticed Vic for the first time. That a wounded man lay sprawled and bleeding not ten feet away from him in such a genteel setting didn't seem to alarm or surprise him much. With a pessimistic sigh, he lurched from the chair for a closer look.

"What happened?"

"Kyler's going to be three short the next time he takes roll call. Four, unless you take care of this one."

"What did you do?"

She tapped the butt of her gun with her fingers. "What do you think? This wasn't a shopping trip to the five-and-dime ribbon counter. Some of his boys got in my way. They're dead."

He pursed his mouth. "I hope you're not in over your head, girl."

"Just do your job, Doc."

"Sure, sure. Newton, go get my bag."

Newton trundled out. Doc went to a cabinet and made himself a fast drink. Fast, because he didn't bother to mix it with anything. He perked up a little after his first bracing gulp and looked at me with polite curiosity. My own scrutiny took in his bleary blue eyes and red-veined nose. I knew him, sort of, having met him for a few minutes one busy night last August. He'd been pretty drunk at the time, and now I was hoping like crazy that he wouldn't remember me at all.

I relaxed with inner relief when he turned to Angela and asked, "So who's this guy?"

"The one Kyler's after," she replied, lacing her voice with obvious patience.

His eyes flashed with awakened interest. "Fleming?"

"You tell me. You're the one who was there that night."

He stood and came closer, giving every evidence of a careful examination, but anyone could tell he wasn't certain of himself. "It was a long time ago, this *could* be him. . . ."

Angela nodded to her men. "Search him."

They loomed close, ready to handle any arguments from me, but I stood up, holding my hands out in a calming gesture. They weren't buying any tonight, though, and each grabbed for an arm. I sidestepped one, getting the chair between us, and shoved a fist into the gut of the other. He folded and fell with a low grunt, totally out of breath. By the time his partner got around the chair I was ready for him.

He dodged my punch, tried a short fast one of his own, but I caught his hand in my palm and twisted hard. He cried out once—it was almost enough to cover the snapping bones—and then crumpled to the floor.

I straightened to check on Doc and Angela. He was frozen, but she had her gun out and ready. Her eyes were wide, but she wasn't the type to go into hysterics over a little scuffle.

"You think I'd be dumb enough to carry anything for the cops to identify?" I asked, directing the question at her. "Besides, Kyler's goons have already picked me over."

"Then why bother?"

It had, indeed, been a risk, but better than having them find that telltale money belt. "I got fed up with being pushed around. So would anybody. If you're that interested all you have to do is ask. My name is Fleming, Miss Paco—if that's who you are."

"It is," she said, her big eyes narrowing.

"Charmed, I'm sure. Now, what do you want with me?"

Doc smiled and put in his two cents' worth. "Watch yourself, my dear. It looks like this one's got balls."

"That would make a change," she murmured. "He'd need 'em to go up against Kyler. Except he wasn't doing so well when we found him."

"He seems to be doing just dandy right now, and that's what really counts. Sheldon, you okay?" he asked one of the men on the floor.

Sheldon, who now had some bones to match his broken nose, muttered something obscene.

"Now, now, there's a lady present. Lester, help him up."

The guy with the burn scar nodded vaguely, looking more in need of help himself. He wheezed a few times and eventually made it to his knees.

Unassisted, Sheldon staggered to his feet, clutching his arm and biting back the pain each movement cost him. Doc got him into a chair and clucked over the damage.

"You didn't answer my question," I reminded her. "What do you want with me?"

"Sit down over there and you might live long enough to find out," she said.

"And you're irresistible, too." But I was willing to wait. Lester had gotten his breath back by now, though he looked far from well. He was standing, but in no shape to do much more than glare at me. I could survive that.

"Tell me why Kyler wants you dead," she asked.

"I crossed him a couple of times—for that he thinks I'm dangerous."

"Maybe he's got something there," observed Doc. "He's got a hell of a grip. Shel's going to need X-rays for this mess."

She kept the gun level and steady. "What did you do?"

I demonstrated, forming a fist and closing over it with the other hand. "It's all in the leverage."

"I mean against Kyler."

"You don't have to do anything to get on his bad side. I exist and he doesn't like it. That's all that matters to him. Now, what's your angle?"

She didn't bother to reply to that one. Newton came in just then with a black bag and paused, uncertain about the changes made in the last few minutes.

"Trouble?" he asked, nodding at Angela's drawn gun.

"Yes. Watch him and watch yourself. He's faster than you'd think."

He gave his burden to Doc and took up a post behind and to the left of me. Doc went to work, rooting around in the bag, finally pulling out a syringe.

Alarmed, Sheldon shook off some of his pain. "What're you going to do with that?"

Doc smiled as he squinted at the printing on a small bottle. "You just look the other way and trust ol' Doc. We'll have you playing the piano again in no time."

"But I don't play the piano—*ow!*"

"I'm only rolling up your sleeve, Sheldon."

"Oh."

Angela ground her teeth, not from Doc's ministrations, but at the time spent over them. He gave the fretting Sheldon an armful of something to kill the pain, fixed up a temporary splint, then told him to go to bed. As he wandered out, Angela all but steered Doc over to his next patient.

"Nasty, but not fatal," he concluded. "Not yet, anyway. Let's haul him to the gymnasium so I can clean him up. The light in here stinks."

"I want him awake and able to talk," said Angela.

"Do my best." Doc got Vic to stand, and with Lester's shaky aid, they wobbled toward the door like a trio of chummy drunks. "One thing about all this, Angela, did you get away from there clean?"

She nodded. "Nobody saw but these two and they're not going anyplace."

"Kyler'll be mad as hell about it, though."

"We'll see."

"You can bet on it, girl." He guided Vic and Lester from the room.

Angela shut the door, turning to stare at me. She had that hungry cat expression on her face again and I didn't think it was because she thought I was attractive.

"Alone at last," I said, then glanced at Newton. "Well, almost. So why are you taking on Vaughn Kyler? Tired of living?"

She laughed, unpleasantly, and put away her gun. Somehow, I still didn't feel very safe. "You were here last summer, weren't you?"

"I don't know, I get around a lot."

"You were here the night of the fire. You set it, didn't you?"

Uh-oh. "You seem to think so."

"A young guy calling himself Fleming broke in the house that night—"

"And my name's Fleming so that closes your case. What are you going to do, send me to prison?"

"How 'bout we break his face for having so much lip?" suggested Newton.

"Maybe later," she said. Newton took that to be a promise and subsided with a satisfied nod. Angela walked behind the desk and dropped into the massive red leather chair below the portrait. Despite her small size, she looked like she belonged there.

But things were still up in the air for her and she had trouble staying in one place for long. She lighted a cigarette, quickly smoking it down to nothing. When she smashed it out in an ashtray, she started tapping her nails against the top of the desk. Possibly out of self-defense, Newton tried to open a conversation with her, but she wasn't in the mood to talk. It distracted her from the nail tapping at least, but she got up and began pacing again, checking her watch at short intervals.

The desk phone rang, startling her.

"Who's calling this late?" asked Newton.

"Probably Mac."

"Mac?"

"I've had him and Gib watching the Travis Hotel. . . ." She fairly pounced on the phone and we were treated to her side of the conversation. It wasn't too informative from my point of view, but the news was good, to judge by her pleased expression when she hung up.

Newton was just as interested. "So what'd he say?"

"Chaven went out in a big hurry a little while ago. Mac followed him to where we picked this bird up. Cops are all over the spot like flies on fresh meat, but they don't seem to be doing much."

"So they're not looking for us, then."

"Mac also said that Chaven hung around long enough to go green at all the sights, then ran straight back to the Travis."

"That means Kyler knows what happened."

"But he won't know *who* did it."

"Not yet."

"Not yet," she agreed, looking at me. "Bring him along, I want to check on Doc."

Newton was cautious, but I willingly cooperated this time around and followed Angela down the hall to a different door. It opened onto a spacious and well-lighted gym that had everything but a boxing ring. Filling the room were Indian clubs, weights, punching bags, padded mats, and several odd machines that looked more suitable for torturing people than keeping them fit.

The bloodsmell hit me square in the face. Human, of course, not animal. There's a difference—especially to me. I'd learned to discern that difference early on in my changed life. One was food and the other a complicated mix of emotion and memory guaranteed to inspire some kind of reaction within. Right now it conjured the ghost vision of a dark street, the flash of guns, and men falling around me.

Off to one side was a high table overlooked by sunlamps. Vic lay on it, flat and unmoving. His upper clothes were off and Doc was busy working on his shoulder under the hot lights. Lester was his reluctant nurse.

"I wanted him awake," said Angela, striding over. She was oblivious to the gore.

Doc didn't bother to glance up. "This fella had other ideas. He conked out so fast we almost didn't get him on the table. It's just as well or he'd be making an awful noise at what I'm having to do."

"How much longer?"

"Until I'm finished. Now stand back so I can work."

Fuming, she subsided for a whole minute before drifting over to watch his progress. With a grunt of satisfaction he straightened, holding something in one of his fancy tweezers.

"Got the bullet," he announced. "Pesky things, especially this size. Which one of you carries a forty-five?"

"That's mine," said Angela.

Doc eyed her up and down. "Like to pack a punch, don't you, girl?"

"It does the job."

"You didn't smear it with garlic, did you?"

"Don't be an idiot."

Doc laughed out loud, dropping it into a metal dish. "Just checking," he said, continuing his work. "Bullets are generally pretty clean, but they can force a lot of stuff you don't want into even a minor wound. If the bullet doesn't kill you right away, the infection can sneak up on you later. Hope this guy believed in washing his underwear."

"When can you get him moving again?"

"In a while, give him a chance to get over the shock."

"I don't have the time and you know it. I want him awake and able to talk to Kyler."

"Why?" I asked.

They all looked at me as though I'd committed a major social crime by asking a reasonable question. Angela's eyes flashed fire, throwing a signal to Newton. She pointed to a metal door set in the far wall. Newton urged me toward it. I wasn't too worried and went along with things; I could always find a way to sneak out later and eavesdrop.

I was shoved into a dim chamber with slick white tile covering the floor, walls, ceiling, and built-in benches. Frank Paco wasn't one to do things by halves. Rather than cram himself into a cabinet, he'd installed a full-sized steam room to sweat away his troubles. It was turned off, fortunately, but still smelled like old socks.

Newton slammed the door solidly behind me. The only other exit had to do with the ventilation system, such as it was, and was far too small for a human to squeeze through. I could probably give it a shot but my ingrained claustrophobia inspired me to look for something easier.

The door was locked; I tried the knob anyway, giving it a good rattle for the benefit of my captors. It was the sort of thing they might expect and I didn't want to disappoint them. That obligation out of the way, there wasn't any reason why I should hang around in their improvised cell. Just at eye level, the door had a small window, letting in the only light. My view was limited to a wall full of Indian clubs and Newton's back as he walked away. That was good news; people tend to get upset when I vanish right in front of them, and I had no intention of upsetting this crowd. Not just yet, anyway.

I slipped out and floated free in the open space of the gym, locating the others by memory. It was easy enough to get close and listen, only no one was talking, not even Doc. Somewhat disgusted, I found the hall door and bumbled my way back to the office to make a phone call.

"Charles?"

"Speaking." His voice was tight, guarded. "Are you all right?"

"Yeah, but I got sidetracked. Are things quiet at the club?"

"Yes . . ."

"Hear any sirens in the last hour or so? Close by?"

"Yes, we did, but—"

"I'll tell you all about it later."

"What about Kyler?"

"I never got near him, so don't relax just yet. I need a ride out of here before I run out of night."

"I'm entirely sympathetic; where are you?"

"Remember that spot off the road to Frank Paco's house where you had me wait last summer?"

"Good lord, man, what are you doing out there?"

"I said I got sidetracked."

"This sounds more like a derailment."

"There's something in that. You remember the spot?"

"Vividly."

"Great, 'cause that's where I'll be waiting for you."

"With a full explanation?"

"Cross my heart and . . . hope to see you soon."

This resulted in a noise that might have been a snort or a laugh. With Escott it was sometimes hard to tell. I hung up and took a second look around the empty office.

It was unchanged, plush as ever—except for some bloodstains on the sofa where Vic had rested. High above, Frank Paco's portrait glared at something across the room, probably his oversized fireplace. I thought briefly about Paco, the thought running in a familiar circle about where the bastard was and what he was doing. As always, I ended up with the conclusion long confirmed by Escott that my killer was drooling the rest of his life away in some loony bin. I felt distant pity for him, but no regrets.

Out of habit, I went through the desk drawers in search of anything interesting. Most were locked, but one of the open ones contained a large checkbook just begging to be flipped through. The last six months had been expensive ones for the household. The medical bills to various head doctors were high, but nothing compared to home repairs. Couple those with the fact that Vaughn Kyler had moved in and taken over Paco's operation, cutting off a ready source of cash, and Angela Paco would have more than enough good reasons to want to take him on.

Present was the temptation to swipe the checkbook and give it over to Escott, but in the end I decided not to bother. If he really wanted the thing, I could always come back later. Tonight, or rather this morning, I was more concerned with getting to a place of daylight safety.

Staying solid so I could see and hear things, I returned to the hall, tip-toeing silently on the rough carpet. I was ready to vanish in an instant, especially as I approached the closed door of the gym, but no one jumped out to recapture me.

I had plenty of time yet before Escott arrived; a look through the house would be more comfortable than standing out in the cold waiting for him. Once past the gym, I became cautiously nosy, opening doors and generally poking around where I knew I'd be unwelcome. This job wasn't without its favorable points.

Some of the rooms were empty; perhaps the furnishings had been ruined in the fire or they'd been temporarily moved out for the painters. One of them was lined with tarps and stuffy with the stink of fresh paint; another was still tainted by smoke and water damage.

The kitchen at the other end of the house had been pretty much restored. Curiosity lured me to the basement door and down the steps to seek out the "laboratory" I'd destroyed last summer. The stairs were new, the wood sharp and clean. They led into the kind of sealed-in darkness that even my eyes couldn't penetrate. I felt around for a light switch before going any farther. Vampires—this one at least—don't like the dark any more than the next person.

I found a button and the place became less oppressive. A string of bare bulbs marched away along the ceiling, bravely fighting the gloom, only there wasn't anything for them to shine on. The basement that had once been divided up by a wine cellar, laundry area, and old furniture was now open and bare. The old walls were gone, replaced by rows and rows of pillars to support the floors above. There was no sign of the lab, only some vague scarring on the floor to indicate where the walls had stood.

Having gotten my fill of nostalgia, I returned upstairs for more prowling. The second floor boasted more restoration, or had received less damage, and several bedrooms showed signs of occupation.

Many of the doors hung open. I proceeded very carefully here, listening before poking my head inside to check each room. One of the

larger ones held a comfortable jumble of feminine gear, apparently Angela's. Discarded stockings and lace-trimmed step-ins littered the floor,
dresses were flung across handy chairs, and enough cosmetics crowded
the dresser top to indicate that she had a softer side. She kept no important papers or correspondence, probably reserving that business for the
downstairs office and the locked drawers of its desk. A brief examination
of a side table confirmed the occupant's identity; there I found a gun-
cleaning kit, several boxes of .45 ammunition, and a couple of spare car-
tridge clips. Mixed in with the hardware were several tiny bottles of nail
polish and some well-thumbed women's magazines.

Quite a gal, I thought, and repressed a shudder.

I paused in my poking around, picking up a vague sound nearby. It
did not repeat, but was enough to distract me into investigating.

Down the hall I found its source: Sheldon. He was rolled up on one
of the beds, treating his broken hand with another kind of medicine. In
addition to whatever Doc had shot into him, he'd imbibed plenty of liquid painkiller of his own. He was so far gone as to not be alarmed at seeing me.

"How you doing, Shel?" I asked.

He squinted, grunting with annoyance. "Sonnova bitch. You busted
me good."

"Sorry about that. Hope it gets better."

His eyes were rolling all over the place. "Pay you back. In spades."

"Did you work for Frank Paco?"

"Still do. Not like some wise guys." His good hand closed around the
flat amber bottle on the nightstand. He pulled the cork out with his teeth,
spit it to one side, and drank deeply.

"What wise guys?"

"Vic. Sonnova bitch wen' over t' the big K."

"No loyalty, huh?"

"You said it."

"Are you telling me that Paco still runs things?"

"Hah?"

I repeated the question more slowly.

"He's sick fer now, but his kid's doin' okay."

"What's Angela's angle in all this?"

"She's number one, y' jerk."

"What about Kyler?"

"He'll be sunk soon enough. She's got it all figured. Gotta cute little
ass, too." His mouth twisted around in a sappy leer.

"What's she got figured?"

"The whole thing," he murmured. "And her legs . . ."

"Sheldon . . ."

He woke up a bit, but his mood had soured. I was too much of an intrusion on his dreams of romance. "What're you doin' here, anyway? Newton should be beating yer head in or somethin'."

"Yeah, we have an appointment first thing tomorrow."

"Hah?"

"Never mind, Sheldon."

"Okay," he said cheerfully, and dropped off into instant sleep.

Damn. I hadn't been influencing him, either. It had to have been the combined effect of the booze and the drugs. He might not even remember our conversation the next time he woke up, which would not be soon. Any chance of getting useful information from his wandering brain was long gone. I rescued the bottle from his lax grip, returning it to the stand, and decided to get going myself.

I found the back door and quietly slipped away, hoping the occupants wouldn't be too mystified by my disappearance. Ah, well, Houdini used to be able to walk through walls; if asked, I could always claim him for a distant cousin.

The cold felt good in my underworked lungs and I was glad to flush the smell of the place out with sweet, clean air. My feet crunched on the white gravel as I walked along the drive toward the front. No outside lights were on, nor were there any guards with dogs patrolling the grounds as on my last visit. Excluding the two watching Kyler's hotel, there seemed to be only four men in Angela's army. Three, now that Sheldon was among the wounded. Maybe she had reserves hidden elsewhere. She'd need them to hold her own against his kind of money and organization.

But that wasn't my problem; if I had enough night left and any kind of chance to get at him, then Kyler would cease to be anyone's problem. The survivors, Angela included, could go to hell in a handbasket for all I cared.

Once up on the road, I increased my pace. I wasn't worried about missing Escott; it just felt good to *move,* arms and legs swinging freely as though I'd never really walked before. My long strides quickly ate up the distance, getting me to the right spot in a disappointingly short time. I looked back with regret, not at Paco's house, but the road running past it. To turn now and walk away from the mess I was in, to just keep going until I was lost to everyone but myself . . .

Get behind me, Satan, I thought blasphemously. Stay, and at least one man would die; go, and he would certainly kill my friends and who knows how many others with them. I would stay, of course. I'd made my decision earlier and would stick to it, but damn it all, why me?

The wind was working its way through the pea jacket and really starting to bite when I caught the low murmur of a motor coming my way. I was fairly sure the headlights belonged to the Nash, but kept my head low until it downshifted and coasted to an easy stop. The bullet dents decorating its thick metal hide were clearly visible in the starlight, almost homey in their familiarity, and I emerged from my thin cover in the brush.

Escott seemed relieved to see me and waved me over. Gratefully, I opened the passenger door and climbed in, shutting out the cold. He worked the gears, wresting a U-turn out of the big car until we were on our way back to the city.

Once up to a decent speed, he took the time to give me a good look. In light of some of my past escapades, he was probably checking for damage.

"I'm all right, Charles," I assured him.

"I was rather expecting—"

"Yeah, I just figured that out. Believe me, they're in worse shape than I am. One of them, anyway."

"Indeed? Now about that explanation . . . ," he prompted.

So I started talking. Somehow, it did not shorten the trip back.

"Well, this does throw a spanner into the works," he said when I'd finished.

"Don't see how. Angela and I seem to have pretty much the same goal of getting rid of Kyler, I just have a better chance of doing it."

"Ah, but now you've two gangs to dodge and previously the one was quite enough."

"Yeah, but Angela doesn't really know what she's up against with me. Kyler's had time to read a whole library on folklore and get prepared." Not that it would do him much good, I silently added.

"You may yet find her to be a formidable force."

Formidable. That was the word for her. I'd never be able to forget how deliberately she'd blown open the back of that man's head. "No arguments there. She's her father's daughter and then some."

"And you think her plan is to regain control of the organization Kyler took over from him?"

"Yeah. That's how it looked from what little I saw. I think she wanted to use me in the bargaining, but damned if I know how. It's not as if I'd be a valuable hostage. If she threatened to kill me, Kyler'd be in the front bleachers cheering her on."

"Unless you were meant to be some sort of bait to draw Kyler into the open," he suggested.

"The problem with that is Kyler wouldn't be dumb enough to do it."

"Only if one chooses to underestimate Miss Paco. She's been able to retain the loyalty of at least some of her father's men, quite a feat for anyone, much less a young unproven woman."

"How do we know she's so unproven?"

"Point taken," he admitted. "In certain underworld circles, this is the smallest town in the world when it comes to gossip. I am making an assumption based on the sole fact that I've simply heard nothing about her until now."

"Maybe she just got back from finishing school."

"I shall endeavor to find that out."

"But carefully, Charles."

He took that point as well with the bounce of an eyebrow and a single nod.

"You've heard my version of the shootings," I said. "What about yours?"

"I've little to add that would be useful. We heard the sirens, of course, causing us to wonder whether they had any connection to you."

"You didn't go out to check things, I hope?"

"That was the subject of quite a lot of debate between us."

"You and Gordy?"

"And a number of his men."

That must have been a show to see. I was sorry to have missed it.

Escott continued, "He was most reluctant for me to investigate personally since he felt he'd accepted the responsibility for my safety. We reached a compromise when Ernie volunteered to go just to satisfy his own curiosity. He returned quickly enough with a report on the casualties. He recognized them as belonging to Kyler's gang and concluded that you had dispatched them."

"But I—"

"We, or at least I, know that now, but you may find your reputation has grown considerably in the last few hours with Ernie and his cronies. Be prepared for a bout of hero worship on arrival."

"Hero worship," I repeated numbly. "What about the cops? Do they have any idea about what really happened?"

"According to my own sources within the department, that matter is 'under investigation.' Gordy made a few calls himself and the unofficial conclusion has to do with gang vendettas."

"Which isn't far off the mark where Angela's concerned." I checked my watch. Dawn was only an hour away, but we were within a mile of the club and its sanctuary. All too soon I'd be forced to seek the safety of my lightproof trunk. Another day would flash by with God knows what happening outside and me totally oblivious to it. I had extraordinary advantages over the rest of humanity, but the frustrating price of them was that daily ration of death that could never be ignored.

Escott drove in silence, perhaps sensing my glum mood, or more likely he was tired himself. Between his usual insomnia and the long wait for my call, he wouldn't have gotten any sleep tonight. I was about to make some kind of comment or other to him about it when his head snapped off to the left as though he'd been given a jolt of electricity.

"Damn," he said in a soft, strangled voice and slammed the gas pedal down as far as it could go.

5

THE Nash shot forward, but too slowly for Escott. He came out with another curse and I joined him, hardly knowing why. Past his head I glimpsed the black blur of a car rushing up on us. Yellow-white flashes from its open windows raked my eyes. There was noise: stuttering explosions coming so fast that they merged into a single horrifying roar that deafened all thought, stifled all movement.

Escott kept saying "damn" over and over again—somehow I could still hear him—as he fought to dredge more speed from the Nash. He clawed at the wheel and cut a right so hard that I would have tumbled into him except for a timely grab at the dashboard. The explosions stopped only briefly, then resumed as the gunman came even with us once more. Huge pockmarks clattered across the windows.

My own throat went tight and my leg muscles strained against one another, trying to run where running was not possible. I had to trust Escott to get us out and he had to trust his car. Its big engine pulled us ahead a bare two yards and the shooting abruptly ceased for a few heavenly seconds, started, then stopped again.

Escott swerved to the left; I grabbed the top of the seat so hard that the covering ripped. We tapped something and bounced away in reaction, then hit it again more decisively. The Nash shuddered, but kept plowing forward at top speed until Escott hauled us to the right and we emerged from a narrow street to a larger one on two shrieking wheels. When the other two landed heavily on the pavement, I was nearly blasted into the backseat by the sudden acceleration.

Through the rear window I glimpsed the other car sideswipe a lamppost and not recover from the impact. It lurched and faltered, then swung out of sight as we took another quick turn, running like hell through a stop signal and ignoring the horn blasts of an outraged trucker. He missed broadsiding us by a cat's whisker.

Escott's teeth were showing and his eyes were wild as they darted from the rearview mirror to the front, to the sides, trying to cover everything at once as we tore along the early-morning streets. He wasn't interested in using the brakes just yet. For that, he had my wholehearted support.

After the second red light he began to slow down to something like a normal speed. I pried my hands loose and watched them shake—hell, I was shaking all over after that—and asked if he was okay. He came out with one of those brief, one-syllable laughs that had nothing to do with his sense of humor.

"Did you know them?" he asked, but didn't wait for an answer. "The driver was that rat-faced fellow who took my Webley last night."

Chaven. I groaned inside. "Kyler thinks I bumped off the men he sent after me."

"That would be a logical conclusion for him to draw. It appears that Miss Paco has not taken the opportunity to inform him of his error."

"Goddammit, Charles, it came that close to killing you!"

"Yes," he agreed, and that's when I noticed the tremor in his hands as they worked the wheel and gears. His knuckles were white, the tendons taut. I faced around front and pretended not to notice. He was handling his fear in his own way and didn't need me to point out the obvious.

"I should never have let myself get sidetracked," I muttered.

"As if they gave you much choice in the matter. If you wish to put the blame for this incident upon anyone, let it be Kyler."

"Incident?" But I canned the rest of it since he was right. Except for having all but the shit scared out of us, we were unharmed. If he wanted to reduce an attempted double murder down to the level of an "incident" that was his business. Mine, I knew, was to eliminate all possibility of it happening again. Bobbi, Escott, and even Gordy were far more valuable to me than bug-house bait like Kyler. Better him and his whole organization than my only real friends.

An unpleasant but necessary job.

A shudder crawled up my spine at that thought. The last time it had brushed through my brain, I'd been out of control. To kill the way I had killed, you had to go crazy for a while. My main fear was that once there, I might not be able to find my way back.

"The sun will be up soon," Escott reminded me. "We cannot risk returning to the club."

"And home and your office are out," I concluded. "We have to find a bolt hole somewhere in this town that Kyler won't look into."

"Or even suspect. I think that might be arranged."

"Can you arrange it before sunrise? If I have to I can hide out in the trunk of the car for the day, but . . ."

"Yes, I'll see what I can do," he promised, and we picked up speed again. Then he stared into the mirror and said, "Oh, bloody hell."

"What?" I asked, looking out the back window with a fresh dose of alarm. If a simple "damn" was his reaction to a machine gun hit, "bloody hell" could only mean an earthquake was sneaking up on us.

Not quite, as it turned out. The car closing in had flashing roof lights and a siren.

"Can we lose him?" I asked, hoping he'd say yes.

Escott shook his head. "He's in a radio car. If we run, he'll only call in others to track us down. Perhaps we can reason with him."

Translated: I would be the one to "reason" with him. Wonderful. "You sure about that? I wasn't all that good at debate in school."

"My dear fellow, this night has been quite busy enough for both of us. I, for one, have no wish to top things off by collecting a traffic citation."

"Okay, okay." This was only his way of saying that I owed him one.

Escott came to a gradual stop by a streetlight and gave the motor a rest. The cop pulled up behind us and got out cautiously, hand on his gun. Escott tried to roll down his window, but something was wrong with the mechanism. He gave up and opened the door instead, which made a terrible creaking, cracking noise that echoed off the nearby buildings. It almost sounded like a gunshot and startled all of us for a moment. Escott remained seated, doing a fair imitation of polite innocence. The cop looked him over carefully, and told him to come out. Escott complied.

"Is there a problem, officer?" he asked, using his blandest tone and most formal accent.

"Your license and registration," he ordered. They attended to that ritual, then I was ordered out of the car to take my turn. "You two wanna tell me what happened here?" He gestured at the car.

Escott followed the gesture, all ready with a distracting story so I could move in for the dirty work, but he hauled up short. It was one of the few times in our association that I had ever seen him totally speechless. He couldn't have not known that the car would be a mess, but there's a wide difference between knowing in your mind and seeing with your eyes.

"Oh, bloody *hell*," he repeated, full of sincere anguish and anger.

The thick windows on his side were nearly opaque with chips and cracks where the bullets had struck; many of them were exactly level where his head had been. A fresh pattern of dimples, dents, and a long ugly scrape ran along the door panels. The paint job was a disaster, but the heavy steel glinting through it was still good for a few more miles and then some. About the only difference between his armored Nash and a tank were the headlights, wheels, and lack of mounted guns.

And if Charles Escott loved anything, he loved his car. This had left him stunned as few things would.

"Well?" The cop raised his voice to penetrate Escott's shock. No reaction. The cop then looked to me for an answer. I had enough light to work with; I smiled and got his undivided attention.

Blithely unaware that he'd ever stopped, the cop drove away. We wasted no time taking another direction until Escott spotted an open gas station and parked a little past it. He said something about a phone call and walked back to place it. I got out as well to work some of the stiffness from my tense muscles. I'd only given the cop straight inarguable suggestions—better than getting caught in the trap of deep hypnosis— but it was still disturbing for me. Walking around the car a few times and letting the icy air clean out my lungs helped ease things until Escott's return.

He walked back quickly enough and I was glad to get going again. My imagination was working too well visualizing what could happen if we didn't find a hole to pull in after us.

"I called the club and let Gordy know we wouldn't be back tonight," he said.

"You told him about the hit?"

"Yes, though he was not especially surprised. That machine gun made a devil of a row; they had no trouble hearing it."

"What about Bobbi? Is she all right?"

"Miss Smythe is still sleeping soundly. No doubt her interior room muffled most of the noise."

Between that, her club performance, and our lovemaking, it'd take more than a greeting card from a Thompson to wake her up. It was okay by me; I'd rather have her sleeping through the storm than worrying about us.

"Gordy and his men will remain on guard today. With this shift in the situation from a quiet kidnapping to an outright attack, he deems it to be the safest course of action. This presumes that you still mean to go through with—"

"I will," I said shortly, interrupting before he could put it into words and bring it that much closer to being a reality. He caught the hint and dropped the subject without further comment.

"Now, as for our own shelter, I've set something up, but we must hurry. You're running out of time."

He was right about that. The sky was starting to lighten. Invisible to Escott, perhaps, but very noticeable to me.

We headed south and kept going. I was tempted to ask him where, but he was concentrating on street signs and it was in my own interest not to disturb him. He took us into a stark section of the city that was full of the kind of shadows that could out-wrestle even the noonday sun. I began to get my own general idea of what he'd planned, and as we traveled more deeply into the area, I breathed a sigh of relief.

He slowed as we approached a block full of aggressively drab buildings that only a bulldozer could have improved. Some broken windows were boarded up, others had been left to gape helplessly at the deserted street. We coasted to a silent stop and Escott flashed the headlights once, frowning with tension.

"There." I pointed. "Is that it?"

Halfway down, the double doors to a decrepit and outwardly abandoned garage swung open, guided by two vague figures wearing overalls. One turned and waved us forward. Escott worked the gears and we quickly slipped into a cramped and greasy repair bay. Even as he cut the motor and lights, the tall doors closed, shutting us into a pitch black limbo.

"This is it," he confirmed in the sudden quiet.

A flashlight came out of nowhere and blinded me as the man holding it checked first my face, then Escott's. We must have passed because it swept down to the stained floor and we were told to get out. Escott did so without hesitation and I copied him. I didn't know the man's voice, but it sounded reasonably polite, and no one seemed to be pointing anything lethal in our direction.

We followed the flashlight beam through several tool-littered workrooms and a place that might have served as an office. It connected with a short bare hall that led directly to an outside door. Waiting in the narrow alley beyond was a newer version of the Nash we'd just left, minus the bullet scars. The back door opened for us and we piled in, leaving our escorts behind.

Two men were in the front seat; the tall one on the passenger side turned around and extended his hand.

"Charles, how the hell are you?" asked a rich voice, an actor's trained voice that confirmed my earlier guess about Escott's arrangements.

Escott's white hand was engulfed in Shoe Coldfield's black one for several seconds. "Better, now that you're here, my friend. Thank you for coming."

"Wouldn't have missed it. How're you doing, Fleming?"

I couldn't help but grin as we shook hands in turn. "Just fine."

"Not from what I hear. Isham, get this buggy moving," he told the driver. The big heavy car did not roll from the alley so much as sail, like a graceful ship on a smooth sea. We glided down the streets, hardly making a sound.

I figured Escott to be the likely source of Coldfield's news. "What have you heard?"

"That Vaughn Kyler's looking to turn both of you into fish food the first chance he gets. Talk about grabbing a tiger by the tail. How did you manage to catch on to this one?" he asked Escott.

"It wasn't all that easy . . . ," he began, and gave Coldfield a summary of most of the fun and games.

Coldfield rubbed a thumbnail against the carefully trimmed beard edging his jaw. "Shit. In a way this is almost my doing. If I hadn't recommended you to Griff—"

"Someone else with fewer advantages working for them would undoubtedly be feeding the aforementioned fish."

"Let's hope they keep going hungry. And now Angela Paco mixed herself into things, huh? I knew old Frankie had a daughter, but I didn't know she was looking to take over the family business. Sounds like she's making a good job of it, too."

"If you were unaware of that, then it's unlikely for Kyler to suspect her involvement, hence his misdirected attack on us."

"That's what it looks like. You sure you're okay, both of you?"

Escott nodded. "We're only a trifle shaken, but my poor car is in fearful need of repair."

Coldfield laughed briefly. "As long as it did the job. That thing's the best investment you ever made and I'm glad I talked you into getting it."

"As am I," Escott agreed with humble sincerity. "Are we going to the Shoebox?" he asked, referring to Coldfield's night-club in the heart of Chicago's "Bronze Belt."

"Not private enough. Kyler's going to have everyone but mediums working for him to find out what happened to you two, but I've got a spot that should be all right."

"But will you be safe as well?"

"Safe as I ever am," he replied. I got the impression that Escott wasn't all that reassured. "How long you need it for?"

"For the day at least," I said. "I don't want to make any moves until nightfall."

"And then what are you planning?"

My voice was thick. "Then I'll take care of Kyler."

A lot of obvious questions crossed Coldfield's face, but never came out. He glanced at Escott, who simply nodded.

Even through the extra thick windows, I could sense the oncoming light. I hoped that our destination was close by or Escott would have an apparent corpse on his hands to explain away when the sun came up.

We had all of five minutes to spare when the driver brought us to a gentle stop in another alley, next to another anonymous door. Coldfield got out first to deal with the lock, then hustled us inside. I reveled in the soothing darkness there, but still felt the approach of day creeping into my bones.

Coldfield led us upstairs. The place was old and could have been designed for anything: an office, a hotel, or apartments of some sort. Perhaps he used it for all three at one time or another, but not recently. The air was cold and stale and our shoes left revealing tracks in forgotten grit on the steps. And it was quiet. I listened hard when we paused on the landing and heard no one and nothing else moving within the building.

Our host noticed and approved of my caution. "I tell you two, the lines between black and white are pretty solid in this town, each on his own side and neither caring much about the other except during elections. I know plenty of people who wouldn't mind seeing you white guys kill each other off and be glad to help things along, so you keep your heads low—and I'm talking about down to the ground. This place is just between us and Isham downstairs and he won't talk, but you don't want to take any chances."

"Words to live by," I said. "What is this place, anyway?"

"A private way station for people in trouble."

He ushered us through the first door on the right and turned on a lamp. We stood in a small, windowless room, containing four ancient folding cots, an oil heater, a pile of dusty magazines, and a lonely old telephone. Though we were out of the wind, it seemed colder in here than in the street. Coldfield lighted the heater right away to start taking the edge off the worst of it.

Always fastidious about himself and his surroundings, Escott favored the stark place with one of his rare smiles. "This is quite an improvement over those rooms we shared at Ludbury."

"Good God, yes," agreed Coldfield.

"Ludbury?" I asked.

"A railroad town in Ontario," he explained. "The noisiest, smelliest, coldest pit we ever had the rotten luck to fall into. The pulp mills were bad enough, but add on the creosote and sulfuric acid plants and you could choke to death if the wind started blowing the wrong way. It was full of workers and miners, every one of them tougher than the next, uglier than most, and itching to prove it come Saturday night."

"What were you doing there?"

"*King Lear.*"

"It went over surprisingly well, as I recall," Escott put in brightly.

"Oh, yeah, they just loved the scene where Cornwall is tearing out Gloucester's eyes. They wanted an encore to that one. Maybe this kind of work is one hell of a lot safer."

"You may be certain of it, old man." Escott warmed his hands in front of the heater, flexing his long fingers. They were no longer shaking. "Given those circumstances, I would think twice about taking up acting again. An audience like that one would have convinced the most rigid Fundamentalist that Darwin had, indeed, some insights about our origins."

Coidfield chuckled, but it faded when he looked at me. "You all right, kid?"

Escott glanced at his watch and correctly interpreted my situation. "Yes, Jack, you must be dreadfully tired after all this. Why don't you have a lie-down?"

"He really should keep moving until this place warms up some more," Coldfield advised.

"I'll be fine," I told him, dragging my stiffening legs over to the nearest cot. Pulling a damp blanket over my shoulders, I stretched out on the old canvas, turning to face the wall. The cot swayed and creaked, but decided to hold my weight. In a few more seconds the whole thing could drop through to the basement with me and I wouldn't notice any of it. The money belt with my earth dug soothingly into my side.

"He's had a busy time . . . quite exhausted himself," came Escott's voice as I started to drift away from the daylight prison of my inert body. "Probably sleep for hours . . ."

That's for damn sure, I thought, and then I was gone.

With my condition, bunking down in a strange place is always a risk. The next time my eyes opened, I was relieved to note that the same wall was still a mere foot away from me and that all was quiet.

Escott was on a cot closer to the heater; he looked up from his magazine and nodded to me. Since his breath wasn't hanging in the air anymore, I could assume the room had finally warmed up. I usually know offhand whether any given place is hot or cold, but it takes a while for excesses to become uncomfortable.

"Easy day?" I asked, cautiously sitting up.

"Exceedingly so. I found it to be a welcome respite. Isham came by several hours ago with some sandwiches. I persuaded him to let you sleep. If he should ask if you enjoyed your late lunch, you'll know to say yes."

I spotted the sandwich wrappings, neatly folded, on a stack of old papers. "How did it taste?"

"A little heavy on the mustard, but otherwise quite nutritious."

"Any news?"

"A Manhattan criminologist has proposed establishing a criminal identification system based on the pattern of blood vessels in the eye. In these days of plastic surgery, it sounds most—"

"I meant here in town."

"Ah." He put away his two-week-old magazine. "Nothing, really. I filled Shoe in on everything, including your remarkable escape from Angela Paco—not to worry, I did not reveal the actual details, only that her people were looking the other way and you seized the opportunity. I also gave Shoe a message to pass on to Gordy and Miss Smythe to the effect that we are well and safe and they are not to worry."

"That's good, but I'll want to call her when I can. Jeez, I could use a bath and a change of clothes. What about you?" I stood and stretched out a few muscles, rubbing my chin. Escott also wore some uncharacteristic stubble, but it didn't seem to bother him. He even looked rested. Our rough surroundings must have suited him.

"Both would be welcome were they obtainable. You'll find a washroom across the hall, but the water is freezing."

And we were fresh out of towels, I discovered after rinsing my face off, but no complaints—not aloud, anyway. We were still moving and kicking and for that I was grateful.

A door creaked open downstairs. Escott and I were in the hall at the same time, both looking and listening. His revolver was ready in his hand, his heart beating a little fast.

"It's me," our visitor called.

Escott sighed in relief, but didn't put the gun away until Coldfield was actually in sight.

He stopped on the landing and raised one hand, palm out. "Hey, I'm on *your* side."

"Indeed you are. Do come up."

Coldfield carried a covered basket. "Want any supper? Straight from the club kitchen."

The basket was stuffed with the basics of a portable feast, more than enough for all of us; even the coffee was still hot. The no-doubt savory smells only inspired the usual pang of queasiness for me, though, and I had to beg off.

"Still got that bad stomach, huh?" Coldfield asked as he set out food.

"Yeah. Must be slow digestion or something. There was a lot of mustard on those sandwiches."

Escott kept a straight face, but it was a struggle.

Coldfield didn't notice. "I keep tryin' to tell Isham that not everyone likes that much heat, but it never seems to sink in. It's where he was raised. He's from Louisiana, y'know, and that kid's eaten things I wouldn't step on."

Escott nearly choked on his coffee. "This from a man who has partaken of jellied eel?"

"Only because you told me it was really salmon."

"The light was poor."

"Uh-huh."

I was tempted to ask for more details, but it would have to wait for a better time. "Anything going on outside?"

Coldfield shook his head. "Kyler got back to his hotel around two in the morning and stayed there, but his men are still looking for you, so I wouldn't get hopeful. He's got the top floor of the Travis blocked off and nobody, but nobody's getting up there."

"Not even the cleaning staff?" Escott put in.

"You figure."

"And Miss Angela Paco?"

"No one's heard a peep from her. The papers are going crazy playing up last night's shootings and so are the cops. They've got no witnesses and the bodies sure as hell aren't talking."

"What about the prisoner she took?"

"Maybe she's still holding him. If he's the same Vic I know of, he'll be lucky to come out of things with a whole skin. He used to work for her daddy and changed sides when Kyler took over. I can imagine how that's made him real popular with the old crew."

"I'd just like to know what they wanted us for," I said.

"It's bound to be for something lousy, kid. By now every hood in the Midwest knows your name. The best favor you can do yourself is to get out of the area. Mexico is just peachy this time of year. Both of you can probably use the sun."

Escott and I exchanged openmouthed looks, then broke up. His own laughter was brief and subdued, mine bordered on the lunatic. Coldfield was disgusted. Escott made a placating gesture.

"My apologies, Shoe. It is an excellent idea, but not really practical for either of us."

"And letting Kyler chop you into fish food is?"

I sobered up fast. "It won't come to that. I'm going to settle things with him tonight."

"How? Kyler's locked in his own private fort with men all over it like ants on a sugar cube. You going to ring the front bell or come down through the chimney? That's about as far as you'll get before they cut you in two the long way."

"I'll be all right." *I think,* I silently added.

Escott backed me up. "He knows what he's doing, Shoe. Otherwise, why else would Kyler be taking such elaborate precautions?"

"Elaborate, hell. He's like that all the time. It's how we all survive, and you should know it more than most after what nearly happened to you this morning."

"We both know it," I said. "But I'm handling this one and I will be careful."

"If you want to go that bad, I can't stop you, but I'd like to know what the hell you have in mind."

Not that he could be blamed for his skepticism; in his place I would have felt the same, but I could give him no real answer. Eventually I'd find Kyler, but beyond that point my imagination stopped working. It was a form of self-protection. I simply did not want to think about what would have to be done until the time came to do it.

Coldfield measured me up with a dark expression that had nothing to do with his skin color. "Charles, are you going to tear out there as well to get yourself killed?"

"Not necessary this time, Shoe. Jack should be able to handle things."

"How? What are you not telling me?"

I shrugged. "I can't go into it now and don't want to. I have to get moving, anyway."

Coldfield's frustrated curiosity could have burned a hole right through me, but he kept it under control. Maybe he was thinking of questioning Escott after I'd left. "You gonna need a ride?"

"Thanks, but I'll find a cab. Safer for all of us. Does that phone work?"

"Yeah."

I crossed over to it and memorized the number. "I'll call when I have any news."

Escott nodded slowly, correctly interpreting what I meant by "news." I tried unsuccessfully to swallow a hard knot of something that had suddenly formed in my throat. A good thing I didn't have to breathe regularly or I might have choked on it.

The time had come to leave. Coldfield led us downstairs and unlocked a different door than the one we'd come in by. I emerged in another alley, buttoning the pea jacket against the wind.

Escott wished me luck. Nobody shook hands; it wouldn't have been appropriate. As I slipped away, he murmured, "Don't underestimate him, Shoe. He'll be all right."

"Uh-huh. Where do you want to send the flowers?"

I wasn't looking forward to any of it, but the process of actually getting started made it seem like the worst was over. Not exactly true, but I was better at lying to myself than to other people. I wondered how successful Coldfield would be at getting information from Escott.

The cab could wait; I needed a walk to limber up my muscles and clear my brain of clutter. I flushed city-tainted winter air in and out of my lungs like a normal man. It had a harsh taste but I liked it. The knot in my throat began to loosen.

After a mile or so, the character of the neighborhood improved from bedraggled buildings and empty lots decorated with broken glass to small shops and other businesses. Foot traffic was light and my earlier optimism about finding a cab waned. A line waiting at the next corner told me that a bus was on the way. I stood with them, commiserating with an old lady about the weather. The talk didn't last long. I was the wrong color for the place and with my business hanging over my head, I didn't feel much like conversation no matter how banal.

The bus came, we boarded; I didn't know or care about its destination, it was enough to be moving. Pieces of the city glided by one block at a time. People crowded around me, their bits of talk and tired silences passing over my head as though I wasn't there. I stared out the dark glass of a window that gave back everyone else's reflection but my own.

It was already here, waiting, the sweet isolation that had once carried me into the darkness of my own mind. The muscles in my neck tightened for an instant as I began to resist it, and then relaxed just as abruptly. What was the point? I was going to kill a man; better to accept the fact now and get through the job quickly than fight it and have a dangerous internal distraction.

And damned if we didn't drive right past the Travis Hotel just then. The carved stone letters of its name jumped out at me like a dare. I felt a smile twitch to life in the corners of my mouth.

A respectable four-story structure on a regular city street, it gave no outer indication of inner skulduggery. Maybe I was expecting to see sinister guys with black hats and machine guns lounging around the entrances smoking cheap cigars. They were probably all waiting in the lobby. I got off at the next stop and backtracked.

This required caution; I had to keep my eyes open for Kyler's people, but not look conspicuous. Lost cause. My clothes and stubble were fine for a soup kitchen or a dockside riot, but here they only drew unwelcome attention. I crossed the street so I could view the place from a discreet doorway without offending innocent citizens.

The spot I'd picked out offered some shelter from the wind, but the awkward placement of a streetlight left me a little too visible for comfort. Since the store it led to was closed for the night, I took a chance and vanished, re-forming inside. The place sold ladies' clothes and the front windows were a busy display of some of their best items. I bent low so that my head would more or less blend in with the phony ones showing off the latest in hats, and studied the hotel opposite. Undignified, but it was out of the cold and away from immediate sight, and didn't seem to have any rabid guard dogs.

People passed back and forth across my field of view, cars did the same. The place was disappointingly normal. Except . . . the top-floor windows were all lighted. No exceptions. Kyler might have thought that leaving the lights on would scare away the boogeyman; that, or draw him into a trap. I didn't like the idea, but nothing would be resolved until I made a move. I went out the back of the shop and took the long way around to one of the hotel's service entrances.

Working with Escott had helped me develop something of an instinct for spotting the kind of human predators who would work for Kyler. I looked for them now, anticipating he'd have an army of hoods scattered around the area. Sometimes they're pretty obvious, but often it's not what you see as much as what you feel, like the way your skin creeps when a bad storm is coming. Right now, I was aware that I could not rely on that instinct. The last few nights had left me so jumpy that I was reading sinister motives off every face up to and including a couple of nuns rustling by to make their bus at the next corner.

The alley running behind the Travis had the usual loading areas and doors for the staff. It was deserted now, which surprised me; I would have expected Kyler to have someone watching his back. Again, they could be waiting inside for trouble to show up.

Invisibility has numerous advantages, but I was having second thoughts about using it now. I could—literally—slip through a door and feel my way around the place. However, there was always the chance of materializing in the wrong spot at the wrong time, giving some bystander heart failure and the hotel a reputation for harboring stray ghosts. No, thanks. On the other hand, I wasn't too crazy about the alternative I'd just thought of, given my fear of heights, but it would be better than wasting time blindly creeping through the halls.

I'd done this sort of thing before, but never for such a height. That knot in my throat, which was a solid symptom of my own fear, returned as I looked for a likely place to start.

The fire escape was promising, but too obvious. If Kyler was expecting me—or anyone else, for that matter—he'd have men covering it. Instead, I chose to try the east side of the place. The lighting was brighter, but the next building over showed only a blank face, with no inconvenient windows.

Pressing close against the hotel's outer wall, I vanished and moved slowly upward.

Distances can be very deceptive in this form, but I was prepared for that and not too surprised when it seemed to take only a moment to find the first irregularities in the wall marking the ground-floor window. I

drifted over the smooth planes of glass and bumped into the next out-
crop of brick above the opening. The wind got stronger the higher I
went, whipped up by the narrow channels between the city's artificial
canyons.

Second-floor window. If my pores had been intact, I might be sweating badly by now, fingers slick and slipping. Did human flies have this
problem as they worked their stunts? Concentrate. A gust of wind hit
hard just then and was gone, free and careless. I'd read somewhere that
the Windy City appellation had more to do with Chicago politics than
the weather. From this insecure perch, the writer would have undergone
severe revision of that opinion.

Third floor. I was like a snail, sliding on an invisible foot up endless
tiers of bricks. Keep going. Hold tight against the persistent tug of wind
but don't go through the wall just yet. If I got dragged away I could tum-
ble for miles, unless I panicked and went solid, which would mean a long
drop lasting a very short moment. I'd survived some terrible things since
my change, but that was one experience I did not want to test.

Fourth floor. The window was shut fast. Didn't matter. I plowed
through it and was inside with something solid beneath me once more.
Oh God, but I hate heights.

I wanted to re-form for some badly needed orientation, but couldn't
chance it just yet. Waiting and listening, I swept slowly through the
room, looking for company and finding none. I poured back into reality
again, grateful to have a body once more, even if it was shaken and shaking.

The window had led me to a luxurious hotel room. The Travis had
not stinted on comfort when it came to the owner and his guests. The
bedspread looked like real silk and the carpet was thick and new, its nap
still at attention from the last cleaning. Mine were the only footprints on
it, magically beginning in the middle of the floor.

Behind the curtains, I noticed that the window was indeed protected
by steel shutters, open now as if in invitation. That wasn't right. Kyler
wouldn't be stupid enough to leave himself so vulnerable . . . not unless
he'd unquestioningly swallowed Stoker's novel whole. He might just believe the stuff about vampires being unable to enter a dwelling without
an invitation. Escott had—before I set him straight on that and other
myths.

I checked the sill, but found no sign or smell of garlic, mustard seeds,
or salt.

The place was unnaturally quiet. Some sounds of living seeped up
from the other floors, but nothing else, nothing close.

Damnation, I thought as I cautiously poked my head outside the
room to check the hall. A carpet with a hypnotic pattern of stylized fans

stretched away in both directions. The doors on either side were spaced
well apart, indicating sizable suites. I stepped out, taking it slowly, listening for any activity behind them. Nothing. No talk, no radios playing,
not even a toilet flushing. I went through one after another, but the
rooms that were supposed to be crowded with Kyler's people were
empty.

I should have figured he wouldn't wait around for me to come after
him. The odds were strong that he hadn't left any forwarding address,
though I'd search just to be certain.

Down the hall in an unexplored room, a phone began to ring. I
closed on it, then hauled up short, paranoid for a trap. Better to go carefully than quickly. I vanished.

The bell drew me on like a snagged fish until I was nearly on top of
it. I was about to take a turn around the room to search for company
when the ringing stopped, interrupted as someone finally answered the
thing.

6

"HELLO?"

A feminine voice; flat, impatient. "I *am* hurrying. . . . No, it's quiet
here. . . . I tell you, I'm just finishing up. If you hadn't called I'd be in the
elevator now. . . . He's down warming up the car. . . . All right, I'm on
my way."

She hung up with an exasperated sigh and moved off. I returned to
the hall once more and went solid, regaining sight and better-than-
normal hearing. The muffling quality of the carpet and the many intervening walls had prevented me from picking up her soft movements
earlier. Now I crept to the edge of the doorway, peering around for a
glimpse at my unknowing hostess.

Her back was to me as she busily shrugged into her overcoat. She already had her galoshes on; both struck a chord of recognition in me. For
a few seconds I debated on how to make an approach without scaring
her to death, finally deciding that it couldn't be done. I simply rapped a
knuckle against the door panel.

"Keep your shirt on, Chick, I'm c——" She froze in midturn. It was bad enough that I'd come out of nowhere, but I was still dressed for a dockside riot.

I put on a friendly smile and pretended hard that I was clean shaven and in a natty tux. "Opal, isn't it? We met the other night."

No bells rang for her.

"I'm here to see your boss."

"He's gone," she blurted.

"I noticed. Where is he?"

"I don't know. I don't pay attention to things like that."

Too much explanation coming too fast. "We're not off to a very good start, are we?"

No comment to that one. Maybe I wasn't her type—or Kyler had primed her with dire warnings to look out for a bloodthirsty monster. Her nervousness was understandable, but scaring women has never appealed to me. I could calm her down, influence the fear right out of her, but shied away from that all-too-easy ploy.

We stood in a well-furnished living area. Like the rest of the place, it was cleaned out. The only personal item left was her handbag, clutched protectively in white-knuckled fingers.

"Come on," I said, deciding that any action was preferable to waiting.

"What?"

"Down to the car. Chick's probably wondering what's keeping you."

The reminder that possible help was at hand wasn't enough to encourage her to move. "But I . . ."

"Come on, Opal. I'm not going to hurt you."

She took a tentative step forward on stiff legs, then balked. "No. I'm not going anywhere with you."

"You'll be all right. I'm just going to walk you to your car." I moved toward her, slowly; she was faster and backed away. Since she was determined to keep a maximum distance between us, I used that to herd her from the room.

The elevator was something of a dilemma for her, being too small for comfort. She scurried to the end of the hall and took the service stairs instead. I followed, but not too closely. I didn't want to crowd her too much or she'd trip and break something. She was wheezing badly by the time she'd reached the bottom landing. She burst into another short hall and out a metal door to the outside, going fast despite her short breath and slipping galoshes.

A new-looking DeSoto was idling across the narrow street, a heavy cloud of exhaust streaming from its tailpipe. Opal charged straight for it, screaming Chick's name.

Chick must have been primed and ready for trouble; he came boiling out of the driver's door, gun in hand. He wore a few visible lumps from last night's encounter with Udo and Jürgens, but they weren't slowing him down. He recognized me instantly and got the gun up and aimed, but Opal plowed right into him, spoiling his shot. He cursed and shoved her headfirst into the front seat to get her out of his way, then brought the gun to bear again.

I was moving too fast to stop, grabbing the gun and pushing it to the outside with my left, throwing a desperate gut punch with my right. The breath whooshed out of him and he doubled and fell, nearly dragging me down, too. But I hadn't hit him hard enough. He landed on his side and turned around just enough to sock me a solid one in the jaw with his free hand.

As socks go, it was a good one, because I felt it. I was already bent over and off balance, trying to wrest the gun away and making a lousy job of it. This one jarred me to my knees, leaving my butt up in the air. Chick seized the opportunity to awkwardly smash one of his size twelves into the seat of my pants. I sprawled, still managing to clutch the gun, and collected another punch in the ribs.

That's when I lost my temper and put the pressure on his hand. He gave out with a yell right in my ear. I kept twisting until something snapped. The yell turned into an honest-to-God shriek, and he finally let go of the gun. I swatted it well away and staggered to my feet, but he wasn't ready to give up yet and tried to belt me once more.

"Stay down, dammit," I roared at him, slapping at his head the way you do an annoying bug. He suddenly dropped flat onto the pavement and stopped moving.

Oh, shit. Had I broken his neck? I knelt next to him to see.

Fingers shaking from exertion and sheer nervousness at what they might find, I checked his throat for a pulse. Thank God. His heart was working fast, but it *was* working. Good. One less thing to worry about. Even as I straightened, he began to moan, getting ready for the second round.

Opal's initial screams had drawn a few people toward us. Three men stepped from the rest, trying to decide whether or not to interfere. They had me outnumbered, but I was a rough-looking customer. Maybe I'd had a good reason to accost an obviously respectable citizen and flatten him.

Opal had recovered and was sitting up in the seat. Once she'd realized how the fight had come out, she screamed again, nothing articulate, just earsplitting and attention-drawing. The three heroes made their decision, surging forward to protect her. Time to get the hell out.

I forced my way into the waiting car, pushing Opal over. There was a bad moment fumbling with the gears before the thing finally responded. One of the men almost caught at the handle, but I hit the gas just in time. The door swung loosely shut as we lurched forward.

Opal made a lot of noise and attempted to crawl out the other door. I got a handful of her coat collar and yanked her back. She clawed blindly, fingers jabbing into my vulnerable neck. I gave her a rough shake to stop that nonsense. She did, but the distraction was nearly enough to smash us into an inconvenient wall. I got the wheel pulled around in time, but overcompensated. We missed the driveway and bumped violently over a high curb into the street. Opal bounced halfway to the roof, came down hard, and slipped under the dashboard with an outraged squawk.

I yelled at her to stay put as I fought to keep a straight course. We managed to swerve away from an oncoming car, miss a parked one, and pick up more speed. I'd need it. As far as those people in the street were concerned, I'd just kidnapped an innocent, albeit noisy girl, no doubt for some horrible purpose. They were probably calling the DeSoto's license number in to the cops right now.

It had finally penetrated to Opal that this would not be a good time to make an exit. She crouched under the dash, holding on to the seat for balance and glaring at me, anger overriding fear for the moment.

"Your glasses are crooked," I told her.

She straightened them automatically. "Where are you going?"

I surprised her and myself with a laugh. "Damned if I know, sister. Your boss has made this town too hot for me to be anyplace."

"Let me out. I mean it. Let me out right now."

"Uh-uh." But I checked first before answering to make sure she didn't have a gun to enforce her demand. More complications I did not need.

She climbed from under the dash, straightening her clothes with jerky, frustrated movements.

"Sit on your hands," I ordered.

"What?"

More slowly. "Sit on your hands, Opal. If you don't, I'll have to deck you just like I did Chick."

She was smart enough not to argue. Grumbling, she squirmed around on the seat.

"Get them well under, put your weight on them."

"Okay, okay."

We were approaching a stop signal; she settled in just in time. The line of cars ahead indicated we'd all have a long wait. She simmered and looked longingly out her window toward escape, but behaved herself until the signal changed and our turn to move came up. While I was busy with the gears and wheel, she wrenched her hands free and tried to get out the door.

I grabbed her arm at the last second and hauled her back. "Relax, sister, or it's beddy-bye time." The threat wouldn't have fooled a ten-year-old, but worked on her. She chewed her lower lip into a fine shade of pink with her small teeth.

"Please let me go." Just beginning to understand her new situation, she was hard put to keep the whine out of her voice.

"That sounds like a good idea, honey. Where shall I take you?"

She came that close to blurting it out, but her mouth snapped shut before she could betray her boss.

"All right," I sighed. "Then we'll have to do it the hard way."

"What do you mean?"

"You'll find out." Eventually, I located the perfect spot, coasting to a stop in front of a closed gas station with an outside telephone box. Opal squeaked when I took her arm again and tried to shrug away.

"Leave me alone."

"At the first opportunity," I promised. With a little forceful coaxing, I drew her out of the car, squeezing us unhappily into the phone box. She kept as far away from me as possible, which was not easy, given the circumstances. I blocked the door and fumbled out a nickel.

Escott answered before the first ring had finished.

"It's me."

"Are you all right?" he asked cautiously. It was a loaded question. Translation: had I killed Kyler yet?

"Just peachy. Kyler's flown the coop, but it wasn't a total waste of time. I've turned up a new angle."

"What sort of angle?"

"Remember the other night at the Satchel? Kyler's accountant, Opal?" Opal glared at me, her jaw working.

"Certainly."

"I've got her."

"You've—" He broke off as the implications soaked in.

"Yeah, and I want to bring her over, but you need to warn our temporary landlord to keep out of the way so he doesn't get drawn into this mess. The fewer people she sees, the better. You know what I mean?"

"I understand perfectly."

"Okay. I'll come by in the same door that I used to leave. We'll be there in about ten minutes."

"I'll be prepared."

We hung up, then I had to expend some effort to wrestle Opal back into the car without hurting her. She started to screech, leaving me with no option but to clamp a hand over her mouth and lift her bodily up and in. She ran out of breath before I ran out of determination. The street was momentarily deserted, but enough noise could change that in short order. I hauled ass out of there.

"This stinks and I hate you," she announced, verging on tears.

"And you're the light of my life, too. Now get under the dash."

"What?"

"Just do it, Opal!" The tone of my voice got through to her. She ducked down, fast.

After a peaceful interval, she complained, "This thing's digging into my back."

"Then stop trying to sit up."

"Why can't I?"

"You don't need to know where we're going."

"But I'm getting carsick down here."

"Fine. If you puke, be sure to keep it on your side."

"You . . ." But she was too nice a girl to use that kind of language. She tried another tack. "I can sit on my hands again. I promise I won't make any trouble."

I didn't answer.

"Really, I won't. I'll even keep my eyes shut."

"Better if you stay put."

"You—you won't think so in a minute," she gasped.

Alarmed, I checked on her. A person doesn't turn that shade of light green voluntarily. She was gulping, too. I hastily pulled to the curb and rolled down my window to give her air. "Better?"

She shook her head, her eyes desperate. Damnation. I leaned over and opened the passenger door. She crawled forward and got her head out just in time. I gripped her collar to keep her from bolting, but it wasn't really necessary. When she finally finished and I pulled her back onto the seat, she was exhausted and puffing like a beached fish, tears streaming down her swollen face.

"You all right, kid?" I found a handkerchief and offered it. She glared and wrinkled her nose. "Go on, it's clean." I pushed it into her hand.

"Why don't you leave me alone?"

"Just blow your nose."

She did, several times.

"You can keep the handkerchief," I said, suddenly inspired to generosity.

"Will you *please* let me go?"

I ignored the subject. "Feel better now?"

Sniff. "I guess so."

"Good. Get back under the dash."

Her mouth popped open and as quickly snapped shut. She looked ready to burst into real tears now, not just the by-product of being sick. "You're *mean*."

"Yeah, I cheat old ladies and kick dogs all the time."

"This stinks. Vaughn's going to get you for this." But she got back down and I resumed driving.

To keep her mind off getting carsick again, I asked, "How'd you come to work for a guy like him, anyway?"

She scowled as though I were a total idiot. "I'm a great accountant. You ask me anything about numbers and I know it."

Off the top of my head I asked: "The square root of pi, what is it?"

"Pi is a transcendental number, you can't take its square root. Ferdinand Lindemann's already proved that. Since it's an irrational number its numerical representation can only be an approximation of its value, and those numbers' square roots will also be approximations. That's algebra, anyway. I can do it, but accounting's better. In a correctly balanced ledger, numbers are always sensible and clean."

I gulped, knowing that I'd seriously underestimated this little gal. "Ah . . . whatever you say, but doesn't it bother you how Kyler makes the money you're adding up for him?"

She shrugged, indifferent.

"Or that he kills people?"

"Will you let me go? I won't tell on you."

"No."

She crossed her arms, resting them on the seat cushion, and stared at the door handle. "This stinks. Vaughn's going to get you good for stealing his car. He'll get you good for doing this."

I shot her a look. Somewhere along the way I'd missed something and it was just now catching up with me. "What's fifty-six times eighteen?"

"One thousand eight," she replied in a bored tone.

"Fifty-six divided by eighteen?"

"Three, remainder two or three point one one one one . . ."

"I'll take your word for it."

"Told you I was good," she said smugly.

"How old are you?"

"Twenty-three years, four months, and eleven days."

"Now you're just showing off."

"Am not. That's the truth."

I tried a few more sums and the answers poured out of her as fast as she heard the questions. It kept her occupied until we reached Coldfield's building. I backed the car deep into the alley shadows. Just as I cut the motor, Escott opened the side door for us. I urged Opal to come along, aware that I sounded like a dog owner working with an especially difficult pet. Hugging her purse, she finally climbed out, and I guided her inside.

"Opal, this is Charles . . . Charles, Opal," I said once he'd locked the door.

"Delighted to meet you again, miss," he responded, with a slight inclination of his head.

She pouted at him, suspicious. "You were at the Satchel. You didn't have a black eye then."

He glanced at me. I gave him a "be careful" expression. "Yes. That's where we met."

She put a disapproving twist to her lips, but decided not to hold it against him. "We only just met *here;* the Satchel was where I *saw* you," she stated, then pointed a finger straight at me. "*He* won't let me go. Will you?"

He instantly came out with a thin but charming smile. "Won't you come inside and warm yourself first? It's much too cold for traveling right now." He gestured upstairs, managing to get her there with no more fuss.

She glared at the sparse furnishings and kicked at the empty packing crate that served as a table. "This stinks."

I told Opal to be quiet and read a magazine. We backed out the door, but kept it open to make sure she left the phone alone.

"Jack . . ." he murmured from the side of his mouth. "I know. At first I thought she was just acting cute, but it's no act."

"And you're certain she's his accountant?"

"Oh, yeah. I don't know how, but she's some kind of a genius when it comes to numbers."

"Even if she is a bit wanting in the social graces. You're sure about her being the new angle you mentioned on the phone?"

"Mostly she got dragged along for the ride, and now I'm kind of stuck with her, but I think she may know where Kyler is."

"In which case it should be easy enough to persuade her to part with the information."

"I was thinking maybe you could charm it out of her with that Ronald Colman act of yours."

Instead of bristling with his usual reply to the joke, he said, "You really don't want to hypnotize her, do you?"

No use trying to hide anything from him; he was too damn sharp. This was a talk I'd been dreading, but would have to have sooner or later. God knows, I owed him an explanation.

"Something's happened," he said. He was trying to make it easy, but I was wincing inside.

"It's too dangerous."

He paused over that one. "For you or the subject?"

"Both."

"How so?"

"It's a trap. The last . . . the last time I was talking—starting to talk, starting to get information . . . I lost control."

"In what way?"

Dammit. "I nearly killed her."

"Miss Grey?" He kept his tone low and neutral, a vocal counterbalance to my obvious twitchiness.

"Yeah."

That answered a lot of questions for him, but not all. He waited for me to go on.

"We were alone in her studio and I'd just put her under to get some answers. Then it just . . . took me over. I got caught up in something I couldn't control. That's when I stopped thinking."

Stopped thinking and began feeding, draining the blood from her as though she were one of the cattle at the Stockyards. Helpless, but uncaring, she'd been swept away and submerged in the sensual pleasure of that joining. I had played upon it, used it to satisfy an appetite and desire blended together to the point of destruction for us both. She'd have lost her life and I . . . what? Illusions about myself? My sanity? My soul? None would have mattered; she'd have still been dead.

"I . . . broke away before it was too late, but it was tough, I almost didn't."

"This aspect of your condition has always bothered you," he pointed out.

"Jesus, Charles, *every* aspect of it has bothered me at one time or another; I may never get used to being what I am. But this . . . I don't want to put anyone through that risk again."

"But you've done it many times before, what made this particular one different?"

That I'd been alone with her, or mildly attracted to her, or feeling the first inevitable pangs of hunger? "It doesn't matter."

"It does, my friend, because there are other lives than your own or even hers to consider." He wasn't indifferent to Opal, or using guilt to pressure, only stating facts that I'd already considered. Opal watched us from the windowless room, trying to read our faces for a clue to her future.

"Which puts me right between a rock and a hard place," I grumbled. "So what do I do?"

"I cannot decide for you. There are other ways of finding out what we need. Shoe or Gordy can probably help, but this will be quickest."

I turned away and paced down the hall and back. My choice was no choice, not when it came between promises to myself or protecting my friends. Opal would be safe enough with Escott acting as chaperon, but it was cold comfort at best.

My hands were starting to shake.

Opal hadn't liked waiting and said as much when we came in to sit with her. With that very clear opinion out of the way, she hunched down in her coat and crossed her arms protectively against any possible counter argument. Escott gave me a silent nod to indicate that it was my show, content to melt into the background.

In an attempt to change the subject and to get her more relaxed, I said, "You know you never really answered my question about how you came to work for Kyler."

She sensed some less obvious purpose than curiosity behind the question, and used her earlier answer. "Because I'm a great accountant."

"That tells me why, but not how. When did you meet him?"

"Two years, two months, and fifteen days ago."

I should have been prepared for that one but wasn't. My expression amused her. "That's very good."

"I know."

"How did you meet him?"

"I was a cashier at a restaurant. They wanted a singing cashier, but I didn't sing, I did numbers instead."

"Did numbers?"

"Like I did for you in the car. People'd ask me to add and subtract and stuff like that in my head. I'd do numbers for the customers to make tips. Vaughn ate there one day and asked if I could do bookkeeping and I said yes."

"If you knew bookkeeping, why weren't you doing that?"

"Because bookkeepers make eight dollars a week and no tips when they start out. I was making fifteen at the restaurant . . . plus tips."

"So Vaughn offered you a new job and you took it?"

"For a thousand dollars a month."

Wow. "What's your family think of your work?"

"They don't care about me. When I finished school, they told me to move out."

"Just like that?"

She shrugged. "They never liked me."

"Your own parents?"

"I'm smart, but in my own way. I wasn't smart in the way they wanted, so they didn't like having me around. Everything I said and did was wrong. I was glad to leave."

"I'll bet you were, kid."

"Don't call me that." She pulled her shoulders tighter, the corners of her mouth turning sharply down. "You're like them, too. Treating me like I'm a baby because I'm different from everyone else. They'd talk about it and think that I didn't hear or care, but I did."

"How does Kyler treat you?"

"He doesn't laugh at me or act embarrassed or talk like I'm not in the room, or talk out in the hall so I don't hear anything." She glared at us. Justifiably so, I thought.

"I'm sorry we have to do this, Opal. We—"

"Nuts to you. This stinks." She turned her back and stared at a dingy wall.

"Yeah, it does. Kyler's probably the best thing that ever happened to you."

"He's okay."

"Even when he kills people?"

"I've never seen him do that."

"Or talk about it? He wants to kill me, you know."

She looked around sharply. "So you're the one."

There went my plan to relax her. "Yeah. He ever say anything about me?"

Her eyes went solemn; her little mouth clamped shut.

"What'd he say?"

But she only shook her head, preferring refusal over lying. At least she didn't seem to be frightened of me. It would be easy enough to push her into answering.

Too easy, as I knew it would be. Always far too easy.

We soon learned that Kyler had forsaken his downtown fortress in the Travis for a more isolated roadhouse he'd recently bought. The purchase had been so far under the table that only a select few in his organization knew about it. Opal, fortunately, had been one of them and freely parted with details on the price, location, and normal hours of operation. It was open now with business as usual to avoid attracting attention, but tonight they would have an extra patron dropping in on them.

"It is most likely that he knows about Opal's disappearance," Escott pointed out. "And he may act upon it."

"Probably so. Chick wasn't that far gone when I left, but this is all I've got for now. I'll give the place a going-over and see what's there. Kyler can't hide forever."

"He's really mad," Opal volunteered in her flat voice as she drifted softly between consciousness and sleep.

No new information there, but was she talking about Kyler's mental state or his feelings? "Mad at me?"

"Oh, yes. Really mad because of last night. Those men you killed."

"I didn't kill them."

"Okay, the men the big guy had killed for you."

"Who? You talking about Gordy?"

"Uh-huh. He's going to get it bad tonight."

"What do you mean?"

"Vaughn's going to get back at him."

I flashed a look at Escott, but he was already on the phone, dialing the Nightcrawler's number. "What's he got in mind?"

"I don't know."

"You have to, Opal. Tell me everything he said."

"I didn't hear the rest. I was busy packing to leave."

Escott had gotten through to Gordy by then. "Yes, we're all right, but we've learned that Kyler's made plans for some sort of reprisal against you . . . Because he thinks that you were involved with the shooting of three of his men last night when they tried to kidnap Jack . . . No, I don't know what it could be."

"When will it happen, Opal?" I asked.

"I don't know."

I shrugged at Escott. She had an exceptional memory, but there was no way I could get information that she didn't have. He relayed it to Gordy and hung up after a minute. "He's been expecting something like this since last night, when they went after us. But he appreciated the additional warning."

"What about Bobbi?"

"He said for you not to worry."

"I'm going over there, anyway."

His eyes glinted. "I rather thought you would. Your presence may be of considerable help."

"Only if I get there in time. Will you be okay baby-sitting her?" I jerked my chin at Opal.

"She seems quiet enough."

Something that wouldn't last until my return. I knelt close by her, taking care not to touch her, and did what I could to ensure that Escott would have a peaceful evening.

Her lids slid shut and she curled comfortably upon the cot. Asleep, her pinched face smoothed out, easing the creases of determined concentration that were already gathering around her mouth and brow. Escott pulled a blanket up over her legs, then removed her glasses, folding them neatly on the packing crate.

"Are you all right?" he asked.

It hadn't been as bad as I'd anticipated, but my gut felt like jelly and he could see the tremor in my hands. I balled them into fists and shoved them into the pockets of the pea jacket. Car keys scratched my knuckles. "Go ahead and call Shoe. Let him know what's going on. I'll take the DeSoto over to the club."

"But—"

"Yeah, I know it's hot, but I'll have to chance it. I'm not waiting around for a cab."

He nodded, then I was out the door and down the stairs.

I had to fight to keep within the limits of the traffic around me. Running into another cop I could handle, but it would cost time. My too-fertile imagination worked full blast throughout the trip, coming up with a variety of attacks that Kyler might try. He could strafe the place with machine-gun fire, as with Escott's car, or lob grenades through any of the windows. The aftermath would bring out the Feds like flies on a corpse. Between them and the local law . . .

And Bobbi was smack in the middle of it. I sneaked up the pressure on the gas pedal and tore around a slow truck.

Things must have also gone wrong for Angela Paco. Vic might not have been in a condition to carry whatever message she had for Kyler. He could have died on her by now or she had needed both of us and I'd slipped out and spoiled it all. Whatever the reason, Kyler didn't know about her involvement and had logically blamed Gordy for the mess she'd left in the street. That's why his goons had been waiting near the club and opened up the moment Escott's Nash showed with me in it.

But that had been last night and a full day had come and gone with no further trouble. If he was spooked enough by Gordy's apparent involvement, why had he decided to wait? It would only give his opposition time to set up defenses or a counterattack. His hope might be that Gordy would leave rather than risk an open gang war, but he couldn't count on it.

Or maybe he was just waiting for me to turn up again and knew that would happen only after dark.

I left the car in a deserted spot a block away from the club. Going by foot was slower, but it gave me plenty of time to check the area. I kept to the shadows, becoming invisible whenever I had to cross an open space or pass under a streetlight. Halfway there, I had to quit because other people were turning up, well-dressed men in polished shoes hurrying along with their polished ladies. Some looked worried, glancing back over their shoulders, others giggled with tipsy relief. Club patrons, then, and too rushed to wait in the lobby for a cab to come for them.

It looked like Kyler had started without me.

Ahead, the flash of lights played along the high walls of the buildings. I picked up the busy commotion of human voices and the grunt of car engines and moved faster against a thin tide of people flowing from the club.

Cops and cop cars everywhere, their lights snapping in endless circles. No ambulances, at least not yet, but a couple of paddy wagons blocked the front entrance and were doing a good business.

A raid?

Gordy had been through this drill more than once, but he was a good businessman and paid his bribes like everyone else to avoid such problems. But Kyler had used the police before, trying to trap me at the warehouse, so why not again to get at Gordy?

The cops were probably all over the casino tagging the slot machines for evidence or pounding them to junk with sledgehammers just for the hell of it. Some sawhorse barricades were up to keep out the public, including me. Fat lot of good it did them as I slipped around to the side of the building and picked out a window on the club's second floor.

I re-formed in an unoccupied bath and shot out to the adjoining bedroom. Bobbi's room was just across from it. The door was wide and her things scattered about, but she was gone. That could he good or bad.

Staying solid, I left the outer bedroom for the hall. It was empty for the moment, but I heard voices coming from Gordy's office. Time to get some answers.

Three men looked up at my sudden barge through the door: Gordy standing by the far wall, a uniformed cop next to him, and a plainclothes man in front. All but Gordy jumped a little. He was deadpan by nature, but there seemed to be a hint of relief in his small eyes and an undeniable sheen of sweat clung to his temples. Something was wrong, wrong, *wrong*.

The uniform had his gun out and it hovered uncertainly between me and Gordy. I fanned both hands up in a placating gesture.

"Take it easy, boys, I'm just here to cover things for the *Trib*."

"You sure as hell don't look it," said the other man.

At least he didn't question the presence of the press, however seedily it was clothed. On raids like this, the cops don't mind having reporters around; it made good publicity for the department. "I was working a skid-row story and saw the ruckus. You can't blame me for wanting to drop in for a look."

"And that's all you'll get. Beat it."

"Aw, c'mon, Sergeant." I had to guess at his rank. "Gimme a break, I gotta wife and kids to feed. How 'bout a short interview? I'll make you the hero of the day. What's your name?" I fumbled for my notebook and pencil, stalling for time.

"That's Lieutenant Calloway, you asshole." He was keeping himself on a short leash; I'd read that from him the instant I'd walked in. The tension washing around the room was thick enough for swimming. The uniformed man was as cool as Calloway was hot. On the desk was a gun, taken from Gordy no doubt, and a stupid thing to leave lying around. There was more going on here than a simple arrest. These guys had other things on their minds.

"Lieutenant Calloway asshole. . . ." I repeated, pretending to write it down. I shouldn't have done it that way, but he'd left himself open and I couldn't resist. It was one way to bring things to a head.

"Baker, get him outta here!"

"Just joking, Lieutenant," I said as Baker closed in. "Okay, you're Officer Baker and what's your badge number?"

Baker started to hustle me out. There was no time to think up anything fancy; once I was out of the room anything could happen. Shrugging off his grip, I turned for a parting shot. "And how much is Vaughn Kyler paying you for this hit?"

Calloway's eyes got big. Baker froze solid. I didn't catch Gordy's expression, but he made a small noise in the back of his throat to communicate that I'd just thrown an appallingly large hunk of shit into the fan.

"Bring him back," Calloway said. "And this time lock up."

BAKER swung the door firmly shut and slid home the inside bolt. I didn't like having him behind me and instinctively turned and backed away to keep him in sight. If he decided to shoot, I wanted to see it coming. Calmly alert, he remained in place, a professional wearing a cop's uniform, but not a cop.

"Who the hell are you?" Baker's face was as blank as a store window's dummy. I wondered if he was a close relation to Kyler.

I looked past them and said, "Bobbi." It sounded like a statement, but Gordy took it for the question I meant it to be. To my relief, he shut his eyes briefly and gave a minimal nod. She was okay, then, wherever she was. That concern off my mind, I was more ready to deal with these clowns.

Baker was on the ball and noticed the interplay. "He's lying."

"Search him."

He closed in cautiously. I let him slap me down without any fuss because Calloway was standing there with his hand inside his unbuttoned coat expecting trouble. The car keys, some loose change, a pencil stub, and a thin notebook were tossed on the desk next to the gun. The money belt stayed in place; he wasn't looking for money.

"He's clean." Baker sounded disappointed as well as suspicious. If I'd been one of Gordy's men, I'd have been packing something lethal as a matter of course; if a legitimate reporter, then a wallet with some kind of identification.

"Doesn't matter," said Calloway, who was coming out of his initial shock. "What do you know about Kyler?"

I kept my eyes steady. "Enough to spot a couple of his stooges while they trip over themselves. He's picked the wrong target this time. Gordy had nothing to do with last night's hit."

"So we should take your word for it? Get him over there, Baker." He gestured at Gordy's end of the room.

"But it's a pretty sharp plan," I continued, as though he hadn't spoken. "Using a real raid as cover, you two come up here for the big fish. Only you'll invent some kind of problem and be forced to kill him, say, while he's resisting arrest. His New York bosses won't pull any reprisals against the official Chicago Police because you were just doing your job. Baker can disappear in the crowd and the whole business leaves Kyler totally clear of the blame. So . . . how much are you getting to do his dirty work?"

Calloway looked ready to drop back into shock again, but picked his jaw up faster this time. "What's it to you? What's your angle?"

"I figure you can lay off of Gordy, which is okay since he's not behind that shooting like I said, and just take me with you to see your boss."

"Why should we?"

Baker interrupted my answer. "Shut up, Calloway, it's him. It's Fleming."

Calloway was quick enough to understand and react; God knows what Kyler had said about me. He pulled his gun free and centered it on my chest. Baker's was already out but there was just enough of a difference in his manner to warn me that he was going to take it one step further. Having been there myself, I instantly recognized it in another. His eyes went blank as he slid into that place of non-thought that makes it possible to kill.

As his gun leveled and centered, he darkened into a gray blur. The rasp of his lungs faded and surged again as I hurled at him, fast as thought. My hands became solid once more to fasten onto his. Momentum carried us into the wall and that put an end to the fight before it could really start. His skull bounced once, he grunted out a thick breath in reaction, and slithered to the floor with his eyes rolled up.

I turned to take care of Calloway, but Gordy was there first and making a short job of it. He'd wrestled him down, using his weight to good advantage to keep him pinned. I stepped in and relieved Calloway of his gun, then dropped to one knee to better focus on him. It might not have been too safe since I had to step up the pressure to get through, but it was fast and we needed speed. He stopped struggling after a moment; seconds later, he was deeply asleep. I broke away and backed off.

Gordy looked down at Calloway, then up to me. "How'd you do that?"

"Beats me, but it works."

"Sure as hell does, kid, and that disappearing trick . . ."

"Comes in handy once in a while, I know. Are you all right?"

He found his feet and dusted his knees. "Yeah. They were all set, you came just in time. I owe you one."

"We'll call it even if you tell me where Bobbi is."

"Locked in the basement."

"Locked?"

"It was her idea. There's a hidden room down there for emergencies."

"And a secret tunnel, too?" I joked.

"How'd you know?"

"I didn't. You mean you've really got one of those?"

"Only to the building across the street. The basements connect up."

"Maybe you and Escott should compare notes."

"Yeah? Why?"

"It's sort of a hobby with him. What d'you have one for?"

"When things were jumping hot in this town between Big Al and everyone else during Prohibition, it seemed like a good idea to have another way outta the place."

"It still is. You should use it until this blows over."

"First I make some phone calls." He gestured at the two unconscious men. "Maybe they're crooked, but this raid was real enough and I'm needing my lawyer to start putting things back together."

"You got any plans for these guys?" I asked thoughtfully.

"I'm for dumping them out the nearest window, then getting away. You got something better in mind?"

"Yeah. I want them to take me to Kyler."

He shook his massive head. "Dangerous, kid. You'll end up showing your face to a lot of other cops who don't need to see it."

Nothing like an example to illustrate a point. I vanished, reappearing a few feet to his right. An ear-to-ear grin was my automatic response to Gordy's open-mouth stare. "Think again. These mugs won't even know I'm along."

After some quick phoning to start things rolling in the legal department, we unlocked the door and cautiously checked the upper hall for invaders. Clear. Gordy locked it from the outside to keep out any importune visitors, then we hustled down to the ground-floor landing. The activity here was casual; just one cop passed us and he only nodded, not so much at me but the uniform. I'd borrowed Baker's hat and overcoat, one too small and the other too short, but it had just proved its effectiveness as cover.

Oops. Wrong assumption. The cop paused, turned, and gave me a tough once-over. "When's the last time you had a shave, kid? Just because you're working this end of things doesn't mean you can run around looking like that."

"Uh . . ."

"And those ain't regulation shoes, neither. What's your name and badge number?"

I locked eyes with him and hoped for the best. It was draining to do it like this and tough on my conscience, but in for a penny, in for a pound, as Escott might have said. "Jack Sprat could eat no fat," I babbled.

"What?"

The distraction of the rhyme took him off balance. The harder he focused to understand what the hell I was talking about, the easier he made it for me. "You didn't even see us, Officer. Go on with what you were doing."

"Okay," he said reasonably, and walked off, just like that.

Gordy let out his breath. "Jeez."

"That goes double for me. Let's move."

For a big man, Gordy knew how to be light on his feet; we fairly shot down the next flight of steps.

The deserted basement was as the raid had left it, with the door open, only a couple of dim lights on, and a mess littering the floor. We dodged around some overturned crates and smashed bottles, working toward the south wall. The farther we went, the happier I was to have company. Unlike the homey familiarity of my own underground room, this one was too large for comfort. The ceiling pressed close and the silence was like a vast monster watching us from the shadows.

Damn my imagination, anyway. I swallowed it back with private embarrassment. Bobbi was stuck down here with no way of knowing what was going on and I was the one trying not to be afraid of the dark. I'd once invented a mythical Vampire's Union as a joke; this kind of nervousness would be enough to get me tossed out, fangs and all. Holding on to that crumb of lunacy got me through the next few minutes.

Gordy stopped over a dip in the floor with a large square drainage grate set into its lowest point. He braced himself and lifted it out.

"My God, you put her in there?" I whispered, staring at the black pit he'd uncovered.

"Not as bad as it looks."

He sat, swung his legs over the edge, and carefully placed his feet on some thick iron rungs set into the smooth cement of the walls. The descent was short, the bottom not more than eight feet down. The hole wasn't much bigger than a phone booth. Gordy fired up a match with one hand and used the other to grip something and push. A narrow door opened away from him. He stooped low and was gone.

I scrambled down the ladder, cracking an ankle against the last rung. Gordy, holding the door for me, waved me in. I ducked and followed and he let it close up behind. His match went out.

I worked spit into my mouth. "You got another light?"

"Jack? Is it you?"

Bobbi's clear, sane, and extremely welcome voice seemed to dispel the crushing atmosphere in my overactive brain. A distant flashlight blazed smack into my face, blinding me as effectively as the total darkness. I didn't mind.

The flash wavered from side to side as she trotted up. "Jack, Gordy, is everything okay?" She threw herself into my arms and I gathered her up in a tender bear hug.

"For the moment, honey." I reluctantly eased her down. "What about you? This place is terrible."

She almost echoed Gordy's earlier comment. "It's not so bad. I just pretend I'm a Becky Thatcher who's given Tom Sawyer the slip. C'mon." She took my hand to lead away with the bobbing light down a cement tunnel with smooth walls and a level floor. It turned once to the left and went up a step. The cement changed to ancient brick and pressed closer.

"Slick's mob built all this?" I asked.

"Not Slick," Gordy answered somewhere behind us. "Pearly Garson. He was scared of Big Al, but wanted to be like him. He heard that Al had an escape tunnel, so he had to have one, too."

"Take long to dig?"

"Nah. He tied it into an old rail delivery system that the city forgot about, even got some of the labor for free. They've tightened up on some of the graft these days, but back then you could get away with murder."

True, and he wasn't just speaking figuratively. "What happened to Pearly?"

"Got shot by his girlfriend's husband, then they took off for Canada.

Never did catch those two. Cops still have the case open, but Slick moved in and made sure nobody kicked about it too much. It was one hell of a funeral."

The walls widened to a circular space that resembled a hub of some kind. More cement sealed up what had once been other branches leading off to goodness knows where beneath the city. I could have sieved through and gone exploring, but that would have to wait until sometime after hell froze over.

"All the comforts of home," Bobbi said cheerfully, gesturing at a portable lantern burning on the grit-cluttered floor with a camp stool next to it. She turned the light up, revealing all the dreary details. It was fairly dry, which was the best that could be said about the place.

"Aren't you freezing down here?" I asked. I was getting cold just looking at the endless rows of brickwork encircling us.

She gave herself a hug within her heavy coat, its high fur collar bunching up her bright blond hair. "Haven't even thought about it. What I want to know is if it's safe to leave now."

Gordy shook his head. "The raid's pretty much over, but we're gonna get out of the way for a while. I called the lawyer and fixed it. We'll go to his place. He'll have a spare room for you."

"Jack, too?" she asked hopefully.

"Not yet, sweetheart," I said.

She read my face, her own clouding up in response. "Then it's not over, is it?"

"It will be soon."

"For Kyler or you? You don't look so good, Jack."

I rallied for her sake. "I just need to clean up and shave."

She nodded slowly, accepting the offered illusion, but not at all fooled by it. "What next?"

"We get you the hell out of here."

Bobbi wasn't all that in love with the place. Gordy took the flashlight, I picked up the lantern, and we started hiking. It seemed like a very long trip. I began to wonder if the tunnel ran down the length of the street instead of crossing it when a slab of iron loomed out of the dark to block our path. I hoped that it was a door; it had a handle but nothing like a lock or bolt on this side. Gordy gave it a hard twist, lifting and pulling at the same time. The thing gave and abruptly came away toward him, revealing the yawning darkness of what I could assume to be the other basement.

"Cozy," I croaked. Both of them remained diplomatically oblivious to my nerves.

"Goes up through a furniture store," Gordy laconically explained. "The lawyer's car'll be waiting for us."

"Sure it's safe?"

"Better'n any bank."

"I'll be fine," Bobbi assured me. "Will you?"

That helped to straighten me up. Once again, she read my face right and we came together like a magnet and an iron, each giving the other what was needed to hold on a little longer.

Bobbi and I weren't in any hurry to say good-bye, but Gordy pointed out that there was no telling how long the two cops would stay in dreamland. Sooner or later one of them would wake up or some enterprising member of the raid might decide to break into the office to see what was on the other side. I had things to do before that happened.

We reluctantly broke off. She gave me a last smile and squeeze on the arm and ducked through ahead of Gordy. He handed me a spare key to his office and followed her. A shift of metal and a heavy clang and we were solidly separated with very different directions to take. Armed with the lantern and trying to hold my mind on more important things than claustrophobia, I quickly returned to the Nightcrawler's basement.

Neatly dropping the grate back into place, I all but galloped across to the stairs. I left the lantern behind, making a point of turning it out, then vanished and floated upward.

It was safer in this form; any cops on the lookout for trouble would miss me, and I didn't have to worry about making noise while whipping around the landings to the second floor. I reached Gordy's office and went on through. The place was quiet. I materialized.

Thankfully, Calloway was still on the rug, sprawled on his back, and just starting to snore. Baker was where I'd left him. I shrugged out of his coat. It wasn't easy wrestling it back on him again, but things had to look right. If he noticed, he'd probably attribute his rumpled condition to our brief run-in. At least he didn't wake up, which didn't worry me too much; Calloway was my prime concern.

His snores were in full swing. It seemed a shame to disturb him, except he wasn't all that aware when I started talking to him in a low, persuasive tone. He took the orders without question, same as the other cop had, and lay there like a zombie while I quietly unlocked the door from the inside. After dropping the key in the top drawer of Gordy's desk, I stood a moment to take in a last bracing breath, then snapped my fingers.

That was Calloway's cue to wake up. I disappeared just as his eyes flickered open.

He moaned, groaned, and cursed whatever aches his body had provided for the occasion, but eventually got to his feet. I kept clear of him, not wishing to advertise the least hint of my presence. He made a trip out to the hall and back, presumably to the nearby washroom for water. I heard a soft splash followed by Baker making outraged sputtering noises.

"What the hell . . . !"

"On your feet, Baker. We gotta get moving."

"What happened?"

"You let that jerk-off kid mop the floor with you, that's what happened." He'd somehow overlooked the fact that Gordy had also fallen on him like an avalanche.

"Shit, I didn't even see it coming."

"Well, too bad for you."

"Where'd they go?"

"Out. C'mon."

"Where?"

"Kyler's. He's gonna want to know about this."

"Criminey, couldn't you just phone him?"

I'd anticipated that alternative and smiled invisibly.

"He'll want to see us personally," he said, repeating my instructions to him, word for word. He made them sound normal.

More grouse, more mild objections, but in the end they straggled downstairs with me in their wake.

Calloway collared one of the regular cops and asked after Gordy.

"You kiddin', Lieutenant? We've been tearing the place apart for him. You'd think a guy that big would have turned up by now."

I recognized the voice of the officer who had stopped us on the way to the basement.

"What about another man, tall, dark hair, needs a shave?"

Long pause, or so it seemed to me. "Nah, no one like that. Check with the boys out front. Maybe they bagged him with the others."

"Got away," Baker muttered when the cop left.

"Can't help it now. Let's get out before someone spots you instead."

"You still going to . . . going to see him?"

Calloway answered by walking off. Baker reluctantly followed. I stuck with them as they went through a regular obstacle course to their car. Like a slightly colder blast of wind, I whipped inside one of the open doors and settled on the floor behind the driver's seat. With my long legs crammed up over the drive shaft hump, I cautiously went solid again, the better to get an idea of our destination.

The ride was tense for me; I had to stay alert, ready to vanish any second should one of them happen to glance back. It was also silent with Baker nursing his bruised head and Calloway concentrating on the road. Plagued as I was by occasional motion sickness, I felt a strong pang of sympathy for Opal's difficulty earlier tonight. At least I wasn't riding with my back to the motor, though being stuffed in sideways couldn't have been that much better.

And so I occupied myself with internal complaints over minor discomforts. The idea was to keep my mind off the near future and a job for which I had no enthusiasm.

A lot more driving, starts and stops, then a long steady stretch which helped to ease my stomach. Turn, then turn again onto a bumpy surface that threatened to undo everything. I had to brace myself to keep from rattling around too much and betraying my presence. We crunched to a final stop, tires sliding over gravel and gravel sliding over mud. Calloway cut the motor. I soaked in the comparative silence for only a second before disappearing. Calloway and Baker got out and I gave them plenty of time to get well away. Solid once more, I cautiously lifted for a peek out the window.

As a roadhouse, it could have qualified as anyone else's mansion, but I wouldn't have expected Kyler to invest in a shack, not after seeing his setup at the Travis. This one had a couple of sprawling stories' worth of white-trimmed brown brick with an extra-wide porch running all around. In the summer it probably sported tables, with romantic couples wanting to watch the moon rise over the surrounding trees. Music leaked out from within. It was the kind of place I'd have taken Bobbi to for a nice dinner and some close dancing. Too bad about the new owner. . . .

Never mind that for now.

I quit the car and circled the house. The front parking lot was full; the back was less crowded, but more informative. Kyler's twin Cadillacs were parked together next to the rear entrance, noses out, prepared for a fast exit.

This was the right place and the time had come, but I hesitated to move, held back by the blankness of the immediate future. No specific plan of what to do during that final confrontation had descended upon me. To be practical, not knowing the layout or circumstances ahead meant that improvisation would be a necessity . . . but the time had come, the time had come.

Before, I'd dreaded slipping into the efficient madness that had carried me through one murder; now I was afraid of not finding it again. It was far preferable to be borne comfortably along in a soothing haze of insanity than to have each action and detail burned clearly into memory as a conscious choice. If banging my head into a wall would have helped, I'd have done so; instead, I took a deep breath and walked right through it.

I usually floated in through cracks below doors or around windows, but picked the more difficult way for distraction. I felt the graininess of the mortar and the hard blocks it held together. Perhaps one night I would find a wall that I couldn't seep through and stay trapped there like Fortunato, forever out of reach of his Amontillado. But this time the bricks gave way to plaster and strips of lath and I was in the free air of a large room. I could fumble around and try to guess my location, but now that I'd started, it was better to keep going and to go quickly. Since it seemed quiet enough to be deserted I found a corner and slowly materialized, eyes wide and ears straining.

The dance music, along with voices and the clink of dishes, grew louder now that I had real ears again. I was in a really nice billiards room. The lights were low and the cues and multicolored balls were stored in their cabinets, but one of the tables was still very much in use. A young man and woman with most of their clothes off were happily thrashing away on its sea of green felt like nobody's business—nobody being myself.

My mouth popped open and an unexpected blush seared my face. I had enough presence of mind to disappear before either of them noticed me and got the hell out. I'd long ago lost my virginity and had seen enough of life not to be a prude, but encroaching on the privacy of courting couples was not a hobby I planned to take up just yet. The temptation to return and study another's technique was very strong, though. One peril—or bonus—of my changed condition was the danger of becoming an incurable Peeping Tom. Maybe later, I told myself firmly, and left them to it.

The accidental intrusion did serve to remind me that Kyler would probably be upstairs away from the . . . uh . . . entertainment areas. I pushed up through the ceiling and drifted around enough to guess that I was in a long hall. Invisibility had its drawbacks, with no vision and limited hearing. I could be methodical and start at the back, checking out each room, which would only take half the night. Nuts to that.

Calloway and Baker would certainly be talking to Kyler by now. I floated softly along, alert for any voices, and eventually found them. The confused verbal blur sharpened into speech as I slipped into a room.

Bingo. I recognized Baker's voice.

I brushed by several people, creating a momentary chill for each . . . hard to tell how many were scattered around the room and any of them could have been Kyler. No one moved as they listened to Baker giving his story. It was very interesting to hear things from another point of view; the facts were essentially the same, except for me being larger and more ferocious, and the fight, such as it was, lasting longer.

"The next thing I know is Calloway telling me to get up," he concluded.

"Gordy and Fleming got away?" Kyler's voice. I surged toward him.

"Yeah, boss."

"And you came all the way out here just to tell me that?"

"It was Calloway's idea."

"I figured you'd want to see us personally," Calloway added from across the room.

Kyler took a while before speaking again, either to think, grind his teeth, or to make them sweat or all three. "Use the phone in the future. You could have been followed."

"Yes, sir."

"Otherwise you saw what Baker saw?"

"What do you mean?"

"About Fleming."

"I couldn't really say. Things were jumping and I was busy with Gordy . . . but it was him and he said he wanted to see you."

"Did he say why?"

"Baker interrupted before he could tell."

I had a mental picture of Baker squirming before Kyler's unblinking eyes.

"Calloway, you may leave. Better luck next time."

"You still want Gordy hit?"

"Yes, but you're off of it. We'll have to try something else."

"But I—"

"You'll get your usual payment, but without the bonus since you were unable to complete the job. I think that's fair enough."

"Yes, sir." Calloway sounded relieved. There was some shuffling and the door opened and closed.

Kyler lowered his voice, concentrating it. "All right, Baker, I want an exact account of Fleming's attack on you."

"It's just what I said. He was fast. I hardly seen him coming."

"Hardly, or did not? Give me more detail."

"I guess I must have blinked. It was like he wasn't there for a second. He was *fast*."

"Almost as though he vanished and reappeared again?"

Baker hesitated. "Yeah . . . but that can't be right. Can it?"

Kyler didn't answer that one. "You may go, too. Change out of that uniform before you frighten away the customers."

"Yeah, boss." More shuffling and door noises. I made a fast, blind sweep of the place. Only two men were left. The odds were getting better for me.

"Well?" said Kyler.

Chaven's voice: "We still don't know how he does it. Is it mass hypnosis, like those Indian guys with the rope trick, or what?"

"The method is not so important as the fact that he is capable of doing it."

"Great, so how do we deal with something like that? If he can turn it on and off like a light bulb . . ."

"Light bulbs can be broken."

"When you can see to hit 'em. How you going to hit this guy? How you going to keep him from hitting you?"

"By being prepared. We must also prepare against Gordy."

"He'll be on guard himself, thanks to those assholes screwing up."

"No doubt."

"What about that stuff about Gordy not being behind getting Red and his boys? And what happened to Vic? If Gordy didn't get 'em, who did?"

"There are others who have the means to do it, but they would know better than to try. We'll find out for certain later. As for Gordy, we'd have had to deal with him eventually. This business only caused us to move a little faster."

"But are you ready to take on him and his backers in New York?"

"I'll have to be."

"How?"

"By hitting him again, before he can hit back. This time we make sure it works. We move in and offer New York a five-percent increase on the profits. Taking over Gordy's territory will increase our present income by about four hundred percent. That will make the expenditure of the extra five worth it."

"First you gotta find him," Chaven pointed out.

"Give it to Deiter. Where is he?"

"Downstairs someplace."

"Get him."

Chaven left. The odds would never be better: one to one and no witnesses. I went solid.

The room was on a level with the rest of the place: opulent with its velvet curtains, grass-thick rug, and overstuffed furniture. All the comforts and then some, though I'd halfway expected him to have at least a few crosses and a garland or two of garlic up in his sanctum.

Kyler had his expensively dressed back to me. He looked smaller without his vicuna overcoat, but snakes can come in all sizes and still pack enough poison to kill. He stood before a well-appointed bar. The usual mirror behind the bottles was missing, replaced by a wall of tufted black patent leather. Too bad, I could have used it to keep an eye on the door. I moved to one side to cover it. Kyler heard the shift of my clothes and whipped around, a gun ready in his hand. It was Escott's Webley. Though not fatal to me, it hurt like hell to get shot, and the .45 bullets this weapon could spit were nearly half an inch in diameter. I decided not to provoke him into anything I might regret.

"So you did follow Calloway," Kyler said after the first surprise wore off. "What do you want?"

"Same as before: a truce, but now I don't trust you to keep your word. Is that something you only reserve for people who can't threaten you?"

That, as Escott might have said, touched a nerve, but Kyler made an effort to hold his voice even. "I kept my word last night. I was not the one after you. Lieutenant Blair—"

"Was your patsy, yeah, I figured that much."

"He was having me watched. My hands were tied."

"So tight that you couldn't have found a way around him? Never mind, it worked out fine for you. You set me up and got the cops looking someplace else for that girl's killer and we all had a good laugh."

"Some of us. You killed Hodge, so that balances things. But I'm out the price of the bracelet."

"Turning it in got you off the hook with the cops. Cheap at the price as far as you're concerned."

He acknowledged the logic with a small nod. "Perhaps, but three more of my men are dead and another's missing along with little Opal. Where is she?"

"Safe enough. You're out the bracelet and some soldiers, but you came that close to killing my friends; we could play I-did-you-did all night. What do *you* want, Kyler?"

He usually kept a poker face, but couldn't quite suppress a minute glitter from his dark eyes. "You may have noticed that the police still don't know who you are. I could have told them, but did not. I will continue to be silent."

I still hadn't lost my initial revulsion for the man, but it was under control, more or less. He was playing me, but I knew it and was willing to go along. "In exchange for what?"

"Information about yourself."

Not unexpected. He must be eaten up with curiosity, and the questions he asked would give me a clear idea of how firmly entrenched he might be in old superstitions. "Why do you want to know?"

"I think we can be useful to one another."

"I thought you wanted me dead."

"For a situation like this, I can be flexible."

He got a cautious nod from me on that one and I experimentally paced the room. The Webley never once wavered, but he didn't try anything, giving me time to think. My real purpose was to get my easy-to-read face turned away from him and orient myself in case I had to leave fast. That's what I told myself; I was *not* trying to stall.

Bullshit.

It was that damned wall in my head. I'd gone through a real one not ten minutes ago; time to face the internal one and get down to practicalities. Get through it, get through *with* it, then get the hell out.

I could easily take away the Webley, but it would be a bad idea to use it against him: too noisy and the thing might be traced to Escott. Maybe we could alibi each other, but he wouldn't thank me for pulling off anything so clumsy.

Perhaps I could arrange for Kyler to jump out a window. Better. That way his death would at least look like a suicide. The idea of methodically breaking his neck or stabbing him sickened me. I had no desire to touch him. It's different in the heat of a fight when the instincts to survive take over and the adrenaline pushes you past thought and over the edge. I might try arranging some kind of confrontation, force him to make the first move. . . .

How? I thought sarcastically. Look him straight in the eye, insult his immediate family, and hope he'll lose his temper?

"Flexible . . . ?" I prompted at last.

"I'll stop the hit on you," he answered readily.

"And my friends?"

"All included."

"Gordy as well?"

He didn't like it, but finally nodded.

"And listening to my life story is worth losing that four-hundred-percent increase in your profits?"

That set him back a bit as he realized I'd been there for his conversation with Chaven, but his eyes continued to glitter. "I would expect it to be instructive."

I'd been down this road before and wasn't about to make a second trip. This time I turned away to pace around his desk, looking for an idea, or maybe a blunt instrument. My eyes swept over a single book lying on the blotter. A few seconds later its title impressed itself onto my busy brain with an inner jolt. I kept going as though I hadn't seen it.

"And along with the truce I am prepared to generously compensate you for your efforts," he added, inspired, possibly, by the shabby clothes I now wore.

The book changed nothing, but it did explain the dearth of crosses and garlic. Though I'd read the story as a kid, I remembered little of it; the visual impression from seeing the movie three years ago was much stronger. The sight of Claude Rains swiftly unwrapping the bandages from his apparently missing head was not something one could easily forget. Kyler wasn't chasing after Stoker's *Dracula,* but *The Invisible Man* of H.G. Wells.

I almost laughed out loud and had to disguise the intake of breath as a heavy sigh. He'd miscalculated this one, but it did make a kind of sense, considering he'd only seen me vanishing and coming back, not lurking around the Stockyards for a meal. He was close enough to the truth and deserved a few points for choosing even crazed science over superstition-ridden vampirism. But it made no difference. The information he wanted would still be useless to him and as soon as he realized that . . .

"How much?" I asked, not looking at him.

"Five thousand."

"Make it ten."

He hesitated.

"It's worth it, Kyler." I let myself fade, moving on ghostly legs until we were closer than before. Eyes filling his face, he renewed his grip on the gun. I faded completely for just a second to drive home the point, then returned. "It's well worth it."

He'd had plenty of time to dwell on the potentials in the last day or so. My demonstration only confirmed the beginning of endless advantages. "How?" he whispered.

I said nothing. His own inner arguments would persuade him better and faster than any I could invent.

"Is it a chemical process?"

It should have been Escott standing here; he was the one with an actor's training and judgment. I had to go on instinct and hope to make it work. "You'll find that out if and when we make a deal. Call off the hits, leave my friends alone, and ten thousand in cash. In exchange, I'll show you how to . . ." I illustrated by vanishing briefly once more, returning that much closer to him.

Kyler's greed hadn't been so obvious before. Moment by moment, I was learning to read him better, and now he seemed hooked. "All right." His voice was very soft. But the last time I'd heard that tone Chaven had been holding a gun to my head, I was hard put not to glance behind me.

"Deal?"

"Yes. But five thousand down, the balance when I'm able to do what you do."

"Then we start now," I told him. "The sooner we start, the sooner I get out of here."

He had no objections to that. This was his last chance and mine as well. If I couldn't break through to him he would have to die and I would have to live with that death. He was as vulnerable now as I would ever find him.

"You must listen to me very carefully. . . ."

I put everything I had into it, focusing onto his stony eyes, shutting out all other distractions. The room we stood in, the people at their games and dances in the rest of the house, the stark winter woods surrounding the place all ceased to be. The changes within that frightened me, that I had promised to keep under control, took over and rushed free once more.

"Listen to my voice. . . ."

The air was very still except for the even thump of his heart.

"You will listen and do what I tell you."

I concentrated, willing his face to slacken into blankness, quietly demanding that he hear me.

"Do you understand?"

His jaw sagged. I almost mirrored him, surprised by sudden hope. This time it just might work.

"You must listen to me."

His eyelids flickered.

"You *must*."

But he drew a steady breath and held it, giving a sharp shake with his head. "Like hell," he said thickly. "What are you doing?"

Losing the battle. "Kyler . . ."

But the harder I tried to hold it, the quicker it slipped away. Whatever it was about him that set him apart from other men and repelled me—an especially strong will or carefully controlled insanity—worked in his favor. He was throwing off my influence, waking up, and stubbornly fighting. My own concentration wavered. Details ignored before, but necessary to survival, abruptly intruded on us.

I was aware that Chaven and another man had entered the room. They'd padded in as softly as hunters after any skittish prey. If I hadn't been so mentally bound to Kyler, I might have had a chance to do something more than just sluggishly notice their presence and start to turn. But that chance came and went like a ghost's shadow. Chaven's hand darted into his coat, dragging free his first and final answer to problems like me.

Wide awake now, Kyler looked past me. His face opened with sudden horror; one arm came up in futile protection.

"*No!*"

But if Kyler had anything more to say, it was lost in the ongoing roar of Chaven's gun.

8

KYLER yells a last inarticulate denial. His voice blends with my own hoarse cry.

Orange-and-white flames explode from the muzzle. Endless, unbearable thunder clogs my ears to the bursting point. Doubling, tripling, the shocks tear into my side and out again.

He falls back against the bar, nodding with each bullet's impact on his body. His cold eyes suddenly blaze to life, but it's an illusion. They turn inward to fix on a place where I cannot look—where I don't want to look. He slides to the floor.

I stagger away from the dying man. Smoke and bloodsmell overtake me. We merge into nothingness, turning, tumbling, free of gravity, free of thought, free of the first awful crash of agony. I twist and soar high in blind flight.

Chaven circles below. He and the other man cast about with broken questions, curses, and anguish. Drawn by the shots, more people rush in. Like a detached spirit with only vague interest in their little problems, I hover above the confusion. Their voices fade. I seep through a wall, seeking another, more tranquil place, away from their alarms and fears.

Stumbling awkwardly into a pink marble counter, I came back to myself with a stomach-lurching jolt. Gravity reasserted its claim on my body, trying to drag me into, and perhaps through, the floor. I fought it, needing to feel my own solidity, my own movements, needing the instinctive assurance that I still lived. My hands clawed at the cool marble as though it were a life preserver. I stayed and was numbly thankful for the privilege.

I'd wound up in a fancy lounge. A huge mirror over the counter reflected gold walls where brass lamps clung like glowing cicadas. As usual, it missed me, but I had no interest in knowing what I looked like. Turning from its emptiness, I was busy just trying to keep my shaky legs under me. I'd been shot before, but not so many times all at once, not to such a point of shattering, sickening weakness.

The bloodsmell clinging to me was my own. Morbidly, I counted four holes going into the right side of my pea jacket and another four raggedly emerging from the left, the fabric soaked with warm red stains, and my guts still churning sharply from the aftershock. Chaven had made a good grouping—too bad he couldn't have known they'd go right through me and on to kill Kyler.

He's dead.

I braced more firmly against the counter, locking my knee joints to offset their tremors. The initial shock threatened to turn into a nauseous disaster, but I gulped it back and sucked stuffy air into my neglected lungs. It shuddered out as soft, nervous laughter that did not want to stop. Some distant part of my brain was aware that it didn't sound quite right, but the restraints were broken down. It hurt too much to hold back and continued for as long as the air lasted, ugly, mirthless whispers of relief. After too many frantic nights crowded with uncomfortable thoughts, I needed the release badly. It washed over me, a wave of sweet, soothing balm for a troubled soul. It washed over and past, leaving me weary and drained, but at peace.

I was finally free of the bastard.

A last little surge of laughter flowed away from me, soft and secret.

He's dead.

He was someone else's problem, now. And I was just cynical enough to be glad about it.

Next door, the clearly audible aftermath of Chaven's mistake was just beginning.

But he was quick to adjust to the new situation, especially since his own skin was at risk. Within a very few minutes he managed to invent a plausible story of how I'd burst in with a gun to fulfill my own contract on Kyler and escaped. The room quickly cleared as he sent his cronies out to search for me and to explain away the commotion to any roadhouse patrons who might have heard something odd happening upstairs.

Then I had to disappear for a time as two of his goons charged in to check the stalls for my presence.

"You believe that b.s. he fed us?" one of them asked as they crashed around.

"Long as we get our cut of the profits, who cares? We do what he says and make him happy."

"And if we find this guy he was talking about?"

"Then we give him a bad case of lead poisoning. C'mon, what's the holdup?"

"Just lookin'. I never been in one of these places before. I thought the pots'd be shaped different or something."

"The only difference is that some of ours are on the wall and all of theirs are on the floor."

That explained the pink marble; I was in a ladies' lounge.

"Live 'n' learn."

"C'mon."

The door banged shut.

When I came back I felt much more tired than before, but better able to think. If those two were a typical example of the kind of loyalty Kyler had inspired in his troops, Chaven had little to worry about in the reprisals department from underlings. But he was still one to watch out for as far as I was concerned, since more than ever he had a damn good reason to keep it a personal fight between us. On the other hand, there was every possibility that he wasn't the same kind of crazy as his deceased boss. I might be more successful reasoning with him.

I pressed an ear to the adjoining wall to see if he was alone yet, but no such luck, and no wonder. With an invisible God-knows-what wandering around the house he'd want to have an army around him for protection. As it was, he'd settled for one man—one too many for the moment. The kind of hypnosis that I had in mind required a certain degree of privacy. I'd have to wait.

To better hear what was going on I went back through the wall, giving the spot where Kyler had dropped a wide berth. It wasn't out of respect for the dead; nervous superstition was a better description for my caution. There was no telling what, if anything, I might encounter in this ethereal form and I had no desire to find out. I found a quiet corner and listened to the hollow voices of the living that remained.

"Now what?" asked one unfamiliar to me.

"What d'ya mean?" Chaven returned. He seemed to be standing near Kyler, perhaps looking down at the corpse.

"I mean about him. You ain't callin' the cops on this. . . ."

"Hell, no."

"Then wake up and start thinking."

Chaven's voice was ragged. "Can it, Deiter, I *am*."

During the shooting, I'd had only the barest glimpse of a man standing behind Chaven. He had to have been Deiter, the specialist Kyler had ordered up to take care of the hit on Gordy, and now the only other witness to the strange circumstance of Kyler's death. One more name to put on the roster of people to be persuaded to forget all about me.

"We take him out to the boat," Chaven finally said. "We get a box and weights and sink him just like any other job. We take him way out and we do it tonight."

"What about your gun?"

"What about it?"

"The bulls got ways of tracing bullets. If they should ever—"

"Yeah, okay, it goes in the drink with him. I can always get another." Pause. "Like maybe this one."

"What the hell is it?" Deiter had to be talking about Escott's Webley. It was a unique-looking hunk of hand artillery.

"Something that shoots. I don't think the boss'll mind me taking it back again."

"Fat lotta good it did him. What happened, Chaven? How could you shoot that guy and hit the boss? What happened to the guy? I had both eyes right on him and he just stopped being there."

Chaven moved away toward the desk where the book lay. "Here. You figure it out."

Deiter followed. "Invisible? You pulling my leg?"

"The boss was checking into it. He said the guy in the book made himself invisible with chemicals. He had the idea that this guy Fleming knew how to do the same thing, only he could turn it on and off like— like a light bulb, clothes and all."

"That's crazy."

"If it ain't this, then what else?"

"You can shoot through ghosts, can't you?" Deiter hazarded.

"I don't believe in ghosts. You saw what happened. Well, didn't you?"

"Yeah, I already said so. I just wanna know what I saw."

"A guy disappearing."

"But it don't make sense."

"It don't have to—but that's how it is. And the worst part is that bastard could be in here right now."

That ominous idea must have made Deiter a sudden believer. Things got very quiet for a while. "What are you going to do about him?"

"One thing at a time. First we clean up this mess on the floor."

"You got a story ready for Kyler's bosses?"

"Just what I told the boys here; he put a hit out on Fleming, only Fleming got him first. We stick to that and we keep our skins."

"What about his family?"

"He didn't have any that he wanted. He told me he left them behind and wanted to keep it that way."

"Maybe the wife skipped to Reno," Deiter sniggered.

"Who knows? I think any skirt would have been crazy to get cozy with him. I was the closest thing he had to a friend and I didn't like him all that much."

"Guess it's just as well we're gonna sink him. You'd do a lousy job talking at his funeral."

"Can it, Deiter. In fact, you can everything you heard and saw in here. If you want to stay out of the loony bin you don't say a word about invisible men to nobody."

"This mean you're running the show now?"

"Until and unless the other bosses say otherwise. The boys'll follow my lead long as they get their money as usual . . . oh, shit."

"What?"

"We gotta get Opal back. She's the only one who can make head or tail of the books. Without them, I'm crippled."

"But you don't know where—"

"I'm laying odds that Fleming's got his partner holding her, and this town ain't so big that they can hide forever. I'll have Calloway look into things from his side. Wouldn't it be something if we got the cops to do our work for us?"

"If you can trust him."

"He's in too deep and likes the money too much to turn on us now."

"You hope. What about the problem down the hall? We can't keep that spook in private stir forever."

Chaven's new responsibilities were starting to irritate him, "Jesus, why don't you just make a list? I'll get to him when I can."

"Right, boss."

The use of his new title mollified him somewhat and they left the room to set things in motion. I went solid almost as the door shut.

Kyler had fallen on his face, but they'd rolled him over, presumably to check for signs of life, and left him that way. His eyes were still open. The rug was thick with his blood, and the cold, dizzy scent of it teased my nose. I tried to ignore it as I borrowed the phone on the desk.

It was a relief to know that my call to Escott wouldn't be long distance and therefore traceable. I'd been worried that Calloway had driven over the state line to Indiana or had at least left Cook County. The other end of the wire began ringing for attention.

And kept on ringing. Where the hell was he?

I dialed the number again, more slowly in case I'd gotten it wrong the first time. And again, to make sure. No answer. My mouth had grown very dry. Then I had to hang up and disappear when a couple of Chaven's men came in to dispose of the body. From their lazily bickering conversation, they would be taking their time on this job. I hurled out past them to find another phone. One of them complained miserably about cold drafts and began sneezing.

Random searches are neither fast nor efficient and that much more difficult when you can't see where you're going. There might have been any number of phones handy downstairs, but I wasn't dressed for fancy socializing. I'd be spotted in short order and either thrown out on my ass by the bouncers or shot again. Both possibilities would prevent me from letting Escott know what was going on, and worse, from finding out what had happened to him.

I took a turn up the hall, bumped through a door, and swept the room for occupants. Clear. Solid again, I checked the place in one fast look. No phone, dammit. I did the same thing once more, twice more, finding either people or not finding a phone. Jeez, when you're making love or taking a bath the damn things are ringing off the wall for you, but when you really need one they vanish like roaches when the lights come on.

One more try. I materialized in a vacant meeting room with a long dark table and padded chairs all around. Some unsung genius had thought to install a phone and I took immediate advantage of the fact.

Or tried to. Just as I was dialing the last number, a door at the far end slowly swung open. There was nothing else to do but drop the ear-piece back and disappear. I clearly recalled that in the movie, Claude Rains had himself endured a frustrating lack of privacy.

The impromptu investigator seemed to be alone and only I stayed long enough to check the place and maybe puzzle over its emptiness. Un-happily for me he left the door ajar, the better to hear any more suspicious noises. I gave out an internal and quite silent sigh and materialized to do some listening for myself. He was alone. I decided that it wouldn't hurt for him to enjoy a short nap while I completed my call.

Taking a direct and low-key approach, I just walked in on him. Leap-ing out of thin air might have been more dramatic, but for this kind of work, the less ruckus, the better.

My unsuspecting victim stood in the middle of a square of rug, star-ing at it. I was ready for him to hear me and turn, but he took no notice. He was a stocky man, but his cheap hickory shirt and rough pants hung loose on his frame as though he'd lost a lot of weight. His clothes didn't fit this place any more than mine did. Head still down, he traced the out-line of the rug's pattern with the blunt toe of his shoe. This simple and childish activity in a middle-aged man brought a rush of prickles to the back of my neck. Deiter had mentioned a "spook"; maybe I'd found him. If so, then he might prove to be as immune to suggestion as Kyler.

Deciding to not take the chance, I began to quietly back out. The man, still tracing, had gradually turned. I froze, held fast by wide, wasted eyes and a scraped-out expression. He glanced at me without concern, his pasty face and subdued manner much too calm. To him, I was just another part of the furnishings, somewhat less interesting than the rug, for he continued with his infantile game.

Recognition reluctantly burst upon me. Last summer, while subject-ing a man to hypnotic influence, I'd lost control of my emotions. The anger, frustration, pain, and roaring hatred buried deep by the shock of my own death had been released like a lightning bolt into another's mind, with predictable effect. This soft, helpless husk before me was all that was left of Frank Paco.

I was frozen with apprehensive shock . . . and fascinated.

"Paco?" I ventured, not really knowing why.

"Yes?" he unexpectedly replied.

After a minute I was able to speak again. "Do you know me?"

His toe began to trace a different pattern in the rug, one that only he could see. He paused to give me a good look. Something flickered over his face, perhaps the corpse light of a dead memory. "You were on the boat."

So he recalled my last hell-filled days aboard the *Elvira*. "Anywhere else?"

He shrugged. I rubbed a hand over my rough jaw. Maybe my unkempt appearance now was misleading him. He might not be able to link me with the younger-looking intruder who had dynamited his basement and subsequently blasted away his sanity. On the other hand, why was it so important to me for Paco to recall that encounter? The answer came even as I thought up the question.

Here was Kyler's other source of information on me.

I fought down the sudden tremors running out from my spine and backed away from him without thinking. Stupid reaction, I thought, and made myself stop. Paco didn't seem to notice.

The boardroom phone was as safe as any for the moment. Paco was too far gone to be much of a danger to me now. I dialed the number once more and this time got an answer, but not the one I expected. It was Shoe Coldfield and I didn't have to hear the tone of his voice to know that something was wrong.

"This is Fleming. Where's Charles?"

"Shit if I know. When he didn't answer the phone I came over to check on him and he's not here. Where the hell are you?"

"A roadhouse somewhere outta town. Was the building broken into?"

"Looks it; I don't think the s.o.b. got bored and took off leaving the door hanging open."

Damnation. "No, he wouldn't, not unless he was on the run, and my guess is that he'd call you for help at the first chance." My belly churned as the right idea hit me. "If he had one."

"What do you know, Fleming?" he growled.

"Did Charles tell you about me finding Opal?"

"Kyler's accountant? Yeah, he told me all about her and the hit on Gordy. Maybe he decided to follow you—no, if he was watching that girl, nothing would have budged him outta here."

"They must have been watching the Travis Hotel for Kyler when I showed up. They had to have followed me while I was busy trying to keep Opal quiet—then they got in and got to Charles."

"Who followed you? Who got in?" he demanded.

"It has to be Angela Paco's people."

This time he said nothing and I couldn't blame him. The situation was rapidly growing beyond words.

"I've found out why Angela put herself in the middle of things last night. It's her father. Kyler's been keeping Frank Paco under wraps."

"Frank Paco? What the hell for?"

"Pumping him for information about me, I guess."

"But Paco's been bughouse crazy since that fire. What can he know that would be of any use?"

"Doesn't matter anymore—Kyler's dead."

He paused a long time on that one and there was a hint of respect in his reaction.

"Took care of him, huh?"

"Not me, his lieutenant. Chaven did the honors. Right now I'm busy keeping my head down while he's covering things up."

"How the hell did you arrange it?"

"Believe me, it was an accident. Chaven's still after my hide, but forget him, Angela's our main worry now. I think the reason she kidnapped me the other night was to make a trade for her father. She might be trying to do the same again, but this time with Charles and Opal, so there's a good chance that they're all right." I purposely skipped over the fact that of the two, Opal was the more valuable hostage.

"Only now she won't be dealing with Kyler—if this is what you think it is."

"You just said that Charles wouldn't budge otherwise. Check around, see if there's anyone else besides the Kyler and Paco factions that are after us."

"I know there aren't. Yet."

"Right. My bet's that Angela's probably got them both and will be making her demands soon. Chaven's got his hands full at the moment and I don't know which way he'll jump on this, but he'll want Opal back because he needs her for his business."

"But Charles will be in the soup if she makes that deal. How long will it take you to get back here?"

"I'm not, I'm going straight to her place."

"If she's still there."

"You know any other bolt holes Paco had that Kyler didn't take over?"

"Okay. But I'm coming out, too."

Fine with me. I wouldn't mind having Coldfield guarding my back. We made quick arrangements on where to meet and I told him to give me at least an hour to get there. I hung up, ready to race for the nearest car.

Frank Paco stood in the doorway, his eyes narrowing and a little less empty than before. "What's all this about *mia Angelina*?"

"Nothing."

"Nothing, what?" he rumbled, a faint shadow of his old authority returning.

I made a bald guess on what was expected. "Nothing, Mr. Paco."

"You goddamn well better believe it. You boys don't say nothing against Angela. She's a good girl and I taught her how to stay that way."

"Yes, Mr. Paco. Have you seen her lately?"

"She's around the house somewhere. What d'you need to know for?"

"Uh . . . I heard she had an errand for me, is all."

"You go find her, then. You don't have her look for you. Remember that working for Angela is the same as working for me."

"Yes, sir."

"What're you doing in here like this, anyway? I don't pay you punks to dress like bums. Get out and get a shave."

"Yes, Mr. Paco." I wished for the time to question him myself, but he was getting loud, and I had to be elsewhere fast. I made my escape while I could.

Initially, I thought of "borrowing" a car from some randomly unlucky patron, but once outside, Kyler's twin Cadillacs popped back to mind and were too much of a temptation to pass up. I found them as they'd been parked, nose out and all ready to go. Locked or not, I slipped inside one and fumbled around with the wires to get it started. The soft, secretive purr of its well-tuned motor was an added bonus; no one in the house would hear my departure. While it warmed, I devoted some attention to the other car.

Both were beautiful machines; it wasn't their fault they'd caught the eye of someone like Kyler, so I drew the line at breaking the headlights off or any other obvious, crippling vandalism. Deflating tires was easy and effective enough; I stuck with what I knew best. The angry hiss of compressed air was loud, but nobody came out to check things. As soon as the rims were flush with the gravel, I took off, leaving behind the roadhouse palace and its dismayed and murderous senechals.

It took a full hour and then some to get there, and then I had to cruise slowly so as not to miss the spot off the road where Coldfield said he'd be waiting. In the summer it was sheltered by thick shrubs; now only black, branchy skeletons remained, clutching their tattered leaves like precious memories being dragged along to the grave. Despite their thin ranks and my excellent night vision, I had to look carefully before finding Coldfield's Nash.

My headlights were on so as not to annoy the traffic cops, so he naturally spotted me first. But I was startled at how fast he emerged from his car and downright alarmed when he crouched behind the armored door to point his gun in my direction. One of his men dropped out the driver's side, nervously copying him.

Maybe stealing one of Kyler's highly identifiable Caddies hadn't been such a good idea, after all. Belatedly, I hit the brakes, doused the lights, and rolled down the window to shout at him.

He recognized my voice and cautiously emerged. "You alone, Fleming?" he demanded, meaning that I'd damn well better be.

"Yeah," I wheezed, recalling how he hated surprises. I cut the motor and got out slowly. "Just me, myself, and I."

He finally put away the gun and came over to glare at the Caddy. "How the hell did you manage this one?"

"The other car had bad tires."

He harked out an unexpected laugh and thumped me on the back so hard that I nearly fell over. "All right, let's work out what needs to be done."

It seemed pretty plain to me. "First I find out if they're there, then I go get them."

"While I twiddle my thumbs?"

"I know the inside of the house."

"So does Isham," he said, with a brief gesture toward the Nash, where his driver waited. "He helped with the catering of a lot of parties there once."

I could see that we were heading for a long argument, so I gave in, up to a point. "Okay, but we can't all three go in or Angela will have more hostages than she knows what to do with." *Or targets,* I added to myself. "How about Isham comes with me and you hang back and cover us?"

"Not too far back," he rumbled. "We'll move up close to the front gate with the car. I'm not crazy about a walk through the woods in this weather."

The wind was light, but dismal to stand in. We hustled into the temporary protection of the Nash and Isham got it in gear.

"Just how did you take care of Kyler?" Coldfield asked.

I gave him an almost truthful story, leaving out a few important points about invisibility, failed hypnosis, and saying that I ducked and ran when Chaven started shooting. It was one of my more demandingly creative efforts.

"You must know how to run pretty damn fast," he commented, but left it at that. We'd once shared a nasty street brawl together and he apparently remembered that I could really move when sufficiently inspired.

Isham stopped and set the brake. "Ready," he said, his inflection so neutral that I couldn't tell if it was a statement or a question.

We got out and checked the lock on the front gates. It wasn't much, just a length of chain with a padlock holding it together, a bit down in the world from the armed guards and dogs that once patrolled the place. Maybe Angela could no longer afford them. Isham got some large bolt cutters from the trunk and snapped open a key link. Coldfield took charge of them and wished us luck as we slipped inside.

It was a long trudge down the gravel drive to the house, or perhaps the wind only made it seem so. I didn't mind much, but Isham looked pretty miserable, and things would only get worse for him before too long.

Lights glowed in some widely separated windows, but we paid more attention to the dark ones. If Angela had anyone on lookout duty, they'd be hiding here. Nobody yelled, though, so we moved on like we belonged until we came to the inadequate shelter of a work shed. It was locked up, but the clapboard sides of the building cut the wind down to nothing, which was very fortunate for Isham. Our parting conversation was brief, onesided, but absolutely necessary. I left him awake and alert, but had persuaded him to stay behind. Better for him to wait for my return than to have both of us in the house dodging around for cover that might not exist. It worked out fine for him; he thought it was all his idea. As for me, all I got was the start of a really nasty headache.

Free of Isham, I was able to move much faster and had no need to conceal my supernatural abilities. Rounding the nearest corner of the house, I vanished and forced my way through one of the many windows. Glass isn't my favorite material to sieve past; it's like falling through the ice in a pond, only the ice doesn't actually break. I always expect it to, though, which is why I usually avoid it. Tonight I was in too much of a hurry to bother. Wish I had; the extra effort took its toll on my head when I materialized on the other side.

The room I stood in was unfamiliar, but deserted. The lights were out in this wing of the house. Angela was either saving on the bills or the repairs hadn't gotten as far as fixing the wiring here yet. I picked my way around water-damaged furniture and eased open the door. The hinges creaked, but not too loudly. The hall was clear.

Trusting my ears and eyes to keep me out of trouble with the tenants, I checked likely and unlikely rooms on the ground floor. Some were untouched by fire and water, others were still a mess, and a few were in a halfway stage of repair. None of them were presently occupied. I blamed the late hour and could guess that Angela's boys were upstairs tucked away in their beds.

Wrong. Two of them were raiding the kitchen icebox for beer and sandwiches. They sounded oddly domestic as they cut bread and searched for the bottle opener, but their talk gave no clue about Escott. I was about to slip off when instead of sitting at the table to eat, they loaded everything onto a tray and went down another hall.

Long experiences had taught me that it was anatomically impossible to kick oneself. I settled for giving them a good start and cat-footed after them.

They were going to the private gymnasium. Vanishing, I rushed ahead to scour the place and found two people there, one stretched out on a table and the other sitting close by. Neither was doing much of anything. Fine and dandy. I whipped into the steam room where Newton had stashed me earlier and got my hunch paid off.

"Jack?" came Escott's inquiring whisper as I brushed past him.

He was alone. With some difficulty, I re-formed; this time my head was so bad that I staggered smack into one of the benches, barking my shins painfully against the wood. Twisting, I dropped onto the seat with a jolt. Rough landing, but at least I was still in one piece.

"That sudden chill was not my imagination, then," he said. "Are you all right?"

"Dizzy. All this Houdini stuff takes it out of me."

"Well, it is good to see you, my friend."

I was surprised that he could. In addition to the scrapes and black eye he'd already collected, his other eye was swollen shut and he held one arm protectively against himself. His long legs were drawn up on the bench, helping him to keep his back braced in a tiled corner. He was white to the hairline and looked about as steady as a guttering candle.

I forgot about my own troubles. "Holy shit, what happened to you?"

His mouth twitched. "Opal," he said dryly. "And, to a lesser extent, Miss Paco. I fear that one day a woman may prove to be my ultimate downfall."

"It's my fault, Charles. I wasn't careful enough about watching for tails when I brought Opal in."

He gave a minimal shrug with his eyebrows. "So I deduced when they broke into the building."

"Jeez, what else did they break? Your arm?"

"I think not, bad bruise at the worst, but I've a devil of a pain along the ribs. They'll need taping, I'm sure."

"Who hit you?"

"Opal . . . with a packing crate. Damn good luck for me that she did or I'd have come to a bad end then and there. Angela Paco was that close to blasting me into the next world."

"Good God."

"No doubt. He has spared me for some other purpose for which consideration I am truly thankful. No, please don't try to help, I've just got comfortable."

"I'm sorry." An apology had never seemed so inadequate before.

He waved it away. "Hardly your fault, old man. It's part of the job. I hope that you're here to help get me away from this place?"

"Only by the shortest possible route. Isham's just outside the house and Shoe's got a car waiting at the gate."

"Excellent," he sighed with quiet approval.

"Where's Opal?"

"With Miss Paco, I think. They left me in here some time ago. Is Gordy all right? And what about Miss Smythe?"

"Yeah. They're fine."

"And Vaughn Kyler?"

It was hard work to talk about that subject, but I did give him a very short summary of what I'd been through. "Chaven must have gotten the worst surprise of his life when Kyler dropped," I concluded.

Escott exhaled a long breath and tilted his head back against the wall. "What a gift for understatement the gentleman has."

"It's still not over."

"True. But you sound better able to handle it."

"I sure as hell don't feel it."

"You do look rather done in. Perhaps Shoe was right about taking a vacation. A few weeks in the Mexican sun would surely be of far less harm to you than all this bother has been."

If I'd had the energy, I might have laughed at that one. Instead, I got to my feet with a groan and went to work again.

He watched me through one slitted eye as I prowled to the small set-in window to get a look at the mugs outside. The door was secured shut this time; I had to settle for a sideways glance through the little square of double-paned glass, but it was enough. Newton, Lester, and some other guy out of the same mold were draped on various exercise benches, putting away the beer and sandwiches. They were making too much talk among themselves to notice our whispered conversation. Near them on the massage table lay Vic, lone survivor of last night's interrupted kidnapping. He was wrapped up in a ton of bandaging and looked asleep.

"Now what about you?" I asked, turning back. "What's your story?"

He frowned. "Well, it's all so bloody embarrassing, isn't it? Though I'm content now that things turned out as they did. The alternative Miss Paco had in mind hardly bears thinking about."

"Charles . . ."

"Yes. Well. They broke open the door below, and that awakened Opal from her slumber. I must say the girl recovered herself rather well. She immediately assumed that it was her employer come to rescue her and delayed me for a few crucial moments. She made a devil of a row and that brought the intruders straight up the stairs."

"No time to shoot?"

Another grimace. "More like a catastrophic lack of inclination. The first one up was Miss Paco herself. I was ready, but damn it, I just couldn't bring myself to kill a woman . . . a girl, really. While I hesitated, Opal hit me from the side with that bloody packing case and inadvertently saved my life by getting in Miss Paco's line of fire. I'm not sure what followed, but the next thing I knew I was at the bottom of the stairs with the breath knocked right out of me and unable to move. Eventually Opal realized her mistake, Miss Paco got things sorted out, and we were all bundled into a truck and brought here."

"They say why?"

"No." He correctly read my expression. "You've learned something?"

I told him about Frank Paco.

"Well, well," he said after a moment.

"Is that what you'd call 'a spanner in the works'?" I asked.

"More like the whole tool kit. No, strike that. Frank Paco's involvement only lends complete logic to his daughter's actions. If anything, it's Kyler's unexpected death that will cause the greatest disruption."

"That's what I came up with, but it might not change stuff that much. Chaven still needs Opal back, and I figure he'll want to bump you off just to make a neat package, so you two have got to get out of here before all hell breaks loose."

He readily agreed. "To that end I suggest you locate Opal next, and from there we may work out a practical exit from this place."

I wasn't crazy about leaving him alone now that I'd found him. "I don't know about that."

He made a deprecatory gesture at the bare walls. "The decor is somewhat lacking in interest, but I can survive it a while longer. As for those fellows outside, I'm content that they shall continue to ignore me as long as I remain quiet. Do go on and find the young lady; I'll be safe enough here."

My friend, the optimist. Movement outside caught my eye. I pressed my face against the glass for a better look.

"What is it?" he asked.

"Doc just came in. I may have to get scarce."

Out of his bathrobe and into a suit, Doc gave the illusion of sobriety until you saw his face. His eyes were bright but wandering, and his arms swung long and loose. His legs were still steady, so he was probably good for a few more miles, yet.

"It's time," was all he said.

Newton and Lester finished off their beer and got up. Without hurry, they went to Vic and pulled him to his feet. He wouldn't stay there. His head rolled, dropping to his chest as they dragged him out. Doc trailed after them.

I glanced at Escott. "They just took Vic for a walk. What say we do the same?"

"And Opal?"

"I'll come back for her later. Right now there's only one guy watching things. A better chance might not turn up again."

He gave out with a twitch of the lips and a very small nod. I think he was too done in to argue much on Opal's behalf; that or he figured she owed him one for braining him so hard.

I started to slip away, but the familiar dissolving of self into weightless nothing would not come. The effort brought back the dizziness, and I had to grab my now thundering head with both hands. It felt like someone had rammed a spike right into my brain.

"What is it?" Escott demanded softly.

"Tired," I mumbled. I could hardly hear myself. After a few moments, the roaring subsided a little and I pushed out a few more words. "Been doing this too much. Tired."

"Perhaps a trip to the Stockyards would not be amiss," he suggested, an uneasy tone to his voice.

"Yeah." Simple to say, hard to fulfill, but a long drink was what I needed. I thought of that while giving myself a minute to figuratively catch my breath. When I felt ready, I tried again.

Nothing.

I'd anticipated either vanishing or more pain, but not this. For the first time in months a layer of sweat broke out on me, flaring over my entire body, and settling around my flanks and groin. "They turn the heat on in here?" I whispered thinly.

But Escott could see something was seriously wrong and that the joke was meant to cover my fear. "Sit down, Jack. You look ghastly."

I didn't have much choice in the matter. My legs sagged all on their own, and with my back to the door for support, I slid right to the tiles.

Despite his damaged ribs, Escott got over to me. He knew better than to check for a pulse, but did get a hard look at my face. It must have been bad news.

"How do you feel?"

"Like hell with a hangover." I raised a lax hand to swipe at the sweat on my forehead. An abrupt whiff of my own scent came to me from the motion. It was faint, but unmistakable. You know it by instinct and you never, never forget it: the warm, sweet, rotten stink of death.

9

ESCOTT may have noticed it or not, but knew instinctively that I was in more than ordinary trouble. "Come, get up on this bench by the door."

I slowly obeyed. It was better than giving in to the cold clot of fear creeping up my throat. My body seemed heavy, as though it were sunrise already, with my limbs stiffening and mind slowing. I tried to shake out of it, but that made me dizzy again.

"You're unable to vanish? Is that it?" he asked, once I was settled.

"Guess so." I was reluctant to admit it and thus make it real.

"Has this ever happened to you before?"

It was difficult to think. "That time I got stabbed. And wood does it, too."

"What about those shots you took earlier? Would they have this kind of effect on you?"

"Maybe. Lost some blood then . . . shook me up bad. It's never hit as hard as . . . I've been doing too much of the Cheshire cat stuff tonight." Far too much, I thought unhappily.

"Perhaps you've discovered your limits, after all," he mused, but he wasn't trying to be funny.

I again mopped at the uncharacteristic and disturbing sweat. Its deathsmell remained, clinging to the sleeve of my coat like some perverse perfume. "I feel like a squeezed-out sponge."

"You look it."

"Thanks."

"Right, then let's see about getting out of here for that trip to the Stockyards. I've no doubt that you need to replenish your internal supply as quickly as possible."

He started knocking on the door to get the guard's attention. It took forever. Escott kept himself close to the window so the man wouldn't see me.

"I say there," he began loudly to make himself heard. He was putting on his broadest English accent. It was a parody of his normal pattern of speech, different enough to tip me off that he was up to something, but only because I knew him. The other guy didn't.

"Yeah? Whatizit?"

"I've been in here for hours, old man, and very much need to relieve myself."

"Yeah? Well, you'll just have to hold it."

"That's exactly what I've been doing and I won't last much longer."

"Yeah? Well, too bad."

"Indeed? I don't think Miss Paco would be too terribly pleased were I to . . ."

The guy laughed. "Okay, okay. But don't you try nothing."

"I assure you that I can barely move with these ribs. I shall make no trouble at all."

Outside, the man juggled with whatever they'd fixed up to lock the room and pulled the door open. Escott was still effectively blocking the guard's view and mine as well so I couldn't see what was going on. He shuffled forward, his breath straining and his heartbeat high, so it wasn't all acting. The man kept him in front as they started across the gym.

My turn. If I could take it; but walking was less tiring than vanishing, and the chance of escape inspired me to throw off some of the weakness. I dragged to my feet and managed to get out. A few steps away was a tempting rack of Indian clubs. I gingerly lifted one out and tiptoed after Escott, who was moving slowly and complaining about his injuries. His talk was enough to cover any small noises I made.

"Yeah," said the guy with a minimum of sympathy. It must have been his favorite word. It was also the last thing he said for the time being. I thumped him once with the fat end of the club and once was more than enough. He dropped flat.

"Good man," approved Escott. "Now, let's try that window." Moving a little faster than before, but still obviously uncomfortable, he beelined to the far side of the room.

I felt marginally better but didn't want to rely on it lasting and wasted no time in raising the window.

Somewhere, something that sounded like a continuous telephone bell went off. Escott cursed and tapped at a metal plate set into the windowsill.

"Burglar alarm. That's torn it. They'll be here straightaway."

I popped out the copper screening. The drop to the ground was only four feet, nothing to me, but awkward for Escott.

"I can manage," he assured me, as though reading my mind, but said it through his teeth as he shifted painfully on the sill to get his legs out. He bit off a strangled noise in his throat when he jolted to the ground, throwing a hand against the house to steady himself.

"Isham's waiting over there," I said, pointing at the clapboard shed across the yard.

He hugged his aching chest with both arms and shambled ahead. I crawled out after him. The alarm bell seemed louder outside than in; the night air vibrated from it. Behind, somebody called for me to stop. I glanced back and saw Newton fast struggling out with Lester following.

Isham was ready to cover us. He stepped clear of the shed and waited for Escott to pass his line of sight before taking a potshot at the pursuit. It was purposely wide in order to miss me, but I found myself ducking anyway. Newton growled something obscene and followed it up with a shot of his own. Several shots. With me smack in the middle.

I dropped and rolled, hoping the dizziness wouldn't kick up again, but was disappointed. The night world whirled and twisted; earth, sky, and earth. My stomach and head spun with them.

More gunfire. Over me. Passing me. Then a horn blowing, coming closer.

I was on my stomach and gulping air. My toes dug into the damp earth. I levered upright. Newton and Lester were ahead of me now, using the shed for cover.

Horn.

Coldfield's Nash tore over the grounds toward Escott and Isham. He swerved around them, the heavy car skidding sloppily as he put it between them and the shooting. He leaned across to open the passenger door for them. They dived in. Escott pointed at me, yelling something. Coldfield was nodding.

He slammed gears and hit the gas. The engine roared, the wheels slipped, gouged, and caught. He was coming straight for me. I moved more to the right, ready to make a grab for a door handle when it came.

Lester broke from the shed and began firing at the car. With all its armor he'd have had better luck stopping an elephant with a peashooter. Newton was more on the ball and decided to shoot at me, instead.

I dodged and staggered to make a more difficult target. He was too damned close.

Then the car was in front of me. I seized a handle and got a foot on the running board. Coldfield hardly slowed down and I could hear him cursing through the thick glass as he fought with the wheel.

Except for the handle, I had nothing else to hold. Inside the car, Isham threw himself over the backseat to get to me. He popped up immediately and rolled down the rear window. He got a handful of my coat collar and shouted for me to climb inside.

It might have worked if I'd had my full strength and if circumstances hadn't suddenly changed.

I didn't hear it so much as feel it, a heavy shock like a drumbeat hitting me from the outside in, going right through me. My bones literally rattled from it. My muscles gave in to it. Dozens of fire-hot bee stings tore at my back. Red dots splashed the car and spotted Isham's face. Involuntarily, he winced away from it. Blood. My blood. Then Isham wasn't there anymore, though I had a last impression that he'd made a futile grab for me as I slipped away.

Hard ground hit me all over. Lights too bright to exist flashed within my brain.

Silence. The thick, ringing kind you get after something's deafened you.

I raised my wobbling head and saw the red taillights of the Nash bump along and close together as the car swung around. Searing white beams from the headlights replaced them. Coldfield was coming back for another try, but I knew it wouldn't work. I got as far as my knees and frantically waved him off, telling him to get out, to get the hell out. I couldn't hear myself shout.

Something arced over my head and bounced toward the car. It was oblong, about the size of a potato. I waved once more, screaming this time.

The Nash swerved away from it. Coldfield must have known what it was, too. His car wasn't that heavily armored. I threw myself flat and covered my head the way I'd been taught in the army. Despite the deafness, I heard this one go off. Once more the shock pulverized me. I felt like an ant under a hammer.

It struck.

Heavy clods of earth hailed on me.

Something smashed into my hand.

Silence.

I couldn't see the car anymore. The blast had flipped me right over. Groggily turning, I was just able to see its lights skimming away. Coldfield was trying to put some distance between us, correction, between himself and them. He couldn't help it and I wasn't blaming him for going. That had been the idea behind all the waving and shouting, after all.

Movement. I followed it.

Angela Paco darted past me. Her legs flashed below the flowing hem of her dark skirt. She had something heavy in one hand. She stopped, fiddled with it, and drew her arm back. The thing arced high like the others but didn't fly far. She was small and probably not strong enough to throw it with much safety for herself. As soon as it left her hand, she rushed back.

Her face was unnaturally bright. Her breath smoked freely from her open mouth. She was laughing as she dropped on the ground not ten feet from me.

Drumbeat.

Farther away. Not so bad, but enough to shake us. When I looked up again, Angela was just dragging to her feet, still laughing with childlike delight.

The last grenade hadn't landed anywhere near the retreating Nash, which was just as well. Angela had thrown it as a parting gift to keep them moving, or maybe just for the sheer fun of it. Coldfield had taken the hint. The car bolted around the bulk of the house, heading for the front gate. They were gone.

I sighed and let my head fall back onto the earth. Clouds marred the wide sky, blocking the stars. I shut my eyes miserably against their gray monotony. It would have been nice to see the stars one last time.

They stood all around me, looking down. Angela was smiling. Newton scowled. Lester slammed another clip purposefully into his gun and chambered a bullet. I had no doubt that he was planning to use it on me.

The belated realization that my condition had limits shouldn't have surprised me, but did. Tonight I'd pushed myself too far, used up too much of myself. The raw strength and powers that I'd come to take for granted were either dampened or gone.

I felt betrayed, by myself, by my changed body.

I felt hunger. I needed blood.

With that thought, I could almost taste it again. The smell was all around me. My canines budded. I brought my hand up to cover them.

Bloodsmell. My own.

There was a gash on the back of my hand. Precious life that I couldn't afford to lose seeped out. What would otherwise be a negligible annoyance easily taken care of was now too threatening to ignore. The red stuff, even my own, had its expected effect on me.

No, don't let them see.

They were talking. I could catch a word or two as the deafness slowly faded. Lester held his gun ready, but Angela stopped him with a curt gesture. When he put it away, I felt safe enough to turn over as though to stand up. Better to be on the ground with my back to them than for them to see. Distinct points of pain flared along my back. I'd been hit by shrapnel. It had gone through me, compounding the blood loss from Chaven's bullets. Not needing to pretend weakness, I rested a moment with my wounded hand right under my month.

No good. The taste was wrong. Filtered through my body and the changes within that made it so different also made it wrong. I might as well have tried drinking my own sweat to quench a bottomless thirst.

Hands under my arms, lifting me. I did nothing. They dragged me into the house. Lights. Hall. Doors. Lights burning through me, burning me up.

Heat lamp. I was in the gym, sprawled on the same massage table where they'd worked on Vic. Doc loomed over me and asked a question. I couldn't answer. Didn't dare. He'd see the teeth.

Angela stood next to him, her big dark eyes interested, but without compassion. Her dress didn't have much of a collar. I stared at the slender lines of red life rushing beneath the flushed skin of her neck.

Doc peered and poked, then pressed fingers on my wrist to check the pulse. I jerked my arm away. He shrugged and let it pass.

"Just a little stunned," he pronounced, his voice distant as though coming through a wall. "Still got some fight in him, though. Should be all right after he cleans up."

So much for his medical expertise. If I closed my eyes and kept very quiet, he might declare me fit for a six-day bicycle race.

"Good," said Angela. "We can use him."

"And just what the hell were you thinking lobbing grenades all over the place, girl? This isn't the Fourth of July by a long shot."

"I had them, so why not use them? That car had more steel than a battleship, or couldn't either of you figure that out?" She looked expectantly at Newton and Lester.

Both shrugged. "Not our fault," said Newton. "Things were jumping too fast. I think it's a good thing you came in when you did."

"Uh-huh." She saw through the flattery, but in a good-natured way. "All right, get things put back together here. Lock that window shut and set the alarm again. I don't want them creeping back on us."

"There's still a hole in the works somewhere," Doc said. He nodded at me. "How else could he have gotten through?"

"Okay. Check the rest of the house, too. What I'd like to know is how he got out last night."

"Maybe your daddy put a secret passage in the steam room," he deadpanned, pulling out a sizable drinking flask. He drank deeply. I watched with a terrible envy.

"Don't be an ass. Go check on Mac. See if he's okay."

He pocketed the flask. "Yes, ma'am."

She crossed her arms, studying me narrowly. "How *did* you get out?"

I barely opened my mouth. "Wasn't easy."

"How?"

"Waited 'til no one was looking." It was the truth, more or less. I studied her in turn, drawn by her brown velvet eyes and cupid's-bow lips. Drawn by her . . . no . . . I can't do that again.

"What's wrong?"

"Nothing. Just . . . you're very beautiful." I squeezed my lids shut and tried not to breathe in her scent.

"Oh, ho," she said. "At death's door and still able to flirt. You guys are all crazy."

"Yeah. I'm crazy. Go away."

"When I'm ready, Fleming. You've cost me, so there's going to have to be a payoff and you're it."

"Only part of it."

"What do you mean?"

"Opal's the other part. She's what matters. You don't need me to make a trade for your father."

Her voice lowered and sharpened. "What do you know about him? Kyler's had a lid on the whole business from the start. Tell me."

"Wasn't on that tight. He's got your father—you want him back. You first figured to trade me and Vic for him."

"But then you got away."

"Vic's not important enough to trade?"

"Vic makes the arrangements. He thinks he'll be traded. He'll be lucky if he survives another day, the lousy, two-faced rat."

"Used to work for you, huh?"

"That's the problem, he decided not to—" She caught herself. "Why are you so interested?"

"I just want to get out of here alive, Miss Paco."

She smiled, offered a short laugh, and turned to check Doc's progress with Mac. The latter was sitting up, head between his knees. Doc probed at the damage and got a moan of outrage from his patient.

"He'll be all right. Just needs an ice bag. What'll you do with that one, Angela?" Doc gestured at me.

"Same as the other. Put him away until we set a deal with Kyler."

"You think he'll be interested in dealing after what you did to Red and the others?"

"He can buy more soldiers. And he'll deal. Opal is one of a kind for him. He doesn't dare let her go."

"Or maybe let you get away with it. It's one thing to trade somebody he wants dead for your daddy, but another to grab one of his own people. He might not be very forgiving."

"Once Daddy's back and safe, I'll be able to fix that."

"Go easy, girl."

"Ha."

Lester returned just then. "Telephone, Angela."

"Is it Kyler?"

He shrugged. "Won't say who he is."

She pushed past him to see for herself. Doc watched her leave with a fond smile, which he turned on me.

"You need anything, kid?"

"A blood transfusion?" My teeth were safely retracted by now, but I was still weak and impossibly hollow inside.

He shook his head. "Fresh out. Better luck next time. 'Course you had some luck tonight or you wouldn't be talking now."

"And how long will that last? She doesn't need me to get her father back."

"True, but Angela and I have an arrangement: I don't try to run things and she doesn't practice medicine."

"She might listen to you."

"Don't count on it." He went away to another room for a moment, returning with a damp towel, which he used to clean up my face. "You are quite a mess, boy, you know that?"

"Mm."

"Now let's see what the rest of the damage is. You've got more holes than a sweater full of moths."

I waved him off. "I'm all right."

But he was evidently used to protesting patients and Lester was there to back him up. I couldn't fight them both. The shrapnel hits in my back were closed up by now. The metal had been moving too fast and gone right through, presumably to bounce off the car's body. I hoped the stuff had missed Isham. Doc compared the holes and stains on my clothes to the unmarked skin below and asked me an obvious question about the discrepancy. I made an uncooperative grunt to indicate that I had no answer. Thankfully, he shrugged it off for the moment. I silently blessed his lack of medical skill and the booze dulling his brain.

Doc washed off the gash in my hand. It had stopped bleeding, but still looked nasty and raw. Perhaps some flying fragment of wood had caused it.

"How about some stitches?" he suggested cheerfully.

"Never mind. Just bandage it."

"You'll have a scar."

Lester laughed. "Doc, the kid ain't gonna be 'round long enough for that."

"I know, but I need the practice. I'm not so steady as I used to be." He spread his fingers flat and exaggerated a tremor.

Then they looked at me for a reaction and found much to amuse them. Doc tied some gauze around my hand, finishing up just as Newton came back.

"I couldn't find where he got in," he said. "Everything's shut and locked. He musta come in the window there." He pointed across the room.

From the floor, Mac groggily disagreed. "Then the alarm woulda gone off."

"The alarm did go off."

"Yeah, but it wasn't going when I got hit, and the only one who coulda hit me was this guy." He jerked a thumb at me.

"Maybe the other guy socked you and you don't remember. Why the hell'd you let him out?"

"He said he hadda use the can."

"Oh, great."

"You'da believed him, too. Besides, he could hardly walk."

"Yeah, he was saving it up to run."

"If you'd seen that fall he took down the stairs . . . ah, forget it. What I'm tryin' to say is that he was in front of me the whole time and I got hit from behind. It was this one, all right. So how'd you get in the house, kid?"

"Through a window," I answered truthfully. "Maybe the alarm's busted in one of 'em, huh?"

"Oughta bust you myself, smart-ass."

"Lay off," said Newton. "I mighta missed something. You and Lester go check it again. And check on Angela, too. Make sure Vic's behaving himself."

"Where's Opal?" I asked.

"Why you want to know? She your girlfriend?"

"Just wondered if she was okay, is all."

"She's just peachy. Come on, you mugs. Get the show on the road."

Lester got Mac to his feet and helped him wobble out.

I appealed to Doc. "She all right?"

"Don't worry about her, kid. She's being looked after. She likes this place a sight better than where we found her."

Angela barged in just then, her brows drawn together and her little mouth tight with a frown. "Newton, bring him along to the office." She pointed at me and whipped out again, skirt swirling.

Newton got me off the table, but my legs were not cooperating too well. The shift from horizontal to vertical didn't help my head. The ceiling swooped down, or seemed to, and I ducked in reaction.

"Hey, this ain't a marathon dance, dummy," he complained. "*Walk.*"

I did my best, but God, I was weak, like a battery out of juice. My cure, I desperately hoped, was simple enough. I needed blood, but was I too far gone to get it? And where to get it?

Newton grunted as he hauled me along. His heartbeat was steady and strong.

No. I stumbled away from that one.

"Doc, f'cryin' out loud, gimme a hand with this wet noodle."

Doc came up to take my other arm. "Sure he's not malingering?"

"Huh?"

"Faking it."

"Wish I were," I gasped.

"What's wrong with you, kid?"

"Angela dropped a grenade on me, what d'you expect?"

"Got a point there," he admitted.

We reached the office and they hurried across the last few yards to dump me onto a sofa. It was crowded. Next to me and unmoved by the ruckus was Vic. He looked like I felt.

"Jeez, he's heavy," said Newton, puffing. Doc grunted agreement and headed for the liquor on the other side of the room. He poured out some whiskey and brought it over to me. I turned my head away from it, lips sealed tight with revulsion.

"Do you good, kid," he advised.

My throat constricted. "Later. I . . . I couldn't keep it down now."

"I can believe that." Doc decided not to let it go to waste and finished it off for me.

"What's the matter with him?" demanded Angela, who was at the desk.

"Bad stomach," I mumbled. "I'll be all right."

"Probably a case of the shakes," said Doc. "Just a little reaction to what he's been through."

That's for damn sure. I closed my eyes so things wouldn't slip around so badly. If only the inside of my head would stop lurching as well.

"What's going on?" he asked her.

She sank into the big chair under her father's portrait. "I got a call from that English guy who says he's Fleming's friend."

"The guy that just broke out? He's got some nerve. Where is he?"

"He'd hardly let that slip, would he?"

"You never know. What's he want?"

"He said he's got information that's going to affect my deal with Kyler. He'll trade it for Fleming. I stalled him and told him to call back later."

Doc put the glass back next to the bottle. "Must be a lie or else he'd have been using it to bargain for himself when we had him."

"That's what I'm going to find out. So what is it he knows, Fleming?"

"I couldn't say."

"Uh-huh. You'd better come up with something. I'm setting up a deal in a few hours that's going to go right or else nobody's walking back from it."

Doc added, "That includes your friend Opal, kid."

Angela picked up on his cue. "Newton, bring her down."

He lumbered out. No one said anything while he was gone. Vic seemed to be asleep or passed out. Doc poured another drink and found a chair. Angela drummed her nails on the desk. When I shifted to a somewhat more comfortable position, she opened a drawer and drew out a gun. I behaved myself, being incapable of much else for the moment. Some of the nausea passed off, but I was still light-headed.

"This stinks," came a familiar flat voice from the hall.

Newton pushed Opal into the room, still in her coat and galoshes, and shut the door, leaning against it. Opal glared at him, at all of them in turn, then, with some surprise, at me.

"You again?"

"It's your lucky day, honey."

She crossed her arms in disgust, her face set and hostile. "No, it's not."

I'd forgotten how literal she was.

Angela played with the gun, looking thoughtful. "Since she's an accountant, she doesn't need to walk much, does she?"

Opal's attention shifted. Her eyes went wide.

"Now how about you tell me a few things before I blow off one of her kneecaps?"

She was her father's daughter, all right. "Okay, you've made your point," I said. "You can put that away."

"When I'm ready. What is it your friend's talking about?"

"I figure it has to do with Kyler."

"So could any grade schooler. What is it?"

"Look, I don't care anything about your deal with him. I just want to get away from this place and be left alone. I'll trade what I know for a fast route out of here."

"That depends on what you know." Her tone was cautious, but she was interested.

"It'll help you all right. None of this is really my show now, but I'd like to see Opal back where she belongs—"

"Then *talk*."

My lids suddenly shut down. Instant day. I wasn't there for her to yell at anymore.

(*Talk, Fleming.* I swam in my own sweat, sick from fear and the stink of Morelli's damned cigar and Frank Paco breaking my ribs and laughing about it. . . .)

My head twitched, as though I'd been lightly slapped.

Liquid fire seared my tongue. A few drops got down my throat before I suddenly choked and coughed explosively.

"Shit," complained Doc, who had been in the way. "What a waste of good booze."

"What's wrong with him?" Angela irritably demanded.

"Damned if I know, girl."

Like the room, time had shifted, tossing me back to last summer for a hellish second. There's nothing in the human experience that can be fairly compared to the memory of one's own death. I'd remembered mine just then because I was facing it again.

Doc looked me over, his expression growing long and serious as he peeled back my eyelids. He tried to get my pulse again, but I yanked my arm away. He settled for putting the back of his hand on my damp brow. That's when he must have caught the deathsmell scent coming from me. If a smell could have a color, this one was *yellow*. Nothing to do with personal courage, that's just how it seemed to me.

Maybe to both of us; he straightened and turned to Angela and didn't say anything. She got the message. She came around the desk to see better. It confirmed what she'd read from Doc, and her manner changed somewhat.

Her voice softened, no longer resembling her father's buzz-saw snarl, which had helped push my memory down its unpleasant path in the first place. "Come on, Fleming. You tell me what you know and I'll send you back home, safe and sound." A softer voice and her eyes . . . Lord, I could get very seriously lost in those big brown pools.

Then it seemed as though my deafness returned for a few moments. I forgot about all the others around us. I could hear only Angela's heart, sense only her light breath whispering in the air between us. She caught and held it and leaned closer to me. Her eyes went dull, gaze locked solidly upon mine.

This was as different from my normal hunger as a bonfire is to a candle. She was entirely desirable, but not as a woman, as food. I recognized the feeling well enough, but was too far gone to worry about the immorality of it. A starving man doesn't care much about such details; he just knows his need, and the hell with everyone else. My instinct to survive had simply taken over, trying to reach her, to bring her to me.

"Angela?"

And so Doc inadvertently cut the link I'd almost established with her. Half hypnosis, half sexual desire for beautiful Angela, all desperate, screaming appetite for me. I'd grown that hungry.

She, of course, had been unaware of any of it. "What?"

"You gonna talk with him or kiss him?"

"Don't be an ass." She automatically dismissed his suggestion rather than make a conscious admission that something out of the ordinary may have touched her. Just as well.

He gave a small shrug to indicate it was her business, not his. The damage had been done, though. The effort, slight as it was, had tired me further. Now I had just the one card left, the one Escott had managed to slip in through Angela.

She smoothly picked up where she'd left off. "How about it, Fleming? You're right, I really don't need you to pull this off, but if you can give me an edge over Kyler . . ." Then she began to shovel the snow on thick and deep and went to some trouble to pack it down solid.

"Deal," I croaked, before her generous promises to preserve and reward me for my help got too embarrassingly out of hand.

Angela smiled, sunshine with dark eyes. And for me now, in this weakened state, sunshine was a guarantee of irreversible death.

I turned from the thought, concentrating on the real business. "Okay. Just a couple of questions: have you talked to Kyler already?"

"Yeah. We used Vic to get things rolling. Kyler's thinking things over."

"And you called him just a little while ago, right?"

She nodded.

"But did you actually talk with him?"

Her face darkened. "What are you getting at?"

I glanced at Opal, but couldn't think of a way to make it easier for her. "Kyler's dead. He's been dead since before I came here."

Opal made an indignant squeak of disbelief. Angela and Doc shifted with more subdued reactions.

"How do you know?"

"Because I was there when Chaven shot him."

"*Chaven?*"

Then they crowded in to demand more details, first as total skeptics, then as half believers. I gave them the version I'd told Shoe Coldfield. There were a lot more questions and interruptions from them, but I had no trouble keeping my facts straight. I would not be forgetting what had happened for a very long time—if I had any left to me.

Angela may have known she wasn't getting the whole story, but looked almost ready to accept what she had. "Can you prove this?"

"Not directly. If you send someone up on the main road to town they'll find one of Kyler's Cadillacs parked on the left-hand side. I hotwired it to get clear of them."

"Anyone can grab a car," Newton pointed out from his post by the door.

"Sure," I agreed. "Nothing direct, like I said. You tell me, Miss Paco, who *did* you talk to on the phone?"

"With Chaven," she cautiously admitted.

"As valuable as Opal is to Kyler's organization, do you think he'd trust something as important as getting her back to one of his lieutenants?"

Her eyes got a lot brighter. "No. That's the last thing he'd do."

"I'd say that this is what Escott meant about it having a direct effect on things, wouldn't you? Who you're dealing with is just as important as what the deal's all about. And if you're still using Vic as a go-between, I'd watch him a little more closely than before."

She glanced sharply at Vic, who had woken up at the news.

"He's gotta be lying," he mumbled out. "Chaven wouldn't dare kill the boss."

"Maybe not," I said. "But he's running things now and he needs Opal back."

Opal sputtered, then found some words. "I don't want to work for *him!*"

"Pipe down, cutie," Newton told her.

"No. I worked only for Vaughn. I'm not working for Chaven."

"You can hash things out with him yourself," Angela snapped. "I'm getting my father back. You're my best chance at it."

Before Opal could open her mouth and possibly make trouble for herself, I interrupted. "I saw him tonight, Miss Paco."

That grabbed her attention far better than the announcement of Kyler's death.

"They had him off by himself in one of the rooms at Kyler's road-house. He seemed okay."

"You're lying."

"I've got no reason to. He's a little thinner and thinks he's still running all this." I waved vaguely. "He called you *mia Angelina.*"

That tore it. Angela erupted from her spot, the energy all but sparking from her. She rapidly paced the office end to end; Doc and the others backed off to give her room to move. She stopped just as abruptly in front of me, her jaw working.

"Okay," was all she said, talking more to herself than to the rest of us. She hated the fact that I'd seen him and she hadn't. She hated it, but it was the proof that she needed. I was telling the truth, or as much of it as was good for me. I got the feeling that if her deal to get her father back didn't work, she'd either keep me alive to drag out more details about him or use me as a target for another round of grenade tossing.

My distinction wasn't enough to put off Opal, though. "Miss Paco?"

She turned a hostile face toward the girl, who was quite oblivious to her irritation.

"I said I don't want to work for Chaven."

"That's your problem."

"I thought I could work for you, instead."

Angela's jaw dropped. So did a lot of others, including my own. Angela wasn't the only one who could toss a grenade. "You . . ."

Opal anticipated the first questions, her ready answers coming out in a monotone rush. "You can trade me, but I could come back. I'm good at numbers. I'm the best, that's why Vaughn hired me."

Doc came out with a noise that could be mistaken for laughter. "I'm sure that was very generous of him, little lady, but we've already got—"

"But I'm the best. You ask me anything about numbers and I know it."

Doc nearly spoke again, but Angela waved him off. "Kyler wouldn't waste his time on . . ." She struggled to come up with another way to finish her sentence.

Opal calmly finished for her. "An idiot. I know what you think. A lot of people think that way. All except Vaughn. He knew different. He *was* different. He could scare people for no reason. I'm different, but if it scares people, they hide it. That's why they've always made fun of me, to show they're not scared.

"He tell you that?" asked Angela.

"I figured it out. But I don't want to scare people. I just want work where I can do numbers."

"Damnedest job interview I ever heard of," Doc muttered. "I'm sure you're real good at those numbers, hon, but there's more to it than that."

Opal's eyes narrowed with disgust. "Don't call me 'hon'."

He sketched a mock salute. "Yes, ma'am."

The sarcasm was lost on Opal. She turned her attention back to Angela. "What about it?"

"Doc's right. In this kind of business you can't just change sides without making a lot of trouble for yourself." She looked significantly at Vic, whose jaw was still dusting the floor. "You can make a lot more trouble for me, because Chaven's not going to be happy when he learns what you've got in mind."

Literal as ever, she said, "I don't care how he feels. I don't want to work for him."

"You've got my sympathy, but there's nothing I can do to help you. No offense, but you're just not worth the trouble you'll cause."

The idea that clicked on in Opal's head was almost audible and certainly visible to all. She lobbed in her second grenade. "I can fix that. I could bring all the organization's books out with me. That would make me worth the trouble, wouldn't it?"

10

"DOUBLE-CROSSING bitch," said Vic in the middle of an awful lot of silence.

"You should talk," snapped Newton.

" 'S not my fault. I did what I had to do. I didn't want to work for Kyler."

But Angela waved them both down, all of her attention focused on Opal. "You're serious?"

Opal nodded. "I worked for Vaughn because he didn't make fun of me. Chaven does. I don't like him and I don't want to work for him. I can take the books and bring them to you and you can run things, instead." I think we all knew that she was telling the truth. Opal's absolute literalness could be trusted.

Angela settled into an unexpected stillness, but her brain was probably racing along like a new adding machine, working out the debits and credits of Opal's offer. Then she laughed. It was the same joy-filled shout she'd burst with outside amid the destruction she'd so casually tossed around.

Opal scowled. "Don't laugh at me."

Angela caught her breath. "Oh, no, honey. I'm not laughing at you. It's Chaven. You work things right with me on this and we'll both be laughing at Chaven. Can you imagine the look on his face?"

"Then you'll hire me?"

"You're on probation," she said decisively.

"What do you mean?"

"Pull this off and you'll never have to work for a piece of scum like Chaven ever again. We'll treat you good as Kyler did. Better."

Ever practical, Opal stated, "He paid me a thousand a month."

"Get away with those books and I'll guarantee you fifteen hundred."

"You're going to trust her, just like that?" asked Doc.

"Why not? I said she's on probation. She'll get a chance to prove herself when the time comes. Besides, I've met Chaven and I don't blame her for wanting to get away from him."

"And what if she decides she doesn't want to be here, either? Don't you think she might just as easily walk out on you like she's doing with Kyler?"

She swung back to Opal. "What about it?"

"I worked for Vaughn, not for Chaven or any of the others, just Vaughn. He's dead, so I'm not walking out on him. Here, I'll work for you, but not for him or him." She indicated Doc and Newton.

That made points with Angela. Doc only shrugged. "Well, you can't beat that with a stick, but aren't you moving just a little too fast, girl?"

Angela grinned. "That's how you get ahead of the others. I'm not going to sit on my keester waiting for people; it's up to them to catch up with me. If Chaven can't move fast enough, then too bad."

"Long as you know what you're doing."

"Long as Chaven doesn't. And he won't. Isn't that right, Vic?"

Vic turned a gray face on her, a dead man's face, though he was still breathing. "Angela, I'll do anything you want. . . ."

"Yes, I know you will. It's the only chance you'll get from me. You screw this deal up and anything happens to my father because of it, I'm going to make sure you live."

Vic puzzled over that one, his mind too foggy to make much sense of it. "Huh?"

Doc leaned forward. "What she means is that if you make a mistake, you'll wish you were dead before we're finished with you."

"I'll do whatever you say. Promise, Angela. I promise . . ."

Her mouth twisted. "Save the whining for later. Screw up and I'll be in the mood to hear it then."

He was sweating freely. "I won't screw up—"

"Save it," she ordered, with a dangerous edge to her voice.

He shut his mouth and saved it.

Doc chuckled. "So . . . what's next?"

"I'd like to go home," I said, by way of suggestion.

He looked surprised. "Would you now?"

"Later," said Angela. "First I deal with Chaven, then with you. Understand?"

I nodded wearily. It hadn't hurt to try. If Escott called back, maybe she'd have him come pick me up, but I wasn't going to bank on her goodwill.

"God, he looks terrible." She frowned as though it were somehow my own fault.

Newton eyed me unhappily. "You don't think he's got anything catching, do you?"

"Doc?"

Doc shrugged at them. "What about it, kid?"

"No. I gotta bad stomach is all."

"You want anything for it?"

The answer to that one would only complicate things. I kept my mouth shut and shook my head.

"Maybe he wants to see your diploma from medical school," Angela said, her plump lips marred by an unkind smile. "If you haven't hocked it yet."

Doc only shrugged again. It seemed to be his ready answer for a lot of business.

"Why do you say mean things like that to him?" Opal unexpectedly asked.

The query didn't bother Angela. Her reply was simple enough. "Because I can get away with it."

Opal next turned to Doc. "Why do you let her say mean things to you?"

Doc glanced at Angela. She looked interested in the answer, as well. "Because, my dear, I can't afford to have pride these days."

"Why not?"

"Pride doesn't buy you stuff like this." He pulled out the flask and drank from it. "Once you get a taste for the old demon rum, a little thing like pride only gets in the way of your enjoyment."

"That stinks."

"I suppose it does, but you haven't got much of a leg to stand on, either."

"What do you mean?"

"Didn't you just sell yourself out to Angela so you could work with your precious numbers? I've got booze, you've got numbers, where's the difference?"

Opal took the point right away, scowled, and turned back to Angela. "Does that mean you'll be saying mean things to me?"

Angela shook her head. "No, I won't. And neither will anyone else here." She gave her men a significant look. They all acknowledged it one way or another. No one cracked anything like a smile.

The scowl abruptly relaxed. Labor relations satisfactorily settled, Opal took off her glasses to polish them against the hem of her dress. "I'm hungry," she announced to no one in particular.

Angela nodded at Newton. "Kitchen. Give her whatever she wants."

"Sure. Y'want anything yourself?"

She glared at the phone with disgust and waved them out.

"When's Chaven due to call?" I asked.

"Soon." Hardly an answer, so she might not know. Chaven could stall her all night if he wanted. She'd wait. I couldn't. Come morning and . . . no, I didn't want to think about that horrific possibility just yet.

"Angela?" This from Vic, who stirred painfully next to me.

She sounded bored. "What?"

"I . . . I'm in a pretty tough spot, I know that."

"All your doing, Vic, not mine."

"Yeah, I know that. I just wanted you to know that I really didn't want to go over to Kyler."

"Uh-huh."

"Honest. The man was . . ." He avoided saying "crazy," perhaps remembering at the last second about Frank Paco's own unfortunate condition. "Well, he didn't give us much of a choice. He'd just as soon skin you alive as look at you. We—"

"Uh-huh. 'Didn't want to go over.' "

"There's others who feel the same. Mort, Gabbo, lots of others. They was too scared not to. Once word gets out about Kyler being dead, they'll want to come back to work for you again."

"Like the way you want to now."

"On the level, Angela. I know the spot I'm in. After the deal you just made with Opal, you can't send me back for fear I'll queer her coming back with the books."

"Looks like the boy's finally grown some brains," commented Doc.

"But I don't want to queer things, I swear to you. I'll work with you, do whatever it takes to help you get Mr. Paco back."

Her face was stone.

"Then when it's over, I'll just tell Chaven that I'm staying on with you. When the other guys hear that, they'll come back themselves. I could talk to 'em, tell 'em about the books. They won't want to work with Chaven. They know he won't be able to hold things together the same way. Not the way you can."

The stone cracked a little. After a long pause, she sighed. "All right, Vic, you get a second chance."

Vic could hardly believe it, sputtered, and started gushing his thanks.

"Screw it up and you're dead," she added, which helped sober him.

He relaxed back on the sofa. Less subtle than the deathsmell coming from me was the stringy scent of his nervousness and white-faced fear. He desperately wanted—needed—to take her at her word, but I didn't think she could afford to keep it. It being no business of mine, I kept my mouth shut. Only last night he'd been too ready to assist in taking me to certain doom. If he could pull this one off, good luck to him. I had my own worries.

The phone rang. Angela pounced on it.

"Yes, it is. What's he decided? . . . Yeah, he's here. Just a minute." She held the mouthpiece against her body. "Chaven wants to talk to you, Vic. Watch what you say."

He nodded, as pale as his bandages. "I'll be careful."

Doc helped walk him to the desk. He slumped into the chair. Angela had picked up the gun once more and nudged it gently against Vic's temple.

"You just remember that you don't know Kyler's dead and turn things back over to me first thing."

Another nod. " 'Lo? Chaven? Yeah, it's me . . . I'm okay. Yeah, they're treatin' us fine. Opal's mad as a wet hen, but fine. Angela wants to deal, what about the boss? Okay . . . Okay." He gave the earpiece over to Angela and wearily put his head down on the desk. She grabbed it and hunched over the phone to make herself heard, juggling untidily with the gun.

"All right, what's Kyler decided? Uh-huh . . . uh-huh. Yeah, we can be there by then, but why there? Uh-huh. I want to talk to my father first and make sure he's all right . . . Then I want to talk to Kyler so he can explain. . . ." She muffled the earpiece. "The lazy so-and-so didn't want to bring in Daddy."

"Bet he wants to bring in Kyler even less," mused Doc.

She tossed me a wink of acknowledgment for the news I'd given her. I didn't bother to return it. After a moment her eyes refocused and she stiffened, struggling for breath. "Daddy! Are you all right?" She laughed at his reply, sounding a little forced. "Well, those mugs will get theirs, soon as you come home again. We'll make sure. What was that? Daddy? *Daddy!*" Her expression abruptly went cold, reflecting the change in speakers. "Okay, you just keep him happy or I'll know the reason why." Angela slammed the earpiece back on its hook.

"What's the story?" asked Doc.

"We meet at the old boat dock in an hour."

"Why there?"

"He's coming in by way of the lake. He'll be in that big yacht that belonged to Morelli and will send a boat out from it. Daddy'll be in the boat."

"Why the hell does he want to do it that way? If we wanted to we could pick them off like sitting ducks when they return. Kyler would never take a chance like that." He glared at me, full of drunken suspicion. "Unless *he's* working with him, misleading us on this whole thing."

"I'm not," I answered faintly. "And you'll talk yourself into a real circle with thinking like that. Go for the simple and obvious reason behind it all: Chaven's taking the yacht so he can dump Kyler's body into the lake. As long as he's out there, he can use it to make a fairly safe exchange. He's not worried so much about you, Miss Paco, as about the cops finding him with a stiff."

It both annoyed and amused, but also reassured her. She gave out with a short laugh that turned into a sharp gasp of shock. Without warning, Vic erupted from his chair and fell onto her. They dropped out of my view behind the desk. Doc froze with indecision for a crucial moment and then I heard Angela's bellow of outrage.

Vic staggered up. He'd gotten her gun. He looked almost as surprised about it as the rest of us. He put his back to the wall and crab-walked toward the door.

"No trouble," he gasped, eyes wild. "No trouble. I just want outta here."

Angela's reply was anything but genteel.

He ignored it and kept going for the door. He made it, made a clumsy but successful scrabble to open it, and was away. As soon as he was out of sight, Angela was on her feet and ripping open one of the desk drawers.

Doc gave a start. "My God, girl, you can't—"

"Yes, I can," she grated. She straightened, with a grenade in each fist. "Watch him!" Meaning me. Then she charged after Vic.

Doc made a halfhearted start to follow, but gave it up. He found lengthy solace in his flask.

"Quite a handful, isn't she?" I observed, seeking calm conversation in the middle of all the insanity.

He nodded tiredly. "Her whole life. Why Frank didn't raise her to be a nice girl, I don't know."

"When I saw him—at Kyler's—he said he did just that."

"You know what I mean, kid. She's no floozie, but she's sure not a regular kind of girl. Maybe it's a sign of the times."

More likely a sign of Frank Paco's skill as a father. God help Vic.

The burglar alarm bell went off. Doc jumped.

"That'll be Vic leaving the house," he concluded. He walked to the window. "He's making for the cars. I sure hope she doesn't . . ."

Drumbeat.

The glass vibrated the way it does during a bad thunderstorm. Doc blanched and let the curtain fall back. He rubbed at his eyes as though they were sore, then looked at me. He seemed about to say something, but swallowed it back like a mouthful of vomit. He cleared his throat with another long drink.

"Want one?" he asked tonelessly.

I said no. Several minutes crawled by without another word. The alarm stopped ringing, then we heard footsteps at the door. Sheldon, his hand and arm in a proper cast and sling, poked his head in.

"Hey, Doc, what the hell's going on here?" His eyes were heavy and fogged from whatever painkiller he'd had that day. He wore a rumpled pajama shirt, carpet slippers, and a hastily pulled on pair of trousers.

"Angela's out taking care of Vic," said Doc with a pale grin.

"That double-crossing—hey!" He had caught sight of me, waking up quite a lot. "What's *he* doing here?"

"He's helping us get Frank back."

"Like he was supposed to last night, huh? That'll be fine by me. I owe this bastard a good one for this," he said, indicating his shattered arm. "Wish I could be there to see what Kyler's going to do to you."

Doc didn't bother to give him the latest news. We heard more footsteps and Angela came in with Newton and Opal.

Angela's eyes were half closed and she wore the smooth and untroubled smile that often goes with contented accomplishment. There was a bright splash of blood on her cheek. Not hers, she explained to Doc in a brisk voice when he asked about it. She was breathing hard, but I got the impression it was from her running, not as a reaction to what she had just done. She had one grenade left and neatly shut it back into its drawer.

Watching her with something like awe, Newton and Opal kept extremely quiet. Angela observed us each in turn and liked what she saw.

"Well, I solved that problem," she stated.

I could see her point, since Vic had just shown he couldn't be trusted. Better to completely remove him as a threat than to explain why he was staying on with people who considered him a traitor. Even Chaven wouldn't have swallowed a story like that for very long without suspecting something else was brewing. I could, indeed, see the point very clearly, and concluded that I'd been hanging around this crazy house for far too long.

"What are you doing downstairs, Sheldon?" she asked, noticing him.

He was a little nervous, having correctly picked up on the tension coming off the rest of us. "I was sleeping and heard the alarm go off again. Thought I'd check things."

"Good. I'm glad to know that you're on the ball. Newton, you'll find Mac and Lester outside. I want you to help them clean up the mess there, but first put this one on ice." She indicated me. "I don't need any more surprises tonight."

"Yeah, sure thing, Angela."

"Opal, you stay with me."

"Okay."

Her eyes sharpened. "You still want to work here?"

The question genuinely puzzled Opal. "Yes, I do."

She made a gesture toward the window to indicate Vic. "Even after that?"

Opal was indifferent. "I work with numbers. That's what I'm best at. That's what I want to stick with."

Angela broke into a grin of sly delight. "You're okay, Opal."

Still indifferent. Opal simply nodded, but some of the stiffness went out of the rest of us. Doc drank some color back into his face and assumed a semblance of his version of normality, and why not? Murder was business as usual in this household.

The phone rang again. Angela snapped it up.

"Yes? What? Oh, it's you." Her big eyes rested on me, giving me an accurate idea of the caller's identity. "Uh-huh, I've thought it over and I'll accept your offer. Uh-huh? Well, you're welcome. Now, what's this information you've got? No, it doesn't work like that. You get your friend back after I hear what it is."

Escott said something to make her smile.

"He wants to know if you're all right," she relayed to me. Great, I was expected to hobble over to the desk with words of reassurance.

I spoke loudly, hoping he could hear. "Tell him I'm fine, but"—I almost added "thirsty" but decided against it—"need some rest."

"You get that?" she asked him. "Good. Now what's your story? No, first you talk. Take it or leave it."

Escott took it and Angela listened, watching me the whole time. I didn't have to ask why she was playing such games; she was only trying to confirm what I'd told her. If Escott was on the ball—and I expected he would be—he'd interpret her lack of reaction to his news to mean that she already knew about it. That's what I fervently hoped, so he'd give her the same information. If not, then the consequences were yet another subject that I didn't want to think about.

After a few minutes, I was almost able to relax. Angela nodded restlessly, as if bored with the conversation, and finally broke in on him to cut things short.

"Okay, okay, I got all that and you'll get him back, but later tonight. Call here in two hours and we'll set it up then. No, that's the best I can do and I think you know better than to bring in the cops. Good." She hung up and frowned at her watch.

"Busy night," Doc commented.

"I can handle it."

"Never said you couldn't, girl. You'll get Frank home again."

"If they know what's good for them. Newton, I told you to get this one out of here. And don't forget about Mac and Lester."

Newton stepped forward to take me away. Once more, he had to call on Doc for help getting me down the hall.

"Third time's the charm," he said as they dragged me to the steam room. "We'll see if we can't keep you here, eh?"

"Your bedside manner stinks," I muttered, not looking forward to being locked up.

"So they keep telling me."

Someone had installed a couple of eyebolts on either side of the outward-opening door since my last stay. Propped in a corner was a steel rod borrowed from a rack of barbells and stripped of its weights. Thread the rod through the bolts and you'd have to break the door itself to make an escape. In my present state, I had serious doubts about my ability to break so much as an egg. They dropped me onto a tile bench and Doc lifted and straightened my legs along it. His face was serious again. He tried to take my pulse. I jerked my arm away.

"Lemme 'lone, will you?"

"You're mighty sick, kid. I can't fix it if you won't let me."

"Then don't bother."

He acquiesced with a pitying shrug. Maybe there'd been one too many lapses to his Hippocratic oath for him to take any extra trouble over an obviously dying man. "Come on, Newton."

Newton all but raced him out in his haste to get away. He couldn't have been in much of a hurry to help Mac and Lester; perhaps he'd caught a little of the deathsmell coming from me. They shut the door and fixed the rod between the eyebolts.

Their steps faded. Silence. Not even the sound of my heart for company, but I'd long grown used to that. I breathed every few seconds just to make sure I still could. It was more than Vic was doing.

Two hours to go. Two hours plus whatever time it might take to drive to the Stockyards; I had to last that long. The waiting would be pretty awful, but at least Angela had set a definite limit for it . . . if I could take her at her word. No doubt she'd be glad to be rid of me, dead or alive.

Despite the lack of real air circulation in the room, the sweat eventually cooled and dried except where it had soaked into my clothes. Unpleasantly damp, but nothing I couldn't put up with. I drifted in my cocoon of skin and resisted the urge to check the time every other minute. Doing that would only make the wait seem longer.

Dry, painful swallow. My throat and mouth might have been coated with dust. I stopped the irregular breathing to conserve what little moisture remained. Shut away from the others, I had no distractions from the internal discomforts. The cut on my hand burned, my stomach was knotting up again, and my head kept wanting to float off by itself.

Since I was still stuck here, Escott would know that I was in a bad way. Maybe he could manage to have some blood on hand for me, as he'd done before when I'd been in trouble. Of course, he was hardly fit for climbing fences at the Stockyards himself. It was nice to think about, but not something I could count on. Coldfield was very much in the way on that one. He wouldn't be fobbed off with a made-up story about a rare medical condition. On the other hand, tell him the truth and he might take it as an insult to his intelligence.

Someone quietly slid the rod from its eyebolts. I allowed myself a glimpse at the time. It was still far too soon. Angela wouldn't even have left to make her meeting with Chaven yet. Hope jumped within me. Perhaps Escott's call had been meant to test things out. Coldfield or Isham could have somehow slipped past the alarm system. . . .

Sheldon walked in.

So much for a daring rescue.

He stood high over me and stared down and said nothing and he did this for a very long moment. Sweat popped out on the back of my neck, making it itch. I didn't move, because in his good hand was one of those damned wooden Indian clubs.

"Doc says not to worry, but I know better," he informed me, lifting his cast a little so I'd know what he was talking about. His voice was as flat as Opal's, but subtly different. Where she instantly said what was on her mind, he'd been thinking things over. He wanted to be certain I understood him.

I said nothing.

He leaned in close. The thick stink of booze was on his breath. "I can tell when that quack is feeding out a line of bull. I seen him makin' those kind of promises to other guys that didn't come true. You know how that feels when it's your turn?"

I tried to focus on him. No good. He was just too drunk for it to work, even if I'd been up to full strength.

"It's a lot of shit. They're already startin' to call me names for it; Lefty, Crab Claw. They think it's pretty damn funny when a guy needs help to get dressed. You think it's funny?"

An answer to that one would only make things worse. I kept my mouth shut tight.

"It ain't funny at all. Can't do anything worth doing now. Takes twice as long for everything else. And it hurts. Don't think it doesn't. That's how I know. It hurts deep down in the bones, in between the bones. Doc says I'll get better but I know I won't. Won't be able to handle a gun as good, sure as hell can't fight. About all I've got left is this."

He hefted the club and tapped it experimentally against the white tile near my head. It made a small, hollow echo in the little room.

"Don't take much practice for one of these. You crippled me, you son of a bitch, and I'm gonna pay you back."

I caught his eyes once more. I had to break through or die. That sickening realization didn't help my concentration, but did heighten the emotions involved.

He wavered. I pushed.

This was worse than it had been with Kyler, infinitely harder. Even with his drunkenness getting in the way, Sheldon was easily the more vulnerable, but I was weak and getting worse as I used up what little was left to me. Fear kept me going.

He shook his head, eyes blinking as though struck with a too-bright light.

"Wha . . . you . . ."

I spoke his name. Softly. Names have power, more than we care to admit to ourselves. I spoke again, steady whispers to cloud his brain with dreams of rest and peace. He stopped blinking. I stepped up the pressure, keeping my voice even and low the way I did with the cattle in the yards. Eyes fixed and growing dull, he began to gradually slip into sleep.

The club dropped as his fingers relaxed, making a shattering crack as it landed. He jumped as though from an electric shock, snapping wide awake, tearing free of my influence.

No. I was too near it now to give up. The blood pulsing through his veins was *mine*.

Before he could make another move, think another thought, I had both hands on his neck. It was like another shock to him. He tried to pull away. I held on. He tried to break my grip. I held on. A minute was all I needed to knock him out, maybe less. He heaved backward. I held on. This was as even a fight as I'd ever had with a man since my change. The sheer terror of what would happen to me if I lost this one kept me going. A minute, just a minute more of strength . . . a few . . . seconds . . . longer . . .

But he got his good arm up between us and managed to pry one of my hands loose. I instantly grabbed his arm before he could slip away, and despite the poor leverage and bad angle pulled him over and down. His slippered feet went out from under him on the smooth floor. The crown of his head smacked solidly into the wall on my left.

He dropped flat across my chest like a bag full of anvils. Any breath left inside me whooshed out and stayed there; it was just as well that I didn't really need it. His cast dug into my gut. I tried to shove him off, but couldn't budge him.

This was it. I was too far gone to move now. Within a foot of his throat and I hadn't the strength to reach it.

Wait. Rest.

God, the bloodsmell was coming right through his skin and clothes. I was going crazy from it.

Rest. He's not going anywhere, either.

His uninjured arm was close enough. It would do. Better a trickle than nothing at all. I worked first one hand free and then another, resting from each effort, but not for long; a disturbing mental picture of sand streaming out of an hourglass kept popping into my brain.

I twisted his arm up, pushing back the thin cloth of his sleeve. My teeth were out and ready. Considering my haste and desperation, I made a surprisingly clean cut on the inside of his elbow.

I drank without thought, without control. Bitter hot strength slowly soaked into my exhausted body, killing the hunger, easing the thirst. I was blind and deaf to everything as liquid life flowed into me from toes to fingertips.

Instinct combined with long practice told me when I'd had enough. I drew away, leaving behind little more than a red mark and two small holes hardly worth noticing. All would fade away soon enough. He was alive, but wouldn't be feeling well for the next few days, not so much from the blood loss, but from a concussion. The tile wall I'd slammed his head into was unforgivingly hard.

With a thankful heave, I boosted Sheldon's limp body off, letting him slump to the floor. I could almost smile at him. He'd come in to either kill or cripple me and ended up saving my life. Perhaps that was why I felt no guilt taking human blood for food this time. I wasn't proud of it, and not about to make a habit of it, but the crushing weight of conscious irresponsibility wasn't there now. I'd done what was necessary. No regrets.

Besides, I had other things to worry about, like getting the hell out of here.

My head felt heavier than before; not uncomfortable, but not normal. As I got to my feet, the feeling became more pronounced. It didn't stop me from stumbling out the door, though.

Decision time. Try the window again, or sneak out through one of the doors? Walls. I could walk through them now, but didn't like doing that, to seep through the wood and plaster like some kind of water leak. . . .

I shook my head. It would have to be practicality over preference. Going out any other way would set off the alarms. Okay, right through one of the walls, and Angela and her merry men could spend the rest of the night trying to figure it out. Jack Fleming, the new Houdini, special midnight shows only, children half price. . . .

Bumped into Doc's makeshift operating table. Bloodsmell lingered on it. My own. Vic's. Somehow knew the difference. Poor old Vic, blown to bits . . . bit . . . no rhyme there. Blown to bit . . . bit . . . bit right into . . . bit off more than I could . . . poor old Vic, dead and no one to mourn him. A sudden tear burned down my cheek, followed by another, and a groan of despair that seemed to belong to someone else.

I pushed the table away, staggering into a bicycle with only one wheel mounted on a special stand. It teetered and crashed over. I stared and decided it wasn't my fault. The owner shouldn't have left it out like that.

Maybe he'd been trying to fix it; the damn thing wouldn't be going very far until he put the other wheel on. The groan changed into a sluggish laugh that only ran down after I forgot what was so funny.

Time. Wasting time. Gotta get away.

The air had become thick and heavy, like water. The harder I plowed through it, the more resistance I met. Had to ignore it. Had to find a wall. I blundered into one, knocking down some framed pictures and a plaster ornament. Wrong spot. Needed one to take me outside the house. Which? I'd known a minute ago. Maybe the guy in the steam room could tell me.

I called to him a few times before giving it up as a bad job. He was out for the count, dead drunk, or drugged. Doc had probably shot him full of something to keep him quiet.

Oh, God.

A small portion of my brain that hadn't yet succumbed screamed out a belated warning against the poison I'd so gratefully taken in. Too late now to cough it up. It was in me.

I tried to vanish, with some idea that it might help. Nothing happened. The heaviness in my head traveled down my neck, into my arms, tugged at my legs. My eyes rolled up and closed with artificial sleep. Fresh fear clogged my mind when they refused to open. I tried to force the lids back with my hands, but my fingers were clumsy and wouldn't work right. Once I used to have a nightmare about being unable to wake up, but now I seemed to be in the middle of the worst of it: asleep, knowing I was asleep, and fighting to get out of it.

Hardly able to stand, I felt my way along the wall, with no real thought left to guide me beyond the desire to escape. And then even that was lost as I fell over some obstacle and fought to untangle from it. It won.

My bones were like lead. I had no strength left to move anymore. There seemed no reason to do so. I was content to lie still and wait for . . . I forget what. I forgot everything, how to move, breathe, think.

Voices.

Men came into the gym.

"What the hell's going on here?"

Newton. He could find his own answers. I was fresh out.

"Shit. Come look at this."

He'd found Sheldon in the steam room.

"Is he okay?"

Lester.

"Out cold. Go get Doc."

Footsteps. I forgot them as quickly as they faded.

Newton returned to me, finished the untangling. I sprawled on the floor, unable to move, not wanting to, not caring about it.

Footsteps. Exclamations of surprise. Questions. In his role as a healer, Doc took over, checking Sheldon first.

"Out cold," he pronounced.

Newton snorted. "No kiddin'. Can you do something for him?"

"Hmm." Doc made a longer examination. "What do you want me to do? Bring him around?"

"Well . . ."

"First he gets his hand torn up and because he thinks he knows more than I do about what's good for him starts topping off his morphine shots with his favorite rotgut. Now he seems to have run headfirst into a truck. Next thing you know someone's gonna drop him from an upstairs window. If you ask me—and I'm taking it that you have—he's better off missing out on the rest of the evening. Got some pennies for his eyes? The way he's going, he'll need 'em."

"You just gonna leave him there?"

"Of course not, but you can't expect me to wade into a mess like that without my bag. Jeez, much more of this and I'll have to hang out a shingle and start charging for house calls."

"How did this happen?"

Angela.

"Looks to me like Sheldon came in to work off a grudge. He opens the door, but the kid's waiting for him, gets the jump on him."

"Uh-huh. So what's Fleming still doing here?"

"Probably ran out of gas, girl. He was looking pretty bad when we left him."

She gave an exasperated sigh. "Too tough for him, then. Newton, get Sheldon up to his room."

Doc's hands poked and prodded me. He noisily sucked a tooth, making a loud "tch" sound.

"What is it?" she demanded irritably. "Lester, lock this one up again and stick around to make sure he stays put."

"Too late for that sort of thing," Doc drawled.

"What d'you mean?"

"Girl, this kid's deader'n Dixie."

11

I could have laughed, but that, of course, was impossible.

Angela came over to see for herself. "What killed him?"

"Hard to say. It's funny, but he looks better than when he was alive. He was sweating buckets and his color was all gone and now look at him."

"Okay, so he makes a handsome corpse; we've still got to get rid of him."

"Give him back to his English friend, then."

"Sure, and he'd have the cops out here tearing the place apart. There's tire tracks all over the place, holes in the ground from the grenades, and the mess Vic left of himself. . . ."

"Okay, okay, I take it back. Do what you like."

Angela paced rapidly a few times, coming to an abrupt halt. "I've got it, but the boys will have to hurry if we're going to make it out to the dock in time. Lester, go find Mac and get some really sharp knives. I want you to cut up a couple of big sections of the hall carpet. The stuff's going to be ripped out anyway, we'll get a start on things. Make 'em long enough to hold—"

Lester interrupted, a grin in his voice. "Yeah, I know, that old rug bit."

"I want them long enough so that the ends can be tied off and roomy so we can load them with weights. You'll need plenty of rope or some heavy twine."

"Okay, I got it now. You wanta sink 'em both in the lake, huh?"

"No, I thought we could stick wings on 'em and drop 'em off the Wrigley building. Get moving."

Chuckling, Lester got out.

"Two down, one to go," said Angela.

"What one?" asked Doc.

"The English guy. I still expect him to raise a stink when we don't turn over his friend, so he'll have to be shut down, too."

"Angela . . ."

"No lectures, Doc, I know what I'm doing. Anyway, go help Newton and I'll check on Lester. We're running out of time."

She whisked off one way, Doc ambled another, and I was left like so much luggage where I lay. None of it mattered to me. The idea of being rolled up in a hunk of rug like an overgrown hot dog caused no alarm. I was already comfortably wrapped in a sweet cottony cushion of well-being and couldn't care less about the things that happened beyond its limits. The people walking and talking around me were no more important than some radio left on to make noise in an otherwise empty house.

So I drifted and dreamed without sleep on Sheldon's poisoned blood while he was carried out and tended. Newton was then drafted to help with the carpet cutting. Their voices blended together in a pleasant, meaningless drone, occasionally punctuated by a laugh or Angela's urgings to hurry. They were all easily ignored as I floated in and out of the black and purple mists spinning lazily in my mind. No thoughts, no needs, no problems, no pleasures, no pains.

Angela and Newton returned and dropped something large on the floor near me. It made a mushy thump and I was treated to a puff of stale, dusty air. They took a moment to arrange it properly, then knelt next to me and rolled me over onto it. I didn't resist, couldn't resist, didn't care.

"He hasn't lightened any," Newton grumbled. "Gonna be hell getting him out to the truck."

"More than you think," said Angela. "Help me with these barbell weights."

"Easy, now, that one's too heavy for you."

"I'm just undoing the thing, you can carry it. How many will we need?"

"At least three of the fifty-pound ones for Vic. Maybe four for this guy. It's gotta be more than their own weight or they can float once they start to rot."

"Okay. Start taking 'em out to Mac and Lester, I'll roll these over to this one."

"But that's too—"

"No, it's not. I can handle fifty pounds if I have to. Get moving."

Newton got moving, puffing hard as he carried out Vic's share of iron. Angela worked to unlock the weights from their crossbars and rolled them over to me one at a time. With a small grunt and a heave, she got the first one placed high on my chest, just under my chin.

I didn't like it.

She placed the second one just below it. By the time she was ready with the third, Newton had come back and was able to take over.

I didn't like any of it. The discomfort was an unwelcome intrusion in my cobwebby dreams. I tried to push the things away, but nothing happened.

Angela lifted her side of the rug, flopping it over me. Dust and fibers smacked against my face. Newton did the same for his side, increasing the weight and discomfort.

With no need to breathe, I couldn't suffocate, but no matter what changes the body has undergone, some instincts cannot be forgotten or suppressed. The pressure on my chest and the stiff carpet folded so tightly around me brought up old nightmares and even a few fresh ones of pain and death.

"Tie it up good," came Angela's muffled voice. "I don't want the weights slipping out when we drop him in."

Newton muttered something, busy with his work. They tied off the top end of the rug just above my head and wound the rope fast around my feet and legs. The latter made me think of my last, my very last, moments of life when Fred Sanderson had tied a weight to my ankles, just before Frank Paco had . . .

"You hear something?" asked Newton.

"Like what?"

"I heard something . . . like a whimper or a moan."

"Coming from him? Doc may be a drunk, but he knows a stiff when he sees one. I've never seen him so cross-eyed that he—"

"But I was sure I heard . . . maybe this guy had some kind of fit. He could still be alive."

"And so what if he is?" she asked pointedly.

"Okay," he said after a moment. "I get you."

They finished the job without further talk.

Lester walked in. "We got Vic loaded into the truck, Angela."

"Good. Where's Mac?"

"On his way."

"Soon as he's here, the three of you get this one out and wait for me. I have to find my coat."

"What about Doc? Is he comin'?"

"Yes. He'll be looking after Daddy when we get him back. Your job will be to look after Doc. Keep him on his feet until this is over."

That got her a laugh as she dashed out.

Mac came in and the three of them puffed and cursed and carried me with all the barbell weights to the truck. Throughout, I said nothing, did nothing, I was totally helpless, a bundle of bone and muscle unable to respond to my chaotic brain. They dropped me onto the metal floor of the truck. The fifty-pound disks had each slipped a little out of place. The one on my chest bumped painfully under my chin. Much more shifting and I'd have a crushed windpipe.

A long wait and then a stream of voices as they climbed into the truck. Its big motor turned and coughed to life, and with a rough shift of gears lurched away. I caught the full effect of the uneven road and was unable to protect myself from unexpected dips and turns.

No orderly, reasoned thoughts came to me. I was operating strictly on emotion, the primary ones of fear and anger. Each added a certain strength to my unconscious internal fight, but neither was generating any workable ideas for escape. Had I been able to vanish, no doubt I would have done so. Had I been capable of movement, I would have struggled. But my body was quite separated from my brain and my brain was barely awake. Just enough of it worked to acknowledge danger, but that was all.

Newton's voice was pitched to be heard above the rumble of the truck. "So what about it, Doc? You sure this guy's really croaked?"

"You sure you haven't been into Frank's home brew? Course he's dead."

"But what about what I heard?"

"Probably just some air wheezing out of the lungs. When you move a body around that can happen. Spooky the first time, but you get used to it."

"Maybe you are. I thought that he might still be alive, but just had some kind of a fit."

"Like catalepsy?"

"I guess."

"No, he didn't have those symptoms or he'd have been stiff as a board when you found him. No signs of epilepsy, either."

"Then why'd he die?"

"Still worried that it might be catching?"

"Yeah, why not?"

"Good question, my friend. Wish I had an answer for you. I don't know what killed him: catalepsy, concussion, or cussedness, and I'm not ready to ask Angela if I can perform a quick autopsy just to satisfy your curiosity. None of it really matters, he's still going into the lake and the fish can worry about him for you."

"But the way he just dropped dead . . ."

"Newton, sooner or later we all drop dead, 'specially in this business. My advice is not to think about it and drink enough of this stuff down so you don't give a damn when it finally does happen."

Newton growled a dissatisfied disagreement to that and subsided.

My fingers suddenly twitched. Since my mind wasn't up to coherent thinking, I didn't notice at first, and attached little importance to it when I did.

"Think he's gonna haunt you, Newton?" asked Lester with a laugh.

"Don't be a wise-ass."

"That it, Fleming? You gonna haunt him?" He nudged me with his foot.

The weight on my chest moved, settling more firmly against my windpipe. A gagging sound that only I could hear escaped. I tried to turn from it and succeeded in easing the pressure a little.

"I think Newton reads too much."

"And you don't read at all."

"Yeah, that's why I ain't gonna be haunted like you. What's the point wasting your time on something that ain't real? You won't catch me noodling around with that kid stuff."

"Knock it off, Lester," ordered Doc. "Everyone knows what you noodle around with."

"What's that supposed to mean?"

"What do you think? And if you keep it up you'll go blind. Did you know that?"

"You drunken lush. I oughta—"

"Lay off, all of ya," complained Mac. "My head's killin' me."

"Then have a drink," said Doc. They passed the flask around, which helped restore peace.

My hands had progressed from spastic twitching to controlled clenching. As far as was possible within the mummylike wrappings of carpet and rope, I formed fists and flexed muscles. Some of the wordless fears spinning in my brain ebbed away.

"You see that?" asked Newton.

"More haunting, huh?"

"Can it, Les. I saw his feet move."

I went very still, which was a conscious decision, the first real one I'd made in what seemed like hours.

"It was just the truck bouncing," said Doc.

"But did you see it?"

"Yeah, and it was the truck and this lousy light playing around."

"You wanna really be spooked, you shoulda helped me and Mac with Vic. What a mess. Had to line his rug up with old newspapers to keep the blood from soaking straight through."

"Les, will you shut the hell up about it!"

"Sorry, Mac," he snickered.

The gears ground and we slowed and turned. The road got worse, distracting them from their conversation. I took the opportunity and chanced a limited stretch. No one noticed.

"This is it," said Newton. "Everyone check your hardware."

The truck rolled to a stop, the brakes squealing crankily. The motor cut off and the front doors opened and slammed.

"Douse the light."

The back doors were also opened and the men filed out. Their voices became fainter and less identifiable.

"See anything?"

"Yeah, he's already here. There's the running lights of the yacht."

"For what we are about to receive . . ."

"They're putting out a boat."

". . . may we be truly thankful."

"Can it."

Their attention elsewhere, I flexed and stretched again, reveling in the return of feeling. Because of the weights and rug, it wasn't at all pleasant, but I knew I was still alive.

"Wish they'd hurry."

"Spread out and check the place for anybody who don't belong."

Then their voices faded altogether. I was alone in the stuffiest, most claustrophobic darkness that I'd ever known. Oddly enough, I no longer minded. The imminent alternative was Angela's completion of the job her father began last summer—dropping me to the bottom of Lake Michigan.

Without Newton and the others bickering around me, it was easy to lose track of time. I lay quietly and waited for more of my mind to clear. It was like struggling awake from a thick and restless sleep, the illusion compounded by the stuff I was wrapped in.

"Sez you, I want to see for myself." Chaven's voice, coming up fast. My muscles tightened.

"And I want to see my father," said Angela, equally demanding.

"Don't worry, he's in good hands."

"He better be or I'll—"

"First things first." He climbed up into the truck. "Which one is he?"

"There."

He began tugging at the ropes. Then I heard the snick of a knife and a snap as he sawed through one.

"You're messing it up," Angela complained. "We had him all ready to—"

"Save it, babe. If this is him, I'll do you a favor and take him off your hands."

"What?"

He cut quickly and forced apart the top half of the folded-up rug. I wisely remained as still as possible. Orange stains flickered over my eyelids as he checked my face with a flashlight. The cold, damp air coming in from the lake felt absolutely wonderful.

"It's him, all right." He slapped my face once, then removed a glove and checked my neck for a pulse. Nothing there, of course.

"Satisfied?" she asked.

"More than you think. Ever since I laid eyes on this s.o.b. he's been nothing but trouble. How'd you get him?"

"I didn't. We found him like that."

"Like what?"

"Dead, lame brain."

"Just like that?"

"Uh-huh."

"You mean he just waltzed into your house and dropped dead?"

"That's how it looked to Doc."

"That quack. Listen, Angela, nobody just drops dead. It's too convenient."

"Miracles happen."

"Come on, you plugged him and just don't want to say."

"I didn't and if I had, I wouldn't need to hide it from you. He looked god-awful for a while, said he had a bad stomach, and then he must have keeled over."

"A bad stomach? Who dies of a bad stomach?"

"Who gives a damn?" she said, her voice rising. "We're here to make a trade, so let's get on with it."

But he was still digesting the news and tapped me again for assurance. "Don't know how you did this, Angela, but I owe you one."

"Then get my father."

"You got him and welcome to him. Who's the other stiff?"

"Never mind him."

"I'll just bet it's Vic. Ah, don't worry, I never trusted the creep, anyway. Here, you have your boys load these two up on the boat and I'll save you the trouble of dumping them."

"Why are you so anxious to help?"

"Because it's something the boss wants to have done. I'm all set up for it and I think it's about time things got a little nicer between us—your bunch and mine, that is."

Angela had a smile in her tone. "Don't you mean my bunch and Kyler?"

"Yeah, that's what I meant. What d'ya say?"

"I'll talk it over with my father when he gets back."

"You got a one-track mind, but that's okay. I'll get things started. Deiter, give these guys a hand, just to show we're all friends."

First Vic was dragged away, then came my turn. Bumpier and less secure than traveling in the trunk, they carried me to the dock. The top barbell weight finally slipped, coming out the top end of my rug. I was nearly dropped as the guy lugging my shoulders got his feet out of the way with a sharp curse. Somewhat out of breath, they agreed to keep going and come back for it later. My eyes were shut tight, but I knew when we'd moved out over the water. Right then and there I attempted to vanish and damn the consequences, but I hadn't quite recovered enough for it to work.

At least it was faceup, but the shock of impact against the wood was pretty bad when I landed, especially with the remaining weights on top. It was an effort holding in the grunts and groans resulting from their carelessness; now was not the time to effect a miraculous resurrection.

When it seemed safe, I cracked an eyelid for a peek at things. No one was in view, so I opened both and drew in a full breath of sweet, damp air. The clouds had broken up; I could see the stars I'd missed before, a thousand tiny suns to dispel the last shadows in my mind. I wasn't free yet, but they gave me hope.

Crowded next to me was Vic, anonymous and shapeless in his improvised shroud. If nothing else, I knew him by his bloodsmell. Despite the inner lining of newspapers, the stuff was seeping through, creating huge red patches on the outer side of the rug. Rest in pieces, I thought, and promptly had to stifle my own sudden gagging.

"What's that?" came Newton's sharp voice.

"Another ghost?"

"Lay off, or I'll bust you one. I heard something."

"Yeah, the water gurgled, is all. Keep your eyes open, we ain't exactly home free with these guys."

"Ah, don't tell me my job."

Bad reaction on my part. Black humor and some stinking memories of the war that I thought I'd forgotten. Damn Angela and her grenades. Damn my own imagination for telling me what Vic must look like. Damn the Kaiser, too, and the joker who shot Archduke Ferdinand. Damn, damn, damn, damn, damn. Unable to vanish, I wrestled around to get my arms free of the rug.

Newton was pacing around on the shore and I had to watch out for him in case he decided to check on the gurgling water for himself. He and Angela had done a good job with the ropes, though, and Chaven hadn't cut away nearly enough to make much of a difference. I'd made no progress by the time he'd marched onto the dock with Opal, Angela, and the others.

Chaven clapped his hands together for warmth. "Okay, let's get things started. First trip, I take Opal back; next, I bring in your father; the last, I clean up your garbage."

Angela agreed, but only up to a point. "Two of my men go with Opal, you stay here."

"Hey, now . . ."

"We're all going to be friends, aren't we, Chaven? Doc and Newton go along to help with my father. Deiter goes with them to keep things smooth."

"They leave their gats here, then."

"No, they don't, or I'll have you leave yours, too. Let's keep things even."

"All right, but no trouble or everyone goes in the drink."

I made another attempt to vanish, a futile one. It should have been easier than this, especially since I was over water, but nothing happened. I was as solid as ever. I damned myself for a total idiot for taking in Sheldon's polluted blood, but there'd been little else I could have done. Was it permanent or did I just need more recovery time? The way they were pushing things, I wouldn't have very long to speculate.

Opal was guided forward. She was short on complaints, perhaps preoccupied by her new employment and making plans on how to leave her old job when the time came. She was helped down into the boat, followed by Doc, Newton, and Deiter, which thinned down the crowd. I'd been concerned about getting stepped on, but everyone managed to avoid it. The oars creaked and water splashed as they shoved off.

Chaven heaved a sigh that verged on the theatrical. "I'm glad this is working out so well for all of us, Angela."

Since it was a rather obvious conversational gambit, she spared him a return comment.

Chaven bulled ahead without her cooperation. "Look, I need to talk with you."

"So talk."

"In private, not with a lot of others around. Since you don't trust me, we can stay out here and your boys can watch us from the land. We'll be in plain sight the whole time."

She thought it over. "All right."

"Angela . . ." said Lester, warningly.

"I'll be fine. Besides, I've got my chaperon with me. If Chaven tries anything I don't like, I plug him. Got that, Chaven?"

"I never argue with a lady."

Lester grumbled, but he and Mac retired to the land end of the dock.

"Okay," she said brightly. "What is it?"

"This whole deal about kidnapping your father . . . I just wanted you to know that it wasn't my idea, that I didn't want any part of it."

"Uh-huh."

"I mean that. It was all Kyler's doing. I told him not to, but he wouldn't listen."

"And now he's come to his senses with this trade?"

"You could say that. The truth is that there's a lot of changes going on right now that you don't know about."

"Really? What changes?" She sounded interested, but wary, playing it just right.

"I wanta give it to you straight about Kyler—just between us." Chaven lowered his voice slightly. "He's on the way out."

Angela took her time before saying, "Uh-huh."

"That's the straight stuff. He's . . . well, he's going nuts."

"Not funny, Chaven."

"I don't mean it to be. If you'd seen him tonight, you'd know. That Fleming guy got him so jumpy that—"

"What?"

Chaven bumped his toe against me. "Well, Kyler got the idea that this mug could turn himself invisible. Now you can figure what the other guys thought."

"I can also figure what I think."

"Hey, I said *he* was crazy, not me. I never said *I* believed him."

Liar, I thought, and had half a mind to tell him so, but was too interested in finding out his game to interrupt.

"Anyway, there's some big changes coming and you need to know about it."

"Why?"

He hesitated. "With Kyler going out, someone else has to come in."

"And you're it?" She was unimpressed.

"I know how you feel, how things were after your father's . . . accident. They really shoulda put you in charge of things, but the big boys said no, thinking that a broa— girl couldn't cut it. I know that Frank had it planned for you to take it over a few years down the line."

"Which didn't pan out."

"Yeah, but that don't mean it couldn't now."

"What's your game?"

"With Kyler out of the way, I move into the top spot, but I need more than just Deiter and Opal to hold things together. A lot of the boys di— don't like Kyler, but they don't dare quit."

"So what's that to me?"

"It means this is your chance to come in on the deal. We can work together on this."

"Oooh, what's next? A box of candy and a ring?"

"I'm serious, Angela. I want to cut you in on the business."

"Why do you need me?"

"For what I just told you. To hold things together."

She was quiet for a long time, probably thinking it all through very seriously, indeed. I could tell because she wasn't pacing.

"So what d'ya say?" he asked.

"Call me when Kyler's out of the way, then we'll really talk."

"Why not now?"

"You already said it: I can't trust you and I know you don't trust me."

"Of course I do, or I wouldn't be giving you this stuff."

"You don't or you would have told me right out that Kyler's dead and on that boat."

Despite the constant lap of water masking over the more subtle sounds around us, I could have sworn that I heard his heart jump. It took him a while to settle down and find his voice. "How did . . . ?"

"Your 'invisible' friend here mentioned it. I got the whole story of how you killed Kyler and put the blame on Fleming. I like the way you tied it up, but I don't like being lied to and I'm not going to forget it if and when we do cut a deal. Are you sure you want to work with me?"

He bumped me with his toe again. "Dead and he's still making trouble. Okay, Angela, you caught me out on Kyler and I'm sorry, but it was pretty important news and I had to know which way you were pointed before I could—"

"Uh-huh. You want to talk or give excuses all night?"

"Talk," he blurted, then shut up. I could almost sympathize with him on how she'd jerked the rug right out from under his generous offer and put him on the defensive. If they did manage to work something out, I had a good idea on who would be the senior partner.

The boat came back just then and Angela's attention instantly switched to it and its passengers.

"Daddy? Are you all right?"

No answer.

"Doc, what's with him? What's the matter?"

"Nothing, he's just a little tired and boozy. They were giving him some of the hard stuff to keep him quiet. Let him sleep it off and he'll be fine."

She wasn't too reassured and fretted until he was safely out of the rowboat and up on the dock. With Doc and Mac's help she was quick to get him away into the truck. Newton and Lester remained behind.

"Last trip and then we can call it a night," said Chaven. Deiter held the boat steady while the other three struggled to lower Vic into it. "Jeez, why did you have to pack the weights inside with the stiff? You coulda tied them on afterward."

No one bothered to answer. My turn came up. They refolded the carpet over my face and hefted and heaved. I was dropped on top of Vic without ceremony or much respect for the dead. The only reason they weren't rougher was worry over tearing up the boat. The barbell weight that had slipped out was handed, not dumped, in then Chaven climbed down and we were pushed away.

The oars scraped in their locks, then Deiter got down to rhythmic rowing. The nasty, corkscrewing motion of the boat abated a bit, but my stomach still wanted to turn itself inside out in reaction.

"What's the holdup?" asked Chaven.

"Nothing, just a heavy load. I'm getting tired and these stiffs must weigh a ton. How'd Angela take your pitch?"

"She's got more brains than what's good for her, but I think we can swing something after she cools down. Give her some time with her dear old dad, then I can start sending her posies, though if that broad's anything like Frankie, money would work better."

"You're going to *give* her money?"

"No, but I'll make sure she knows the stuff is there and waiting if she wants to work with me."

"Still can't figure why you want to risk it. I'd rather sleep with a tarantula than trust her, especially after what she did to Red and the boys."

"I'm not sleeping with her and I'm not trusting her, but she is necessary. She may not have much pull yet, but she does know how to work with people and knows what people to work with. Kyler played it too close to the chest for me to get enough of a handle on things."

"But what about Red? And Vic here? You wanta end up like them?"

"No, and as long as I keep my eyes open, that won't happen. The nice part is that Angela knows she needs me, too."

"And when she don't need you no more?"

"Then she can go on a nice cruise of this beautiful lake."

" 'Less she bumps you first."

"She won't."

Deiter applied his full attention to rowing and was quite out of breath by the time one of the *Elvira*'s crew hailed us. Ropes were thrown and instructions passed. Deiter and Chaven gratefully turned the problem of unloading us over to them. After some discussion, a rope net was thrown down and wrapped around us and we were hoisted up with the help of one of their loading cranes. So I deduced from their talk and the complete discomfort and sick-making swinging around that I was subjected to before they were finished.

The steadier deck of the yacht was an improvement over the rowboat, but my back hairs were still on end and the effect of all the acrobatics on my already sensitive stomach was predictable. Vic and I were rolled from the net like so much fish and a protective tarp thrown over us. He didn't mind, but I did and began fighting to get free, not caring who saw; this was pure survival.

At least my strength had returned. After enough wriggling to tear up a straitjacket, I got one arm free. This created some space for the other to come out, and I clawed at the carpet, pushing it from my face. The tarp hadn't been tied down and fresh cold air came up under it to ease the revolution in my gut. Such frantic activity had dislodged the barbell weights, which was something to celebrate.

I was freezing. My fingers could do little more than fumble at the knots, which I could barely feel. All this was by touch, with me folded in

two to get to the ropes on my ankles. It was the kind of work designed
to teach a person patience in the most exasperating way possible. I was
a lousy student and went on another silent cursing streak. Finally, one of
the less likely loops came loose, but it led to another that was a dead end.

With an idea of turning up something sharp, like a convenient knife,
I took a cautious look from under the tarp. No one around. Lucky them.
I was in a pretty foul mood by now and more than ready to work it off
on anyone handy.

They'd left us piled on the aft section. Beyond the rail was a vast line
of the city's lights floating above silver and black ribbons of water—not
far away, but too far for me. All I wanted was to cut loose, get to the
rowboat, and get to shore and to hell with everybody else.

Except that it didn't work out like that. I'd forgotten that Chaven
had more to throw overboard than me and Vic. He still had Kyler on his
hands and wasn't about to waste time getting rid of him. Just before
ducking back under the tarp, I saw one of the crew and Deiter struggling
along with a blanket-wrapped bundle of unmistakable weight and shape.
Chaven was right behind them.

"Get the rail off," he ordered.

"I still think we're too close to the shore," Deiter complained.

"Opal's starting to bitch about going home soon. I have to stay on
her good side until I can get her to hand over the code key for the books.
So let's move it."

"A punch in the kisser would work just as good."

"Come on, give us a hand."

They yanked away the tarp. I played possum once more. With my
feet still tied up, I couldn't get to them, they'd have to come to me. Deiter
grabbed my ankles and hauled me almost to the edge of the deck. The
water was much too close. I flinched involuntarily against the uneasy
movement of the yacht.

"Hey, what the hell?" He let go as if I were a hot brick.

"What is it?"

"Chaven, look at this. He's . . . come loose . . . or something."

"Who're you kidding? He's dead."

"Maybe not so dead as you think. See?" Deiter shuffled nervously
back.

"Douse that light, you jerk." His voice was thinner, harsher. "The
ropes didn't hold, is all."

"Don't be a stoop. *Look* at him! He had to have done it. Who else?"

Chaven looked. "This is crazy. He's dead. I know he's dead."

"Angela put one over on you, is what it is. You gotta do something
about him."

"Oh, hell, get outta the way."

It was dark enough for me to risk cracking my eyes. Chaven crowded in close, right where I wanted him, but he drew his gun—Escott's stolen Webley—which I could have done without.

As I suddenly sat up and reached for him like some long-dreaded retribution, he let out an honest-to-God shriek that I didn't think could come from a human throat. Deiter and the other guy also joined the chorus, stumbling all over one another in their hurry to get away. It might have been funny if I hadn't truly been fighting for my life.

I got both hands on Chaven's arm and shoved the gun to my right. He tried to pull himself away. The damn thing went off, again and again and . . .

Chaven threw himself backward. I didn't dare let go of his arm. I was dragged along.

The bullets flew wide.

Couldn't use my legs for leverage, they were still caught up in the rug. Concentrated on the gun. Another shot.

Then I got one hand over his. The Webley bucked and roared as I twisted it up. This time the bullet struck. The side of Chaven's throat exploded. Blood burst from the wound, spraying me. The gun's sharp recoil took it out of his grip; it dropped on the deck with a thud. Then there was a horrible weightless second with both of us screaming as we crashed headfirst into the lake.

Headfirst into hell.

Water.

Free-flowing water.

Free-flowing death.

Chaven pushed away, the last thing he ever did. In four seconds all the life went out of him, flooding the shifting shadows around us with the black cloud of his blood.

I was upside down, my legs tied fast in the rug and the thing spreading above me, buoyant in the water. Arms out as though flying, Chaven's body drifted past in a slow downward spiral, a thick trail streaming from his throat. The darkness took him . . . and reached out for me.

It bubbled and burned like fire, tearing right through the top of my skull.

It seared and clawed and ripped at my frail flesh like a starved monster.

It smashed and smothered, crashing my final wailing hope of escape.

Ears stuffed with it, eyes blurred from it, mouth gagging on it, bones shrinking from its freezing touch . . .

I kicked and writhed and fought and howled and strangled against it.

▲ Epilogue ▼

I'M alive.

It was the first real thought to surface in my cobweb-clogged brain since I woke up on the beach. I'd been groggy then, with only enough stuff working in my head to shakily stand and blink down at my soaked clothes. It never occurred to me to question why I was on a beach and in such a condition, and I was still in a thought-numbing state of shock when I climbed a short, sandy rise and found the road.

Loose-limbed like a cartoon scarecrow, I walked, head bowed to watch my feet because I couldn't feel them. I looked up once to check that the lights of the city were still ahead, and tripped on something, sprawling flat. I immediately scrambled up again, not daring to rest. The icy wind was cutting me in two; if I stopped moving now, I might stop moving for good.

Teeth chattering, arms clutched tight around my chest, I bowed my head again in a wordless prayer for more strength and staggered forward. I'd been down this road before, only then it hadn't been so damned cold.

I had been colder . . . out there . . . shuddering in the water, my ankles bound together . . . not suspended between heaven and hell, but very definitely *in* hell.

Headfirst.

For an age.

Until the press of water became too much and began to crush me into something that wasn't me and yet was.

I floated, just another bubble compressed into a moving plastic sphere by the water. I was going to float to heaven.

I made it as far as the surface.

Then the trip, an endless rush over a liquid desert. Realization that heaven wasn't my destination, after all, but then neither was hell. Perhaps another time, if ever.

I shivered. It was a memory now, but memories have a way of hurting you far worse than the original experience.

Road. Watch the feet. Think of other things.

Like Angela Paco, a dark little angel of death, every bit as lethal as her father had been. If not already, she'd be making plans to get rid of Escott. Not at all nice. I'd have to have a serious talk with her.

Escott. Might want to mention it to him, too.

Chaven. Better not to think about him at all.

Same for Kyler.

Dear God, it's cold. The wind sliced through my wet clothes, cutting at my puckered white skin.

Road. The one I'd taken that first night, when Sanderson tried to run me down. I'd stuck my thumb out, hoping for a ride. . . .

Motor. This time the sound coming toward me from the city, not from behind. Too bad. Could have used the lift.

Headlights separating, growing larger, had to shade my eyes from them. Not wanting to tempt fate, I moved closer to the shoulder of the road to give the driver plenty of room to pass.

He slowed instead.

Not again.

I waited for him to shift the gears, hit the gas, and hurtle down on me as Sanderson had. I waited and shook miserably in the Arctic blast off the lake.

The car coasted to a stop, motor idling softly.

It was a Nash.

The passenger door opened. A tall, lean man got out, moving slowly, his bony face pinched with concern. I glanced behind me to see what he was looking at, but saw nothing of interest.

"Jack?"

Yeah. That's my name. His was Escott. I had something to tell him. . . .

He came closer. "Shoe and I had arranged a meeting with Miss Paco—we were just en route to pick you up. Are you . . . ?"

"B-better not g-go," I choked out. My words tasted of lake water.

He stiffly shrugged out of his overcoat. "My God, man, you're freezing to death."

I grinned, which alarmed him even more. "N-not this t-time."

I'm alive.

He draped the thing over my shoulders and guided me toward the waiting car.

P. N. "Pat" Elrod, best known for The Vampire Files and the Jonathan Barrett: Gentleman Vampire series, coedited *Time of the Vampires* and has stories in several other anthologies. A great fan of the television series *Forever Knight*, she collaborated with actor Nigel Bennet (LaCroix) on the Lord Richard, Vampire series. She is currently working on a new set of toothy titles and branching into the mystery and science fiction genres.